Dancing on Thorns

REBECCA HORSFALL

Dancing on Thorns

A Novel

BALLANTINE BOOKS

NEW YORK

Copyright © 2005 by Rebecca Horsfall

Published in the United States by Ballantine Books, an imprint of The Random House Publishing Group, a division of Random House, Inc., New York.

BALLANTINE and colophon are registered trademarks of Random House, Inc.

Library of Congress Cataloging-in-Publication Data

Horsfall, Rebecca.
Dancing on thorns : a novel / Rebecca Horsfall.
p.   cm.
ISBN 0-345-47978-5
1. Ballet dancers—Fiction.   2. London (England)—Fiction.   3. Friendship—Fiction.
I. Title.
PR6108.O77D36 2005
823'.92—dc22
2005041041

Printed in the United States of America

www.ballantinebooks.com

2 4 6 8 9 7 5 3 1

First U.S. Edition

Book design by Dana Leigh Blanchette

ACKNOWLEDGMENTS

MY THANKS TO Kate Elton for her superb, tireless, and tactful editing, and to my agent Judith Chilcote for her valued support and encouragement. And huge thanks also to Allison Dickens, Ingrid Powell, Gilly Hailparn, Kim Hovey, Bert Yaeger, and everyone at Ballantine Books.

Many thanks, too, to Georgina Hawtrey-Woore, Jo Wheatley, Rebecca Ikin, Emily Cullum and all at Random House UK, and to Paul Marsh, Camilla Ferrier, Caroline Hardman, Christiaan van Raaijen and all at the Marsh Agency for their international expertise, and a special thank you to Cressi Downing.

Thanks to the following for help during the research for this novel: Christine "Quee" Woodward, Philip Feeney, Frances Guthrie, Richard Herriott; the dancers Rachel Lopez de la Nieta, Hironao Takahashi, Omar Gordon, Martin Lau, Claire Fielder, David Gorman, Sarah Hanley, Shizuka Koizumi, Konrad Simpson, Shinobu Suwa, Charlotte Talbot, Gail Morris, Mika Kato, Samantha Claypole, Jorge Morro, Vanessa Donkin, Abigail Cowan, Sarah Bennett, Kathryn Alcock, Fiona Chivers, Julian Lopez, and the staff of British Gas Ballet Central; Kathryn Wade and the English National Ballet School; the Royal Ballet; and Sonia Boddy of the Dance House, Horncastle.

I also owe heartfelt thanks to Cassandra Manning, Caron Ottewell, John Gore, Kate Bright, Hannah and Krishna, Christian and Tessa, Patrick and Myra Woodrow, Noël Horsfall, Vanessa and Steven Garratt, and especially to my parents, Jane and Bernard Horsfall, and to Douglas Woodrow.

Part One

1

ONCE A YEAR, in the spring, Nadia Petrovna cleared her desk. She scooped the piles of unpaid invoices and tax demands into drawers with a long sigh of relief and escaped London for a fortnight to revisit the beloved Europe of her youth.

This year, as always, Paris laid out the red carpet for her. At the airport she was met by the Minister for the Arts, and stopped on the pavement beside his black limousine to beam at the select band of press photographers who showered her with affectionate greetings. The Minister's secretary presented her with a bouquet of spring flowers and her wrinkled face lit up in delight.

"How lovely!" she said, more delighted by the daffodils than all the other combined attention. "They're absolutely my favorite."

Nadia Petrovna adored Paris. She went out to lunch with the director of the Opéra and then attended a gala performance on the arm of a great dancer who had taken his first classical steps under her tuition—and who had now, in his turn, retired to become one of France's foremost choreographers.

At the Académie Française de la Danse, a little girl in pink tulle and satin slippers presented the dowager *étoile* with a bunch of pink roses, curtsying deeply as she had been instructed by the junior ballet teacher. Every year it was exactly the same; Nadia Petrovna Sekova had been making these visits for so long they had become part of the tradition of the dance world. Only the faces of the children changed; little girls who had once presented that annual pink bouquet were now dancing in the company, or had become teachers in their own right, or were married and had children.

"Nadia Petrovna," said her old friend Henri, taking her hand. Like everyone in the ballet world, he addressed her in the old-fashioned Russian style, adding the feminine form of her father's Christian name to hers. "You look younger every time I see you."

The ancient woman smiled in reply and shook her head. They both knew she couldn't go on making these trips forever. Already she relied heavily on her walking stick and this year, for the first time, she had taken a taxi to the Académie from her hotel instead of walking. Even the journeys to and from the airport exhausted her now.

"Paris always makes me feel young," she said with a courageous sparkle in her old eyes.

Madame de Sancerre, the school's director, accompanied Nadia Petrovna on her traditional tour of the classes, pointing out favorite young dancers with her long fingers. The atmosphere in every studio they entered prickled with nervous unease. Whenever Madame walked into a room it was as though an icy wind swept in with her through the open door. One by one, they went into each of the studios, sitting on wooden chairs at the front of the class while the anxious students performed their rond de jambe exercises, adages and allegros for the great dowager prima ballerina of the Diaghilev era.

Nadia Petrovna sat upright on her chair—alert and attentive—with her knotted, arthritic hands folded over the handle of her walking stick.

"That tall boy at the back," she said, picking out one of the students at the barre in a large class of boys. "Why does his teacher not correct his position? Here . . ." She indicated on her own body a line between her shoulder and her hip. "Here, this is all wrong."

Madeleine de Sancerre glanced sharply at the boy and turned to her guest with a gesture of irritated dismissal.

"There's no point correcting him. He won't be taught. It's not his teachers' fault: the boy is unteachable. He's one of the ones we're getting rid of this term. He was a promising child—extremely promising—but, like so many, puberty has ruined him. He's sixteen now, and quite beyond salvage. Instead of improving, his technique just gets worse and worse. As you see, everything is out of place. Look at his feet and hands."

Nadia Petrovna looked. Carefully. The light-haired boy was tall; his gangly limbs seemed too long for his narrow body, giving him an unbalanced, coltlike air. There was something very forlorn about him as he danced halfheartedly behind the other boys, not even attempting to keep up with the exercise. Nadia Petrovna studied him through pensively narrowed eyes. His technique was a disaster. Every movement he made was wrong. The question that puzzled her was why they hadn't got rid of him sooner. Competition for places at the Académie was extremely fierce.

Madame went on, with pursed lips, "See how he keeps his eyes down? Henri has told him a hundred times that he can't balance if he gazes at the floor. And yet look at him. I haven't made up my mind whether it's from stubbornness or sheer stupidity."

Nadia Petrovna was still watching him with calm interest.

"Perhaps it's just fear of heights."

"No," Madame snapped. "He's deliberately obstructive. And the other boys take heed of his rudeness. He's a nasty, destructive influence in this school and the sooner we're rid of him the better. I hate that boy."

The old woman turned her head to look at her in surprise. Madame de Sancerre looked down at her clasped hands as she apologized mutedly for her outburst.

"Forgive me," she muttered. "It makes me so angry."

Nadia Petrovna nodded her sympathy. There was no need to explain. She knew from her own experience that nothing makes a ballet teacher more bitter than wasted talent.

"Madeleine, I'm sure the poor boy has no idea he's caused you so much frustration."

"Oh, he knows," she replied acidly. "He doesn't speak—won't even answer direct questions. Never looks you in the eye. Never smiles. Never frowns. No expression at all. He does it on purpose just to infuriate us."

Nadia Petrovna doubted that even a stubborn teenager could keep that up, day after day, merely for the satisfaction of annoying his teachers. But she kept her own counsel and tactfully pointed to a different student.

"That boy there, with the black hair, has the most beautifully polished feet. You've done a marvelous job with him."

"Yes, he's a very dedicated worker," Madame said with relief. "Only fifteen. Henri thinks he might go into the Upper School a year early."

A few minutes later she rose from her seat and led her aged guest out of the studio to continue their tour of the classes. At the door Nadia Petrovna stopped and looked back along the row of boys as they swept their feet over the floor in rapid unison, all in identical green dance uniform. At the far end of the barre, the willowy boy with the blond curly hair and invisible eyes was marking the exercise listlessly, his arms and feet moving mechanically in time to the thumping of the pianist's hands, his technique floundering on every step. Nadia Petrovna's heart went out to him.

In the afternoon, after lunching with Madeleine de Sancerre and Henri Renoir, Nadia Petrovna escaped from her companions and stole a pleasant half hour to wander alone through the school where she had taught for so many years. In the pillared foyer she lifted her face, still radiant despite its great age, to look at the Rococo paintings on the curved ceiling of the huge dome. She had always loved that dome. Such grandeur. Like classical dance at its best—untouched by the pettiness and the humdrum of the lives that passed beneath it.

She walked slowly through the corridors of the school, leaning on her walking stick, thinking of all those children she had taught so long ago in these echoing studios. She still remembered every face, every pair of feet, every heartbreaking injury that had destroyed a promising career. Silently, in one of the empty studios on the top floor, she ran her hand lovingly over the barre remembering a time even before her teaching days. Her hands were misshapen and white now, crippled with arthritis, fragile skin stretched over them like parchment. Once they had been described as the most beautiful hands in Europe.

She stopped outside one of the small studios, resting both hands on top of her stick, and looked through the little window in the door. The tall, fair-haired boy was standing alone in the studio, his back propped indolently against the barre with his arms folded and his feet, in long white ballet socks and ballet shoes, crossed at the ankles. Through an open window at his side the sound of piano music drifted in from across the courtyard. He was gazing through the window, listening, lost in abstraction.

Nadia Petrovna opened the door quietly and went in.

When the boy saw who had entered he unfolded his arms and shifted his weight away from the barre in an unconscious gesture of respect. Nadia Petrovna permitted herself a small smile. Hostile and undisciplined he might be, but he was still a pupil of the Académie Française.

"Excuse me," she said. "Am I interrupting you?"

He looked at her warily and glanced at the door behind her to see who might be about to follow her into the room. "No, Madame."

"A little bird in the staff room whispered to me that I would find you up here. Under strict instructions, as I understand the situation, to spend an hour working on your pirouettes."

He made a small explanatory gesture toward the window, indicating the music.

"Chopin," he said. "*Les Sylphides.* I was listening, Madame."

Nadia Petrovna smiled at that.

"I see. And can you not listen and dance at the same time?"

"I can't even dance and dance at the same time." He looked away. "As you saw in class this morning."

The old woman walked slowly across the wooden studio floor to stand beside him at the barre. She peered up at his face with shrewd interest.

"How tall you are. I think I should be rather frightened to be so tall. Do you get vertigo all the way up there?"

He looked down into her sympathetic eyes, not fully comprehending her meaning. His own gray eyes were a little perturbed. It wasn't every day that a pupil of the Académie found himself face-to-face with a genuine *danseuse étoile* of the old Russian school.

He cleared his throat. "Shall I get you a chair, Madame?" Despite his height and his sixteen years his voice was not yet quite settled in its precarious baritone.

She shook her head, amused. "No, thank you, child. I know I look dreadfully feeble but I'm not quite so decrepit that I can't stand for a few minutes." She saw that she had embarrassed him and immediately regretted her flippancy. What, after all, could a boy of sixteen be expected to know about such great age as hers? "Tell me," she said, "what's your name?"

He answered her reluctantly: "Jean-Baptiste St. Michel."

Nadia Petrovna managed to hide her surprise. She looked him over slowly, recognizing now the extraordinary familiarity of those fair curls and those guarded gray eyes. St. Michel—yes. Oh yes, that explained a great deal. Indeed, she thought, that name must be quite a burden for a boy to bear in the world of dance. With a profound tact born of almost half a century's experience with teenage students she pretended not to recognize his family name.

"Jean-Baptiste," she said. "What a charming name."

"I'm always called Michel."

"May I ask why? Or is it a secret?"

"It's not a secret, but I can't tell you why. I don't know."

"Then it's a mystery. I love mysteries; there should be more of them in life. They keep us young." Her gleeful smile vanished and she looked him firmly in the eye. "Your teachers tell me you're lazy, Michel. That you're unfocused and make no effort to take corrections. That you're rude and undisciplined. Why is this?"

He grappled with her question in discomfort but he couldn't find a reply. Watching him closely, Nadia Petrovna saw in his troubled gray eyes something she couldn't define; something that had no place in the eyes of any sixteen-year-old boy.

"Let me ask you a different question," she said. "Do you love dancing?"

"I've lost the facility, Madame. I can't do things that came easily to me at twelve or thirteen. I can't even turn anymore."

"That was not my question. I asked if you love dancing."

Again he struggled to find an answer. His withdrawn gaze turned involuntarily for a moment toward the window, toward the piano music that was still drifting up across the courtyard.

"I don't know," he said.

Nadia Petrovna's old eyes sparkled softly. He couldn't know how eloquent that simple glance had been.

"Sixteen is a good age," she said, with a plucky cheerfulness that defied her physical frailty. "A splendid age. It's the age of choice, Michel.

Choice! Do you realize what a wonderful word that is? It's an age when you can be who you want to be. Even when being sixteen is ghastly it's still absolutely wonderful. And the best news is it gets better as you go along. Dancers always whine terribly about getting older—take no notice of them. I'll tell you a secret: being old and white-haired is tremendous fun. The only thing that's not fun about it, apart from arthritis, is the unfulfilled dreams you've left behind you."

She paused to let Michel speak if he wanted to, but he said nothing. He just watched her with quiet, interested eyes.

"You're not a great talker, I see. You prefer to listen."

"I can't learn anything when I'm talking."

Nadia Petrovna nodded slowly.

"I think you are rather a bright young man."

He looked at her in surprise. No one had ever called him a young man before. And certainly no one had ever suggested that he was anything other than patently dull-witted.

"I don't read or write very well," he said doubtfully.

"There are different kinds of intelligence and different things you can do with it." She raised her chin with a proud smile. "Did you know I have my own little company in London?"

"Yes, Madame. Charles Crown is your choreographer."

"Good! You have heard of him! Excellent! What have you heard? Be frank."

"That his style's very modern. And his ballets are controversial." She saw the flicker of a dormant personality steal into his eyes for the first time. "And that he's dangerous, Madame."

"Dangerous?" She clenched her fragile fist and shook it in excitement. Her ancient eyes blazed with enthusiasm. "Is that how he is known in France? Hurrah!"

"The other boys say he's clever," Michel said. "Some of them went to the summer school he gave on choreography last year."

"And why didn't you go?" she demanded.

"I wasn't allowed to. I had to attend the classical summer school here at the Académie to work on my technique."

"Well, you missed a great opportunity. Did you know that he is also a very fine dance teacher? Between you and me, I think he's the best."

He was puzzled: "But you don't have a school, Madame."

"No, but we have students within the company. A few boys and girls around your age who come to finish their training and learn to perform onstage." She smiled mischievously. "It allows us to have our little stake in the future of dance. And, to be truthful, I'm afraid it helps keep our company solvent. Now what do you think of our scheme?"

Michel shook his head quickly.

"I could never afford it. Apprenticeships like that are very expensive."

Nadia Petrovna stopped herself from replying that a course of study at the Académie was hardly cheap. The faint flush that had stolen over his face warned her against it. And yet, she thought, someone must be paying for his education.

"I am sure we can find a solution if we try," she said, and then, seeing his uncertainty: "Think about it, Michel. I will be in Paris for three more days. The office downstairs can give you the address of my hotel."

As Nadia Petrovna made her way slowly to the door Michel gazed after her.

"Excuse me, Madame . . . ?"

She stopped to look back at him. "Yes, child?"

"Is it true that you danced in the first production of *Les Sylphides*?"

Nadia Petrovna laughed. "I am very old, Michel, but I am not that old. It was first performed in 1907 in St. Petersburg. The first time I danced in it was here in Paris in 1913, with Pavlova and Nijinsky. I had only just turned fourteen." Her eyes softened for a moment, gazing into the past, and then she smiled at him. "You can work out my present age for yourself."

The front hall and corridors of the Islington Ballet's headquarters in London were alive with bustling dancers on their way to and from the studios, and up to the wardrobe room for fittings. In the large ground-floor studio Charles Crown was auditioning young women for the corps.

Nadia Petrovna walked very slowly along the short corridor, leaning on her stick as always, to peer through the reinforced glass in the studio doors. Eyeing the rows of hopeful girls at the barres, she shook her head. She knew the artistic director's taste.

"No," she told herself. "Not one."

She went back to her office and filled the electric kettle, exhuming the files of unpaid invoices from her desk drawer with a sigh. They couldn't stay buried forever.

One by one, she turned over the bills, dunking a peppermint tea bag in a bone-china cup of hot water. Before long, through the wall of her office, she heard the foyer reverberate with the violent crash of a door being slammed. A moment later angry footsteps thudded on the linoleum floor of the passage.

Nadia Petrovna squeezed out her tea bag and laid it on the saucer.

"Come in, Charles," she murmured quietly.

The door flew open and the short figure of the artistic director exploded into the room. His dark eyes were spitting black fury.

"Mindless bloody elephants!" he bellowed, closing the door behind him. "Waste of a whole fucking morning!"

"Charles," she said calmly, "you swear so terribly. Were they really no good?"

"No good?" Crown lit a cigarette and flung the spent match into the bin in frustration. "Nadia Petrovna, what do those girls think about?" He waved his hand in front of his eyes to indicate a blank stare. "Nothing! Nothing going on in there at all! And what, for Christ's sake, do they eat?"

"Sit down, Charles, and have a cup of coffee."

"I haven't got time to sit down." His dark eyes glared at her as he plugged in the kettle. "Did you have a good trip?"

"Very pleasant."

"You look tired. You said you were going to take it easy."

Nadia Petrovna passed him the sugar bowl.

"I had a marvelous time. I saw two ballets in Paris, had lunch at Maxim's with Rudy . . ."

"At your age? You should be ashamed of yourself."

"And I saw Béjart's new piece in Brussels—naturally I didn't have a clue what it was about. I sent you a postcard. Did you get it?"

"I don't know; probably."

He paced the office with his coffee, frowning as his thoughts moved on to the thousand and one details for the new ballet awaiting his attention. Charles Crown was a very small, powerful man with strong Latin features and black hair, and ferocious black eyes that blazed with concentration, never resting for a moment. As he paced back and forth he managed to half listen to Nadia Petrovna's chatter, even while his mind was tugging away at the host of problems waiting to be solved.

"Charles," she said, aware that he was distracted, "I managed to see the Arts Commission in Brussels."

The piercing eyes turned toward hers, instantly attentive.

"And . . . ?"

"They are considering our application. The grant committee doesn't meet again until October."

"October!" He ran his hand through his black hair with a growl of anxiety. "October! How are we going to survive until then? The print for *Aeneas* ran way over budget, by the way; there was nothing we could . . . Jesus! I forgot to tell you; Alf got out the rest of the touring floor last week. Four rolls are completely perished. God only knows what we're going to do."

The old woman smiled confidently. "Don't worry, Charles, these problems will resolve themselves. They always do."

"No," he spat. "No, they don't! I resolve them. Me!"

"Sit down. You make me nervous with all your pacing and fidgeting. There's no question of buying any more flooring this year, so we will just have to find another way. How about The British National Ballet? Maybe it's time to call in a few favors from Martyn Greene?"

Crown had sat down but he was now pulling apart a paper clip with vigor.

"I called Martyn; he's in New Zealand until Tuesday."

"So we will just have to practice the virtue of patience."

"Patience!" The dark eyes flashed fiercely. "Nadia Petrovna, have you any idea what's been going on in this place while you've been gallivanting around Europe? I've got ten days until *Aeneas* opens. Seven of the girls . . ." He held up seven fingers for emphasis. ". . . *seven* aren't dancing on pointe; three of them with serious sprains. I've got Carlotta and Ingrid at each other's throats over the role of Dido; it's like bloody Armageddon in rehearsals. I've had to get the whole print run redone, which is going to make it next week before we get handbills, and the

Theatre Royal in Margate is trying to shove us two weeks further into July which will screw up Chichester. Boris is in hospital—did you know that? It transpires that what we thought was depression and flu is actually an incurable compulsion to stick needles in his arm, full of some shit whose name I can't even remember . . ."

"Good Lord!" said Nadia Petrovna.

"And what's more, the set's come out six inches longer than Alf calculated so it won't fit in the scenery truck we've leased from Brownings. So, Nadia Petrovna, don't—and I repeat *don't* sit there lecturing me on the virtues of fucking patience."

"Poor Charles."

His aged colleague made the words sound like a caress; her mournful Russian accent, which had never faded even after all her years in the West, gave even her most commonplace remarks an exotic flavor.

They were interrupted by a knock on the door and Carlotta, one of the company's leading dancers, stuck her head into the room.

"Am I intruding?"

Crown looked up at her from his chair with a tense frown.

"What is it, darling?"

"I've just been up to wardrobe to try on the frock for Act One. It's above the knee. I'm sorry, Charles; I don't mind on the knee but I can't wear it like that."

"That's the way it was designed."

"But it's utterly hideous."

"I'm sure it's fine." Carlotta was a very highly strung ballerina and Crown was keeping his temper admirably. "I'll look at it on you once everyone else is in costume, darling. That's the only way to tell."

"I'm not wearing it. I absolutely refuse."

Crown exploded. "Carlotta, I'm the artistic director of this company and you'll wear a fucking *beard* if I say so! Understand?"

The door slammed behind the departing ballerina and Nadia Petrovna smiled dryly, sipping her tea.

"Very tactful, Charles."

"Don't start."

"Oh, but I meant it." She did mean it. On one of his bad days Crown would have told the girl to learn to dance before she started criticizing the rest of the creative team. "I watched part of the rehearsal upstairs when I arrived this morning," she told him. "The choreography's beautiful."

Crown nodded and shrugged. There would be time to talk about all that once the tour was up and running.

"That reminds me," the old woman said after a moment's careful thought, "do you remember, long ago, back in Paris before we went to Rotterdam, when you spent—how long was it?—at the Académie?"

"Two years."

"Yes, two years. There was another boy there at the same time; a tall fellow with blond curly hair; rather handsome and really quite talented. He may have been a few years older than you. He became a principal at the Opéra; very popular with the French fans. He's in America now, making quite a name for himself, I understand, as a choreographer . . ."

"Jacques St. Michel," Crown said, picking up the printer's invoice from Nadia Petrovna's desk to check through the figures. His strong features twisted into a scowl of derision. "Yes, I remember him very well. He was an arrogant shit, even then. I saw him give a workshop in New York when I was over there in eighty-two; thinks the sun shines out of his own arse. His choreography stinks too—although the Americans love all that surreal crap. We were deadly enemies at school." He looked up at her. "Why?"

She ran her tongue over her thin, dry lips.

"Nothing important. I think I . . . someone mentioned him, that's all."

At the end of that same long day, shortly after nine o'clock, Nadia Petrovna climbed up the stairs, step by step, to the second floor and walked into Crown's cluttered office. The busy man was sitting behind his desk surrounded by piles of disordered papers, thrashing through schedules with his head resting on his hand and a cigarette burning in an ashtray next to his elbow.

Crown frowned at her in surprise.

"What are you doing still here?"

"I've been catching up on the bookkeeping. How did your day go?"

He stood up to clear a stack of files from an armchair, throwing them on the floor so she could sit down, and shook his head. She didn't want to know.

"What was the rumpus with the apprentices?" she asked.

"Oh, that; nothing. I caught the boys smoking in their changing room."

"Well it's hardly surprising. You really shouldn't smoke in front of them, Charles."

"Why not? They should have more sense than to follow my example. They're supposed to do as I tell them, not copy me like mindless chimpanzees. You ought to get home; you can't go on staying in the office all hours like this. What time is it anyway, for Christ's sake?"

"Don't fuss," the old woman told him. She seated herself in the chair he had cleared for her and hooked her walking stick over the edge of his desk. "I have something I want to discuss with you: some news from Paris."

"Fire away."

"While I was there I found a boy for you."

"A boy?" He frowned. "Are you talking about an apprenticeship?"

"Yes."

"Okay. What age is he?"

"Sixteen."

Crown nodded and raised his eyebrows. "Alright. Sixteen's good. So when's he coming to audition? It can't be in the next ten days; I'm up to my neck in it."

"Ah. I'm afraid I have done something a little rash."

"Now, wait a moment." He held up his hand to stop her. "Don't imagine I'm going to go tearing over there to look at him. I simply haven't got time."

"No, it's not so bad as that. The fact is, Charles . . ." She folded her gnarled hands tightly together on her lap. ". . . I have offered him a place here and he has accepted."

He stared at her.

"You offered him a place? Without consulting me?" He didn't believe it. "To be my student?"

"It seemed wise. I'm not sure he would have come if I had invited him to audition. I acted on instinct."

"So who is he? Where did you find him?"

"At the Académie."

"The Académie," Crown repeated. "Alright, Nadia Petrovna, let me ask you something; why does a boy want to leave one of Europe's leading dance schools to serve an apprenticeship in a tiny, obscure company that tours number three venues in England?"

She clasped her hands together and her face glowed with pride.

"Because he has heard of you! You, my friend! He knows about your work!"

Crown closed his eyes and shook his head. That was just like her. She let herself get so carried away by enthusiasm she'd offer the moon to any idiot who had a good word to say about him or his choreography. Luckily, few praised him.

"You'd think, if I'm to sweat my balls off teaching this kid to dance, you'd at least let me have some say in the matter. If he's so great, isn't the Académie furious?"

"I never said he was good. He's grown a lot in the last year or two; I should guess as much as ten or twelve inches."

"That's tough luck," Crown said ungraciously. "He's not the first boy who's done that at his age. What does he want; to end up five-foot-two? It's no bloody advantage in this game—you can tell him that from me. What do his teachers say about him?"

It had never been Nadia Petrovna's way to mislead Crown and it didn't occur to her to start now.

"His teachers believe he's finished. They're glad to see the back of him."

Crown looked into her eyes, scrutinizing her.

"But you saw something in him, right? What was it? A strong basic technique? A special facility? He's particularly musical?" He frowned at Nadia Petrovna's unresponsive face. "Christ, has he even got feet?"

"Of course he has feet, Charles."

"You know exactly what I mean. Come on," he prompted, rotating his hand in the air impatiently. "Charisma? Style? Brains? Something!"

"I liked his face."

"Great," sighed the artistic director. "Nice face." He lit a cigarette and got up from his chair. "Okay, Nadia Petrovna, I'll take on this boy of yours for one reason and one reason only: because we desperately need the money. Six months and then if I don't like him he's out, agreed?"

Nadia Petrovna was so naturally pale that he couldn't see her blanch at his words. There was no help for it.

"Charles, I have offered him a scholarship."

Crown had started pacing the small space behind his desk. Now he stopped dead and stared at her, his cigarette hanging from the corner of his half-open mouth.

"A scholarship," he said.

"Yes, for a year."

He actually laughed, a small strangled laugh of hysteria, and then, taking his cigarette out of his mouth, he slammed his fist down on the corner of his desk so hard that the old woman's walking stick crashed to the floor. His face was like thunder.

"Are you insane? A scholarship? What fucking scholarship? We can't even afford to pay our own bloody dancers!"

"I'll find the money somewhere, Charles."

"What are we running here, some kind of charity? Why don't we set up a collection? Nadia Petrovna, you're out of your mind!"

"There are student grants he can apply for."

"No there aren't. This is a professional institution; you know that as well as I do." He sank into his seat and ran his hands over his face. "This boy of yours; does he even speak English?"

"I've no idea; we spoke only French."

"Oh, for God's sake. So what's his name?"

The old lady looked him steadily in the eye. There was a limit, she decided, to what either of them could bear.

"I'm afraid I can't recall it offhand."

2

Michel arrived at the Islington Ballet on a bright morning in late April, three weeks after the start of the company's spring season. He stopped on the pavement on the busy Goswell Road to gaze up at the front of the narrow Victorian building. On this sunny morning the windows on all three floors had been thrown wide open and a hubbub of chattering voices, laughter, and resonant piano music drifted out onto the street, mingling with the noise of the passing traffic.

Michel watched the self-assured dancers who strolled up the three stone steps beside him and in through the open door.

The atmosphere at the Islington Ballet had relaxed considerably over the past fortnight. The first performance of Charles Crown's new piece had come and gone with no disasters and the dancers were settling into the familiar routine of touring the home counties: a few days out, a few days back in the studio. This morning they breezed into the building greeting each other with boisterous good humor, exchanging gossip and updates on injuries after the weekend. No one took any notice of a solitary boy of sixteen standing on the pavement outside.

Michel's heartbeat quickened as he walked up the steps. He stood in the small lino-tiled foyer, looking around for someone who could take control of his immediate destiny. But other than the dancers who came in from the street and vanished up the stairs there was no one in sight. Both the reception desk and the untidy office behind it were deserted. At last, spotting a boy who looked around his own age, he plucked up the courage to ask for directions.

"Excuse me, please."

The boy turned to look at him, neither friendly nor unfriendly. "Yeah?"

"I'm looking for Mister Crown's class. I was sent a schedule." He held out a photocopied page to prove the truth of his claim. "I believe there's a class at ten o'clock today."

The boy looked him over with suspicion. "Si," he said, with a cursory nod toward the stairs. "Changing rooms is up there. You a new apprentice?"

"Yes."

The boy was four or five inches shorter than Michel, with shining black hair and rich brown eyes. Michel guessed, from his accent, that he was Italian. The brown eyes gave Michel another critical once-over and then he shrugged, turning away to examine a noticeboard.

"Everyone here's goin' to Charles's class. You can follow me or you can follow anyone else. It don't make no difference."

Michel thanked him, although he wasn't quite sure what he was thanking him for, and moved away toward the staircase that wound up to the floors above. As he climbed hesitantly toward the first floor the Italian's voice yelled after him up the stairs.

"Hey! You want the apprentice changing room! Is second floor, turn right, last door on the left! An' don' take the seat under the window—is mine, okay?"

The second-floor changing room was empty apart from a row of battered gray lockers and a few bags strewn on low wooden benches along the walls. Michel walked out into the corridor and back in again twice before he convinced himself he had got the right place. For the first time, he changed into practice dress for class without the restriction of a school uniform. Gone were the loathed knee-length white socks he had worn over his green all-in-one for the past seven years. Gone were the hated regulation criss-cross elastics on his ballet shoes. Gone was the detested white elastic belt—he extracted it from his bag and dropped it ceremoniously into a black-plastic-lined bin next to the shower cubicle. As he sat down on one of the low benches to pull on his shoes, adjusting the single strip of elastic that now held them in place, he felt adult and independent for the first time in his life. The unfamiliar atmosphere of the unknown building filled him with tingling optimism.

The studio wasn't hard to find: a large, airy room on the ground floor. Already it was crowded with dancers gossiping at the barres next to the open windows or stretching in yawning groups on the sunlit floor. Michel had never seen such a dazzling assortment of dancewear: woolly jumpers and leggings of every color and shape, and eccentric headgear ranging from berets to headscarves and even old tights which some of the women had pinned over their hair. He sat down on the floor, well away from the other dancers, and began to stretch, averting his eyes from the curious glances of all these strangers who seemed to know each other so well. Among the thirty or so dancers gathering in the studio he spotted the Italian boy who had given him directions in the foyer. He was leaning with both arms folded on the barre, flirting lazily with one of the girls. The boy hadn't glanced in Michel's direction even once.

Suddenly, in one coordinated movement, the assembly came to order, melting into a single row along the barres that lined three walls of the studio. Michel saw in an instant what had prompted this transformation; a short dark-haired man with hawklike features, in jeans and a black sweater, had come into the studio. The great man himself. Michel looked around in alarm; everyone seemed to have their own predetermined place at the barre. But before he could find himself standing alone and conspicuous in the center of the studio, a tall boy with a kind face caught Michel's eye and stepped backward to make space for him. Michel thanked him with a glance and slipped into the offered, vacant place.

If Charles Crown hadn't been preoccupied his sharp eyes would have instantly spotted an unfamiliar face amongst the crowd. But he was turning over the pages of a notebook with a frown and only looked up briefly, feeling the slight breeze.

"Close those windows, will you?"

A chorus of murmured protest greeted this command but the dancers obeyed him.

"You can open them again when we get to the center."

It was hard to place Crown's age. With his athletic build and strong face, radiating fierce energy, he could have been any age from thirty-five to fifty-five. But the weight of his authority was unquestionable, even to a complete stranger.

He closed his notebook.

"Right, let's do it. Pliés: two demis in second for four, two for two, one full for four, two for two, two demis in first for four, one full for four, relevé, repeat—you know the routine."

Michel's hand trembled on the barre as he followed the dancer in front of him, copying the gentle series of knee bends. He hoped no one could see his heart thumping under his sweatshirt. Crown was standing next to the piano in front of the mirrored wall drinking coffee while he chatted to the pianist.

"Okay, tendus glissés," he said, as the exercise ended. He put his cup down on the piano to mark out the beats with his hands: front, back, front, back, rond de jambe, close to fifth. And so on. All, thankfully, familiar territory to Michel.

A few bars into this exercise, the moment Michel had been dreading came. Crown's piercing eyes, sweeping along the rows of briskly sliding feet, spotted a foot he didn't recognize. His gaze froze, staring at the unknown foot for several long, painful seconds, before he looked up, straight into Michel's anxious eyes. Michel couldn't even take refuge in a defensive gesture; he was halfway through a rond de jambe with his arm stretched out in second position. Crown's eyes traveled slowly over Michel's vulnerable body, lingering on his shoulders and arms with a frown, before they returned to his working foot and then passed on to the next dancer.

When the music ended Crown singled Michel out with a nod.

"You, the new boy at the back there . . . you! Roly, give him a shove, will you, son?" The boy who had stepped back to make room for Michel touched him gently on the shoulder. "Yes, you. What's the matter with you? Don't you understand English?"

The Italian boy called across the studio, "Si, he speak English, signore; I heard him."

"Let him answer for himself, Primo." Crown walked over to Michel. "Well?"

"I am English, sir."

"Oh, you are. How long since you did class?"

Michel was acutely aware of the eyes of the whole company watching him. "Five days, sir."

"Well it shows." Crown gave Michel's shoulder a push, positioning him square to the barre, and reached up to lift his chin. "Wake up—neck and shoulders. I know it's Monday morning but that's no excuse." He walked back to the mirror. "Same goes for the rest of you."

Several bars into the next exercise Crown called to him again, snapping his fingers to attract his attention.

"You again, the new boy. Look up. Eyes on the mirror, not on the floor."

Michel made an effort to keep his eyeline raised but he had grown used, at the Académie, to being invisible. All those strange eyes, staring at him across the studio, burned into his skin like lasers.

Five minutes later Crown halted the first adage in mid-exercise, waving to the pianist to stop. His frowning eyes were fixed on Michel.

"Hold on a minute, Max. You—what the hell do you call that?"

Michel looked at him in alarm.

"Call what, sir?"

"This." He leaned over in a rough approximation of a very sloppy arabesque.

"Uh . . . arabesque croisée fondue."

"Are you trying to be funny with me?"

"No, sir."

Crown stared at him hard for a few seconds and then nodded slowly. "Alright, show me."

Michel tilted his body obediently into the arabesque. None too gently Crown pushed him into the correct position, twisting his hips and shoulders between his hands and adjusting each of his limbs.

"Okay, relax," Crown said. "How long have you been dancing?"

"Eight years, sir."

"As long as that? You're having me on. How long at the Académie?"

"Seven years." He saw Crown's eyebrows shoot up and added earnestly, "When I was twelve I took first prize in the junior section of the *Concours National de Danse*."

The company laughed good-naturedly at this boast. Michel looked down at his feet. It had been a ridiculous thing to say. Stupid. He had just wanted Crown to know he hadn't always been last in his class. A few of the dancers, who could remember what it was like to be sixteen and blurt out completely the wrong thing in front of a group of strangers, exchanged smiles of pained sympathy.

Charles Crown was laughing too.

"Did you, by God? Well you wouldn't win it now, believe me. Alright, tell me your name, son."

Michel gave his surname first, as they did in France.

"St. Michel, Jean-Baptiste, sir."

Crown had started to rub his eyes but he stopped and looked at him quickly.

"St. Michel? Really?" The black eyes scrutinized his face with sharp interest. A slow smile gradually replaced Crown's astonished frown, and it was a smile that was very far from reassuring. "Well, well, what do you know? A celebrity—a member of the French royal family of dance, no less." He turned away, back toward the mirror at the front of the studio. "Alright, St. Michel, let's see you murder my adage again, shall we?"

"Take no notice," whispered the boy behind Michel. "He's just seeing if he can wind you up; trying to embarrass you."

He had succeeded. Michel danced through the rest of the barre mortified, with his gaze riveted to the wooden floor. Although he couldn't see them, he was aware of Crown's sharp black eyes watching his every move.

Once the class moved into the center to begin floor work, Michel was completely out of his depth. The exercises were far more difficult than anything he'd encountered at the Académie, and the physical vocabulary included modern steps he'd never even heard of. But Crown was making no allowances.

"St. Michel, turn your feet out," he shouted. "Out! And get your eyes off the fucking floor! Come on, let's see what they taught you at the Académie!"

Once again, in Michel's honor, Crown stopped an exercise in mid-flow.

"What's this?" he asked, as the other dancers spiraled to a surprised halt. "Is a double pirouette beyond you, St. Michel, or is it just too much effort?"

In fairness, Crown's question was justified; Michel hadn't even attempted it, substituting a simple chassé for the turns. The artistic director saw Michel's lips move but his words were inaudible.

"I can't hear you, St. Michel. Speak louder."

"I said I can't do it, sir."

"Then do a single pirouette. But do something. Don't ever ignore a move I give you; you won't learn anything that way."

Michel felt a rush of panic as the pianist started playing again. He knew what Crown would say when he saw him attempt even a single pirouette. He simply didn't have the balance. Sure enough, after the company's second go at the exercise, Crown folded his arms.

"This is a historic moment," he told the class. "We have in our midst a dancer who not only cannot manage a simple double pirouette but who executes a single pirouette staring at the floor, wondering why it is he's about to fall over. St. Michel, show your new colleagues how not to do a pirouette."

"Charles," protested one of the women, "don't be a bugger."

"Why not?" Crown asked. "If the boy's going to be my student I need to see what he can do."

"For Christ's sake have a heart," agreed another of the girls, but Michel was beyond the solace of their sympathy. He stared fixedly at his own reflection in the mirror and executed a dangerously unstable single pirouette, putting his foot down to steady himself before he closed his feet into fifth. The company watched with sober faces. Only one girl, a very tall girl with striking green eyes, let out a shriek of laughter, clapping her hand over her mouth to smother her giggles. Michel turned scarlet.

In the final grand allegro Crown pointed at Michel, even before the music started.

"You," he said. "St. Michel. No turns in the air; I can't face it. One pirouette for each double *tour* the others do, got it?"

Michel nodded blindly, aware only that this was the last exercise. Even before the last notes of the accompaniment died away, without waiting for the traditional révérence, he snatched up his discarded sweatshirt from under the barre and fled the studio. At the door he raced past Nadia Petrovna, who had been leaning on her stick watching the class for the past twenty minutes. He didn't even see her.

In the apprentices' changing room he threw his sweatshirt on a bench, ripping off his shoes, and dashed into the single shower cubicle. When he had closed the door and pushed the bolt across he turned his face to the wall and pressed his cheek against the cold white tiles.

Mistake. Coming here. Terrible, terrible mistake.

That was all he could clearly distinguish from the muddle of misery and humiliation that spun around his mind. He turned on the taps of the shower, heedless of his stretch-cotton all-in-one, and leaned his back against the wall, closing his eyes. His sense of isolation was so deep that he literally ached with loneliness. But this at least was a feeling he recognized. Michel had developed a very efficient "off switch" for dealing with pain and he tried to operate it now. He stood very still and let the hot water stream over him, soaking his hair and clothes. Perhaps if he stood here long enough everything would simply go away.

Through the shower door he could hear the Italian and another boy conversing in low voices. Other voices, louder and distinctly adolescent, joined them. Michel couldn't understand them; too many English words jumbled together, too many years hearing nothing but French. He closed his mind to shut out the sounds and concentrated on the feeling of the hot water hitting his face. He pictured himself spending a year in this company, always an outsider, always wandering around lost in the maze of corridors that filled the building.

Gradually, one by one, the voices disappeared until at last the changing room was silent. Michel waited a couple of minutes and then turned off the taps and unlocked the door.

He wasn't alone in the changing room. On a low bench under the window his Italian acquaintance was sitting threading laces carefully into a pair of trainers. When Michel appeared he put the trainers down on the bench beside him.

There was a silence while the two boys looked at each other.

"You okay, amico?"

Michel nodded.

"Yes."

He peeled off his dripping all-in-one and dance belt, and hooked them over the end of the old-fashioned radiator. The Italian watched him in curiosity.

"Say, that ain't such a bad idea you know, showerin' in your dance gear. Save on washing. I wish I'd thought of it."

"Would you pass me my towel?"

The boy leaned over to pull a towel out of Michel's open bag and chucked it to him. Michel caught it with one hand. "Thanks."

"So how come the maestro got it in for you? What you do to make him so mad?"

Michel rubbed his towel over his wet blond curls.

"I didn't do anything. Is he always like that?"

"Pretty much. Was he like it when you auditioned?"

"I didn't audition. I met Nadia Petrovna Sekova in Paris; she invited me to come and study here."

The Italian whistled, a long, low warning whistle. His eyes widened ominously.

"Man, he ain't gonna like that! No wonder he's mad. He don't let no one interfere with his teaching. Us boys is *his* business, you know? Hey, you really won the *Concours National*? That's some serious fuckin' shit, amico; no joke."

Michel draped his towel around his neck and pulled on the bottom half of his gray tracksuit.

"It was four years ago."

"I entered that. Fell flat on my arse in the first round. Hey, you know what?" The boy's brown eyes sparkled with expressive interest. "I was watching you in class, amico. You dance like shit but you got a real ear for music—not so much as me but you got it anyway. You play piano?"

"I used to." Michel sat down to pull on his socks and shoes. "I'm not very good. Do you?"

"Sure, in my family everyone play piano. But me, I'm a dancer." He spread his arms with a wide, beaming smile. "*Il grande ballerino,* that's me. Hey, you got a girl back in Paris?"

Michel clicked his tongue, shaking his head as he leaned over to tie his shoelaces. The other boy looked dismayed.

"What? You mean you ain't even in love?"

"No."

The Italian's frown of appalled disbelief turned to one of dark suspicion.

"You ain't a fairy, are you?"

It took Michel a moment to understand the question.

"Oh. No, I don't think so."

"Then how come you ain't in love? Me, I'm always in love. You see Belinda, the girl I was talking to in class?" Michel nodded. "That's who I'm in love with. It ain't healthy you don't think about sex at your age, amico."

Michel knotted his shoelaces with a grimace that was almost a smile. He thought about it all the time.

When the last of the company had filed out of the ground-floor studio Charles Crown walked along to the front office with a typed sheet of paper in his hand. The office was empty apart from Nadia Petrovna, who was looking for a lost invoice in the secretary's in-tray.

"This had better be the last version of tomorrow's cast list," Crown said, turning on the photocopier. "If anyone else goes off injured I'll have to pull the show, not that it'd make much difference with the number of seats we've sold."

"You can't pull the show," Nadia Petrovna replied. "We couldn't possibly afford the cancellation fee."

Crown humphed under his breath. He knew that as well as she did.

The old woman watched in silence as Crown laid the cast list facedown in the photocopier and pressed the copy button. Her pale eyes followed him as he lifted the first pile of copies out of the tray and put them on a nearby desk.

"Charles, he is sixteen years old."

"Let me handle this my own way, Nadia Petrovna. If he's tough enough he'll take it. If not let him leave."

"No sixteen-year-old boy is tough."

"I bloody well was."

"No you weren't, Charles; you just pretended to be. You were vulnerable and confused, just as he is."

There was a marked silence while Crown took another stack of copies from the tray and shuffled them into a pile.

"You never told me his name," he said coldly.

Nadia Petrovna made no answer to this. She knew that Crown knew exactly why she hadn't told him.

"I don't like him," Crown said. "I don't like his attitude. He looks at you with those placid eyes but behind them he's stubborn and arrogant."

"But you admire rebels, Charles."

"I admire rebels who can dance. This one's got the technique of a twelve-year-old. Years of damage. Christ knows what's gone wrong there—it won't be the fault of his teachers; they know what they're doing at the Académie. No, somehow that boy's managed to fuck up his technique all on his own. It's too far gone to put right at this stage."

The old woman's eyes were anxious.

"But you will have a closer look at him—to make sure?"

"Obviously." He picked up his photocopies and switched off the machine. "Before I kick him out."

Nadia Petrovna was so tiny and frail it sometimes seemed a light gust of wind might blow her away. But she had a will of iron.

"Charles, you must not bully him! You must give him a chance. It's only fair."

Crown grunted at that and left the office.

The boys' changing room was L-shaped and from where Michel was sitting he couldn't see the door. It was the young Italian who saw who entered as it swung open.

"Hey, signore," he said, shooting Michel a warning glance, "you ain't allowed in here. This is private property."

Crown closed the door behind him.

"Not while you and Roly and the others go on smoking in here, it isn't."

"It weren't Roly," the boy said. "He don' smoke. It was only me an' Dan."

Crown ignored him and turned toward Michel. Michel stood up slowly and removed the towel which was still draped around his neck.

"Alright," Crown said. "Now listen carefully, St. Michel: this is how it's going to be. This is not, as I said to Nadia Petrovna, a charitable institution. You turn up late for one class, one tutorial, one rehearsal, you're out. Understand?"

Michel nodded.

"Yes, sir."

"You disobey one instruction, you're out."

"Yes, sir."

"Miss one company class: out."

Michel hesitated: "Even if I'm injured?"

"Hey!" the Italian interrupted cheekily. "You answer back, amico, you're out."

"No," Crown said, "you answer back and I thump you, and that goes for you too, Primo. If you're injured—you damage something or you have pain in any part of your body—you tell me or you tell Karl Redman, the company physio. Have you got any kind of injury now?"

Michel was wildly tempted to invent one on the spur of the moment but he shook his head reluctantly.

"No, sir."

"Right." Crown glanced at his watch. "Primo here will tell you the rules. You do classical classes with the company when they aren't away on tour, and we fit in other classes—contemporary, pas de deux, allegro, whatever—where we can. The rest of the time you watch rehearsals or work on your own if there's a free studio, which there generally isn't. You go to acrobatics and eurhythmics classes in Covent Garden: no other outside classes without my permission. No dangerous sports, no football, no rugby, no skateboarding, et cetera. Fencing class on Tuesday evening is compulsory for boys. See Karl on Wednesday morning; tell him I want a complete physical and X-rays, details of past injuries, allergies, and so on. Ask him to arrange a BCG for you if you haven't had one. See Anita in wardrobe about shoes, though you'll have to make them last; she's got better things to do with her budget than waste it on apprentices. I'm too busy to deal with you now—I've got rehearsals and performances all week—but I'll try and sort out a tutor for you before the weekend, so keep an eye on the board. Got all that?"

Michel wasn't sure he'd got any of it but he nodded.

"Yes, sir."

"So this is it. I'll give you until the start of the company's summer break in August to convince me I'm not wasting my time."

Michel felt himself coloring; he could think of no response. Crown cast his eyes disparagingly over Michel's skinny naked chest and shoulders.

"And I'll level with you, St. Michel, I'm going to take some convincing."

"Yes, sir."

Crown frowned. "Look, what's with this sir thing?" he asked, irritated. "What did you call your teachers in Paris?"

"Monsieur."

"All of them?"

"Or Madame."

"Well, I hate that kind of shit. As long as you're here you call me Charles, understand?"

Michel looked down at him without expression. He moistened his lips slowly before he answered.

"Yes, sir."

Crown's piercing black eyes narrowed sharply. For several seconds neither of them moved. From his seat beneath the window Primo was watching them both, his brown eyes moving attentively between the two of them.

"Alright, St. Michel," Crown said at last, "we can play it that way if you like. But I warn you, I'll win. I'm a lot more experienced at that kind of game than you. Don't fuck with me, son. This isn't the Académie where your name entitles you to special privileges. You can change your name to Nijinsky for all I care, and it won't make a damn's worth of difference if you cross me." He folded his arms. "By the way, what is your relationship to Jacques?"

"Jacques?"

"I'm talking about Jacques St. Michel, the choreographer."

"Yes, I know who he is," Michel said. "Every student at the Académie knows who he is. I've never met him. He's no relation to me."

Crown's intelligent gaze passed slowly over Michel's distinctive mousy blond curls. And those all-too-familiar gray eyes. Michel could see the dislike in the dark eyes that scrutinized him.

"Alright," Crown said, with a single nod of his head. "So he's no relation. We'll leave it at that. So who are your next of kin?"

"Next of . . . ?" Michel didn't understand.

"Your family. I'll need an address for them."

Crown was extremely adept at reading body language—especially adolescent body language. His sharp eyes took in Michel's uneasy shift of posture as he answered.

"My mother lives in Devon, sir. I'll look up the postal address and bring it tomorrow. I've got an uncle in London too. You . . . won't need an address for him, will you?"

"What about your father?"

"I don't have a father," he said.

Crown nodded, accepting that.

"Alright. As I said, the August break. That's a little under four months. And let me make it very clear to you, St. Michel, you're free to leave at any time. All you've got to do is pick up your bag and walk out." He gave Michel's puny chest another contemptuous glance as he moved toward the door. "It's time you did something about that body. If you're still here in a week's time we'll get you started in the gym. In the meantime I want you to swim. Primo will show you where the local pool is."

"Bad luck, amico," his new friend commiserated. "An' just when you thought it was all going to be a piece of cake."

Crown turned to frown at him from the doorway.

"Come to think of it, it wouldn't do you any harm either, Primo. Thirty lengths, the pair of you, every morning before class. And I mean thirty lengths each."

The Italian looked horrified.

"I can't swim, signore."

"Then learn," said the artistic director.

When he had gone, closing the door behind him, Primo shook his head mournfully at Michel.

"Now look what you done, amico."

"Sorry," Michel told him. But he had problems of his own. He sat down on the bench and rested his head against the wall, closing his eyes. Somehow he was going to have to survive this. He had burned his bridges at the Académie and no other school would take him, especially as he couldn't pay. But the thought of four months in this terrible place, or even four days, was almost more than he could bear.

"Hey," Primo said, jumping cheerfully to his feet, "you're gonna need a locker." He opened several gray lockers, screwing up his nose at each in turn. "Here, have this one; is the one next to mine. Just let me clear out this junk."

Michel watched him as he started tossing old ballet shoes, crisp packets, and bits of paper over his shoulder.

"What did he mean about sorting out a tutu for me?" he asked him. Michel didn't like the sound of that at all.

"Man, not a tutu—a tutor. We get like private coaching. Is usually from one of the injured dancers who ain't on tour. My tutor's Marcus. Marcus is okay; him an' me got the same sense of humor." He pulled a dance belt out of the locker and held it up in surprise. "Hey, this jockstrap's mine! I was wonderin' where that got to." He threw it in his own locker and continued his excavation of the locker next door. "Anyhow, Marcus has got hyperextended knees too, which is a comfort."

Primo arranged his feet in first position with his hand resting on the open door of the locker for support. His locked knees bent backward like a horse's knees. He looked down at them, pulling a comical, tragic face.

"Tough luck, eh? You got Charles on your back an' I got these. You wanna swap?"

"I wouldn't mind," Michel said.

"Is my dad's fault; I inherited them from him." Primo frowned at Michel in sudden curiosity, forgetting about his knees. "Hey, amico, tell me something, yeah? Was you lyin' to the maestro when you said you ain't got no father?"

Michel pulled the top of his gray tracksuit over his head, vanishing underneath it. He looked at him as his eyes appeared through the neck hole, and pushed his arms through the sleeves with a shrug.

"Maybe."

3

MICHEL HAD NEVER ADMITTED to anyone that he had no recollection of his father. As a child he hadn't even known he had a father, nor ever wondered why he was the only child in the Devonshire village without one. The first time it dawned on him there was something important missing from his life was when he was eight years old, the day his mother had come in from collecting the post with a tense face.

"Michel, do you remember Papa?"

He remembered the anxiety in her eyes as she asked the question. It was late spring and she was standing in the farmhouse kitchen wearing a floral-print pinafore dress, her dark fringe hanging low over her forehead. Early morning sunshine was pouring through the open kitchen windows. Michel had been wolfing down his breakfast, in a hurry to meet his friends on the way to school, but now his cornflakes lay forgotten in the bowl, his spoon suspended in midair in front of his open mouth.

"Don't you remember him at all?"

When he slowly shook his head Caroline Eastleigh sat down at the long pine table. "Haven't you ever wondered why your surname isn't the same as mine? We all lived together, the three of us, in a very small cottage—it was old, made of stone, and the windows leaked—near a city called Paris. You used to run down to the gate to watch the trains go across the road. And we had a cat called Petipa. I'm sure you can remember if you try. It wasn't very long ago."

But four short years for Carrie had been half a lifetime for Michel. He laid down his spoon and screwed his eyes tight shut, trying to recall a time before he had lived here in Devon. His mind was so full of the present it seemed his whole life had taken place between this farmhouse and the local junior school in the village.

He remembered fields, darker than the chalky fields in Devon, and gray flagstones that turned black when it rained. And grapes; purple grapes that hung down from the wall and were fun to squash with your fingers. He thought he could remember the cat—a thin tabby with sharp claws—but there were so many cats in his life; Mrs. Dean at the post office had five and there were two right here in the barn.

He chased the image of a tall man around his mind. There had definitely been a man; Michel sensed his presence in every corner of the cottage that presented itself to his struggling memory. Yet every time he thought he could picture him the man slipped out of focus, remaining as a vague, uneasy shadow just outside his field of vision.

"No," he said, opening his eyes, "I don't remember him."

"It doesn't matter. He's written you a letter; look."

Carrie forced herself to smile as she handed the letter to him across the table, but her green eyes were apprehensive.

"What does it say?"

"I haven't read it. It's addressed to you, not me."

Michel took the blue airmail envelope in his hands and looked down at it, mystified, running his fingers over the unfamiliar stamp. His father meant no more than that to him; a new stamp for his collection. His lips moved slowly as he studied the postmark, spelling out each letter to himself.

"Los Angeles; that's in America," he informed her knowledgeably. "Why did he write to me?"

"I don't know. Probably because you're his son."

He held out the unopened letter to her.

"Will you read it to me?"

"No, Michel, you're not a baby. Try and read it yourself; I'll help you with the difficult words."

Obediently he opened the envelope and pulled out the single sheet of blue paper. He stared at the first few words, furrowing his brow in concentration and sucking his soft lower lip entirely into his mouth. After a few seconds he cast his eyes quickly over the rest and refolded the letter, tucking it back into the envelope with a casual shrug.

"It doesn't say much."

Carrie reached across the table to take it from him and looked at it herself.

"Oh, it's in French! I'll read it for you and tell you what it says." Her fingers folded and unfolded the corner of the paper as she started to read the handwriting which had given her such a violent shock when she saw it in the postbox beside the gate. "*'Dear Jean-Baptiste,'* he says—that's because he doesn't know we call you Michel—*'by now you must be eight years old and a very big boy. When I was your age I went to dance school in Paris. If you . . . want . . .'*" Carrie's voice trailed away as she read the rest of the sentence to herself. Her eyes filled with rage. She read on, translating hurriedly.

"*'If you want to be a dancer or a choreographer like me you must go to school like I did. I will write to my friend Henri at the Académie and ask him to look at you. I am becoming famous now; has she told you?'*" Carrie repeated the word in disbelieving fury—"She!"—and muttered through the rest: "*'I will pay for you to go to school. Be good. From Jacques.'* That's all, Michel." She folded the letter quickly and put it back in the envelope.

Michel stared at her. There were tears of anger in her eyes.

"What does it mean?"

"Nothing!" she cried. "It means nothing!" For once, the bitterness she always hid so well erupted from her in a burst of passion. Four years without a word or a sign and now this. This! And addressed to Michel instead of her! "He's being cruel, Michel. Cruel and spiteful. He's trying to take you away from me. You wouldn't want that, would you?"

Michel's eyes widened in alarm.

"No." The idea terrified him; his mother was his whole world. He got down from his chair and ran to her side. He was small for his age and his head barely reached her shoulder as she sat there with the letter crushed in her fist. "He can't make me go away, can he?"

"No, of course he can't." Carrie reined her emotions in quickly, wiping away the tears from beneath her made-up eyes. It was her day for giving piano lessons at the college in Exeter and she couldn't afford to go looking like a panda. "Of course not." She straightened his school tie with an artificially merry smile. "What a silly idea. Imagine if you went away when you've just started learning the Chopin, and we've only just bought your new school uniform; you haven't even grown into it yet."

Michel looked doubtfully into her eyes. He was too young to have any notion of the heartbreak and disillusionment that had ended his mother's early love affair, but he sensed the anguish his father's letter had aroused in her.

"Let's throw the letter away, shall we?" he asked earnestly.

She looked down at the crumpled letter as though tempted to thrust it into the stove, but after a moment she handed it to him.

"No, keep it, Michel. Put it away somewhere safe and forget about it. When you grow up you might be glad to have it."

Michel took it upstairs to his bedroom and buried it in the bottom drawer of his wardrobe under his winter jumpers. When he came downstairs again Carrie was humming cheerfully over the washing up.

That night when he should have been asleep he heard her sobbing in her bedroom. The lights upstairs were all off and he stood in the dark on the landing and listened to her cry. His helpless gray eyes scanned the dark surface of her closed door as he stood there in his pajamas. Eventually he went back to his room, walking softly across the floorboards in his bare feet, and opened the drawer of his wardrobe to look at the letter again in the dim light from his bedroom window.

In the weeks following the arrival of Jacques St. Michel's letter Carrie saw with perturbed eyes the gradual change that came over her son. His sunny smile grew more hesitant, and his keen interest in everything around him dulled to the point where he no longer even looked up in excitement when Concorde flew overhead. Carrie saw how his gaze followed his school friends when their fathers came to collect them at the school gate—and how he stood alone on the village green instead of playing with the other children, and watched the boys kicking footballs with their fathers. She heard him playing imaginary games in his bedroom, where it was always "Papa's turn next," and "Papa says I have to go now."

"Talk to him about it," advised Michel's schoolteacher, Margery, when Carrie consulted her. "Don't let it turn into one of those awful things that isn't mentioned between you or he'll think about it all the more."

But Carrie didn't know how to broach it with him. The subject was fraught with emotional difficulty, and her world, for the past four years, had been a brisk, practical one. If she secretly dwelled on her betrayal by the man for whom she had thrown away both her independence and a promising musical career, she hid those feelings firmly from herself and everyone around her, and concentrated instead on the details of her life as a busy working mother, hoping Michel's preoccupation with his father would fade of its own accord in time.

When he was older, Michel had no recollection of what went through his mind during the weeks after his father's letter came. All he could remember was the shock in his mother's eyes when he came home from school one day almost two months later and informed her, "I've decided I'm going to Paris to be a dancer."

She dropped her pen on the table where she was busy correcting students' music tests, and stared at him.

"You can't."

"Why not? Daddy says I can."

"Daddy? What do you mean Daddy? What have your school friends been saying to you?"

Michel's friends had, in fact, said nothing at all; he had simply put two and two together.

"Why can't I go to Paris if my father says I can?"

"Because it's not up to him. He's not the one who's bringing you up. You don't even know what it would mean. You'd have to go a long way away and not see me for months at a time; you'd be terribly homesick." She got up from the table and started clearing things away noisily from the draining board beside the sink. "Besides, you wouldn't be any good at dancing, Michel. You aren't a very graceful little boy."

"But I want to."

"No you don't. You just think you do. Now, I don't want to discuss the idea anymore. Go upstairs and change out of your school uniform."

Later, when Michel was sitting at the kitchen table making fork-shaped holes in the crust of his shepherd's pie, he asked her, "Why doesn't Papa live with us?"

Carrie's mouth twitched as she washed up the pie dish. She was a small woman with a full, soft mouth like a child's, and clear, intelligent eyes.

"Because he wanted something different from living with me and bringing up a family, that's all. Jacques wanted to go to America and do his dancing and I wanted . . ." She looked determinedly out of the kitchen window. "I wanted to come and live here with you on my brother's farm and teach the piano."

"Why didn't he want a family?"

Carrie turned her head to look at him. She was awkward in expressing her love for him but she wasn't insensitive.

"It wasn't your fault, Michel. You mustn't think he went away because of you. That's not the reason."

Michel's innocent eyes looked into hers hopefully.

"Did he like me?"

"Of course he did. Of course he liked you."

"Would he like me better if I was a dancer?"

"No, if he saw you he'd like you just the way you are. You wouldn't want to be a dancer. You'd have to give up too much for it: far too much. And you'd have to go around wearing tights; I don't think you'd like that, would you?"

Michel screwed up his nose doubtfully at this revelation.

"Tights? Like a girl?"

She nodded soberly.

"What kind of dancing is it?" he asked, realizing he hadn't quite thought his plan through. "How can a boy be a dancer when he grows up?"

Carrie thought of something that should cure his fascination for the subject permanently, and she laughed, ruffling his hair as she stood up.

"I tell you what, come with me tomorrow morning when I go and play for Mrs. Baldwin's ballet class. You can join in, then you'll see for yourself."

Michel watched her uncertainly as she went to finish the washing up.

"I won't have to wear tights, will I?"

"No, not this once."

"Promise?"

"Promise."

Carrie was right in guessing the ballet class wouldn't be to Michel's taste. His face was pink with disgust as they walked home from the village the following morning.

"Didn't you like it?" she asked.

"It was stupid. It was all girls." Michel was fiercely anti-girls. "I was the only boy there. I felt like a twit."

She laughed at his vehemence.

"Did you like Mrs. Baldwin?"

"No. She's fat and sweaty and she goes up really close to you and squashes her bosoms against you on purpose when she leans over you. And her breath smells."

"You shouldn't talk that way about anyone," Carrie reproved him, although she had to admit his description was an apt one. "So what did she teach you then? I couldn't see you from the piano."

He stopped walking and held on to the railings outside the post office while he showed her, very matter-of-factly, the five positions he had been taught by Mrs. Baldwin. Carrie watched as he waved his arm like a bored traffic policeman.

"See?" he said. "It's really drippy stuff. That's why girls like it."

She let him hold her hand as they continued walking down the street toward the lane.

"So you don't want to come again next week then?"

"No." He shrugged dejectedly. "But I have to. Otherwise I won't be ready to go to school in Paris."

Carrie stopped dead on the pavement and put her hands to her head.

Michel's obsession might have lacked the force of an adult passion but his tenacity was incredible. When Carrie told him she could no longer afford the fifty pence for the Saturday ballet class he went out and earned the money for himself washing cars in the village. When she said there'd be no more ice cream until he stopped talking about Paris, he said he didn't think ice cream was good for dancers anyway. She told him he obviously didn't love her anymore and he locked himself in the barn, shouting that she was right and she didn't love him either. She sent him to his room in disgrace— and sat gazing at the kitchen ceiling in despair with her hands over her ears while he practiced jumping in fifth position in his bedroom above.

Week by week Michel wore his mother down.

At last, in sheer desperation, she took him to Bath to see the Royal Ballet's tour of *Swan Lake*; praying that three hours of swaying tutus would bore him out of his mania. Michel sat through the whole ballet with his mouth open in awed delight, his soft eyes shining with the magic of it, away in a wonderful world of make-believe. Carrie watched him, expressionless. She could feel him slipping away from her.

When Uncle Jim drove down from London for the weekend Michel lay awake in his bed in the little orchard room, listening. Carrie often put him to bed early when her brother was coming on a Friday evening. In the kitchen downstairs he could hear the rise and fall of their voices as they argued. Michel heard his uncle's chair scrape against the stone-tiled floor.

"Is this about you? Is this some scheme to drag that monster back into your life?"

"Shh. He's sleeping above us; he'll hear you." Carrie's voice was muted but crystal clear. "That's not the reason. You know it."

"Do I? Why then? What can it possibly do but harm the boy?"

"He's set his heart on it. I'm not going to stop him doing what he wants the way you tried to stop me when I wanted to go to music college."

"I was doing what I thought was best. And anyway, that was different; you were seventeen years old. He's only eight. Besides, I was right to try and stop you, wasn't I? Look what came of it. Caroline, the man walked out on you with no warning, no explanation, leaving you penniless in a crumbling hovel with a four-year-old brat; when will you acknowledge that? If I hadn't come over to France and bailed you out you would have starved."

"Jim, please don't drink any more."

Michel heard the clink of a bottle against glass. It was always a bad sign when his uncle started on the subject of how much Carrie owed him. James Eastleigh was a bitter, disillusioned man. A remnant of a faded rural gentry the modern world had no use for, he ran an antiques business with his partner in London. He was fifteen years older than his sister, and her only close relative since their parents' early death.

"Do you realize," he said, "how much damage it will do to the boy if you let that man drive a wedge into his affections? Or are you still so infatuated that you—"

"I hate him," Carrie interrupted. "I hate him, do you hear me? I hate him for what he did to me and I hate him for what he's doing to Michel now."

"Then stop him doing it. He has no rights over him. Exert your authority. Don't let the child tell you how to run your life."

"He's not trying to run my life. He's trying to run his own."

"He's educationally retarded, for God's sake. He's barely capable of writing his own name, much less making a major decision about his own future. And what happens to you once he's off your hands, eh? You pick up your career where it left off, I suppose."

"Don't you dare suggest I don't love my son," Carrie said savagely. "D'you think I'd even consider letting him go if I didn't know for a fact he'll be on the phone to me within a week screaming blue murder to come home?"

"And what if he doesn't? What if he wants to stay?"

"He won't; I know him. He can't even bear to be away from home for a night. He'd be miserable; he'd miss me and he'd miss his piano lessons—I'm teaching him the Chopin études. He'd be devastated by homesickness."

"Then why let him go at all?"

"Because I won't let him grow up thinking I kept his father from him!"

There was a pause while the bottle clinked again, and Carrie remonstrated, "Jim . . . remember what the doctor told you."

When Jim spoke again his voice was lower.

"Look, has it occurred to you that if you tried showing him a bit more affection he might not feel the need to go rushing off to Paris to look for his father? He's going to be bloody disappointed, that's all I can say. Why send him off on a wild-goose chase? You're all he's got; he may as well face up to that."

"He's all I've got too," she said. "And at the moment he isn't mine. I know he's going to be disappointed but I want my son back, Jim."

There was a firm clunk as Jim thumped his whiskey glass down on the table.

"And you think sending him to school on the other side of the Channel is the way to achieve that? Carrie, listen to me! If you send that child to school in Paris you will *destroy* him."

"Don't talk nonsense."

"You think I'm wrong?"

"I know you are. He'll come home a little wiser, that's all."

For a while neither of them spoke. Eventually Michel heard his uncle sigh.

"Listen, why not just give it up, Carrie? Put your foot down; tell the kid to quit whining. I'll play the heavy uncle, give him what Daddy used to call a damn good thrashing, and that'll be an end of it."

Michel's eyes opened wide in the darkness of his bedroom. His uncle's belt was more terrifying even than his mother's tears.

"Don't you touch him!" she said fiercely. "He's my son, not yours."

"Thank goodness." Jim sipped his drink with a short, exasperated laugh. "Ballet. Honestly, do you want him to grow up into another Jacques St. Michel? It wouldn't surprise me. The little bastard's already the spitting image of the bastard that fathered him."

There was a pause before Carrie spoke.

"He does look like Jacques," she said quietly, "although he's got my mouth. But thank heaven he's got something of his own as well because, God only knows, he's going to need it."

The Académie audition at the Guildhall in London was nerve-racking. There were nine other boys there, all older and far more advanced in ballet—the Académie took very few children under the age of eleven. Michel performed his simple exercises at the barre: the five positions, pliés, and tendus. He was examined by a doctor, pushed and prodded in all sorts of uncomfortable places. The Académie teachers, who spoke only French, talked him over amongst themselves, shaking their heads with dubious faces. But at the end of the morning, when he traveled back to Paddington with Carrie on the tube, he clung to her hand, victorious.

"Will you write to Papa and tell him I got accepted?"

Carrie coldly withdrew her hand from his.

"No, Michel, the teachers at the Académie will tell him. They know he'll be paying your fees and board."

Michel was petrified—literally shaking—as he walked beside her along the platform at Charing Cross six weeks later. He put his hand into the hand of the waiting chaperone and looked at Carrie with a white, tear-stained face.

"Don't be silly," she said crisply. She was determined not to let him see her cry. "You're only going to France. Go along and don't make a fuss. You can come home anytime you want, I've told you."

As he let himself be dragged away by the chaperone to their seats at the front of the train he turned his head, craning his neck to look back at his mother. But she had already turned around and was hurrying away along the platform toward the ticket office.

The first shock awaiting Michel when he arrived in Paris was that he couldn't communicate with anyone—not with the master who ran the boys' boardinghouse. Not with the other children. Not with the teachers or the housekeeper or the dinner ladies. He was stranded on a linguistic island of his own. During the first few days, as he followed the other infants through the daunting labyrinth of corridors, he sometimes heard other students speaking English. But they were fully fledged juniors; they didn't mix with children his age.

At night, in the infants' dormitory, he lay in his bunk bed and sobbed quietly into his pillow. The boy in the bunk beneath him kicked the bottom of his mattress whispering—

"Eh, Michel, *qu'est-ce que t'as?*"

Michel didn't answer. He didn't understand. He pulled the bedclothes over his head and continued to cry.

At the end of a week, just as Carrie had predicted, he was so homesick he was ready to ask the alarming director of the school to phone his mother and tell her to come and collect him.

Madame de Sancerre wasn't in her office when he knocked so he stood under the dome in the foyer and waited for her, looking at the big black-and-white photographs that decorated the marble walls. He gazed up forlornly at a photo of twenty-four ladies—he counted them—all perfectly aligned in arabesque. There was only one male figure in the picture, beautifully stretched in a wonderful leap. The school's principal male teacher, Henri Renoir, came and laid a hand on Michel's shoulder, looking at the picture with him.

"Is *magnifique,* yes? You like to dance like that, *mon petit?*"

Michel just stared at the picture sadly. Monsieur Henri tapped his finger on the image of the flying man in the middle of the picture.

"*C'est ton père,* Michel—Is your fazzer."

Michel twisted his neck to look up at his teacher wide-eyed.

"My father?"

Henri clicked his tongue and nodded; "*Oui*. Is a great man. He study here. You 'ave to work very 'ard you want he is proud of you. He will come to Paris wiz 'is *companie* in ze spring; maybe 'e come see you zen, eh?" The tall man looked down at Michel and winked. "He write me— ask I 'ave my eye on you. But don' tell ze ozzers, *hein*?"

Michel pointed to another photograph.

"Is that him too?"

"No, is Nureyev. But here . . ." He indicated another picture; a masked man and woman dancing. "Zat is Jacques. And also here."

Michel gazed at the photographs in awe. Monsieur Henri looked down at him with a quizzical frown.

"What you do down 'ere, Michel? Is class time, yes?"

"Yes, sir," Michel said, backing away slowly with his eyes glued to the photographs of his father. Everything had changed. "I'm going, Monsieur."

He turned around and sprinted off toward his ballet class.

Once his homesickness vanished, Michel was quickly accepted by the small group of nine- and ten-year-old boys at the Académie. They couldn't speak to him but they communicated on a more basic level. They ran around together screaming in the infants' playground. They giggled together in the changing room over the appearance in their lives of the dance belt, an item of apparel none of them had ever encountered before.

Very soon he was not only laughing with the other boys but chatting to them as well. In fact, French had been his first language, although he had buried it deeply along with his other memories of his first few years. Now it came springing back to his tongue in a matter of weeks.

The boys at the Académie were mostly French: little Parisian boys whose wealthy parents had apartments overlooking the Seine. For most, enrollment at the Académie was merely a manifestation of their mothers' frustrated childhood dreams. They cared very little about ballet. They enjoyed the exercise. Some enjoyed the competition. A few remained faithful to their parents' dreams, staying in dance all their lives, but the majority plodded reluctantly through daily classes only to slip away at twelve or thirteen to normal schools. Michel alone was a boy with a mission.

Day after day he slogged away at his dancing, chewing his lower lip in concentration as he struggled to master the rudiments of classical technique. Since the life-changing discovery that his father was a god not merely in his own eyes but in the eyes of the whole world, his attention was focused on one thing only: his father's visit to Paris in the spring.

Michel worked with such determination that he very quickly overtook all the other boys of his age; even those who had been dancing for years. It was the first time he had ever been good at anything and, from a feeling of shy humility, he soared to an extraordinary level of arrogance. His teachers fostered his conceit. He was a perfect little carbon copy of his gifted papa. No one cared that he was far behind all the other children in the rest of his education. This was a ballet school. Here only one thing mattered.

When Michel went home for Christmas he was full of the excitement of his new life. He had blossomed, in the few months of his absence, into a confident, bright-eyed chatterbox. He didn't see how his mother's hopeful smile of welcome faded into bleak expressionlessness as he launched, at the station, into a stream of enthusiastic babble about the Académie.

Carrie let him chatter on about his teachers and his friends, interrupting only occasionally to remind him to speak in English. He failed to notice how tense her eyes were as she pottered around the kitchen with saucepans and potatoes, listening to him. Nor did he notice that her mouth became firmly pinched whenever he talked about Papa's eagerly awaited visit in the spring.

On Christmas Eve Uncle Jim shut up his antiques shop in Camden and drove down to Devon through the rain. He brought his partner, Toby, with him. Michel liked Toby, he was quiet and kind, but he had always been a little wary of his uncle. On the evening they arrived Jim sat in an armchair by the open fire with a glass of whisky at his elbow and beckoned to Michel.

"Come here. Let's have a look at you."

Michel rubbed the end of his nose with his fingers and went to stand shyly in front of him—no nearer than was absolutely necessary. Jim had once been lean and handsome but now his face was bloated from too much whisky, and his light brown hair, which flopped over his forehead in a long fringe, was turning prematurely gray. He reached out and took

Michel's face in his hand, examining him with a languid smile. Jim was never completely sober.

"You still look like a girl."

Michel shrugged his shoulders. With his blond curls and full mouth people often mistook him for a girl, especially here in England where they thought his name was Michelle.

"I can't help it," he said apologetically.

"No more you can," said his uncle, releasing his face and sipping his whisky. "Well I daresay that'll change as you get older. So you're enjoying Paris, eh? Not fed up yet?"

"No, I like it. I'm working very hard. I have to be ready for my father when he comes to see me in April. I don't want him to be ashamed of me."

Jim looked gravely at his sister.

"I see," he said. "And what if he doesn't come? What if he's too busy to see you? Have you thought of that?"

"Oh, he'll definitely come," Michel said with confidence. "He has to; I'm his son."

"And what about me?" Carrie demanded, losing patience at last. "Aren't you my son, too? Why do you talk and talk about him? He's done nothing for you!"

"I'm his son," Michel repeated stubbornly, and then he closed his mouth tightly and didn't mention his father again.

On the train back to Dover, at the end of the Christmas holidays, Michel was miserably homesick again. He wanted his mother and he wanted his safe little bedroom in the wonky old Tudor farmhouse. But within a few hours of arriving in Paris he was sucked back into the language and the environment and the circle of friends which had become so familiar to him. He put out of his mind the sadness he had seen in his mother's eyes on the platform at Charing Cross. April was only three months away and suddenly the time seemed very short.

The fervor with which Michel threw himself back into his dance classes was so intense that his teachers grew alarmed and tried to persuade him not to push himself so hard. His popularity among his classmates dwindled; competitiveness was acceptable but no one liked a teacher's pet. Michel worked on undaunted. Only one person's approval mattered.

In the third week of April the Los Angeles Festival Ballet came to Paris for a fortnight of performances. And with them came their new choreographer, the rising star, Jacques St. Michel.

Michel spent the entire two weeks in a state of feverish excitement, unable to eat, refusing to venture out into the playground with the other boys in case his father sent for him during the lunch hour. When the Los Angeles Festival Ballet returned to America at the end of a fortnight without the long-expected visit from Jacques St. Michel, Monsieur Henri sought Michel out in the infants' schoolroom.

"Are you very disappointed, little one?"

Michel's face was pale as he raised it from his folded arms on the desk. But it was pale with relief.

"I wasn't ready," he said. "I knew I wasn't ready, Monsieur." He smiled despite his pallor. "Now I've got a whole year to get better at my barre before he sees me."

Henri Renoir laughed and shook his head.

"I never saw a child your age who could focus on an event a month away, let alone a year. You're a single-minded little fellow, Michel, I'll say that for you. That's important for a dancer."

A month later Michel was promoted to the ten-year-olds' class. And a few weeks before his tenth birthday he was promoted again to dance with the eleven-year-olds. When, the following spring, Jacques St. Michel came again to Paris without finding time to contact his son, Michel sat blank-faced in his dormitory, hearing nothing and responding to nothing, for an entire afternoon. But the next day he was back at the barre, hurling himself back into his dancing with even greater determination. There would be a good reason why the choreographer had been too busy to leave his company for as long as it took to drop in at the Académie. He might be training up an urgent replacement for an injured dancer, or even in the middle of creating a new ballet. Whatever it was, it was a good reason. Next year he would come for certain.

The following year Jacques stayed behind in America when his company came to France. And the year after that the company made only a whirlwind two-night stop in Paris before moving on to Lyon and then Toulouse. Michel worked on patiently, trusting in the relationship that made the younger boys look at him with awe and his teachers treat him with special favor. His father's name had made him a celebrity at the Académie.

While he was still twelve years old Michel won first prize in the junior section of the prestigious *Concours National de Danse.* The school talked about nothing else for days. He wrote a letter to his father, slowly and painstakingly, telling him the good news. In reply he received only a kind note in English from the secretary of the Los Angeles Festival Ballet, enclosing an international check for a hundred francs. He also wrote to his mother asking if he could stay in Paris for the summer to attend a series of dance workshops, although he had already stayed in Paris for Christmas and had spent most of the previous summer with a friend's family in the south of France. Over the years he had been in Paris, Devon had come to seem more and more distant.

Rather than let an entire summer go by without seeing him, Carrie traveled to France herself and arranged to spend five days with him by the sea in Brittany, but their time together wasn't a success. Between Carrie's antipathy toward the ballet school and his father, and Michel's stubborn refusal to hear either of them criticized, the five days were filled alternately with sharp conflict and long, awkward silences. The next Christmas, when Michel again asked her if he might remain in Paris for the holiday, Carrie replied that as far as she was concerned he could do as he pleased.

Michel had once enjoyed every moment of his dance classes at the Académie—always pushing himself to jump a little higher, to stretch his feet a little farther, to catch that one extra beat on an entrechat. But when the Los Angeles Festival Ballet came to Paris for the fifth year running without a call or a visit or a single word of acknowledgment from his father, he lost heart. The child who had once been the soaring butterfly of the Académie retreated into a motionless chrysalis. Michel simply gave up trying. There no longer seemed any point.

4

THE QUALITY OF THE FILTERED COFFEE in the common room at the Islington Ballet was the first encouraging sign to temper Michel's bleak view of his new surroundings. The dancers in the impoverished little company would put up with scenery that was recycled from production to production, cramped studios and scant wages, second-, third-, fourth-hand costumes dyed for the umpteenth time and covered in patches, but they drew the line at Maxwell House.

The dancers' common room was, strictly speaking, off-limits to the apprentices. They had their own little den on the second floor decked out with blue carpet tiles and orange plastic chairs. But the second-floor den was the exclusive property of the girls; the boys preferred to risk Crown's wrath in the company common room rather than trespass on the female territory upstairs.

Charles Crown's savage treatment of Michel on his first day had one consoling outcome: Michel was an immediate favorite with the company women.

"Don't you listen to him, duck," said a girl in a purple headscarf and long false eyelashes, laying a sympathetic hand on Michel's knee. "He's just being a tosser."

"He's a moody old bugger," agreed another.

Of course they all wanted to know what relation he was to Jacques St. Michel.

"Nah, he ain't a relative," Primo butted in, answering for him. 'Cept for maybe a, like, fourth cousin twelve times removed or somethin' what Michel don't know about." He dragged Michel away toward the coffee machine. "You just bin talkin' to rumor control, amico. You want anythin' spread round the whole company, that's who you talk to: Janine an' Chloe."

There were only twenty-three dancers in the company, including the walking wounded who spent the day lounging in the common room wallowing in self-pity, but it seemed a vast multitude to Michel as he sat beside Primo in the main studio watching rehearsals. Each time Primo pointed out a dancer, giving him the lowdown on their company status and sexual indiscretions, Michel instantly lost sight of them again amongst the Lycra-clad throng.

The studio was buzzing with activity. Some of the soloists were rehearsing with the ballet master while others practiced sections of choreography on their own or in groups, and the majority of the girls' corps sat on the floor around the edges of the studio stitching their pointe shoes.

In addition to the men in the company there were four male apprentices.

"Five now," Primo told him, "an' seven girls, only Heidi got shin splints an' Lucy mostly goes on tour with the company, which leaves five." He smiled at Michel and his brown eyebrows rose suggestively. "One each, amico."

The two older boys strolled into the studio. They were already in the second year of their apprenticeship and consequently too lofty to talk to the first-year boys.

"They reckon they're big shots," Primo whispered to Michel. "You watch Daniel over there. That boy ain't never walked past a mirror in his life without stopping to admire himself." Right on cue the Oriental-looking boy turned to smooth his sleek black fringe in the mirror. Primo snorted with laughter. "Ain't so fuckin' much to admire neither," he added nastily.

Michel sipped his coffee, watching as one of the men—a slim, muscular dancer with peroxide-blond spiky hair—executed a superb series of turns in one of the sunny spots on the far side of the studio. He wound up his turns with a deep curtsy and a ladylike flutter of his eyelashes.

"That's Marcus," Primo said. "You know, our tutor? Most likely he'll be your tutor too."

"I thought you said the tutors were dancers who were injured. He doesn't look very injured to me."

"Yeah, I ain't sure what his injury is; he don't talk about it. He ain't been on tour for months." He screwed up his nose in disdain. "Daniel heard from someone it was a nervous breakdown but me an' Roly reckon that's bull."

Michel watched the bleached-blond man chatting and joking with the tall apprentice called Roly. Really, Michel thought, he wouldn't mind having Marcus for a tutor. But on the whole, his future here looked pretty grim.

At the front of the crowded studio Charles Crown was working on a solo with an elegant, long-limbed woman. Michel's gaze followed her as she glided gracefully through a series of slow arabesques. Her technique, with her slender, powerful arms and long, proud neck, was awe-inspiring.

"Who's she? A ballerina?"

Primo rolled his eyes.

"Company big cheese. A real snooty bitch. She don' talk to us apprentices—reckons she's somethin' really special."

"She is."

"Yeah, she ain't bad. No common sense though. Totally dippy. In Weston-super-Mare she grand-jetéed right off the stage into the woodwind. If it had been the trombones she'd'a bin off work for a week." Primo leaned over to pick up his coffee cup from the floor. "She was a principal at the Royal till they sacked her. Name's Carlotta di Gian-Tomaso."

Michel repeated the name slowly to himself. Primo's accent was so strong it wasn't always easy to tell where his Italian ended and his English began. He turned his head to look at Primo with a puzzled frown.

"That can't be right, can it? I got Carlotta the Giant Tomato."

Primo's legs flew up in the air and his mouthful of coffee sprayed everywhere. He rolled onto the floor howling with laughter.

A long-absent flicker of amusement kindled slowly in Michel's reserved eyes.

"You won't . . . you won't tell anyone I thought that, will you?"

Primo was clutching his sides.

"Fuckin' Giant Tomato," he squealed in agony. "Is bloody brilliant!"

At the front of the studio Carlotta adjusted the strap of her leotard with an irritated ping.

"Charles, can you please make those boys be quiet? How can I feel the music with that noise going on?"

"Primo, shut up!" Crown roared. "In fact, get out! You too, St. Michel; the pair of you—out! And stay out!"

"What do we do now?" Michel asked, once they'd been evicted from the studio.

Primo shrugged his shoulders with a beaming grin.

"What d'you think, amico? We go over the road to the café. They got a real pretty new girl workin' there, started last week. Man, you wait till you see her."

London. It was all new to Michel. The unfamiliar Victorian architecture, the squealing brakes of the black taxis, the international bustle on the streets, cafés that smelled of vinegar instead of coffee. On Monday morning on his way to the Goswell Road Michel had drunk it all in with a sense of joyous homecoming: an English boy once more on English soil.

But in the evenings, as he sat in his hostel room behind King's Cross station, the city that surrounded him felt foreign and hostile.

Everything was strange to him: the dingy little room with its threadbare, stained, brown carpet and graffiti-covered desk; the pop music on the radios blaring from different rooms around the hostel; the glowering city skyline. Even the language was alien—he'd had to strain to catch the meaning of what people said to him in shops and on buses, asking them to repeat more slowly the words of his own mother tongue.

Sitting on his narrow bed, his back resting against the wall, he twiddled a pen between his fingers and looked down at a blank sheet of paper, trying to compose a letter.

"Dear Carrie . . ."

It was a task he had been putting off ever since he accepted Nadia Petrovna's invitation to come to London, and it couldn't wait any longer.

"I have come to London to study as a sc . . ." He looked up the next two words in his French-English dictionary. *"Scholarship apprentice at the Islington Ballet. I have a room at King's Cross. Here is the address."*

He twiddled his pen and wondered what else he should write. He considered telling her about Primo or Charles Crown but what were either of them to Carrie? Over the past few years their monthly phone calls had grown increasingly stilted and, since Christmas, they had ceased altogether. They hadn't met face-to-face since he was fourteen. For several minutes he toyed with different ways of saying he would like to pay her a visit. Or that he would call her. Or that they might meet up if she ever came to London. At last he wrote, *"I hope you are well—Michel,"* and folded the letter, climbing off the bed to look for an envelope.

When he had laid the sealed envelope on the desk he picked up a ragged pair of old ballet shoes from the top of his bag and leaned against the windowsill, looking down at them. The suede was shiny from dozens of hours of contact with the floor, the handwritten name almost completely rubbed away. Michel had never worn them. They had lain forgotten for almost twenty-five years at the bottom of a lost-property box in a cupboard at the Académie before one of the secretaries had found them and given them to Michel by mistake.

He ran his fingers over the familiar smooth texture of the soles. He didn't know why he had lied to Charles Crown about Jacques St. Michel. But it didn't matter. No doubt he would be long gone before someone from the Académie, or even Jacques himself, put the record straight.

Michel opened the square window beside the bed and folded his arms on the sill, looking out at the dark alley below. On that day, more than seven years ago, when he had let go of his mother's hand on the platform at Charing Cross and set off on his first solo adventure, it didn't cross his mind he might one day have to choose between his parents. He certainly never dreamed he might end up with neither.

Outside the window, in the gaping black arches behind the railway station, the sordid nighttime commerce of the King's Cross backstreets was under way. At the end of the alley a woman in a short skirt and denim jacket was waiting despondently for a rendezvous, checking her watch every minute or two in the light of a streetlamp. From time to time Michel watched as a lone figure hurried along the pavement, emerging from the shadows for a moment to pass beneath his window before it turned the corner toward York Road and the bright lights of the city. For one lonely, sixteen-year-old boy the London night ticked by very, very slowly.

Michel had comforted himself with the thought that at least his position at the Islington Ballet couldn't get any worse. But he was in for a surprise.

As the dancers assembled at the barres for company class, Crown summoned him with a sharp gesture.

"Now, this habit of yours of staring at the floor, it's over, you hear? I daresay your teachers in Paris have told you that hundreds of times. I'm not that patient and frankly, St. Michel, I don't care enough. I'm going to tell you once, understand?" And Crown dismissed him with a careless half wave.

Michel tried. He really did. He knew his chances of making it to the end of his probation period here were slim, but he didn't intend to make it any easier for Crown to throw him out than necessary. Flanked for protection at the barre by Primo and Roly, he made a concerted effort to keep his gaze on his own eyes in the mirror. But the comforting obscurity of the floor was magnetic. During only the third exercise he heard Crown shout his name and clap his hands to make him look up.

"You! St. Michel! On your face; twenty press-ups." And when Michel just stared at him in amazement, he added, "Now!"

Still Michel didn't move. The company turned to stare as Crown walked slowly across the studio toward him.

"I gave you an instruction, St. Michel."

Michel just stood there, blank-faced.

"Look, Charles," protested a female voice from the front of the studio, "if you don't mind, this is a company class and I have to dance *Dido* tonight."

Crown raised a hand to silence her without taking his gaze from Michel's eyes.

"This is my class, Carlotta, and I'll run it how I want to." He lowered his voice. "St Michel," he said quietly, "I think you should know that you're about ten seconds away from the termination of your apprentice-ship with this company."

Seconds passed. Michel felt Primo kick him. At last he looked away, his face tight with humiliation.

"I don't know what it means."

"Oh Christ," Crown sighed. "Okay, Roly, show him."

As soon as the tall boy began to push himself up effortlessly on his fists on the studio floor Michel nodded.

"Yes, I know." He dropped to the floor to obey Crown's command.

After struggling through only six press-ups, Michel collapsed flat on his face. He couldn't lift himself another inch. Crown folded his arms and looked down at Michel's prone body. He was surprised he had managed even that many.

"Dear oh dear. Well it looks like you're going to have to ask one of your new friends to finish them for you, doesn't it?"

"Is no problem," said Primo, glowering at Crown darkly. "I'll do 'em."

Michel looked on helplessly while the young Italian completed the press-ups he was too weak to manage himself. Never had he longed so desperately to be invisible. He continued, scarlet-faced, with the class—his eyes rooted desperately to the mirror—until he heard Crown yell his name again. He looked up in guilty horror.

"Roland, son, you want to give St. Michel twenty press-ups?"

Michel wanted to sink into the floor. If it weren't for the friendly wink Roly gave him as he lowered himself onto his fists, he would have fled the building there and then.

Twice more before the class moved into the center Michel had to watch either Primo or Roly pay the price for his lack of self-control. After the first adage in the center Crown addressed the class with a smile; he was enjoying this.

"Someone else's turn? How about one of you two second-year boys? Obviously not. Someone in the company? Any of you men want to help St. Michel out here?"

Peroxide-blond Marcus stepped forward with a good-humored smile.

"I'll do it, Charles. I'm so tense with all your bitching I can't dance anyway."

In the changing room after class Michel slumped onto the bench and put his head in his hands.

"Oh God, I am so sorry."

"Forget it," Roly told him as he pulled off his ballet shoes. "We're on your side."

"Yeah," Primo agreed with a comical grimace, rubbing his biceps. "Just learn to look up soon, okay, amico? A few more sessions like that's gonna kill me off."

Roly laughed. At seventeen Roly already had the broad-shouldered, muscular body of a man. He had a funny face, not at all good-looking, and an unruly mop of wavy straw-red hair, but his blue eyes were so frank and amiable it was impossible not to like him.

"A few more sessions like that wouldn't do you any harm at all, Vincenti."

"Man, don't listen to him," Primo said in disgust. "He ain't normal. The boy's a fuckin' workaholic."

One disheartening class followed another. It seemed Michel could do nothing, but nothing, to satisfy Crown.

"Hey, come on," Primo consoled him, "there gotta be somethin' the maestro didn't pick on this morning."

"Yes," Michel sighed despondently. "He didn't say anything about my pliés."

"So, okay." Primo threw out his arms with an ecstatic smile. "You got the perfect plié! What more you want after only three classes, eh?"

"I expect he's only waiting to tear them apart tomorrow."

Primo's brown eyes rolled ominously.

"Amico, did you see that man's face? You seriously reckon he's gonna wait till tomorrow to savage your plié if he could'a done it today?"

Michel managed a lame smile. There was almost nothing Crown could do to him that didn't seem less awful once Primo had subjected it to his crazy brand of humor.

During those first difficult days, Nadia Petrovna kept a worried eye on Michel, watching him in classes through the little window in the studio door. His technique was worse than she'd realized, and Charles was right: there was something in the way criticism seemed to bounce off him that was very disquieting.

One morning, while the company was still in class, she climbed the stairs slowly to the first-floor library, one frail hand on the banisters and the other on the handle of her walking stick. Outside the door of the library, she stopped for a moment to think, and then turned the handle and went in.

The library was little more than a wide corridor with shelves lining one wall, stacked with books on dance history and human anatomy, biographies, musical scores, pamphlets on diet, even a few battered novels.

The wall facing the bookshelves was made of plate glass; a huge window overlooking the main ground-floor studio. Nadia Petrovna stood in front of the glass wall with both hands resting on her stick and looked down at the company in the studio below. Her pale old eyes glowed with calm pleasure as she watched the graceful rows of dancers perform a flowing adage which Crown had concocted, as always, on the spur of the moment.

"Beautiful adage," she said. She turned her head to look at Michel. "Don't you think so?"

Michel was sitting on a low chair with his arms folded, gazing stonily down through the glass wall. He had lowered his feet from the edge of a coffee table when she walked in, but otherwise he hadn't moved.

"Yes, Madame."

"Tell me, Michel, what have you been thinking about, sitting here all on your own?"

"Mister Crown threw me out of his class for not remembering a correction he gave me yesterday."

"I did not ask why you are here, child. I asked what it is you were contemplating with such angry eyes."

Michel was still staring fixedly down at the studio.

"Frankly, Madame, I was wondering why you bothered bringing me here."

Nadia Petrovna's hair was white and her skin was brittle and translucent with age, but her eyes still shone with the beauty and intelligence which had made her a goddess throughout Europe in the first half of the twentieth century. She turned back toward the window with a shrewd smile.

"Good," she said. "Let me know when you have found the answer."

At the end of his first week in the Goswell Road, Michel was faced with a new ordeal. The girls.

"Hey, look at that!" Primo said, his handsome face lighting up as he pointed to the noticeboard in the foyer. "I'm partnering Ruth this afternoon. Ruth's the one I'm in love with."

"I thought you were in love with Belinda."

"Yeah, but that was before. Actually, I ain't made my mind up."

Primo's black hair, still wet from his morning swim, was plastered to his head, several glossy strands dangling over his eyes. Michel's damp hair had already twisted back into obstinate curls. His hair had been cropped close, under Crown's orders, and the fair half-curls stuck up forlornly from his head like the coat of a newly shorn lamb. He ran his fingers through his short, unfamiliar mane and looked at the list. Although his literacy was poor he had no trouble spotting his own initials, J.B.St.M.— paired with the initials L.F.

"That's Lynne over there," Primo said, when they were upstairs in the library spying on Nadia Petrovna's pointe work class with the girls. "You see the small one with the blue leotard? That's her."

Michel looked down at her. The prospect of partnering a girl daunted him. At the Académie, segregation had been strict; the teachers believed ignorance was preferable to the chaos that would ensue if the junior boys were allowed access to the girls.

Lynne was executing a series of small jumps and turns with three of the others. Michel had never noticed her before. He could see her face but not her eyes; she seemed to keep them deliberately averted.

"She's pretty," he said.

"Royal Ballet arms," Primo told him. "You can spot 'em a mile off. But looks ain't everything, amico. Lynne Forrest is hell in pointe shoes."

"Is she?"

She didn't look it. Michel watched her for a while; she had a strong, accurate technique and her style was light, seemingly effortless. With her delicately arched feet and her flyaway light-brown hair escaping from its bun at the nape of her neck, there was something almost elfin about her.

By now the girls had become aware they had an audience. Only Lynne kept her face hidden; the rest danced primly for the mirror, arching their pretty eyebrows and ostentatiously ignoring the boys—except for one girl, the tallest and most elegant, who was darting sly glances up at the library with a provocative smile.

"Ignore her," Primo advised. "That is one seriously dangerous signorina."

Michel fully believed him. He hadn't forgotten the tall girl who had laughed so mercilessly at his pirouette on his first morning here. Her eyes met his for a moment as she reached the end of the exercise, smiling with an almost demonic self-confidence.

"She's a good dancer, though," he said, avoiding her gaze.

"Sure, so long as you ain't got to partner her. She weighs a ton, an' she's got no strength in her back at all—like tryin' to dance with a dead horse. You know, I heard she gets through six pairs of pointe shoes a week, just with classes—six, can you believe that? Pounds them into mush, she does. Lucky her parents can afford it. Boy, I tell you, you ever get put down to dance with her, you call in sick. Lucky for the rest of us, Roly's the only one tall enough." He frowned at Michel, looking him up and down critically. "Come to think of it, you better not grow no more, amico, or you could be in trouble."

Roly had accompanied the two friends. He was standing beside them, leaning against the wall where he could just glimpse the girls through the window. He too was watching the tall girl.

"Annette's not so bad," he said. "She's only young yet; she'll get stronger."

"Man, don' take no notice of him," Primo told Michel. "Roly's crazy in love with her."

"No I'm not," Roly protested.

"You're blushing, amico. Hey, Michel, ain't he blushing?"

"That's bullshit," said Roly, really turning red.

The pas de deux class took place at half past two that afternoon in the big studio. The apprentices had the building to themselves; the company were away performing in Dartford under the supervision of the ballet master. Only the caretaker, Ralph, and one or two administrators still buzzed around the ground floor. The few other staff had disappeared; it was Friday afternoon and the past few weeks had been long and hard.

Charles Crown, however, was as snowed under with work as ever. He strode into the big studio at two-thirty on the dot and threw an armful of files on a chair in front of the mirror.

"Right, let's get on with it. Girls, come away from the barre. Daniel, put the comb away."

The boys and girls eyed each other suspiciously. In the institutionalized ballet world, teenagers hung out in single-gender gangs long after their peers out in the real world had discovered the opposite sex. The girls were clustered in an aggressive huddle at one end of the studio, swathed in a thick armor of sweatshirts and woolly leggings. Only Annette displayed her statuesque figure brazenly, wearing nothing over her leotard to conceal her body except a pair of plastic sweatpants rolled down to her hips at the waist.

Gradually the girls ambled away from the barre with scowls which warned the boys not to do themselves any favors; this was strictly business. Ruth clumped toward Primo in her pointe shoes, glaring at him while she pulled the hem of her leotard further down over her bottom. Annette hitched up the shoulders of her leotard unconcernedly as she joined Roly. Two other bland girls took possession of Daniel and Felix. Only Michel was left alone.

Lynne was still standing at the barre, facing the wall, and she showed no sign of moving. At last, because he seemed to have little choice, Michel walked over to her.

"Hello? . . . Lynne?"

There was no response.

"My name's Michel. I think we have to do this class together."

He leaned over slightly to look at her. He could see her pixie face in profile but her downcast eyes were hidden behind long lashes. At the front of the studio the pianist started playing the Bluebird pas de deux from *Sleeping Beauty*. Michel put his hand on the barre in front of Lynne where she couldn't help but see it.

"I said I think we have to dance together this afternoon."

Nothing. Not a murmur. The light-brown bun didn't even twitch. Michel looked over his shoulder at Primo in consternation. Primo spread his hands in a shrug. Whispered conversation began to develop between the boys and the girls until Crown shouted at them—

"Listen to the music, for Christ's sake! This is for your benefit!"

Suddenly, taking him by surprise, Lynne ducked past Michel, scurrying across the parquet floor to stand alone and withdrawn in an unoccupied spot at the back of the studio. Michel followed her, followed in turn by the black eyes of the artistic director and those of every apprentice in the room. He recognized in Lynne's downcast face the desire to hide from all those eyes—to disappear. But he didn't recognize what came next. As he tentatively rested his hand on her waist, she sprang out of his reach, hunching her shoulders and protecting her body with her arms. Her eyelashes fluttered in panic like two trapped butterflies.

"For God's sake!" snapped Annette, glaring at him.

Michel stepped backward in amazement.

"What did I do?"

"Just bloody well leave her alone."

That was all very well for Annette to say—Michel would have liked nothing better than to leave Lynne alone—but this was a pas de deux class; it wasn't an option. Primo signaled to him with a grin to try again. Michel shook his head in alarm.

At last, however, he stepped forward and laid his hand very gently on Lynne's waist. She started crying. Michel took his hand away and rubbed the back of his head in perplexity. Crown was watching him with his piercing black eyes.

The class started without Michel and his unwilling partner. The apprentices listened again to the music and then walked through the choreography in their pairs. "Keep it light," Crown told them, "just as Ingrid and Peter showed you last week . . . okay, that's not bad; let's try it again." Lynne and Michel were still standing in their corner, several feet apart. Neither of them had moved a step.

Michel watched the other boys with their partners and waited for the axe to fall. But Crown said nothing, either to him or to Lynne. He let them be. As he stood there, Michel's eyes were drawn to Annette, berating Roly about his partnering technique at the front of the studio. Annette wasn't like any other dancer he had ever seen. At five-foot-nine, she was virtually a giantess in the world of ballet. On pointe she was as tall as Roly. Michel watched her as she spiraled into Roly's arms, her magnificent green eyes smiling scornfully into his, one long leg bent in an elegant tiré-bouchon. But her real glory, more than her figure or her eyes, was her hair: massive near-black curls that flowed all the way down her back when they weren't crammed into a knot on top of her head. Michel had seen that hair in the corridors and in the café across the road and had marveled at it. Even now jaunty ringlets escaped from her bun to curl around her heart-shaped face with Grecian playfulness. Annette Potter was beautiful and she knew it.

Michel's attention was brought back to earth by a light touch on his arm. While he had been gazing across the studio, a small brown-haired figure had crept toward him until it had plucked up the courage to nudge his arm with a shoulder. Cautiously—very cautiously—Michel looked down at the top of her head and laid both his hands on her tiny waist. Lynne spun round in a neat double pirouette and stopped, facing the front.

Gingerly, without exchanging a word or a glance, they began to follow the choreography behind the other couples. Lynne was like ice between his hands, a frozen statue, thawing for a moment to make a step or a turn and then instantly freezing again. She needed very little support; her turns were neat and exact, and her fingers on his shoulder exerted scarcely more pressure than a feather. To Michel's surprise he found he could even lift her; she was so strong and light she almost seemed to lift herself. For more than ten minutes they managed to keep up with the others, surviving even a dangerous wobble on Lynne's *développé,* which brought Crown's keen gaze instantly to Michel's supporting hand.

It was only when Michel was convinced that Lynne was over the worst of her fear—or excessive shyness, he wasn't sure which—that disaster struck. In his inexperience, he caught her by the waist and lifted her up without giving her time to prepare. Her arm flew out, knocking him off balance, and her tense little body buckled with a jerk as she tumbled, all arms and legs, to the floor.

He clasped his hands to his head in horror.

"My God! Are you alright?" His accent, for once unthought of, sounded embarrassingly French. He had dropped her. He had actually dropped her. Crown was there in a moment, crouching beside her and shooting furious glances at Michel. When Crown tried to touch her, her eyelashes started flapping wildly and she burst into tears. She huddled whimpering on the floor, cowering away from him.

It was Annette who finally pulled Lynne to her feet and dusted her down, without apparent gentleness. It seemed no lasting damage had been done.

"She's alright," Annette said, giving Michel a filthy look as she handed Lynne back to him with a little shove.

Crown's hard stare was even filthier.

"For Christ's sake, St. Michel, try not to break her neck."

Lynne returned to Michel's side like a dead person but she made no fuss when, a minute later, he laid his hands back on her waist. For the rest of the class she danced like an automaton, her little body secure and strong in its technique, hiding her face from him whenever she turned toward him.

In the boys' changing room Michel sank onto the bench with a long, long sigh of relief.

"You see why the Royal Ballet School threw her out," Primo said. "Ask me, you should have dropped her on her head, amico; would have been humane."

"What about you?" Michel asked. "Haven't you ever partnered her?"

"I try twice. Is more than enough; *Cristo!*"

"How about you, Roly?"

Roly was tossing his ballet shoes into his locker.

"Not a hope. The poor little kid's scared stiff of me."

Martin and Felix, for once condescending to talk to their inferiors, both shook their heads.

"Charles had to separate us; I was ready to bash her."

"I never got near her."

Michel pulled off his sweatshirt.

"Does she ever speak?"

"Not to us. I don't know if she's ever spoken to the girls."

"Yeah," Primo said, well informed as ever, "Ruthie says she sometimes speaks in the changing room. But when there's boys around she's . . . whassitsname."

"Dumb?"

"Yeah, that as well."

Michel stood up to take off his all-in-one. "Anyway, I've had my turn. At least they won't let me try and dance with her again."

On Monday morning, the list of partners for the week's three pas de deux classes went up on the foyer noticeboard.

Primo gasped when he saw it: "*O Dio!* Amico, don' look!"

But it was too late. Michel had looked. He slumped against the wall closing his eyes. He couldn't believe it. Surely not even Charles Crown could be that vindictive.

But there was worse news to come as Primo pointed out the list of the week's private coaching sessions. Primo's tutorial with Marcus was on Tuesday evening.

"Hey, is great! I'm gonna miss fencing practice."

Michel looked down the typed list for his own name and found it. His initials had been added to the bottom of the list in an untidy black scrawl—J.B.St.M. Monday 5pm, studio 4—C.C.

The two boys turned slowly to look at each other.

"Jesus, amico, you're gonna die."

"I know."

5

AFTER AN HOUR AND A HALF'S private tuition with Charles Crown, the death Primo had predicted for Michel would have been welcome.

"Did I say we were stopping?" Crown demanded when Michel stopped to drink water from the plastic bottle he had brought with him. "I said drink, not rest! Move it—back on your feet!"

"Please," Michel groaned. "No more, please!"

He was slumped over the barre, his scalding forehead resting on his arm, with his water bottle trailing from his drooping hand. Every muscle in his body hurt; his legs hurt, his feet hurt, his shoulders hurt. Even his breath, sucked into his lungs in great painful gasps, stung his burning throat. His eyes were smarting from the sweat that had been pouring into them. Crown hadn't allowed him to stop to wipe the perspiration from his face—he'd had to make do with his sleeve, snatching a moment to brush his arm over his face each time his eyes stung so much he could hardly see.

"Let's go, St. Michel—turns in second. Feet in fourth, arms in second."

"I can't."

"On your feet." Crown snatched the bottle from his hand and threw it on the floor under the barre. "We can spend ten minutes on this or we can stay here all night; it's up to you."

"Please . . . just two minutes."

"Feet in fourth!" He gave Michel a firm shove toward the center of the little studio.

"Don't do that!" Michel cried; he'd taken all the shoving he could bear from Crown for one evening. "Stop pushing me around!"

"If you don't like it, walk away." Crown gave his shoulder a deliberately painful prod, following him as he staggered backward on his exhausted feet. "Go on, St. Michel, turn around and walk out."

Michel was damned if he'd walk out when Crown told him to. He wiped his sleeve over his burning face.

"No."

"No one's keeping you here. No one's making you go through this. I told you you're free to leave at any time you like, so why not walk away now?"

"No."

Crown's hand flew out and slapped him across the ear so hard Michel felt his dehydrated brain rattle inside his skull.

"Walk away!"

"No, sir!"

Crown looked at him intently for a few seconds and then walked over to the piano to pick up his cigarettes.

"Feet in fourth, St. Michel. Arms in second."

After only another ten minutes of torture Crown finally sighed, "okay, enough; relax."

Michel dropped to the floor like a stone.

Crown looked down at his prostrate body with grim, unimpressed eyes.

"One day," he said, "I'm going to realize I've got better things to do with my time than waste it on kids like you who don't want to be here anyway. There are four things you need, St. Michel—what we dancers so illiterately call the four Fs: the feet; the face; the facility; and the physique—either you're born with them or you're not. Some dancers are born with only one or two and still manage to make a career for themselves, and others are born with all four and never get anywhere. Why? Because there's a fifth F, St. Michel, more important than all the others put together. It's called Fucking Hard Work."

Michel was still breathing too hard even to open his eyes. Crown folded his arms.

"You think the last couple of hours were painful? Well I've got news for you: the pain gets worse. And if, by some miracle, you make it into a company one day, there'll be endless hours of rehearsal and performances on top of classes, week in, week out for the rest of your career—immense physical pain, frustration over injuries, intolerable personal sacrifice, and nothing at the end of it all but certain heartbreak. Give it up, St. Michel. You're not tough enough. What are you trying to prove?"

"I don't have to prove anything to anyone," Michel panted.

"Is that right? Well, that's just changed. Because from now on, if you want to last here, you've got something to prove to me—every single day until the day you leave. But I don't think you'll stay. You're lazy and you're arrogant. You think that having the same name as some poser of a chore-ographer in America gives you a God-given right to a place in the dance world. Well it doesn't. The man's a narrow-minded, shallow phony."

Michel opened his eyes and looked at him. He had never in his life heard anyone speak that way about Jacques St. Michel.

"Go on," Crown said, turning away to gather together his files and papers on top of the piano, "get out. I've had enough of you for one evening."

Michel dragged himself to the door. His body was so numb he could scarcely coordinate his arm to raise his hand and turn the handle.

Primo was waiting for him in the boys' changing room. He stubbed out a half-smoked cigarette quickly as the door opened, waving away the smoke.

"Oh, is you," he said in relief. "Man, I bin waiting here hours—well, not all the time; me an' Ruthie went to the girls' changing room for a bit. Hey, they got two showers, properly tiled, an' the paint ain't falling off the walls either."

Michel sank onto the bench, his limbs lying lifelessly where they fell. When Primo saw his deathly pallor the chirpy smile faded from his face.

"Santa Maria! What did he do to you?"

Michel didn't answer. He covered his face with his sodden sweat-shirt. He was shaking.

It was very rarely that Charles Crown paused in his work, even for a moment. There were a hundred things always waiting for his attention.

But for once, when Michel left the little second-floor studio, he leaned on the windowsill and lit a cigarette, looking down at the Goswell Road through the half-open window. It was after eight o'clock and the building was finally quiet.

The studio door opened almost silently and then closed again. Crown heard the familiar soft thud of a walking stick as a pale, ghostly figure crossed the studio toward him.

"Charles." The apparition stopped by his elbow. "What on earth do you think you are doing?"

"What am I doing? I'm having a calm, quiet cigarette at the end of an extremely long day before I go back to my office and try and cut another ten grand off the touring budget so that we stand a slim chance of making it to October without going into liquidation; that's what I'm doing, Nadia Petrovna." He rubbed one eye. He was exhausted. "Have you had the latest advance through from Maidstone yet?"

The old woman nodded slowly.

"Yes, the theater phoned just after six. The advance is standing at just over nine thousand pounds."

He turned his head to look at her over his shoulder and they gazed at each other with sober eyes.

"Nine," Crown said.

"It will pick up, Charles. The piece is magnificent: the word of mouth is certain to be good once we open. And you said the Sunday *Times* promised to send someone to Croydon this week. If their review comes out this Sunday it's bound to make a difference."

"Depends what it says really, doesn't it?"

"Whom are they sending, do you know?"

Crown nodded: "Boyle."

"Ah." The old woman looked down at the handle of her walking stick. Well, that was that.

After some seconds of silence, she asked him—

"How do you feel your tutorial with Michel went?"

He turned his head back toward the open window.

"Hard to tell. I'll have a better idea once I see whether he turns up for class tomorrow or not."

The old woman watched him as he drew on his cigarette and flicked his ash out of the window.

"Charles, he's only a child."

"No, he isn't. Not in this profession. If he's not ready in two years' time to take up a professional position in a company, nobody's going to take any pity on him then."

"Yes," she said. "You're right, of course, although it does seem so unfair."

Crown's tired eyes looked down at the quiet street. It was raining outside and the few people who walked along the street-lit pavements were hidden under umbrellas.

"Whoever said the dance world was fair?" he said wearily. "Of course it's not fair; it's not fair on any of them. Other kids, at eighteen, are just setting off to college where it's taken for granted they'll fuck up everything, workwise and emotionally, for the next three years. But these kids have to be ready; ready to shoulder adult responsibility, to keep their emotions under control while they take strain after strain on their bodies, day after day. And yes, Nadia Petrovna, maybe I'll end up pushing this boy of yours so hard that he'll break a leg—and that won't be fair either."

Nadia Petrovna folded both her hands on top of her stick.

"How about his technique? Do you think you can fix it?"

"Not unless he's prepared to fight and fight hard. It's in a terrible state and the body's too weak to make any real progress on."

A small sparkle appeared in the ancient ballerina's eyes.

"He does have a nice face, though, doesn't he?"

Crown grunted. "All sixteen-year-old boys are hideous. I suppose he'll be alright once the spots go and he fills out a bit."

"And what about his feet? Do you think they'll do?"

"They'd be better if he made an effort to stretch them. And the way they turn in every time they leave the floor is shit. He'll have to get that under control if he wants to stand any chance at all of scraping into the back row of a corps somewhere in two years' time."

"You can help him overcome that, Charles. Is he musical, do you suppose?"

"So-so." Crown ran his hand over his tired face. "Yes," he conceded, "probably. It might help if he listened to what the pianist was playing. He can pick up the exercises alright; there's nothing wrong with his memory. Though I wouldn't be surprised if his English isn't quite as fluent as he'd like us to believe."

"And how about his . . ." Nadia Petrovna's arthritic fingers twitched on the handle of her walking stick. ". . . you know, his sensitivity for dance? His instinctive line?"

"You've seen him move, Nadia Petrovna. You can judge that as well as I can."

"But I want to know what you think, Charles. I want to know what you think of his fundamental dance quality."

Crown frowned out at the rain in the semi-deserted Goswell Road. He breathed out a slow, pensive stream of smoke. After a few seconds' thought he tossed the butt of his cigarette through the open window and turned to pick up his files from the top of the piano.

"It's unique," he said, and he walked out of the studio.

Two evenings later, Crown was working late as usual. The dancers had all left at five because of the early start in Croydon tomorrow and Crown had the building to himself to work in peace.

At half past nine, as he walked through the foyer on his way home, he nodded to the caretaker who looked up from his newspaper.

"Night, Ralph. Sorry to keep you so late."

"That's alright, Mister Crown. I'm paid till ten. Often stayed later. Anyhow, you're not the last."

"Aren't I?" Crown glanced over his shoulder. The building behind him seemed silent and empty. Most of the lights had already been switched off.

Old Ralph closed his newspaper on the reception desk and nodded toward the stairs: "One of the youngsters is up in studio three doing a bit of practice on his own. Been there all evening. The tall lad with the fair hair."

Crown was checking his pockets for his wallet and cigarettes. "That'll be Roland. Kick him out when you want to go home."

"No, not Roly, the other lad; the new one."

Crown looked up at Ralph. And then he turned around to gaze up the stairs with a thoughtful frown.

"Really," he murmured to himself. "Interesting." He nodded to the gray-haired caretaker again as he walked toward the door. "Night, Ralph."

"Night, Mister Crown."

On a warm Sunday morning in mid-May, Primo and Michel were sprawled in the living room of Primo's home. Beside them, one of Primo's younger brothers was tuning his violin to the grand piano that took up almost half the room. Michel had been in London for a month now, and it was the fourth Sunday in a row that he had spent with Primo's family in their five-bedroomed house in Hackney.

"Mauro, you want to take that racket somewhere else?" Primo put his feet up on the sofa. "Is bustin' my eardrums."

"Go away yourself if you don't like it. I asked Dad; he said I could."

"Well, I'm telling you not to, little brother. You can use the piano in my room—go on, beat it."

Primo was the eldest of seven brothers and sisters, all with the same shining black hair and brown eyes, and all inheriting their mother's beauty. It was a madcap, noisy household. As Mauro reluctantly tucked his violin under his arm and left the room, Michel tilted his head to look up at the ceiling. A cacophony of music and voices came from the floors above.

"How many pianos have you actually got in this house?"

"Four, but only one grand." Primo grimaced at him expressively. "The walls is soundproofed, you know? But not the floors."

Michel propped his hand on his fist and looked around at the cozy room; the crammed bookshelves and the stacks of music scores that covered every surface including the floor, the giant cheese plant in its ceramic pot by the piano that was trying to claw its way out into the garden through the French windows. He had grown to like this room. After a while he sank back in his chair with a sigh and closed his eyes.

"What you sighin' for?" Primo asked. "You got somethin' to be pissed off about?"

"He hates me," Michel said. "I mean—I don't know. I know my turns are bad but, after all, they're not as bad as Roly's. What have I done wrong? I work on his corrections, I practice in the evenings, I swim like he told me to. And he's still going to throw me out in August."

"He ain't gonna throw you out," Primo said, without sympathy.

"Yes, he is. He told me twice last week he couldn't wait to see the back of me."

"Nah, he's just pullin' your dick to scare you, amico. He has far too much fun chewin' your head off to throw you out."

"In my last tutorial he spent half an hour just attacking the way I *think* when I'm dancing."

"Exactly," Primo said. "What for he's gonna bother rearrangin' your brain now if he's only gonna chuck it out with the rest of you in three months' time? You're worryin' about nothin'."

Michel wasn't reassured. He'd done everything he could think of to earn Crown's indulgence—everything! He had slogged with determination through every one of Crown's tutorials. He'd borne patiently with the nightmare Lynne Forrest for eight hideous pas de deux classes. He'd taken every insult, every humiliation, every push and shove, without rebelling. Whether he was working on his pirouettes in one of the small studios in the evening or learning the repertoire behind the company men in rehearsals, whether he was lifting weights in the gym or doing press-ups in his room at the hostel, Michel's every waking moment for the past month had been spent trying to get Crown off his back. But with every day that passed Crown's persecution became more venomous.

"Anyway, you think you got problems," Primo grumbled. "At least you got a tutor."

There had been changes in the company over the past month. And the latest, the vanishing of Marcus from the company, had been completely unexpected. No one knew what had happened; one day he was there and the next he had simply disappeared. The apprentices were stunned. Peroxide-blond Marcus, with his wonderful pirouettes and flamboyant good humor, had been a favorite with all the boys. Even Primo, with his mistrust of homosexuals, had liked him.

"Where am I gonna find another tutor with hyperextended knees?" he lamented, looking glumly at his knees on the sofa.

The smallest member of Primo's family was sitting on the floor beside the arm of Michel's chair. Little Maria was only four but she was already in love. She knelt up and tugged on Michel's sleeve, looking at him with adoring eyes.

"You want to hear me play something?"

Michel looked down at her.

"Okay. What do you want to play?"

She jumped up and ran to the piano stool, turning the knob with both hands until the seat was fully raised, and then hoisted a stack of Schubert scores onto it. Once she had seated herself laboriously on top, she selected a Mozart minuet from a pile on the piano and opened it on the stand. She stared at it for a while and then turned her head to look doubtfully over her shoulder at Michel.

"You do it."

"Hey, baby," Primo protested, "ain't everyone can play the piano, you know."

"It's alright," Michel said. "I'll have a go. I'm pretty rusty but I can bash through it if she likes."

He shifted Maria, Schubert and all, along the wide piano stool and sat down beside her, flicking through the pages of the Mozart score. He began to play through it slowly, grimacing at his many mistakes. As he glanced at Primo while he turned the page, he caught sight of Primo's father in the doorway and stopped halfway through a phrase.

Roberto Vincenti maneuvered his wheelchair farther into the room. He was an impressive, serious-eyed man, with the aristocratic features of his ancient Florentine family.

"Don't stop, Michel. Is true, is pretty rusty but is also talented I think. Where you learn to play?" His Italian accent was even stronger than Primo's.

"My mother used to teach me," Michel said. "She was—is, I mean, a piano teacher."

"She studied where?"

"At the Conservatoire in Paris. She won a scholarship to go there when she was seventeen."

"Ah yes," he said. "I know the Conservatoire very well, of course." Roberto Vincenti had been principal conductor of the Roma Filarmonica until illness had forced him to resign his podium and accept a post as

Professor of Music at the University of London. "The Conservatoire is a fine school, though perhaps a little traditional."

Michel had met Primo's father only once or twice. He very rarely left his study. Now that he had taken the unusual step of interrupting his work he turned to his eldest son.

"Roberto, play for me." He was the only member of the family who called Primo by the name with which they had both been christened.

"I don' want to play, Babbo."

"Play! Play!" The imperious man wheeled his chair around closer to the piano. *"Subito."*

Primo swung his feet off the sofa. He leaned over Michel's shoulder and played "Chopsticks" with a set face.

"There, I played. Okay?" He closed the lid of the piano.

"Play for me Prokofiev 21 B flat."

"No, Babbo, the neighbors already had enough punishment for one morning, eh?"

"Play, Roberto."

Primo's father was not someone you could argue with.

Grudgingly, Primo searched through the piles of scores for the Prokofiev and took Michel's place on the piano stool. He opened the score at the first page and pushed up the sleeves of his sweater with deep reluctance.

Michel had never heard Primo play the piano, though he knew, of course, that he did play. As Primo launched into the first bars of the piece Michel's eyes widened slowly. He stared at his friend's hands as they flew up and down the keyboard filling the room with sound, and realized he didn't know Primo at all. Michel was no expert in music but he knew enough to recognize that Primo was unnaturally gifted; he played with as much skill and sensitivity as many a concert pianist three times his age.

What amazed Michel most was the continuous criticism Primo's father leveled at him while he played. For Primo's fingers the piece was effortless, but the stream of complaints and commands was so relentless he had to screw his face up in concentration so as not to lose his place. Michel couldn't understand why he was so scathing. He had heard Primo's father lavishing praise on his other children's musical skill, and Primo outclassed them all a hundredfold. Michel knew nothing of the subtle technicalities that prompted Roberto Vincenti's complaints. He only knew that his friend was a prodigy. He was born to play.

"Don' give me that shit!" Primo ordered, when the two boys were alone upstairs in his bedroom. "I told you I ain't interested in music."

"But if I could play even half as well, or a quarter . . ."

Primo's temper flared.

"You shut up! I'm a dancer!" He executed a sloppy pirouette on the bedroom carpet. "*Sono ballerino! E tutto!* Finish! Got it?"

"But why waste your time on dancing with a talent like that?"

"Don't!" Primo rounded on him frantically. There was a depth of passion in his eyes that startled Michel. "Don' tell me I'm wasting my time! Listen, Michel, you want me an' you should stay friends, don' you ever tell me to give up dancing and play piano. Never, right?"

Michel's gray eyes took a moment to digest this.

"Alright," he said at last, "I won't." And yet the thought of Primo struggling in classes with his hyperextended legs and inflexible tendons when he had such an extraordinary gift for music was rather sickening.

Primo picked up a football from the floor and started bouncing it angrily against the bedroom wall. Then he flung it on the bed in frustration and flopped onto the chair at his desk with a disgruntled sigh. After a few seconds he turned his eyes apologetically toward Michel.

"Forget it, amico, okay? You know our problem? You an' me, we need to get laid, that's our problem."

Sunday lunchtime in the Vincenti household was chaos. Primo's mother ferried dishes back and forth between the kitchen and the dining room with the smaller Vincentis always under her feet. Even after bearing seven children, Primo's mother retained a sensuous, girlish beauty, and her soft brown eyes smiled kindly at Michel as she gestured, amidst the hubbub, for him to sit down next to Primo.

No sooner were the children finally seated around the table than two of the older boys arrived home from football, causing further pandemonium. Mamma and Babbo both had to be kissed. The little ones had to jump down from their chairs and run excitedly round the table. Primo, too, kissed both his brothers, although the elder, Paulo, who was fourteen, accepted the salutation only grudgingly. Michel watched the spontaneous exchange of greetings in embarrassed fascination. An awful lot of kissing seemed to go on in Primo's family: not the kind of kissing he'd seen so much of in France—vacuous, insincere kisses which embraced only the air—but loving kisses, full of warmth. The uninhibited affection of Primo's family disconcerted him, giving him a sense of leaden discomfort even while he was hopelessly attracted to it.

While they ate, Primo waved his bread at Michel, speaking with his mouth full.

"You got to shout if you want to get heard in this family, amico. Wait till August; is gonna be even worse: my auntie's comin' for the school holidays with five of my cousins. You got to be here to protect me."

"I will if I'm still in London."

Maria, who had insisted on sitting next to Michel, was shrieking at Mauro, and Mauro was shrieking back that she was making too much noise. Primo waved at them both to be quiet. "What's that?"

"I said I'll come if I'm still in London. If I'm thrown out of my apprenticeship, I won't be able to afford to stay at the hostel over the summer."

"I already told you the maestro ain't gonna throw you out. You're talkin' shit, amico."

"Shi-it!" screamed Maria in delight, "Mamma, Primo *ha detto Merda*!"

"Button it, you little squirt." Primo gave her ponytail a tug by way of persuasion. As he leaned toward her behind Michel's chair he saw his father's table napkin fall to the floor, and stood up quickly. "I'll get it, Babbo."

Despite the general ease amongst the family Michel had sensed the deep, bristling tension between Primo and his father. And yet the tenderness with which Primo spread the napkin over his father's knees and positioned his wheelchair closer to the table was unmistakable.

"Thank you, Roberto," his father said coolly. "After lunch you come to my study and we look through prospectus for music colleges for you, yes? To start in October is time you apply now."

Primo returned to his place at the table.

"I'm not going to music college, Babbo."

"Of course, is only one or two places in England are any good. Is maybe better you go to Vienna or Rome, I think."

Primo's pursed mouth twitched.

"I told you I ain't goin' to study music. It ain't up to you. It was different when I was seven or eight an' you could make me sit at the piano till I played the Mozart D major perfectly—"

"You played it like a child," his father interrupted scathingly.

"I *was* a child, Babbo. But I ain't a child now an' you don' run my life no more. I was four years at the Royal Ballet School; I ain't about to give that up."

Roberto Vincenti reached calmly for the salt.

"We'll see" was all he said.

In the late afternoon when Michel left to catch the bus back to King's Cross, Maria accompanied him faithfully to the door. She clung shyly to Primo's trouser leg and looked up at Michel with solemn eyes.

"Are you going?" she asked.

Primo grinned. "You got yourself a real fan there, amico." He crouched down to talk to his little sister. "Hey, you like my friend, bambina? You want to give him a kiss? You got to kiss her, Michel, or she's gonna think you don' like her."

Maria held up her arms to be lifted and Michel bent down to pick her up. She wrapped her arms around his neck.

"Come next Sunday," she whispered with the blend of coyness and intimacy so instinctive to her sex.

"Alright, I'll try," he said. "Only next time you've got to play for me, okay?" As he held her he felt the same unease he had felt at lunchtime: the same discomfiting mixture of yearning and repulsion. He kissed her dark, shining head quickly and put her down.

"I don't know the first thing about children," he said, laughing to cover his embarrassment.

"Nah, kids are great, amico. You just got to kiss an' cuddle them a lot, and smack 'em when they don't do what they're told."

Michel shook his head. Families were a mystery to him. He didn't envy Primo the chaotic rituals of his home and family life; he had grown too used to the freedom of having his independence for that. All the same, walking along the road toward the bus stop, as he thought about Primo's noisily loving household, the mother's warm eyes and the feel of little Maria's arms clinging tightly to his neck—and even the intense conflict between Primo and his father—he felt a pang of regret. The shabby hostel room in King's Cross that awaited him suddenly seemed very drab and empty.

On a morning in mid-June, some four weeks later, the Islington Ballet receptionist stuck her head around the door during Charles Crown's class and waved her hand cautiously to attract his attention.

"What?" Crown snapped. He hated interruptions to his classes. Even Nadia Petrovna had to watch her step if she wanted to sneak into his class after the first exercise had started.

"Sorry, Charles; there's a girl on the phone for Michel. She says it's urgent."

Crown's gaze turned sharply toward Michel. If there had been a trace of self-consciousness in his eyes, Crown would have yelled that she could damned well wait, whoever she was. But Michel merely looked baffled.

"Go on, then," Crown said, "and make it quick. And put a sweater on," he added as Michel started moving toward the door. "Have a bit of common sense!"

Michel shoved his arms into his sweatshirt as he followed the receptionist into the corridor.

"Where's the call?" he asked her.

"Front office."

"Did she say who she was?"

"No. She didn't really say it was urgent but I knew Charles wouldn't let you come otherwise. She did sound in a bit of a flap though."

The front office was deserted when Michel went in and picked up the telephone receiver that was lying on the company manager's desk.

"Hello?"

"Michel, is that you?" The female voice sounded breathless.

"Yes, this is Michel. Who's this?"

"Michel, it's Carrie." And then, after a pause, a shade colder: "Eastleigh."

He flushed instantly, unable to believe he hadn't recognized his mother's voice.

"Carrie! I'm sorry. How are you?"

"I'm alright, Michel. You sound different."

"Well, yes, I suppose I must. Is everything okay?"

"My brother died on Saturday."

"Uncle Jim?"

"He's been ill for months but it was still sudden. The doctor told him to stop drinking years ago but of course he wouldn't listen. He was only fifty-one."

Michel sat down on the edge of the company manager's desk and tried to make sense of the fact that his uncle was dead. But he felt nothing; Uncle Jim was too distant a feature in his life. The few memories he had of his uncle were all unhappy ones. Vainly, he searched for something appropriate to say.

"Is Toby alright?" he asked at last.

"No, of course he isn't. He's down here at the moment, staying with me until after the funeral tomorrow afternoon." She waited for Michel to respond and then said, "I think you should come, Michel. Jim was your only uncle. I don't suppose it's too much to ask, do you?"

"No. No, of course I'll come if you want me to."

"I think Toby would appreciate it."

When he rejoined Crown's class, picking up an adage halfway through, Michel was too distracted to concentrate on dancing. He tried to shut out the conflicting emotions Carrie's call had roused in him, focusing on the adage instead, but his skin prickled with discomfort as though tiny wedges were being driven into the tightly closed seams of his new life here in London. His cheeks flushed hot like a child's. He was going home to Devon to see his mother.

6

IT WAS EARLY EVENING when Michel walked down the wooded lane
from the bus stop at the village green to the old farmhouse where he had
spent his brief childhood. The farm courtyard was slippery after the recent heavy rain and he stepped carefully over the uneven paving stones
toward the house. Three years had passed since he had last crossed this
courtyard.

Michel could see the shape of his mother's figure moving around behind the misted kitchen windows. He lifted the latch of the kitchen door
and went in, ducking under an oak beam that unexpectedly appeared in
front of his eyes. When he straightened up he was astonished at how
much smaller the kitchen seemed than he had remembered it to be.

Carrie was bent over the Rayburn, putting a dish in the oven. She
stood up and turned to greet him with a prepared smile of welcome, but
when she saw the six-foot youth who stood before her she froze and her
smile drained away. She stared at him without speaking, her green eyes
moving in shocked recognition over his changed face and close-cut fair
curls. Michel remained standing just inside the door, his hand still resting on the edge of the beam beside his head, and watched his mother's
expression change from horror to confusion, and then from confusion to
bitterness. He moistened his lips slowly.

"Hello, Carrie."

She twitched her mouth into a small, tense smile.

"Hello, Michel." The smile forced its way to her eyes. "It's kind of you to come."

Michel sat at the end of the long pine kitchen table and drank a cup of tea that Carrie had made for him, while she busied herself over the evening meal and talked about the arrangements for tomorrow's funeral.

She dried her hands on her cotton summer skirt as she crossed from the sink to the stove.

"So you decided to move back to England," she said. "I'm surprised; I'd have imagined you'd feel more at home in France after all this time."

"It wasn't really a decision," Michel told her. "It just seemed to happen. And I wasn't making much progress at the Académie."

He explained about meeting Nadia Petrovna at the Académie, and about his scholarship, describing how the two-year apprenticeship scheme worked at the Islington Ballet and about the probation Charles Crown had put him under. And as he spoke, although she had her back to him, he could feel her bristling resentment at every word he said. After a few minutes he stopped talking.

Carrie stood at the counter with her lips pressed tightly together, taking cutlery out of an open drawer. Michel was mistaken in thinking she resented his choice to study dance. It was the dance world she resented—passionately and bitterly—for taking her son away from her, as it had already taken her son's father.

In the silence that followed, each of them waited for the other to say something to mend the break in the conversation. Carrie moved around the kitchen very quietly while she waited, laying knives and forks noiselessly, one by one, on the table. But neither of them knew what to say. It was a relief for them both when they heard Toby's sad, light footsteps on the narrow oak staircase.

Later, after supper, as Michel sat with them in the low-ceilinged sitting room beside the bare hearth, Carrie poured out three cups of coffee from a jug. Since the three of them had sat down to eat, she had scarcely taken her eyes from Michel's face.

"Michel, Toby wants to talk to you about your future." She glanced at the thin middle-aged man sitting listlessly in the corner of the sofa. "Unless you'd rather wait until after the funeral."

"No," Toby said, rousing himself with a smile that only partly succeeded in hiding his sorrow. "Let's talk about it now."

"My future?" Michel leaned over to take the cup his mother handed to him. "There isn't much to say. I'm afraid I don't know very much about it."

"How about London?" Toby asked him. "Are you planning to stay there?"

"I hope so. I don't know. If I'm not allowed to continue with my apprenticeship after August, I won't be able to stay. I won't be able to afford it." He voiced something that had been on his mind for some time, and which he had been trying all evening to find the right way to say. He turned toward Carrie but couldn't quite meet her eye. "If that happens, I'm afraid I'll probably have to come back here for a while. I don't want to at all, and I'm hoping it won't come to that, but I'm afraid I wouldn't have any choice." He was so anxious not to sound as though he felt he had a right to a place in her home he failed to realize how hurtful his words had been. He saw her mouth pinch tightly and he looked down at his coffee, misunderstanding. "Hopefully it wouldn't be for very long," he said.

With a fierce effort of self-discipline, Carrie hid her deep pain at his rejection behind a brisk, set face. She stood up and crossed to the mahogany bureau in the corner beside the upright piano, pulling open the top drawer.

"That won't be necessary," she said. She came back holding out two Chubb keys on a ring toward him.

Toby frowned at her in concern. "Carrie, that's not what was intended."

Michel took the keys. "What are these?" But Toby was still looking at Carrie.

"Carrie, it was intended for you to rent the flat out and keep the income, or give it to Michel as you choose, until he's eighteen."

"He may as well have it now," Carrie said resolutely. "He's old enough to make his own decisions." She saw that Michel was looking down mystified at the keys in his hand, and explained, "Jim left his flat in Pimlico to you in his will. He meant that you shouldn't have possession of it until you're eighteen but I don't see any reason to wait."

"A flat in Pimlico?" Michel was astonished; he hadn't even known it existed. "But . . . surely it should be yours, Toby."

"Jim left me the freehold of the shop in Camden Passage and the flat above it. We had a joint portfolio of stocks and shares which all come to me."

"Well, Carrie, then."

"I inherit this farm and the property in the village."

"I thought they were yours anyway."

"No, it was all his. He just allowed me to live here. That's the way our parents decided it should be. The rent from the land and the old Manor will be enough for me to live on. The flat's yours, Michel. I don't need it."

He looked down again at the keys in his hand. He had always known his uncle was well off but he had certainly not expected to be remembered in his will.

"But I don't understand. Why should he leave anything to me? I mean, he didn't even . . ." He stopped; he had been going to say he knew his uncle had despised him.

In the lull left by his unfinished sentence Toby stirred his coffee, the spoon tinkling gently in the cup.

"Accept Jim's legacy, Michel. You're his only nephew and it's what he wanted." He stood up slowly and took a box of matches from the oak mantelpiece to light his pipe. "The flat won't be much use to you as it is, I'm afraid. It's a terrible great barn of a place on the top floor. We never lived there. Jim bought it cheaply in the sixties as an investment; it used to be the headquarters of some defunct political organization. We generally used it to store antiques. I'll help you sell the flat. Find yourself a little pad somewhere sensible and invest what's left over. There are still a few thousand pounds to pay on the mortgage but the sale of the contents ought to cover that. The contents of the flat are yours. Most of it's junk but there are one or two decent pieces. I'll go through the stuff with you so long as you give me first refusal on it, right?"

Michel nodded blankly. It still all made very little sense.

When Toby excused himself and went to bed, Michel and Carrie sat silently on either side of the empty stone hearth. They had nothing to say to each other. After a few minutes Michel stood up.

"I know it's early but I think I'll go to bed too if you don't mind."

"Yes, go ahead. I put you in the front bedroom at the top of the stairs. Will you be able to find the bathroom?"

It was a subtle dig, and Michel felt himself blushing.

"Yes, I remember where it is. Good night, then."

"Good night, Michel."

The next afternoon, in the small medieval church that held so many memories for Michel, James Eastleigh was brought home for the last time to the village where he had been born.

Carrie and Michel sat through the service, withdrawn and dry-eyed. Only Toby wept: kind, patient "Uncle" Toby, who had been Jim's closest companion and business partner for more than twenty years. When they left the gaping grave in the churchyard, Michel walked beside Toby with his hands in the pockets of his rainproof jacket. It had been raining during the service but the shower had stopped and the sun was shining weakly behind the clouds.

"I didn't have an address for you and Uncle Jim in London or, you know . . . I'd have come to see you."

"Yes. Thanks." Toby blew his nose and then smiled. They both knew it was a lie.

In the evening Michel and Carrie said good-bye awkwardly at the kitchen door.

"Maybe I could come down again sometime," he said. "I've got a friend who plays the piano; he could come with me."

"Yes, of course. Whatever. Just let me know."

She no longer seemed interested. She didn't even look at him. She just seemed impatient for him to be gone.

Michel walked back along the lane to the bus stop through the dull evening on his way to catch the eight-fifty train from Exmouth. When he reached the churchyard, instead of walking past, he pushed open the gate and walked in, following the path between the dripping yew trees until he came to the mound of fresh earth that had been there only since the afternoon. He stood for a while looking down at it.

In the damp silence of the shadowy graveyard he made his peace with the uncle whom he had never liked and who had never liked him. It seemed strange that his uncle should vanish from his life so soon after unexpectedly entering it again.

On the train, while the darkening fields and villages flew past the window, Michel looked at the keys of his uncle's flat in the palm of his hand. He understood that in giving him these keys, Carrie had knowingly severed the last bond of his dependence upon her. As the train sped toward the city, Michel's disappointment at his mother's detachment began to fade from his thoughts. London, with its busy streets, crowded dance studios, and Primo's boisterous companionship, lay ahead of him. That was where he belonged.

The following Saturday afternoon, Michel and Primo walked along Warwick Way in Pimlico and stopped in front of a row of tall Georgian terraced houses: grand white-fronted houses, each with identical white pillars on either side of the large front door, and black iron railings guarding the steps that ran down to the door of the basement flat. Originally built for wealthy families, they were kept in pristine condition by their current owners, with tidy paintwork and BMW sports cars parked outside. Two houses in the row had been converted into hotels.

The black front door that Michel opened with the larger of the two keys on the ring belonged to a house that was slightly shabbier than the rest. Inside, in the resonant stairwell, as they climbed upward they lowered their voices, feeling as though they were breaking and entering.

"You do it," Michel said, handing Primo the keys when they reached the fourth floor. The stairs had come to a sudden end at a landing. Primo looked at the big paneled door and handed the keys back.

"No, you. Is your bloody flat."

Michel turned the key in the lock, half expecting to be confronted by a roomful of residents glaring up at him indignantly from their armchairs. But, instead, the door opened into a square hallway, easily twice the size of his hostel room in King's Cross, with smooth marble floor tiles and a high ornately molded ceiling. The hall was crammed with old furniture: chairs with broken legs, two tables—one upside down on top of the other—a standard lamp; a stack of frameless oil paintings standing on end in a corner, their faces turned to the wall. A thick blanket of dust covered everything.

Primo opened a door on his left and screwed up his nose.

"Bathroom," he said. "Pretty old-fashioned."

There was a large square room next to it, undecorated, with bare floorboards and a tall window that overlooked the street at the front of the house. The kitchen opposite was very long, a huge table taking up three-quarters of its length. The window over the stainless-steel sink was so grimy it was only just possible to make out the shape of the buildings on the other side of the tiny courtyard behind the house.

"Who on earth's going to buy a place like this?" Michel asked, looking at the peeling paint under the kitchen window.

"Ah, some mug'll want it. Some City type who can afford to get the place done up." Primo went out into the hallway and opened the last door. He stopped in the doorway, calling to Michel over his shoulder, "Hey, amico, come an' have a look at this!"

Michel stood in the hallway looking into the room over Primo's shoulder. The room was colossal. Absolutely vast. And so packed with junk—furniture, crates, paintings, and bric-a-brac, all brownish-gray with dust—there was no way through the room except by clambering over precariously balanced wardrobes, tables, and boxes.

"Man, where'd he get all this stuff?" Primo wanted to know.

"He was an antiques dealer. His partner said most of this is rubbish."

The two boys mountaineered their way across the piles of furniture, covering themselves in dust, examining the odds and ends they passed on their way. "Look at this thing." Primo brushed the dust off a bronze icon with his sleeve and passed it to him. Michel ran his fingers over the detailed engravings of the saints and then put it down, picking up a broken cuckoo clock. They were two children again, let loose inside an Aladdin's cave. It didn't matter that half this jumble was worthless.

"I never saw anything like this place," Primo said. "What is this, a ballroom or something?"

"I think it was used for political meetings or something like that, I'm not sure."

"Man, if you took all this stuff out of here it would be . . ." He stood up straight and looked around, trying to visualize it. The room must be at least forty feet long and twenty-five feet across. It was filled with natural daylight that poured in through two huge sash windows at the far end of the room, each set into an arched alcove and reaching almost from the floor to the high ceiling.

"It would be a dance studio," Michel said.

The two boys looked at each other.

"Amico, you thinkin' what I'm thinkin'?"

"It's crazy. We could never afford the rent on a place this size."

"Rent? What fuckin' rent? You own this place. There'd just be, like, bills an' poll tax an' stuff."

"I suppose it might be possible. I wonder if this junk is really worth enough. My uncle's partner said there's still about seven thousand pounds to pay on the mortgage."

"So there ain't no harm finding out. All these paintings an' shit got to be worth something."

They explored the room further, looking at it in an entirely new light. The idea of becoming a homeowner of any description daunted Michel. It belonged to that range of intimidating adult activities he had always reserved for the distant future.

Primo pulled back the dust cover from an upright piano and lifted the gleaming lid to touch the keys. It was badly out of tune.

"Is a crime to leave a decent piano covered up like this an' not keep it in tune. Don't do the instrument no good." He lowered the lid and caught sight of the maker's signature: *"Cristo!"*

"What?"

"Is a Steinway."

"Is that good?"

"Amico, you're kiddin' me!—I mean, is a *Steinway!*"

He played a few more notes and then replaced the green dustcover lovingly, running his hand over the corners to smooth it down.

"I guess you're gonna have to sell this too," he said, looking wistful. "It'll help with the mortgage, anyhow."

It took Michel, with Toby's help and Primo's high-spirited hindrance, a fortnight of evenings and weekends to sort through the contents of the flat. Much of it was saleable and a few items were very valuable. The bronze icon alone was worth almost two thousand pounds. Such vast sums of money were mind-boggling to Michel; he had been living for the past few months on twenty-eight pounds a week after he had paid his rent at the hostel.

At last, on the second Sunday evening, when the flat's contents had been sorted into things Toby would buy for his own shop, things to be sold at auction, and things to be thrown away, Toby sat down at the big table in the dusty kitchen and reckoned up the value of the whole lot.

There was a long, nail-biting wait while Michel filled the kettle from the corroded tap in the sink to make coffee and Toby checked and rechecked his figures.

At last, as Michel brought three full mugs to the table, Toby said, "Okay, if we assume you're keeping this table with the chairs, and disregarding the two Staffordshire figures which may or may not be worthless, it'll probably come to about thirteen thousand."

Michel puffed out his cheeks. Thirteen thousand pounds! It was as unreal to him as if Toby had said a million. But more important, it was enough. He had a home of his own.

Primo was looking at Toby in an agony of suspense.

"This thirteen thousand is . . . including sellin' the piano, right?"

Toby smiled and shook his head.

"No, I didn't include the piano. I got the feeling someone here had set their heart on keeping it."

There was a loud thud as Primo collapsed, flat on his back, on the floor. His feet hovered dramatically in the air for several seconds before they plummeted, lifeless, onto the cold kitchen tiles.

"Looks like that third cup of coffee's going to be wasted," Toby said, taking the mug Michel handed to him. "I'm afraid your friend seems to have fainted."

"I think, perhaps, if we can afford it," Michel said, "it might be a good idea to keep one of the beds as well."

"Two," said Primo's voice from the floor.

Michel looked down at him. "Two?"

Primo opened an eye.

"Are you havin' me on, amico? You seriously reckon I'm gonna live in a house with six noisy kids when I got somewhere better to go?"

Once the flat was cleared, the enormous front room looked even bigger. Now began the real labor. Together, working in the evenings and at weekends, the two boys plastered over the cracks in the front room ceiling, ripped up the uneven floorboards, replacing them with chipboard underlay, and scrubbed down the walls. Michel had no instinct for the work; Primo was in charge of everything. Michel just followed instructions and paid for the materials.

"How much money we got left?" Primo asked, chewing the end of his pencil as he sat in the kitchen browsing through paint catalogs. "Man, I never knew there was so many shades of white!"

"About five thousand pounds, unless you want to sell the Steinway."

"Five thousand's gonna be enough, amico. I'll make sure it is."

At the Islington Ballet they crouched on the studio floors examining the parquet tiling like a pair of archaeologists. When the older dancers leaned over their shoulders in curiosity, Primo shooed them away.

"What does it look like we're doing? We're looking at the floor. So quit bothering us; this is complicated stuff, okay?"

The two friends were camping in the Pimlico flat, living in what was essentially a building site while they worked on transforming their studio. As for the other rooms, they had given no thought at all to their decoration. They hadn't even thought of cleaning them; they simply brushed the dust off a surface when they wanted to use it.

As the weeks passed and the end of August drew nearer, more of the work fell to Primo as Michel stayed later and later in the Goswell Road studios, trying to appease his nemesis, Charles Crown, who was still on the warpath. The end of Michel's probationary period was approaching fast and Crown showed no signs of relenting.

Michel's position at the Islington Ballet had improved very little in the months he had been there. Pas de deux classes, in particular, were an unceasing headache. Not only did Crown still make him partner Lynne Forrest in every class, he no longer left them alone as he had in the first few weeks; every promenade and supported pirouette was picked apart ruthlessly, and it was invariably Michel who bore the brunt of the attack. After more than three months, Lynne had still not spoken more than a few whispered words to Michel. Their pas de deux classes were conducted in frigid silence, apart from Crown's critical comments raining down on them after every few moves.

They had, however, made some progress. In the absence of the conventional forms of communication they had begun to develop an instinctive physical dialogue: Michel could tell, from the way her muscles contracted, if she was uncomfortable in a lift or whether she felt secure in a partnered balance, and she, in turn, was beginning to trust his support and know how to distribute her weight to make the lifts easier for him. It was very far from ideal—and Michel would have given almost anything never to partner her again—but he supposed it was better than nothing. Each week, when the list went up on the board, he couldn't believe that Crown had done it to him yet again. But, in truth, Crown had little choice. By surviving those first few classes with Lynne, Michel had sealed his own doom. There was simply no one else she would allow near her.

However, if the trials of Michel's pas de deux classes weren't Crown's fault, the misery of his classes and tutorials certainly was. Crown grew more exacting and implacable with every day that passed. By the time Michel got home from practicing in the evenings, often well after nine o'clock, he had no energy left for DIY.

The final week of August came and Michel had his last tutorial with Charles Crown before the company's three-week summer break. At a quarter to ten, exhausted and dispirited, he let himself into the Pimlico flat to find Primo still hard at work.

"Hey, amico," Primo said, beaming at him from the top of his ladder as he walked in. Primo had already painted all four enormous walls of the studio—three coats of brilliant white emulsion—and was busy putting a coat of primer on the window frames. "Guess what. I tuned the Steinway. Is *magnifico*!"

"Yourself?"

"Sure, myself. You reckon I'm gonna let anyone else do it?"

"Do you know how?"

"That's a joke! You think my parents are rich or somethin', they can afford to pay for my apprenticeship with seven kids and no help from me? Who do you reckon tunes the pianos at the Islington Ballet?"

Michel dropped his bag wearily in the hall and went to fill the kettle. He learned something new every day.

From the kitchen he yelled out, "What happened in here? I hardly recognize it."

"Man, don' blame me!" Primo yelled back. "Annette and Belinda came over an' spent the evening flapping mops and cloths about—well, Belinda did; Annette just gave orders. Typical, ain't it? I ask 'em over here for sex and what do I get? A clean kitchen. By the way, I got news for you."

"What's that?"

"Annette's decided to paint the bathroom green."

"Is that right?"

"Yep, avocado."

Michel opened the fridge with a glum sigh. He didn't see why Annette shouldn't paint the bathroom green if she wanted to—just as long as she didn't expect him to help her. When he walked back into the studio with a glass of milk, Roly looked up at him from the floor at the side of the room. Roly had followed Annette here after one of their routine falling-outs in pas de deux class, and had stayed to help Primo paint the skirting boards.

"How did you tutorial with Charles go, Shel?"

Michel sank down on one of the wooden crates that served as chairs.

"I screwed up," he said. "I forgot everything he told me last week: every single correction. I didn't even remember what he told me in class this morning about my épaulement and port de bras. There's no chance he'll let me stay now."

As the months had passed, the idea of being thrown out of his apprenticeship had grown harder and harder for Michel. He didn't want to leave. The Islington Ballet was his home. But there were only three more days between now and the summer break. Sometime in the next three days he was going to hear the worst.

"You know what?" Primo said, pausing in his painting and looking down at him from the ladder with a frown. "I reckon is maybe best you go an' see Charles tomorrow an' ask him if he's gonna let you stay."

"Go and ask him? You have to be joking."

"No, Primo's right," Roly agreed. "Better ask him when he isn't in one of his moods. You don't want him suddenly remembering about your probation in the middle of one of his rages."

Michel nodded reluctantly. They were probably right. But the idea of the interview wasn't one he relished.

The next morning, before class, Michel knocked on the door of Crown's second-floor office.

"What is it?" Crown asked curtly when he glanced up from his paperwork and saw who it was. "I'm busy, St. Michel."

Michel's mouth was so dry he had to moisten his lips twice before he found his voice.

"I, um . . . you told me you'd let me know at the end of August whether I could stay and finish my apprenticeship. And as the summer break starts on Thursday . . ." He left the sentence unfinished.

"August? Did I?" Crown frowned at him, nonplussed, unwilling to be distracted from his paperwork. "Oh." He stared at the wall for a while, pondering, and then went back to his paperwork. "I didn't say August, I said Christmas."

"That's an utter lie!" Primo cried, as Michel dropped disconsolately onto the bench in the changing room. "Man, he did say August, I heard him!"

Part Two

7

JONNI KENDAL WAS CLIMBING STAIRS in the middle of the night. Up and up, turning corner after corner of a winding staircase she had never seen before. On a small landing she stopped and puffed out her cheeks looking upward. Everest!

Off she set again, her red high-heeled shoes dangling from one hand, padding up the concrete stairs in her stockinged feet. Her clinging jersey dress, pillar-box red, rode up over her thighs as she climbed. When she paused on a stair to pull the hem down, swaying precariously, the tall man who was following close behind her rested a steadying hand on her back.

"Only one more floor."

She twisted her neck to look back at him. He was two steps below her but his gray eyes were almost on a level with her own. Jonni smiled what she considered to be a very sober and mature smile.

"Did I tell you I was an actress?"

"Yup."

She swayed again, holding on to the handrail. "And did I tell you I'm rehearsing a play at Stratford East with Grant Noble?"

"I believe you did just mention it, yes. Come on, up you go."

He gave her a gentle shove to get her moving again—as though she were a child, she thought. At nineteen, Jonni took healthy umbrage at any grown-up making fun of her.

Up she went, one laborious step at a time, while he followed patiently. Jonni was in no hurry to get to the top even if it was after one in the morning. She had never done anything like this before—not that she was doing it now, she reminded herself quickly. She was only going home with him because she had left her house key at the theater in Stratford and Auntie June would go berserk if she woke her up at this time of night.

On the top-floor landing she leaned against the wall while he punched a code into a keypad next to the paneled door.

"Don't you have a key?"

"Yes, but we don't use it." He pressed the last button and turned the handle. "This is easier."

"Michel; isn't that a bit of an odd name for a man?"

He smiled at that. "This from a lady who goes by the name of Jonni. Are you coming in or are you going to stand out there all night?"

Really she wouldn't mind standing here for a while. The cool cement felt wonderful under her hot stocking-clad feet. But she tore herself away from the wall and walked through the door. In the wide, square hallway she stopped and gaped at the marble floor and elaborately molded ceiling, and the shining brass fittings on the paneled doors.

"Heavens! Are you terribly rich?"

"No, 'fraid not. Sorry to disappoint you. It takes all my earnings just to pay the bills on this place."

Michel left her standing in the hall, walking past her into the kitchen while Jonni stood staring at the pictures on the walls. There was a framed photograph: five bodies clumped in a heap under what looked like Waterloo Bridge. She could pick out Michel amongst them, much younger-looking and skinnier than he was now. They looked happy.

"What was here?" she asked, pointing to a rectangular patch above the photograph that was paler than the rest of the wall.

Michel came out of the kitchen to look, a jar of coffee in his hand.

"Where? Oh, a picture that came with the flat. An old watercolor—I quite liked it. One of the girls in the company had her nose fixed last year, and we sold it so she could get it changed back again."

He went back into the long kitchen and Jonni wandered after him, wondering who "we" were. The huge central table was so cluttered with papers, magazines, dirty cups, and overflowing ashtrays that the tabletop was invisible. Every surface in the kitchen was covered with junk; even the backs of chairs were draped with assorted garments and carrier bags, hooked over the corners.

Michel cleared a space on the table and set down two cups of black coffee.

"I don't usually drink coffee at night," she said.

"Trust me, you need it."

"Mmm . . . okay." Jonni sat down. She wasn't in a fit state to argue. "Have you got any milk?"

"Uh-huh."

He kicked the fridge door shut with the side of his foot and stuck a carton of milk in front of her on the table. Jonni looked at the odds and ends that were scattered around her, picking up different things to examine them. There were some objects whose functions she couldn't even begin to fathom.

"What's this thing?" She held up what looked like an oversized, ribbed sticking plaster.

"False metatarsals. They aren't mine."

"No, I'm sure they're not." Jonni didn't know what metawhatsits were, and she wasn't sure she wanted to.

She picked up a satin pointe shoe that had once been salmon pink but was now splodged with deep yellow stains where it had been painted with something nasty. The leather sole was encrusted with shiny black dirt and the toe was grimy where the satin had been snipped away and roughly stitched. It was extremely unpleasant. Even the long ribbons dangling from each side of the shoe were no longer pink but gray-black where they had been twisted out of shape and knotted repeatedly. Jonni peered inside the shoe to look at the toe block. To her amazement it wasn't a block at all but a hollow cavity: a rigid box. Imagine squeezing your toes into a pair of torture chambers like that! She squirmed at the mere idea.

"Whose are these?"

"I don't know. What size are they?"

The size was still just visible on the sole, imprinted in dirty gold lettering.

"Four and a half F."

"They'll belong to my practice partner. Chuck them on that bag over there, would you? She'll probably want them."

"They look past wanting. They're very old."

Michel clicked his tongue and shook his head, reaching across the table to take the shoe from Jonni's hand. He thumped the toe against the edge of the table to test its hardness and then tossed it carelessly, along with its mate, onto the bag on the floor by the kitchen door. "Good as new," he said. "Or they've got a rehearsal or two left in them anyway."

"So you really are a ballet dancer, then."

"Uh-huh. What did you think I was?" He took a cigarette from a packet that was lying on the table amidst the mess. "Do you want one?"

Jonni took the cigarette he held out toward her wanting, oh so badly, to appear adult and sophisticated in the eyes of this unknown man who had brought her home. She tapped the end of the cigarette on the edge of the table just as she had seen him do and held it poised in the air, studying him critically. What had she imagined him to be?

There had been lots of dancers at the party in the foyer at the South Bank; girls with perfect features and straight backs—all, alas, much slimmer than Jonni—and boys in flamboyant waistcoats with extrovert mannerisms and loud voices. This Michel didn't fit the bill at all. He was looking at her now with calm interest as he lit his cigarette unhurriedly, not at all perturbed by her scrutiny. He was tall and, as far as she could judge, well built. Handsome in his own way. But his whole manner—and his face with those quiet eyes—was too private somehow to suggest a performer. The sleeves of his black sweater were pushed up to his elbows. She looked at his strong forearm where it rested on the table and the broad hand that held his coffee cup, his fingers lightly curved around it in repose. His hand looked as if it had been built for swinging an axe rather than leading a ballerina daintily across a stage. Jonni leaned forward with what she hoped was great panache to light her cigarette from the match he held out toward her, inhaling deeply—and then collapsed against the back of her chair, startled out of her stylish pose by a paroxysm of violent coughing.

Michel reached across the table and took the cigarette out of her hand, stubbing it out in an already overfull ashtray while she continued to choke. He fetched her a glass of water and she sipped it slowly between splutters, trying to regain her dignity.

"Oh gosh," she coughed, "sorry. You see, I have to learn to smoke on-stage."

"Don't do it. It's not worth it. We boys all started at the Islington Ballet when we were kids. I wish I'd had more sense."

"Have you been doing ballet long?"

"Of course. All dancers have."

Jonni beamed at him in tipsy fascination as her coughing subsided.

"Are you terribly important? Do you dance all the big roles and solos? Are you famous?"

Michel shook his head slowly.

"I'm in the corps; not even a coryphée. I dance ensembles, usually in the back row. I've been there ever since I finished my training."

Jonni looked down at her scarlet jersey cleavage. Oh dear, her and her infallible knack for asking the wrong question. She always asked too many questions; it was her number one failing—or one of her number one failings anyway. Without thinking she fired another question at him.

"Why were you sitting on the radiator under those stairs at the party?"

"Well, I wasn't there through choice. Were you?"

"No, Sir Christopher Bell put up the money for our play so we had to go. No sponsor, no show, Grant says—Grant Noble, that is. He's starring in the play I'm rehearsing in Stratford, did I tell you that? So we all had to turn up to the reception."

Michel nodded and drank the rest of his black coffee.

"Sir Chris throws a soirée like that every time the Islington Ballet premieres a new piece in London; it's part of our sponsorship deal. I didn't have time to come home and change before the performance and it's a sackable offense to be seen front of house in jeans." He smiled at her. "Unfortunately it's also a sackable offense not to turn up to one of Sir Chris's receptions—hence my retreat under the stairs. So what were you doing under the stairs?"

"Me?" Jonni smiled foolishly. "I was hiding."

"Ah."

"You see Grant's a wonderful actor. Working with him is a tremendous privilege, it really is. But, well, it does have its drawbacks."

"Yes," said Michel. "Grant Noble's got a bit of a reputation for his drawbacks."

It was true; Grant Noble's romantic escapades featured regularly in all the tabloid gossip columns. It wasn't Jonni's fault if she had never heard about them before she landed this job; her parents never allowed any newspaper in the house that wasn't the *Telegraph* or the *Financial Times*. Besides, Grant was old enough to be her father.

"We actresses have to take the rough with the smooth," she said with a deep sigh of worldly wisdom. She stretched out her hand to pick up Michel's cigarette packet, barely noticing when he moved it out of her reach. She was enjoying herself. Sitting in an untidy, gigantic flat in the middle of the night, chatting away happily to a complete stranger; this was something like life. This was adventure! For three whole weeks she had been in London on what should have been a whirlwind voyage of new discoveries and experiences, and so far nothing had happened to her at all. Despite her new job and despite living with Auntie June she had been lonelier in London than she had ever been in her life. Tonight, drinking coffee with this unknown man in his kitchen, she felt mature and intrepid. She only wished her head would stop spinning.

"You know, I'm really only an assistant stage manager," she confessed, "with two small scenes in the play. But I'm going to be a star before I'm twenty-one. I've decided."

"Oh, surely not so old as that," Michel said, unable to conceal a smile. The telephone in the hall began ringing and he stood up. "That's my best friend calling to yell at me for leaving the party without him—watch yourself; you're going to fall off that chair in a minute." He picked up the receiver, speaking into it before he had time to hear who was on the other end. "Hi, Primo."

Jonni beamed, righting herself on her chair. Michel was standing in the kitchen doorway holding the receiver away from his ear at arm's length. She could hear the loud, complaining male voice even from here, fifteen feet away.

"No," Michel said at last into the telephone, "I don't want you round here in that state; I'm dog-tired . . . What? . . . Oh, I met someone . . . No, a woman." Michel's gaze traveled over Jonni's face and seated figure. "Yes," he said. "Yes, she is, very."

Jonni felt herself blushing. Was she? Of course he was joking—her legs were ridiculously short and her chest was too big for her height and her mouth was far too wide, ditto her backside, not to mention her nose which was freckled and small and turned up like a ski jump. But the smiling gray eyes were still turned toward her, as though looking at her gave him pleasure.

"I don't know, Primo. I haven't asked her yet."

Her color deepened. To her great surprise Michel held out the receiver toward her.

"He wants to talk to you."

"Me?" She stood up cautiously, alarmed to find the floor rocking under her feet like the deck of a boat, and navigated slowly along the side of the table. She hoped her unsteadiness wasn't visible to her host.

He handed her the receiver and she held it to her ear.

"Hello?"

"Bella, is me! Hello, bella. You havin' a good time?" The voice was so slurred and so Italian that Jonni could only guess at what he was saying. "*Senti*, bella, you ain't got to keep Michel up all night, *va bene*? And don' let him have no more coffee."

"Why don't you take some aspirin?" she suggested. "And drink lots of water."

She rested her hand on the door frame, steadying herself. Who was she to be offering advice?

"You got a nice voice, bella. I like to . . . Oh, *Cristo*, I don' feel so good. I'm gonna go to sleep on the sofa. *Ciao, bellissima. Ciao.*"

The phone went dead and Jonni hung up. Michel was leaning against the door frame beside her. He was still gazing at her.

Suddenly she found herself growing flustered under his stare.

"Your friend says you're not to have any more coffee."

"Does he?" Still Michel's eyes watched her. "Do you have to get up in the morning, Jonni?"

She hesitated. "Uh . . . no. We don't rehearse on Saturdays. Not yet, anyway."

Michel laid his hand on her stretchy red waist—touching her, she felt, as intimately as if the fabric weren't there at all. Now that his eyes were so close, looking down into hers, she could see it was tiredness that made him look so much older than she guessed he really was.

"There's only one bedroom," he told her, "but the bed's king-size."

She pressed herself as far back against the door frame as she could, smiling up at him awkwardly.

"Ah—right. One bedroom. Do you live here alone then?"

"Yup."

"Oh, that's nice. I wasn't sure. Yes, well, I'll just . . . go to the loo, if that's okay."

Michel nodded to one of the doors in the hallway.

"The bedroom's the one on the right."

"Thanks. I won't be a sec."

She dashed into the bathroom and bolted the door. She was insane! Totally one hundred percent stark crazy! Here, alone, with a man she'd never met before in his flat at half past one in the morning. And there was absolutely no doubt what had been in his mind when he was looking at her in the doorway—not that it meant he wasn't planning to rape and murder her into the bargain.

Sitting on the avocado-green loo seat, she pressed her knees together and clutched her little red handbag tightly. She was sobering up alarmingly quickly. How could she have been so naive? This was London! What had she imagined? That a man would pick up a strange girl at a party in the middle of the night and take her home just for a chat? She could still feel the intrusively sexual tingling of her skin on her waist where his hand had touched her through her red dress. It was flattering to be fancied but—Oh God—not here! Not now! Not alone with him at the dead of night when there was no one she could call for help.

What did other girls do in situations like this? Miserably she reflected that other girls probably weren't stupid enough to get themselves into this kind of situation in the first place. Oh, why had she drunk so much champagne? She didn't even like the stuff; it made her sneeze.

She stared wide-eyed at the back of the bathroom door. Okay, it was time to examine her options. She could make a run for it—dash out of the flat without saying good-bye—but what would she do then? She didn't have enough money for a taxi back to Auntie June's house in Clapham, and she supposed it was too far to walk even supposing she could find her way. Besides, she'd have to go back into the kitchen for her shoes. Suppose he was lurking there in the dark, waiting for her?

Jonni tried to stay calm. After all, what was the worst that could happen? She knew perfectly well he wasn't going to rape and murder her; that was nonsense. Ballet dancers didn't rape and murder people. But how could she put him off? Heaven knows she ought to have had enough practice with Grant Noble, but this was very different. This was Michel's flat and she had come here of her own accord—worse: she had practically invited herself! She gazed helplessly at an open box of Tampax on the floor next to the loo, vaguely registering how out of place it looked in a bachelor's bathroom. There was nothing for it but to tell him the truth: she was just a silly little girl from Gloucester with no experience of anything and she hadn't meant to lead him on—so please would he take pity on her and send her home or let her sleep on the sofa? And if that failed she supposed she'd have to scream the house down. One way or another she was resigned to making a complete fool of herself.

She stood up and looked at her reflection in the mirror over the sink with a sigh. Her mouth was still too wide. Her shoulder-length hair was pinned in a sloppy pile on top of her head, apart from one reddish-brown strand that had escaped, falling rakishly over her ear. She reached under the neck of her red dress and pulled up her bra strap, which had slipped off her shoulder.

Preparing to meet her doom, she opened the bathroom door and stepped into the dark hallway, expecting him to jump out at her at any moment.

The flat was silent, as it had been since she first arrived, but now the darkness made it seem silenter still. The only light came from behind the bedroom door, which was standing ajar. She stopped outside for a moment and then pushed it open.

"Michel, listen . . . I'm really sorry . . ."

The square bedroom had bare white walls and very little furniture. Plain sanded floorboards glowed soft orange in the dim light from a lamp on the bedside table. Jonni stood in the doorway looking in. Michel was lying facedown on top of the duvet, fully dressed, with both hands buried beneath his pillow. He was sound asleep.

Jonni stood without moving for a while and watched him. On the far side of the room the uncurtained sash window stood open, letting in the warm summer night air from the street.

"Michel?" she whispered.

There was no reply. Jonni crept toward him and leaned over to turn out the bedside lamp. She crouched down beside the bed and scraped her loose lock of red hair behind her ear with her finger, looking at his sleeping face in the shadowy light from the window.

"Are you awake?" she whispered.

The even rhythm of his soft breathing didn't change.

He looked very peaceful lying there in the darkness, and quite different. His half-open mouth was squashed innocently against the pillow, his clean-shaven face almost childlike. He slept very quietly. Jonni watched him in silence, still crouched beside him.

On the other side of the bed, beside the open window, she crossed her arms to pull her red dress off over her head and dropped it on the wooden floor. She threw her tights and hairpins after it. Lastly, she popped out her contact lenses and stowed them carefully away in the lens box that she always carried in her handbag. When she lifted one corner of the tan-covered duvet and slipped underneath it, Michel frowned in his sleep, murmuring in protest, and tucked his hands further under the pillow. Jonni froze, waiting until he was still again before she wriggled slowly down under the bedclothes. The cool cotton, pinned over her by Michel's sleeping body, smelled faintly of eau de cologne.

With her head on the pillow beside his, Jonni lay in the semidarkness with her eyes open, looking at him. The effects of the champagne had worn off during her panic in the bathroom and her mind was now quiet and calm. She could see the fair hairs on his forearm inches from her face where they caught the dim rays of light from the window.

Oddly, she was closer right now to this unknown dancer who had rescued her, picking her up like a stray puppy in the middle of the night, then she had been to anyone since she had come to London. In the morning when she woke up to find herself in a stranger's bed she might be embarrassed and wish she'd never come here. But for the moment she would just enjoy the unexpected intimacy of lying awake in bed beside a sleeping man she'd never seen before. Perhaps she might even meet him again one day. She hoped so.

Jonni Kendal knew all about hope. When she had first left home to go to drama school in Cheltenham she had been full of hopeful dreams of newfound freedom. Sadly her liberty was short-lived. Home came with her. No sooner had she settled blissfully into her crummy one-room bedsit in Cheltenham than her father's firm moved, bag and baggage, from Oxford to nearby Gloucester and she had no possible excuse not to move into her parents' new house less than two miles from the college.

But she never gave up hope. Hadn't she been the very first student in her year to get picked for a summer job in a holiday camp? The job never happened—her mother had a hysterectomy and Jonni had to spend the summer shopping and cooking at home—but at least she'd been picked.

Hope had blossomed anew with the unexpected offer from Stratford East to act with Grant Noble in *Forty-Love*. It all happened so quickly; Grant and his director, Leum, saw the school's showcase in April. The offer came less than a week later. Admittedly it was only a semi-acting role—she had to look after the props as well—but it was a real theater job. And with a real star. Against all advice, despite the funereal warnings of her mother and the pleas of her teachers who wanted her to finish her three-year course, Jonni disdained caution and set sail for London and freedom. After all, if she was going to be a star why wait another two years? Why not start now?

It was midsummer and Jonni had been in London three whole weeks. The rehearsals were going very slowly but she hoped the director would get to her scenes next week. Of course it didn't help that Grant never gave her a moment's peace. At the first read-through, when Grant had smirked at her across the room, a middle-aged actress sitting next to her had hissed under her breath, "Don't smile back! Don't smile back!" But it was too late; Jonni had smiled. Now she was paying the price. She hoped—oh, how she hoped—he would learn to appreciate her for her acting skills and leave her bottom alone. And though it was dreary living with Auntie June she hoped she would save enough by the end of the summer to rent a room of her own. And though London was a lonely place for an outsider she hoped she would soon make some friends. She hoped . . . hoped . . .

Jonni's eyes had closed without her noticing. Her last unspoken hopes vanished with her into sleep.

8

JONNI OPENED HER EYES in bright, gleaming daylight to find herself confronted by Margot Fonteyn decked out in white feathers and smiling down at her from a framed poster on the white wall. She knew it was Margot Fonteyn because it said so in swirling gold letters large enough to read even without her contact lenses.

For a few moments she gazed blankly at the photograph without a clue as to where she was.

And then it came back to her—the party, the man in the shadows under the stairs, a slightly befuddled memory of discovering she had left her door key on the prop table in the theater. But here . . . this room . . . ? She raised her head from the pillow and looked around, squinting against the piercing sunlight.

The other side of the bed was deserted, the smooth cotton crumpled from the weight that had lain upon it all night. Her outlandish nighttime adventure had unaccountably survived to take on the reality of the morning but it seemed appropriate that her mysterious companion had vanished, vampirelike, with the golden sunshine that streamed over the bed and walls in vivid, sloping rectangles. She snuggled down under the duvet, closing her eyes, and listened to the clatter of cheerful morning noises coming from the kitchen. Her recollection of the night before was hazy but at least she still had her bra and knickers on which was a comfort.

Suddenly the bedroom door was thrown open with a triumphant cry.

"Ta-da!"

She jerked her head up, clutching the duvet to her chin, and stared in amazement at the joyous face which had burst in. He was holding a tray bearing, amongst other things, a tall red rose in a glass of water. Jonni blinked firmly. Even allowing for her poor eyesight and the changes wrought by natural daylight, this was definitely not the same man who had slept beside her last night. That man had been taller, for a start, and fair. The fellow who was standing in the doorway beaming at her over the tray had shining black hair and rich, glowing eyes.

"Morning, bella! Is a beautiful day, no? Just like you!"

Jonni's head sank back onto the pillow and she smiled up at the ceiling. Of course! Primo! How could she have forgotten?

He sailed into the room, setting the tray on the foot of the bed, and snatched the rose out of its glass, presenting it to her with a flourish.

"For you, signorina—pinched from my landlady's garden with my very own hands."

Jonni sat carefully up in bed holding the duvet over her chest and took the flower from him. It seemed this was a household where mad things just happened.

"How's your head?" she asked, smelling the rose cautiously.

"Is *magnifico,* bella. I never slept so well in my life." He made himself comfortable, sitting on the far side of the bed, and started pouring coffee into two cups from a tall red jug. "You like it *alla francese,* with milk, or *al'italiano,* without?"

"Oh, with, please." She drew her knees up to her chest under the duvet. She must look like a scarecrow with her hair unbrushed and last night's makeup smudged around her eyes, but she didn't care. "To be honest, I feel a bit underdressed for a breakfast party."

The Italian stared at her in comical horror.

"What? Ain't you got nothing on under there?"

"Not an awful lot."

"Mamma mia!" He clapped his hand over his eyes and stood up to grope his way with exaggerated clumsiness to the pine wardrobe. When he pulled open the door a pair of suede ballet pumps held together with an elastic band fell off the top shelf. He caught them deftly in his hand and turned them over to look at the soft leather sole. "Hey, the thief!

These are mine. What's Michel doin' with a pair of seven and a halfs, eh? Jesus, you can't trust no one these days."

He tossed the shoes through the open doorway into the hall and pulled a folded T-shirt off a shelf, throwing it to Jonni. She wriggled into it, keeping her body concealed under the duvet. The T-shirt was huge on her; gray with "Islington Ballet" printed across the front in elaborate blue lettering.

Primo made himself comfortable again, handing her coffee across the bed and starting to butter a pile of toast.

"Bella, you got to taste my mamma's damson jam. You ain't lived till you've experienced this. I got to come over here for breakfast 'cos she sends it all to Michel; ain't that typical?"

"Where is Michel?" she asked, sipping her coffee.

"Gone to class. He'll be back in an hour or so."

"Class?"

"Yeah, class—you know."

Jonni didn't know. She frowned, puzzled, and Primo narrowed his smiling brown eyes, equally puzzled.

"You ain't a dancer, bella?" He glanced involuntarily at her chest. "No, you ain't a dancer. What are you, then?"

"I'm an actress."

The handsome Italian's brown eyes widened in ludicrous horror, suggesting all manner of dreadful sins inherent in such a wanton profession. "An actress?" He whistled. "Boy! Your mamma know about this?"

Jonni laughed.

"I think so—I did tell her. But she set Auntie June on me just to make sure."

"Ah," Primo said knowingly, "Auntie June. Yeah, you can't hide nothing from Auntie June. She's got eyes everywhere." He handed her a piece of toast. "So how did Michel find you?"

Jonni smiled, embarrassed. "I sort of found him, actually."

"That figures. I wish I knew what that guy's got that I haven't."

"Oh, it wasn't like that at all."

Between mouthfuls of toast and mouth-watering damson jam, Jonni told him all about her meeting with Michel under the stairs and the forgotten key. When she recounted the story of her desperate flight from the lascivious clutches of her famous colleague, Primo waved his toast at her, interrupting with his mouth full, "*Sì*, that man, Grant Noble; I see him throwing up in the gents' at the end of the party. Me, I am also so drunk I nearly piss on his head."

Jonni laughed so much she spilled her coffee on the pristine tan duvet cover.

"Oh, no! Look what I've done. Won't Michel be furious?"

Primo waved the mishap away with his toast. "Him? What's he care about a thing like that for? Ain't nothing worries him, 'less you ruin his ballet shoes."

Jonni and Primo made a riotous breakfast in the warm sunlight on Michel's bed, munching through the whole pile of toast and drinking a second jug of coffee. Jonni hugged the duvet to her knees, blissfully happy to be giggling like a schoolgirl with a complete stranger in another complete stranger's bed. She liked wearing Michel's T-shirt. It smelled of washing powder and a man's deodorant.

Jonni held the rose Primo had brought her under her nose, sniffing the heavenly summer smell luxuriously.

"Will your landlady mind that you pinched her rose?"

"What?" Primo pulled a crazy, skeptical face. "You reckon she goes out every morning an' counts them?"

"My mum would notice," she said grimly.

"She'd phone up Auntie June an' tell her."

"Yes, I'm afraid she would. Where do you live? Is it far away?"

"Nah, not far." He turned away, leaning across the bed for the coffee jug. "I used to live here with Michel when we was students, after he inherited this place from his uncle. I got my own flat now, just round the corner." As he sat up with the jug he winked at her. "This bedroom's great for two, but it ain't got room for three or four, you know? You want another cup? There's still some left."

She held out her cup eagerly although she was already swimming in coffee.

"I suppose I really ought to go," she said at last, looking forlornly at the sunlit window, "Michel won't want to find me here when he gets back if he has to dance tonight."

"So what, he's got to dance? It's his job. Besides, he ain't got to do nothing tonight 'cept drag Lynne across the stage by her feet a few times. Is no big deal."

"Don't you have to dance tonight too?"

"Me? No, I danced last night. We got two new ballets, see? Last night and tonight. I ain't in this one. Last night was the important one. Didn't you see it?"

She screwed up her nose and shook her head.

"Uh-uh. I'm not much of a fan. Was it good?"

"Yeah, course it was, it had me in it. Anyway, you can't leave, bella. What's Michel gonna think, eh, if I let his new girlfriend run away?"

Jonni grinned and tucked the bedclothes more tightly around her knees.

"I'm not really his girlfriend, you know."

"Course not. No one's ever really Michel's girlfriend." He yawned and stretched lazily, tipping over his coffee cup which luckily was empty. "So you got another name besides Bella?"

"Jonni."

"No kiddin'?"

She laughed. "No kidding. But I think I prefer Bella. Have you got another name besides Primo?"

"Sure, I got three. But in my family is so many of us we just get given numbers. It's easier to remember that way who gets to boss who around. No, I'm havin' you on—I was named Roberto after my dad 'cos I'm the eldest. But everyone called me Primo so we'd know which one of us Mamma was yellin' at."

By the time Michel returned from class Jonni and Primo were sitting in the kitchen drinking yet more coffee. Miraculously, the kitchen had been transformed overnight. The cups and ashtrays were all clean, stacked neatly on the draining board, and the junk that had littered the table and work surfaces had been arranged into tidy piles. Even the floor was shining.

"It was my turn," Primo said, stuffing the duvet cover into a washing machine next to the sink. "Michel ain't no good at housework anyway."

Jonni had given herself a brief tour of the flat, gasping slowly as she walked into the vast studio, with its beechwood floor and floor-to-ceiling mirrors covering one long wall. The only furniture in the room, apart from the black upright piano, was a coffee table and a pair of black leather sofas, dwarfed by the empty space around them. She walked slowly around all four sides of the studio, mouth open in awe. It was as well she hadn't known it was here last night; she would have felt swamped by it.

"It's incredible," she said. "I've never seen a room in a house this big."

Primo was smiling at her from the doorway, drying the coffeepot with a tea towel.

"We did it up ourselves, just five of us. It took us over two months just to tile the floor."

"Imagine having somewhere like this all your own."

Jonni's hand ran lightly along the polished wooden barre on the white wall opposite the mirrors. The studio was spotless and beautiful in its simplicity. Only the brilliant sunlight pouring through the two tall arched windows and a large rubber plant in a china pot saved the room from being austere. Jonni retied the cord of Michel's gray jogging trousers at her waist—she had rolled up the bottoms a good ten inches—and wandered into the middle of the parquet floor in her bare feet looking up at the molded ceiling. She could stay in this room all her life.

Michel came home shortly after one, dropping his bag beside the kitchen door and squeezing Jonni's waist lightly as he walked behind her.

"Hello, darling, my clothes suit you better than they do me. Primo, where the hell were you? The boss did his nut."

Primo was chopping tomatoes on the kitchen counter next to the stove. It seemed it was his turn to cook too.

"I only gotta do four classes a week. Equity rules say so."

"Yes, I know." Michel plugged in the kettle. "But it's not Equity who decides who gets a contract next year."

"Bullshit," Primo said. "I ain't on again till Tuesday so what's Charles growlin' about? Just 'cos he's wired about these new ballets ain't no reason to take it out on me." He saw Michel look at his watch. "What's the hurry, amico? You ain't called till six."

"Change of plan. Rehearsal on stage at two-thirty, though I doubt the new set will be in by then. Coffee, Jonni?"

"No thanks, I've got it coming out of my ears."

"Okay, chuck me that teaspoon, would you? Thanks."

That was all? He seemed barely to have noticed she was still there—or rather, he accepted her presence as though she were part of the furniture. Jonni sat with her chin propped on her hand and watched Michel sew gray elastics onto a pair of gray-dyed ballet shoes. His coffee was by his elbow and his feet were up on the edge of the table. He looked different today; rested and fresh-faced, newly showered after his ballet class. Wearing a T-shirt identical to her own—and which fitted him much better—she could see how athletic and muscular his body was. Now he did look like a dancer.

Primo was watching him too, frowning at him uneasily over his shoulder from the gas cooker while he stirred his tomato sauce with a wooden spoon. He had been subdued for the past few minutes.

"Listen," he said, "you want to do me a favor, amico? If Charles mentions me again, you want to tell him my groin's still hurting me after last night?"

"It's okay," Michel told him, biting off his thread without looking up, "I already did."

"Hey, I owe you one!" Primo's face bounced back to its former joviality in an instant and he whistled tunefully to himself, tossing handfuls of dried herbs into his pasta sauce. "This is goin' to be one seriously fuckin' great salsa napolitana, amici. You ain't gonna believe this!"

Jonni watched Michel snip off a length of gray elastic for his second shoe.

"It makes a change meeting a man who can sew," she said, smiling.

"All dancers can sew." He picked up his needle, glancing at Primo. "Though that doesn't mean they all actually do."

"Hey!" Primo protested, "The girls love sewing my shoes. You want I should deprive them of one of the simple pleasures of life?" He tasted his tomato sauce from the wooden spoon. "So class was okay then, yeah?"

Michel clicked his tongue.

"No, C.C. was in a filthy mood."

"I can tell. I was expectin' you back over an hour ago. How come you got to go to the theater this afternoon? I thought Charles said he weren't going to rehearse the new piece no more before tonight."

"Last minute cast reshuffle. Erik was rushed to hospital in the middle of the night with suspected appendicitis."

"You ain't serious." Primo paused in his stirring to look over his shoulder at Michel. "Boy, no wonder Charles is pissed off. Peter ain't goin' to like that at all—not after last night; his knee was killing him after the show."

"No, Peter's not up to it. He didn't even make it into class this morning."

"So who's dancing Paulo?" Primo asked. "Don' tell me is Daniel. No way. I s'pose it'll have to be him—ain't no one else knows it. Unless Anton can get it down in a few hours."

"No, I'm doing it."

"*WHAT?*" Primo's wooden spoon flew up in the air, splattering tomato sauce on the ceiling. He stared round-eyed at Michel, clutching a green pepper for support. "*Cristo!* Oh, God! Is okay, nobody panic! Nobody panic!"

No one apart from Primo was panicking in the least. Michel continued stitching calmly.

"It's no big deal. I know the steps; I've been dancing them at the back of the studio for weeks. It just means we have to rehearse it onstage this afternoon, that's all."

Primo was frantic: "But I mean, what? Charles really said you're gonna do the pas de deux? No way! You? Who with? Irena?"

"No, Lynne."

"*Mamma mia!*"

When Primo had calmed down enough to serve up his pasta—which had unfortunately got overcooked in all the excitement—Jonni sat with them eating quietly while they talked over Michel's unexpected new role in tonight's premiere. She was fascinated. Their discussion was complex, full of foreign vocabulary and jargon—and behind everything they said lurked the unmistakable presence of the ominous master whom they feared and obeyed, hovering over their heads like the Prince of Darkness.

"What about the triple?" Primo asked, waving his bread at Michel and talking with his mouth full. "I saw you trying that out at the back of the studio. Are you gonna put it in? What did Charles say?"

"That he'd sack me if I even attempt it." Michel added more salt to his soggy pasta. "He says there isn't enough time between the two steps to get a good enough preparation on it. He's probably right: I tried the triple in the combination twice after class this morning and fell on my arse both times. He told me to stick to the double, same as Erik and Peter."

"Man, you better then," Primo warned, "or you're gonna be singing effortless high Cs by the time the maestro's finished with you—I ain't joking, amico."

Jonni listened, wrapped in the mystery of the keyhole world which she was gazing into by pure chance; two dancers casually discussing the details of their obscure trade in the relaxed privacy of their own flat—at least, it was Michel's flat but Primo seemed equally if not more at home here. She felt like a spy, covertly observing the hidden universe of ballet into which she had stumbled accidentally. If it weren't for the fact that Primo and Michel had moved their chairs into positions at the table that included her naturally as the third corner of a triangle she would have felt invisible.

Michel chatted unhurriedly while he ate, with one foot propped on a chair beside him and his elbow resting on his knee, gesticulating calmly with his fork between mouthfuls as he talked. If he was nervous about the role he was dancing tonight it didn't show.

"C.C.'s worried about the one-arm lift; Erik was having trouble with it."

"Yeah, but that's 'cos Irena weighs a ton. Man, I'll bet Charles is absolutely spittin' mad he's gotta let you dance this role tonight."

"He didn't look best pleased, it's true. But Lynne and I know it so he doesn't have any choice. No, Carlotta's the one who's really furious. She was bitching about it all morning; she doesn't think I'm up to it—nor Lynne, for that matter."

Primo screwed up his mouth disparagingly.

"She's just jealous."

"Come off it," Michel laughed. "Carlotta wouldn't be caught dead dancing with me."

"She let you shag her."

"That's different. We didn't do that in front of eight hundred people."

"Look, amico, there's only one reason the Giant Tomato don't like you an' Lynne dancin' this pas de deux. An' that's because she's shit-scared you're gonna show her up. She likes the rest of the cast to be good, but not too good, you know? She's been countin' on havin' tonight all to herself."

Jonni propped her elbows on the table, letting her chin sink onto her hands again. She was intrigued.

"What's the ballet about? The one you're dancing tonight?"

"Hell," Michel said, as he pushed away his empty plate and lit a cigarette. "Dead sinners writhing in eternal torment."

"Crumbs! That's a bit heavy, isn't it?"

"It's very short. It's in a double bill."

"Can I come and see it?"

"I thought you hated ballet." He reached across the table for an ashtray, smiling. "I thought it was an outdated, meaningless relic, full of narcissistic men who look like women, and neurotic women who look like pipe cleaners."

Jonni felt her cheeks begin to turn pink.

"Oh Lord, did I really say all that? Goodness, I *must* have been drunk."

She wished Michel had told her he was a dancer before he let her shoot her mouth off like that. Abashed, she realized that if she'd given him a chance he probably would have. Primo, who was stacking the dishes in the sink, was shaking with laughter.

"To be honest," Jonni confessed, smiling guiltily, "I've never actually seen a ballet. Just snippets on the telly. It would be interesting."

Michel clicked his tongue and shook his head.

"Not tonight. Anyway it's sold out." He looked over at Primo. "You aren't coming, are you?"

"Nah, I've seen it so often I'm sick of it. An' like you say, the pas de deux ain't such a big deal."

"Just as well you think so. At the rate the boys are dropping you'll probably be dancing it yourself on Monday." He smoked the rest of his cigarette, chatting calmly to Primo about the "triple" he'd been ordered to miss out on pain of instant unemployment. As she listened, Jonni's view of their mysterious world became embroidered with colorful sketches of temperamental and eccentric dancers—and someone called Roly who was driving all the way to Gravesend between class and rehearsals just to see his grandmother for ten minutes on her birthday, and who hadn't minded in the least that Primo had accidentally bashed him on the nose with his elbow on stage last night.

"Mind you, Roly's nose could do with a bit of flattenin'," Primo admitted, but he said it with the loyal reluctance of friendship.

Jonni knew she should leave—go home to her cramped room at Auntie June's—but how could she? This flat, Primo's instant affection and crazy smile, the calm eyes of the man who had picked her up and put her in his pocket last night, they all anchored her here. She didn't want to walk out of the bubble she had unintentionally stepped into; it was round and multicolored and far more interesting than anything her own life had to offer. These people had ties to one another and to their profession. For all her dreams, Jonni was still gazing hungrily at life from the outside. Besides, hadn't Michel put his hand on her waist last night and looked deep into her eyes, claiming her? Although, for what she didn't know. For a moment of human contact? For a simple smile because he had taken pity on her? But Jonni was wearing his clothes; his rolled-up jogging trousers and his company T-shirt next to her skin. She felt attached.

Michel stood up to go to his rehearsal, searching through the tidy piles of papers on the table until he found a white paper bag containing a new pancake of makeup foundation. He ruffled Jonni's unbrushed hair as he passed her chair.

"See you around, darling. Primo, put her on the right bus for Clapham, will you?"

"We're goin' for a walk in the park," Primo told him as though it were all arranged. "Is too beautiful a day for sitting on a bus to Clapham."

Indeed it was; a glorious, warm summer's day—late June in full bloom. As Jonni walked over the grass in St. James's Park in her bare feet, carrying her red shoes in her hand, she felt the great depth of the ground under her feet: London, this huge city that linked her own little life with Primo's and Michel's. Even if she never saw them again they would still have this in common: this soil and the hard city pavements.

With the warm grass between her toes and the smell of freshly cut lawn in her nostrils, she strolled beside Primo, distractedly listening to his cheerful chatter. Suppose Michel hadn't been asleep when she crept into his room last night—there was no dread in the supposition now.

What would she have done? What would he have done? But her imagination failed her. Michel was still a sleeping mystery to her.

"Is tonight's premiere very important?" she asked, walking gingerly as they crossed a gravel path.

"Not so much as last night. Tonight's only a short piece. Like an afterthought for the *Paradise* ballet we premiered last night. Is unconventional, two new pieces in a row, you know. Though that don't bother the maestro none."

"Is he the man you're so afraid of?"

"Afraid? Nah, we ain't afraid of him. We just got to make sure he don't notice us. He's like a grizzly bear; you keep your head down and don't make no noise, he leaves you alone. 'Cept Michel—he don't never leave Michel alone." Primo grimaced, laughing. "Man! I wouldn't want to be in Michel's shoes this afternoon."

"Is Michel a good dancer?"

He grinned at her.

"What you say we go an' find out?"

"Tonight?"

Primo's shining brown eyes ignited in mischief.

"You reckon I'm goin' to miss Michel's first pas de deux—an' in a London premiere as well?"

Jonni blushed with pleasure at the invitation and the thought of seeing further into the secret world she had discovered. And to watch Michel dance.

"But you told Michel you weren't going."

"Sure; who wants their friends in the audience when they're nervous? But what he don't know ain't goin' to hurt him—an' afterward he ain't goin' to care."

"I thought you couldn't get tickets."

"Bella, I can always get tickets. Trust me."

She beamed at him.

"Can I go like this?"

Primo looked at the rolled-up bottoms of her gray jogging trousers and the T-shirt that hung tentlike from her shoulders.

"Yeah, why not? You better swap T-shirts with me though, if you're gonna be seen front of house."

Jonni looked down at her own chest—the Islington Ballet logo boldly stamped in blue—and then at Primo's plain green T-shirt. She would be sorry to lose her little stake in Primo and Michel's ballet company but it couldn't be helped. She watched as Primo pulled his T-shirt off over his head without inhibition, standing half naked in the park like the sunbathers who surrounded them, his narrow chest brown and muscular. He held the T-shirt out to her with a grin that dared her to follow suit.

"Wait, I can do this," Jonni said, laughing.

They sat on the luxuriant grass together, Primo stretched out lazily watching as Jonni wrestled with two T-shirts, wearing both at once, freeing her arms from the inner sleeves, scrabbling between the two layers to put her arms through the outer sleeves and, finally, dragging Michel's company T-shirt off over her head, apparel and dignity both intact.

"Victory!" She held it triumphantly aloft and then chucked it at Primo as a consolation prize. Primo sat up to put it on.

"Is a good trick."

"D'you think I'll make a contortionist?"

His eyes, peeking over the neck of the shirt, considered this for a moment.

"Nope."

"Pity. Can you do the splits?"

"What sort of question is that? Course I can, I'm a dancer."

"Show me."

Primo parted his legs into second position on the grass, flexing his ankles in his trainers.

"No, bugger it," he said, pulling a face. "I didn't do class this morning. I'm cold."

"You can't do it!"

"I bloody well can! That ain't fair! I got a groin injury!"

Jonni laughed until she fell over, burying her face in the fresh green grass.

In the warm golden glow of the summer evening, gorged on ice cream, Coca-Cola, and pizza slices from a stall in the park, Primo and Jonni walked along the South Bank. Pale orange ripples streaked the surface of the Thames beside them, reflecting brilliantly in the windows of the buildings that overlooked the river. The pavement, warmed all day by the hot sun, cushioned Jonni's bare feet, carrying her along on a carpet of dusty comfort. She lifted her face contentedly basking in sunlight.

"What a wonderful afternoon."

"Yep." Primo too was basking. "You want to sit on one of these benches while I go pick up the tickets?"

She nodded, choosing a bench in the sun not far from a statue that resembled a stick of celery.

Primo was gone for more than twenty minutes and by the time he returned Jonni was looking for him eagerly, missing his companionship.

"I thought you'd forgotten me."

"You think I got these tickets easy, bella? I bin chatting up the girl in the box office. I had to take her to the staff cloakroom for a bit of persuasion."

Jonni opened her mouth, only half believing him.

"Primo, you're terrible! You didn't!"

"It's the sexy Italian charm that does it. She couldn't resist my big brown eyes." He flashed her a wicked, provocative smile, his eyes sparkling. Jonni had to admit that he was probably right. His eyebrows wiggled cheekily as he waved two tickets in front of her nose: proof of his infallible powers of seduction.

"Easy, see? That's the best thing about being a dancer. You get to practice on all the pretty girls."

"I thought all male dancers were supposed to be gay."

Jonni felt a sudden jar between them. As so often, she had spoken without thinking. Primo's dark eyes were tense, offended.

"Bella, there ain't no queers at the Islington Ballet."

"Oh, I didn't mean . . . !" She backtracked anxiously. "I mean I wasn't saying—well, I was but . . ."

But Primo's high spirits were made of India rubber. Even as she dug herself deeper into her hole they bounced back, leaving the insult behind and forgotten.

"Hey, you look beautiful with the sun in your red hair, bella."

"Oh, Lord! It's not red . . . is it?"

"Aha! *La bella donna*'s weak spot. Her hair!"

"It's not my weak spot. Just tell me it isn't red! Please!"

"Alright, it's . . . *castano* . . . *châtain* . . ." He snapped his fingers. "What's the fuckin' English?"

"Auburn?"

"No, you eat it."

"Chestnut?"

"Yeah."

"Thank you."

"S'okay."

Jonni smiled into his warm, laughing eyes. The low golden evening sunlight was blinding.

"D'you think we ought to go in?" she asked. "It's after seven."

"You want to put your shoes on?"

"No."

"Carrot head?"

"Oh, alright." She squeezed her warm feet into her red high-heeled shoes and unrolled the bottoms of Michel's gray jogging trousers a few inches. "How do I look?"

"Original, anyhow. Come on then."

The foyer of the Queen Elizabeth Hall was beginning to fill up and Jonni followed Primo to the bar, remembering her frenzied flight of the night before when Grant had been pursuing her. She half expected to see his immaculately coiffured head appear from the crowd.

In her high-heeled shoes Jonni was almost as tall as Primo. She felt conspicuous walking beside him. There were dancers everywhere and they all seemed to know him. He stopped to speak to many of them as they passed, his arm protectively around Jonni's waist.

"Nah, she ain't mine," he said to an inquisitive girl who stared at Jonni very rudely, "I'm just lookin' after her for Michel." Primo patted the girl dancer's backside affectionately as they walked away. "Don' mind them," he told Jonni, "they're just nosy. They can't bear to think there's anything they don't know."

"I thought you said you had a girlfriend."

"Sure. I got half a dozen."

The auditorium was already half full when they shuffled along to their seats in the middle of the stalls. It was hot in the theater. Jonni was surrounded by a sea of waving programs as the waiting audience fanned themselves, talking noisily and waving to friends. The sea gradually gathered force as more and more people filed in. Some of them were dressed for a premiere, sweltering in evening dress, but there was also a strong contingent of young people, sensibly dressed in cool floral prints and short-sleeved shirts. The air buzzed with anticipation; the audience conferred knowledgeably over their programs or rose in their seats to point people out to each other across the aisles. Jonni's skin prickled at the atmosphere of excitement.

"Is it always like this at a first night?"

Primo looked around unimpressed.

"I suppose so. Look, you see that woman?" He pointed to a very ancient lady, white-haired and frail but still resplendently beautiful, being helped to her seat at the front by two middle-aged women. A small throng of elegant people paid court around her. "Is Madonna Nadia Petrovna Sekova: great Russian ballerina. She's our goddess."

"Does she belong to the company?"

"No, the company belongs to her. Tough as old boots she is too; even the maestro sits up an' listens when she speaks—sometimes."

Other dignitaries of the ballet world floated in and Primo pointed them out to Jonni as they appeared.

"That's Ernst Zuroff. Hotshot choreographer guesting at the Royal. Full of shit but the press like him 'cos he quotes Brecht in his program notes."

"What do you think Michel will be doing now?"

"He ain't on till after the interval, bella, so he'll still be at the barre."

Jonni twisted her head around to look at the steady flow of people still drifting into the auditorium. She could do with a drink herself.

"Cazzo!" Primo's face suddenly contorted in annoyance as a grossly overweight bulldog of a man lumbered down the aisle. "What's he doing here? He weren't here last night."

Jonni stared at the new arrival in distaste. The obese figure was sweating profusely in a mammoth tweed jacket and chewing on an unlit cigar.

"Who's that? You aren't going to tell me he's ever been a ballet dancer."

"Boyle," Primo said gloomily. "Big-time freelance dance critic; writes for the national press. The maestro ain't goin' to be pleased about that.

Boyle ain't never got a good word to say about nothing. You watch, bella; he'll sit right down the front next to the aisle so he can make a big exit ten minutes before the curtain. He's already made up his mind he hates the piece anyway."

"I come to bury Caesar, not to praise him," Jonni said with a sympathetic grimace.

"Yeah, and he's got a memory like an elephant. When Boyle decides he hates someone he hates them forever."

"Who does he hate in your company?"

"Charles Crown, of course. All the critics hate Charles. Bad news is, he hates Michel too."

"Oh no! Why?"

" 'Bout five years ago, when us apprentices were standin' in 'cos the company boys all had flu, Michel fell flat on his arse in one of the ensembles. Ain't no way Boyle'll have forgotten that; he wrote an entire review gloating about it."

"The bastard!"

Jonni detested Boyle. Lowering her eyes so she wouldn't have to look at his hideous bulk squeezing itself into a seat half its size, she studied the photocopied sheet in her program listing the casts for the two ballets.

"Why isn't Michel's name here?"

Primo turned her sheet over and pointed to his name halfway down the list of dancers: Francesca and Paulo: Lynne Forrest and Jean-Baptiste St. Michel.

"Jean-Baptiste?" She pulled a dubious face. "Is that real?"

"I suppose so; is what it says on his driving license."

Jonni read the program notes. The new ballet was an adaptation of part of Dante's *Inferno*. Skipping the background she read up on Francesca and Paulo; illicit lovers slaughtered in the guilty act by her husband, doomed forever to . . .

She never found out what their doom was. The houselights went down as a bald man in a black tailcoat stepped onstage to a burst of applause and took his seat at a grand piano.

The first half of the evening confirmed all Jonni's fears about ballet. *Les Sylphides*—twelve girls in frothy white net frocks floating around interminably in a moonlit wood to the accompaniment of Chopin on the piano. There was only one male dancer: a drippy, droopy chap in white tights and black waistcoat, with a white bow at his throat so enormous it covered almost his whole chest, reminding her of a huge cabbage-white butterfly. To make matters worse, halfway through the piece, one of the corners of the massive bow became detached from his waistcoat, leaving it flopping unbecomingly over his breast.

As far as Jonni could see there was no story, just a lot of gliding about and leaning over. The girls' movements were so identical it might as well have been done with mirrors. Every time the music came to a halt, Jonni was ready to burst into applause out of sheer relief. And each time it started again she sank back in her seat with a suppressed sigh. She began to believe it would never end.

Her only source of interest was Primo. He was staring at the stage, rapt, taking in every movement. His hand moved gently on the arm of his seat in sympathy with the music. Jonni watched his face with puzzled curiosity. Once or twice, she saw the muscles around his eyes contract in disapproval and his gaze drop sharply to the pianist's hands. But most of the time his eyes were fixed excitedly on the dancers. Mystified, Jonni glanced from his riveted eyes to the row of girls onstage. Yup, they were still gliding.

Twenty minutes into the ballet, when the lumbering figure of Boyle waddled up the aisle, Jonni turned her head enviously to watch him leave. She wouldn't mind betting he was heading straight for the bar.

At long last the ballet finished to an enthusiastic ovation, and Jonni slumped in her seat dying of relief.

"That was savage," Primo told her joyfully as he clapped and clapped, "Marcia's solo specially—you see those beautiful penchés?" He shouted ecstatically as one of the girls was handed forward by the droopy boy to take a solo bow; "Brava! Brava, bella!" Every member of the eight hundred–strong audience was in raptures, cheering and whistling. Jonni gazed around at them in astonishment. She had never felt so out of her depth in her life.

In the crowded bar amidst a deafening hum of conversation Primo handed her a glass of white wine and took a gulp of his stiff brandy.

"Man, I need this," he said.

Jonni raised her glass to her mouth lamely.

"So do I."

While the audience were queuing for the loos, and the critics swigged their free champagne, Charles Crown tracked Michel down in the dark wing at the side of the stage where he was waiting for the crew to finish the set change. As always before a premiere, Crown was rigid with fear, his whole body taut.

"You know what you're doing then?"

"Yup."

"Confident in Lynne?"

Michel was bouncing lightly on the balls of his feet to keep his muscles moving. His gaze was focused on the stage in steady concentration.

"Totally."

"Keep it simple and accurate. You're not here to impress anyone or to prove yourself, understand?" Crown's hands searched the pockets of his jacket for his cigarettes. He was terrified of letting Michel perform this role tonight in front of an invited audience of critics and the top brass of the profession. The few solos he'd allowed him to perform in the past had been in remote provincial venues well away from the eyes of the industry. And this pas de deux was a technical showpiece—a monster. If there were any alternative, even now, Crown would have pulled Michel out of it. It had even crossed his mind, for a few insane moments, to dance the role himself.

"Take it gently and concentrate on the lifts. I want it low-key; no fireworks."

Michel nodded still looking at the stage. "Got you."

"Nice easy turns—and a clean, straightforward double cabriole into the last combination. Right?"

"Right."

Crown's worried face twitched as he watched him, but there was nothing else he could say. After a few moments he turned around and went away.

———

Jonni was back in her seat beside Primo in plenty of time for the second part of the evening. In the orchestra pit a dozen musicians were tuning up. If someone at last night's reception had told Jonni she'd be sitting here tonight eagerly waiting for a ballet to start she'd have sent for the men in white coats. Boyle had taken his seat early, she noticed. This, after all, was what they had all come for.

The Premiere. Charles Crown's second new ballet in as many days.

"Oh, God, what if he falls over again?" Jonni whispered to Primo.

"Nah, he won't," Primo whispered back. "He was hungover that time when we was kids."

The ballet started strangely, arresting Jonni's attention at once: a black stage; a single dark note from the orchestra, very low. Then a pinprick of light and a hand reaching out. She watched the stage with a deep frown, puzzled and interested.

As the slow creaking notes grew from the orchestra pit, a lone cowering man was summoned into the darkness by a statuesque woman shrouded in white chiffon. Together the two figures descended into night.

Crown's interpretation of Dante's vision of Hell was intensely unpleasant. Gray-clad dancers drifted in their own form of misery across the stage, their movements jarring. Nothing went together. Each character moved with its own kind of pain. Jonni didn't like it but neither could she take her eyes off it.

In particular she watched the white chiffon lady. The role of Virgil, played by a woman, had caught her eye instantly in the program. Carlotta di Gian-Tomaso. Noble, elegant, unspeakably beautiful with vivid, lustrous eyes and a proud neck. Jonni wondered, awestruck, if Michel had really slept with her. She certainly didn't blame him if he had. She almost envied him. Carlotta moved like a bowing poplar, her shining eyes seeing far into the distance or the past. Jonni felt horribly, horribly ordinary.

Her mouth turned down in aversion as a tall, well-built man, shadowy in his gray costume in the dim streaky light, hauled a long, dead woman across the stage by her feet. Stolid step by stolid step he lugged his macabre burden, both her feet tucked under one arm. Her body trailed behind him, lifeless arms and long hair dragging pathetically after her, her chiffon dress rucked up around her breasts. Another sad spirit was trying to pull its own face off. The stage was filled with sagging souls writhing on the ground, or flailing helpless arms, dancing monstrously deformed ballet steps while Dante wept. Jonni could feel the audience around her cringing in physical and emotional discomfort. They just wanted the ballet to be over.

Her eyes were drawn to a couple dancing in the shadows at the back of the stage, almost unlit. Virgil summoned them and the girl came—a tiny, sorrowful creature draped in gray chiffon to her knees—to dance a slow classical lament alone. Jonni felt Primo's hand tighten its grip on the arm of the seat between them. The ethereal figure was bending backward to the ground, willowlike in her despair. Then, with a crash from the orchestra that nearly shook Jonni out of her skin, her forgotten partner flew out of the shadows in a huge, terrible leap and gathered her up in his arms, whirling her off into a tormented dance.

Jonni watched as Michel flung his little partner around. It was Michel who had flown out of the shadows, though she didn't quite believe it. How could this anguished, flying maniac be the same man who had slept so childlike and tranquil beside her last night? How could Michel, with the quiet eyes and the relaxed body, transform himself into this . . . this thing? She didn't even know if he was any good or not—she had nothing to compare him with. She only knew this couldn't be Michel. She didn't like it.

Her eyes followed him as he uncurled his body from an arching spin and launched himself off the stage, throwing his feet up in front of him and striking them together in the air—once, twice, three times—defiant of gravity.

"Jesus!" Primo whispered in horror, "he's dead!" He turned his head frantically to search for Charles Crown's face in the dark auditorium but Crown wasn't in sight.

The pas de deux was over almost before it had started. The couple went off to writhe together in the shadows, Michel bearing his partner away as though she were no heavier than an empty dress in his arms while Dante fainted through pity. Other ghastly punishments were paraded and wept over by the poets. People on the stage were eating each other's bodies. Boys squirmed together on the floor, bodies locked. At the back Michel was having undisguised intercourse, passionate and contorted, with the tragic Francesca. Jonni decided it was altogether the most explicit thing she had ever seen—aside from two minutes of a blue movie some prankster had edited into a video of *King Lear* at drama school, which still made her blush when she remembered it.

The whole ballet, from its start to the moment when the two poets emerged—to Jonni's great relief—into the light at the end, lasted no more than twenty-five minutes. And whatever anyone felt about the ballet nobody had been bored, that much was certain. As the lights came up the audience's reaction was one of bewilderment. There was a long stunned silence before the first smatterings of applause rippled from the front of the house. It was a strange reception that greeted the dancers who lined up to take their bow. The audience clapped steadily but no one felt like shouting. Even Primo was blank-faced, applauding automatically rather than with enthusiasm.

A slight crescendo greeted Carlotta as she stepped forward to make her deep curtsy. Now the audience remembered their manners. There was polite applause for the conductor and for the dripping man who had played Dante. Onstage everyone except Carlotta looked exhausted. Jonni watched Michel; he was breathing heavily, shining with sweat, dropping occasional swift glances at his partner's head as he stood with his protecting hand on her tiny waist. At one moment, as he looked out into the blinding lights from the auditorium, Jonni was almost certain he had deliberately looked right at her—but, of course, it was impossible.

How strong his body looked, like a classical statue. The flowing chiffon shirt that should have made him look effeminate only emphasized the masculinity of his hard body. And yet there was something fine about him; something light. She glanced at Primo. He was gazing loyally at his friend, his brown eyes glowing with pride.

"C'mon," Primo said as the curtain came down, "let's go meet him at the stage door."

"Won't he be ages?"

"What for? He's only got to shower and get changed. He'll be out in five minutes—unless Charles gets to him first."

"What will he do to him?"

"I don' know, but it's gonna be bad. *Cristo,* an' at the premiere, too."

Primo grinned at her as they shuffled along the row of seats in a queue. "It was worth it though, weren't it?"

"I don't know. Was it?"

Michel came out as quickly as Primo had promised, bright-faced and wet-haired from the shower, dressed in an outfit identical to the one Jonni had been wearing before she'd swapped T-shirts with Primo. He was more animated than Jonni had seen him before, laughing and chatting with the dancers who emerged from the stage door with him. His petite dance partner had possession of one of his hands, keeping his arm draped around her shoulder with her own small fingers intertwined with his, but he slapped his free hand into Primo's hand and squeezed Jonni's waist without interrupting his conversation. He didn't seem at all surprised to see her.

In the foyer bar Michel was so much the focus of attention and affection—and so fiercely guarded by his dance partner—that Jonni felt embarrassingly superfluous. A dozen different topics of discussion bounced back and forth around the crowd of dancers, all of which excluded Jonni. Even Primo, despite his friendly efforts to include her in the social mayhem of in-jokes and banter, became distracted by the familiar faces that shared his daily life.

Jonni began to creep away unnoticed, sipping her white wine with a fixed smile as she drifted farther and farther from the laughing group near the bottom of the stairs. One step at a time she retreated, still watching them with smiling eyes, until she had almost reached the shaded alcove where she had first met Michel less than twenty-four hours ago. It seemed she was destined to leave his life through the same door by which she had entered it. Her smile faded and she gazed wistfully at the happy group who were engrossed in the issues that linked their lives, picking up the threads of conversations that had started yesterday and the day before, the complex web of relationships and balletic jargon that was their world.

Behind Jonni, in the dark recess under the stairs where yesterday Michel had been unwittingly waiting for her, today there lurked only the familiar bugbear of her loneliness. She looked again at Primo, his laughing, expressive eyes deep in communion with his own kind, forgetful of his impromptu guest. And Michel with his back toward her, relaxed and mobile, still closely attended by his little partner, his hand absent-mindedly caressing the girl's shoulder.

As Jonni braced herself to take the final step back into the engulfing shadows she saw Michel turn his head, his eyes placidly scanning the bar. Instinctively he turned toward the alcove under the stairs. His eyes found hers and he looked at her, not communicating anything, just looking. For a long moment, while they stared at each other, the bar, the other dancers, the whole of the South Bank complex simply seemed to vanish.

At his side Lynne noticed his abstraction and twisted her slender neck to follow the direction of his gaze. Jonni saw her frown up at him and ask who she was. Michel turned away, back to his crowd of friends, giving her a brief dismissive answer. But Jonni didn't care. He had looked.

9

As the opening night audience poured out of the auditorium into the foyer, Charles Crown walked very slowly down the stairs toward the bar. He was totally washed out, oblivious to everything and everyone around him. The public streamed past him on the stairs, the tide of bodies parting to flow around him, taking no more notice of the short, dark-haired man than if he were a stone in their path. They were all talking loudly about the choreography but he didn't hear them.

The first performance of a new ballet always left Crown feeling like a wet, trampled dishcloth. For weeks, sometimes months, he poured his life's blood into the creation of a piece, tearing his hair out over it, raging at the dancers; black eyes blazing night and day in a fever of obsessive concentration. The struggle for perfection overwhelmed him during rehearsals but never, until the extra dimension of the audience was added, could he tell what the nature of the work would really be. At the first performance, a piece was lifted entirely out of his hands to take on a life of its own. Throughout the premiere Crown had sat rigidly at the back of the auditorium, teeth clenched, staring unblinking at the stage. Now he felt drained, lifeless, ready to melt in a puddle on the floor of the theater foyer.

At the bottom of the stairs an old friend was waiting for him, smiling and shaking his head over the choreography.

"Charles, you mad bugger; you've started a riot."

It was all Crown could do to lift his arm and shake the hand that was offered to him.

"Hello, Martyn. I didn't know if you'd be here tonight." Crown's eyes were still glazed. "Buy me a brandy, will you? I want to find a cigarette machine."

Martyn Greene was the artistic director of the British National Ballet; a slim, silk-voiced man in his mid-fifties who had been a celebrated principal of the Royal Ballet and one of the most flamboyant darlings of the ballet world until Nureyev defected from the East and knocked him off his pedestal. Now his still boyish face was engraved with intelligent, authoritative lines, and his camp mannerisms were given weight by his status as the director of one of the country's largest and wealthiest ballet companies.

When Crown rejoined him at a table in the bar, Martyn Greene was sitting back comfortably on his chair, unpeeling the transparent plastic from a long, slender cigar.

"You're a scary bastard," he said as Crown sat down opposite him. He clicked the button of his gold lighter, watching the flame for a moment before he held it to the end of his cigar. "Of course the critics will hate it."

Crown shrugged, too weary to reply in words. The critics hated anything they didn't understand, and they certainly wouldn't tolerate the mixture of classical and contemporary styles in this piece. He picked up the double cognac that Greene pushed toward him and swallowed a large mouthful. As the strong liquid burned on his palate his hawklike eyes watched Greene's face anxiously. Greene's was one of the few opinions he knew he could trust.

"What did you think—really?"

"Oh, it's a masterpiece. No question. I wasn't quite sure about the set, though. I thought you could have risked a bit more color. Jules's design, wasn't it?"

"Yes, but he didn't have a budget for it. It was mostly a recycled *Giselle*—not the last production, the one before."

Greene smiled to himself and sat back even further in his seat, cigar in hand, looking at Crown.

"The situation's not worthy of your work, Charles. You know it isn't.

Come on, isn't it time you stopped playing tiddlywinks at the Islington and started doing your choreography justice?"

Crown looked down at the table, swilling his drink slowly around the bottom of his glass. This was nothing new. Greene had been badgering him for years to forsake the Islington Ballet for the far greater opportunities and kudos that the British National Ballet could offer him.

"Resident choreographer," his old friend said. "Total freedom to make whatever pieces you want. A hundred-, a hundred-and-fifty-thousand-pound budgets. Full symphony orchestra. Arts Council support. Vast studios. Massive technical and administrative backup. The choice of the best designers and composers in Europe. Instant recognition in the international dance arena. Think about it, Charles: seventy-eight of the finest dancers creamed from schools and companies all over the world."

Crown thought about it. The money worries at the Islington Ballet and the practical hardships; the constant battle just to keep the little company afloat. Twenty-six dancers, groomed and shaped by his own hand: a faulty, problematical crew of rampant individuals . . . compared to Greene's magnificent seventy-eight. Every few months Greene waved the same fat carrot in front of his nose. One day, no doubt, either Greene would give up or Crown would give in. And Crown was pretty damned sure he knew which would happen first.

He knocked back the rest of his drink.

"Thanks, Martyn; I'll stick to my twenty-six."

Greene laughed. "You're a stubborn son of a bitch." He sipped his martini looking at Crown, taking his time. "Charles, my love, you've been keeping something from me."

A shadow of unease crossed Crown's face.

"Yes? What's that then?"

"The boy."

"What boy would that be?"

"Come on." It was a gentle, amused reproach. "You know which boy I mean. The boy who danced the short pas de deux in the middle of your piece."

"Oh, him."

"Yes, him." He took a cast sheet from his pocket and glanced at it.

"St. Michel; now there's a name to conjure with. Where have you been hiding him?"

"I haven't been hiding him."

"A new acquisition?"

"Not at all. You just aren't very observant. He's been around; he was my student."

"Ah, he was. Yes, I thought I recognized your signature on his technique." Greene raised his eyebrows. "Nice job, Charles."

Crown lit a cigarette, tapping his heel rhythmically under the table. "Thanks."

"He's not a soloist yet?"

"Fourth-year corps. He'll make coryphée next year. He's only twenty-two; there's no hurry. I'm still working on him."

"Yes, of course. That's some very serious equipment though—extraordinary. Where the devil did you find him?"

"Paris." The heel of Crown's black shoe was still tapping against the floor. He didn't want to discuss Michel. "At the Académie."

Greene nodded pensively. "Figures. What relation is he to Jacques?"

"I don't know. He says none."

"He's lying, of course."

"Probably. I wouldn't blame him, would you?"

Greene twisted his mouth into a grim smile and shook his head. St. Michel's ruthlessness and arrogance were becoming almost legendary in the dance world. It was largely stories of his outrageous behavior, gleefully reported by the press, that kept the public flocking in their thousands to see his work.

"I heard on the grapevine that Jacques has a nephew somewhere in Europe. This is the boy, I suppose. It's a remarkable body. Beautiful proportions."

"Good feet," Crown conceded reluctantly. "It's the feet that catch your attention."

"Yes, and the face; lovely mouth."

"He's not so special."

Across the packed bar behind Greene's shoulder, Crown could see Michel amongst a crowd of dancers near the stairs. Even in unconscious repose Michel's face and body stood out naturally from those around him. He had his back to Crown but he had turned his head to look at someone across the foyer: a girl—Crown didn't recognize her. Crown looked down at the cigarette in his hand, not wanting to direct Greene's gaze toward Michel.

"He's just like any boy, Martyn. He has his good times and at others he can be bloody frustrating."

"Brave of him to stick in that triple at a premiere."

"Fucking irresponsible!" Right now Crown could have killed Michel for that stunning triple cabriole. "He could easily have buggered the whole thing up."

"Looked to me like he had no doubt he was going to pull it off."

Crown was becoming increasingly agitated.

"Look, he's my dancer, Martyn. I know him. I know how he ticks and I know his body. Don't overestimate him. Now let's change the subject."

"I see." Greene looked at him with sly amusement. "Something of a personal possession, is he?"

"What's that supposed to mean?"

"Fresh . . . youthful . . . a real Adonis."

Crown's face clouded over in rage.

"I do not fuck my dancers! Of either sex!"

"I want him, Charles."

"Well, you can't have him."

"I meant for my company."

"I know what you meant. And you still can't have him."

"But I will."

"Jesus!" Crown stared at him. "You wouldn't do that to me!"

"To you, Charles? What about him? Think what I can do for him. Immediate exposure. The very finest partners. A proper platform for his talent."

Crown clenched his fist slowly on the table in front of him.

"Look, Martyn, if you're trying to wind me up it's working. The boy came to me with very serious problems. His technique was completely screwed. I've broken my fucking back getting him sorted out. I told you I'm still working on him."

"He looks pretty solid to me."

"But he can go farther. Much farther!" Crown raised his dark eyes urgently to Greene's face. "Martyn, listen to me. He needs time. His body's still getting stronger. And his style hasn't developed yet. He knows he's good but he's got no idea of what's really in there waiting to come out. He mustn't be rushed; he needs to be brought out slowly. He needs the focus of the studio, you understand?"

"But if he isn't stretched—"

"Stretched? Christ! Mornings, evenings, weekends—in classes and rehearsals, alone in the studios with him at night, for six years I've done nothing but stretch him. And plan for him. You've seen him, Martyn—how often does a teacher get a chance like that? What you saw on that stage tonight is nothing to what I can get out of him if I have the chance. Let me finish with him first. Martyn, Jesus! You and I have been friends for years!"

Greene shook his head.

"Charles, you've never put friendship before your company's interests, and nor can I. Besides, how much longer can you hide him in the corps? It isn't fair on him; you know that."

"Give me two years with him. One year! For Christ's sake, at least let me keep him until January."

"I can't, Charles. I'd gladly give him a year or two, but by then Royal or English National might have nipped in before me. My checkbook's big but it's not as big as theirs."

"He can't be bought," Crown said savagely.

"Yes he can. All dancers can be bought, my love, especially young ones; if not by the money then the bright lights and the chance of fame. He'll accept my offer, don't doubt it."

Crown closed his eyes and ran his hand slowly over his knotted forehead, trying to settle his frantic brain.

Of course Michel could be bought. Greene was right. What boy of Michel's age could not? Any dancer would be lured by the opportunity to partner women of the standing of Marie Gillette and Tatjana Kieskewicz at the BNB. Crown knew what would happen once Greene got Michel into a studio and saw what he could do: the explosive leaps, the wild turns in second, that intense sexual magnetism, all at close quarters. Greene would put him on in everything: Albrecht, Corsaire, Don Quichotte, Romeo; all the bravura roles one on top of the other. Michel was hungry and ambitious just like any young dancer. Of course he would accept Greene's offer. And Greene would make a circus performer out of him, showing off his tricks to the world until Michel either broke an ankle or wore out his ligaments. Crown gave him five years, maximum.

"You don't have to lose him," Greene said. Crown opened his eyes and looked at him, weary but attentive.

"Come with him, Charles. Come to the BNB. You can keep an eye on him; I won't put him on in any role against your advice. Create your ballets on him. Continue teaching him. The offer's there."

Crown was silent for a moment and then he leaped to his feet, slamming both his fists violently on the table. His brandy glass and a slender vase of carnations toppled to the floor with a crash of breaking glass. The dancers by the stairs all turned their heads to look.

"Get the fuck out of my hair!" he yelled. "Keep your government-sponsored claws out of my life and out of my fucking company!" And he stormed out of the foyer, charging through the crowd like a torpedo, knocking startled onlookers out of the way.

Greene rescued his drink from its position precariously near the edge of the table and finished it calmly. His eyes scanned the foyer looking for one particular face but he didn't find it. The area where the crowd of dancers had been standing at the bottom of the stairs was deserted.

In the small hours of the morning Michel drove Lynne home from his flat in Pimlico to her tiny bedsit in Camberwell overlooking the green. She stood by the window watching him with her hazel eyes while he drank the coffee she'd made for him; strong and black with two sugars. Michel held his coffee cup cradled in the palm of his hand between gulps, his other hand still in the pocket of his tracksuit bottoms with his car keys. He was in a hurry.

"What do you think that explosion in the bar was about?" Lynne asked him.

"I don't know. Could be anything, you know him. Especially when he's wired after a premiere."

Lynne knew he was thinking about the illegal triple he had thrown into his solo.

"What are you going to do?"

"There's only one thing I can do. I'll tell him the truth: that I didn't mean to do it, it just happened—assuming, of course, he doesn't beat the shit out of me before I get the chance to say anything."

"Michel, he wouldn't hit you!" Lynne's smooth forehead furrowed in concern. It was far from impossible that Crown would hit Michel. It wouldn't be the first time.

"Well, if he does, I reckon I can give as good as I get."

Lynne's eyes widened. Charles Crown was simply not someone you could hit back. Michel saw her alarm and smiled. "I wouldn't, Lynnie. Besides, how could I? He's smaller than me."

Her elfin, childlike face relaxed when she saw she was being teased.

"Oh, God, I thought you meant it. He'd kill you, smaller or not."

"I'm sure you're right."

They both knew what would really happen. Whatever form Crown's fury took it would be short and sharp, Michel would apologize, and it would be over. For all his ferocity Crown wasn't the man to bear grudges.

Michel set his empty cup down on the mantelpiece.

"Anyway, Lynnie, you've got nothing to worry about; you danced perfectly tonight."

Lynne blushed at the rare compliment from her partner. She turned away to toy with the corner of the curtain hanging at the side of the window.

"Do you really have to go?"

"Yes, I must. Primo and the others will have gone by now. I can't leave Jonni back at the flat on her own."

She laid her face against the cool glass of the window. "Are you going to make love to her?"

"Yes, if she'll let me."

"Why?"

"Because I fancy her. What other reason?"

"You spent all that time in the kitchen with her this evening ignoring the rest of us."

Lynne raised her hand to wipe away the mist that her breath had formed on the black windowpane. She knew quite well it was her own bitchy comments that had driven Jonni out of the studio, and that Michel had followed her only to console her.

"She's not one of us," she said tensely. "And, anyway, she's appallingly fat."

"Both of which you made abundantly clear to her."

Lynne could hear that he was smiling and closed her eyes in frustration. In the six years that she'd been Michel's partner, and intermittently his lover, she had never seen him angry. Oh, how she'd love to see Michel, just once, blow his top—to see that placid smile wiped off his face; to know she had at least the power to move him that far. She had more or less given up trying except for occasional moments of nastiness such as this.

"She probably screws around more than you do, seeing she's an actress. She sounds just your type. And her boobs are as big as mine were before I had them fixed. I'm sure she perfectly reflects the depth of your values when it comes to women."

She waited for him to speak but she was answered instead by a silence that grew and grew. She looked at his reflection in the window where she had wiped the condensation away; he was standing patiently with both hands in his pockets, rocking gently on the balls of his feet.

"Did you kiss her while you were with her in the kitchen?"

"Yes. Is that alright?"

"Oh, fine."

"Look, I'll see you tomorrow. Come over early if you like and we'll do some work on the Tchaikovsky piece."

"Oh, Michel." She turned around to show him the two big tears that were running down her cheeks smearing her mascara. "Our first pas de deux! After all this time, all our hard work. All the years we've been dreaming and talking about being allowed to dance a duet on stage. And we finally did it."

Tears sometimes worked with Michel but they weren't infallible. He jiggled the car keys in his pocket, uncomfortable.

"We'll dance the pas de deux together again on Wednesday, I hope.

C.C.'s not expecting Erik back on his feet before Cardiff, if then. And there'll be lots of times in the future."

"But our first, Michel! Our very first! How insensitive can you be? It's got nothing to do with anyone else. This is our night. I thought you would want to spend it with me."

He took his hand from his pocket to rub the back of his head, running his fingers slowly through his fair curls. Looking at her vulnerable eyes and quivering mouth he couldn't help but remember how vastly she had changed since they first danced together, and what a long, hard struggle it had been for them both. Lynne gazed at him plaintively, crying while she watched him change his mind.

He walked to the window and put his arms around her slight body, resting his chin against her hair and looking over her head at the buses waiting at the traffic lights on the far side of Camberwell Green.

"I didn't mean to be thoughtless," he said. "You know me, Lynnie; I'm no good at all that sentimental stuff."

Lynne hid her wet face happily in his shoulder.

"Will you stay?"

"Yeah, of course I will."

He bent to kiss her and, as she raised her eager mouth to his, he put his hand under her thin sweater feeling for her breast.

"Don't, Michel. I hate having my boobs touched."

"No, you don't," he said. And he kissed her again. In many ways they knew each other better than they knew themselves.

When Primo went home to his little flat in Lupus Street leaving Jonni alone to wait for Michel, she washed up the cups and glasses from their little unplanned party and then wandered from room to room, delighting in having Michel's flat to herself. After only twenty-four hours she loved this flat more than anyplace she had ever been. She loved the high ceilings with their corner moldings and the tall Georgian windows, and the sparse furniture that left the flat full of big empty spaces. And the life this flat saw! People came and went as they pleased, making themselves at home, raiding Michel's kitchen, and taking over the studio with a nonchalance that seemed to Jonni thoroughly bohemian. Jonni had seen enough of Michel and his friends to know a little more about them by now. She had heard them talking earnestly about their craft curled up on the black sofas in the studio. She had listened in wonder to Primo playing Liszt on the piano, her contact lenses swimming in tears of sheer surprise. Nothing in the laughing frivolity of the madcap Italian had prepared her for the shock of his skill and sensitivity as a musician. He could play absolutely everything—from memory and in any key you liked. And she'd discovered he was something of an intellectual as well; he spoke all sorts of languages, had read Nietzsche, Plato, and Koestler and knew more Shakespeare than she did herself.

But most of all she had seen Michel dance.

When she grew tired of wandering through the rooms of the flat she brushed her teeth with the same toothbrush Primo had found for her that morning and tucked herself up under the duvet in Michel's bed, turning on the bedside light to leaf through a copy of Dante's *Inferno* which she had found lying on Michel's chest of drawers. The pages alternated between Italian and French—no use to her at all. She looked up as the telephone rang in the hall.

The clock on the bedside table said ten past two. She decided to let it ring. When the ringing stopped she turned off the lamp and lay in the unlit room looking at the cross-shaped shadow of the window frame on the wall, where it targeted Margot Fonteyn's shoulder like a badly aimed rifle.

In the silence of Michel's bedroom she tried to remember how she had felt when he lowered his face to hers in the kitchen, his eyes near and intimate, and enclosed her lower lip softly between his own lips. Remembering the warmth of his mouth, and with the smell of his cologne aftershave on the pillow under her head, she closed her eyes and died very quietly.

When she opened her eyes again Michel was sitting on the edge of the bed smiling at the sight of her warm sleeping face. It seemed only a moment ago that she had closed her eyes. The physical memory of his kiss was still in her mind, confusing her.

"Oh, God; hello," she said, awake but disorientated. "I must have dozed off."

Daylight had once more stolen into the bedroom to dispel the dreamlike clarity of nighttime; a black-and-white film unexpectedly flooded with Technicolor. She blinked at Michel, befuddled, as he picked up the small leather-bound volume of Dante still lying open on the duvet under her hand.

"I'm not surprised you fell asleep."

"What time is it?"

"Nine-thirty, quarter to ten."

"In the morning?"

"Yes." He creased up his eyes apologetically. "I'm sorry. I did try to call you."

"I heard the phone but I didn't dare answer it." She gave him a sleepy smile. "I was afraid it would be the terrible Charles Crown ringing up in the middle of the night to tell you off about the triple whatsitsname."

Michel laughed aloud. "I wouldn't put it past him."

"Are you coming to bed now?"

"No, I've been to bed. Lynne's in the kitchen."

"Oh."

Jonni's face fell as she remembered Lynne. It all made sense now. He had gone to take Lynne home and he had never come back. She understood.

"She's okay, Jonni. She didn't mean those things she said last night. That pas de deux at such short notice was a really tough pull for her."

"I'm sure she's very nice."

Jonni was certain that Lynne was perfectly ghastly. Pretty, super-thin Lynne, with her bitchy comments and even bitchier smile, was the one person she'd met this weekend whose acquaintance she could happily have done without. But it couldn't be helped. As Michel had said to her in the kitchen last night, you take your friends as you find them.

"It's quite cozy in here," she said, smiling. "I'm beginning to feel quite at home in your bed. Oh!" She grabbed the edge of the duvet and pulled it quickly over her face. She hadn't meant that to come out sounding the way it did at all.

When she peeled the duvet back gingerly his eyes were alight with laughter.

"Really?" he asked.

"Oh, don't! I can't believe I said that. I'm sorry, I must have taken my brain out last night with my contact lenses."

"Don't say you're sorry. I was hoping you meant it." He laid his hand on her waist through the duvet. "Come and join us in the kitchen. Help yourself to my clothes; you know where to find them."

In the kitchen Lynne was making coffee, filling the jug slowly from the kettle through a filter. She glanced at Jonni when she appeared in the doorway but didn't speak to her. Michel was turning over the pages of a newspaper on the table while he munched a croissant. It was a very Sunday-morningish scene.

"Where's Primo?" Jonni asked.

"Gone to Mass."

"Mass?"

"He always takes his mother when we're in London. He'll be here soon. Help yourself to croissants." He pushed the open paper bag toward her.

There was a sudden crash from the studio next door; the sound of something heavy landing on the floor. Michel and Lynne turned their heads quickly to look at each other in alarm. They both cocked their ears, listening, toward the wall of the studio.

"She's alright," Lynne decided. "She'd have yelled if she'd hurt herself."

Michel saw Jonni's puzzled expression and smiled.

"Annette," he said. "She's warming up."

A few minutes later the handle of the studio door rattled cheerfully as it opened and Annette sauntered into the kitchen, resplendent in a black leotard and turquoise shiny tights, with a blue silk scarf twisted through the dark curly hair that was piled haphazardly on top of her head.

"Oh God, I'm so virtuous," she moaned ecstatically. "I've been working out for a whole hour. I deserve a stack of doughnuts." She looked at Jonni, straightening her neck in surprise. "Oh! Hello!"

"Annette, Jonni—Jonni, Annette," Michel said without looking up from his paper. Annette was apparently satisfied with this limited introduction and leaned over to kiss Michel before plonking herself on a chair with an air of complete exhaustion. She fanned her warm cheeks with a copy of *Dance and Dancers* that had been lying on the table.

"Michel, darling, you have the face of a man who got laid last night."

"Well, you of all people ought to know what that looks like, darling."

Instead of taking offense, Annette seemed to consider his quip a huge compliment. She snorted delightedly and accepted a cup of black syrupy coffee from Lynne's hand. If Michel had the face of a man who'd got laid, Annette certainly wasn't in any doubt as to who the lucky girl had been; Lynne was radiant with smug, complacent happiness. Jonni's cheeks began to tingle with embarrassment. She realized what a fool she must look, waiting alone for Michel all night in his bed while he was with another girl.

"Oh, bliss!" Annette sighed, sipping her coffee, "God, this really hits the G spot, I can tell you."

Jonni laughed to cover her mortification.

"I thought it wasn't supposed to exist," she said. "Isn't it a myth?" She smiled timidly at Annette. Annette was the most glorious creature she had even seen. What wouldn't Jonni give to be so tall and elegant with round, exquisite eyes, perfectly balanced heart-shaped face, and such magnificent hair?

Annette turned her decadent, confident gaze toward Jonni.

"What's a myth? The G spot? Lord, no, of course it isn't, lovey. It'd be a pity for us girls if it was. Get Michel to point it out to you; he knows all about those things."

Jonni turned an immediate, horrified crimson but Michel merely raised his eyebrows, continuing to study his newspaper.

Annette laid her cup on the table and took a croissant from the bag as she turned to Michel.

"Did you see the notes I left you by the phone?"

"No. Who rang?"

"Oh, everybody. They were determined not to let me do my barre in peace this morning. Let's see . . . someone named Carrie Eastleigh."

He glanced up at her in surprise.

"Really? What did she want?"

"I couldn't quite work it out. I think she wanted to know the best route to Croydon from Yeovil—something to do with a chicken shed." She looked at Michel oddly. "Is that possible?"

"Yes, I suppose so."

"Who is she?"

"Oh . . ." He turned the page. "A relative. What did you tell her?"

"I told her to take the M6."

"Oh, you didn't. For God's sake, Nettie." He stood up, closing his newspaper. "I'd better call her."

"No, no!" Annette laughed. "I didn't really. I told her I didn't know and she said she'd ask a neighbor. She said not to bother calling."

Michel sat down again, shaking his head at her.

"Who else phoned, then?"

"Martyn Greene."

"Who?"

Annette's huge green eyes were provocative and mysterious. "Martyn Greene."

"*The* Martyn Greene?" asked Lynne, stunned.

"Well, of course, *the* Martyn Greene! How many Martyn Greenes are there? Mister British National himself."

Michel looked dumbfounded.

"Christ Almighty! What would he phone me for? And here?"

"He wanted to invite you to the BNB's do on Monday week. He knows we don't have a show that night because Primo and Roly are already going. You know, Primo played for those classes at the BNB in January."

Michel was still dubious.

"Why would he ask me?"

"Who knows, darling? He said he'd pop an invite in the post." She put her hand dramatically over her eyes. "My God, I had a conversation on the phone with Martyn Greene! I must have been hallucinating."

"Perhaps you were," Lynne suggested.

"Don't talk cobblers, of course I wasn't." Annette was her down-to-earth self again. "Anyway, I told him you'd be delighted to accept."

"Oh, thanks!"

"Don't mention it. This could be it, Michel. You're on your way up."

Michel smiled, amused, and went back to his newspaper.

"I don't believe a word of it. It's a wind-up."

"Ha! You wait and see."

Ten minutes later Primo turned up, with a large oily bag of jam doughnuts, filling the kitchen with craziness and laughter. And not long after him, the fifth and final member of Michel's little family arrived, letting himself into the flat with a cheerful singsong greeting from the hallway.

"Hi, gang!"

Jonni shrank against her hard kitchen chair as she looked at the stranger in the doorway. Roly was rather scary at first sight; too muscular for comfort, his body pumped-up after a grueling two-hour dance class in Shaftesbury Avenue, and too tall. When he walked into the kitchen, pulling off his sweatshirt, he seemed to fill the whole room.

"Everyone okay?"

He walked around the long table, clasping the hand Michel held out amicably toward him, and bent down to kiss first Lynne's mouth and then the top of Primo's head.

"Who was teaching this morning?" Michel asked him.

"Medallion Man."

"I'm glad I didn't go, then."

"No, it was good. I liked his allegro this time."

Jonni braced herself for the inevitable introduction but, instead, Roly walked straight over to her chair.

"Stand up, chicken, and let me have a proper look at you."

Before she knew it she had been pulled to her feet and she shrieked in surprise as he picked her up between his strong hands, holding her tightly under her arms as he lifted her like a toddler toward the ceiling. She looked down at his face, some two feet below her own, blinking in astonishment.

"Hi, Jonni," he said smiling.

"Hello."

Roly gazed up at her—examining her, as he had said, properly. His smiling eyes traveled slowly over her, taking their time. Roly's face had none of the fine-featured beauty of Michel's nor the romantic dash of Primo's. His coarse wavy hair was reddish-blond, quite without dignity or style, and his skin was slightly marked with the scars of ancient acne. But what his face lacked in physical graces was more than compensated for by the kindness in his blue eyes. Roly was clearly as soft inside as he was hard outside.

"Jesus, Shel," he said in dawning wonder, not taking his eyes from her face. "You said Jonni was pretty; you never told me she was so . . ." he gazed at her wide mouth searching for the word, and then he laughed, ". . . delicious."

He put her down, holding her against his body as he lowered her the last few inches to the ground so her feet wouldn't jar against the floor. Jonni couldn't help smiling, even when he kissed her mouth before releasing her from his arms.

"Watch him, bella," Primo warned. "He's a wolf."

"I recognize you," Jonni said shyly, "from the ballet last night. You were dragging a dead body across the stage. It quite upset me."

"Corpse," volunteered Annette, raising her hand to nominate herself without looking up from the color supplement she had pinched from Michel's paper. "It upset me too, lovey, I assure you. My ankles are still killing me."

Roly frowned at her. "Do they hurt? Honestly?"

"Well, no; not at the moment. But they should after the way you pulled me around so roughly. Really, you might try and be a bit less cack-handed; it's a bloody painful thing, you know, being yanked along by your ankles."

Having heard the material answer to his question, Roly ignored the rest of Annette's complaint. He laid his hand on Jonni's shoulder.

"I'm not really a wolf, darling."

Jonni wasn't sure she believed him.

Once the group had polished off Primo's doughnuts with yet more coffee, Annette yawned expansively, unfolding her arms swanlike into the air above her head.

"So are we going to do this bloody pas de deux then, or what? Or did I spend an hour warming up for nothing?"

Roly nodded and pushed back his chair. "Yup, okay." But Annette wasn't ready yet.

"Hold it. Let me get my clogs on."

Jonni watched as she stuffed the toes of her pointe shoes with paper tissues and put them on, tying the ribbons round and round her ankles and tucking in the ends.

She stood up and knocked each of her toe blocks indifferently on the floor to test them, pulling her leotard further down over her shapely bottom before she clomped off toward the studio with a long-suffering sigh.

"I suppose we may as well get on with it. Though I expect you'll only drop me."

"You're probably right," Roly agreed. "Only don't make the mistake of thinking it'll be an accident." He winked at Jonni as he followed Annette out of the kitchen. "Welcome to the family, chicken."

In the studio Jonni stood beside Michel and Primo. All three were watching Roly and Annette work through the pas de deux that Michel and Lynne had performed last night. Lynne was sitting on the piano stool in front of the mirror clapping her hands as she counted out the beats for them. She did know how to smile, Jonni discovered, and she could even be quite funny. But only if she liked you. Lynne still hadn't spoken a word to Jonni since the night before.

The pas de deux was a completely different matter in Roly and Annette's hands—Annette so magnificent and statuesque; Roly gravely trying to cope with the tricky lifts. Jonni watched with bright, interested eyes while the movements which had looked so simple last night were broken down into their complex, problematical components.

Nothing had changed between Roly and Annette, even after more than six years of dancing together.

"You'll have to help me more," Roly told her, putting her down after a lift.

"What do you want me to do, for Christ's sake? Fly?"

"Come on, love; even little Jonni pulls up more than that when you lift her."

"Dance the fucking pas de deux with her then!"

Michel was standing with his arms folded, watching the pair of them gravely. He turned his head to murmur to Primo, "She's going to break that guy's back one of these days."

Primo nodded. "Yeah, that or his heart."

Jonni smiled at the idea. Brawny, robust Roly, with his muscular shoulders and tolerant if somewhat sarcastic good humor, didn't seem in imminent danger of suffering damage to either.

Suddenly she felt as though she were watching them all from a great distance. Annette lording it over her partner in the middle of the studio with her beautiful, arrogant eyes. Roly nodding patiently, trying to catch his breath with his hands on his hips. Lynne's small fingers tapping out the rhythm of the music. Primo laughing at them, his arms folded in unconscious imitation of Michel.

And in the midst of them Michel himself; his body relaxed, watchful face in repose, clear eyes deep pools of thought.

Later, when Primo was at the piano accompanying Roly and Annette, and Michel and Lynne were stretching at the barre, Jonni slipped quietly out of the studio and changed into her red dress, leaving Michel's clothes neatly folded on the bed. On her way to the front door of the flat she paused outside the studio with her red bag and shoes in her hand.

"Yes, that one's a real bugger," Michel was saying to Roly. "You've just got to go for it, there's no other way. Get your hand under her bum and give her a really good shove—Lynnie, come here a sec. I'll show you."

Jonni closed the front door silently behind her as she left.

10

ON MONDAY MORNING, before an early class—the Islington Ballet had a busy week ahead—Michel presented himself in Charles Crown's office prepared to submit to the full force of his anger.

"Can I have a word?"

Crown looked unusually weary, depressed even.

"Well, what is it?" He lit a cigarette and looked at Michel with spiritless eyes, waiting. Michel moistened his lips, nonplussed at this bland reception. He had fully expected to be yelled at the moment he walked through the door.

"I'm sorry about the triple. I know you said not to try it. It just came out that way. I honestly meant to stick to the double." When Crown didn't respond Michel laughed uneasily. "I bet I gave you a bad moment there."

Still Crown said nothing. Michel ran his tongue over his lips a second time.

At last Crown flicked the ash from his cigarette into an ashtray.

"When you launched into the triple were you sure it was going to work?"

"Yes, certain."

Crown shrugged: "Well, that's alright then, isn't it?" He waved the two fingers holding his cigarette at the door. "Go on, St. Michel, off you go. I've got work to do."

Michel went away, but he was puzzled. Crown's passivity didn't deceive him. He'd been Crown's dancer for six years and he knew that disobedience, even accidental disobedience, didn't go unpunished. Michel had hoped to forestall the blast by bringing it down on his head in one early explosion—it had always worked in the past. But this time it seemed Crown intended to choose both the time and form of Michel's castigation for himself.

Walking slowly down the stairs toward the men's changing room, Michel tapped out an uneasy rhythm on the banisters with his fingers. Crown had told him on Saturday morning he'd sack him on the spot if he was stupid enough to try for a triple at the premiere. Michel didn't believe it. But then he didn't believe Crown's placidity either.

The reviews for the two new ballets came out over Tuesday and Wednesday, pinned up on the noticeboard by Nadia Petrovna's secretary as they appeared. For once the national dailies had all sent representatives, intrigued by the sheer insanity of launching two new ballets on consecutive nights.

As expected, the critics unanimously damned both *Paradise* and the *Inferno*. Carlotta, however, received measured praise. Even Lynne got a few mentions. She was described by various critics as "lithe and ethereal," "aerial," and even "delightfully pretty," which last comment she considered offensively ambiguous.

Michel received only one mention. Boyle's contemptuous review in the *Telegraph* noted that Lynne was "partnered adequately by the inexperienced Jean-Baptiste St. Michel." There was certainly nothing ambiguous about that.

Michel shrugged off the snub. Everyone at the Islington Ballet made it a matter of pride to shrug off reviews. The ferocious independence of their artistic director had rubbed off on them all. No matter how many tears were shed in private over the reviews, the dancers made light of them amongst the company. It had become traditional for Charles Crown to stroll up and down the studio in the mornings before class with a newspaper in his hand picking out the rudest bits to read out loud.

This week, however, Crown said nothing about the reviews.

He plowed through rehearsals with a set face, stalking forbiddingly around the corridors in the Goswell Road building, or hid himself away in his office with paperwork, dogged and uncommunicative. Everyone was aware something was wrong. The dancers kept out of his way. The company manager and administrators stepped around him gingerly as they pulled together the last-minute arrangements for the tour. Nadia Petrovna watched him with puzzled eyes. For once Crown wasn't the loud driving impetus at the center of the company; he was a brooding, dark force skulking in the shadows.

By Thursday Crown had still not so much as growled at Michel. On the contrary, during a rehearsal of the *Inferno* duet he shrugged and told Michel to use his own judgment about the cabrioles.

"You're not a child, St. Michel," he said, and turned away to attend to something else.

A cloud hung over the whole company. Nobody said so but they all felt they had somehow let him down—except for Carlotta who informed the entire common room tartly that she, for one, had danced like a bloody prima and if Charles didn't like it then it was the fault of his eff-ing choreography, wasn't it? Everyone longed for next week when they would be out on the road.

"You know that dinner at the BNB?" Michel was sitting with his friends in their usual corner of the common room during a break in re-hearsals. "I was thinking I might give Jonni a ring and ask her if she fan-cies going."

"I thought you were taking me," Lynne said quickly.

"It doesn't make any difference. You can go with Primo. We'll still all be together."

"Yeah, come with me, bella. Hey, Michel, how you going to find Jonni? She vanished without leaving no address or anything."

"She's working at Stratford East. I'll track her down there."

Annette was reclining in luxury with her feet in Primo's lap while he massaged her insteps with his strong hands.

"Yes, there—there! Ah God, that's better than sex!" She twisted her elegant neck to look over her shoulder at Michel. "Actually, I was hoping one of you buggers was going to ask me."

The boys glanced at each other. Annette: of course she couldn't be left behind. But there was no question of her going as Roly's guest. The two of them would only bicker all evening and, besides, she'd almost certainly refuse.

Roly finished his coffee and threw the plastic cup in the bin, bouncing it expertly off the metal rim from a distance of ten feet.

"Primo, why don't you take Annette?" He laid a diplomatic hand affectionately on Lynne's arm. "Lynnie, love, you come with me. That'll work best."

Lynne leaped to her feet, shaking off Roly's hand and glaring at them all in fury.

"I feel like bloody pass the parcel! Let me know when the music stops." And she stomped off inelegantly across the common room, flapping her feet like a duck in her pointe shoes.

At lunchtime, in a café near the theater at Stratford East, Jonni sat stirring a cup of coffee and gazing into space.

The small café was quiet, even at lunchtime. It was a quaint place, self-consciously cottagey, with square gingham-draped tables perfectly aligned along each side of the room, and a white vase of pink carnations on each table. The paintings on the walls were slim-framed watercolors of blooming gardens with white garden furniture.

Across the table from Jonni, toying with a paper-wrapped lump of sugar, sat the elder of the play's two leading actresses. Maggie Lane had been in the business twenty-five years and she had learned how to ride the overweening egos of actors like Grant Noble on a wave of wry cynicism. Maggie had a glamour all her own: deep-red hair always piled high on her head and a plump, hearty figure that wouldn't look out of place striding across a field in wellies. She was forty-seven going on sixteen, and her eyes twinkled with wit and intelligence. She watched Jonni with raised eyebrows.

"I think that coffee's stirred by now, Jons."

"What? Oh . . . yes, of course. Sorry." She laid her teaspoon on the saucer beside her cup. "I was miles away."

"I could see that."

"I was trying to understand what Leum was saying about letting my own emotions feed the character. I do wish I wasn't so stupid."

Maggie snorted, picking up her own teacup.

"The reason you don't understand, love, is not because you're stupid; it's because Leum is full of bullshit."

"But Grant agreed with what he was saying."

"That's because Grant is stupid."

"Oh, Maggie." Jonni bit her lip, amused and scandalized by such heresy. "How can you say that? He's a great actor."

"Yes, and so's my left foot. Don't believe everything the critics tell you. And, for heaven's sake, don't let Leum get you all worked up about emotions. Decide what the character wants and what she's afraid of, that's the key. Once you know that, decide what brand of toothpaste she uses, what she reads in the loo, and leave the rest to instinct." She swigged her tea like an alcoholic knocking back a stiff gin. "That's all you need to do, Jons. Take it from an old ham."

Jonni smiled. Maggie was the best person in the company. Jonni adored her.

"You don't really think Grant's a bad actor, do you? He always makes me feel terribly small."

"Oh, this play's just a big wank for him. He doesn't give a monkey's about your emotional realism or anyone else's. As far as he's concerned this is the Grant Noble Show, and that's all that matters to him. You watch him: he'll always find little, sneaky ways to keep the rest of us in the background—making sure he's doing something very interesting downstage when it's anyone else's turn to say a line; not listening to you; always keeping just a couple of feet behind you so you have to turn your back on the audience to talk to him. They're all old time-honored tricks. But it's not fair on you, love; you're not experienced enough to take him on."

"What about you? Do you do the same to him?"

"Heavens, I'm far too old to fight back. Let him have his day, I say." She looked at Jonni with a malicious sparkle in her eyes. "I'm a fine actress, Jonni, and I've met plenty of insecure actors like him before. I could demolish his performance single-handed if I fancied the battle."

Jonni looked dubious for a moment and then beamed at her.

"I bet you could too, Mags."

"Oh, don't doubt it."

Their toasted cheese sandwiches were brought to the table by a motherly waitress in a floral overall, and they set aside their professional grievances in favor of hot molten cheddar. Jonni wolfed hers down; she was ravenous. Long after she had pushed away her empty plate and picked the last pieces of watercress off the rim, Maggie was still eating at a far more dignified rate. Eventually Maggie patted the dark lipstick that remained on her mouth with a paper napkin and then folded the napkin and tucked it under the edge of her plate.

"Okay, out with it: who is it?"

Jonni looked up guiltily, startled.

"Who's what?"

"Who's the man—at least I assume it's a man—whose face you've been staring at in that vase for the last ten minutes? And whose hand you keep feeling touch your face?"

Jonni whisked her hand away from her cheek, trying to pretend she had just been rubbing it absentmindedly.

"No," she said. "There's no man, honestly."

"Aha! I knew it!" Maggie slapped her hand triumphantly on the table. "Then it must be that dancer fellow you met at the weekend."

"Goodness, no! I wasn't thinking about him. I didn't even realize I had mentioned him to you."

"Mentioned him? Jonni, love, I know what the fellow has for breakfast. Oh, Lordy, there you go again, only this time it's your lips."

Jonni lowered her fingers from her mouth.

"Don't be ridiculous."

"Oh, dear." Maggie tilted her head sympathetically. "Is it very bad? We couldn't be dealing with a little infatuation here, could we?"

"I'm not infatuated with him."

"It's not . . . Oh my God! It couldn't be the dreaded . . . dare I say it? It's not . . . love?"

At last Jonni gave in and smiled. There was no hiding anything from Maggie.

"Alright, I like him, okay? He was nice to me and he kissed me once, that's all. I don't suppose I'll ever see him again."

"So phone him up and ask him out to dinner!"

"Don't be absurd."

"Why absurd?"

"Oh, Mags. He doesn't want me. I'm just an ignorant, awkward stray he found wandering around lost in a cheap red dress from C & A. He was just being kind. He's got a life of his own. I haven't." She was still smarting at the humiliation of having so obviously waited for him in his bed while he was with Lynne. It was he, after all, who had suggested she should stay the night—she really wasn't sure whether to feel indignant or just plain silly.

"Well, give me his number," Maggie said, "and I'll phone him. I've got a husband and three kids and if that isn't a life I don't know what is."

Jonni shook her head.

"It's really not important. I had a wonderful weekend with a bunch of people I've never met before. I should be glad. It's just that . . ." She looked down at Michel's face in the reflected sunlight on the vase, her eyes becoming wide and abstracted. ". . . Oh, I don't know."

"He must have liked you. He did kiss you."

"I don't suppose he meant anything special by it." She looked up at Maggie with a sheepish smile. "I think he was going to make a pass at me but he ended up spending the night with another girl instead."

"Ah," said Maggie. "I'm afraid that's not such a good sign."

"It sounds weird, doesn't it? But it didn't seem as odd as it sounds at the time. It was like being . . . in a film."

Maggie chuckled. *"Gone With the Wind."*

"Oh, no. An arty French film."

"Worse and worse. That always happens when you fall for a man." She shuddered dramatically. "Your perceptions become heightened and real life goes all tingly. Beware *l'amour!*"

She uttered these pearls of wisdom with such melodrama that an elderly couple on the far side of the café turned their heads to stare. Jonni put her hand over her face, laughing.

"You make me feel like such a fool, Maggie."

"Why? I'm the one who's behaving appallingly—and loving every moment of it." She waved regally at the staring couple and then leaned across the table to whisper to Jonni, "In a minute I'll stand up and dance a fandango just to see their reaction."

Jonni looked at her, pulling a funny, sorrowful face.

"I wish I was like you. Oh, Maggie, why am I such a child; daydreaming all over the place, desperately trying to pretend I'm sophisticated when I'm really ugly and gawkish. I only have to open my mouth and I make an idiot of myself. I wish I had style and confidence. I wish I was like other people."

Maggie's laughter faded. She looked at Jonni with frowning compassion and moved over to sit on the chair next to hers, reaching out to lay her hand on her cheek.

"Jonni, love, you're beautiful. And you have a beautiful face. Don't try to be like other people. You're fresh and young. Your spontaneity is enchanting; it makes you special. And never be ashamed of innocence. It's splendid that you daydream—I hope to God no one ever takes that away from you."

Maggie was so much in earnest that Jonni lowered her eyes, smiling, to the table.

"I still wish I wasn't so fat."

"Fat? Your figure's heaven. Where on earth did you get that idea?"

"Someone told me—well, she sort of told me. That's what she meant, anyway."

"Then she's either insane or a stick insect."

Jonni contemplated that, frowning thoughtfully.

"Actually," she said, "now you come to mention it . . ."

The meager hour allotted for lunch had slipped away all too quickly. Reluctantly the two women pushed back their chairs, leaving the money for their lunch on the table.

"Ah, well, back to the male chauvinist pigsty." Maggie fanned herself with her tattered copy of the script. Summer had turned the East End into a blinding furnace over the past few days. She hoisted her heavy handbag onto her shoulder. "Girdles on, girls!"

In the middle of the afternoon in the sweltering rehearsal room, a run-through of Jonni's uncomfortably intimate scene with Grant Noble was interrupted by a telephone call being put through from the stage door.

"Oh, panties!" sighed Leum, the director. "What a time to interrupt the flow!"

"Saved by the bell," Maggie murmured to Jonni as she went to answer it. A moment later she put her hand over the receiver, waving it at Jonni in a frenzy of excitement.

"It's him! It's him!" she hissed in a high-pitched whisper that was almost a squeak. "My God, he's got the sexiest voice I've ever heard in my life!" She took her hand away from the receiver and spoke into it again with dignified grandeur. "Do hold on, please. Miss Kendal won't be a moment. She's just finishing her iced tea."

Jonni dug her in the ribs in wide-eyed laughing outrage and held out her hand for the telephone. Her whole body from the waist down had turned suddenly to jelly and she felt something go clunk in her stomach. She held the receiver to her ear.

"Hello?"

"Jonni? It's Michel. Where did you run away to?"

11

MONDAY WAS AN ODD NIGHT of the week for a party, but the British National Ballet had finished their summer tour on the previous Saturday in Southampton so the week ahead was, for the BNB, a week of comparative rest.

Jonni heard nothing of her acquaintances from the dance world over the weekend. They were busy with their last London performances and working all day Sunday to prepare for their own tour, which was just about to begin. Jonni's weekend was quiet and lonely but even the loneliness had a thrilling tingle to it; she sunbathed on Clapham Common in the blazing heat, reading over her lines, which she already knew perfectly, and watched television with her aunt in the evenings. Auntie June liked to watch political debates and documentaries, so Jonni went to bed early to lie awake and dream. Monday night crawled toward her as slowly as the leisurely ladybirds that mooched around in the grass on the common.

Jonni went to rehearsal on Monday morning with her plans carefully laid. If—worst-case scenario—her rehearsal ran on until six, she would just have time to hare to the Underground station and leap on a tube, dash through Pimlico's wide streets to Warwick Way, and scramble into her stretchy red dress and high heels before it was time to leave at half past seven. She would be hot and sweaty but it was the only solution.

All morning while Maggie, loyal conspirator that she was, complained of exhaustion and sunstroke, Jonni hoped against hope for a miracle. And for once, against all odds, fate was on her side. The afternoon's rehearsal was canceled at an hour's notice so that Grant and Leum could give a live radio interview at the BBC.

"Sorry, lovelies," Leum said, "afternoon's a write-off."

Jonni didn't need telling twice. Squeezing Maggie's hand for luck she dashed out of the rehearsal room at half past twelve into the brilliant sunshine of Stratford's busy Broadway.

"Knock him dead!" Maggie called after her.

Outside the stage door Jonni closed her eyes and sniffed the heat-soaked air of the beautiful afternoon. It was all hers. The day was too glorious to be cooped up unnecessarily on the Underground so she took a bus into the West End, sitting on the top deck with a carrier bag containing her red dress, shoes, and makeup clasped on her lap. She was aggrieved at having to wear the same cheap jersey dress that she'd worn last week but it was all she possessed—apart from a green satin ball gown her mother had bought for her which made her look like a Christmas tree. She had a horrible suspicion that Lynne Forrest would have oodles of clothes—magnificent, expensive evening dresses: Jaeger, Dior, Chanel; stuff by Italian designers she'd never even heard of—and that her own stretch-polyester would look unbearably tawdry. No matter, she told herself bravely. It couldn't be helped. At least her frock was freshly dry-cleaned.

While the bus inched its sweltering way down Oxford Street, along with what seemed like every other bus and taxi in London, Jonni gazed through its hot windows at the crowded shops. London was half dressed at the moment; the city had thrown itself wholeheartedly into the joy of the heat wave. Even the businessmen carried their jackets slung over their shoulders, hooked jauntily onto one finger, their collars and ties loosened in a rare fit of unorthodox homage to the weather. Half the world was in shorts and sleeveless tops. Oxford Street glowed with sunburned necks and faces, and Jonni was as brown and glowing as the rest. She had spent the whole weekend outdoors in just her shorts and yellow strapless bikini top.

Suddenly Jonni got up from her seat and hurried down the stairs at the back of the bus, stepping off onto the pavement. A turquoise dress in one of the shop windows had spoken to her, calling her name.

She certainly couldn't think of buying it, especially once she saw the price tag. She had only two hundred and twenty pounds in her bank account and payday was almost a month away. But it wouldn't hurt just to try it on. It was a sunny day, after all, and she had all the time in the world.

In the communal changing room, concealing her body self-consciously from the other women shoppers, she wriggled into the dress, twisting her arms like an escapologist to do up the zip at the back, then turned to look at herself in the mirror. It really was a splendid dress: vibrant turquoise linen, beautifully shaped to hug the curves of the body, with a plunging neckline and demure calf-length hem. With a heartfelt sigh she took it off and returned it to the rail with its identical twins. There, alas, it must stay. It gazed after her reproachfully from its hanger as she left the shop.

Ten minutes later Jonni was walking dazedly along the blistering pavement, amid the crowd. It was by far the most she had ever spent on one garment—eighty pounds! She was shocked at her own temerity. Stopping on the pavement in front of another shop window, her eyes widened in horror. Her crime was even worse than she had realized. Of course, she would have to have turquoise shoes as well! Even Jonni with her limited dress sense knew she couldn't possibly wear her tatty red shoes with this frock.

The search for shoes took her a further thirty-five minutes and decreased her bank balance by as many pounds. It was dreadful but they really were lovely shoes; one shade darker than the dress with slim, elegant high heels. She blushed at the sheer joy and wickedness of such rash expenditure.

Having sinned thus far Jonni abandoned all caution. She bought a beautiful choker of dark blue beads at John Lewis and then went back to buy the matching bracelet. Enticed into the ladies' wear department at Selfridges by a sign advertising massive reductions, she chose a lacy, white strapless bra and—as there was twelve percent off—decided to buy the matching knickers and suspenders too, along with two pairs of shimmering tan stockings. Last but not least, she bought a dazzling red lipstick called Femme Fatale; just the shade she had always wanted.

She stood at the bus stop clutching her purchases and trying very hard not to think about the fact that she had only seventeen pounds, plus what little she had in her purse, to last her the rest of the month. It would mean getting a sub from the theater or, worse, borrowing from her mother—but it was worth it.

On the bus Jonni's heart misgave her. She was plagued with doubts. The dress wouldn't fit properly. It was too classical to suit her. And turquoise, for heaven's sake! And she was sure the shoes were the wrong color, besides which she'd be certain to turn her ankle at every step. And the beads would look tacky, which they weren't, defeating the object of the whole exercise. What was the object of the exercise? she wondered. Oh, dear! Her mother would have a purple fit if she knew she'd bought a suspender belt.

At least she was certain about the lipstick. She took it out of its paper bag and tested the rich crimson color on the back of her hand. No one would convince her that this lipstick was not perfect.

By the time she rang the doorbell of Michel's flat in Warwick Way, it was almost four o'clock. No one answered, so she sat down on the wide front doorstep to wait. The sun, bouncing off the cream and white walls of the tall Georgian houses, was scorching, more like Mediterranean sun than English sun, and the black railings lining the pavement were too hot to touch.

Jonni only sat and basked for ten minutes before someone came out of the building and let her in. She climbed the winding concrete stairs to the top landing and tapped out the code on the keypad next to the door, her heart racing because she remembered this landing so well and because she had thought she would never see it again.

The flat was empty. Its emptiness filled it like a ghostly presence. She had three and a half hours to get ready for the party, and with any luck Michel wouldn't be home for ages. She reacquainted herself with each room, making a slow circuit around the sunlit studio and experiencing again the childish delight of the first time she had seen it. In the bathroom she touched the things on the shelf under the mirror: Michel's shaving foam, Michel's razor, Michel's soap and toothbrush and cologne.

In Michel's bedroom she stashed her purchases guiltily behind the door in case anyone should come in unexpectedly and rumble the embarrassing secret that she had bought new clothes especially for this evening. Then she locked herself in the avocado-green bathroom and ran a deep bath, helping herself from a large bottle of pine-scented bubble bath and sinking down under the suds until only her nose and eyes were poking out. She was here in Michel's flat, wallowing prenatally in warm soapy water with the smell of pine in her nostrils. All other things, even Michel himself, could wait.

As Jonni soaked with her eyes closed she was startled by a sudden bang in the hallway and an urgent thumping on the bathroom door. Her head shot up, protruding from the suds like an alarmed rodent as a voice called out to her, "Jonni! Is that you in there?"

Her shoulders sank back into the water limply as she recognized Lynne's voice. The very last person she needed to complete her enjoyment of the afternoon.

"Jonni! Hurry up and let me in, will you? I'm absolutely dying for a pee."

Jonni wasn't quite sure what to make of the unusual request, but she couldn't very well refuse. She hauled herself reluctantly out of the bath and, like a dripping snowman, leaned over to unlock the door. Inhibited, she plunged back into the water, covering her breasts with foam as Lynne burst in.

"Hello," Jonni said, suspicious and unwelcoming.

But Lynne was too busy unzipping her jeans and pulling them down past her knees with a sigh of anticipated relief to notice Jonni's restrained greeting. Jonni looked away tactfully until the other girl stood up and fastened her jeans over her impossibly small waist.

"Hello, lovey. Did Michel tell you we got a massive round of applause for our pas de deux on Friday? It was incredible. We've really got it cracked now. D'you want a coffee?"

"Thanks." Jonni was still cowering under the suds.

"Righto, I'll stick the kettle on." She breezed out of the bathroom leaving the door open and shouting, "Charles let us off early today so he could spend the afternoon beating the boys into shape—isn't that blissful?"

Jonni could hear her running the tap in the kitchen sink. Lynne's unexpected friendliness had confused her. A few moments later Lynne came back into the bathroom clutching a yellow taffeta dress.

"What do you think of this? I got it in a secondhand shop in Tachbrook Street on the way here. There's a stain on the waist but I thought I could cover it up with a black scarf for a belt. Do you think I could get away with it or is it absolutely ghastly?"

The dress was tightly boned in the bodice, strapless, and flared below the waist—an original 1950s jitterbug dress. Jonni found herself grinning.

"I think it's gorgeous."

"You're sure? It's not too garish?"

Within minutes the girls were sitting in the kitchen together, Jonni wrapped in Michel's white bath towel, drinking coffee and examining each other's purchases. One by one the pieces of Jonni's new outfit came out of their carrier bags to be held up for inspection.

Lynne groaned over the dress.

"You bitch! I'm going to look like a frump beside you!"

The shoes received modest approbation, and the jewelery, after long contemplation and holding up to the light with the dress and shoes, was finally passed as suitable. After a lengthy debate on the important issue of underwired bras, Jonni finally produced her *pièce de résistance:* the Femme Fatale lipstick.

"Oh, no," Lynne said, putting her hand earnestly to her chest. "No, Jonni, I'm afraid not. It would be quite wrong with your complexion and hair color."

"Oh." Jonni's face fell. She looked mournfully down at the lipstick in her hand. "Would it suit you?"

"Yes, I expect so." Lynne stowed the lipstick cheerfully away in her makeup bag and rummaged around until she found one that would be right for Jonni. "Here, try this one. It's not so orange. You must let me do your whole face for you. I'm frightfully good at it."

Without apology or explanation Lynne was as amiable and generous today as she had been unpleasant and selfish last week. The two girls took over Michel's bedroom, turning it into a beauty salon, while Lynne applied foundations and lipliners to Jonni's face and experimented with different hairstyles, her pretty hazel eyes frowning in concentration as she surveyed the results of her creative efforts.

"This is really awfully kind of you," Jonni said, looking at Lynne in the mirror.

"Oh, it's fun. I get bored having only myself to play with—if you'll pardon the expression."

Jonni smiled, trying to keep still while Lynne combed out her fringe. She wished she had the courage to say things like that.

"Is Annette going tonight?"

Lynne took several hairpins out of Jonni's hair, sticking them between her lips for convenience and talking out of one side of her mouth.

"Yes, of course. There'd be hell to pay if she got left behind."

Nervous that, in her curiosity, she might be presuming on her new-found intimacy with Lynne a little too far, she asked, "Has Michel slept with Annette?"

"Oh, loads of times. Everyone's slept with Annette—even, believe it or not, a real live cabinet minister."

"Has Primo slept with her too?"

"We've all slept with each other in our gang—apart from Roly who does his own thing, whatever that may be. I know it seems appalling but we've spent six years together, all day every day. We know each other terribly well. We're a family."

Jonni tried hard not to let Lynne's admission shock her.

"You all seem very fond of each other."

"We are—well, except Roly and Nettie, of course; they spar all the time. They've never got on. It's inevitable; Roly's the only boy in the company tall enough to partner her, and she's hell to partner, by all accounts. She bitches at him terribly, as you've seen. But then all partnerships are tough."

"Do you fight with Michel?"

"Heavens, no. Michel never fights with anyone. If I get on his nerves he just goes away and has a cup of coffee. But it doesn't happen often; he's terribly patient."

"That must make him wonderful to work with."

Lynne raised her eyebrows because the pins in her mouth precluded any subtler facial expression. Her hands were busy with Jonni's hair.

"Oh, yes, he is. I'm incredibly lucky, Jonni. I'm really a very good dancer—did you know that? But I'm not in Michel's league. None of us are."

Jonni twisted her neck to look up at Lynne's face.

"Really?"

"Why do you think he's been invited to this BNB do tonight?"

Jonni pondered this for a moment.

"But Primo and Roly are invited too."

"Yes, Primo plays for occasional company classes there, just for the extra cash—they pay awfully well—and Charles lent Roly to them to help out with a tap number for a charity gala."

"A tap number?" Jonni laughed incredulously.

"Yes, he's won prizes for it. Roly went to a stage school before he came to the Islington. But for goodness' sake don't mention it; it embarrasses him. Stage school's a bit of a dirty word in the ballet world."

Jonni was silent for a while watching Lynne's busy fingers in the mirror. At present she was trying the effect of a tight French roll—too formal and adult to suit Jonni's face. When the French roll came down to be replaced with a soft, fluffy bouffant, Jonni turned her head to look up at her again, passing hairpins one at a time over her shoulder.

"So do you think the British National Ballet might offer Michel a job?"

"Oh, possibly, but he wouldn't take it," Lynne said easily. "Keep still a minute—Michel wouldn't leave the Islington."

"Why not?"

"Because of me, of course. And also, I suppose, because of Charles."

"But I thought he and Charles Crown detested each other."

"Oh, they're infuriating, the pair of them. When I was an apprentice it used to make me cry when Charles shouted at him. These days it just makes me want to bash their heads together. Charles treats him like shit; he even barks at him when we're practicing privately on our own in the corner of the studio. It's a pain in the neck; he never leaves him alone. Poor Michel gets terribly frustrated—I'm not sure I like this droopy bit at the front here—but of course it's all nonsense. They're nuts about each other. They're both absolutely passionate about dance; you should see the way Michel hangs on his every word in the studio, as though it were Gospel." She repinned the last strands of Jonni's hair expertly. "It's one of those mysterious man things—nothing's ever said. If you asked Michel how he felt about Charles I've no doubt he'd put his hand on his heart and swear he hated him, and vice versa. You know, in six years they've never had a single conversation about anything other than dance technique." Lynne gathered up her hairdressing equipment, laughing as she remembered suddenly: "Actually, that's not true. Michel told me that Charles once sat him down, years ago, and ordered him to ask me out on a date."

"Why would he do that?"

"Because of . . . my problem."

"Problem?" Jonni wasn't sure she should inquire further. The smile had vanished from Lynne's lips and she was tidying hairgrips and combs away busily.

"I'm sure Michel told you, after the things I said last weekend."

"No, he didn't."

"Honestly?" Lynne's elfin eyes met Jonni's hopefully in the mirror. "He didn't tell you? My God, what a pal! It's nothing really, just that I'm an idiot about dieting—a bit obsessed. It used to be serious. I'm over it now."

"Oh, Lynne, I'm glad."

Lynne shrugged. "Well." She wasn't looking as cheerful as she had earlier. Jonni watched while the wraithlike dancer applied her own makeup, carefully smoothing on foundation and blending four different shades of eyeshadow before she painted her long brown lashes with mascara. Remembering how devastated she'd been when Lynne had implied she was fat, Jonni felt a swelling surge of compassion in her chest.

"Lynne, can I ask you something?"

"Go ahead. No secrets here, Jonni."

It seemed an incredibly forward question but Jonni genuinely wanted to know.

"Have you been in love with Michel for a long time?"

Lynne's hand, holding her mascara wand, fell to her side. She turned to look at Jonni. After a few moments she sighed, her mouth turning down in sympathy.

"Let me tell you something about Michel, Jonni. He's the best friend you could ever hope for; really the best. And as a ballet partner he's—oh God, he's unbelievable. We've been practicing that horrific pas de deux together for weeks and, look!" She lifted up her yellow skirt to show Jonni her slender white thighs. "Not a single bruise. Not even a thumbprint. That chap has the gentlest hands. And you know, he'd break every bone in his own body before he let me fall and injure myself. He believes in our partnership too. He jokes that we'll dance *Romeo and Juliet* together one day on the stage of the Coliseum or La Scala. But I know he'd never leave me. As I say, he's a marvelous friend. He even asked me to marry him once."

Jonni's eyes widened in surprise. She hated to admit it to herself but, if she were honest, she felt a little deflated as well.

"What did you say?"

"Oh, I turned him down." She laughed quickly. "I knew he didn't really want to. It was a few years ago when I put myself in hospital with that problem I told you about. Perhaps he felt he'd let me down. He watches me very carefully, I know. They all do in their own way. Nettie can be vile sometimes; she bitches me out horribly if I'm underweight, but it's just her way of showing she cares."

She sat down on the edge of Michel's bed.

"Michel's a nice guy, Jonni, truly he is. But when it comes to women I'm afraid he's a bastard. That's the only way I can think of putting it. He's a fantastic lover; you might as well know it now. He has this amazing sort of physical empathy; it's the same thing that makes him such an extraordinary dancer. And he absolutely adores sex. Oh yes, I know all men do, but he's different. He makes you feel that having sex with you is the only thing in the world that matters to him. Annette gives him the most tremendous press. According to her you haven't been laid until you've been laid by Michel St. Michel. Ask any girl in the company. They'll all tell you."

"Any girl?" Jonni said, unbelieving.

"Almost any." Lynne looked at the mascara wand in her hands, rotating it between her fingers for a few moments, then raised her head to look at Jonni. "You know, he really wants you."

"Me?"

"It's not often that he goes to the trouble of phoning someone. He doesn't chase girls at all. They're just there in his life ready to sleep with him if the moment's right. That's the way he likes it. He'll make love to you so passionately you'll believe he really means it—and he does mean it; that's the terrible thing. But one day, before long, you'll come to his bed and find someone else already there. Like you're a piece of chewing gum he's spat out and discarded because the flavor's gone." She tucked her mascara away inside the open makeup bag beside her on Michel's bed. "As though you'd never mattered to him at all. You'll cry and smash the crockery and call him every name under the sun but it won't make any difference. He'll be terribly sweet to you and do his best to comfort you, and then just when you think you're winning he'll pat you on the backside and tell you to run along and find yourself a real boyfriend. And you know what'll be the worst thing of all? The worst thing is you won't even be able to hate him, because he never lied to you. He told you right from the start it wasn't going to be anything more than it was." A tear ran down her cheek and she wiped it away under her chin with the back of her hand. "But somehow you just never believed him. I fell in love with Michel the first time Charles made us dance together. Poor Michel. It must have been terrible for him. I had so little confidence when I left the ballet school. I was so afraid of putting on weight, and I felt such a failure—I was so shy, Jonni, you wouldn't believe it. Michel looked so horrified at having to partner me. But he was so beautiful and so kind. I thought he seemed the loneliest boy I'd ever seen."

She smiled at Jonni bravely, blinking away the tears that were coming fast into her eyes. What, after all, was a mere broken heart compared to the tragedy of spoiled makeup for a smart party?

"I'm really sorry," Jonni said. But Lynne shook her head.

"Don't be. I wish you happiness, I really do. Enjoy it for what it is if you can. You won't take him away from me, Jonni. Nobody can do that."

When the two girls were dressed and ready they stood side by side in the huge studio looking at themselves in the mirrored wall. Jonni didn't recognize herself. That sophisticated woman in the elegant turquoise cocktail dress couldn't possibly be her. Her beautifully piled hair looked as though it had been casually and perfectly pinned up in a moment, and her face—she looked like an advertisement for cosmetics or hairspray.

"I'm afraid to smile in case my face cracks," she said.

Beside her Lynne looked dazzlingly pretty and, although she was twenty-two—which to Jonni seemed a ripe old age—her petite figure and long, childlike eyelashes made her seem much the younger of the two. How different their figures looked standing beside each other. Of a similar height, though Jonni had just the edge in her high heels, Lynne's sylphlike body was slender and reedy while Jonni's waist only existed at all thanks to her round breasts and hips—like a stunted saloon singer, she thought.

As they walked through the hallway to the kitchen Lynne put her arm around Jonni's waist and Jonni, touched by the gesture of friendship and acceptance, smiled at her awkwardly. She found the tactile affection of the dancers discomfiting; none of her family or her friends at drama school had ever touched her so freely.

"You know, Lynne, I think Primo really likes you."

"Course he does, lovey. He adores me and I adore him. Anyway, we've had our fling if that's what you mean."

"But don't you think it might be more than that? I thought he seemed to have a special soft spot for you."

Lynne took her arm from Jonni's waist and stepped back frowning at her, puzzled. They were standing under the hall light and her hazel irises both reflected the outline of Jonni's face.

"Jonni, I thought you understood. Didn't you realize? Primo's in love with Michel."

"With Michel." Jonni repeated the words quietly, gazing at the telephone on the hall table. "No, I didn't realize."

"It's his curse. He's used to it by now, although he still finds it hard to come to terms with, I'm sure you've noticed that."

"How does Michel feel about it?"

Lynne laughed and put her arm back around Jonni's waist.

"Who can tell? Who ever knows what Michel feels about anything?"

When the boys arrived, after a punishing four-hour rehearsal under Crown's tempestuous surveillance, Jonni and Lynne were drinking tea in the kitchen, sipping carefully so as not to damage their makeup.

Michel arrived first, dropping his bag in the hall and calling out a greeting as he vanished into his bedroom, pressed for time.

Primo was only a few minutes behind him. He came into the flat whistling and slamming the door, breezing into the kitchen cheerfully in his smart black dinner suit and bow tie. He looked very handsome.

"Mamma mia!" he cried, staring at the girls in exaggerated despair. "What you women trying to do? Is too much for a good Catholic boy

like me to bear!" He turned to yell back through the kitchen door, "Hey, Michel, we better watch it tonight! These girls really got it in for us!"

He was in the midst of taking a large bite out of Jonni's wriggling neck when Roly strolled in, kicking the front door shut behind him. He too was immaculately dressed in a black dinner suit, and if he didn't exactly look handsome, he looked nice. His funny face wore a smile for each of the girls as he kissed them, and his broad hand caressed Lynne's shoulder while he and Primo discussed their grim afternoon in the studio.

Where it had taken Jonni and Lynne over two hours to get themselves ready for the party it took Michel no more than twelve minutes to shower, shave, and change into the cotton ivory suit which was the only one he possessed. He draped three ties over the back of a chair in the kitchen and put one foot up on the seat to tie his shoelaces, checking his watch.

"Where the hell is she? Which one, Lynnie? I don't have a clue about these things."

Lynne eyed the three ties critically, tilting her head.

"The blue," she decided. Michel obediently picked out the mist-blue tie and buttoned his collar. Jonni gazed at him. Beside him Primo and Roly looked overdressed in their starched shirts and bow ties. Michel's relaxed body scorned the bondage of a jacket and tie but the clothes seemed to worship him. He looked unbelievably sexy.

"I wish you could wear jeans to these things," he grumbled, throwing the long end of his dangling tie over the short end. "I just hope the hotel's air-conditioned."

Annette sauntered into the flat bang on half past seven, timing her arrival to perfection. As she appeared in the kitchen all conversation ceased. Her friends just stared in silence. Michel's mouth opened and so did Primo's. Roly raised his hand to scratch his shoulder slowly. Annette towered, Grecian and statuesque, in a calf-length strapless dress of clinging black velvet with a velvet choker and long black gloves. Her magnificent dark curly hair tumbled down her back like a frozen waterfall. Her made-up face was stunning. Jonni stared and stared. She wanted the floor to open up and swallow her.

"Jesus," Primo murmured. He closed his mouth with a low whistle.

Annette raised her eyebrows and blinked at their dumbfounded faces, the picture of innocence.

"Is there something wrong with me? Michel, darling, you're so gauche. Couldn't you have worn a dinner jacket, just for once?"

"Not a chance," Michel said, recovering. "I couldn't afford to, anyway. Let's go."

Outside on Warwick Way, strangers turned smiling to watch them as they walked in a group to the corner: six attractive young people in evening dress strolling along the pavement in the golden evening sunlight. They traveled to the hotel on the Bayswater Road in two taxis: Michel, Jonni, Primo, and Annette in one; Roly and Lynne in another.

The grandeur of the hotel foyer silenced them all.

"Blimey, this is a bit posh," Roly whispered, pulling a face at the gleaming chandeliers and gilt paintwork. Lynne was holding on fast to his hand.

At the end of a long corridor, through a series of fire doors, the pink-carpeted banqueting hall was already crowded with people, all in their smartest evening outfits. Heads turned as the dancers from the Islington Ballet entered; some to smile and wave at Primo and Roly whom they recognized, some to gape in awe at Annette—but mostly they turned to stare at Michel.

Rumors had been circulating around the BNB all week about Martyn Greene's miraculous new find at the Islington Ballet. He had discussed it confidentially in the company office and the story had spread to the principals and down through the ranks of the dancers. When Greene's secretary had leaked the information that this discovery had been invited to tonight's dinner, the dancers exchanged significant nods. They all knew their artistic director was planning a hit.

They looked Michel over as he handed his printed invitation to the doorman, no doubt in their minds that this muscular young Apollo in the pale suit, with his innocent curls and handsome face, must be Greene's intended prey. As Michel strolled down the short flight of steps from the doorway, one hand on Jonni's back, the dancers of the BNB leaned closer together, conferring in whispers.

Jonni was conscious of nothing but the intense sensation of Michel's hand touching her through the fabric of her dress, but Annette, following them down the steps hand in hand with Primo, murmured to Michel, "Don't look now, darling, but I think this lot are rather curious about you."

Michel remained cool as he walked down the stairs, but his skin tingled under the unsubtle scrutiny. Once he had accepted two glasses of dry white wine from a waiter he turned his back on the crowded room and looked down at Jonni with a secret, pained smile.

"I hate smart parties like this. I'm useless at them."

Jonni's face relaxed in relief.

"Me too, but then you already know that. Perhaps we should find some stairs to hide under."

"Unfortunately, I don't think I can this evening."

"Is it very important?"

"Maybe for the future; I'm not sure." His eyes traveled over her face, contemplating her glamorous new image a little skeptically. "I'm glad you could come."

Jonni caught Lynne's eye beyond his shoulder. Lynne smiled at her from the protective shelter of Roly's black-clad encircling arm.

"I'm glad I came, too."

The British National Ballet's annual summer dinner was an expensive, formal affair, although Michel warned Jonni it would deteriorate into a bunfight before the evening was over; you couldn't keep a bunch of dancers on best behavior for long. Jonni had never seen such a sparkling array of glamorous designer dresses. Almost three hundred people sat down to eat at long white tables, beautifully arranged with spotless linen, shining silver cutlery, and long-stemmed wineglasses. Every few yards the table was arrayed with a display of orchids and frilly ferns, but to Jonni's disappointment she found that she and Michel were seated separately from his friends. The other four were together at a table on the far side of the vast pink room.

Michel pulled out Jonni's chair for her and sat down beside her. The gilt-edged name card on her plate said, "Guest of Mister St. Michel, Islington Ballet."

Michel reached across the table in idle curiosity to pick up the name card for the vacant seat opposite Jonni. When he had read it he dropped it back on the plate very quickly.

"Jesus Christ!"

"What?" Jonni whispered.

He didn't have time to answer her. A handsome middle-aged couple arrived, pulling out the two chairs on the other side of the table. As the elegant lady sat down, Michel rose half out of his seat with the courtesy that had been drummed into him at the Paris Académie. Martyn Greene had an athletic, pantherlike grace which belied his age. He shook Michel's hand, presenting him to his wife with urbane charm. Once the introductions were over Michel's hand found Jonni's knee under the table and stayed there very firmly.

Martyn Greene sat back and surveyed the assembly around him with complacent satisfaction. This was his party and he had every intention of enjoying it, whatever other concerns might preoccupy his calculating mind.

Jonni smiled timidly at the beautifully dressed woman sitting opposite her. Greene had introduced her as, "Sedefka Gentcheva, my wife."

"Were you—I mean, are you—a dancer too?"

She felt Michel's hand tighten on her knee but the world-famous ballerina smiled serenely.

"Yes. In fact I was a quite good one." Her eyes glinted in amusement. "You, I suspect, my dear, are not part of the dance world."

"No, I'm not. I'm an actress."

"How fine. You must tell me all about it. I used to plague dear Larry—Larry Olivier, that is—with questions, but he was frightfully secretive about it all."

All through the soup and fish courses Sedefka Gentcheva exchanged anecdotes about the rich and great with a slim man sitting on Jonni's left. He had introduced himself as the ballet master. Jonni listened politely, smiling at the funny stories and frowning over the shocking ones, while Michel talked ballet jargonese with the artistic director. Michel ate with one hand, keeping the other under the tablecloth, his thumb unconsciously caressing Jonni's thigh.

On the far side of the packed room Michel's friends leaned closer together over their plates, speculating excitedly. They kept their voices low; they were surrounded by the dancers and musicians of the BNB.

"You reckon he's going to offer Michel a place in the company?"

"God, I hope so; I'd love to see Charles's face."

"Don't! He'd go apeshit."

"He's already apeshit. I reckon Greene's just pumping him for information."

"Or trying to get him into bed."

Across the ocean of clinking cutlery and hovering glasses, Jonni made eye contact with Roly, telegraphing her desperation through the camouflage of a fixed smile. Roly winked at her encouragingly.

When the main course arrived Michel took his hand from Jonni's knee to pick up his knife. Without that reassuring contact she felt hopelessly abandoned. She still smiled and nodded automatically at the right places in her neighbors' anecdotes but her fingers began to twist the stem of her wineglass nervously. Without looking at her, Michel moved his knee under the table so that it rested against hers. Instantly she relaxed again.

After her second glass of wine she found the confidence to sit back, pretending to listen to Sedefka Gentcheva's story about dancing *Swan Lake* during a power cut, and eavesdrop on Michel's conversation with Martyn Greene.

"Soloist," Greene was saying, lighting a cigar as a waitress took away his plate. "Promotion to senior soloist in six months if all goes well. There's no reason why we shouldn't be looking at a principal post within eighteen months or two years."

Jonni's ears would have been standing out on stalks if such a thing were possible. Michel hesitated before he responded.

"How many performances do your soloists dance in a year?"

"Seventy, eighty. I'd expect you to cover the principal roles in *Nutcracker* and *Sleeping Beauty* next season; maybe fourth or fifth cast."

"I see."

"I know what you earn at the Islington. You'd be starting on roughly twice that with us. A little more, in fact."

Jonni's attention was called away by the punch line of the *Swan Lake* anecdote so she didn't hear Michel's reaction to the promise of such riches. While the laughter subsided around her she glanced at Michel furtively. He was rubbing the back of his neck, looking rather worriedly into Greene's eyes. Their conversation had changed tack.

"The one I partnered in the *Inferno* pas de deux. She's here tonight somewhere, with Roland Kovak."

"Ah, yes," Greene said, "I know the one you mean. Pretty girl, tiny, tremendously loose. Yes, it's a nice, expressive facility. I'm not sure where I could put her at the moment but it's not an impossibility. Does she have a weight problem?"

Michel lit a cigarette and blew out a stream of smoke.

"Yes."

"But you'd keep an eye on her, I'm sure. Well, what do you think, Michel? You're interested, at least."

Michel laughed. Who wouldn't be interested in an offer from the BNB? Let alone one that included covering principal roles. It was fairy-tale time.

"I'm not sure Charles Crown would be happy about the idea."

"Really? What sort of promises has he made you for the future?"

"None."

Greene raised his eyebrows significantly. "It's not up to him how you structure your career, you know."

"I feel I owe it to him to stick around for a while. I was a scholarship apprentice."

"Yes, I understand where you're coming from." Greene's eyes were se-rious. "But teaching isn't like that, Michel. We all train dancers; that's what we're here for. They go into the common pool and enrich the pro-fession. Dancers I've trained have gone off to dance in companies all over the world, some of them never having set foot onstage with my com-pany. And dancers who have been trained in other companies come to me. That's the way the system works. It keeps things healthy."

"I don't think Crown would see it that way."

"You underestimate him." Greene shook his raised hand at a waitress who stopped by his chair, refusing the dessert that was offered to him. "Charles knows perfectly well that I can offer you exposure and opportu-nities he can't. What would you say if I told you Charles and I have al-ready discussed the plan of your coming to join us here at British? You look surprised; do you suppose we artistic directors don't talk to each other?"

Jonni wished she dared turn her head to look at Michel. He had shifted his position slightly on his chair and his knee was no longer touching hers. He cleared his throat.

"You mean my moving to British was Charles Crown's suggestion?"

Martyn Greene was no more deceitful than most people in his position but he knew how to put a bit of spin on the facts to make sure they fell in his favor.

"Put it this way, Charles was very anxious for me to see this new piece of his. And, yes, he's obviously concerned about your future."

Greene was looking him straight in the eye.

"Of course he'll kick up a fuss if you resign; that's his job. But the Islington isn't financially secure. And if it were, what security do you personally have within the company? Is there any guarantee you'll even get a contract for next year? What I'm talking about at the BNB are firm, structured promises—and by the age of twenty-four, twenty-five you'll be in a very strong position from which to consider the next stage of your career. Where will you be if you stay at the Islington? I've got to have an answer on this soon, Michel. I need to start planning the coming season."

"I'm contracted to the Islington until February."

"The betterment clause in your contract covers your move to the BNB as long as you're joining us at a higher rank. The only way Charles could stop you, even assuming he wanted to, is by promoting you from the corps to senior soloist. And I don't think that's likely, do you?"

"No."

On the other side of the room Lynne was staring abstractedly at the plate of filet de veau, broccoli, and potatoes that was sitting in front of her virtually untouched. Roly caressed her cheek, drawing her out of her reverie.

"Eat a little more, darling. Go on, just for me."

Lynne gave him a wan smile and ate a forkful of broccoli to please him, then she handed her plate to a waitress who walked past with a pile of empty dishes. Primo and Annette were howling at an obscene joke one of the company pianists was telling about the ballet master.

When a waitress stopped beside Annette, offering her dessert, Roly leaned across the table and laid his hand on her wrist. Annette wasn't renowned for her tendency to undereat.

"Do me a favor, Nettie, and have the fruit salad, this once—as a gesture of goodwill."

"What goodwill?" she said tartly, and turned around to take a plate heaped with profiteroles and chocolate sauce. When she had eaten only one, however, she slammed her fork down and pushed the plate away furiously, scowling at him and folding her arms.

Roly raised his eyebrows and mouthed "Thank you" to her across the table.

She held up one finger to tell him where he could stick his gratitude.

"When are you off to Glasgow?" Martyn Greene asked, stirring his coffee.

Michel reached in front of Jonni for the sugar bowl.

"We travel up tomorrow and stay until the weekend."

"Then give me a ring on Monday when you get back. I'll put something down on paper and fax it to you at the theater."

"No, don't fax it, for God's sake. Can you stick it in the post?"

"Of course. I understand." Greene unwrapped the plastic from another cigar and very wisely changed the subject. He glanced at Jonni and leaned forward to rest his elbows on the table, speaking low. "Knockout face. Where did you find her, you lucky dog?"

"Hmm?" Michel wasn't listening.

"Your girlfriend."

"Oh." He looked up and smiled, his face clearing. "Yes, you're right, she's beautiful. And I don't think either of us should say any more because she's been listening to every word we've said for the past twenty minutes."

Jonni was suddenly deeply engrossed in Sedefka Gentcheva's story.

"Did she really?" she asked, "Goodness! How on earth could she manage it wearing all that tinsel?"

"I'm sure she's not listening, Michel."

"Oh, yes, she is."

"Say something pornographic and see if she laughs."

Jonni put her hand to her chest, staring wide-eyed at her host's wife.

"No! Not the same man who had been sitting in the front row every night for the past month?"

"Indeed it was."

"That's terrible!"

Inexperienced in her trade she might be, but Jonni was not an actress for nothing.

After the coffee Martyn Greene made a speech to the whole assembly praising the company's work over the last year, flattering his ballerinas and even thanking Primo and Roly amongst others, by name, for their help as guests of the company. He was looking forward to the coming year, he said: seasons at the Coliseum, the biggest houses nationwide, Rome, Berlin, Sydney, Japan . . . new repertoire . . . new faces. The gathering applauded rapturously with hoots and whistles and then rose from the tables in a body and adjourned to the ballroom where the party began in earnest. Michel and Jonni rejoined their friends who plied them for news.

"Was he after your body or your triple cabrioles?"

"On balance I'd say the latter, though I wouldn't swear to it."

"Did he say anything specific?"

Michel shook his head. This wasn't the moment to share the details of Greene's offer.

Annette vanished, embarking on the evening's trail of seduction, while the four remaining Islington dancers made their way to the bar. When Michel described how Jonni had made the social gaffe of the century with one of the world's most celebrated ballerinas, Roly, Lynne, and Primo howled with laughter.

"You poor darling," Roly consoled her. "Was she horribly offended?"

"I'm not sure," Jonni confessed. "She threw Laurence Olivier back at me. I don't suppose that was a very good sign."

Primo, not surprisingly, was expected to play for his supper. Martyn Greene, doing the rounds of his guests with his illustrious wife on his arm, made a particular point of stopping to speak to him.

"You must play for us, Roberto." He turned to his wife. "This handsome young fellow is a remarkable pianist."

Primo's expression darkened in anger. He didn't like being labeled a pianist by anyone, and especially not by the director of one of the country's leading ballet companies. He kissed the famous ballerina's hand with elaborate formality as she gave it to him.

"I am a classical dancer, signora."

"Yes . . . I can see that you are."

"*Grazie.* In that case, if I'm going to play something I'd better do it before I get any more pissed. What would the signora like to hear?"

She glanced at her husband, not sure how to cope with this half-inebriated Italian boy.

"What do you know?"

"Try me, madonna."

"Something by Rachmaninoff."

"Something particular?"

"Oh, anything."

Primo gave her a curt little bow.

"Anything by Rachmaninoff coming up, signora."

He marched to the nearby piano, a white baby grand, and took off his jacket, rolling up the sleeves of his dress shirt with businesslike promptitude. There was a big red "danger" button attached to Primo's generally amenable temper and Martyn Greene had just inadvertently pressed it. Primo adjusted the height of the piano stool and sat down, lifting the lid with an aggressive frown.

A dozen people around the piano had already stopped talking, turning their heads expectantly toward him. Jonni watched as he clenched his strong hands into fists over the keyboard. She was half-afraid he was going to break the instrument. And then she saw him catch his breath, his fingers hesitating for an instant above the keys, before he launched into Rachmaninoff's second piano sonata with total control.

The room gradually fell silent until there was almost no sound but the piano and the occasional clink of glass against glass as the waiters went about their business. Jonni stood, with Michel's hand on her waist, unable to take her eyes off Primo's hands, terrified he was going to make a mistake. But she didn't know Primo. Sure, solid, unimpressed by their own ability, Primo's fingers flew securely up and down the keyboard thundering out Rachmaninoff's torrent of semiquavers without a flaw. And at some moments he played with such gentleness it was impossible to believe he was the same person who had seemed so angry only minutes ago. In the final wild allegro, while his right hand was negotiating a devilish solo passage, Primo even managed to undo his bow tie and loosen his collar before bringing his left hand back to the keyboard, not a second too soon, to pick up the tempestuous bass line.

When he finished to huge applause—and yelling and thumping of beer glasses from the company pianists—he picked up his jacket and returned to Sedefka Gentcheva. He smiled apologetically.

"Please forgive me, signora. I was very rude to you."

She held out her hand to him. "That was beautiful. Thank you. You have an immense musical gift; that's so important for a classical dancer."

Primo's dark eyes glowed with pleasure.

"It was a privilege to play for you. But I am afraid the piano needs tuning."

"I really couldn't tell."

Greene laid his hand on Primo's shoulder.

"If you ever need a job—"

"I have a job, thank you," he interrupted politely, and with a final nod to the great ballerina he went back to join his friends.

12

THE SIGHT OF MORE THAN EIGHTY ballet dancers and as many musicians and stage technicians letting down their hair in earnest is one that should only be administered to the uninitiated in very small doses.

As the evening progressed the assembled company of the British National Ballet grew wilder and wilder, all inhibition thrown away, shoes and handbags kicked to the side of the room, jackets discarded as the energetic crowd hit the dance floor. Hair came tumbling down, alcohol flowed in copious quantities, the hot, summer-crazy air became filled with shrieking laughter and adrenaline. Tonight the company was not on show; this was their one night of total license and they indulged themselves immoderately.

Jonni's head reeled with the atmosphere of debauched hedonism. The dancers writhed on the dance floor like dervishes. Never had she seen so much life in one room: so much liberated, flagrant participation. But beneath the waves of revelry there was a distinct undercurrent of tension. Internal politics were fierce in the big national company; envy and resentment were rife, even on the seething dance floor. There was a large homosexual contingent at the BNB: beautifully groomed young men flaunting their healthy, athletic bodies; screaming with laughter; perching on each other's laps and flirting outrageously on the dance floor. Martyn Greene, liberated from his duties as host—and from his wife— cavorted amongst his minions like an aging satyr.

Annette created a sensation on the dance floor and off it: a flowing river of sexuality; sensual, isolated by her beauty, rejoicing in her power. Wherever she went a throng followed adoringly in her wake, women as well as men, longing not to possess her but to be like her. Jonni lost sight of her very quickly from her secluded seat near the bar.

Every few minutes Lynne and Primo came into sight, twisting together on the dance floor or chatting amongst a group of Primo's acquaintances, fanning their sweating faces with their hands. Roly was engaged in a laughing tap-dancing challenge with some of the younger BNB dancers near the bar. He was tapping out an easy time step on the wooden floor in his black dress shoes with a beer glass balanced on his head. Roly had spent only a week with the corps of the BNB but they all loved him. He was a capable ballet dancer with plenty of technique, which was the reason they forgave him for his years of training in tap. Now a dozen or so of the youngsters were goading him good-naturedly, cheering his challengers on to beat him. But Roly was easily the winner. When his glass finally fell he caught it in midair and raised his hand in a smiling gesture of defeat. But it was good enough for the youth of the BNB. They whisked him away onto the dance floor in their midst, claiming him as one of their own.

Only Michel didn't dance. He sat at the small table with Jonni, chatting with company members who had been introduced to him very selectively by Martyn Greene. Jonni sat beside him silently while he talked in French with the BNB's leading ballerina, Marie Gillette. They were, he told her, comparing notes on the Paris Opera School and the Académie. Michel's face was more mobile when he spoke French, punctuating his conversation with affirmative intakes of breath, expressive shrugs, and little negative clicks of his tongue. Jonni watched him, mesmerized. As he talked his eyes were appraising the renowned ballerina's strong, beautiful body, but whether as a man or as a dancer Jonni couldn't tell. It was clear Marie Gillette couldn't tell either; she stretched her slender neck and posed decorously beside him, fiddling self-consciously with her pearl earrings.

"He's fucking privileged," whispered an unknown girl into Jonni's ear. "Gillette wouldn't be caught dead talking to one of the corps in our company."

By two in the morning the atmosphere at the party had become heavy and sodden with alcohol. The lights were low and people danced drunkenly, groping each other, or lounged around in groups exchanging home truths and whispered confidences.

Michel caressed Jonni's waist, looking thoughtfully over her face. "Shall we go?"

She stopped breathing, although she tried to smile. She knew he was visualizing her naked and in his bed; his eyes made no secret of it.

"Alright."

"Are you coming back to Pimlico with me?"

"Well, I need to, really—if that's okay. I left all my things there."

He widened his eyes, teasing her for her diffidence, and then smiled. "Okay. Don't forget your bag."

"Shouldn't we say good-bye to the others?"

"No, they'll work out we've gone."

Lynne watched them leave. From a concealed spot behind a pillar where she had been standing observing them for the past half hour, her hazel eyes followed them slowly across the room as they walked together to the door.

Primo saw them leave too. He was sitting on a table at the end of the bar telling dirty jokes with the BNB's pianists. As Michel caught his eye and nodded toward the exit, Primo raised his eyebrows in acknowledgment. Less than a minute later, when his attention was once more engrossed in a bawdy anecdote about Martyn Greene, his eye was drawn to Lynne's distraught figure scrabbling in her handbag for a tissue as she ran across the dance floor. He put his drink on the table beside him and swung his feet down onto the floor.

"Don' forget the punch line," he said, "and don' steal my drink. I'll be right back."

Twenty minutes later he caught up with Roly in the gents' loos. Primo's face was somber.

"Listen, amico, I think I got to take Lynne home. Michel left with Jonni . . ." He grimaced. "You know what I mean. Anyway, she's hysterical. Ain't nothing I can do to calm her down."

Roly rinsed his hands under a tap, shaking them over the sink before he turned to dry them on a towel.

"Poor little Lynnie. She's going to cry her pretty eyes out over him one of these days. What it is to be a Michel, eh?"

"Yeah," Primo said bleakly, "tell me about it. I know she came with you but I reckon is better if I take her home myself."

"Sure. Put her to bed and give her a cuddle. See if you can cheer her up."

"Yeah, I will. I don' suppose it'll do much good, though. I ain't no substitute for the real thing."

They weren't alone in the gents'. Two boy dancers were snorting cocaine off a copy of the *Guardian,* talking away in high, excited voices. They ignored Primo and Roly. They weren't even listening to each other.

"Look, amico, I'm sorry to leave you with . . ." Primo tossed his head, nodding toward the party beyond the door, ". . . you know."

Roly smiled. "It's okay. I'll look after Medusa for you. Where is she, have you seen her?"

"Last I saw her she was over by the potted palm trees, flirting with the BNB ballet master big-time."

"Far that'll get her, from what I hear about him. Still, it sounds about her measure. Don't worry, I'll see she gets home safely—unless she makes other arrangements of course. You go off and take care of Lynnie."

Roly sat on his own at the bar with a Scotch and soda watching Annette toying with the emotions of a tall, handsome boy who was standing beside her—she had evidently drawn a blank with the BNB's ballet master. The boy was flushed and clearly way out of his depth. Annette was an expert; leaning gracefully against the wall with her hands clasped behind her back, huge millpool eyes glancing sideways at him; half-timid, deerlike; half-seductive. Her long spiraling curls hung down her back framing naked white shoulders.

"He doesn't have to bloody well lift her," Roly murmured to himself, knocking back his drink and ordering another.

Half an hour later he saw her pick up her tiny handbag from the back of a chair and crane her neck looking around the room for Primo. He hauled himself off his bar stool and walked to her side.

"He's gone," Roly said. "He took Lynnie home; she was in a bit of a stew."

"Charming!" She glanced around the room as though she didn't quite believe him. "So he just buggers off and leaves me here alone."

"He didn't leave you alone. Shall I get you a taxi?"

"No, I'll walk. It's only across the park."

"Hang on, I'll get my jacket."

She looked him up and down scornfully, amusing herself with the image of Roly as a protector, despite his six feet two inches.

"It's alright, thanks. I'll be perfectly okay on my own."

Roly shook his head. "Wait here for me, I won't be a sec."

They walked through the brightly lit, pink foyer together. Roly carried his jacket draped over his shoulder, the ends of his bow tie dangling around the open collar of his shirt. A rogue lock of his coarse straw-red hair, damp from the sultry heat in the airless hotel, hung over his eyes, and he brushed it away with his hand.

"Isn't Kensington Gardens locked at night?" he asked.

"I know a place we can get over the fence." She gave him a caustic look. "It's nice to know you'd actually care if I got mugged or raped."

Roly opened the huge glass door for her and followed her through it with a dry smile.

"Primo would never forgive me."

The air outside on the Bayswater Road was warm and balmy. Exhaust fumes mingled with the smell of hot tarmac and summer pollen. Annette shuddered in her strapless evening dress as they walked down the wide steps onto the hotel forecourt.

"Do you want my jacket?"

"No, it was just chilly coming out of that boiling hotel." She pointed. "We can get into the park down the road there."

Across the street, at a gap in the thick hedge, Roly jumped up onto the wall and threw his long legs over the spiked fence, extending a hand to pull Annette up behind him before he dropped down easily on the other side. He picked up his jacket from where he had thrown it onto the shadowy grass and waited for Annette to climb the fence—a much trickier job in her calf-length evening dress.

Despite the niggling animosity between them Annette didn't think twice about dropping into Roly's arms as he held them up to lift her down from the wall. These were, after all, the relative positions in which they had spent so much of their working lives for the past six years. He set her on her feet and held her elbow firmly as she walked over the treacherous grass in her high heels.

When they reached the path Roly let go of her arm. He let her stride ahead into the darkness of the unlit avenue, strolling behind her at his own measured pace. Forced to stop and wait for him, she folded her arms.

"Has anyone ever told you you're an inconsiderate pig, Roland?"

"Often, darling: usually you."

"I am not your darling."

"Thanks for the reminder."

They walked a hundred yards in silence under massive beech trees, thick with foliage, black against the luminous sky. The grass on either side of the avenue was invisible, robbed by the night of everything but its faint, warm smell. Roly walked pensively, looking down at the dark path as it vanished beneath his feet. His friends were so wrapped up in their complex lives that they had always taken his good-humored contentment for granted, but he had his own hidden troubles.

Once they had passed the ghostly bandstand he pushed his damp hair off his face again.

"Nettie, listen; can I talk to you about something?"

"Oh, look, not now, alright? It's half past two in the morning. This isn't the time to start nagging about my weight or pulling up my muscles."

"It's nothing to do with that, truly." His hand, in the pocket of his black evening trousers, turned a coin over and over. This was probably the first time in all their years as partners they had ever been alone together for more than a moment or two. "I just wanted to say that . . . well, those games you used to play, teasing me, flirting, and then running away again; they stopped being funny a long time ago."

"I stopped playing them a long time ago."

"Yes, you did, I know. It's just that . . ." He stopped, not knowing how to go on, and looked at her anxiously. Annette paused for a moment on the path, staring at him, astounded. And then she opened her mouth and tilted back her head to look up at the trees in laughing disbelief.

"My God, a pass! And from you of all people!"

She strode off ahead angrily.

"Nettie, wait, I'm trying to talk to you!" He caught up with her. "Annette!"

She stopped walking and put her hands on her hips.

"Well, what then?"

"I just want to tell you what I feel."

"You're pissed!"

"No, I'm not." He dismissed the idea with a wave of his hand. "I had a couple of Scotches; I'm quite sober."

"A couple of Scotches would finish me."

"Yes, love, I'm nearly twice your size."

"That's not what you normally tell me—alright, alright!" She could see her bitching was annoying him. "Say whatever you've got to say and get it over with."

He looked at her face, cast into shadow by the overhanging trees, and nodded, grateful for the few moments thinking space she had allowed him. This was more nerve-racking than even the most terrifying performances he'd given on stage. He laid his hand on his chest to steady his emotion.

"You know me pretty well by now, Nettie. We're probably friends, for all we do nothing but fight all the time. Look, I realize I'm not such a great-looking guy—I'm no Michel, I know that."

"You've got a great body," Annette suggested helpfully. She wasn't stating a personal opinion but a professionally acknowledged fact. And, indeed, Roly ought to have a good body after all the hours he'd spent sweating in the gym until he had the physique of a young Goliath to cope with partnering a dancer of Annette's weight and undisciplined musculature.

"Thanks," he said. "Anyway, I'm not such a bad dancer. Again, I'm no Michel but I'll make a career for myself. Charles told me I'll make soloist next season. That has to mean something. As I say, I'm not much but I work hard, I love ballet, I'm as honest as I can manage to be. What else can I tell you?—I don't smoke, I adore oysters, I've got a full no-claims bonus on my car insurance—"

"Look, what is this, a proposal of marriage?"

He looked earnestly at her half-shadowed face.

"I care about you, Annette, that's all."

"Oh, no!" It was the last thing she needed.

She turned and stomped quickly away. When he called after her she threw out her arms, raising them to the trees and sang out loudly, trying to drown out the sound of his voice: "This isn't happening! I'm not hearing this!"

He laid his hand frustratedly on his head for a moment and then hurried after her. When she refused to stop he caught her arm.

"Nettie, for God's sake stop running off, will you?"

She snapped at him in fury, "You've got a bloody nerve!"

"No, I haven't; that's where you're wrong. If I had any kind of nerve at all we'd have had this conversation long ago. That's something I obviously forgot to tell you: I'm a complete coward."

"Let go of my arm!"

"You won't run away?"

"That's up to me, isn't it?" Her eyes were sharp and angry. He released her arm slowly.

"Yes, you're right. Sorry."

"You're wasting your time, Roly. I don't fancy you."

He looked at her, so near and so real in front of him on the dark path and so beautiful in her black dress. If he stretched out his hand he could touch her—as he had touched her so many times before, but never when they were alone together and never at night in a lonely avenue. Her eyes were hidden, gazing down at the blackness of the grass, but he didn't have to see her eyes to see the scorn in them. That scorn was imprinted on his mind like a wound torn open again and again every time she had glanced at him during the past six years.

"Will you look at me?" he said.

Her face, as she stood in her high-heeled shoes, was only a couple of inches below his own. She lifted her heavy, sensuous eyelids, their lashes sweeping up like the fringe of a theater curtain, and raised her green eyes slowly to his. There was anger there and some apprehension, but for once, blessedly, no scorn. Roly took that as a good sign.

"Nettie, I know this is awful for you. I'm making a complete fool of myself but I'm past caring. This isn't something new for me. I've been living with this for six years. I can't sleep. I can't concentrate in the studio. I never look at other girls. I've never even kissed a girl except onstage."

"That's a lie: you snogged Ruthie at Belinda's seventeenth birthday party."

"Yeah, so I did. You've got a better memory than I have." He shook his head in despair. "The way I feel about you, Nettie, it's not your fault but it's driving me up the bloody wall. I wish you could give me some kind of answer."

"I already did. You just weren't listening."

"I know you don't have any sentimental feeling for me. I don't even know what I want, except that I want to get rid of this terrible fixation. I keep thinking that . . ." He pushed his hair slowly away from his forehead again. ". . . perhaps, if we made love it might go away."

"I see." Annette stared at the buttons on the front of his shirt. "A moment ago you were in love with me. Now it appears you only want to fuck me."

Roly was taken aback. He had heard that word a million times, but coming from Annette as a verb relating him to her, it hit him like a slap in the face. The image of instant, raw physicality that it conjured up sent a sudden flush to his cheeks and a rush of blood to his groin. He raised his hand to rub the back of his neck slowly.

"To be honest with you, right now I can't really tell the difference."
Her face was hard.

"Does it turn you on when we dance together?"

"No, of course not!" He looked down at his shoes and told her the truth reluctantly. "Sometimes, when we dance together onstage."

Of course when they danced onstage. When else did she ever smile at him? When else did she turn her beautiful, beckoning eyes toward him and step into his arms without a scowl? He forced himself to look at her, his cheeks pink with humiliation.

"I'm sorry."
It took her a few moments to make up her mind.

"Oh, forget it; it doesn't matter. Christ, Michel gets a hard-on every

{189}

time he stands in the wings waiting to go onstage. And Primo gets horny listening to Beethoven. All you boys have your passions. I've always thought it must be rotten having a penis."

"I've never looked at it that way but I suppose you're right. Mine's never done me much good."

With a sigh that deflated her shoulders, Annette climbed down from her position of moral superiority and looked at his flushed, miserable face with genuine contrition.

"Look, I'm sorry about the way I used to tease you when we were apprentices. It was shitty of me. Honestly, I've felt dreadful about it for years. It was—the girls dared me. It was a huge joke amongst us all in the changing room—oh, not Lynne; she used to sit silently in her corner glaring at me—but it was a great joke with the others. You're a decent bloke when you aren't growling at me about my weight or about pulling up my muscles. But I don't love you. And I don't fancy you. That's the truth, Roly. I'm afraid I never did."

His eyes were fixed on the tarmac path. A faint breeze lifted the sultry air of the hot night and, from the dark tree-lined avenue in Kensington Gardens, the traffic on Queensway sounded very distant. Still looking down at the path, Roly screwed up his face, rubbing his forehead slowly.

"You've had so many boyfriends, Nettie. I mean so many. Men you haven't known from Adam. Men you've even disliked; you've said so yourself. I don't suppose you could find it in your heart to spend just one night with me?"

She was silent. Totally, totally silent. When at last he looked up at her and saw the extent of her rage his eyes widened in alarm.

"Can you afford it?" she asked, with icy calm. "I'm very expensive!"

"Oh, Jesus. I didn't mean it like that."

"Then how did you mean it? You want me to screw a man I've already said I don't find attractive?"

"No, listen—"

"So what's it worth to you? I've screwed a lot of men but no one's ever taken me for a whore before. What are we talking about, a fiver's worth in the back of your car?"

"Nettie, don't."

"No, come on, what's it worth to put your cock inside me? A grand?

No? Not worth as much as your Escort then! Two hundred? A hundred? Forty? What, not even the cost of two sessions with the osteopath? Come on, Roly! A tenner?"

"Stop it," he said. "Please stop, Annette."

She turned on her heel and strode off, leaving him standing mercifully alone on the dark path. When she was well ahead of him he followed at a distance, his hand in his pocket and his jacket slung over his shoulder, keeping her just within his sight until she reached the bright lights of Kensington Gore opposite the deserted Albert Hall.

On the pavement next to the Albert Memorial Annette stopped to wait for him. He walked to her side and stood in silence waiting for her to speak.

"So are you going to apologize or what?" she asked stonily.

"Yeah, I was out of order. Sorry."

She glared at the park fence for a few seconds and then sniffed huffily, playing up her role as the injured party.

"Well, alright then."

"Come on, I'll walk you home."

Annette lived in a bedsit just around the corner from the Albert Hall. As they walked along the pavement together without talking, he gently hitched up the strap of her little handbag when it started slipping off her shoulder. At the door to her ornate redbrick apartment building she turned and looked at him.

"Look, Roly, do you think we should try not being quite so bloody to each other all the time?"

"I suppose we could give it a go. It'd be a break for the others if nothing else."

"I do feel sorry for you about your crush on me. It's not worth it, really it's not. I can think of two—no, three girls in the corps, right this moment, who'd give their pointe shoes to hop into bed with you. Do you want me to tell you their names?"

He shook his head. His blue eyes were their usual kind, soft selves again.

"Don't feel sorry for me, Nettie. There's really no need. I knew exactly what your response was going to be even before I started this row tonight. I just needed to get it off my chest." His smile brightened slightly. "Actually, I feel much better. I think it's almost gone away just from getting it out in the open."

Her face fell in visible relief and she half smiled in reply.

"Good night then. I'll see you on the train tomorrow."

"Yeah, half past twelve. Goodnight, love."

When the front door closed behind her he stood perfectly still and pressed the palms of his hands tightly over his eyes. A middle-aged woman, entering the block not long after Annette, had to squeeze past his motionless body to reach the door but he didn't notice her. When he took his hands away he ran them both through his unruly hair and sat down on the stone doorstep, looking at the redbrick and stone façades of the buildings opposite. One or two lights were on in the windows of the ornate Victorian apartment blocks and, now and then, a pedestrian walked past the end of the cul-de-sac, but otherwise the pavements were deserted. After watching the quiet street for a couple of minutes, Roly shook his head slowly and closed his eyes, putting his head back in his hands.

13

Soft yellow light from a streetlamp on the pavement below slanted through the window into Michel's unlit bedroom. It was after three but still the breeze that gently rocked the blind above the open window blew warm air over Jonni's face. She knelt on the varnished floorboards with her arms on the white sill inhaling the faint summer odors which drifted up from the garden in the hushed Pimlico square. It was London's silent hour. The streets were deserted apart from an occasional car slowing down to change gear as it turned the corner into Warwick Way. Jonni's face was clean and her hair hung straight and unadorned to the base of her neck. She was wearing nothing but the striped collarless shirt Michel had given her to put on when she came out of the shower.

"It's so hot," she said, closing her eyes to feel the warmth.

Behind her Michel was hanging up his jacket and tie.

"Yes, it gets much hotter in here than the rest of the flat."

Jonni stood up and turned to watch him as he moved across the uncluttered room in the dim light from the window. The cross-shaped shadow of the window frame passed over his face as he walked to the side of the bed unbuttoning his shirt.

He unbuttoned his cuffs and pulled off his shirt. As he threw it on a chair he glanced at her across the wide bed and saw that she was gazing at him, her eyes moving slowly over his chest and shoulders. He stood still for a moment, rubbing the back of his hand with his thumb, and then turned his head away toward the white wall and let her look at him.

Jonni had never looked at a man's body before, never really looked. Michel's body didn't have the huge bulk of a bodybuilder's but the fine, sculpted musculature of a dancer. His shoulders were naturally broad, each curve of their surrounding muscle and the muscles of his upper arms thrown into stark relief by the shadowy light from the window. She looked slowly down over his chest and narrowing rib cage to where his flat, strong belly vanished under the waistband of his trousers. Strangely, for she had imagined herself in love a number of times, it had never occurred to her that a man's body could be beautiful.

His face complemented the power of his body; clean features like cut crystal balancing the softness of his mouth and his boyish cupid's curls. Michel had an awesome, untouchable beauty like the dome of St. Paul's or a painting by Botticelli.

"If you'd rather not," he said, "it's alright."

"No."

"No you'd rather not, or no you rather would?"

"Yes."

He smiled as he unclasped the metal watch strap that was hanging loosely around his wrist and laid it on the dark bedside table. He took it that yes meant yes.

"Are you a virgin?"

". . . No."

The luminous glow from the window fell full on his face as he lifted his head to look at her. He had caught the note of hesitation in her voice.

"Is that true?"

"Yes. But I'm not very experienced."

She didn't know why she had told him that. She couldn't tell him that her two brief previous encounters with sex had been dreadful, humiliating disasters, both with narcissistic drama students who had inspired her with passionate infatuation. Seized by a burning desire to give something to each of these paragons she had given herself. Those limited forays into her own sexuality had left her with a sense of deep anticlimax and the fear of frigidity.

Michel held out his hand to her and she walked around the end of the bed to join him—it seemed quite natural: women came to Michel, he did not come to them. He put his hands on her body above her waist and caressed her through her cotton shirt as he looked down at her. His face was in shadow but she could see the dark rings around his gray irises and the black, dilated pupils flitting between her two expectant eyes.

"Jonni, listen . . ." She was listening. She knew what was coming even without Lynne's warning. "If you're looking for romance I'm the wrong guy for you. I don't have time to get involved; my work takes up my whole life. I don't have girlfriends. I just have friends—and some of them are friends I sleep with. If that isn't right for you, just say so."

"I don't want anything except to be here now," she said. It was true. She was glad she didn't love him. Being here with him like this felt liberating and life-affirming and intriguingly grown-up. She knew the time she spent with Michel was nothing more than that—a little time. He wore his emotional independence like a cloak. Solitary, self-sufficient, he reminded her of the story of the cat who walked alone. She didn't want to fall in love with Michel. But she wanted to be here and do this with him.

He had lifted her face and was kissing her, his hand on her neck. His other hand, unbuttoning the front of her long shirt with practiced fingers, made her feel, to her surprise, safe and confident. He would look after her, she knew he would. She could feel it in his careful hand on her neck and his slowly moving mouth.

Michel made love just as he danced: with flowing certainty and concentration, unstoppable, using all his strength to control himself as he moved on top of her, completely absorbed and yet aware. His arm under her waist on the cotton top sheet—it was too hot for a duvet—lifted her bodily from the bed and turned her over, pressing her against him, uninhibited, erotic, soaked in the combined sweat from their hot limbs.

Jonni was only nineteen and she wasn't a dancer. She was only just beginning to realize that her body was actually a part of her. She didn't know how to respond physically but she was drawn into the intimacy and abandonment of the situation. She exclaimed softly, more aware of Michel's immersion in the moment than of any sexual feelings of her own. Jonni had never had an orgasm and as far as she knew never would, but she had discovered heaven and it was Michel's mouth between her legs and his hands moving slowly over the inside of her thighs. When he looked up at her face, pausing to remove a hair from his mouth, Jonni laughed disbelievingly.

"This isn't me. I'm going to wake up in a minute and find myself in the middle of a rehearsal."

Michel laughed too, wiping his forearm over his drenched brow.

"Well, you'd give Grant Noble a hell of a surprise; that's for sure."

Later, when Michel had finally collapsed, Jonni knelt beside him on the bed holding the damp, crumpled top sheet over her breasts with her arm and looking at him. His face was turned away, thrown into dark shadow by her body as she knelt between him and the window. He was smoking silently. She thought she had lost him already.

"I like this room," she said.

"Do you?"

"Especially at night. It's white and mysterious; I love it." She could barely see him but she could sense that he was miles away, deep in thought. "Are you thinking about the British National Ballet and Martyn Greene?"

He turned his head in the darkness to look at her.

"Were you listening to our conversation at dinner?"

"You know I was. You must be ecstatic. Were you expecting it?"

He didn't sound very ecstatic. "No, I wasn't expecting it at all. I knew he was vaguely interested; I heard he'd made some inquiries about me last week. It's a big opportunity." He shook his head at the shadows. "Soloist in one of the majors—unbelievable. Anyway, he doesn't know Charles Crown as well as he thinks he does. No one gets away from Crown that easily, more's the pity."

"But Martyn Greene said he couldn't stop you. And surely it was his idea in the first place."

Michel said nothing, finishing his cigarette silently in the shadow of her kneeling figure. When he had put his cigarette out he turned the clock on his bedside table to face him, tilting it so he could see the hands.

"Are you around next weekend?"

"Yes, except for Saturday morning; we've got a run-through."

"I'll be back from Glasgow on Sunday afternoon. If you feel like coming over, do. You know the code if I'm not in. There are a couple of spare front door keys by the phone in the hall."

Jonni laughed out loud. She couldn't help it. He wanted to see her again. She stretched her arms above her head in lazy happiness and squealed in surprise as Michel reached over suddenly and grabbed her by her waist, pulling her down beside him and rolling on top of her. They made love again as the dawn crept slowly over London, replacing the shadows with clear gray light.

Jonni was woken by the alarm after only two hours' sleep. She sat bolt upright with a jerk and hit out at the clock without thinking. The alarm was for her: she had to be in Stratford by ten o'clock. Brilliant sunlight poured through the window. It was going to be another scorching day.

Michel slept through the alarm without stirring. Sleepily Jonni blinked at his prostrate body. He was facedown, his limbs splayed out like a lopsided swastika, legs tangled up in the twisted sheet. He was comatose—completely wiped out by his night's exertion—and so drenched in sweat that Jonni could almost see the steam rising from his burning body. She wanted to touch his long muscular back and sleeping arms but she didn't dare. Instead she climbed off the bed and put on his collarless shirt over her jeans and went to the kitchen. On her way out of the bedroom she glanced at the wardrobe mirror. Her face was puffy, her eyes were deep-set and hollow, and her hair was everywhere.

She knew Primo was already in the flat. She had heard him humming as soon as she switched the alarm off. Primo was an early riser. He was sitting at the kitchen table with his back to the door reading a piano score and drinking coffee, kitted out for Glasgow with his leather jacket hanging on the back of his chair and his bag on the floor beside the fridge.

"Morning, bella. You sleep good?"

"Great!"

With a confidence that was rare for her, Jonni put her arms impulsively around his shoulders and leaned over the back of his chair to kiss his cheek. Delighted, he reached up to encircle her neck with one arm and turned his head to smile up at her. As he did, his eyebrows shot up.

"Jesus, bella! What did he do to you? You must have had a good night, eh?"

Jonni went to switch on the kettle, a smiling Mona Lisa. She wasn't giving anything away.

"What happened at the party after Michel and I left?"

"Nothing, bella. We all got pissed and went home."

When she arrived in Stratford for her rehearsal an hour and a half later she had reluctantly showered away the sweat and fluids that had soaked her during the night, but her face was still glowing and her eyes were still bright.

"I don't believe it!" Maggie said, whispering to her at the door while the stage manager laid out the shape of the Act Two set on the rehearsal room floor in sticky tape. "You seduced him! That's wonderful. Was it beautiful?"

Jonni beamed, blushing.

"Oh, crumbs. It was terribly dirty."

"My God!" Maggie stared at her with frank envy. "How absolutely marvelous."

"We didn't go to sleep until after dawn."

"This chap's beginning to sound like pure heaven. Dirty sex till dawn! What's the hitch?"

"No emotional involvement. Totally forbidden."

"All the better. At least he's honest."

Leum called to them, clapping his hands at the front of the big room. A relic from the seventies, he was a camp, mincing faun with a goatee beard, open-breasted silk shirt, and flared trousers.

"Come on, pussies! It's run-through week."

"If he calls me a pussy one more time," Jonni whispered, "I swear I'll brain him."

"Do what I do," Maggie whispered back, "out-pussy him," and she swept toward the director, raising her voice with an elaborate smile; "We're coming, tiddles! Don't get your little G-string in a twist!"

Anyone less like a forty-seven-year-old ex-RSC actress Jonni couldn't have imagined. Between Grant and Leum and bitching in the ranks this wasn't a happy company, but Maggie made it all worthwhile. Jonni slid into her seat behind the stage management table, half-drunk from her short night and her happiness. She could still smell Michel's body on her wrists. It was going to be a long week.

On the hot InterCity train, rattling north from Euston toward Glasgow, Michel made his way along the central aisle between the pairs of seats looking for Charles Crown. The train was crowded. Yawning dancers, some reading or chatting, some half-asleep, were interspersed among the other passengers, spread over several carriages. Michel nodded at the dancers who caught his eye as he walked past.

In the first carriage he passed through, Primo was sitting with his back to the engine, listening to music through headphones with Lynne's feet on his lap. He had left the Pimlico flat an hour before the train to go and collect her from Camberwell. Michel leaned over a plump middle-aged woman next to the aisle, smiling an apology at her, to kiss Lynne.

"Hi, darling. You okay?"

Lynne looked hollow-eyed and drained but she gave him a limp smile.

"I feel like a lumpy steamed pudding. I got my period this morning."

"Poor babe. You'll feel alright by Thursday night. Do you want any painkillers? I've got aspirin."

"Primo already gave me some."

Michel moved on, watched by Lynne's neighbor. At the end of the compartment, surrounded by strangers, Roly was gazing absently out of the window watching the Midlands fly past with expressionless eyes. He didn't see Michel. Michel walked on through two more carriages, pausing beside Annette who was so hot she declared she was going to die before they reached Glasgow. She was wearing shorts and the skimpiest of skimpy halter-necked tops, attracting wallowing gazes from surrounding male passengers. She lifted her mouth automatically when Michel stooped to kiss her. As he walked away an off-duty British Rail guard tore his gaze from Annette's cleavage to give him an envious, helpless glance. Michel winked at him.

He found Crown in a seat near the front of the train working out the final casting for the week's performances, scribbling away at lists on the table in front of him. Opposite, a mother and her wriggling child were gazing through the window pointing at horses and cows. Michel rested his arm on the high plastic headrest that separated Crown's seat from the seat behind, letting his body rock gently with the motion of the train.

"Have you got a minute?"

Crown turned his head and looked up at him, surprised.

"I'm up to my neck in casting. What do you want?"

"Just a word. I was at the BNB's annual dinner last night. There's something I need to talk over with you."

The change in Crown's mood was instant. He returned to his paperwork, his brow contracting.

"Not now. It'll have to wait until we're open in Glasgow. I've got to get this stuff finished. Have you heard about company class this evening?"

"Yes, six-thirty onstage."

"Correct." He waited obstinately for Michel to go away. "Go on, St. Michel, didn't you hear me? I'm busy. See me after the show tomorrow if you like."

Michel waited a further few seconds, swaying as the train flew smoothly around a bend in the track. He could see his own name on the list on the table, his initials marked down in Crown's scruffy handwriting against the list of boys' corps for Thursday night. A change of plan— Thursday he had been supposed to dance the pas de deux with Lynne.

"Yes, okay," he said at last, and went away, puzzled.

When Michel walked away Crown put down his pen and raised his head, staring straight ahead with such alarming intensity that the young Glaswegian mother opposite gathered her squirming child close to her side, watching his face in unease.

It had happened. That was it. Michel was gone. Crown shut his eyes tightly; he might as well go back to his casting and forget about him. He seized his pen with the same suddenness that he had just laid it down and went back to his work.

But he couldn't concentrate. He put his pen slowly down again and propped his elbow on the narrow armrest, letting his cheek sink onto his fist. The woman opposite was still watching him warily. His piercing eyes looked straight into hers.

"I've just lost my best dancer."

"Oh, that's terrible. I'm sorry."

"So am I." He turned his head to look out of the window. "I'm sorry for me and I'm sorry for him."

It was hard to bear the thought of seeing Michel's unique sensitivity absorbed into the huge machine of the BNB where his technical prowess would be exploited at the expense of all else. The depth and subtlety, the inner fire which Michel was only just beginning to bring to his work, would be snuffed out in a huge company where competition was fierce and triple *tours* were all that mattered.

At the BNB Michel would be worshipped for his soaring elevation, his quick feet, his incredible pirouettes. In no time those athletic gifts would become all in all to him. He'd get cocky—he'd been cocky as an adolescent and it would happen again. He'd listen to the voices around him, delighting his audiences with fine-tuned acrobatics, and hold out his arms at the curtain calls while his fans threw roses at his feet, quite forgetting he had once bled passion in the tiny roles in which Charles Crown had cast him. The thought of Michel turned into a sideshow—a feral tiger performing circus tricks with his teeth and claws filed down to render him harmless—made Crown's blood boil.

As he sat there brooding, while the train plowed through the English countryside, he tried to envisage the Islington Ballet without Michel. No Michel in classes to be watched and obsessively corrected. No Michel to be yelled at in rehearsals or criticized while he doggedly learned the principals' choreography at the back of the studio. No Michel on tour chatting up the usherettes and bedding the theater barmaids. No Michel onstage when the curtain went up. It was unimaginable.

And as for all Crown's plans for him . . . Crown lit a cigarette, looking bitterly out of the window.

Crown had never examined his relationship with Michel very closely. It had always been straightforward: he shouted at Michel and Michel did what he was told. It had worked. He could bully Michel into staying at the Islington Ballet. It would be easy. But he wasn't going to do it.

If Crown thought Michel's talents would be best served by his remaining at the Islington Ballet, he was probably the only person to think so—except perhaps Nadia Petrovna. However well he hid it under that nonchalant smile of his, Michel was as hungry and ambitious as any other dancer his age. Greene's company could offer him opportunities and facilities that Crown could only fantasize about. At the BNB Michel would partner some of the finest women in Europe—no, the world! Technical deities. He would dance on the greatest international stages; work with dozens of top choreographers. He'd earn money, perhaps achieve fame—maybe even great fame. It was more than most dancers dared even dream of. Who was Crown to dictate the values of a twenty-two-year-old man?

Charles Crown couldn't, in conscience, advise Michel to turn down Martyn Greene's offer. And nor could he bring himself to advise him to accept it. He sighed as he crushed his cigarette out with his heel and went back to his cast sheets. Whatever advice he gave Michel, either to move to the BNB or to stay at the Islington—whatever influence he exerted either way—he would probably regret it for the rest of his life.

On Wednesday night, after the first performance in Glasgow where Michel had danced alongside Primo in the corps of *Paradise,* Charles Crown was nowhere to be found in the foyer or backstage. Michel walked slowly through the stalls and circle bars looking for him. Marina, the ballet mistress, was fairly sure he'd already gone back to the hotel.

In the foyer of the run-down hotel Michel asked the receptionist to telephone up to Crown's room. There was a loud disco on in the adjacent bar and he had to shout to make himself heard.

"Crown! With the Islington Ballet!" He screwed up his face against the racket. "C-R-O-W-N!"

The girl seemed quite happy conducting her business against a background of deafening pop music. She looked up the number of Crown's room and dialed up to him, keeping an interested eye on Michel's waiting figure. He saw her speak into the telephone but her words were drowned out.

"He says he can't see anyone!" she yelled, with her hand over the receiver.

"Tell him it's St. Michel!"

"Who?"

"SAN—MEE—SHELL!"

There was a pause while she conducted another inaudible conference with the telephone. She looked up at Michel and bellowed, "He says you see him tomorrow after class!"

"What?"

"After class!"

"No, wait . . . !" But she had hung up.

He leaned against the reception desk frowning, even more puzzled than before. Crown was clearly avoiding him and he couldn't understand why.

"Are you okay?"

"What?"

The girl moved closer to shout in his ear, "Are you okay?"

"Yeah, fine!"

"Do you fancy a drink?"

"A what? Oh, a drink!" Michel was still Michel. The frown in his gray eyes melted and he looked her over with candid appreciation. "What's your name?"

"Tina!"

She was leaning over the high desk, her face very close to his. She was pretty. And available. He thought about it for a few moments. And then he smiled into her eyes and touched her cheek.

"No thanks, Tina. I'll see you tomorrow."

"What?"

"Tomorrow!"

And he went to bed.

Thursday passed and Friday but still Crown hadn't managed to find a free moment to talk to Michel. On Friday evening, after a dismal performance where half the audience left at the interval because of the heat, Michel sat on a rickety chair backstage removing his makeup slowly in front of the mirror. The Glasgow theater was hellish. Twelve boys, including Michel, were crammed into one small dressing room. There was no Tannoy. There was no wing space; the dancers had to scramble over one another to get onstage. The stage was steeply raked—even the Giant Tomato's perfect pirouettes sent her spinning like a child's top down toward the footlights. And Max, the company pianist, not only had to change into his penguin suit in a corridor, he had to accompany *Les Syl-*

phides on a piano which Primo described as a parrot with a whore's bed-springs up its arse. Added to all this, it was nearly a hundred and ten degrees onstage under the lights. Peter had fainted when he came off after *Les Sylphides.*

Michel was oblivious to the grotty conditions. Like all the Islington dancers, he'd learned to take cramped, uncomfortable theaters in his stride. At present he had the dressing room to himself; most of the boys had shot off to the bar and Primo was in the shower humming a concerto.

Michel sat back in his chair and folded his arms musingly, frowning at himself in the mirror. Martyn Greene couldn't be right, surely, that Crown actually wanted him to take this contract. The BNB, for all its wealth and its status in the dance world, was an old-fashioned company; an unadventurous one, the object of Crown's scorn. He couldn't believe Crown would make a decision like that on his behalf without consulting him.

"Hey, Primo!"

Primo stopped humming and called out to him over the hiss of the shower. "*Dimmi,* amico! *Tell me.*"

"D'you think Charles Crown would throw me out of the company?"

"Yeah! Throw you straight out the window of his office upstairs."

"No, I'm serious."

The noise of the shower dwindled and stopped and Primo emerged, flicking his towel down from the top of the broken shower door.

"I don' reckon it's likely. But then it weren't likely he'd let Annette dance the pas de deux either an' that happened."

Some days you just couldn't get a serious answer out of Primo.

"Come on, amico. You getting dressed or what? We're goin' out to a club with the stage crew."

"I don't think I'll bother," Michel said. "I'll head back to the hotel and get some sleep."

Primo looked at him askance, pulling a face.

"You been odd all week, boy. You sick or something?"

"No, I'm just tired. I don't know, maybe I ate something that didn't agree with me."

"You got the shits?"

"Yeah."

"You want me to come back to the hotel with you? I ain't so keen on goin' out tonight anyway."

Michel pulled off his dance belt and headed for the shower. He couldn't talk to Primo about Greene's offer. It was too inflammatory and too unreal. And if Lynne got to hear of it there would be hell to pay. Michel urgently needed to talk to Crown. But Crown wasn't talking.

"It's alright," he said, turning on the taps of the shower, "you go to the club. I'll catch you later."

When Michel got home from Glasgow on Sunday afternoon Jonni was sitting in the kitchen of the Pimlico flat reading an old copy of the *Dancing Times.*

Primo and Roly arrived with Michel from the station, all three of them with faces filled with their week in Scotland. They dropped their bags on the floor and Roly headed straight for the kettle while Primo collapsed into a chair. Michel threw his wallet and a newspaper onto the table and caught hold of Jonni's arm.

"Make me a coffee, will you, Roly? I want a quick word with Jonni."

Jonni let herself be led out of the kitchen and across the hall.

"How was your journey?" she asked, laughing.

"Okay—long." He kicked the bedroom door closed behind them. "How did your run-throughs go?"

"Not bad. There was an awful row on Thursday. Grant wanted to cut half a scene with Maggie and Russell, and everyone took sides. The writer had to be brought in and everything."

Michel was already kissing her, taking large, slow bites from her neck. He pulled the strap of her summer dress off her shoulder and Jonni's eyes widened.

"Heavens!"

"Don't say no."

"I'm not going to."

She had hoped Michel would be pleased to find her there but she hadn't expected his welcome to be quite so . . . *Continental.*

Michel's lovemaking was very different this time. He seemed less aware of her vulnerability, more concerned with his own hunger. His arms held her tightly and urgently, and he kissed her mouth while they were making love, which he hadn't done before. Jonni knew she was giving him something he needed and it felt wonderful. Miraculously, and to a mental fanfare that trumpeted her triumph to the skies, Jonni had her first orgasm while she lay naked beneath his body. It wasn't much to shout about, merely the briefest local quiver of flesh, not even a terribly comfortable experience, but she was as proud of it as if she had been Lady Chatterley consumed in flames on her bed of bluebells. She looked at the white ceiling, opening her mouth in silent, incredulous laughter while Michel's arms tensed around her, shuddering.

When he lay panting beside her with his eyes closed he laid his hand on her damp belly.

"You're getting there."

"Oh. I didn't think you noticed last time."

"Of course I noticed." He turned his head on the pillow in surprise to look at her. "What are you crying for? I didn't hurt you, did I?"

"No." She wiped the tears from her face with her wrist. "I just didn't think I liked sex, that's all."

Michel held her hand between their bodies on the sheet and closed his eyes again. Her tears made him uncomfortable.

"I've known girls do some very strange things in bed but I've never had one cry on me before, at least not over an orgasm."

"Will you teach me about sex? I don't know anything about it."

She heard him smile. "Yes, alright. Just bear with me a couple of minutes, okay?"

It was dark outside by the time they went to join the others in the studio. By then Annette had arrived with a good-looking boy dancer Jonni had never seen before.

"Coffee's cold," Roly said, smiling as Michel appeared.

Primo looked round from the piano stool, continuing to play as he shook his head and winked at Jonni.

"You got to be good for that boy, bella. He ain't looked so happy all week. First time I seen you smile, Michel, since we caught the train on Tuesday. Seems it weren't your gut makin' your dance belt too tight for you after all."

Jonni tried hard not to blush. Nothing was too private to be turned into a joke amongst these dancers. They were so uninhibited about their bodies that Jonni, with her nice English upbringing, could never dream of keeping up with them.

Annette stood up and stretched her arms luxuriantly.

"I'm going for a crap. God, it's lovely to be home!"

Early on Monday morning Michel sprang up the stone steps through the open door of the Islington Ballet building hoping to catch Charles Crown before he set off for Cardiff. The ballet mistress was in the company office behind the reception desk checking typed copies of cast lists against a sheaf of scruffy handwritten notes.

"Is the boss around?" he asked her.

"No, poppet. He's already gone. You got my message then."

"What message?"

She glanced up at him over the front desk in surprise.

"Didn't you get it? I left a note on your makeup box on Saturday night. Charles said to tell you he doesn't need you in Cardiff this week."

"Doesn't need me?" He looked at the bag he was carrying, packed and ready for the week ahead. He was astounded. Every able-bodied dancer was needed on tour, usually in several places at once. "How can he not need me?"

"I've no idea but that's what he says." Marina's tone was strangely guarded. "Give Martyn Greene a call, will you? Charles wants you to do classes at the BNB this week."

"Why?"

"I'm sure he's got his reasons." Marina couldn't look at Michel.

"Do you know why?" he asked.

"No—no, I don't know. It's nothing to do with me. Don't ask me, pet. I don't know."

Michel rested his folded arms on the high reception desk, looking at her with a worried frown. Marina was someone he completely trusted. The tall, glamorous ballet mistress, with her shoulder-length brown hair and earthy sense of humor, had been one of his first friends at the Islington Ballet. Back in Michel and Primo's apprentice days there had been loud lamenting when the boys' adored tutor, Marcus, had suddenly disappeared from the company. There had been an even greater stir when

Marcus reappeared six months later with a new name and a new ward-robe, and a distinctly different outlook on life. But as far as the boys were concerned, Marcus in a frock was better than any other teacher. Despite her new sex, proudly displayed on her passport, she could still turn out a mean double *tour* and, in the boys' eyes, that was all that counted. Marina was fiercely loyal to all her boys. She had been a good friend to Michel over the years.

Michel watched her as she hurriedly checked over the cast lists behind the reception desk. She was looking flustered, which was unlike her.

"Marina, have you got a minute? I want your opinion on something."

She went into a flap, her Adam's apple bobbing nervously under her silk scarf as she scrabbled her cast sheets together.

"Sorry, duck, I can't stop. I've got to do these—finish them—and pre-pare for my . . . sorry! No, sorry!" And she vanished in a flurry of waving papers. Michel gazed after her, perplexed.

But if neither Crown nor Marina would listen to him, he knew one person who would.

Nadia Petrovna sat in her ground-floor office looking at Michel with thoughtful eyes. Nothing was ever hurried with Nadia Petrovna. After all her years of work and rushing around she felt she'd earned the luxury of thinking before she spoke. Michel's handsome, freshly clean-shaven face watched her patiently across her desk while she studied him.

At last she said, "You seem so very young to me, Michel, but I sup-pose you are no longer a little boy."

"No, Madame, I'm not."

"You've come a long way since I brought you here from Paris."

"I hope so."

The old woman's eyes narrowed, glinting.

"Oh, yes. You have." She studied his face again, nodding slowly. Nadia Petrovna had aged a great deal in the past six years. Her pure white hair, though always elegantly coiffured, had grown thin, and her limbs were so feeble and emaciated she could no longer walk more than a few yards unaided. Her body's once great strength had gone but the blaz-ing spirit that inhabited it burned on undiminished. Nadia Petrovna's courage was as legendary as her arabesque. It seemed incredible that a woman in her nineties was still working a full five-day week. Some of the many people who hated Charles Crown hated him precisely because he let her keep on slaving for the company—as if even he could stop her.

Nadia Petrovna moved her hand toward Michel.

"Give me your hand, child."

Obediently he laid his hand on the desk and she took it in hers. His hand looked enormous next to her tiny one, so fragile and knotted with arthritis, pale and translucent with age. Nadia Petrovna's eyes glowed as she looked at his broad palm and strong fingers.

"Beautiful hands," she said slowly. "A dancer's hands. It was your hands I first noticed when I saw you at the Académie."

She released his hand and he returned it to his knee.

"Madame, Martyn Greene's invited me to move to the British National as a sol . . ."

She stopped him with an abrupt gesture and closed her eyes.

"Don't say anything," she said. "I can't discuss it."

She already knew all about it. But not from Charles Crown. Oh, no. She'd heard it from her secretary, Barbara, who went to the same aerobics classes as Martyn Greene's secretary. And when she'd broached it with Charles this morning there had been a furious quarrel. He had forbidden her to use her influence with Michel to keep him at the Islington— forbidden her to so much as mention it to him. "Let him go!" Charles had insisted. Still with closed eyes, she shook her white head in frustration. Charles was never so maddening as when he was right.

After a moment her ancient eyes opened resolutely.

"Talk to him," she said.

"He won't see me."

"Well, make him. It's important. Promise you'll talk to Charles before you sign. Promise me, Michel."

"I can't talk to him. I've tried."

"Then try again. He's a stubborn man."

Michel smiled despite himself and scratched his ear.

"I know, Madame."

When he had gone away Nadia Petrovna stood up, easing her weight carefully onto her arthritic ankles, and picked up her walking stick. She made her way slowly to the tall bay window and pulled back the net curtain to look out at the Goswell Road. It was lunchtime and the office workers were striding past on the pavement, huddled under umbrellas. They were all in such a hurry to get somewhere.

The intense heat had broken over the weekend into a series of summer downpours. Wet weather made Nadia Petrovna's joints ache. Every year the stiffness grew worse. But all the same, she wouldn't choose to be young again. Youth brought with it so many fears, so much pressure. Like those people outside on the pavement, the young were all in such a rush to get somewhere; to catch up with the future. No, Nadia Petrovna would not want to be young again. The only thing that brought certainty with it was time.

Yet age brought its fears as well—oh, not death; that had ceased to frighten her years ago. The future was for the children. Nadia Petrovna had never found the time in her own hurried youth for motherhood but she still had hundreds of children spread all over the world: children of all nationalities and creeds. Children who had come and gone, year after year, in the ballet schools of France, Austria, Sweden, Denmark, the Netherlands. They were her legacy to the world. And of all her children, the best and most faithful was still at her side: fiery, passionate Charles Crown.

It was Crown's energy and determination alone which sustained this little company they had founded together. Crown's tempestuous personality pervaded every corner and every crevice of the Islington Ballet. Time after time, Nadia Petrovna had seen him claw the company back from the edge of bankruptcy by dint of sheer willpower and bloody-minded obstinacy. She had watched him fight for the company, rage about it, weep for it, month after month, pouring his life's blood into it, tyrannizing over it with jealous devotion, crushing anything that stood in its way. Charles Crown was the company.

She tapped her stiff fingers slowly on the handle of her stick as she gazed through the window. Michel must stay; he must! Only Michel, his precious creation, could bind Charles to the Islington Ballet. Wasn't that what she had brought Michel here for in the first place? To fuel Charles's creative passion, which was being smothered here without sustenance or recognition. If Michel went, Charles would go too; it was inevitable. The little company they had created together couldn't hold Charles Crown's great talent for long without the inspiration of other great talent for it to feed on.

Nadia Petrovna Sekova was the quintessence of balletic grace and decorum, but like any ballerina worth her salt she hadn't traveled the world without picking up a few choice obscenities on her way. She muttered a few of them now as she gazed out at the wet Goswell Road.

When Michel failed to appear in Cardiff and news leaked out that he was spending the week at the British National, rumors began to pulse frenetically through the veins of the Islington Ballet. On the phone to Primo, Michel had little to say except that Greene had made him an offer. Primo and Roly sat up late with the girls in their tatty Cardiff digs, speculating as to what Charles Crown was up to.

"I hope he ruddy well accepts it," Annette said nastily. "It would serve the old bugger right."

Only Lynne, surprisingly, was serene under the tide of whispers that swept through the company.

"If Michel wants to change companies, why shouldn't he?" She was sitting on Primo's bed, calmly daubing shellac on a pair of pointe shoes that had already seen her through two performances of *Sylphides* and would have to see her through at least one more. "Frankly, I don't see what the fuss is about. If we move to the BNB I'll get eight pairs of shoes a week, so I'm certainly not complaining."

At the British National Ballet's cavernous headquarters in Fenchurch Street, Michel attended classical classes with the company's thirty-seven men, and sat in on rehearsals for their massive production of *La Bayadère,* which was opening at the Coliseum on Saturday night.

Michel knew he had a strong technique but that didn't stop him being nervous before his first class with the internationally renowned company. However, his fear of looking like an amateur alongside them was unfounded. The men of the BNB were good—some of them were very good—but their technique lacked the edge, the absolute biting crispness that set the standard at the Islington Ballet. Charles Crown would have said they were unfit.

As he worked through the exercises in class every eye was upon him. The BNB men were extremely curious to know what Martyn Greene had seen in Michel—aside from the obvious physical attractions. When they saw the size of the flowing jumps and the almost inhuman softness of his landings, eyebrows rose and swift glances were exchanged around the studio.

"No wonder Martyn's got a hard-on for him," whispered one of the soloists to the boy next to him. "That's one seriously fucking sexy pair of Achilles tendons."

At the Islington Ballet the dancers never praised each other. No matter how well you danced, the most you ever got from your friends was a nod and a slap on the back. At the BNB, the dancers showered Michel with compliments. The boys exclaimed wonderingly over his turns, his leaps, his hyperextended feet. The girls cooed about his line and his fluidity until he was dizzy with all the flattery.

After years of penal servitude in the obscurity of the Islington it was very gratifying to be gazed at in awe by the hordes of corps dancers who stepped aside in the corridors to let the soloists pass. And to be sitting in the soloists' changing room chatting casually with dancers of the caliber of Yohihiko Ishimoto and Yuri Rodenkov. Even the suppressed hostility of the other male soloists was flattering. At the Goswell Road the atmosphere amongst the dancers was one of support rather than rivalry—they were all striving against a universal standard of perfection. Here, however, in the competitive world of the BNB, hatred was the highest expression of admiration.

But if the male soloists saw Michel as a threat, the rest of the company, especially the women, were fascinated by him. Wherever he went—in the studios, the corridors, the canteen—interested eyes and whispers followed him.

The BNB was a wonderland to Michel. There was a sunbed room, a body-conditioning and Pilates suite, an immense music library—Primo had talked of nothing else for weeks when he first played here. There were two full-time dance notators, an army of physiotherapists, a whole department dedicated to shoes. The dancers naturally complained about everything: about having only three dress rehearsals with the orchestra, about photo calls that ran on past 5:00 p.m., about the dreary three-star hotels on tour . . . Michel shook his head, smiling at their grumbles. They had no idea. None.

It wasn't just the dancers who kept an interested eye on Michel that week. Martyn Greene sat at the front of morning class with a smile of smug satisfaction. Michel was even better than he'd realized: that long, beautiful line, the extraordinary extension and elevation, and of course those catlike landings. He nodded slowly to himself as he watched Michel turn at the barre with the other boys and unfold his leg into a magnificent développé. Greene was extremely pleased with himself. It wasn't only within the ranks of the dancers that the BNB was fiercely competitive. In spotting and securing Michel, Greene had stolen a march on the other majors and he fully intended to make the most of it. As yet Michel didn't have the arrogance or flamboyance of a star performer; his ego was only fledgling. But with enough flattery and adulation it wouldn't be long at all before he thought he was God in white tights. In fact Greene could already see a marked difference since the beginning of the week.

"How are you finding it?" he asked Michel, walking with him toward the changing rooms after class.

"Good," said Michel. He held a fire door open for Natalia Makarova and turned his head to watch her in wonder as she disappeared down the corridor. "Yes, I think I'm beginning to get the feel of the place."

Martyn Greene sat Michel down in his office and showed him press coverage for the company's coming tour to Japan and Australia. He took him with him in a chauffeur-driven limousine to the Coliseum for a dress rehearsal of *Bayadère,* seating him next to the leader of the Opposition (the Labor party, that is, not the Royal Ballet), and then to an opulent charity dinner where Michel found himself rubbing shoulders with Dame Alicia Markova, Anthony Dowell, and William Forsythe. He took him to watch a televised press conference in front of flashing cameras, where the journalists besieged Marie Gillette with impertinent questions about her much-publicized romance with a famous footballer. Systematically and deliberately Greene took Michel to the highest peaks of the international dance scene and showed him the glittering world spread before him saying, "All this can be yours."

Michel's eyes traveled slowly over the great expanse of opportunity, wealth, and celebrity that lay stretched out in front of him. It was a breathtaking view.

Michel had phoned Jonni to tell her that he wasn't in Cardiff. On Thursday night, while she slept beside him after they had made love, he lay awake in the darkness staring at the bedroom ceiling. He thought back over his six years at the Islington Ballet: those first two hard years of his apprenticeship when he had slaved in vain to win a word of praise or encouragement from Crown, and his four years of servitude in the corps, touring run-down venues with the obscure little company, dancing minor solos in Bridport or Clacton-on-Sea when no one else could face doing them. All the pushes and slaps, the insults and humiliations. Lynne, too, had been held back by his own lack of advancement in the company, he knew it. Martyn Greene wanted him to sign a soloist's contract tomorrow afternoon. And Lynne would be offered a contract from the end of August when the Islington's current tour finished; Greene had given his word on it.

Michel watched the swaying shadows of the leaves of an ash tree on the white ceiling.

Yes. He would sign. But first he had a promise to keep.

Michel would never know what Charles Crown went through that week in Cardiff coping with injuries and the company's low morale playing to near-empty houses—nobody wanted to go to the ballet in this heat. Wherever he went in the theater he was confronted by Michel's absence: Michel's makeup and shoe box unloaded from the van and sitting unused at the stage door. Michel's empty costumes swinging from hangers on the rail in the dock. Michel's name crossed out on a card on the boys' dressing room door. And when he returned to London halfway through the week: Michel's X-rays on the wall of Karl Redman's treatment room, his personnel file on the company manager's desk, his photo on the company notice board. Even at home, the papers and notebooks that littered Crown's sitting room were covered in Michel's initials. He saw Michel's ghost everywhere he looked.

Crown was in a meeting with the accountants when Michel arrived at the Goswell Road building on Friday morning. Michel hadn't brought his dance gear with him but, to kill time, he joined in Marina's class with the apprentices, dancing behind the boys in his tracksuit and socks.

When he rapped on the closed door of Crown's office, shortly after twelve, Crown's brusque voice called out, "Yup, who is it?"

Michel opened the door and went in. Crown was at his desk, deep in paperwork; a foot-high pile of CVs next to his elbow. When he saw who had come into the room he bent lower over his scribbling pen with a frown.

"I'm busy, St. Michel. Go away."

"Just give me five minutes."

"Look, I've got this budget and this whole pile of CVs to get through before two o'clock. Now leave me alone."

The artistic director's fierce eyebrows were knotted obstinately as he went on with his writing. He didn't glance up once. Michel picked up a wooden chair from beside the door and placed it in front of the desk, sitting down. His body was inflated and solid, his muscles still hard from Marina's class.

"Can I put my feet up on your desk?"

"No you can't. Go away."

Michel put them up regardless, resting the heels of his trainers on the corner of the desk to let his legs drain. He picked up a CV from the top of the pile and looked at it.

"You don't want this one," he said, curling his mouth. "She's put ballerina after her name in brackets. And her GCSE grades."

Crown snatched the CV out of Michel's hands and put it back on the pile.

"Don't touch those. And get out, you're interrupting my work."

"I know you know about the offer Martyn Greene made me."

"I don't know about anything."

Michel picked up another few CVs from the pile and cast his eyes over them.

"Looks like you've finally got rid of me, then."

"Good. Go away."

"I'm going over to Fenchurch Street this afternoon to sign."

"I'm not listening to you, St. Michel."

Crown was writing away furiously, glancing at a notebook beside him from time to time. Michel sat and looked around the office. It was small and cluttered, with books and papers stacked on every surface, and a wilted pot plant on top of the filing cabinet. It was a room which had held many terrors for Michel in the past, and with good reason.

Michel had Greene's letter with him. He unfolded it and laid it on the desk under Crown's nose.

"This is the letter he sent me, with the details of his offer."

"I've seen it," Crown said, moving it aside without so much as a glance. "Martyn faxed me a copy to Glasgow."

Michel said nothing for a while. He looked down at his hand on his knee, flexing it slowly as he contemplated it. The arteries of the back of his hand and forearm stood out in bold relief like an illustration from an anatomy book. Throughout the past week he had refused to acknowledge to himself how hurt and resentful he felt at Crown's offhand dismissal, and even now, as he sat there, he told himself that he didn't care.

"To hell with it," he said at last, taking his feet down from the desk. "I'm glad to be out of here. You make such a big show of despising the way the directors of the majors operate. Well, to hell with you and everything I used to think you stood for: you're just as big a hypocrite as the rest of them."

Crown continued writing as though he hadn't heard him. Michel picked up a pen from the desk and began clicking the button at the end with his thumb as he looked at the top of Crown's lowered head.

"I'm taking Lynne with me. I suppose you realize that. It's not going to be easy on her; she's going to be pretty swamped in the corps there to start with. But at least you won't have the chance to betray her trust too."

Crown's pen stopped moving on the page. After a few moments he laid it down on the desk and sat back in his chair, looking at Michel evenly.

"Alright, St. Michel, you have my complete attention."

Now that Crown was looking him in the eye, Michel felt a compulsion, which he resisted, to look away.

"*Danseur noble* in one of the majors. I'll get to wear white tights and have my photo in the program. I'll even be able to afford decent practice dress for a change. You struck a great bargain for me. Thanks."

"It's nothing to do with me. This is between you and Martyn."

"It was your suggestion, though."

"No, that's not true. If I had suggested it, I'd have told you about it."

"But you certainly didn't object to the arrangement, in fact you just about literally pushed me out of the door. Well, that's fine. I'm not complaining. The BNB's one of the top gigs in Europe and, in fact, I think I'm good enough for them. It's great: they're going to Sydney and Tokyo in eight weeks' time—Martyn Greene wants me to go with them, and possibly even dance one or two *Bayadères* while I'm there. I'm going to start rehearsals for it on Monday." He started tapping his foot under the desk. "There is one thing I'd like to know, though, before I leave. One thing I honestly don't understand. Why did you bother beating the shit out of me for all these years if you weren't planning to have me dance in your company? I mean, what was it: some weird sort of revenge because you don't like my name? Or did you just enjoy it?"

Crown drew in a sharp, deep breath.

"This is making me fucking furious. In point of fact, I put a lot of effort into your training."

"Yes, you did. And that's what I'm asking you: why? Why did you take so much trouble putting all that technique on my body if you were only planning to pass me on to one of the majors at the first chance you got? Explain to me how the system works. What's in it for you?"

Crown closed his eyes tightly and ran his hands over his head. This was very, very hard for him.

"Son, I'm not going to have this discussion with you. If you've got something more to say before you leave, say it. Otherwise go. Go and sign your contract. I wish you all the best with it, I really do."

Michel sat looking at his teacher's half-hidden face. He felt he hadn't finished but he didn't know what else he wanted to say. In any case, he had said a good deal already; it would probably be best to go away and leave whatever it was unspoken. And yet something kept him sitting there on his chair. Seconds passed in silence while he tapped the pen slowly on the top of the desk. Eventually he put the pen down and stood up to leave without a word.

In the doorway, with his hand on the open door, he paused for a moment, looking at the corridor wall. Then he suddenly closed the door again and came and sat back down.

"I can work harder," he said. "I'll dance ensembles—anything." He looked at Crown avidly. "I can put in more studio time. I'll cover all the boys in the corps: every single corps position—I'll do it."

Crown's face fell. For a moment he was speechless.

"Good Christ," he said at last.

"I'll coach the apprentices in the ensembles in my spare time," Michel entreated. "I'm good with them, you know I am. I'll earn my keep."

Crown lit a cigarette and stood up to walk to the window, where he stood with his back to Michel. Michel sat and watched him in expectation. After a very long time Crown blew out a slow stream of smoke, still looking out of the window.

"You know the top of Act One in *Swan Lake*? The number with the kettledrums where everyone walks on? Haven't you ever thought that bit of music's wasted? I mean, don't you think someone should be dancing to it? Siegfried, perhaps. Fucking great turns in second."

"Yes, I've often thought that."

"This *Swan Lake* I'm planning for December; do you dare me to re-choreograph the ballet from scratch?"

"Jesus!" Michel helped himself to one of Crown's cigarettes. "Yes, I dare you."

Crown sniffed—a short laugh—and turned away from the window.

"I might just do it, too." He walked over to the filing cabinet, tapping a purple bruise at the base of Michel's neck as he walked behind his chair. "What thoughtless tart was that?"

"It's not her fault; she didn't realize. She's not a dancer."

"Well, tell her next time she marks your body she'll have me to answer to."

"I'll cover it with makeup. It won't show."

"It'd better bloody not." Crown was rifling through a drawer. He pulled out a triplicate sheet of paper and laid it in front of Michel on the desk, handing him a pen. "Sign that."

Michel looked at the printed form. It was an Islington Ballet contract very like the one he had signed in February—but a Senior Soloist's contract. Michel turned his startled eyes toward Crown.

"First Soloist?"

"I got Adrian to draw it up in a moment of weakness. I was thinking of trying to bribe you."

"Bribe me? To do what?"

Crown sat down and stubbed out his cigarette.

"I'd kick you out of the company tomorrow, son, if you didn't pull your weight. But I'd never sell you down the river."

Michel looked down at the contract. His career at the Islington Ballet had moved very slowly but he was prepared to wait. Michel knew what he wanted. Coryphée, junior soloist, soloist; he had expected to work his way up through the ranks by hard work and patience. This was a very big step to jump all at once. It was unheard of. At the Islington Ballet where funds were so limited, you remained in the ranks until you had danced so many solos it was virtually impossible not to be given promotion.

"You don't have to do this. If you want to give me solo work I can do it from the corps. Everyone else does."

Crown shook his head.

"Sign it. It's time. And I warn you, St. Michel, I'm going to work you so hard you're going to wish you'd gone for Martyn's soft option. What do you want to stay here for anyway? I can't make you famous."

Michel shrugged.

"I suppose I thought you hadn't finished with me."

Crown nodded toward the contract.

"I haven't even started. Sign."

As Michel left the office Crown picked up a reference book from his desk and hurled it after him, striking him cleanly on the back of his head.

"Jesus!" Michel said, turning around. "What was that for?"

"That's for that fucking triple cabriole at the premiere. Try a stunt like that again and I'll skin you alive."

Michel laughed and looked up at the office ceiling.

"Thank you, God."

"Get out!"

14

No one at the Islington Ballet, with the exception of Michel himself, was surprised at his sudden promotion to senior soloist. They had all seen it coming. Some, with foresight, had seen it coming for the past six years.

"Hey, we're rich!" said Primo, when he heard the news. "Where you taking us, amico?"

"I don't know. Wherever you like."

His friends planned a celebratory outing to an all-night restaurant in Soho; a late dinner after their last performance in Bromley on Saturday.

"Don't forget Jonni," Roly reminded Michel.

"No, I won't."

It was a mad, wonderful, expensive night out, taking care of Michel's substantial pay rise for at least the next three months. His much-needed new dance gear would have to wait, it seemed.

In the restaurant Lynne threw her arms tipsily around Michel's neck.

"Senior soloist! Oh, Michel, if Charles doesn't let us dance together anymore I'll die of misery!"

Michel put his arm around her and caressed her skinny waist.

"We've got a deal, you and I, Lynnie. We're going to dance *Romeo* together one day, right? Now eat up and don't get slushy on me."

"Don't you worry," Roly said to Lynne, smiling at her across the table, "Charles wouldn't split you two up, chicken; he's way too smart." Roly was thrilled about Michel's promotion. He had performed dozens more solos than Michel—literally dozens—yet it hadn't even crossed his mind that this promotion should by rights have been his.

They were very happy that night, Michel and his friends. Annette even went so far as to put her arm through Roly's as they walked along Frith Street, causing him she knew not what emotional turmoil. Jonni walked hand in hand with Primo. She was family now. She loved them all.

Jonni spent every night that week, after dashing around madly in technical and then dress rehearsals, sleeping at the Pimlico flat with Michel. Usually she arrived before him, collapsing in bed exhausted to wait for his return from Bromley. But on Friday, after her nerve-racking first night, she arrived at midnight to find the whole gang—Michel, Primo, Annette, Lynne, Roly—waiting for her in the kitchen, greeting her as she walked through the door with expectant cries.

"Well . . . ?"

"How'd it go?"

She stood and gazed at them all with a funny emotional smile. They were there for her. Grant and Leum might both have failed to congratulate her on her first professional performance but her new friends hadn't forgotten her.

"Oh, shit," Annette said seeing her tragic smile. "The theater burned down halfway through Act One."

"No," Jonni laughed, "it went terrifically, barring an accidental spoonerism and one blown lantern."

Primo threw his hands in the air.

"Great, let's get pissed!"

"I can't," Jonni said. "I'm called for a ten o'clock rehearsal in the morning."

"No, we can't," Michel agreed. "We've got to get up for class."

When they were undressing for bed Michel asked her, "What's a spoonism?" He had lived in England for ten of his twenty-two years but some of the idiosyncrasies of the language still escaped him.

"A spoonerism?" Jonni gave him a pained look. "I'm afraid, in the last scene, Maggie called Grant her shite in nining armor."

Michel erupted into laughter.

"That was an accident?"

"Oh, I'm certain it was. Maggie's a pro. Grant had just skipped two of her lines and that threw her."

"I'm sure it did." He pulled off his jeans and chucked them on a chair. "My God, I like Maggie's style, whoever she is."

"So do I," Jonni said, and she began to laugh too. Now she came to think of it, perhaps it wasn't an accident after all.

As the show in Stratford settled into its run Jonni spent most of her nights and all her Sundays in the Pimlico flat, trotting up the many flights of concrete stairs and tapping the code eagerly into the keypad next to the paneled front door. Each time the door swung open her heart gave a little leap of joyful homecoming. She adored this flat, along with everyone she might find in it; especially one person, and he filled all her thoughts, morning, noon, and night, except for the minutes she spent onstage.

In the white simplicity of Michel's bedroom Jonni's heart pounded with secret happiness. She learned to love the stream of yellow light that shone through the uncurtained window all night casting its eerie shadows on the walls, and the varnished floorboards, warm and hard beneath her feet. The nighttime furniture became familiar; the plain pine chest of drawers with its rounded knobs, the van Gogh chair, the tall, ghostly wardrobe, and most of all the bed with Michel's strong arms and clear face in shadowy repose, away in a sleeping world of his own but still beside her.

Outside the bedroom Michel never kissed Jonni or treated her with anything other than nonchalant good humor, the same he showed to all his friends. But once the bedroom door closed behind them, then his secret smile came out and his eyes were all hers. Once the bedroom door was closed Michel knew exactly what he wanted.

They laughed like children together, romping and wrestling on the bed, scattering the bedclothes on the floor. Michel teased her, letting her think she was winning and then pinning her wrists to the bed with embarrassing ease.

"Oh, God, I hate that!" Jonni wailed in her humiliating capacity as a prisoner. "It's so unfair!"

"I think it's very fair."

And when he kissed her she laughed and struggled: "Please! Let me take my lenses out first!" But she never struggled for long.

Jonni was making headway in her voyage of sexual discovery. Michel introduced her to her G-spot and taught her how to press down with her abdominal muscles during sex as though she were trying to spit him out—which made her laugh so much the first few times she tried it she completely spoiled the mood. He took her hand and put it between her legs, hushing her frantic inhibitions, and showed her how to arouse herself. He encouraged her to fantasize, helping her over her horrified scruples by offering comical suggestions of fantasies so outrageously lewd they made her own guilty little garden of erotic daydreams seem like a suitable spot for a Sunday-school picnic. She discovered for herself the magical transmutation of her fingertips during lovemaking which made Michel's skin feel like soft, velvety silk under her fingers as she caressed him. And the delectable heaviness of her limbs after one or two of her proudest orgasmic successes. But with all these joyous breakthroughs, it was still the same moment that gave her the greatest pleasure. In the seconds before Michel reached his own orgasm, when his body and face convulsed and control was gone; only then was he vulnerable. Then he belonged to Jonni. And those moments, while they lasted, filled her with an ecstasy greater than his.

Jonni grew used to the riotous life which Michel lived with his friends in the flat: the easygoing humor, the quick quarrels, the unabashed farting and semi-nudity. It wasn't easy to understand how thoroughly these dancers lived through their bodies. They touched her all the time, without thinking, resting their hands on her waist when they spoke to her or patting her bottom to move her out of the way. It was natural to them but to a politely raised girl from suburban Gloucester it was extremely disconcerting. In the studio they clambered all over each other on the sofas like a litter of puppies in a basket. Gradually Jonni learned not to bridle if a hand accidentally made contact with her breast or groin during all this cheerful frolicking.

Life in the Pimlico flat wasn't all noisy hilarity. With their frenetic lifestyle the dancers found it hard to relax but, sometimes, late in the evening when they had exhausted their store of wild energy, they would sit together in the studio listening peacefully to music on the stereo.

Then Jonni would sit on the floor between Primo's feet with her head resting on his knee and he would stroke her hair while his eyes filled at the music. Or, if Primo was playing the piano, she would curl up on the sofa next to Roly and he would put his arm kindly around her, moving his shoulder so she could lean against him. Always in these quiet hours Michel worked on his body, practicing balances at the barre or sitting on the floor with his legs in the splits, twisting slowly from side to side as he listened.

There were times during Jonni's blissful sojourn in the dreamworld of Michel's flat when she still felt painfully excluded from their intimate little family. They talked about almost nothing but dance; it was their craft and their obsession—their life. Jonni listened and tried to understand but they were talking on the basis of ten or fourteen or, in Lynne's case, eighteen years' experience. Jonni's first glimpse of dance had been five weeks ago. And they knew each other so well. They knew everything about each other. So much was unspoken, so much communicated with a raise of an eyebrow or a half-gesture. Often it was impossible to know, with their crazy quarrels and flying insults, whether they were joking or serious.

"*Cristo!*" Primo said, looking aghast at his reflection in the mirrored wall of the studio. "Look at this all-in-one I bought today. Bloody expensive this was. My thighs look as big as Annette's in it."

"Yes," Michel agreed. "Only in your case it's muscle."

"I got one comfort, anyway—my arse ain't so big as hers."

"If you ate as much pizza as her it soon would be."

"You're horrible!" Jonni protested from her seat on a sofa. She could see Annette was offended; she was flicking, tight-lipped, through Michel's CD collection. "Annette, they're talking nonsense, you know they are. They're just winding you up. I would kill to be as slim as you are. And to have such skinny thighs." She saw Michel and Primo exchange glances but took no notice. "You've got a perfect figure, like a model. Ignore them. If you were any thinner you'd be . . ." She caught Lynne's eye and hesitated. ". . . too thin."

"Hah!" Annette beamed triumphantly at Michel and Primo and smugly made a decisive two-fingered gesture to each of them before she turned away to put on a Queen album, pleased as punch.

A few minutes later Roly leaned over the back of the sofa and whispered into Jonni's ear.

"Can I have a word?"

She turned her head and looked up at him.

"Yes, of course. What is it?"

"No, outside."

If it had been Michel she wouldn't have minded—Michel was a god in her eyes—but to be told off by Roly who was usually so easygoing and amiable made her feel like a naughty child who had been sent to stand in the corner. The fact he was so nice about it only made it worse.

"I know you mean well, lovely, but you're sticking your oar in where it doesn't belong."

Jonni looked up at him in the bright light of the hallway, flinching under his serious gaze.

"I'm sorry," she stammered. "But I thought, as they were teasing her so dreadfully and she looked upset . . ."

"They weren't teasing her, they were reminding her."

"Is she really overweight, then?"

Roly nodded.

"Dancing's a confusing, complicated affair, and a careless comment like that can do real damage. Annette isn't overweight for a normal person—of course she isn't. She's slim and beautiful, we all know that. But she's not a normal person. She's a classical dancer. And it's tougher on Nettie than most; tall girls have to be especially thin. You're a sweet, generous girl and you don't like to see people's feelings hurt. But Annette needs to lose weight and if she doesn't it's going to cost her her career."

His hand, while he frowned into her eyes, caressed her arm gently to reassure her.

"We're an insecure breed, Jonni. We believe what anyone tells us, especially if it's what we want to hear. If you don't know what you're talking about don't express an opinion; that's the safest thing. Leave our business to us, eh?"

Jonni knew quite well that Roly had forgotten all about it as soon as their conversation ended, but she continued to feel dreadful about it for hours. Neither Primo nor Michel wanted to discuss it when she went to them for sympathy. It was clear she had crossed the boundaries of her welcome amongst them. They liked having her around. Their eyes lit up when she walked into the flat—all except Michel who greeted her, as he did everyone else, with a calm nod. They kissed her and made much of her. But there was a vast area of their lives into which she could not and never would be able to follow them. She would never be one of them. It was a painful lesson she learned that evening before she disappeared into the consoling comfort of Michel's arms.

One Sunday afternoon when Lynne was dozing on Roly's lap, her face buried in his neck, and Annette was stretched out on another sofa sound asleep with her extraordinary mermaid's hair fanned out over the cushions, Jonni sat alone on the floor at the edge of the studio watching Michel practicing slow développés at the barre while Primo played Chopin softly on the Steinway. Silently, without attracting anyone's notice, she stood up and slipped out of the room, leaving her untouched coffee behind her.

When Primo went to make another pot of coffee he found her crying in the kitchen, sitting with her head bowed over the table and a pile of soggy kitchen-roll accumulating by her elbow. Primo's face puckered in concern. He sat down beside her and smoothed her hair away from her red, swollen eyes.

"*Dimmi,* bella," he said gently, stroking her face. "Tell me, eh?"

"It's nothing. I'm being so stupid. It's just that Leum told me he doesn't want me to go into the West End with the play."

"Ah, bambina." Primo was the world's best big brother. "Poor little Jonni. You don' want to keep on doing this play with the Shite anyway."

"I know," she sniffed, wiping her eyes, "but I must be terrible for him to want to recast me."

"You ain't terrible, bella." Primo had seen the play. He and Roly had been to Stratford together one night when Michel was at Covent Garden watching the Royal Ballet's new *Giselle.* "You're sexy and funny. The Shite's just sore 'cos he can't get you into bed. You knew all along they weren't likely to take you if the show came into town. Anyhow, you got another month in Stratford."

Jonni's mouth widened into a miserable grimace and her tears started afresh.

"It isn't the play."

"Then what, bella?"

"Oh Primo, you must know what it is."

"Ah." A comprehending soberness replaced his frown of affectionate concern. "It's Michel, isn't it?"

Jonni nodded.

"Oh shit. You got it real bad?"

"Pretty bad."

Primo moved closer to her, putting his foot up on the wooden rung of her chair, and let her throw her arms around his neck, patting her back sympathetically as she cried. Sobbing into his shoulder Jonni could feel his sorrow as well as her own. For all his fooling around and his bright Italian smile, Primo wasn't a happy young man. She had heard it in the way he played the piano and seen it in his eyes sometimes when he didn't realize anyone was watching him. Primo found solace in his music and his friends and his pride at being a dancer. And she—where was she to find comfort?

"We just got to hope for the best," Primo told her, caressing her hair.

"What is the best?"

"That you'll stop caring so much about him. That's the only best you can hope for. You've been coming here, what, six weeks—seven? You already outlived any of his other girlfriends."

"Oh, don't say that!"

"I know him pretty well, Jonni."

"You might be wrong."

"Yeah, I hope so. Just don't tell him how you feel about him, okay?"

Jonni nodded into his shoulder. It was good advice.

Charles Crown hadn't been joking when he said he was going to work Michel hard. Suddenly Michel was hurled into rehearsals for all the solo roles in the Islington's current repertoire: roles he had already learned alone at the back of the studios behind the soloists but which needed to be hammered into shape and rehearsed with the rest of the company. Every minute of Michel's day from class onward was filled with study and rehearsal, and usually, in the evenings, performance. He danced the role of Satan in *Inferno* twice in Swansea and performed Dante's love duet in *Paradise* with Irena. After each performance Crown tore him apart. Michel took the criticism in his stride and learned from it. He was having a wonderful time.

Michel loved all his work, even the painful and boring parts, but onstage he was discovering a new freedom he'd never experienced before. Onstage he could be anything: lighthearted, passionate, angry, romantic, even violent—whatever Crown and the role demanded. He could weep, love, fight, frolic, and seduce. It was total liberty. It made him feel sexy and powerful; he reveled in it.

Offstage he was the same undemonstrative Michel as ever: quietly focused in the studio, relaxed and chatty in the dressing room. The flame that lit him up like a beacon onstage was instantly snuffed out once he stepped into the wings. Michel's passion was a hidden passion, even from himself.

The company gathered at the sides of the stage to watch his performances in astonishment. As a performer Michel had seemed to blossom overnight. Suddenly his onstage persona—his authority and sexual charisma—was so vivid they scarcely recognized him. But Michel and Crown both knew that in reality it was far from an instant transition. Years of patient slog and regimented instruction had built the foundations for this newfound artistic freedom. With the unexpected offer from the BNB, and with Charles Crown's act of faith in promoting him, Michel's career had turned a corner and there was no going back.

There was resistance, of course, from the senior women in the company when they were told they had to accept him as a partner. The Giant Tomato, needless to say, refused flatly to have anything to do with him; she wasn't about to stoop to the indignity of dancing with a boy who, only a fortnight ago, had been in the corps—and one moreover who hadn't batted an eyelid when she had forsaken his bed. The rest, however, once they gave in to Crown's dictate on the matter, found Michel's partnering confident and secure. No mistake from his partner ever threw him. No one was ever too fussy for him; no one too dependent on his support.

But the best of his partnering he saved for Lynne. Irena's condescension in laying her dainty hand on his shoulder didn't go to his head. Michel and Lynne had taught each other everything they knew about partnering. They could move together with a fluency that was startling to watch, never once glancing at their own or each other's hands. Michel knew where to find Lynne's waist better than he knew where to find his own. Lynne's body had come to feel like an extension of Michel's body. He sent his arm or his leg a telepathic message to move and it moved; he sent Lynne's arm or leg a telepathic message to move and it also moved.

Crown watched their partnership with sharp-eyed, cautious satisfaction.

"You'll make soloist next season," he told Lynne. "But you're going to have to share him, darling."

Lynne didn't care. She was over the moon.

At Michel's first performance of *Les Sylphides* Lynne danced the beautiful central pas de deux with him. She was perfect: so light and ephemeral that each time he lifted her in arabesque it truly seemed he was trying to stop her flying away. At the curtain call, when the cast stood smiling in front of the audience, Annette dashed impulsively out of her place in the lineup of girls at the back, running across the stage in her white sylph dress to throw a rapturous arm each around Lynne and Michel and kiss them both in ecstasy. In the dressing room afterward Crown gave Annette a severe ticking off but secretly he was amused. As long as his dancers concentrated on their work and didn't screw up performances he rather admired a bit of spirit. And Annette Potter had plenty of that.

Annette, the stately Venus of the company, could be very sweet and funny. But she could also be a monster. Her truce with Roly had survived almost a month, with occasional intervals for altercations over their dancing, but it was too good to last.

Michel and Primo had taken advantage of a rare few hours' break in the day before they had to travel to Dartford for an evening show. Michel was dancing in the corps for *Inferno* tonight—virtually an evening off compared to his recent schedule. It was a peaceful time: bright early-August sunshine lit up the studio while Primo played Bach on the Steinway with scholarly precision and Michel listened, his feet up on the coffee table and his hand on Jonni's knee. The restful scene was shattered suddenly when the front door slammed and Roly strode into the studio, marching straight past them toward the far end of the room. His face was rigid with fury. Jonni had never seen him angry before—could not have imagined it—and she looked at Michel in surprise.

"For Christ's sake don't stop playing!" Roly cried to Primo as he heard the orderly tempo slacken.

Primo carried on playing with raised eyebrows while Roly stood with his back against the barre staring fixedly at the wall. He had pulled on jogging pants and trainers but otherwise he was still in his dance gear, his muscles still pumped up from the rehearsal room. Michel caressed Jonni's thigh reassuringly. They could only wait and give him time to calm down. An explanation would come in good time.

And come it did. Exactly four minutes later, on the next train arriving at Pimlico on the Victoria Line.

The door slammed again even louder and Annette burst in even angrier, if possible. She ignored Michel, Jonni, and Primo, marching straight across the studio toward Roly and punching him in the face. He turned his head quickly to avoid a second blow and caught her wrist furiously in his hand.

"Don't hit me!" he shouted. He caught her other wrist as she went for him again: "I said don't!"

"Let go!" she shrieked, and wrenched her wrists out of his hands. "Get your bloody hands off me!"

"Then lay off hitting me! I'm warning you, Annette, I'm a fucking sight bigger and stronger than you are!"

It was true. With his usual gentleness and his kind smile it was very easy to forget just how powerful Roly's body was. That was far from the case now. His raised hand warned Annette off as she screamed at him in uncontrolled anger and frustration.

"How dare you? In front of half the company and Charles! I should have kneed you in the balls!"

"It wouldn't have been the fucking first time!" He was just as angry and just as loud. "Will you let me cool off before you start on me?"

"I want an explanation now!"

Roly made a valiant attempt to control his rage. He was shaking with the effort.

"Look, I put you down because my back hurt. And I lost my temper because you weren't doing a bloody thing to help me."

"You yelled at me in front of everyone!"

"Yes. I was pissed off, okay? Angry and in pain! I still am! Now leave me alone!"

They were eye-to-eye, glaring at each other.

"It happened, Annette! It just happened, alright?"

"No, it's not alright! You had no business saying those things to me in public! You humiliated me!"

He looked away, trying to collect his wits, and nodded briefly, acknowledging what she said.

Annette stared at his averted eyes in fury.

"Do you want to know why I don't pull up when you lift me?" she demanded. "You always blame me for everything. You complain that I don't use the strength in my back, that I'm a dead weight. Haven't you ever asked yourself why?"

He looked at her.

"I'm frightened," she said bluntly. "Scared. Paralytically terrified." She spelled it out for him: "I do not feel safe with you! Every single time you lift me I'm convinced you're going to drop me. Every time I have to dance with you I think it might be my last. I don't trust you. Does that make things any clearer?"

Roly stared at her, not moving. His lips parted but no words came out. He blinked away the tears of anger and devastation that had filled his eyes and clenched both his fists.

"I don't trust you!" she repeated, staring him out.

At last Roly found his voice. He was looking at her helplessly.

"My good God, I've never wanted to hit anyone so badly in my life."

Primo and Michel exchanged dubious glances and Primo shifted his weight slightly toward the edge of the piano stool.

"Be my guest," Annette said. "Except that you won't."

"No, I don't suppose I will." He unclenched his fists carefully; he clearly didn't trust himself.

"You haven't got the guts. Poor bloody Roly. You haven't even got the guts to get yourself laid."

None of the three observers saw Roly hit her. It happened too fast.

Even Annette didn't realize until it had already happened. But hit her he did, and hard, with a resounding smack that echoed through the studio, and then he walked firmly out of the studio and out of the flat.

"Get the fuck out of my life," he muttered as he left.

Annette stood absolutely motionless. She didn't even cry out at the blow; she was too dumbfounded. None of the others said a word.

At last Annette noticed that her face hurt and raised her hand to her cheek, dazed.

"Why doesn't anybody feel sorry for me?" she asked.

Michel stood up and walked across the expanse of the studio toward her. He put his arm around her waist.

"Let's have a look at your face. It's just a bit red—it was only a slap. There's no real harm done."

"Well, it hurts like hell." She gave Michel a bitter look. "You're a fat lot of use, Michel. Why don't you go and beat the bastard up?"

"He's bigger than me. Besides, I think you probably deserved it."

"I'd have hit you too," Primo agreed, "only much harder."

"Thanks," she said. "What great pals you are!"

Unfortunately Roly had picked a very bad day to quarrel with Annette. They were scheduled to dance the pas de deux in *Inferno* together that evening for only the second time. And that pas de deux, short as it was, was no joke.

To Annette's delight a genuine bruise had appeared on her cheek by the time she reached the theater in Dartford. It was very slight, even after she had bathed it in hot water and prodded it all the way to Dartford on the train, but it was better than nothing. If she was going to get hit she might as well have something to show for it.

Half an hour after she arrived at the theater the whole company knew that Roly had hit her. Those who had seen him lose his temper with her earlier in the afternoon whispered knowingly together in the corridors. The event became company property.

The girls clustered sympathetically around Annette stroking her poor bruise, unanimous in their verdict. That Annette had hit him first and cut his lip was irrelevant. For a big man like Roly to strike his partner was an unforgivable abuse in a professional relationship, never mind any basic rules about hitting women in general.

The boys were divided in their opinions. Those who had fallen victim to Annette's charms in the past were vociferous in their approval of Roly's thumping her—they only wished they'd been there to see it. Others who were still under her spell or had yet to succumb were less certain. All in all, the event caused quite a scandal. Annette had been at the center of many scandals within the company but Roly, never. Roly was always nervous before a performance. He suffered terribly from stage fright. Usually he was good-humored about it, making a joke of it, but that evening he moved amongst the boys in the dressing room silently, keeping himself to himself and frowning at the inappropriate congratulations of his colleagues.

Michel found Roly onstage, stretching alone at one of the portable barres. Peter and Carlotta were warming up in another area of the stage.

Michel put his foot up on the barre beside Roly's.

"You okay?"

Roly nodded. "I'm sorry that had to happen at the flat."

Michel slid his heel along the barre until his legs were stretched into the splits. Where else would it have happened? Wasn't that why Roly had gone there? Surely he had known Annette would follow.

"I took a look at her. She's alright."

"Thanks."

Roly bent low over his stretched foot on the barre and then twisted his spine, rotating his strong shoulders to the left and right. Michel glanced at him.

"Your back still hurt?"

"No, it's fine."

"You should see Karl about it."

"I have. It's nothing serious."

They warmed up together without speaking further. Roly worked steadily and slowly, preparing each area of his body for the big jumps and lifts in the pas de deux. Michel scarcely needed to warm up for his simple part in the ballet tonight, but he stretched calmly alongside him, working through the same methodical exercises. He could feel Roly's nervousness; it radiated from him like electricity. Michel had seen Roly gripped by stage fright many times before, but he had never seen him like this. Drops of cold sweat were trickling down the side of his face.

As they left the stage together to return to the dressing room Roly caught Michel's eye. "Don't worry, Shel. I'll look after her."

Michel shook his head, smiling at him. "I'm not worried."

Annette was wrong about one thing: Roly certainly didn't lack guts.

Roly and Annette didn't speak a word to each other when they met up onstage before the curtain but, like the professional he was, Roly laid his hands on her waist and they went through a few practice steps together, both with stony faces.

Michel watched their pas de deux from the wings, standing with Primo and the other dancers who weren't onstage at the time. Amazingly, it went well; far better than their first attempt.

Michel followed the choreography with his hands while he watched them, marking the steps with unconscious gestures as he willed them to get it right. There were a few fumblings and adjustments of foot position but they were only visible if you were watching very, very closely. Roly jumped into the last combination of his solo variation with a strong, sure double cabriole and Michel nodded in approval. How different from Lynne Annette was in this role: majestic; black hair flying everywhere, especially into Roly's eyes, but that wasn't her fault.

From the dark wing behind one of the flats, Michel watched Roly lift Annette—a "pressage" lift, straight up in the air until his arms were fully extended, his hands securely under her hips: nine stone of unevenly balanced woman horizontal above his head. His arm and shoulder muscles bulged under her weight and his jaw was tightly clenched but he didn't waver even for a moment.

There was no point telling Annette that Roly would sooner break his own neck than drop her. If she didn't know that already she wasn't going to believe it just because Michel said so. Besides, it wasn't Roly she didn't trust, it was herself. She was too insecure about her own technique to feel safe with any partner. Michel shook his head in admiration as Roly lowered her to the floor without even flinching as she put her arm around his neck in what was effectively a stranglehold.

Michel had more respect for Roly than for any other dancer in the company. Considering that Roly, with his stage school background, hadn't had his first ballet lesson until he was fourteen years old, it was phenomenal what he had achieved in only a few years. And it wasn't just the late start which had been against him. Those four Fs Crown always talked about: the feet, the face, the facility, and the physique; nature had cheated Roly of his fair share in every one of them. His feet looked good now, but only at the expense of hundreds of hours of painful persuasion. And his face, however beloved by his friends, was not a handsome face. A special facility, alas, he didn't have either. He had rhythm, edge, a certain virility of style, but a natural gift for ballet, no. Even his physique let him down—not visibly; he was well proportioned and strong limbed—but in hidden traps: short Achilles tendons, tight ligaments, inflexible upper spine. And yet Crown's famous fifth F: hard work—what miracles Roly had achieved with that alone. Hour after hour after hour, working alone in the studios at the Goswell Road, he had turned himself into a dancer worthy of any company in the world. Roly would never set the Thames on fire—he lacked the self-confidence to push himself beyond the boundary of fear that had always restrained him—but neither would he be stuck partnering Annette all his life. Roly would make principal one day. Annette would not.

Onstage Roly reached out to catch Annette as she fell backward into his arms. It had been a serious quarrel. After that slap and the terrible things she had said there was little chance of its being soon mended, if ever. Michel sighed as he adjusted the elastics on his shoes and moved to his position in the wings for his entrance. It was going to make things difficult in the flat for a while.

After the curtain call Roly's hand fell from Annette's waist like lead and they parted without a word, heading toward their separate dressing rooms with set, expressionless faces.

When Michel arrived home that night he opened the door of the flat and called out expectantly toward the kitchen. He was answered by silence.

Jonni had left a message on the answering machine. Her parents had come from Gloucester to see the show and they were taking her out to dinner. She would see him when he got back from Margate on Saturday night, in four days' time.

Michel felt a little knot of disappointment in his chest. He had thought she'd be here, her face lighting up as he came through the door, anxious to hear what had happened during the pas de deux. He shook off his disappointment with a frown and went to make himself a sandwich.

Sitting in bed he gazed at the outline of the pine wardrobe in the half-light from the window. The evening had been an unpleasant one but he wasn't thinking about that; he was thinking about Jonni's soft body, so unlike a dancer's body. And her earnest eyes, vulnerable and trusting, as though she'd give him the whole world if only she knew how and ask nothing in return. The dance world was a closed, claustrophobic world and Jonni brought a breath of fresh air into it. Michel realized he had grown accustomed to finding her waiting here for him at the end of the day.

The telephone rang and he went out into the hall to answer it, hoping it was Jonni.

It was Annette.

"Hello, Michel." She sounded woebegone. "Is Jonni there?"

"No, she's out with her parents tonight."

"Can I come over and sleep with you?"

"Yeah, of course you can. Don't make a racket and wake me up though; I'm knackered. I'll leave the hall light on for you."

He switched on the light and went back to bed.

15

Jonni's evening with her parents was dreadful. They had driven all the way from Gloucester with Jonni's younger sister to see the play for the first time. Her mother was shocked at the subject matter, disgusted by the language, and not at all convinced that her little girl should be sharing a dressing room with someone as red-haired and flagrantly down-to-earth as Maggie Lane.

It was not until they were seated in the restaurant in Stratford Broadway that Jonni found out the real cause of her mother's sour-faced aversion to everything she had seen all evening.

"So, Jonquil, June tells me you've been spending your nights away from her house. I believe you've been seduced by . . ." she dabbed her mouth with her table napkin leaving red lipstick splotches on the white linen, ". . . a dancer."

Jonni smiled. "He didn't seduce me."

"So much the worse."

"Honestly, Mum, don't be so old-fashioned. This is the nineties."

"Morals don't change, Jonquil. At least, they don't change in Christian families. Is he planning to marry you?"

"No, of course not. It isn't like that. He's just a boyfriend."

"But, darling—a dancer!"

"So he's a dancer. What of it?"

"The company that kind of person keeps is hardly—"

"What kind of person?" Jonni demanded, "You don't even know him! His best friend takes his mother to Mass every Sunday morning."

"A Catholic! Oh, Jonquil!"

"Mum, I'm not going to be put off seeing a man I like just because his best friend's a Catholic. Anyway, I don't believe in God anymore."

"That much is very clear."

"Michel's a nice person."

"Men like that always seem nice, Jonquil. Actors are bad enough. You wait and see; he'll cast you aside and take up with someone else before long. And you'll probably catch some kind of dreadful disease, anyway. Maybe his friend would be better, even if he is a Catholic?"

Jonni glared at her sister who was enjoying this scene hugely, smirking away on the far side of the table. Bernadette was sixteen and far from pure. Her mother would have one of her purple fits if she knew half the things innocent little Bernadette got up to. Jonni had half a mind to tell her.

"I can't go out with his friend, Mum. He's gay."

Her mother's eyes widened. "Do you mean homosexual?"

At that Jonni laid down her knife and fork and looked squarely at her shocked mother.

"He has sex with girls too; he's just in love with Michel. Of course, if you prefer, I could always go out with Michel's other friend. He's got a Polish surname; you wouldn't like that, would you? Worse than French! Besides, he smacked his dancing partner in the face today. Oh, don't worry, he's a big softy really. Or I could have an affair with one of the girls; not Lynne—she's anorexic—but Annette, perhaps. She sleeps around so much she'd probably be up for it."

Her mother folded her hands neatly on her lap.

"As far as I'm concerned, Jonquil, the sooner you return home to Gloucester the better. Don't you agree, Gerald?"

"What?" Jonni's father looked up from the wine list over the top of his spectacles.

"I said, don't you agree, Gerald?"

Michel didn't return from Margate until late on Sunday morning. Jonni was waiting for him in the kitchen at Pimlico.

"Michel, I thought you'd be back last night! I came over from Stratford after the show, I hope that's okay."

He dropped his bag inside the kitchen door and went to fill the kettle. His back was to her.

"Yes, sorry. I got delayed. We had a late night so I stayed over at the hotel. Has Primo been in?"

"Not yet." Jonni watched him in uncertainty. There was something unusually distant in his manner. "Roly called round. He was expecting you to be here. He only stayed for coffee; he said he was just passing. I suppose he didn't want to bump into Annette."

"Probably. Do you want one? A coffee, I mean."

"Please. Isn't Lynne with you?"

"What? Oh . . . no." He sounded cagey. "She came back last night, I think."

Jonni wished he would be a little more demonstrative. Although they weren't in the bedroom, it wasn't as though there were anyone else here. He hadn't even looked at her properly since he came in, and she had bought a new turquoise blouse specially because he had said he liked the color on her.

"Did the performances in Margate go alright?"

"Yup."

"Did you and Lynne dance *Les Sylphides* again?"

"Uh-huh."

Annette arrived, only a few minutes behind Michel, breezing into the flat in shorts and a Royal Ballet T-shirt and hailing him archly from the hallway.

"Well, well, the wanderer returns! I thought that blonde in the miniskirt last night was going to eat you alive." She saw Michel's frown and drew back in mock dismay, putting her hand to her heart. "Crikey, don't say she actually did! Michel, you tart! She was a slapper!" As she spotted Jonni she stopped short, looking guilty. "Oh! Hello, Jonni. How's the Shite?"

Jonni's reply was hesitant. "He seems okay . . . full of himself as usual." She was gazing in incomprehension at Michel.

Annette looked down, puzzled, at Michel's bag beside the kitchen door.

"Have you only just got in this morning?" she asked. Her eyebrows rose slowly in amusement as she began to understand. "Didn't you come back last night?"

Michel bent down to put the milk away in the fridge.

"Give it a rest, will you, Nettie?"

Jonni looked from Annette's wry face to Michel's frown of displeasure and jumped to her feet, running out of the room. Michel shook his head slowly at Annette and then followed her.

Jonni was sitting on one of the sofas in the studio with her knees drawn up to her chest, her arms wrapped tightly around them. She didn't look at him when he came in.

"Jonni, look, I was going to tell you about it."

She shook her head very hard.

"You don't have to tell me anything. It's none of my business. You've got a right to sleep with anyone you please."

"It was really nothing. A couple of girls came to see the ballet and they wanted to spend a bit of time with me, that's all. It didn't mean anything."

"Does the time you spend with me?"

He hesitated. "Well . . ."

"Forget it. Don't answer that." She closed her eyes. "You should take care, you know. You might catch something."

"I used a condom. Look, if I'd known you were going to feel this way about it . . ."

"It doesn't matter how I feel."

"Come to bed with me," he said. "I'll make it up to you."

Jonni laughed at that. "No way!"

He sat down beside her and tried to take her hand but she threw him off. "Please don't, Michel. I really don't want you to touch me."

He was silent for a while.

"Alright."

They sat saying nothing while Michel brushed a bit of fluff from the thigh of his jeans. Jonni refused to look at him. At last she tightened her arms about her knees, staring across the studio at the windows.

"What was her name?"

"The girl in the miniskirt? Susan—or Suzanne, I'm not sure."

"You said there were two. Did you sleep with them both?"

He picked another imaginary piece of fluff slowly from his jeans.

"Not at the same time."

Jonni swung her legs down from the seat of the sofa and stood up.

"Jonni, wait . . ."

"I had a lot of fun, Michel. Thanks. Give my love to Primo and Lynne."

Thirty seconds later she was gone from the flat.

Once the door had closed behind her Michel walked back into the kitchen and took a cigarette from a packet that was lying on top of the fridge.

"You're a bitch," he said to Annette as he lit it.

"Don't say you've only just noticed. So that's the end of poor little Jonni, is it? Pity; I rather liked her."

He blew out a stream of smoke and looked at her, more annoyed about what had happened than he cared to admit, even to himself.

"You did that on purpose."

"No, my love, I've got news for you. You did it on purpose."

"What's that supposed to mean?"

"Getting just a tiny bit too keen there, weren't you? You'd got rather used to finding Jonni's willing little body in your bed when you got home from work, with her nice tits and innocent eyes. In fact it was almost in danger of turning into a relationship, wasn't it? Oops! Time to fuck things up before it gets too late. You see, I know you terribly well, my darling. We're very much alike, you and I."

Michel stood by the sink looking at her evenly. Annette screwed guys only to see how much damage she could do them. For her an affair lasted only as long as it took to get a man's neck firmly under her heel.

"We aren't at all alike," he told her.

"Are you sure? Don't tell me you're actually hurt about losing her!"

He shook his head. Nothing hurt Michel. There hadn't been a moment's pain in his heart since the day, when he was thirteen, that he had realized his father was never coming to see him. Since then his heart had belonged to his dancing.

"I feel sorry for you," she said, standing up to walk toward him. "But we all have to do what we have to do. You've always got me, darling."

"I don't want you, Annette."

She put her hand on the crotch of his jeans and caressed him gently. "Are you sure?"

"Quite sure," he said, unmoved. Michel was the only man in Annette's life that she hadn't managed to diminish emotionally, sexually, or materially. He looked at her coolly. If they hadn't been friends, and if it hadn't been entirely outside Michel's nature, they would probably have been bitter enemies.

"You want a fuck?" he asked, still smoking placidly.

"Not as much as you do."

He tossed his lit cigarette in the sink.

"Okay."

He made love to Annette standing up against the kitchen wall without ceremony, which was just the way she liked it. If anything she liked it rougher but Michel wasn't into that kind of thing, even for a friend. When he pulled away to reach into the pocket of his jacket on the back of a chair she protested.

"You don't need that, Michel."

He smiled. "Darling, I wouldn't screw you without a rubber if you were the last woman in London."

In the early afternoon, when Michel was in the studio cracking Roly's spine for him, Lynne poked her head into the kitchen looking around in surprise. An unhappy little quiver had crept into Lynne's smile recently.

"Hi, Netts. Where's Jonni? Isn't she here?"

Annette complacently turned the page of her copy of *Vogue*.

"It's okay, lovey, you can relax. Michel's given Jonni the old heave-ho—and in style too."

Lynne dropped onto a chair at the kitchen table and melted into sobs of relief. "Oh, poor Jonni," she groaned, wiping away her joyful tears with the sleeve of Roly's sweatshirt. "Poor, poor Jonni."

Somehow, although the minutes seemed like miserable hours, Jonni got through the rest of Sunday, and Monday, and Tuesday, and Wednesday.

On Wednesday night, when the curtain had come down and she was taking her face off in front of the mirror in the dressing room she shared with Maggie, there was a knock on the door.

Maggie had her wig half on, half off, hairpins everywhere, as she called out, "Huloo-oo!"

When she turned to see who it was, Michel was standing in the doorway with his hands in his trouser pockets.

"Can I come in?"

Maggie's face fell and she stared at him openmouthed.

"Oh my God," she whispered. "Is that him? He can't be real."

Michel looked at Maggie, amused by her compliment.

"Hello, Maggie."

"Go away!" Jonni said quickly. "I don't want to see you." She turned back to the mirror and continued to remove her makeup, willing herself not to start crying again. "What are you doing here, Michel?"

"What do you think? I came to see the play. We did a schools' matinee this afternoon so I had the night off."

"Well, you've seen it now. So you might as well go home."

"Do you want to go for a drink?"

"Sorry, I've got other plans. Go and find someone else; it shouldn't be difficult."

"Jonni . . ."

"For heaven's sake," Maggie said, recovering from the shock of Michel's good looks, "come in and close the door if there's going to be a scene."

"There isn't going to be a scene," Jonni said, but Michel came in anyway and closed the door behind him. She turned her face away when he leaned over to kiss her cheek. "Don't, I'm covered in makeup."

"You didn't call," he said.

"Why should I?"

"I just thought you might. So I could apologize."

"Shall I leave?" Maggie asked.

"Don't you dare!" Jonni told her. "There's really nothing to apologize for, Michel. You live your life the way you live it. You're perfectly honest about it. I just don't fit into that kind of scene. Please don't let's talk about it anymore or I shall cry and you'll hate that. Did you like the play?"

"Yes." Then he smiled. "Actually, no, I hated it."

"Thanks a lot."

"It's not your fault; you were just fine." He looked over at Maggie. "And you were amazing."

"Yes, I know," Maggie said grandly. "I'm a frightfully good actress."

"I was disappointed you didn't call him a shite, though."

"Awfully sorry. If I'd known you were in I would have done."

Michel put his hand in his pocket and took out a contact-lens box. He laid it on the dressing table in front of Jonni.

"You left this by the bed. Why don't you put your clothes on and let me drive you home?"

"Because it wouldn't change anything."

"How do you know? At least let me try and explain."

"Explain what? The situation's crystal clear."

"Well, if nothing else, come to the bar for a drink with me."

"Oh, for goodness' sake stop!" Jonni cried, and she jumped up from her chair and ran out of the room in her dressing gown, banging the door behind her as she burst into tears. Michel watched her leave in frustration.

Once she had gone there was a marked silence in the dressing room while Maggie pinned up her rich, red hair. It was a long time before she glanced at Michel in the mirror and, when she did, she found he was staring at her. Her hands, fixing the last strands into the loose knot on her head, stopped moving as she met his eye.

"You really are stunning," Michel said.

Suddenly Maggie's fingers were all thumbs. She looked into her own eyes in the mirror, pinning away clumsily. She could see the fine lines around her eyes and the bloated skin beneath them sagging at the edges.

"I've grown awfully dumpy in my old age," she said, artificially merry.

Michel leaned over the back of her chair, resting his hands on its narrow arms, and put his face next to hers, not touching her but so near that she could feel the warmth of his cheek on her own. Maggie's smile drained away and she held her breath. His eyes were gazing at her intimately in the mirror, glowing with soft appreciation as he studied her startled face. Maggie felt her mouth go dry: his sexual presence was magnetic despite the simple frankness of his gaze. It was ridiculous, she told herself; her eldest son was almost his age. Yet still she couldn't break the hold of his gray eyes.

"Oh Lord," she whispered under her breath.

Michel smiled and whispered back, touching her arm to reassure her. "No, it's okay, don't worry."

He stayed close to her, watching her in the mirror, enjoying her face. After a few seconds that seemed like an hour, Maggie raised her chin slightly and narrowed her eyes.

"She's very special, Michel."

"I know."

"If I send her back to you, will you look after her?"

Michel lowered his gaze to the dressing table, thinking about that for a while, and then met her eye in the mirror again.

"Yeah," he said. "Yeah, I will."

"God only knows why, but I believe you."

The run at the theater in East London dragged on, eating up a golden August, but Jonni didn't look at the sunshine or the rich foliage on the trees on Clapham Common or hear the busy, merry chatter of birdsong. She brushed aside all Maggie's hints about Michel, lamenting with downturned mouth that there was no point even thinking about him; there was no future in loving Michel. In the end Maggie stopped mentioning him. It only made her cry.

The Shite discovered or deduced that Jonni had been, as he graciously put it, found, fucked, and forgotten by her boyfriend, and renewed his unwanted attentions toward her with wearying perseverance. He had fame, he told her; experience, money—he glanced in the mirror on Jonni's dressing room wall, running his hand lovingly through his dyed-brown hair—and looks! What else did she want?

"Not you, Grant," she said, closing the dressing room door in his face. She no longer cared about keeping things sweet with Grant for the sake of her career. Her career could go hang in some cold, forgotten corner on the peg next to her heart.

Relentlessly, as she walked on the common or sat in the dressing room putting on her makeup or lay awake in her bed in Auntie June's house, her thoughts revolved around Michel's flat and Primo's laughter and the life that was going on without her. Although that world had been sucked away from her she knew that somewhere in another part of London Lynne was trying to get to grips with Virgil's tricky solo variation from *Inferno;* Roly and Annette either were or weren't talking to one another; and Michel, always Michel, was slapping cool French cologne on his face after he shaved every morning and sitting in the kitchen with his feet up on the table drinking strong black coffee with two sugars.

As the weeks passed she began to smile again and to giggle in the dressing room with Maggie, but in the privacy of her lonely bedroom in Clapham she wondered how she could still feel so bereaved. Surely simply by feeling so bad for so long she ought to have been able to make the misery go away.

The end of the show's run loomed large, just a week away, and Jonni had no idea what she was to do with herself once it had closed.

"You'd be far better staying in London," Maggie told her. "Get a job crewing in the theater, or dressing, and send CVs off for everything in the casting newsletters. Do fringe—do anything. Try and get some Shakespeare under your belt."

"Yes, I will," Jonni said despondently. Maggie already had a telly lined up for the following month and the possibility of a tour in the autumn. Her agent had been busy. Jonni hadn't even managed to get an agent out of this show. "I'll get around to all that soon, Mags. First I'll go home for a while. My mother wants me to."

"That's the worst reason for going home I've ever heard," Maggie said.

That last week of August flew by and before she knew it Jonni was clearing her things from her dressing table, packing her makeup and lens-cleaning fluids and funny good-luck gifts into plastic carrier bags. She took down the First Night cards that were tucked around the edges of her mirror. Michel had sent her a postcard: a black-and-white photograph of Nureyev and Fonteyn dancing in *Giselle.* She held it in her hand, looking down at it for a long time and running her thumb over it gently.

Maggie laid her head to one side, frowning at her sympathetically.

"Go and see him, love."

"I can't. It's over and, anyway, it's been too long now."

"Just turn up and say you've come for tea, and part as friends if nothing else."

"Michel doesn't drink tea," Jonni said, and she put the card away in her bag.

Maggie looked at herself in the mirror remembering how one evening almost a month ago, in this room, a young man had made her feel beautiful in a way she hadn't felt for years. In fact, there were moments when she could still feel the warmth of his admiring eyes.

"I think you're making a very stupid mistake," she said.

Jonni's trunk had been sent on ahead by train. At lunchtime, the day after the show closed, Jonni and a shoulder bag containing yesterday's underwear and a clean T-shirt were at Victoria Coach Station waiting for the one-fifteen bus to Gloucester. It was all behind her.

It was a warm late-summer London Sunday. Outside the bus station an air of laziness hung over the black taxis that chugged past the dusty curb. Jonni had over an hour to wait for the bus. On a sudden whim she decided she would walk down to Warwick Way—just walk down there and back; she had nothing to lose.

At every step of the ten-minute walk she expected to see Primo or Lynne or Roly appear around a corner. It was Sunday lunchtime; they should! They should appear simply because she willed them to so desperately. In her imagination she visualized Roly's kind eyes lighting up in pleasure when he saw her, or Primo's face bursting into a smile— visualized it so clearly she couldn't believe it when it didn't happen.

People strolled past her on the pavement in shorts and patterned summer dresses as she walked slowly down Belgrave Road waiting for fate to give her a helping hand. She didn't want much, only to see them and to pass through their world once more before she slipped away into the obscurity of her own.

On the corner of Warwick Way she stopped and looked across the road at the tall white-fronted house squeezed between two other identical houses behind fanning telephone cables. The top-floor studio windows were wide open and she could hear laughter coming from inside, echoing in the resonant well of the hot street. Someone was playing the piano.

It couldn't hurt just to say hello. She still had her front-door key. She could pop in, telling them she was just passing on her way back to Gloucester. It was very nearly true.

It was strange to be climbing those stairs again. She had climbed them every night for the past month in her dreams and in her imagination. To feel the hard concrete reality of them under her feet was heaven. Outside the flat she hesitated—perhaps it would seem more natural just to stick her head around the door. She pressed the digits of the entry code on the keypad and turned the handle. Nothing happened. She knocked.

The door was opened by a very pink young woman, round-faced and pretty, in pink dance clothes and ballet shoes. She kept her hand on the door, looking at Jonni with an inquiring, proprietorial smile.

"Yes?"

Jonni's heart sank.

"Is Michel there, please?"

"Who?"

Jonni thought she must have misheard, but the girl was frowning, looking perplexed. Jonni smiled uneasily.

"Michel . . . St. Michel?"

The girl turned her head and shouted into the studio.

"Anyone know a Michel?"

"He lives here!" Jonni said in amazement.

"I think you've got the wrong address."

"No, I haven't. He does live here! Look: he's in that photograph on the . . ." Her face fell. The photograph had gone.

The pink girl's expression, however, cleared.

"Oh, him! The guy who owns the place! I'm sorry, I don't think we've got an address for him but I can try and find a number for the solicitor we rented from if you like."

Jonni stared. She was beginning to believe the girl.

"You mean he's just . . . gone?"

"I suppose he must have done." She glanced over her shoulder at the door of Michel's bedroom. "That door's locked. The solicitor will probably have a key if you're looking for something."

"And he didn't leave an address?"

"I'm afraid not. Hold on, I'll find you that number."

"No, it's okay. I can reach him through the Islington Ballet. They'll know where he is."

A tall, skinny man had just walked out of the studio on his way to the bathroom, dripping with sweat. He shook his head.

"Won't find anyone at the I.B., babe, not now. I'm pretty sure that company closes for most of September."

"Oh," said Jonni. "Thanks."

Very slowly she walked down the stairs trying to understand what could have happened. It was surreal. Michel and his whole world seemed to have vanished from the face of the earth. If there was a logical explanation Jonni could not, at that moment, fathom it. He simply no longer existed—perhaps he never had. She was dazed.

As she stepped out onto the bright street, shoulders drooping, a voice called her from above.

"I say!" Jonni looked up. The pink girl was leaning out of the studio window. "Your name isn't Jonni Kendal, is it?"

"Yes. Why?"

The girl waved an envelope.

"Sorry! It arrived yesterday and we pinned it to the back of the front door! I forgot!"

Jonni sped back up the stairs. Round and round the corners of the gray stairwell.

A letter addressed to her, marked "For collection" in Michel's tidy handwriting. Black ink. Her name. Postmarked Paris.

She took the small envelope in both hands and held it tightly.

"Thanks."

"Best of luck!"

Jonni didn't even open Michel's letter as she walked back up Belgrave Road. He had written to her and that was enough. But once she had reached the bus station and bought herself a cup of watery coffee, installing herself in one of the orange plastic cafeteria seats, she turned the letter over in her hands and opened it.

"Jonni—Gone suddenly to Paris to work with C.C. on project here. Would have written before but only just settled. Expect this would miss you in Stratford. Here is address if you want to get in touch. Otherwise back mid-October. M."

It was just like Michel: short and to the point. But his meaning was plain. He wanted her in his life. Or on the edge of it. Or somewhere.

She still had half an hour to wait for her bus and she spent it reading and rereading her letter, her chest swelling inside her as she dreamed up a mad, harebrained plan. Her thoughts must have been transparent because a pair of young Australian backpackers at the table next to hers watched her with comprehending smiles.

"Do it, darling," said the girl. "Whatever it is. Go on; you're only young once."

Jonni looked at them with frightened, laughing eyes.

"What if he doesn't want me?"

The boy grinned at her in his turn. "He will. Believe me."

Jonni bit her lip. Oh boy! They'd better be right!

Her savings, after three months working in London, were practically nil but she had enough money in her bank account to get her to Paris and, if necessary, back again. She hurried to the ticket office and bought a coach ticket to Dover and a ferry ticket to Calais before she could change her mind. Her courage nearly failed her when she dialed her parents' telephone number and heard it ringing, but her tickets were already in her handbag between the pages of her passport, which she had kept with her by pure luck. When her mother answered she gabbled hurriedly into the receiver that she was going to spend a few days with a friend and rang off before her mother could protest.

All the way to Dover Jonni gazed through the bus window and listened to her own heart thumping at the craziness of her scheme. Two hours ago she had made up her mind that she could cope with never seeing Michel again, except perhaps to slip into the back of a theater and watch him dance someday. Now she had to see him today, and at any cost, even if only for a moment.

By three-thirty she was on the ferry, sitting with her shoulder bag beside her, staring at the rugged white cliffs through the salt-splashed picture windows. She fingered Michel's letter as a talisman, thinking of the mysterious foreign land to which she was sailing. Every other adventure of her life seemed pale by comparison. Her previous travels abroad were limited to a holiday in Majorca with her parents and a school day trip to Boulogne.

When they were halfway across the English Channel Jonni stood up and wandered rather unsteadily toward the Bureau de Change, rifling in her handbag. Then she saw her wallet—saw it in her mind's eye, as clear as day, still sitting on the counter at Victoria Coach Station where she had taken it out to buy her tickets. Her head shot up and her mouth opened. It wasn't possible!

But, oh, it was! She was on a boat ten miles off the coast of France without a penny: no checkbook, no credit card, nothing.

The ship's purser was sympathetic.

"Telephone your contacts in France and ask them to pick you up from Calais."

"Yes, I will," she said, nodding automatically like a plastic water-seeking duck. "Thank you very much."

But she wouldn't, even if she could, which she could not.

She sat down to think. If she went and told her story to the port authorities, no doubt they would take pity on her and put her on a ferry back to Dover. Or, alternatively, she could try and busk her way to Paris and to Michel. Onwards or backward—she would have to make up her mind soon; the ferry was reversing slowly into the dock at Calais. She could see the cranes and low port buildings spread out on the quay through the window.

Something Maggie had once said popped into her mind. After one terrible rehearsal when she'd been lamenting, terrified of failure, that she hadn't stayed at drama school, Maggie had hoisted her back onto the rails with a firm pat on the hand.

"There's only one way off a tightrope, love, unless you want to break your neck, so never look behind you. And for Christ's sake don't look down."

With Maggie's words echoing in her head Jonni made her decision. She walked over to a kindly looking elderly couple who were just gathering their belongings and duty-free bags together and leaned over to talk to them, her hair swinging forward over her face and her hands pressed between her knees.

"Excuse me. Do you know if it's very far to Paris?"

The couple were American. They glanced at each other before they made up their minds it was alright to speak to her.

"I guess it's quite a lick if you're planning to walk."

The man laughed at his own wisecrack and Jonni grinned politely. That wasn't nearly as funny as he seemed to think.

"Is it as much as fifty miles?"

"Well, now, no. I should say more like a hundred."

Jonni's ears caught the rattle of metal coming out of his pocket. Ah—car keys! Her eyes glinted. In the space of two minutes she had turned from innocent lost sheep to hustler.

"I don't know what to do. I have to meet my boyfriend in Paris and I've lost all my money. I don't suppose . . ." she showed her white teeth winningly, ". . . you're going anywhere near Paris, are you?"

The couple looked at each other again.

"I guess we could take you as far as Nogent-sur-Oise."

Victory! And with so little difficulty!

"You'll have to call your boyfriend from there. I guess you won't mind sitting in the back with Herman, huh?"

Jonni loved Herman, whoever he was. She followed them down to the boat deck with a wide, happy smile, swinging her shoulder bag gleefully.

She didn't feel quite so victorious once she had found Nogent in the road atlas in the back of their hired Ford. Still, it wasn't very far from Paris—or it didn't look too far. She tucked her loose hair behind her ear as she gazed down at the map, trying to work out the best route to take after Nogent.

"Get off, Herman!" She pushed him away with her arm. Herman was a large Dalmatian. Nancy and Roger were taking him back to Denver via the Continent.

They were a kind couple; kind to Jonni and kind in the tales they told of their two sons grown-up and married; of a daughter living in Canada where the snow covered the ground-floor windows every year, and an ancient school friend battling bravely against multiple sclerosis in Maidstone.

"Herman's too much of a handful for her to manage, aren't you, boy? Still, we'll take good care of you, feller. Wait and see."

Jonni listened to it all with grateful attention, watching the unfamiliar scenery, the bold road markings, the strange place-names flash past the car windows. With every town and village they passed in the early evening sun she felt herself moving nearer and nearer to Michel. It was still only half past five. No—she rotated the hand on her watch with a sense of wonder—half past six.

Almost two hours later Roger and Nancy left her in the center of Nogent with strong misgivings. The sun was sinking rapidly.

"Are you sure your young man will be home? You've got enough money to get the train if he ain't?"

Herman licked Jonni's face enthusiastically as she stuffed his head back into the car so she could close the door.

"Yes, honestly. You've both been so kind already. Thank you."

She waved them off with a bright smile, already regretting her English scruples. She wasn't even quite sure how far it was to the city center. She only knew there was a good inch of white map between Nogent and the red splodge that was Paris. Well, she would set off along the small road that ran, according to the map, along the Oise river and hitch a lift on the way.

The romantic, oddly shaped buildings of Nogent dwindled away almost at once as she set off down the road that was signposted "Précy-s-Oise." Jonni had never hitchhiked before and she let the first few cars go by without making a move to stop them. As long as she was heading in the right direction there was no need to hurry. In fact, she was enjoying her walk. The evening sun was long and golden and the narrow road passed between fields, with only an occasional glimpse of the river in the distance, gleaming white in the bright twilight. The cars that passed her were French. The people inside them were French. The grass that grew by the side of the road was French. Jonni was in heaven.

When she finally plucked up the courage to wave down a car, the bearded man in the driver's seat looked her over appraisingly as she bent down to ask him, "Paris?"

He shook his head; *"Non,"* and drove on, much to her relief. She hadn't liked the look of him at all.

On she walked. The sun vanished behind the horizon, leaving her in a gray, misty half-light in which the trees and buildings became increasingly difficult to pick out across the fields. Before she knew it, it was dark. She no longer dared think of hitchhiking. She just walked, spurred on by Michel's letter in her pocket and the hope that the outskirts of

Paris would appear just around the next corner. She saw signposts where roads joined hers and went up close to them to read them. Sure enough, they guided her toward Paris, giving her confidence, but they didn't say how far.

The night wasn't cold, at least not to Jonni's constantly moving body, but it had grown damp as a thick fog settled over the valley. It gave her the creeps. She made up her mind that she would give in and ask for help at the first open shop or police station she came to but after walking for another hour she changed her mind. She had walked so far now that she must be nearly there. On the edge of a shadowy little hamlet she met a woman carrying a huge basket. She was plump and headscarfed and looked heartwarmingly normal. Jonni stopped to speak to her.

"*Excusez-moi . . .* Paris?"

To her joy the woman smiled and nodded, gesturing with a confident wave along the route Jonni was traveling.

"*Oui, oui, par là. Tout droit.*"

"Is it far?"

The woman continued pointing and gesturing cheerfully.

The fog got worse. The road got worse. Everything got worse. Jonni's feet in two-inch-heeled sandals were killing her and she stooped down to take them off, continuing along the hard, gravelly road in bare feet. At first the gravel pricked the soles of her feet but she soon stopped feeling it. In the security light over the door of a closed-up house she looked at her watch. One in the morning, French time. There was nothing she could do but walk.

Afterward Jonni didn't remember much of that night. Dawn came and the sun burned off the sweetness of early morning as she walked on wide, rough pavements through a heavily industrialized area. The factories gave way eventually to commercial businesses: furniture showrooms, "Monsieur Jardin," the corrugated buildings of an "Intermarché" with its orange musketeer on a huge signboard overhead. When she finally walked across the crowded junction at the Porte d'Aubervilliers and entered Paris she was far, far too exhausted to care.

The world around her was at work, bustling between the shops and ornate office buildings. Traffic roared, billowing out exhaust fumes. The busy life of Paris was under way and Jonni simply wasn't interested. She showed the address on Michel's letter to a gendarme who was directing traffic as it came off the Boulevard Périphérique. He looked at the address and then waved his finger dismissively at a side road.

Jonni followed signs for Montmartre.

Within half an hour she was climbing the agonizingly steep hill toward Sacré-Coeur, pushing the ground determinedly behind her with her bare feet. Now her interest in her future began to revive. Somewhere near here, perhaps within a stone's throw, Michel was living and might even now be putting the kettle on to make coffee. Oh, God, only let him be pleased to see her!

She climbed all the way to the Basilique Sacré-Coeur and back down again without finding the Rue des Soupirs. Near the bottom of the steep road she asked for directions in a boulangerie, nearly swooning at the smell of hot fresh bread, and nearly swooning again when the woman behind the counter pointed firmly back up the hill.

"*À gauche! Gauche!*" Her voice was harsh and grating. Jonni thanked her lamely and set off back up the hill, stopping at a cast-iron fountain halfway up to drink and to rest for a minute.

At long last she found it; a tiny street on the left, winding up and up, nearly to the top of the hill. Outside the wrought-iron double doors of number ninety-two she stood in the cobbled lane and looked up at the shabby building, puffing out her cheeks. She had made it. Her night of hell was over.

The doors stood open, latched back from the street, and she walked into a cold, dark hallway with iron-banistered stairs spiraling up around the four crumbling walls. The tiles beneath her bare feet were freezing after the warm street outside. She half expected to find a concierge, but, of course, her school French textbook had been a very old-fashioned one. When she had waited a few minutes in perplexity a door opened on her left and a big-breasted woman came out carrying a bag of rubbish into the hall. She was middle-aged with a red, bulbous face, and wearing a blue polyester overall and bedroom slippers.

Jonni asked her for information in her best school French, clasping her hands together in supplication.

"*Un homme? Ici? Anglaise? Monsieur St. Michel? Grand?*"

She raised her hand to show a height of six feet. The woman looked at her with an unfriendly stare and shook her head.

"*Un anglais, tu dis? Non.*"

"*Blond.*"

The woman grimaced while she thought about it.

"*Non.*"

"Please!" Jonni begged, racking her brain for GCSE adjectives. "*Très beau.*"

"Ah, *le beau!*" That had struck a chord. She nodded with an affirmative gasp and waved Jonni up the stairs, indicating the very top. Jonni sighed; she might have guessed.

Michel, if indeed the small wooden door under the roof was his, was not at home. She sat down to wait on the chilly stone tiles. The tiles were faded red and yellow, badly chipped, and the once yellow paint was peeling from the walls, bubbling from the damp. With the floor so hard beneath her bottom that she felt it was attacking her deliberately, she closed her eyes and inhaled the musty air. She was so tired she thought she could sleep anywhere, even standing up, but she couldn't sleep here. The cold and the tiles and the knowledge that Michel might come home at any moment kept her awake. She listened for his voice or his step. The stairwell was built for echoes. Every creaking door and every word that was spoken on the stairs resonated throughout the building before the sound was swallowed up by the damp walls.

People came and went. Jonni even came to recognize a few of their voices as she lay curled up on the stone landing with her head on her bag, too weary to move but too cold and uncomfortable to sleep. She tried not to think of the horrors that might still be in store for her. What would she do when Michel came home with some girl? Or if he didn't come at all?

In the early evening a crowd of voices mingled noisily on the stairs, speaking a mixture of English and French. From the floating incoherence of her semidoze Jonni thought she could distinguish Michel's voice amongst the French speakers.

She heard a man's voice nearby, strongly accented.

"Look at zis! Zere's a child 'ere! No, a woman! She looks ill."

Another voice, older and distinctly English, said, "That's typical of you, St. Michel. Been living here a week and the flotsam and jetsam of humanity already starts washing up on your doorstep."

"Per'aps we should call the police?" asked the first.

There was a pause before a hand touched Jonni's shoulder and moved her hair gently away from her face. She heard Michel's smiling voice close beside her.

"It's okay, Paul. She belongs to me."

Jonni stretched out her arms sleepily, like a baby, to be lifted.

"Feed me, bathe me, and put me to bed."

16

JONNI WAS RUNNING THROUGH A DENSE WOOD, except that she wasn't moving and she looked down to find that her feet were buried up to the ankles in stones that were really the sea. A wild boar in front of her was charging at a tree but the tree became Michel and he couldn't run away because of his roots. She tried to cry out but her voice was drowned by the hammering of the boar's feet against the ground.

The boar faded away, and the wood and Michel, and she relaxed as the fog dissolved into clear, ordinary daylight. But the hammering still persisted.

"Hello? Flotsam? Are you there?"

She opened her eyes, squinting against shafts of piercing light that were slanting between the slats of a wooden blind beside her, capturing brilliant specks of swirling dust. She was lying in a window alcove in a huge empty attic with sloping walls and rough unvarnished floorboards. The attic had never been decorated; it was all bare wood and plaster. Jonni thought it must cover the top of the whole apartment building. She lifted her head, blinking and frowning. She was lying on a bed under a white sheet.

"I don't have any clothes on!" she called, "And I don't seem to be able to move!"

"It's alright, darling, I've got a key!"

"Who is it?"

"It's Charles Crown!"

The Prince of Darkness himself! Her eyes widened in alarm as she heard the key turn in the lock of a door on the far side of the attic. She turned her head on the pillow; the attic was L-shaped and she couldn't see what was around the corner but she was fairly certain she was alone.

While she was still wondering how she got here and who had taken her clothes off and what had happened after Michel found her last night—at least she assumed it was last night—the door opened and Crown walked in.

Jonni had expected a giant: a ferocious ogre with a bushy beard and a suit and tie. What she saw was a very short man in jeans and a leather jacket, clean-shaven with dark, Latin features and a hooked nose. If he hadn't been frowning against the light he might even have been handsome. However, that didn't stop him being terrifying. He might have been forty-five or fifty but he moved with an aggressive directness that gave him an air of immense power. His black eyes flashed with fierce preoccupation as he strode quickly over to a battered brown piano that was standing in the corner of the attic.

"I just came to get this," he said, snatching a folder from the top of the piano. "St. Michel will be back around three, and only then because I'm so fucking softhearted."

"What time is it now?" Jonni asked timidly.

"After eleven." He was striding back toward the door but he stopped and turned toward her, squinting against the light as he demanded, "Why can't you move?"

"I don't know. I haven't really tried. I think I'm just stiff."

He threw his folder on a table that was just protruding from the hidden area of the attic and walked over to the bed. Jonni felt her aching muscles contract in fear. She felt very vulnerable lying here with no clothes on. There was nothing she could do, however, but watch while he leaned over her, across the bed, to pull up the blind. As sunlight flooded the attic he grabbed her under her arms, wrapping the sheet around her, and sat her up, swinging her legs down over the side of the bed. He crouched down and took her bruised feet in his hands.

"I saw these last night. How in God's name did you get here, walk?"

"Some of the way. I had to. I lost my money."

He grunted at her stupidity and rubbed her knees and ankles so hard with his strong hands that she wailed in pain.

"Come on, on your feet," he said. He pulled her arm over his shoulder and lifted her by the waist until she was standing. Jonni squeaked in embarrassment as the sheet fell down, uncovering her breasts. He tucked it back under her hand with a growl: "For Christ's sake, I've seen enough women's bodies."

Gradually her legs began to work and she found she could walk, very slowly, without his assistance.

"Boil the kettle and soak your feet in mustard water, hot as you can bear," he told her. Jonni discovered that the area around the corner was a scruffy kitchen. Crown opened a battered-looking cupboard and found a jar of mustard which he put on the table. He picked up his file and looked at her sharply.

"Are you going to stay?"

"I don't know."

"He's here to work, understand? You're not to distract him."

"No, I won't," she promised.

She was sitting at the table, still wrapped in her sheet, and Crown snorted as he went toward the door. She didn't think he believed her.

The recessed windows of the semi-converted attic looked out at the back of another building above it on the hill, with green wrought-iron window grilles and weather-beaten shutters hooked back against the sandstone wall. A row of enormous underpants were drying in the sun on a washing line strung between two windows. Far below on the narrow street, cars hooted as they tried to squeeze past pedestrians: mostly tourists with cameras around their necks and guide books in their hands. Jonni knelt on the bed with the sheet tucked around her and looked down at them through the open window, listening to the babel of foreign voices.

Inside, the attic was strangely empty. The only furniture apart from the table and the upright piano was the bed and half a dozen unvarnished wooden chairs. The kitchen in one corner was makeshift: an ancient gas cooker with broken knobs and an oven door that didn't close, a stainless-steel sink, a couple of shabby cupboards. Even the bathroom with its rough plasterboard walls had exposed plumbing and bare floorboards.

Depending on which way you looked at it, the place was either an idyllic refuge for struggling Parisian artists or a slum. Jonni was definitely of the romantic turn of mind. She wandered about with lumpy steps, munching a baguette she had found in the cupboard and dragging the end of her sheet behind her like a bridal train. She was thrilled at the dilapidation and the sloping walls. Four wide strips of purple rubber covered the floorboards of the huge empty space, taped down securely with black gaffer tape. Jonni knew what the rubber floor was for. It was clear this wild hideout served as a dance studio.

By the time Michel arrived Jonni had bathed—although she already seemed to have been washed clean of the grime that had covered her during her journey—and was dressed in a pair of Michel's jogging trousers and an Islington Ballet T-shirt; an outfit which felt cozily familiar.

Michel strolled through the door with a bright face, exhilarated by his day's work, and dropped his bag and a copy of *Le Monde* on the table. It was an easy meeting. He didn't ask any questions or comment on her blue, swollen feet; he just put the kettle on the gas cooker and asked her if she had slept well.

"Like a log. I don't remember last night at all."

"No, I put you in the bath and you went out like a light."

They drank their coffee on the roof. The roof was something Jonni hadn't yet discovered and her mouth opened in wonder as she clambered up the two wooden steps in the corner of the attic and out through a small door which Michel had unlocked.

"Nice spot, isn't it?" he asked, smiling at her awestruck face.

The terrace was only a few meters square, built into a corner of the roof and surrounded on its two open sides by a very rickety-looking black rail. But the view was unbelievable. Below them the rooftops of Montmartre sloped away down the hill, all piled on top of each other at random angles and all covered with slate and lead. Beyond Montmartre the whole of Paris was spread out before them: miles of roofs, domes, and turrets, all brilliant in the afternoon sun, blending into a haze in the far distance. She could even see the bright water of the Seine curving through the city.

Jonni stood on the asphalt roof with her hand resting on top of her head gazing at the heart-stopping splendor of it.

"It's breathtaking!" she said.

"I can't take credit for it, I'm afraid." Michel handed her one of the two cups he was holding. "Charles Crown found this place. We needed somewhere to work but we couldn't afford a studio. He managed to find a tenant for my place in London so we could rent this."

"There's the Eiffel Tower! And the Arc de Triomphe! Just think, I could have died without ever seeing this!"

"Have you never been up to the Sacré-Coeur before?"

"This is my first time in Paris."

Jonni sipped her coffee and looked down over the city glowing in the clear, warm afternoon. Standing behind her, Michel rested his hand on her waist and pointed over her shoulder with his coffee cup in his hand.

"See there, where the Seine divides at those towers? That's Notre-Dame. And that big square is the Louvre, with the Tuileries gardens in front of it—and over there's La Bastille, with the flag. You see that green dome behind it with the bell tower?"

"Uh-huh?"

"That's where I grew up."

Jonni turned her head and looked up at his face. She realized with surprise that she knew nothing about his background and family at all.

"Do your parents live in Paris?"

"No, that's the Académie. I went to boarding school there when I was eight."

"But you must have been so lonely!"

"Why? I had my friends and my teachers. We had a chaperon." Michel smiled at the memory. "He was very strict."

Jonni looked back at the distant tower of the Académie. It had an austere, mirthless look about it. She wondered if Michel had been happy there. She supposed he must have been; she couldn't imagine Michel being unhappy anywhere. For herself, the moment and the view and Michel's hand on her waist were so perfect she could have stayed there all her life.

"How far away's Nogent?"

"On the Oise?" He clicked his tongue. "I don't know. Fifty kilometers? Sixty, maybe."

"I walked here from there."

"Girl, you're crazy!"

"I wanted to see you."

"Did you?" Michel put his arm closer around her waist and moved nearer to her, still looking at the view. She could feel his breath in her hair. "I'm glad. You were very warm and soft last night sleeping in bed next to me. I lay awake for ages just watching you. It was all I could do not to take advantage of you."

"Why didn't you?"

"I wasn't sure that was what you had come for."

She smiled, glancing down into her coffee cup. "I was afraid you might have met someone—that you'd already have . . . you know, a girl here."

Michel was silent for a few moments.

"Do you want the truth, or do you want me to lie?"

Jonni looked at the sparkling city. It didn't matter. She was here now and Michel was pleased she was here.

"Neither," she said.

When she turned around and reached up to put her arms around his neck he kissed her and then looked down at her sunlit face with a smile.

"Can you stay?" he asked.

"I don't know. I don't think Charles Crown wants me to."

"It's not Charles Crown who's asking you."

Jonni cried when Michel made love to her on his bed in the alcove. As before, her tears discomfited him and he turned away from her in unease. Jonni looked at his body while he got up to pull on his clothes.

"What work are you doing here?" she asked, drying her eyes on the sheet.

"Wait about fifteen minutes and you'll find out."

Half a dozen dancers appeared in the attic almost as soon as Michel and Jonni had dressed themselves. Charles Crown she recognized from the morning but the others were strangers—except for Primo. He scooped her up in his arms and kissed her face all over, rather like Herman.

"Bella! Michel said you were gonna come. I didn't believe him."

Jonni was so glad to see him that her eyes filled with tears again and

Primo wrapped her in his arms, laughing and hiding her face away from the others. The other men were ribbing Michel about his afternoon's activity. She couldn't understand what they were saying but she knew it anyway from their tone of voice—she realized that innuendo sounds the same in any language.

They had brought supper with them: bread and pasta and enormous oval tomatoes. Primo and one of the girls took over the kitchen, boiling large pans of water and making a wonderful mess with onions and bunches of basil. One of the men uncorked two bottles of red wine, leaving them to breathe on the windowsill. It seemed these evening sessions had already acquired an element of ritual.

They were working on a project for a festival of experimental dance. Choreographers from all over Europe and Scandinavia had gathered in Paris with their dancers to make new works related to their national heritage. Crown had been asked to represent Britain—an honor of which he seemed obstinately unaware—and he had decided, at the last minute, to bring Michel with him as the festival coincided with the Islington Ballet's summer break. Primo had condescended to come as Crown's accompanist, and to rewrite the musical score Crown had commissioned from one of the Festival composers. Jonni gasped when she heard that.

"You can't rewrite music someone else has composed!"

"Watch me, bella. The guy's an amateur. He ain't even going to notice. Better keep your voice down; the maestro don't like to be disturbed."

It was extraordinary to watch Charles Crown working. His whole body was taut with concentration and his eyes blazed as they followed the bodies of the dancers, instructing them with gestures and barked commands in a jargon that was pure Greek to Jonni. Michel and his colleagues listened intently, interpreting his instructions cautiously with their bodies. Crown corrected everything again and again—especially, it seemed to Jonni, everything Michel did. Often the choreographer walked out onto the rubber dance floor and demonstrated the steps himself, moving with surprising grace, even in his jeans and outdoor shoes. Jonni looked on in awe. She was watching a ballet in the making.

They discussed the ballet while they ate, waving their bread and forks emphatically around the table while every word that was spoken was translated simultaneously into at least two different languages. The conclave of European choreographers pooled their dancers. Michel was involved in the making of the German, Danish, and Spanish ballets, as well as the British piece, and the assembled group in the attic was correspondingly international. Somehow, between English, French, and Italian, they managed to communicate.

Michel smiled at Jonni across the table.

"Still want to stay?" he asked.

She beamed, her eyes shining, and nodded enthusiastically.

That evening formed the pattern for every evening in the attic. Jonni took over the job of cooking, glad she could do even that much to be a part of their work. Michel was out all day doing classes with different teachers and following a chaotic schedule of rehearsals at the Opéra where the huge event was based.

Jonni was never lonely on her own. She wandered through the sloping streets of Montmartre dressed in Michel's outsized clothes, shopping for ingredients for increasingly adventurous cooking: fresh herbs, cheeses, artichokes, bread, and always vast salads. The men ate enormous amounts of anything they could get their hands on; she didn't know where they put it all. The women were fussy and neurotic about food, worrying about calories and vitamins and combustible carbohydrates. Gradually, with hints from Primo and Michel, Jonni learned to make the high-energy, nonfattening meals that suited the dancers.

All this cooking, often for ten people or more, was expensive. Michel gave her money, crisp hundred-franc notes from the bank, warning her to make it last because there was no more until his next wage check cleared. But most of the money for their communal meals came from Charles Crown. He was getting paid for this work; the dancers were not.

Sometimes Jonni ventured into the center of Paris to look at the streets and houses, or walked in the park around Sacré-Coeur, dodging the African traders who tried to sell her rugs and key rings. But most of the time she spent sitting on the roof in the sun, reading recipe books she had borrowed from one of the French dancers and concocting ever more garlicky meals for her willing victims. The dancers laughed at Jonni's cooking. They were kind to her, accepting her as part of the enterprise, and grateful for the meals she cooked, even the disasters.

Jonni loved watching the creation of Crown's new ballet as it developed. She pottered around the kitchen area humming the music as Primo played it and brandishing shallots, happy because Michel was there even if he was too busy to speak to her.

Jonni began to get to know the dancers who spent their evenings working so feverishly in the huge attic. They were a mixed group, some very affected and highly strung, some more solid and earthy. All except Michel found the mixture of classical and contemporary steps problematical; Crown's choreography was notoriously difficult. The festival had asked for a piece based on British folklore and Crown had decided on a quirky, rather bleak retelling of the Arthur legends: "a fluffy piece" he called it, but Jonni could already see it was far from that. He and the dancers could spend an hour squabbling over Tennyson and Malory, arguing the psychological toss about whether Lancelot would lift Guinevere here or there, or whether she must turn away from him first, or how far Arthur need stand from them for this or that balance. Armand, who was creating the role of Arthur, would sometimes wink at Jonni while these disputes were going on. He was a soloist from the Paris Opéra; a wiry dancer in his thirties who always arrived wearing a brown wool jacket over a white polo-necked jumper no matter how hot it was outside.

"Zat man," he whispered to her, nodding his head secretly toward Crown, "is ze most intense bastard I ever work with."

Jonni fully believed him. She had no one to compare Crown with but surely no one could get more intense than that!

Crown still terrified Jonni. His aggressive energy never slackened, even for a moment. He was always rude and abrupt, never wasting words on civilities, and blurting out whatever seemed the truth to him at the moment. He criticized ruthlessly and without tact. Even during the lighter moments of their work, when the gathering collapsed laughing, Crown's laughter would only last a few moments before it was snapped off with the suddenness of a door slamming shut and his blazing eyes returned to their habitual ferocious concentration.

The first time Jonni saw Crown lose his temper she was petrified. It seemed to come from nowhere. One minute Michel, Armand, and pretty Vittoria were peacefully running through a pas de trois they'd been working on for the past few evenings, and the next Crown was on his feet, his chair crashing to the floor, stopping their pas de trois with the force of an erupting volcano.

"Stop!" he shouted in thunderous rage. "Stop this shit!"

Jonni turned around in the kitchen with a vegetable knife in her hand. Armand's pirouettes wound to a slow halt and Michel lowered Vittoria to the ground with one arm.

"What are you doing?" Crown yelled, principally at Michel but including the other two in his furious stare. "That is amateur dancing! Lazy, fucking amateur coasting! What is wrong with you?"

There was silence apart from the low murmur as Primo translated Crown's outburst into Italian for Vittoria. The small dark-haired woman looked at Primo in alarm.

"I'm waiting for a fucking answer, St. Michel!"

"Oh, don't!" Jonni cried in terror, putting her hands to her face. "Please don't!"

"You keep out of this!" he snapped, whirling round to glare at her.

Michel waved his hand to tell Jonni it was alright.

"We weren't dancing flat out," he said.

"I can see you weren't dancing flat out!"

"We've had a really rough couple of days with the Danish." Michel glanced at the other two. "I think we're probably a bit tired."

"We're all fucking tired! You listen to me, son—listen all of you!" He looked at Primo and pointed sharply at Vittoria. "You tell her. You're either dancing or you aren't; end of story! Are you too stupid to understand that every single step you dance could be your last?" Crown's fist thumped the back of a chair beside him in frustration. "You are only one technical fault away from the end of your career! It could happen to any of you—anytime!" He snapped his fingers. "Like that! Do you want your last dance step to be a lame travesty? Mark if you have to mark. But when you dance, you dance! Or, Christ help you, you might go out on a fucking pathetic note like that!"

Jonni was shaking. Michel had taken off his T-shirt to wipe his face with it.

"Yeah, I got you," he said, nodding as he threw the T-shirt away.

"You should have worked it out for yourself!" Crown yelled. He picked up the chair he had knocked over and slammed it down on the wooden floorboards before he stormed out of the attic, flinging the door shut behind him.

Primo pressed an E flat key on the piano, playing the note several times.

"You reckon I've got time to tune this bitch before he comes back?"

"I shouldn't risk it," Michel said.

While Armand and Vittoria whispered together, shaking their heads incredulously, and the other dancers stood around in silence, Michel went to Jonni and rubbed her arm to reassure her.

"That was harmless, Jons. Wait till you see him in a bad mood."

She managed to laugh, gasping, "It gets worse?"

"He was right, you know."

"But does he have to be right so loudly?"

"Yup." Michel pinched a spring onion from the chopping board and stuck it in his mouth, biting off the stalk. "Can you imagine if he bottled all that up?"

Crown came back about ten minutes later, bursting into the attic with even more intensity than he had left it. But the blazing glow in his black eyes was of a very different kind.

"I've got it!" he cried, pulling off his sweater as he kicked the door shut: "I know where we've been going wrong, it's Armand who should be dancing the allegro; you two should be going against the music. Christ, it's so obvious! We'll scrap these and these," his arms waved descriptively, "and slow those two lifts down into four sets of eight."

"Jesus!" said Michel.

A cacophony of excited debate started up immediately, Primo gabbling to Vittoria in Italian; Michel and Armand sorting out the steps together in French; Crown pointing, counting, and gesturing. They hurried onto the dance floor, discarding sweatshirts and leg warmers in all directions, lost in enthusiasm. The other dancers crowded around, nodding and contributing expert opinions with eager faces.

Jonni decided they were all mad.

Several evenings later, while the dancers moved noisily over to the table to eat an elaborate risotto Jonni had cooked, she plucked up the courage to take Charles Crown a tumbler of red wine. He was leaning over the back of the piano with a cigarette in his hand, frowning intently at his notebook as he turned over the pages. She stopped a couple of feet behind him clutching the glass, not daring to interrupt him.

"Don't hover!" he told her sharply. "If you want something, say so. You're putting me off my work."

"I'm sorry," she said. "I didn't mean to. I—I'm terribly frightened of you, Mister Crown."

His frown deepened for a moment and then he turned his head to look at her, his thoughts half disengaging from his work as he examined her face with his piercing eyes.

"And you thought telling me so might make me less frightening, is that it?"

"I don't know."

"Well, has it?" He stared at her, doing nothing to help her. But the directness with which he had asked the question reassured her slightly. She managed to meet his eye with an awkward smile.

"Maybe. A little."

He took the glass of wine from her hand and turned back to his notes.

"Don't call me Mister Crown, darling; it pisses me off. My name's Charles."

"Crown's got a real soft spot for you," Michel told her later.

"I don't believe that."

"He thinks you're gorgeous. He said so. He told me I'd be crazy not to hold on to you."

They were lying in bed together under the attic window and Jonni looked at him in the stark white light of the huge moon that was taking its last look at Paris before it vanished for the night behind the chimneys of Montmartre.

"Do you think he's right?"

Michel was lying on his side with his head propped up on his hand. He ran his other hand slowly over her waist and hip, following it with his calm eyes. "I don't need Charles Crown's advice on how to run my life, Jonni."

On Sundays, when Michel had a few hours of freedom, he took Jonni into Paris and they wandered through the Louvre hand in hand looking in awe at the paintings and sculptures, or strolled peacefully along the banks of the Seine.

At night when they were alone in the cavernous attic Michel made love to her, murmuring obscenities in French as his face contorted with passion. Jonni gripped the pillow behind her head, dying silently every time he lost himself to her. She wanted to keep him inside her forever.

Afterward they lay awake in the darkness talking about their lives and their childhoods, which were still close enough for both of them to be vivid in their recollection.

"Is your mother nice?" Jonni whispered.

Michel smiled. His hand was resting on the wet, secret place between her thighs. "She seems nice. I don't really know her. I see her maybe once a year, if that. I saw her in April when we were playing in Bath. Primo and I drove over and had lunch with her. She keeps chickens."

"Chickens?" Jonni's head turned toward him on the pillow.

"Yes, why not? She used to teach the piano. I don't know if she still does."

"That's really sad."

"Teaching the piano?"

"No, not knowing your mother. How did that happen?"

Michel closed his eyes. He didn't know the answer to that. But he couldn't think about Carrie without picturing the stricken dismay on her face when she had first seen him that time he had gone to Devon for his uncle's funeral. He blocked out the image from his mind and turned his head, looking at Jonni.

"My mother doesn't like dance so we don't have much to talk about, but why should we? We're two adults who live very different lives. I've never understood why people take their relationships with their parents so seriously. How about your mother, is she nice?"

Jonni grinned.

"She thinks I'll go to hell for living in sin with a dancer. I'm endangering my mortal soul."

"I'm living in sin with an actress; that must be far worse. What about my soul?"

"I don't think Mummy's too bothered about your soul, Michel. In fact I'm not sure, as a dancer, you've even got one."

Michel leaned over and wrapped his arm around her, pulling her toward him on the bed. "In that case I may as well sin as much as I can."

At last, when the pale gray of the false dawn crept over the rooftops of Paris and stole into the attic, Jonni whispered to him, "I love you."

Michel lay perfectly still and didn't reply. He was already asleep—or else he was pretending to be. Jonni buried her face in his armpit and went to sleep too. She was very, very happy.

September rolled on and the ballet started to take shape in those crowded evening sessions in the attic. Sometimes at midnight when the others had gone Michel and Jonni sat with Primo on the warm roof and drank pastis, looking down over the twinkling lights of the city.

"Is quite a sight, ain't it?" Primo said, gazing thoughtfully at the flood-lit arches and churches as he sipped his drink.

Jonni gazed with him. From different streets and courtyards nearby, African drum rhythms and South American dance music drifted up to the roof terrace on the balmy night air.

"Stop the world," she begged. "Stop everything right here. I want everything to stay just like this forever."

Primo shook his head. Below them Paris looked as peaceful as the distant stars that peppered the vast night sky overhead.

"It ain't such a good idea to stop the world, bella. Somewhere down there in all those houses there's someone breakin' their heart. And another person waitin' to die. And there's people down there crying. You can't stop the world just 'cos you're happy, Jonni. It wouldn't be fair."

Jonni looked at him. Primo's solemn eyes were traveling slowly over the rooftops as though he were looking straight through them. He could really see all those things. Perhaps he understood them too.

"Besides," Michel added, "I'd rather not stop the world until I've cracked that bloody pas de deux with Vittoria."

At the end of September the evening rehearsals in the attic came to an end as the dance festival moved into performance. Now there were no more late nights lying awake until dawn; Michel's concentration was focused entirely on dress rehearsals and performances of each of the four ballets he was involved in. At the start of October, Primo went home to London to begin work in the corps for the coming Islington Ballet season. Jonni's heart ached for him when he came to say good-bye to them, his brown eyes turning toward Michel at the door, desperate for a word or sign of affection as they parted. Jonni knew it was neither loyalty to Charles Crown nor creative zeal that had brought Primo to Paris to spend his annual month's leave playing tirelessly for classes and rehearsals all over the city. Michel was leafing through his schedule for the next few days while he ate breakfast. He glanced up at Primo distractedly.

"Yup. See you in a fortnight."

Jonni missed Primo dreadfully. She went to see Michel's ballets alone wearing a long, black evening dress she had borrowed from the daughter of the woman on the ground floor.

The ballets were all very different, although they were all classed as "experimental" ballet. Some were very twee. Jonni didn't like the French pieces; she thought them tasteless, flashy, and arrogant: patriotic colors, dazzling technique, and not much else as far as she could see. She liked the Danish and Spanish ballets; they had more heart. The German piece she liked too; it was spiky and avant-garde.

Sitting on her own in the packed auditoriums of the Opéra, Le Châtelet, and the Conservatoire, Jonni began to realize that Michel was attracting a lot of attention. She started hearing his name spoken around her even before the performances began, and seeing people in the audience lean together and whisper when he came onstage. Journalists began to seek him out at the receptions they attended afterward, wanting to know about his background and his training, and especially about his relationship to Jacques St. Michel. Michel shied away from their cameras and their notebooks, directing them instead toward Charles Crown. Crown sent them back again. Neither of them relished the attention of the press.

"There's a strong resemblance between you and Jacques," the journalists inveigled. "Are you saying he's no relation?"

"No, I'm saying I don't know him. I've seen his work in London, that's all." Michel was flustered by their constant questions.

"What about your parents; are they here?"

"Look—no." He just wanted them to go away. "I'm not involved with them. We live totally separate lives."

"The Académie must be very pleased with your performances here."

"I've no idea. Ask them."

Jonni glowed with pride. It was easy to see why Michel was causing a sensation. His technique was astounding, even to Jonni's untrained eyes: massive leaps, hovering in the air with his legs in the splits, and pirouettes that turned him into a blur. His love of movement was apparent in every tiny gesture of his hands.

Charles Crown, too, was the focus of a buzz of interest at the festival. Not only did his piece throw the rest into the shade, he could also boast the distinction of having brought with him from England one of the finest unknown dancers at the festival and easily the best rehearsal pianist. Charles Crown's name had no impact with the dance-going public of Britain or France, but within the closed circles of the dance world itself, his choreography was notorious. Now, suddenly, it was both notorious and fashionable. The VIP patrons of the French dance scene showered him with invitations to sparkling dinners and cocktail parties. Crown turned down every invitation bluntly. All that stuff just irritated him. As soon as his ballet had been performed for the first time he kissed Vittoria's cheek, shook Armand's hand, told Michel with a grunt that he'd seen him dance a lot worse, and went back to England to start choreographing the ensembles for *Swan Lake*.

When the fortnight of the festival was over Michel followed his employer back to London with a sigh of relief. It had been the experience of a lifetime: eight weeks of concentrated work with some of the best teachers and choreographers in Europe. But Michel was exhausted, as much by the unexpected praise and attention he had received as by the work itself.

With the money he had been given to pay for his single flight back to London he bought two coach tickets. Jonni sat beside him as the bus made its way through the suburbs of Paris to the motorway. She already missed the attic and the little rooftop terrace. It hurt to think that she would never see them again. In his seat by the window Michel was asleep, his head resting on his arm. He slept all the way to London. Jonni nestled down in the scratchy velveteen-covered seat and laid her head against his warm shoulder. Her Parisian idyll was over but her happiness was not. Wherever Michel was, there she was at home.

Michel and Jonni hadn't discussed what would become of her once they returned to London. It was simply understood. As easily as she had crept into his pocket the night they first met at the South Bank, she had crept into his life.

It was strange to come back to the Pimlico flat and find it already full of the friends she had once thought she would never see again. The pink girl and her colleagues had gone, leaving no trace except a cup ring on the lid of the Steinway (which had sent Primo into a paroxysm of fury when he discovered it) and two pairs of sad, dead ballet shoes on one of the studio windowsills. Primo, Lynne, Annette, and Roly were all waiting for them in the flat when they arrived late on Sunday afternoon. Michel was glad to see them despite his red eyes and hot, puffy face—he hadn't woken up until they pulled into Victoria Coach Station ten minutes before. He kissed Lynne and Annette, shook hands with Roly and Primo, and then fell sound asleep on one of the sofas in the studio.

"Stupid bugger," said Annette, "he's wiped himself out."

"That's Charles's fault," Lynne said, looking at his prostrate form with her anxious hazel eyes softening in sympathy.

They sat around him, drinking the bottle of burgundy they had opened to celebrate his return, the five who loved Michel, watching him sleep—Annette on the piano stool with her feet up on the coffee table; Roly on the sofa with Lynne on his knee and a friendly hand resting on Jonni's thigh; Primo perched on the arm of the other sofa next to Michel's feet.

"That boy ain't got no idea what's gonna hit him when he gets back in the studio tomorrow morning," Primo said, keeping his voice low.

"What is going to hit him?" Jonni wanted to know.

Roly put his arm around Jonni's shoulders. "Charles has gone berserk over this new *Swan Lake*. The whole company's broken out in a cold sweat. It's going to be far worse for Shel than the rest of us."

"Why?"

Annette frowned, surprised. "You mean he hasn't told you?"

"That . . . ?"

"That Charles is making the role of Siegfried on him—partnering the Giant Tomato. Principal rehearsals start tomorrow afternoon."

Jonni looked at Michel, gnawing her lip.

"I'm not altogether sure he knows."

Less than half a minute later Michel woke up with a sudden start, his face burning, blinking in confusion while he scrabbled to sit up.

"Oh, Jesus," he said, exhaling slowly in relief as he looked around him. "Christ, I just had the damnedest bloody dream. I thought I heard someone say . . ."

Primo laid his hand reassuringly on Michel's ankle.

"Is okay, amico. It was just a dream. Go back to sleep, yeah?"

17

Michel took the news about his role in the creation of Crown's new *Swan Lake* very calmly. He was glad Crown hadn't told him about it while he was snowed under with his four roles in Paris. The company had all heard about the stir his performances had created amongst the French audiences. He walked into the Goswell Road building on Monday morning to be greeted as a returning conqueror.

"Most of the audience were dance students," he told the boys in the changing room modestly. "You know what they're like; they freak over a simple triple *tour,* especially the French. There was this one girl— thirty-two fouettés, right? And every two turns she's spotting on a different point of the compass—unbelievable!—and her supporting foot doesn't budge an inch. The audience had a mass orgasm."

"Good girl!" said Daniel with a whistle. "Where was she from?"

Michel pulled his Lycra all-in-one over his knees.

"Stuttgart, I think. I'll tell you what else caused total mayhem in Paris: Primo. All the top choreographers squabbling like chickens over who got him for classes and rehearsals. It was phenomenal."

"He never told us," David said, tucking himself into his dance belt.

"Yeah, well, you know how he is."

The boys tutted and shook their heads. Nureyev himself could demand to have Primo play class for him and Primo would brush it off with a shrug, or pretend to.

"Someday," Daniel said, "that guy's going to face up to the fact he's in the wrong job; he's going to have to."

Michel and Roly exchanged glances; they both knew Primo better than that but neither of them said so.

Crown watched Michel with sharp eyes in class that morning, checking him over critically. He knew every muscle of Michel's body.

"Everything alright?" he asked him when the class had finished.

"Uh-huh. The Danish went down well in the end. The last performance of *Arthur* was the best we did."

"I heard. You've been told about Siegfried?"

"Yup."

"Body alright? Nothing hurting? No strains?"

Michel raised his hand to take hold of his left shoulder, rotating his arm slowly. "Seems okay. I was a bit stiff after Saturday but it's fine now."

"A bad lift?"

"Not sure. How does Carlotta feel about making this ballet with me?"

Crown smiled. "You know what, St. Michel? I don't give a fuck how Carlotta feels."

The Giant Tomato wasn't happy. She wasn't happy at all. For the past week while Michel was in France she had thrown one tantrum after another, first with Crown then with Marina and even with Nadia Petrovna.

"My dear girl," Nadia Petrovna told her serenely, closing her eyes, "if you feel Michel is too inexperienced to partner you, I'm afraid you must take that up with Charles. I'm far too old and tired to get involved in such disputes. But between you and me, if you don't want Charles to suddenly change his mind and create Odette-Odile on Irena, I strongly advise you to bite the bullet."

"Bullet?" Carlotta demanded, "What bullet?"

"An English idiom, my dear. It means lump it."

As the dancers filed out of the big studio after class on the morning of Michel's return to the Goswell Road, the supercilious company star clumped over to Michel in her pointe shoes and looked him witheringly in the eye, planting her fists firmly on her hips.

"Studio two," she said. "In ten minutes. Come alone."

Michel raised his eyebrows.

"Shouldn't we have a surgeon in attendance? And seconds and witnesses?"

She didn't dignify that with an answer.

"And don't wear anything woolen. I'm allergic."

Carlotta was a creature of bizarre contradictions. In public or in front of the rest of the dance world her manners and voice were painfully affected, but amongst the company she was foul-mouthed and earthy. She was highly intelligent and yet she lacked even the most basic common sense—to the point where the other dancers had to watch her like hawks in case she tried to make her entrance onstage behind the backdrop or tripped over the fold-back speakers in the wings. On tour her bags had to be checked on and off the train. She even needed her hand held crossing the road; the sight of Carlotta dashing scattily out between two parked cars into the middle of Islington's Upper Street with traffic roaring in both directions was terrifying. Every time she nipped out to the bank or the chemist Crown had to send someone with her for her own protection, which merely added to her sense of her own eminence. But dizzy as she was, and snooty and arrogant, she danced as though she had been touched by divinity.

Alone with Michel in studio two, she instructed him with sharp precision through dozens of standard partnered moves. Despite—or perhaps because of—having slept with him twice on tour, Carlotta disliked Michel intensely. But it seemed she had made up her mind to deal professionally with the ignominy of having to dance with him.

"This isn't too bad," she said, from her semi-kneeling position on his shoulder. "I don't want you to hold my hand though—I'll hold yours. I must have control of my own balance."

"Hang on tight then," he told her, and he held on to her thigh while she adjusted her grip on his hand. "Okay?"

"Yes, better." She frowned at the studio doors in annoyance. "For heaven's sake, who is that peering in? It's very irritating."

Michel turned his head to look.

"It's just a couple of the girls. They're only . . ."

Without warning Carlotta dived headfirst off his shoulder and plummeted toward the floor. Michel grabbed her swiftly with an arm about her waist, catching her just before her head hit the floor.

"Woah!" he cried: "Jesus Christ, Carlotta!" He put her down, staring at her wide-eyed. "You could have broken your neck! Are you out of your mind?"

She pulled the hem of her leotard down over her bottom with a matter-of-fact sniff.

"Good. Now I know you are awake. I must trust my partner."

Michel shook his head in total disbelief. Carlotta certainly wasn't the star dancer of the Islington Ballet for nothing.

Jonni saw frustratingly little of Michel over the next month. Although the Islington Ballet wasn't on tour, Crown's choreographic sessions ran on until nine or ten almost every night. The ballet was scheduled to open in early December and it was a vast project: four huge acts with massive pas de deux and solos in each one. Crown was reworking the entire piece, almost three hours of music to be filled. And Siegfried was onstage for all but five minutes of it.

Alone in the flat poring over casting newsletters and the back pages of *The Stage*, Jonni was beginning to realize just how deluded she had been in seeing her Stratford East debut as a springboard to fame. At every audition she attended, even for unpaid and semiprofessional theater, there were dozens of other young women jostling together in the waiting room like cattle in a market. Nobody wanted her.

While Michel and Carlotta slaved away late into the evenings in the studios at the Goswell Road, Jonni relied on Michel's friends for company. Primo usually finished rehearsals by five or six. He came to the Warwick Way flat to play the piano: beautiful sonatas and concertos, humming as he shook his head slowly over the keyboard—or to gossip in the kitchen with Jonni while they made culinary messes together. Primo was on a wild high. He was creating the comic role of Siegfried's best friend in the new *Swan Lake*. Crown had used Primo in contemporary choreography before, and often in jazz, but never for a classical role. Primo was ecstatic. He taught Jonni to waltz and to dance a paso doble. Jonni was very, very proud of her paso doble.

One evening, while Primo was tuning the Steinway, she leaned over the side of the open piano top, looking down into the mysterious bowels of the instrument in fascination.

"Is it difficult tuning a piano?"

"Not when you got perfect pitch."

"It seems to need tuning an awful lot."

"Nah, she keeps her intonation real good." Primo wouldn't hear a word against his gleaming black darling, with her grand piano action and her ringing, mellifluous tone. "Play me a bottom F sharp, will you, bella? I'm just finicky; it bugs me if she's even a fraction out."

He was so blasé about his gift that Jonni smiled.

"Why did you decide to become a dancer instead of a pianist?"

" 'Cos that's what I am, bella—a dancer. I never wanted to do nothin' else."

"But it seems such a waste."

Primo leaped up from behind the piano, glaring at her in fury. "A waste? Don't you fuckin' tell me my career's a waste! Just 'cos I ain't making principal roles like Michel, you reckon my dancing ain't worth nothing? It ain't a waste, it's my whole life! Now, you want to talk about it some more?"

Jonni recoiled at his explosion. She had seen him lose his temper before but never with her. And never with such fire in his brown eyes. He breathed out his anger slowly.

"Don't get me started on that story, Jonni. Is a whole can of worms you don't understand." Moments later he was himself again, the smile returning to his eyes. "Hey, you look like a little child when you're scared. You don' want to be scared of me, bella—you know I adore you. You want to learn another couple of steps for the paso doble?"

Jonni put her arm around his neck and rested her cheek against his, nodding. She knew Primo had forgiven her.

Sometimes Lynne came to the flat to wander restlessly around the studio marking out the steps of the new *Swan Lake* choreography. She had become reserved and solitary since Michel's return from Paris with Jonni. There was a sadness in the air around her.

"Are you alright?" Jonni asked her, poking her head gingerly through the studio door.

"Yes, fine, lovey. Roly's coming round later this afternoon to go through this pas de deux with me. I'm just getting it settled in my head."

Jonni smiled at Lynne encouragingly.

"You know, all Michel wants is to perform Siegfried with you. He keeps saying so. He's really hoping Charles will let you perform it to-gether."

"Yes, I know he is," she said, gazing absently in the mirror.

Annette came to the flat too, full of loud complaints about the gruel-ling hours they were all working in the studio and bitchy comments about Roly's partnering. Jonni enjoyed Annette's irreverent chatter. It was through Annette, and with some help from Primo, that she kept abreast of all the gossip at the Islington Ballet. And gossip there always was in plenty.

Sunday was the only day Jonni saw anything of Michel, but even then he was working. Jonni sat on the sofa with her feet tucked up under her watching while he showed Roly the new sections of choreography they were creating in rehearsals. The second act of Crown's *Swan Lake* was nothing like the staid lakeside scene of the original ballet. Crown's Act Two pas de deux were massive: horrendous technical scorchers for both partners. Roly burst out laughing as he watched Michel make a double turn in the air, landing with another whipped double turn and coiling his working leg into a tight series of pirouettes. Jonni's jaw dropped.

"Gosh!" she said. "What's that move called?"

Roly was still laughing. "It's called big dick."

Roly shook his head in frustration when it was his turn to try the vari-ation. It wasn't that he couldn't do the steps; there was nothing in it he couldn't manage technically. It was his style that thwarted him: his peren-nial struggle for fluidity and expressiveness.

"Hey, it looks good to me," Primo said from the piano.

"Yes, you're fine," Michel agreed. "No problem with that section."

Roly smiled gratefully at their encouragement but inwardly he sighed. He really, really wanted Siegfried. If Crown decided to have only three Siegfrieds he wouldn't have a prayer; Peter and Erik would be second and third cast. But if he decided on four it would be a toss-up between him-self and Daniel. And if it was Daniel he was damned sure it wouldn't be for lack of trying on his part. Every spare moment of the day, when he wasn't working on his own arduous portering role in the new ballet, he was learning Siegfried behind Michel at the back of the studio with Lynne. But try and try as he might, that extra something—the "it" which all dancers aspire to—eluded him. Lynne had it. Michel definitely had it.

But Roly didn't have it, and he sometimes wondered in secret despair if he'd ever find it.

Often in the evenings Roly came to the Pimlico flat just to rest. His flatmate, an old buddy from stage school, was doing an opera course, he said, and there wasn't a moment's peace. While he slept exhausted in the studio Jonni tiptoed around the flat or dozed with him, curled up on the sofa with his arm wrapped comfortably around her shoulders.

But whoever was with Jonni at the flat, it was for Michel that she waited, half an ear always cocked toward the door, anticipating his arrival at every minute. And when he came home, dog-tired but still buzzing from his work, he would kiss her in the kitchen while she prepared dinner for them both and they would talk about his day. If it had been a good day they would laugh and chat while they got ready for bed. If it had been a bad day, or he had come home too late and too weary to eat, he would cast off his clothes without a word and reach out for her silently and briefly in the familiar shadows of the bedroom. And when they had made love he would turn over, already half-asleep, and yawn, feeling for her hand.

"How was your audition today?"

"Okay. I have to wait and see if I get a recall. I think they liked me, though. I spoke to my mother, by the way. She wants me to give her the phone number here."

He yawned again. "So give it to her. She's your mother."

"I know. I suppose I'll have to. Oh, I meant to ask you, have you seen the nail scissors anywhere? I thought I left them by the bed but I couldn't find them this evening."

Silence. She waited a moment and then touched his shoulder gently. "Michel? Have you seen the red nail scissors?"

Michel stirred and then mumbled, "Yes, they're . . . in studio two . . . behind . . . the échappé battu to fifth."

Jonni laid her head on the pillow beside him and smiled, closing her eyes.

October became November, turning the leaves in the Pimlico square brown and marking the end of their beautiful summer. But Michel didn't have time to notice the change except unconsciously to mark the musty chill in the air as he hurried out of the flat at eight-thirty every morning to stride down Belgrave Road toward the Underground.

By mid-November the choreography for the ballet was all roughly in place but still Crown went on changing everything, reworking all the pas de deux and picking away at the ensembles. Injuries abounded. Some mornings it seemed there were more dancers sitting in the common room with their feet in electro-vibration baths or with ice packs on their metatarsals than there were at the barre in class. Crown cursed and tore his hair in frustration, but he was never without Michel and he was never without Carlotta. For that, at least, he was thankful. Michel and Carlotta worked on dauntlessly through winter colds, blistered feet, groin strain, and premenstrual tension. Often, when a rehearsal was scheduled to finish at seven, it would run on until ten or even eleven. Michel protested only very occasionally.

"Oh, hey, listen," he said to Crown, looking at the clock on the studio wall, "we were supposed to finish at seven-thirty this evening. It's gone eight already."

"Too bad," the choreographer said, preoccupied. "We can't stop here; this is getting somewhere." He frowned at Marina. "Don't you think the link between the adage and the second solo is better? Let's try that section again."

Michel bent down to adjust a thermal knee support he was wearing over his all-in-one. "Yeah, okay. Just let me go and call Jonni. She's cooking something tonight; she's asked a bunch of the dancers over."

"Call her in ten minutes. Just run through the adage and the link first."

The pianist had already started playing the section that led into the adage, so Michel pulled up the sleeves of his sweatshirt and collected Carlotta's waist, arranging his feet in fourth.

When he arrived back at the flat just before midnight Jonni was sitting with both elbows propped on the kitchen table and her chin on her hands surrounded by unwashed plates and glasses. She smiled at him bleakly.

"Was it going really well or really badly?"

"A bit of both. I am sorry, Jons. I did mean to call you."

"I know. We had a great time without you. Are you hungry? I saved you some Stroganoff. It's a bit curdled but it's still pretty good."

"No thanks, I grabbed a sandwich earlier. Can I have a kiss, anyway?"

She reached up to put her arms around his neck as he leaned over wearily to kiss her.

"Happy birthday," she said.

"Thanks."

By the end of November the last details of set and costume were finalized in a flurry of activity while the rehearsals turned into vast company calls—as many as half a dozen couples working on the same pas de deux at once and the entire company practicing every pas de trois and mini ensemble. An air of excitement filled the building. The ballet was being premiered at Sadler's Wells: the first time the company had ever risked such a prestigious opening. Dancers' faces glowed with unusual energy as they scurried busily back and forth along the corridors.

But when the cast list for the premiere was pinned up on the noticeboard the buoyant atmosphere collapsed like a burst balloon. Michel's friends huddled together in the corner of the common room whispering in consternation. None of them could quite believe it. After all his hard work for more than two months, all those late nights in the studio, Michel had been passed over.

"It ain't fucking possible!" Primo whispered, wild-eyed.

Lynne pressed the palms of her hands to her forehead. "It's so unfair; he must be devastated!"

"Of course he's devastated," Annette growled dangerously. "Who wouldn't be? This sort of shit happens at the Royal, maybe, but not at the Islington. It's the most outrageous thing I've ever heard. I'd take a blasted gun to Charles if he cast someone else in my role for the premiere." Annette was quite serious. For the first time in her career she had been raised from her place in the corps to create the role of the frigid princess whom Siegfried was ordered, by his mother, to marry. It was a character role with little dancing—and what dancing there was mostly consisted of sustained aerial lifts in the arms of a faithful rejected suitor—but if someone had told Annette that it would be another dancer and not she who would turn her back on Siegfried and make that long, stately walk across the stage into Roly's long-suffering arms on the first night, it would have been the greatest blow of her career. "Charles is a total shit!" she said in disgust.

Roly shook his head slowly. He understood exactly why Crown had taken this brutal step. The company had a lot riding on this ballet: an initial budget deficit of fifty thousand pounds, for a start, even supposing the week at Sadler's Wells sold out. Crown couldn't afford to risk the hostility of the critics by putting forward a new face in the lead role. The press knew and liked Peter and Carlotta. With Peter dancing Siegfried the critics would give the new ballet a head start.

"Jesus, poor Michel," he said. "Still, he'll have other chances in the future. And he will get to dance two out of every five shows on tour."

"Fucking easy for you to say!" Annette spat. "I don't see Charles relegating you to the ensembles for the premiere. You're quite safe, thank you very much!"

Roly rested his cheek glumly on his fist and turned to look out of the window at the gray afternoon. "Give me a break," he sighed. Roly and Annette rarely spoke to each other these days if they could avoid it.

Even Carlotta was appalled by the news about the premiere. She stamped her little pointe-shod foot on the changing room floor, describing Charles Crown with a range of colorful Italian adjectives that dwarfed even Primo's impressive vocabulary. Peter was so embarrassed he couldn't look Michel in the eye. To spend two months sitting on his backside nursing his overworked knees and then saunter on in the lead role at the premiere was outrageous.

Michel was almost the last person in the company to hear the news. Nobody wanted to be the one to tell him.

When he walked into the common room Lynne threw her arms around him. He smiled and sat her on his knee, caressing her waist.

"Come on, Lynnie, what's the big deal? It's only a premiere."

But Lynne refused to smile. Michel's role! His own creation into which he had poured so much sweat and love.

"Don't be so brave!" she wailed.

"I'm second cast with you and fourth cast with Carlotta. What more could I want? Hey, and you and Roly in fifth cast!" He reached over to clasp Roly's hand. "Fantastic news. You earned it."

"But the insult to you," Lynne insisted. "Peter will get the credit for all your beautiful work!"

"It's not my work, Lynnie, it's C.C's work. He just made it on my body. Peter's entitled to the premiere; it's the privilege of his rank. So I'll dance on Friday instead of Thursday. The music will be the same, the choreography will be the same, the sets and costumes will be the same. What's a premiere, anyway, except a chance to get ripped apart by the critics?"

Lynne laid her cheek forlornly on his blond head.

"Can't you even be a little bit pissed off so I can cheer you up?"

"Come round on Sunday with Roly and we'll work on the pas de deux." He stroked her thigh. "There is one thing you can do to cheer me up though."

She sighed. "I'm okay, Michel."

"Just a few pounds, darling. Or you're going to make yourself ill again. Will you do that for me?"

Jonni could have cried with anger when she heard about the casting for the premiere. That night when Michel sat down on the edge of the bed to pull off his shoes, he flung them slowly, one after the other, into the bottom of the open wardrobe and then just sat there staring at the wall. He felt as small and as humiliated as he had on the first day of his apprenticeship more than six years ago.

Jonni crawled across the bed and put her arms around his shoulders, burying her face in his neck.

"You must be so upset. Don't try and hide how you feel, Michel. Take it out on me if you like. I don't mind."

Michel patted her arm as it lay over his chest.

"I'm not upset. I was thinking about the adage at the end of the first act; we changed a couple of the steps this afternoon."

His neck was warm under Jonni's cheek and she closed her eyes.

"I love you so much; I can't bear to think of Charles doing such a dreadful thing to you."

He got up from the bed in irritation, turning his back on her as he pulled off his sweatshirt.

"Don't get emotional on me, Jons. I've had a long, tiring day."

The following Thursday evening in the wings at Sadler's Wells Michel hitched up the tights of his peasant costume, waiting with the rest of the corps for the overture to start. Peter stopped beside him, grim-faced with fear, and held out his sweating hand toward him.

"Luck," said Michel gripping his hand hard. "Go out there, Pete, and blow them out of their seats. I'll be rooting for you every bloody step of the way."

Peter laughed, pale under his thick pancake foundation.

"Yeah, I know you will. If I fall on my arse in those sodding doubles it'll be your fault."

Michel slapped him on the back, sending him away onto the stage to join Carlotta.

"There's nothing in the role I didn't learn from my elders and betters."

But though Peter danced Siegfried admirably, there was never any doubt in the minds of the dancers to whom the role really belonged. At the second performance the whole company crowded the wings, squeezing against each other and craning their necks, to watch Michel's melancholy solo at the end of the first act. He looked so beautiful and lonely as his body unfolded slowly into each long, yearning arabesque that many of the watching dancers had tears in their eyes. They, if anyone, knew how to appreciate wonderful dancing. When the solo came to an end Peter raised his eyebrows and turned toward Carlotta.

"Fuck," he whispered, puffing out his cheeks, "am I glad I didn't have to follow that!"

The audiences enjoyed Crown's *Swan Lake*—they liked the liveliness and the technical pyrotechnics: they liked the strong characters and the clear story line—but critically the production was a flop.

There was praise in the newspapers for Carlotta's skill and grace, and for Peter's agility, and some for the steps themselves. But the ballet world wasn't ready to have the glass casing broken from around its precious classics. Another decade would pass before the dance critics could handle the concept of a man masturbating over a swan.

And yet the takings at the box office, as the company went out on the road after its expensive week at the Wells, were mercifully hovering just above break-even. *Swan Lake* was still *Swan Lake,* and it was still the biggest box office pull in the business. And the publicity department did its work well. There were photographs and features in every regional paper. Carlotta and Peter gave interviews, they recorded sections of the big Act Two pas de deux for local television, went to gala events, and actually managed to make one or two appearances in the gossip columns of the society glossies. Even Annette, so stunning in her red Princess costume with her magnificent hair flowing over her shoulders, got her photograph in *Dance and Dancers.* Charles Crown rushed around the country doing pre-publicity, and Nadia Petrovna steeled herself to appear on *Wogan,* where she heroically dragged the conversation back, time and again, to her current production of *Swan Lake.* But of Michel there was nothing said, either in the press or in the dance world.

Michel made the best of it. He was touring and working hard, dancing Siegfried twice a week and smaller roles or ensembles on other nights. Though he had created the role with Carlotta, he danced most of his Siegfrieds with Lynne, and she was perfect for the Swan Princess. Delicate, vulnerable, and supple as a green reed, she balanced Michel's strong romantic lover to perfection. Their bodies flowed together like water. Watching them from her seat in the dark auditorium, Jonni believed that even their hearts beat in unison. If ever two bodies had fused to become one flesh she was looking at them now.

With no work to occupy her, Jonni's life revolved around Michel and his friends. As an outsider she became their confidante, ear to their professional frustrations and healer of quarrels and injured pride. She was earning her place in their lives just by being there to listen. Annette moaned to her about Roly's partnering and about all her aches and imagined sprains. Primo ran to the flat to cower under her skirts when he got himself into trouble having affairs with two different dancers at the same time—the trouble mainly being that the two were married to each other. Roly urged her to try and influence Annette to diet; quite apart from his own aching back, she honestly wasn't doing herself any favors. And even Michel asked Jonni to see if she could nudge Primo to turn up to a few more classes.

But though Jonni adored all Michel's friends, her relationship with them wasn't without its tensions. She loved Lynne—and trusted Michel when he said he hadn't slept with her since before he went to Paris—but watching them dance together, so intimate, so passionate, how could she help feeling bitter pangs of jealousy? And if Jonni's jealousy was ruthless, Lynne's was far worse.

It all came pouring out, as it was bound to sooner or later, one Sunday night when all the friends were together at the flat in Warwick Way.

Jonni lost her temper at a deliberately smug comment from Lynne about how well she knew Michel's body, and Lynne snapped straight back, more than ready for a fight.

"I work with his body, you stupid girl! Don't be so possessive!"

"Me? Possessive? Lynne, I watch you climb all over him day after day, pawing him and sitting on his lap and doing . . . doing . . ." she flapped her hand frustratedly, ". . . whatever it is you're doing now."

Lynne was curled up on the floor with her knees tucked underneath her, almost stark naked, while Michel stretched her spine; one strong hand spread over the top of her buttocks and the other between her shoulder blades. Now Lynne pushed Michel away and jumped to her feet, squaring up to Jonni fiercely with her hands on her hips, in nothing but a cotton G-string.

"Our physical relationship is no business of yours."

"It certainly is."

To both girls' annoyance Michel stepped between them, laughing.

"Okay, darlings, when you've quite finished squabbling over my body—"

"It's not funny!" Jonni cried. "Lynne's resented my being here ever since we got back from Paris!"

Lynne shoved Michel aside so she could shout, unobstructed, at Jonni. "You aren't even a dancer! What right have you to come barging into our rehearsals as if you owned the place?"

"I live here, for Christ's sake!" Jonni snapped, and then glanced over her shoulder in alarm to check her mother hadn't heard her bad language, though her mother was over a hundred miles away in Gloucester. "Stop laughing, Michel. And you, too, Roly. It isn't a joke!"

"Fucking right, it isn't!" Lynne yelled, turning to Michel, not at all concerned whose mother heard her. "What's so bloody special about her, anyway? Why don't you ever talk about her weight? It's she who should go on a diet; never mind Nettie!"

Annette folded her arms and looked stonily at the studio wall.

"How can you be such a bitch?" Jonni squealed at Lynne. "You're way too skinny to start criticizing me. And you do it deliberately to get attention. I was born this way!"

Jonni burst into tears and so did Lynne. When Michel tried to touch them they both flung him off furiously, and ran, sobbing, one after the other, from the studio.

Primo winked at Annette.

"They ain't in your class, baby."

Annette just scowled.

Half an hour later Michel told Primo to go and see what had become of them.

"No way, amico. They're your women. You sort 'em out."

"Roly, you go. I'm dead if I try and comfort the wrong girl."

"Which one's the wrong girl?"

"God only knows. Go on, Roly, do me a favor. You understand women."

Annette hooted. "That's a ruddy joke!"

Less than a minute later Roly came back smiling. He picked up his jacket from the back of the sofa, preparing to go home.

"They're in your room."

"Is it safe to go to bed?"

"I couldn't tell you, Shel, but they look very sweet."

When Michel went into the bedroom it was dark. Jonni and Lynne were lying side by side, sound asleep with their arms resting over each other's waists.

"Hey, girls," Michel said, just loud enough to half wake them, "I don't want to intrude but this is my bed too, you know."

They moved apart, grumbling, and he lay down between them, pulling the duvet over their bodies. He put an arm around each of them and went to sleep.

Jonni went home to Gloucester for Christmas. The Islington Ballet was performing all over the holiday season, except for Christmas Day itself which, as always, Michel spent with Primo's family in Hackney. It was a quiet day. Since Primo's father had died two years ago, Christmas had been a subdued festival in the Vincenti household. Primo's youngest sister, Maria, was eleven now. Still faithful to her first infatuation, she had painstakingly knitted Michel a pair of lime-green leg warmers.

After a week with her family Jonni couldn't wait to get back to London. Seven days of her mother's snide insinuations about Michel was as much as she could take.

On the morning of New Year's Eve, a Sunday and therefore a blessed day off for the dancers, Jonni and Michel were sitting in bed together drinking coffee. Their faces were glowing. They had just made love.

Jonni leaned back against the pillows and closed her eyes blissfully. She could feel his semen running out of her in a warm rush of liquid heat, soaking the bed under her thighs. She was so relaxed she couldn't even be bothered to lift her cup to her mouth.

"Mike?"

"Uh-huh?" He was smoking a strong French cigarette.

"Have you thought about the two of us getting married?"

"Good God, no. Not for a moment. Why on earth would I think of that?"

Jonni turned her head toward him in surprise. "Why not?"

"Marriage is something other people do. You know me, Jons. That sort of crap means nothing to me."

"Why not?" she asked again.

Michel looked at her face. His own face vanished for a moment in a cloud of smoke as he exhaled.

"Are you afraid I'm going to get fed up with you and find a replacement?"

"No." She had a vague suspicion he wasn't taking this discussion very seriously. "But I don't see what's wrong with marriage."

"You're here because you want to be. That's good enough for me."

"You asked Lynne to marry you once."

He was silent for a moment and then he shook his head. "No, I didn't. She asked me. I told her I'd do it if it was the only way to stop her starving herself to death. Thank Christ she had the sense to refuse. Marriage is an excuse people use to limit each other's freedom, to tie each other down."

"That's not what it's about at all. Marriage is about letting the whole world see you're a couple. It's about romance."

Michel smiled as he turned away to stub out his cigarette.

"I have no desire to let the world know anything about my private life. And, as for romance . . ."

"Yes?" she demanded, needled.

"I wake up in the morning and there you are next to me. Because you've chosen to be, today. Maybe it's hard work to have to face the same choice every day but we do—and, as you see, we're still in the same bed. That seems pretty romantic to me."

This wasn't what Jonni understood by romance at all. For Jonni romance meant passionate vows and unexpected gifts of flowers, blushing confessions in the moonlight and love blazoned in public for all to see: all so convincingly portrayed by the Michel she saw onstage. But the real man offstage farted in bed, spurned her sexually when he got "jock-rot," a rash from his dance belt, and laughed whenever she tried to become sentimental.

"You know your problem," she said, "you've got a barrier when it comes to commitment."

Now Michel really did laugh.

"That's fantasy talk, Jonni." He shook his head and finished the last mouthful of his coffee. "I've watched lots of people make commitments, and then I've watched almost every one of them break them. I'm not planning to screw up what we've got. It's great; we have a lot of laughs and the sex is terrific. But how can anyone know how they're going to feel for the rest of their life? You might wake up tomorrow and find you don't fancy me anymore. Then you'll be bloody relieved you're free to walk away, I can tell you. You just can't will yourself to want to be with someone."

"Some people can."

"Jons, you're talking bollocks."

"My feelings aren't going to change. I'm not afraid of commitment."

"Nor am I. Commitments are just words."

"So you don't want to marry me then?"

"Not in the least."

It seemed, as far as Michel was concerned, that was the end of the conversation. Jonni stared at him for almost a minute in stony silence.

"Screw you!" she said suddenly, and she threw back the duvet, getting angrily out of bed. "Just forget I exist, Michel!"

Michel laughed at her stroppiness. "Stop sulking, Jons. It's Sunday. Come back to bed."

"Bugger off! Don't talk to me!"

He watched her scramble quickly into her clothes.

"Where are you going?"

"I'm going to Lynne's. And I'll be back when I feel like it."

"Well, don't forget we've got to leave at seven."

"Don't bother waiting for me." She tugged open the wardrobe and took out her blue dress and shoes, folding the dress and stuffing it in a bag. "I'll phone Roly and get him to take me to the party. There's no way I'm going with you."

To her intense frustration Michel was still smiling. She pulled open a drawer and grabbed a selection of underwear, throwing it in her bag.

"Don't you need a strapless bra with that dress?" Michel asked.

Jonni snatched up the white bra from the top of the bag and flung it back in the drawer, grabbing her strapless bra instead.

"I'm going. Good-bye!"

She stormed off noisily via the bathroom and Michel called after her, "Don't pinch my razor! If you want to shave your legs borrow one from Lynne!"

The Islington Ballet's annual party was far less formal than the British National's smart summer dinner. Every year the Islington had a bash on the Sunday between Christmas and New Year's, right in the middle of their busiest season. It was by pure chance that, this year, it fell on New Year's Eve itself. Most of the dancers had dressed up for the occasion. They relished any excuse to indulge their passion for clothes. The boys sported loud waistcoats and paisley bow ties, and the girls were at their wildest.

At the Islington Ballet's party there was no politics and no undercurrent of tension. Like dogs, dance companies eventually take on the personalities of their masters: the Islington was an outspoken, intolerant, warm-hearted company. Competition was up-front and good-humored. The dancers took no prisoners but neither did they scheme behind each other's backs or harbor secret jealousies; their motto was simple: all for one and every man for himself. They were here tonight to laugh and to drink and to sit on each other's laps without discrimination like the close-knit family they were.

Jonni wandered through the crowded hotel bar with her arm tucked under Roly's as he chatted to the dancers. The majority of the boys she knew, at least by sight, but it wasn't easy to tell the girls apart; they looked very different in real life from the prim faces she had learned to recognize onstage with their identical buns and false eyelashes. Roly came to her rescue every time, addressing each girl clearly by name as he met them. Roly was always an easy person to be with. The dancers teased him and made him the butt of jokes, and pulled him around like some kind of overgrown teddy bear, and he just laughed with patient good humor. He was attentive to Jonni, including her in all his conversations and making sure her glass was kept topped up.

Michel met them by the bar. He was looking painfully beautiful in gray slacks, a heavy white cotton shirt, and straight red tie. On anyone else it would have been an inconspicuous outfit. On Michel it could have come straight out of a fashion magazine. He smiled a greeting when he saw them.

"There you are! Have you both got a drink?"

Roly put his arm around Jonni, looking down at her affectionately. "I don't think we're talking to you, Michel, are we, darling?"

"No we're not," she agreed, refusing to look at either of them. Michel and Roly exchanged wry smiles before Jonni dragged her escort away to join Primo in a crowd farther along the bar.

It was a surprisingly well-behaved party. Thirty dancers with assorted partners and seven apprentices—five of them girls who lurked together in a corner giggling and watching Michel—in addition to fifteen musicians, seven technical and wardrobe crew, an administrative staff of five, and the Board of Governors who were mostly members of the Bell Foundation, the company's chief sponsor. In all there were less than a quarter of the number who had been at the British National's party in the summer.

Jonni chatted to the dancers and ostentatiously ignored Michel, glancing over her shoulder no more than once a minute to check whether he was looking at her. Unfortunately he wasn't. He had his back to her and seemed to be having an inappropriately good time. Refusing to admit how hurt she really felt about his rejection this morning, she decided she was just as capable of enjoying herself without him and set about doing so with determination, laughing gaily at anything that seemed funny and plenty that didn't, and eating so many smoked salmon sandwiches she thought she would burst.

Annette was looking radiant, despite the rather superior manner she always assumed when she was accompanied by one of her male victims. She left her latest prey, an expensive-looking banker, sitting alone at the bar drinking himself into an early retirement while she went into a huddle with her friends. She held out a startling green pendant: a magnificent teardrop emerald on a gold chain.

"Look at this," she whispered. "Isn't it out of this world?"

Jonni took it from her, gasping. "Oh, heavens! It's bliss! You're so lucky!"

The pendant was passed around discreetly from dancer to dancer. The girls groaned in envy. Roly whistled and Primo's eyes opened wide.

"*Cristo!* This is a serious piece of rock, bella! Who gave it you? Signor Rothschild at the bar there?"

"Sshh, for crying out loud!" Annette took the pendant back and clipped it around her neck. It matched the vivid green of her eyes perfectly. "It might have been him. It came in the post; a New Year's present. It just said—from Me. I can think of three, no, four blokes who might have sent it." She spluttered with laughter. "Isn't that appalling?"

"What are you going to do?"

"I don't know. I'll have to busk it. I wish to God he'd signed his name."

"Yeah, stupid of him," Primo said. "You should warn them all to label their gifts carefully to avoid confusion."

Annette tutted and rolled her eyes to the ceiling, not deigning to acknowledge his sarcasm. She went off, back to her escort, to exhibit her pendant casually before him, watching closely for any telltale sign of recognition.

Roly shook his head as he walked beside Jonni to the bar.

"That girl's going to land herself in big trouble one of these days."

Jonni tucked her arm further under his. "Do you think you and Nettie will ever be friends again after what happened in the summer?"

"I doubt it. We weren't exactly on good terms to begin with." He looked at Jonni with a grim smile. "At least we don't fight over our work anymore. I suppose it's all been said. D'you want another gin and tonic?"

The Islington Ballet made its own music at the party. There was always someone at the piano and, instead of wild disco dancing, company tradition brought the dancers onto the floor to dance in the old-fashioned way. Later it would become a wilder gathering but while Nadia Petrovna and the Governors were there it retained an atmosphere of friendly dignity.

Jonni sat on Roly's knee with her arm around his neck and her gin and tonic in her hand, watching Michel with wistful eyes across the room while the first quickstep commenced with a mixture of familiarity and strict courtesy. Once Nadia Petrovna had been led onto the dance floor with extreme care by Sir Christopher Bell, Charles Crown offered his hand dutifully to his leading ballerina, making sure she didn't trip over anyone's handbag as she walked between the tables. One by one, the women were escorted onto the floor. The principal dancers paired up with the Governors and their wives. Michel danced with Marina. As the floor began to fill up Roly patted Jonni's knee.

"I've got to leave you for a minute, chicken. Don't go away."

Jonni watched him making a highly formal smiling bow to an attractive Laura Ashley–style woman with short blond hair.

"Who's she?" Jonni asked Lynne.

"The leader of the orchestra."

"How do the boys decide who to ask?"

Lynne shrugged. Even in an informal troupe like the Islington, company hierarchy was etched deep into its members' unconscious.

"They just know," she said, and let herself be dragged off by one of the boys from the corps.

Jonni watched the couples quickstepping on the black linoleum floor. They danced wonderfully; if only they could see themselves. The sight of thirty couples spinning so gracefully while they laughed and talked, not giving the well-known steps a moment's thought, sent shivers of appreciation down Jonni's spine. Michel danced very sexily with Marina, chatting to her all the while and slapping her hand occasionally when she tried to lead.

Later, when Primo took over at the piano, the dances and their execution became more extrovert: flamboyant tangos where the boys dipped their laughing partners almost to the floor and wild foxtrots and rhumbas. As Primo started to play a paso doble, he caught Roly's eye and nodded toward Jonni, raising his eyebrows.

Roly was a marvelous ballroom dancer, easy and relaxed and effortlessly able to put his partner right when she made a mistake without letting her know it. Jonni was very proud of herself turning and stepping through the maneuvers of the dance with haughty detachment, just as Primo had taught her. Roly did his best to make her laugh, unzipping her frock as she danced in his arms.

"Stop it, you sod, you're putting me off!"

"You're very charming when you frown, señorita."

Jonni elbowed him in the ribs as he tried to tickle her, and moved away to spin around at the proper place in the music. A surge of commotion had broken out in one corner of the room and, glancing over, she saw that Michel was in the middle of the shrieking crowd. She moved back into Roly's arms looking over her shoulder, wondering what had caused the uproar.

Moments later Annette appeared at their side with round eyes, trying to drag Jonni away.

"Jonni, come here, woman! Quick, we want you!" For once she turned to Roly without rancor. "Michel and Jonni are getting married, isn't that incredible? Jonni, come on, will you?"

"Go away!" Jonni cried frantically, thrown into confusion. "I'm in the middle of a paso doble!"

She moved closer into Roly's arms and carried on dancing for all she was worth.

"You alright?" Roly asked her.

"Keep dancing," she said through gritted teeth.

Roly could always be relied on. He put his arms tighter around her and continued dancing as if nothing had happened. "The boy's no fool," he said smiling.

Jonni was engulfed by the crowd the moment the dance was over. Her confusion increased as she was swamped from all sides with congratulations and kisses. Primo had abandoned his place at the piano and was trying to crush her to death in his arms. Before she knew what had happened she was standing beside Michel with hot, scarlet cheeks. Michel was sipping his drink and accepting the good wishes of his friends with a cool smile as though he got engaged every day of the week.

"Are you going to have a white wedding?" asked Annette eagerly.

Jonni looked uncertainly at Michel and he shrugged.

"Ask the bride."

"We . . . really haven't decided," she stammered. She had a sense that she should be angry with him—it was scarcely fair, after all, to announce their engagement to his friends before he had announced it to her—but all other emotion was buried under her irrepressible, knee-trembling happiness. "It's all . . ." she looked at him again, "a bit sudden."

"When did he ask you? Was it romantic?"

"Well . . ."

To her relief the crowd was distracted by shouts from the bar as someone turned up a radio so they could hear the chimes of Big Ben. A massive cheer went up all over the room as the new year began. Only Michel didn't join in the emotional orgy of kissing and hugging that followed. He remained where he was, leaning against the wall beside Jonni.

"*Bonne année!*" he said, raising his glass to her. Michel's eyes, when they wanted to, could make a private space in which there was no one but the two of them, no matter where they were. As he looked at her now they were quite alone, despite the hullabaloo around them.

"Are you really sure?" she asked him.

"Yes; of course, why not? If it's what you want that's a good enough reason for me."

"I'm not going to change my name, you know."

"I should think not. What would you want my name for? You've got a perfectly good one of your own. I hope to God you don't want a white wedding. I can't afford it, for one thing."

Jonni buried her face in his shoulder. It appeared she was getting married.

18

AT THE START OF THE SECOND WEEK of January the Islington Ballet broke its winter tour to spend a week rehearsing in the studio. The tour bookers had been keen to fit Llandudno into this week but Crown had put his foot down; after five weeks of solid touring bodies started to get tired and tempers to fray. That was just when accidents happened. He wasn't prepared to risk it, even for an upfront guarantee of forty thousand pounds. The dancers were glad to get back to the mirror after so many classes onstage. The mirror was their lifeline and their guide. Crown and Marina could offer them as many corrections as they liked but it was only in front of the mirror that the dancers could employ the necessary self-criticism to keep their technique razor-sharp. By the end of Monday's class Crown could already see an improvement.

As the company filed exhaustedly out of studio one, well pleased with themselves, Michel caught up with Crown at the door, waving his hand to stop him.

"What?" Crown asked. He had places to go and things to do.

Michel was still so breathless from the final allegro he couldn't immediately speak. He leaned over and propped his hands on his knees, struggling to catch his breath. He was soaked in sweat.

Crown's mouth twisted into a wry little smile.

"You liked those double doubles, did you? I put them in just for you."

"Yeah," Michel gasped, "savage—thanks! Really got my heart pumping. Listen," he straightened up slowly as his breathing became more regular, "can you spare an hour or two on Wednesday after class?"

Crown shook his head.

"Wednesday? Not a chance. I've got to go through figures with the old lady and the accountants before the AGM. Can't Marina help you? What is it you need?"

"It's not work. I was hoping you'd . . ." Michel wiped his dripping face on the shoulder of his T-shirt. "Jonni and I are getting married on Wednesday. It's probably the only chance we'll get for a while, with the AGM being in the afternoon. We were hoping you'd agree to be a witness for us."

"Me?" Crown was dumbfounded. He frowned, trying to hide his uncharacteristic embarrassment. "Good God!"

"Jonni would be thrilled." Michel couldn't quite meet Crown's eye. "We both would. There won't be anyone else there; just witnesses. It shouldn't take long. It's booked for twelve-thirty at Victoria Register Office."

Crown took a packet of cigarettes from his pocket and lit one, nodding curtly as he threw the match into the sand bucket by the studio door.

"Alright. I'll go through the accounts tomorrow. I suppose I'll manage."

On Wednesday morning Jonni waited in the dancers' common room during company class. She had never been in the Goswell Road building before and that, in itself, marked this as a day of new experiences. The common room was deserted. Because of the AGM in the afternoon there were no rehearsals today so none of the injured dancers had come in as they usually did to limp through a few barre exercises in class and then slope off to the common room to nurse their wounds. The building was filled with a holiday atmosphere.

While Michel and Primo changed out of their dance gear after class, Charles Crown went to find Jonni. As he walked into the common room she sprang up from her seat by the window to meet him, blushing with happiness.

He shook his head at her.

"Are you really going to get married in an Islington Ballet sweatshirt?"

"Why not? It's old, borrowed, and blue."

"I hope you've got something new."

"Knickers," she whispered.

Crown raised his eyebrows. "Lucky St. Michel. Come on then, Flotsam, let's go and find a taxi or you'll miss your own wedding."

It was a simple, undramatic ceremony with no flowers and no tears. Michel and Jonni sat side by side spelling out their names and occupations patiently for the gray-haired, bespectacled registrar.

"Place of birth?" the man asked Michel.

"Issy. I-S-S-Y. France."

"Father's name and occupation?"

There was a pause before Michel cleared his throat and answered—"Jacques Yves St. Michel. Choreographer."

He turned his head to look over his shoulder at Crown. Crown was sitting with his elbow propped on the arm of his chair and his hand covering his mouth as he listened. He moved his hand away from his mouth to give Michel a small smile. The lie had never been very strong between them anyway.

When Michel had placed the gold ring he had bought for Jonni on her finger and had kissed his wife for the first time, Crown and Primo each signed their names on the register and the small wedding party strolled through St. James's Park in the cold January sunshine. Jonni couldn't keep still; she and Primo ran ahead together like children, chasing each other around the sleeping, naked trees. Michel smiled as he watched Primo pick her up bodily, dangling her over the edge of the river pretending to throw her in. Her legs were kicking frantically and she was squealing with laughter.

Michel felt very strange; not strange because he had just become a husband but strange because he and Charles Crown were walking slowly through the park together chatting as though they were equals.

"What time do you have to be back in the Goswell Road?" Michel asked, glancing at his watch.

"Not until three." Crown, for his part, seemed perfectly at ease. Michel wasn't sure he had ever seen his frenetic employer relax before. Crown walked with his hands tucked into his jacket pockets to keep them warm. He too was watching Primo and Jonni. "Where are the rest of your gang?" he asked.

"Roly's taken Lynne out for a drive in the country."

Michel didn't say anything to explain this seemingly unfriendly behavior but he found, seeing Crown nod calmly, that he didn't have to. Crown knew a lot more about what went on between the dancers in his company than he let on.

"Roland's a good chap," the choreographer said. "Salt of the fucking earth."

Michel had never heard Crown pass comment on any of his dancers, except to tell them to their faces that they were lazy, unimaginative bores. If anyone in the company deserved Crown's esteem it was Roly. Michel flushed with pleasure on his friend's behalf.

"Nettie's at home with her parents," he added, not wanting Crown to think she was excluded from their nuptial party. "She went home on Sunday so she could keep off her ankle until tomorrow."

"Skiving, you mean," Crown said dryly.

In fact, on this occasion Annette hadn't gone away to shirk classes and rehearsals. She had fled home to Hertford when her liaison with the banker had come to an unpleasant and potentially violent end. Michel had had a desperate phone call at midnight on Saturday and had driven to Sunningdale with Primo and Roly in the dead of night to rescue her. But of course he couldn't explain that to Crown so he said nothing.

"Tell me," Crown asked him, "how are you enjoying Siegfried?"

"Enjoying it? I love every minute of it. You know that without asking."

"Yes, I suppose so. What role would you really want to dance, given the choice?"

"In our rep, d'you mean?"

"No, in the whole international repertoire. What role would you most like to dance or create, out of everything you've ever seen or imagined being made into a ballet?"

Michel smiled.

"I'm sure you wouldn't have much trouble guessing."

"No, I don't suppose I would."

"Romeo."

"You don't say."

Michel put his hands in his pockets, mirroring Crown's easy stroll. "I suppose you've heard me and Lynne talking about it, and seen us messing around with the pas de deux. We want to dance them all: MacMillan's, Cranko's, Ashton's, van Dantzig's, the one Nureyev made for English National. I'd like to have a crack at every one of them. Roly, too: he'd give his right arm to dance Romeo, and I know he could do it."

He stopped talking as Jonni came running toward him, holding out her ring gleefully to show him.

"Look, Michel! Look! I'm a married woman!"

"Never," he said. "Who'd be daft enough to marry a little rat like you?" He put his arm around her and took her hand in his, holding it up to look at her ring finger. "Good God, you're right. Some fool obviously has."

"No way of telling who, though," Jonni said mock forlornly.

Michel caressed her shoulder as they continued to walk along the path together. Jonni had been upset that he refused to wear a ring. But how could he? He'd have to take it off when he was dancing—which was so much of the time he might as well not have a ring at all. And then he would probably lose it which would upset her even more. Jonni had seen the sense of this at last but her disappointment had made him so uncomfortable he had turned his back on her in bed and gone to sleep rather than risk a renewal of the subject halfway through making love.

By now, however, Jonni had forgiven him. In a moment, after reaching up on tiptoe to kiss him, she was off again, scampering along the edge of the lake with Primo in hot pursuit.

"You don't look much like a man who's just got married," Crown commented, seeing Michel stifle a yawn.

"It was Jonni's idea. I've got nothing against it if it makes her happy."

"Sounds like a bit of a one-sided arrangement."

"No, I don't have any doubts about it. Marriage just isn't very important to me."

"Make sure you tell Adrian. You'll be entitled to a bigger tax allowance."

"Good point; I'd forgotten that."

"Wouldn't you rather have a crack at creating the role from scratch?"

"Sorry?"

"Romeo, I mean."

"Of course. More than anything in the world."

"Next summer," Crown said, and he smiled as Michel stopped dead on the path. "Think of it as a wedding present."

Michel's face was blank.

"Are you serious?"

"Why not? I can't afford to pay royalties on anyone else's choreography. Besides, I've always wanted to have a go at making one myself. It's one of the best ballet scores ever written. Arno's come up with a few preliminary designs already."

Michel could feel his own heart suddenly thumping.

"Next summer?"

"Yes. I'll probably start putting it on its feet in August. It might mean working through the summer break again."

"Wouldn't Peter be better?" Michel asked, terrified that Crown might agree.

"I told you I'm going to make it on your body, son. If I thought Peter was the better choice I'd have realized it without your help."

Very slowly Michel started walking again. He was too stunned to speak. A thousand thoughts were racing around in his head. He could already hear the music as clearly as if an entire orchestra were playing it in the park.

Crown grunted. "You know, it's a damned pity Primo hasn't got the technique. If he weren't so bloody lazy he'd make a wonderful Mercutio."

"Yeah. Yeah, he would."

"Do see if you can get him to show up for class a bit more often, will you? Peter will make Mercutio, and Roland will do Tybalt, I think. I haven't quite made up my mind. This is between you and me, you understand."

"Of course," Michel said absently. One idea had taken root amongst the chaos of thoughts clamoring for precedence in his mind. "There is one thing I'd like to ask you though."

"Who's going to dance the premiere?" Crown suggested.

"No, bugger that. I only want to create the thing with you and then perform it. No, I was wondering—look, don't be pissed off at my asking . . ."

"Go ahead."

Michel looked at him anxiously. "Do you think Carlotta is the best choice for Juliet?"

"Do you?"

"That's not really for me to say."

Crown nodded. "No, it isn't. But you're right, Lynne was born for the role."

Michel looked down at the tarmac path beneath their feet, shaking his head in stunned disbelief. "My God, I think this has got to be the happiest day of my life."

He couldn't for the life of him think why Crown seemed to find that comment so amusing.

That night as Michel lay in bed beside Jonni he wanted to tell her about Romeo. She would understand what it meant to him and she would be so happy for him. But a rare sympathetic insight warned him it would be unfair to steal the thunder of her joy at their marriage. Perhaps it would be better to tell her tomorrow.

Jonni snuggled closer to him, burying her face in his neck, and he stretched his arm behind him to turn off the bedside light and made love to her. On the whole he was rather pleased to have married Jonni.

Four days after Michel's informal wedding the Islington Ballet went back on the road with another six weeks of touring to go before the season ended. Many of the venues were within commuting distance of London. At the end of a long day in Croydon, Swindon, or Ilford, Michel would come home to find Jonni bopping around the kitchen with pop music playing on the radio while she cooked him some special dish, or singing loudly in the bathroom while she painted it bright blue. One night, after dancing a grim Siegfried to a half-empty house in Gravesend, with a pulled hamstring aching and Lynne complaining about her pointe shoes throughout all four pas de deux, he came home to find Jonni bouncing around funkily in the studio to a Bob Marley album and reading the script for a fringe play with an apple stuck between her jaws like a roasted suckling pig.

"Hi-hel!" she cried joyfully, and then remembered the apple and took it out of her mouth. "Michel! I've cooked a wonderful cheese sauce! Except it's blue."

"Blue?"

"Yes, I stirred it with my paintbrush by mistake. Don't worry, it's non-toxic; I checked on the side of the tin."

Michel was gladder than ever that he had married her. Things were tense at work at the moment; the physical and mental strain of *Swan Lake* was taking its toll on all the dancers. Lynne had become tight-lipped and reclusive; she hadn't been over to the Pimlico flat for weeks. Even Roly was under so much stress partnering Annette in all those massive lifts on the nights when he wasn't grappling with Siegfried that he seemed unusually weary all the time. With all this, and with Carlotta nursing a ligament sprain, Jonni's bright face and warm body were an extremely welcome tonic at the end of a grueling twelve-hour day.

Not that the early days of their marriage were all smiles. It took Jonni three days to pluck up the courage to telephone her mother and break the news about the wedding. And when she did, Michel came home to find her in floods of tears in the studio, sobbing into a cushion as though her heart were breaking.

Michel wasn't good at sympathy, especially when there were tears involved, but for once he sent Primo and Roly away to the kitchen and sat beside Jonni on the sofa, listening while she told her sorrowful story.

"You got married the way you wanted to," he said. "They'll forgive you, Jons. They haven't got much choice."

"Will you come and meet them?"

"Yes, if you want."

She looked at him with tragic eyes because her mother had already made up her mind she hated him—although Jonni hadn't told him that part.

"Michel? Have you told your mother?"

"No, I didn't think of it. She won't care. Although I'm sure she'll like you. Do you want to drive down to Devon sometime and meet her?"

Jonni smiled and dried her eyes. Now that Michel was home it no longer mattered what her parents thought.

At the start of February the Islington played three nights in Cheltenham, and Michel and Jonni drove up to neighboring Gloucester to stay, for the duration of the company's visit, as guests of Jonni's parents.

"You won't be rude to my mother, will you?" Jonni asked anxiously as she packed the shirts she had carefully ironed for Michel into a suitcase.

"Why should I be rude to her? I'm never rude to anyone. Do I really have to wear a fucking tie?"

"Please. For my sake. And you are rude, Michel; incredibly rude, except you don't notice it. People are different outside the dance world."

"In what way?"

"Well, for a start, please try not to say exactly what you think about everything. I don't mean you have to lie; I just mean you could be a bit more tactful sometimes."

Michel grinned, flipping the long end of his tie over the short end in front of the mirror.

"You mean if I don't like the tablecloth I should keep my mouth shut."

"Oh, don't tease me," she pleaded. This was terrifying for Jonni. "You won't put your feet on the table, will you? And please don't fart at dinner—or anywhere else, for that matter. And for goodness' sake don't swear at all. Damn's okay in a crisis but anything worse would shock Mummy awfully."

"For Christ's sake," he said. "What sort of life does she lead if she never hears anyone swear?"

"She lives in Gloucester," Jonni told him, as though that were explanation enough.

Jonni's parents lived in an expensive, modern detached house in a suburb of Gloucester where the streets were lined with identical tidy front lawns and the lampposts carried signs threatening retribution if your dog fouled the pavement.

Mrs. Kendal was even more straightlaced than Jonni's description had painted her. She reminded Michel of the icy, marble-breasted principal of the Académie. But his years at ballet school stood him in good stead. He behaved impeccably. He complimented Veronica Kendal on her pristine home, listened politely to Jonni's father talking about stocks and shares for an hour without showing the least sign of boredom, remembered not to smoke or swear, and even refrained from stepping on the yapping dogs that were always under his feet.

"I've arranged a luncheon party for tomorrow," Veronica said. "I'm sure you'll enjoy meeting Jonquil's cousins and aunts, Michel."

"I'm sorry but I'm afraid I can't."

"Michel has to work," Jonni said quickly. "I did warn you, Mummy."

"But your performance isn't until the evening."

"It takes me some time to prepare. I have a class from ten until twelve. Then we have to place the ballet; that means we have to rearrange it for this particular stage and cast. It usually takes a couple of hours. Then I have to do two or three hours' work on my own before I get into my costume and makeup."

"All for this one show?" she asked, clearly not believing him.

"Every time I perform, Mrs. Kendal."

Jonni's mother was shocked by Crown's *Swan Lake* when she saw it. The choreography was far too racy for her taste.

"I daresay I'm old-fashioned," she told Jonni, "but ballet wasn't so suggestive when I used to go to Covent Garden as a child. I'm afraid I found some of the movements very improper."

"Oh, Mum," Jonni protested. "It's art. These days people fondle each other's bottoms on the street, for God's sake."

"There's no need to be profane, Jonquil. I presume I'm entitled to an opinion."

Michel smiled and put his arm around Jonni's shoulder.

"Of course you are, Mrs. Kendal. Lots of people are shocked by Charles Crown's choreography."

"I can quite believe it. I'm sure you and that young ballerina must know each other extremely well in order to do such intimate movements together."

If she had been anyone other than Jonni's mother Michel would have told her that onstage chemistry had nothing to do with whether he had fucked his partner or not. As it was, he merely nodded and said, "All the company are good friends—or most of them."

Jonni looked at her mother pleadingly. Veronica was tight-lipped and fifteen-denier tan-stockinged, with humorless eyes and a mirthless, disapproving smile to match.

"Didn't you think Michel was beautiful, Mummy?"

"Don't be foolish, dear. How could a man be beautiful? He looked very fit and healthy, and I'm sure he's very good at his job."

Jonni's younger sister—who had been a bitch ever since they arrived, hiding the fact that she was extremely struck with her new brother-in-law's handsome face and muscular body—smirked at him maliciously.

"I've never met a man who wears tights before."

Michel gave her a flat smile.

"You'd be surprised what some of the blokes you know get up to in private, darling."

"Jesus fucking Christ Almighty!" Michel said, as he walked into the boys' changing room in the Cheltenham theater the next morning.

Primo grinned. "Enjoying your stay with your in-laws?"

He puffed out his cheeks, raising his eyebrows.

"I can see why they call it a long weekend. Jonni's mother has decided to call me Mitchell. She doesn't approve of Michel for a bloke."

"She's probably joking, amico."

He pulled off his clothes, dropping them on the floor. "Primo, I honestly don't think that woman would recognize a joke if it hit her in the face."

"Then where did Jonni get such a great sense of humor?"

"God knows. Not from her parents, anyway. What amazes me is that they actually managed to conceive two children."

"Maybe they had them artificially implanted."

"I wouldn't be at all surprised."

From the moment he woke up on Sunday morning Michel was waiting for the afternoon when he would drive home to London and escape the stifling claustrophobia of his in-laws' house. But first he and Jonni must sit politely through breakfast and accompany Veronica while she walked her dogs on the common. Veronica discreetly looked the other way while her dogs pissed and shitted, pretending to be engrossed by a train that was rattling over the level crossing below them on the hill. She frowned, however, when she saw Michel put his arm around Jonni's waist resting his hand just below her breast.

"We're in public, Jonquil," she whispered.

Michel took his arm from Jonni's waist and held her hand instead.

But nothing about the visit offended Michel as deeply as having to shave and put on a tie on Sunday. Lunch was formal and populated by a number of shriveled relatives whose names Michel forgot as soon as they were told to him. He did his best to behave well for Jonni's sake but he hardly dared open his mouth for fear of upsetting their political, social, or grammatical sensibilities. It wouldn't have been so bad if smoking hadn't been forbidden in the house. As it was, nothing but Jonni's grateful, adoring eyes could have got him through that meal.

"I hope you'll both be coming to church with us this evening," Veronica told Jonni.

Michel answered for her. There had to be a line somewhere and Jonni's mother had just crossed it. "I'm sorry, we have to get back to London."

"It would be good for you to go to evensong. A civil ceremony means nothing until it has been blessed in church, you know."

"You may be right, Veronica, but it isn't going to happen. If Jonni wants to go that's up to her."

"No, you're right, darling," Jonni said, with just a hint of urgency. "We really do need to get back to the flat."

When the lunch guests had gone Michel and Jonni put their cases in the car and were thankfully preparing to leave when Veronica stopped them in the hall.

"Jonquil, I can't let you go just yet. I want you to sort through the clothes in your wardrobe and in the trunks in the attic and decide which ones you want to keep. I'll pack up the rest and take them to the Oxfam shop in town."

"Mummy," Jonni groaned, "I could have done that anytime in the last three days. Why wait until we're just about to leave?"

"Now don't fuss, dear. It will only take half an hour. Three-quarters at most. I'm sure Mitchell won't mind waiting for you while you do that small thing."

Michel managed to smile—just. "No, I don't mind waiting."

"Okay, come up with me," Jonni told him, heading for the stairs. But Veronica shook her head.

"It will take less time on your own, Jonquil. Mitchell won't mind sitting quietly in the study." She turned to Michel with a chilly smile that was intended to be pleasant. "Gerald always naps in the sitting room after Sunday lunch. If you go into the study you won't disturb him."

Michel exchanged expressionless—but, oh, so eloquent—glances with Jonni and obediently removed himself to the study to wait.

The study was on the ground floor; an airy, book-lined room with antique leather-covered chairs and French windows looking out over the garden which was bare and bedraggled now, in winter, but must have been lovely in the height of summer. Michel picked up a Sunday newspaper from a studded leather coffee table and sat down to while away the time reading Boyle's vitriolic review of the Royal Ballet's new triple bill.

Before he had been sitting there two minutes Veronica came hurriedly into the room and closed the door. Michel looked up at her in surprise. He was almost sure he had heard the key turn in the lock.

Veronica's face was set as primly as usual but there was an unusual energy about her that Michel hadn't seen before. She stood with her back against the door looking at him; a mixture of fear, excitement, and determination in her eyes.

"Mitchell, I wanted to see you alone," she said, rotating a gold bracelet quickly on her wrist. "There's something I want to ask you."

"Yes? Go ahead."

She gazed at him intently, her face flushing a violent red and her chest rising and falling as she struggled to control her nervousness.

"Do you know how to make a woman have an orgasm?"

His gray eyes looked steadily at her.

"Excuse me?"

"An orgasm, Mitchell. Do you know how to make a woman come?" A few moments passed in which he said nothing, looking at her with his mouth half open. She ran her tongue rapidly over her lips before she went on, "It's terribly important; much more important than most men realize. Even Jonquil herself won't understand it fully at her age. It's not until she gets much older that she'll feel something's missing. I don't want this to happen to her."

Michel exhaled slowly and passed his hand over his mouth, wiping away his involuntary smile. He folded the newspaper.

"Come and sit down, Veronica."

He took a packet of Gauloises from his pocket and lit one, regardless of the house rules. If they were going to discuss orgasms he was going to smoke. He hesitated as he went to put the packet back in his pocket, seeing Veronica look at it.

"Do you want one?"

She perched on the edge of the chair opposite him and smoothed her skirt anxiously over her knees.

"I haven't smoked a cigarette since before I met Jonquil's father."

"These are very strong."

"Perhaps I will have one."

She coughed as she lit the cigarette, covering her mouth delicately with her hand, and then sat holding it, gazing at him expectantly.

"Listen, Veronica," he said, "if you're worried about Jonni's sex life why don't you ask her? I'm sure she can give you a much better account of what I'm like in bed than I can."

"We don't talk about things like that in our family."

"But you're her mother."

She shook her head quickly. "No, I couldn't. I really couldn't. But it's still important." She took a quick puff of her Gauloise. "Did your mother talk to you about . . . you know, those things?"

"Sex? No. My mother and I have never discussed anything."

He looked at her thoughtfully. For the first time he realized that she must once have been a beautiful woman; beautiful in the way that Jonni was beautiful. He wondered what had happened to her over the years to give her such a shrewish, puritanical veneer.

"Does Jonquil like it when you make love to her?" Veronica asked, embarrassed but apparently resolute.

Michel looked down at the glowing end of his French cigarette. Jonni was still very young and her enjoyment of sex was still physically superficial. Plenty of the women he'd known hadn't discovered orgasms at all until they were in their thirties—he knew that for a fact because he'd enlightened a number of them himself. Jonni was disappointed with her orgasms, he knew she was. They were rarely, if ever, the thunderous explosions of sensation she'd been taught by the folklore to expect. But that would change as she grew older. Their sexual relationship wasn't perfect; of course not. No sexual relationship was perfect. His appetite exceeded hers tenfold for a start, which was frustrating for them both. And there was so much that couldn't be said—so many things neither of them would want to hear. How could Jonni understand the undiscriminating lust that drove the male psyche? Jonni wanted everything to come wrapped in tenderness and emotion and he simply didn't have that in him. She wanted soft words while they were making love and he couldn't give them to her—he couldn't give her any words at all during lovemaking except for a few four-letter ones. However, Michel wasn't about to relate these facts to her mother or to anyone else.

"Yes," he said, "she seems to like it."

Veronica stood up and took an onyx ashtray from the shelf above the fireplace, emptying the multicolored paper clips it held into her hand. She put the ashtray on the coffee table between them.

"There are things a man should know about—about physical intimacy, Mitchell. And so many of them are too selfish or too lazy to bother finding out. I don't say this applies to you. But my daughter's happiness is very important to me."

"Fire away, by all means."

"Well, it's not as easy as you young men imagine. It's not just a question of . . ." she made a tense gesture with the hand that held her cigarette, ". . . you know."

He frowned and shifted his position in the chair.

"No, I'm afraid you've lost me already. Not just a question of what?"

It took Jonni's mother several puffs on her Gauloise and more than one attempt to work herself up to the word.

"Penetration."

"Ah, yes—that." He didn't know where to look or how to stop himself smiling. He rested his cheek on his fist and nodded. "Yes, I do realize there's more to it than that."

"And many men don't know that there are alternatives to the missionary position."

Michel nodded again. Last night he and Jonni had made frantic love on their knees on the rug in her bedroom—mainly because the bedsprings squeaked, admittedly, but that was very tame compared to some of the things they got up to at home.

He decided it was time to put the woman out of her misery.

"Look, Veronica, I know you have reservations about me. I don't blame you at all. I'm not academic and that's an understatement. I have no financial security whatever; if I break my leg tomorrow God alone knows what we'll do for money. I'm no good with words. I'm not always very sensitive to what people are feeling. I can't cook and I'm hopeless at DIY—I can barely change a lightbulb without asking someone's advice. There are only two things I can do with any competence at all. But those two things I do extremely well."

Veronica looked at him gravely. There was the very faintest glimmer of humor in her eyes as she extinguished her cigarette.

"In that case, having seen you dance and having heard you speaking French with that young man outside the stage door, I'm afraid there's very little hope for my daughter's happiness."

Michel smiled. "Alright, maybe three things."

As soon as Michel and Jonni pulled away from the curb outside her parents' house, Jonni turned to him in horror.

"Michel, you were smoking in the house! I could smell that vile French tobacco all the way from the attic. You said you wouldn't!"

"Veronica and I were having a quiet cigarette together."

"Oh, don't be impossible," she groaned. "My mother wouldn't be caught dead smoking. I know you didn't like her but there's no need to be horrible."

"I adore her, Jon."

"Please don't be sarcastic. She does mean well."

"I'm not being sarcastic. Your mother's a giant amongst women. There's nothing she wouldn't do for you, including smoking two-thirds of a Gauloise."

"What were you two talking about in there?"

"Orgasms."

"No, seriously."

"And sexual positions."

"Michel, you can be very frustrating when you want to be. You were not discussing orgasms with my mother. So what were you talking about?"

"Flower arranging," he said, because otherwise she would nag him about it all the way to London. "Can you reach my sunglasses? They're on the backseat."

When Michel told Primo and Roly the story of his conversation with Veronica Kendal, Primo fell off the bench in the changing room and Roly laughed so much his back started hurting, making him squirm in agony and laugh all the more.

"I tell you," Michel said, shaking his head soberly and puffing out his cheeks, "when I heard that key turn and she asked me if I could make a woman come, I've never been so frightened in my life."

19

THE END OF FEBRUARY came with its annual company reshuffle pitching Charles Crown, as usual, into the depths of indecision and despair. The February board meeting where the dancers' contracts for the coming year were finalized never passed without heartache and hair-tearing but there was no help for it, new blood had to run in the company's veins. Without it the Islington Ballet would wither and die.

At the end of what was always the worst day of the year Crown sat in his office bowed over his desk with his forehead resting on the heel of his hand. He was sick of always having to be right. Everyone else in the company was allowed to make mistakes. Everyone else could be swayed by their feelings. Why couldn't someone else make the decisions for a change? Surely it was somebody else's turn to sit behind that desk and hand out the bad news. That afternoon he had told three of his five graduating apprentices that they were on their own; there was no contract for them at the Islington Ballet. The joy on the faces of the two he had decided to keep was no consolation for having broken three hopeful hearts. But worst of all had been breaking the news to six of the older dancers, some of his favorites among them, that their contracts were not to be renewed.

He sat up with a grunt as someone knocked on the door, and called out a curt summons with a cigarette clenched between his teeth.

"Oh, it's you." He flicked his ash. It was only Roly, not one of the interviews he was dreading. "Okay, have a seat." He hauled a file of contracts wearily from the drawer of his desk and started leafing through it. "I've had a real bugger of a day, son. It's the same every year: corps who think they're coryphées; coryphées who think they're soloists; soloists who think they're principals; and principals who think they're Margot fucking Fonteyn. Right, here you go." He pulled out a contract with Roly's name on it and handed it across the desk. "At least you won't complain. Promotion to soloist as I said. Christ knows, you deserve it." It was one of Crown's very few pleasant tasks in a dreadful, dreadful day. Roly had labored tirelessly for years for this promotion. "Now, you've doubtless heard rumors about this *Romeo and Juliet* we're making this summer. I think you're ready to create a major role. At the moment I'm planning to make Tybalt on you. Sound okay? And I'm not making any promises but it's going to be a long tour so I'm going to need four, maybe five Romeos."

Until this point Crown hadn't noticed that Roly was sitting silently staring at him across the desk. But now when there should have been an exclamation of ecstatic delight Crown looked at him with a frown. Roly's contract was still lying untouched in front of him. His expressionless blue eyes returned Crown's gaze for as long as they could before they fell slowly to the cluttered desktop between them.

"Come to think of it," Crown said, "where the fuck were you this morning?" He could have counted on one hand the number of times that Roly had failed to show up for class in the last seven years. Roly's face was unnaturally pale and his breathing was shallow and irregular. Crown looked down at something Roly was holding on his knee. "What's that you've got there?"

Roly passed him the large brown envelope.

"X-rays. I was at the hospital. It's a stress fracture."

"Christ, do you mean your shin? You're kidding, you ought to be too old for—what's this?" He had pulled one of the large X-rays out of the envelope and was staring at it.

"It's my spine."

"I can see it's your spine, son, I have that much knowledge of anatomy, but I thought you said you had a . . ." Crown slowed to a stop and his dark eyes rose from the brown-and-white image in his hand to look at Roly's face ". . . a stress fracture."

Roly reached over the desk and with an unsteady hand pointed to one of the thoracic vertebrae just below the base of the cervical region, averting his eyes as soon as he had located it. Crown looked and saw it: a jagged white line extending from the top of the vertebra diagonally through the bone almost to the bottom. However little he wanted to see it, it was unmistakable. He closed his eyes for a few seconds but the jagged white line wouldn't go away.

"How long have you known?"

Roly tried to moisten his lips but his tongue was too dry.

"This morning. But I've known something was wrong for a while."

"Did you talk to Karl about it?"

"No, I was afraid he'd stop me dancing. I didn't want to believe it was anything like this."

"I noticed you had back pain last year during the summer tour. Has it been hurting since then?"

"Yes."

They both fell silent. Crown stared down at the X-ray trying to juggle a hundred thoughts: the danger signs he should have seen, the grimaces of pain he had ignored because they looked like annoyance, the casting for *Romeo,* the treatment for a spinal fracture, the months ahead of Roly's absence, the great weight of muscular stress bearing down on that fracture during every lift.

Furious with himself, he stubbed out his cigarette and thumped himself on the forehead, gritting his teeth.

"Potter! Fucking Potter! Why didn't I use my brain?"

"It wasn't Annette's fault, Charles, or yours. If I'd been partnering a stronger girl it would have taken longer, that's all." Roly's rib cage was shaking. He was in shock. "It's a congenital weakness in the bone; the orthopedic surgeon told me. It was going to happen sooner or later anyway."

Crown nodded, accepting that grudgingly. "You okay? Want me to get you some water?"

"Maybe . . . yes, if you wouldn't mind."

Crown went out of the little room and came back with a glass of water. He sat down again and watched Roly's blank face while he sipped it.

"So what happens next? What treatment will they give you?"

"They want me to go into hospital on Monday to have some kind of screw put in. I should be in for about ten days. Then I'm in plaster from neck to waist for three to five months. Apparently they change the plaster about once a month so they can manipulate the other vertebrae in case they seize up—and so I can have a shower." He laughed at the ghastly humor of that. "The surgeon assured me the pain gets a lot worse. They've given me morphine."

"How long will it be, do they think, before you can dance again?"

"Um,"—he took another sip of water—"they said I'll be able to do some of the barre as soon as the plaster's off. But it doesn't make any difference. I can never lift a woman above shoulder height again. They said if I put that kind of repeated strain on the vertebra, even after it's healed, I'll risk paralyzing myself for life." He tried to smile as tears sprang into his blue eyes. "I'm through, Charles. A boy who can't lift is no good to you or to any ballet company."

Crown kept his own face under control. He reached for another cigarette and lit it, exhaling the first stream of smoke sharply.

"Right. First we'll talk to Karl, then we'll get you straight to Harley Street for a second opinion."

"I've been to Harley Street for a second opinion. That's where I was this afternoon."

"Can I keep these X-rays? I want to talk this over with Karl anyway."

"Yes, they're copies. But I'm afraid these people know what they're talking about. I'll have plenty of time while I'm flat on my back to think about what I'm going to do."

Crown looked fiercely into Roly's eyes, at the wretchedness they were trying so bravely to hide. Crown's instinct was to fight, but that wasn't the help those blue eyes were asking him for now. Crown sat slowly back in his chair and nodded with reluctance.

"Alright. You'll let me know what I can do to help."

"Oh God, you've done enough already. All your teaching and encouragement and patience for all these years. Thanks for taking a chance on me, Charles. It's meant a lot to me." He looked down at his hand on his lap. "Actually there is one thing. Will you let me do classes with the company occasionally once I'm back on my feet? I won't be able to afford to go to public classes."

Crown laughed. It was a bitter laugh, and God knows he felt bitter enough. "There'll always be a place for you at the barre in any class where I'm in charge, that's a promise. And don't panic about money. You can claim for compensation while you're laid up. Your current contract expires with your next paycheck; we'll sort something out with the insurance company before then—Christ, that reminds me, I'd better call St. Michel and tell him he's dancing Siegfried tomorrow night."

Crown was already reaching for the telephone but Roly caught his arm, stopping him.

"Don't, Charles! Just tomorrow. Please."

The artistic director looked at him, appalled.

"You can't! Even if I wanted to, it would be total negligence to let you."

Roly's hand was still on Crown's arm. The pale blue eyes never left his face. "Please, Charles."

"You've got a fucking fractured spine!"

"Lynne doesn't weigh a thing and I've been doing it for months with a fractured spine. One more won't make any difference. And if it did, it would be worth it."

"I can't allow it."

"Charles, don't stop me doing it!" His tone was desperate. "I've got nothing else left to lose!"

Those were dreadful words coming from a man of twenty-three. For the first time in years Crown found himself unable to meet the eye of one of his dancers. He closed his eyes and rubbed them slowly while he tried to think. All those years of determined work and patience, all that sacrifice and pain, all that hard-earned technique—all now worth so little that Roly only asked for one last performance in return.

"Alright, you've got it."

Roly stood up immediately.

"Thanks." At the door he stopped. "Charles, there's one more thing. There's bound to be talk in the company once this gets out. I won't be around to make sure the story comes out straight. Will you make it clear this injury's no one's fault but my own?"

"You mean Annette?"

"I'd try explaining it to her myself but I doubt she'd listen. We don't get on—but then you already know that." He screwed up his face in miserable self-disgust. "I hit her once, can you believe that? Jesus, what a crummy thing to do."

When Roly had gone Crown walked to the wall of his office and struck his forehead repeatedly against it.

"Fuck!" he shouted. "Fuck! Fuck! Fuck!"

It had been a terrible day.

Crown was more than twice Roly's age but he hadn't learned to cope with the spectacle of despair.

He phoned down to the physio's room and summoned Karl Redman up to his office. He only just caught him in time; Karl was on his way home.

"What do you think of Roland Kovak?" Crown asked as Karl closed the door.

"Roly? I think the world of him, Charles, same as you do. If I had to choose a favorite out of the—"

"I'm talking about his body!" Crown spat.

"Ah, yes." Karl sat down uninvited and unbuttoned his overcoat. "Actually, I've been meaning to talk to you about him for a while. I'm not sure his back's as strong as it should be."

Crown couldn't find a suitable reply. He tossed the envelope containing Roly's X-rays across the desk.

"Take a look," he said. And then he held up his hand like a policeman stopping the traffic. "No, don't. Get out of my office and then look. I don't want to see the expression on your face when you see what's in there."

Roly left Crown's office without any thought in his head except that he needed to be alone. Despite the words of the doctors and the evidence of the X-rays and the searing pain in his back, none of it had become true until he had seen his own disbelief mirrored in Charles Crown's stricken black eyes.

The building was almost deserted. Contract day was always a strange, tense day at the Islington Ballet. He passed the company manager,

Adrian, on the stairs and they exchanged a few murmured words of greeting. Roly had been passing Adrian on the stairs and in the corridors for more than seven years.

He sat on a bench in the changing room, rotating his neck slowly. His mind was numb. The few thoughts that came flying toward him—Who would partner Annette now? Would the insurance cover his rent until he was fit to find work?—he fielded deftly and threw away again. He didn't want to think.

One thought, however, did find its way in. He jumped to his feet and grabbed his jacket from its peg even before the idea had fully registered. He was wrong about needing to be alone. What he needed was to be with his friends.

Coming out of the tube station at Pimlico he lengthened his stride, quickening his pace. The knife between his shoulder blades twisted cruelly as he pressed the doorbell outside the Warwick Way house and ran up the stairs to the fourth floor. Roly ignored the physical pain; he was used to it. When he reached the top landing Jonni was waiting for him, her hand on the open door and her eyes full of frightened misery.

"I'm so glad you're here," she squealed, desperate. "We can't do anything. I didn't know if you'd heard."

His face clouded in confusion and he laid his hand on her waist.

"Heard what, chicken?"

There was a crash in the studio—the destructive peal of breaking glass—accompanied by a howl. Roly turned his head.

"About Primo: Charles hasn't given him a contract for next year."

"Oh Jesus."

He moved her quickly aside and hurried into the flat. Primo was out of control, screaming and hitting out at everything in violent rage. He picked up a half-empty mug, hurling it at the wall, and slammed down the lid of the piano with such force that the strings of the instrument rang out a discordant hum in protest. Michel followed close behind him, reasoning with him, trying to calm him, but he didn't touch him. It was left to Roly to sprint across the studio and grab Primo by the collar, dragging him forcibly away from the stereo before he could destroy it. Primo struggled like a wild animal, lashing out at him with his fists and yelling obscenities, but Roly was the stronger of the two and in a very few seconds Primo was out of the reach of temptation, flying backward into the corner of one of the sofas.

"Get a grip on yourself!" Roly cried, standing over him, arms and hands braced, ready to seize him if he leaped up again.

Primo covered his head with his arms and howled.

"Fucking traitor! He thinks I ain't got no future; he don't know shit! I ain't going to let him destroy me. I'll get a contract somewhere else. I'll go to Germany! Ain't no one can tell me I ain't a dancer!"

"Of course you're a dancer," Roly said. He and Michel exchanged grim looks. The chance of Primo finding a contract outside the Islington was slim, even in a German company. Primo's classical technique would never stand up in an audition. And even if he did find a company that would take him, Germany was a bleak prospect. The provincial companies that might take Primo only used their boys as porters to carry the girls around. The intelligence and charisma which had kept Primo in the Islington until now would be wasted on an endless round of antiquated court ballets.

"Charles has got him a real sadistic streak," Primo growled savagely. "You should have seen the glint in the bastard's eye when he sat there watching me squirm—watching my whole life come crashing down round my ears and he don't say a word. And then!"—he appealed to Roly with outraged eyes—"then he offers me a contract as a fucking pianist! Insult on top of fuckin' injury! I tell you that man gets a big fuckin' hard-on shoving people's noses in the dirt."

"No, he doesn't," Roly said. "He isn't like that. Just take it easy, Primo. Things'll work out okay."

"What the fuck do you know about it? You ever had someone tell you your life's over—finish—just like that? You got made soloist—yeah, I heard!—so there ain't no way you can understand how I feel. So just shut up!"

"Yes, shut up," Michel agreed helplessly.

Jonni sat on the sofa and put her arms around Primo's neck, resting her cheek against his disheveled black hair and blinking away her tears of sympathy.

"Yes, Roly, do be quiet."

Roly sat down silently on the sofa opposite Primo and watched him knock back the stiff drink Michel handed to him and light a cigarette with a trembling hand. The shattering of Primo's dreams had a tragic irony to it. Roly had never known anyone who wanted something so desperately and yet was prepared to do so little to achieve it—and was so little suited to his goal. But Primo had stubbornly refused to accept the truth although it stared him in the face every time he looked in the mirror. Primo was probably the only one among them who hadn't known this was coming. Roly put his hand over his face. Was he not equally unsuited himself? Had he not had to struggle endlessly for every ounce of the technique that sat so naturally on Michel's adept body? Perhaps he too should have seen the writing on the wall. He pitied Primo deeply.

Michel stood uneasily beside the sofa watching Primo as he sat slumped in desolation. Michel hated emotional scenes; his instinct was to walk away from them or to ignore them. But for once he stretched out his hand and rested it cautiously on his friend's shoulder to comfort him. Primo flung his hand off with a violent swipe, springing enraged to his feet.

"Get your fuckin' hands off me, Michel! You ain't got to pollute your precious skin touching a filthy queer like me!"

Neither Roly nor Jonni had ever heard Primo speak like that to Michel whom he so passionately loved. And judging by his expression, neither had Michel. He took a quick step backward, recoiling from Primo's anger.

"Don't do that to me," he said, shocked into betraying the slight French accent he generally kept so well hidden. "What have I done?"

"You ain't done nothing!" Primo cried. "Go back to your great teacher who thinks the sun shines out of your eyes! Go back to the girls who wait outside the stage door for you every night! I know what drives you, Michel. I know how come you ain't got time for nothing in your life but dancing. It's the only thing you got to fill up the terrible silence in there!" He jabbed his finger against Michel's chest, over his heart.

Jonni clapped her hands over her ears as Michel turned away.

There was nothing more the friends could do for Primo. He had shut himself up in the isolation of his despair and he wouldn't let anyone near him. For almost an hour Roly, Jonni, and Michel sat in the studio avoiding each other's eyes while Primo played furious scales of chords on the piano, his fingers flying up and down the keyboard thundering out increasingly rapid chromatic scales. Up and down, up and down, hammering the keys as though he would bash the piano to pieces in his rage, his steel-strong fingers never missing a note. The studio was flooded with such dense sound that Roly could feel it on his skin.

That was a bitter, cheerless evening in the flat. There was no comfort for Primo, none for Roly, none for poor Jonni who was entirely bewildered at seeing the people she loved hurt each other. And no comfort for Michel because he had none to give. But the evening's trail of destruction was not yet complete.

No one heard the front door closing over the noise of the piano. The first thing that drew Roly's gaze away from his knee was a sudden ringing silence as Primo's hands froze over the keyboard in mid-scale. The studio was still buzzing with dying harmonics. One look at the frightened, ghastly expression on Annette's face told the whole story. She took two trembling steps into the studio and stood quite still, staring stricken at Michel.

Roly lowered his eyes. He couldn't be the one to break the silence. He had been afraid of this for many months. Her weight, her lack of discipline in rehearsals, her frequent absences from class, and most of all the growing impatience with which Crown tolerated her behavior, had all warned him there was a distinct possibility he might not be partnering her much longer. But what could Roly have said that he hadn't already been saying for years? Even if there had been something new to say, she wouldn't have listened if it came from him.

It was Primo who broke the silence.

"Well, I hope Charles is fucking satisfied."

Annette seemed to try to speak but a great gasp caught her unawares and she choked on her words. Her round eyes widened in puzzled surprise as the gasp was succeeded by a second heaving gasp, convulsing her chest and stiffening her shoulders.

Michel was already on his feet: "Nettie, love, are you okay?"

Annette could only clutch her chest in alarm as she gasped. Her breast heaved under her hands, rising and falling rapidly as fear filled up her eyes. Roly turned his head away. The pathetic sight of her uncontrolled gasping was more than he could stand. He had no role to play in this wretched scene.

"Roly?"

He turned his head back again when he heard Michel say his name. Annette's wild arms were pushing Michel away, fending him off while she flapped her hands toward Roly in urgent supplication.

When he got up from the sofa and went to her, she seized the front of his sweatshirt with both hands, plunging her face against his shoulder while she gasped frantically for breath.

"Has anyone ever seen her like this before?" Roly asked.

Michel, Primo, and Jonni exchanged quick glances, shaking their heads. No, they never had.

"Anyone know if she's asthmatic?"

Another exchange of glances. No, they didn't think so.

"Nettie, are you asthmatic?" She was strong in her terror; Roly had to use considerable force to prize her head from his shoulder to look into her petrified eyes. "Nod if you're asthmatic. Nod, you understand?"

It was a vast effort for her to muster even that much self-control, so violently was her body shaken by her convulsive gasps, but eventually she managed to shake her head.

Primo was still sitting on the piano stool. He folded his arms with a sardonic grunt. "Perhaps you should smack her again, amico. It worked last time."

Annette's eyes grew even rounder.

"I'm not going to hit you," Roly said. "Primo was joking." He put his arm around her and laid her head back on his shoulder, giving Primo a sharp look. "You just hold on to me; you're going to be okay."

It seemed to take forever for Annette's piteous gasping to subside. Roly held her calmly, moving corkscrew curls of dark hair slowly away from her face with his hand. One obstinate curl kept falling down over her eyes and each time it fell he lifted it away.

When at last her breathing was peaceful and silent, Annette let go of Roly's sweatshirt and took a small step backward. She turned her head to look up at the clock above the studio door, smiled sweetly at Michel, and then collapsed unconscious in Roly's arms.

"Oh, God," Jonni said. "Should we call an ambulance?"

"No, it's okay." Roly put an arm under Annette's knees to lift her. "She just hyperventilated. She'll come round in a minute. Make her a cup of tea, would you, and put loads of sugar in it?"

As he laid Annette on the nearest sofa Primo stood up and took his jumper from the top of the piano. He pulled it on over his head with a derisive growl.

"Is a pity Charles missed that little scene. He'd have really got off on it."

Michel looked at him. "Where are you going?"

"To get pissed: where d'you think?"

"There's brandy here and what's left of the Scotch you opened at the weekend in the kitchen. Or wine if you prefer it."

"Yes, please stay," Jonni pleaded. "Surely you should all stick together tonight."

Primo was checking his pockets for his wallet and front-door key.

"Together is history, bella. It don't mean nothing for us no more. I'd rather drink my own booze, thanks. Michel's don't leave such a good taste in my mouth." He halted by the door and looked back at Michel. "You better watch your arse these next few days, amico. They say bad things come in threes."

Michel clicked his tongue in exasperation and shook his head. Once Primo had gone he sank wearily onto a sofa and lit a cigarette.

"Plonker," he said, tossing his lighter onto the coffee table.

Roly stretched his shoulders with a sigh to loosen them. If it was true that troubles came three at a time he knew Michel was out of danger. But this was far from the moment to bring up his own misfortune. He was leaning over Annette, his hand resting on the back of the sofa and his knee wedged beside her prone body, watching for the first sign of her recovery. When she had passed out he had unbuttoned her blouse without hesitation to unhook her bra. Now he buttoned it back up again with a wistful smile; once she came to she was more than likely to bite his head off for having touched her.

When, finally, Annette did open her eyes she certainly seemed surprised to find Roly's blue eyes looking gravely down at her.

"Oh, hello. What happened?"

"You blacked out. You had some kind of panic attack."

Her eyes registered a flickering memory of the trouble that had sent her into hysteria, misery filling her round green eyes.

"Charles sacked me."

"Yes, love, I know."

She turned her head with a frown to see who else was in the room.

"I don't remember falling down. Did you pick me up and carry me here?"

"No, you didn't fall. I was holding you."

She smiled painfully at that. "That's right. You never did drop me, after all, did you?" Her face creased up. "I wish you had. Then I could have blamed you."

"Annette, that's a fucking monstrous thing to say!"

She made a sudden movement and, for a moment, he thought she was going to lash out at him—he wouldn't have cared if she had—but instead she flung her arms around his neck and clung to him in terror. "What am I going to do? No one will give me a contract, not with my height. And I can't do anything but dance."

"Of course you can: you can do anything you want to." He held her tightly, resting his cheek against hers. "There are a thousand things a beautiful, intelligent girl like you can do."

"Will you teach me to tap?"

He screwed up his face in sympathetic pain as she burst into tears.

"God, no, not tap; not for you. You'll find something much better than that. Please don't cry, Nettie," he said, tightening his arms around her, "it's not like you to cry. Your life—our lives are just beginning. There are other things as good as ballet, there must be."

His mouth found hers and he tentatively kissed her tears away, waiting for a rebuff. But Annette's lips softened submissively under his and they disappeared into the embrace which had been waiting for them both since they had first started dancing together nearly seven years ago.

Michel went out to the kitchen to find Jonni.

"I wouldn't worry about the tea, Jons. Those two are making up for lost time in there."

———

Later, Michel sat in the studio with his arm around Jonni, while Roly and Annette were buried in each other on the other sofa oblivious to everything and everyone around them. The sight of that particular pair kissing so enthusiastically was more extraordinary than anything else this day of surprises had brought. The events of the evening had left Michel dazed. All he wanted was to go to bed. But Primo would come back before the night was over; he knew that for certain.

Michel didn't feel he had any right to an opinion about what was going on between Annette and Roly. Over the years, he had seen Annette snap up scores of men, chew them, and then spit them out again, usually in several pieces. He only hoped they both knew what they were doing.

One opinion, however, was entirely within his right. Whatever Roly's hands were up to under Annette's clothes it was becoming altogether too fruity for public display, even amongst friends. He leaned over and kicked Roly gently with his foot.

"Hey, you two! Take that into the bedroom, will you?"

Roly sat up, willing enough, but Annette wriggled out from beneath him and pulled down her skirt defensively.

"No, really—I don't want to."

"Don't you?" Roly asked despairing.

"I'm not ready. I need some time."

Roly collapsed facedown on the cushions groaning. Michel laughed aloud and even Jonni had to smile.

Annette buttoned up her blouse demurely.

"Will you walk me home?"

"Yeah, alright," he moaned from the cushions. "But you'll have to wait a few minutes."

By the time Primo showed up at the flat Jonni was asleep in bed and Michel was sitting alone in the studio sipping the same drink that had been on the table in front of him for the past hour.

Primo was so drunk he could hardly walk. He lit the wrong end of a cigarette and threw it away, taking another from the packet.

"You know what, amico?" He propped his back against the barre and waved his cigarette shrewdly at Michel. "You know what? I wish I knew what it's like to be Michel. Only for a day. Or an hour." He thought for a while. "Or a minute. It must be wonderful to be Michel."

"It's not so special," Michel said.

"Sure it is. You're a great guy, amico. Everybody loves Michel. Charles loves Michel 'cos he's the best dancer he ever got his hands on. All the girls love Michel. Every dancer in the company loves Michel. The audience loves Michel. The whole fucking world loves Michel! And you know what?" He put his finger confidentially to his lips. "I'm gonna tell you a big secret."

"What's that?"

"Everybody loves Michel. But Michel, he don't love nobody. He don't love the audiences who stand up and cheer his Siegfried. He don't love his sweet little wife. He don't love his friends or his dancing partner. He don't love his mamma. He don't love me. An' you know what's the worst of all? I don't even think he loves Michel."

Primo fell silent, his eyes downcast and sorrowful as he tried to smoke his cigarette. After a couple of minutes Michel stood up and took it from him, putting it out in an ashtray.

"Come on, Primo. We've got class in the morning."

Primo fell over the arm of a sofa, crashing facedown onto the cushions with his feet sticking out over the end.

"I ain't going to class, amico. I got a hangover."

Within seconds Primo was asleep. Michel watched him for a while and then picked up his own jacket from the back of the sofa and laid it carefully over Primo's sleeping arms and shoulders. Then he turned off the light and went to bed.

20

BUT PRIMO DID GO TO CLASS in the morning.

Charles Crown sat in front of the mirrored wall in the main studio watching Marina's class with sober eyes. The whole company was tense with the changes of yesterday's contract announcements; some stricken at the loss of friends, some grudging, feeling hard done by, some elated at their own promotion and struggling not to let their jubilation show. Crown watched them all, his hand gravely covering his mouth, reading and understanding the expressions on all those faces he knew so well.

Primo was rigid with anger. He threw himself into every exercise with murderous aggression, his limbs thrashing in rage. Every sweep of his hand was a tug on a noose. Every battement was a kick to someone's head. Of the six dancers whose contracts weren't to be renewed only Primo and Annette had showed up this morning. Annette was dancing listlessly at the barre behind Roly, scarcely even bothering to lift her feet from the floor on the développés. She had simply given up.

When the company turned at the barres so Annette was no longer behind Roly but in front of him, she lengthened her spine and held up her head, uncoiling her long leg in the air with careful precision. Crown's eyes narrowed in interest as he watched her. So she had turned up to support Roly, had she? That was something new. He shook his head slowly. It was too late for her to start pulling up her muscles for him now. She should have thought of that a long time ago.

Crown couldn't bear to watch Roly stretching his broken back with such immense courage in every arabesque and balance. He turned his head away, sick at heart, to watch the hash the rest of the company were making of Marina's adage. Even Lynne was slack today, which wasn't funny as she was dancing Odette-Odile tonight. Only Michel was on form, working his way through each exercise with his usual focus and discipline.

In the second half of the class, when the dancers moved from the barres into the center, Primo hurled himself into the exercises with such abandoned violence and wildness that Crown stood up after the first exercise, stopping Marina with a raised hand.

"Primo, cool it." He walked over to Primo and held up his forefinger firmly and warningly in front of his face. "What you are doing is dangerous, Primo. Cool it!"

Primo glared at him with hatred.

"Don' you fuckin' talk to me!" he spat, enraged. "Don' you ever fuckin' talk to me, you Hitler!"

On another day Primo would have felt the back of Crown's hand for a retort like that, but today Crown just shook his head, cautioning him with his eyes, and walked back to his chair at the front of the studio. He nodded to Marina to continue with the class.

"If he scares you kick him out."

"You try it!" Primo yelled. "You kick me out of class an' I'll have the fuckin' union all over you! I got a contract says I'm entitled to be here!"

Crown and Marina looked at each other with raised eyebrows. Even Carlotta in her queeniest fits had never dared threaten Crown with the union.

That night the Islington Ballet was booked to perform *Swan Lake* at the Churchill Theatre in Bromley.

In the claustrophobic underground corridor, Crown stopped outside Lynne's dressing room door just as the half-hour call was broadcast over the backstage speakers. He tapped his fist thoughtfully against his mouth for a few seconds and then knocked and walked in.

The small dressing room was cozy but depressingly windowless. Crown nodded to Selina, the soloist who was sharing the double room, and then looked at Lynne's reflection in the dressing table mirror.

"Are you ready, darling?"

Lynne was in a green satin kimono, stuffing her toe blocks with scrunched-up toilet paper. Four pairs of pointe shoes were already spread on the dressing table in front of her. As always, before a performance, the atmosphere in the dressing room was thick with nervous tension.

"Of course I'm ready."

"You're okay about doing this with Roly?"

Lynne frowned in surprise: "Yes, of course."

He ran his hand anxiously over the top of his head. She didn't know; Roly hadn't told her. Crown already regretted his decision to let Roly dance this last Siegfried. The risk to Lynne was as great as the risk to Roly, and he had the company's reputation to think of too. A disastrous performance so near London was something the Islington could ill afford.

But there was nothing Crown could do to stop it now. He sighed in frustration. He supposed Roly's instinct was right: there was no point telling Lynne, it would only terrify her. Even if he told her now and gave her the choice, she wouldn't refuse to go on. How could she do that to her friend? It was best she didn't know, even if it was unethical.

"Look, darling," he said, "I know you're angry with me about Primo and Annette but you have to put that out of your mind tonight. You've got to focus on this performance."

She looked up from her shoes, meeting his eye in the mirror.

"I know that, Charles."

"Lynne, listen . . ." He glanced at Selina. "Darling, can you give us a minute?"

Selina bridled at being asked to leave her own dressing room during the half hour before the curtain. But one indignant look at her volatile boss's face warned her this wasn't the moment to cross him. She got up from her dressing table and stomped out of the room with a peeved sniff.

Crown paced the narrow room a couple of times and then stopped behind Lynne's chair, frowning at her reflection.

"Lynne, you're a strong, consistent dancer but there's something not right at the moment. These past few weeks your performances have been down. Your heart isn't in it."

"Yes, it is."

"No. Even if you can't feel the difference, I can see it. Whatever it is that's weighing you down it's skimmed the edge off your technique.

Look, I'm not having a go and I'm not asking any questions." He was all too aware that her technical discipline had slackened since Michel's engagement and deteriorated with his marriage. "I'm just asking you to put it behind you, whatever it is, and pull something special out of the bag for me, only for tonight if necessary."

"What's so special about tonight?"

He shook his head, looking intently into her hazel eyes.

"You trust me and so I don't have to answer that. But it's important. I want you to go out there, pull up for all you're worth, and shine like I know you can. Just imagine you're on the stage of the Coli dancing for the Queen."

"With Roly?" she asked dryly, despite the fact he was one of her closest friends.

"Yes. With Roly."

Lynne wasn't a stroppy dancer; she was mild and obedient. But neither was she the shy wallflower she had been during her apprenticeship.

"Look, Charles." Her eyes complained to him in the mirror, and not without justification. "This isn't the moment, okay? Don't come into my dressing room at the half putting pressure on me like this. I don't need this from you right now."

"Yes, you do. Tonight that is exactly what you need from me. Or you're going to look back on this performance and you're going to hate me for not saying what I'm saying to you now. Believe me, Lynne, this has to be a special one."

Lynne looked at him steadily for a while.

"Okay."

"Good girl." He pointed at Selina, who had come back in just in time to hear the end of his lecture. "That goes for the rest of you too. I want total concentration tonight." On his way to the door he said to Lynne, "You haven't asked me about next year, darling. Catch me later or after class in the morning. You won't be disappointed."

As he walked away down the corridor he heard Selina slip out of the room behind him and whisper to the girls' corps through their open dressing room door. Within five minutes the whole company would be buzzing with the rumor that there was someone very big out front tonight.

"Like, duckies, I'm talking ginormous! You should have seen the old bugger's face."

Crown nodded to himself. It didn't matter why the company pulled themselves together tonight just so long as they did. They wouldn't say anything to Roly; they all knew Roly was a bundle of nerves before a performance, especially something as huge and technically horrific as Siegfried.

Three doors down the corridor from Lynne, Roly was carefully gluing the heels of his ballet shoes to his feet with spirit gum. Michel watched him out of the corner of his eye while he put on his makeup. Roly had been very strange since he arrived at the theater this evening: withdrawn, unsmiling—he hadn't spoken a word either to Michel or to the dresser who came to hook him into his tunic. And, stranger still, there was no sign of his usual pre-show nerves.

Michel dried his mouth with his towel and reached for his carmine lip color, keeping a puzzled eye on Roly's uncommunicative face in the mirror.

"I hear we've got Dominic in the pit tonight," he said. "That's good news."

"Yep."

There was another silence while Michel made up his mouth.

"So . . . ah . . ." He wiped the carmine from the corners of his mouth with his fingers. "you get laid last night then, Roly?"

"Nope."

Michel nodded.

"Right. Nettie okay, is she? Poor babe, it's a tough break for her."

"She had it coming."

Michel turned his head to look at him in astonishment. Roly's blue eyes, as he leaned toward the mirror to draw brown lines beneath them with an eye pencil, were cold and expressionless. A long, strange silence descended in the dressing room while the two men completed their makeup.

"Bit stuffy in here," Michel said after a while, standing up. "Mind if I open the door?"

"I'd rather you didn't."

"No problem." He sat down again. "You know, Roly, Primo's not good. Marina won't have him onstage. I left him at home trying to bash a hole in the Steinway's keyboard."

"Best place for him. Serves him right."

"That's a bit harsh, isn't it? I mean he's just been—"

"Look, Michel," Roly said abruptly, "is it absolutely necessary for you to keep talking? Can't you possibly just shut the fuck up?"

"Yes," Michel said, reaching very slowly for his shoes. "Yes, it's not necessary at all. Sorry."

Michel laced up his soft ballet boots, mystified. Twice he saw Roly take a brown bottle from his bag beside his chair, and twice he saw him turn it over in his hand and fling it angrily back into his bag unopened.

"You okay?" he asked him cautiously.

"Yup."

Michel was dancing in the Act One ensembles and pas de trois that evening. The dancers loved performing Crown's joyous reworking of Siegfried's birthday party: the wild ensemble piece that was already in full swing when the curtain rose; the flying circular waltz with its great leaps and unison lifts; the huge folk dance which invariably degenerated into a contest between the boys to see who could pinch the most girls' bottoms. The staging was so informal that it wasn't at all rare for one of the girls to stop mid-dance and clout one of the boys around the head. Today the company were discussing Roly while they danced; Michel wasn't the only one who had noticed his strange mood.

"No, he's fine," Michel said, picking one of the girls up with his arm around her waist and spinning her round. Like all dancers Michel had got the knack of speaking without moving his lips down to a fine art. "He's just tired. Didn't sleep well."

At the front of the stage Roly was smiling and flirting with the girls. He seemed to be holding his own. He even stole a kiss from one or two of the peasants when the queen wasn't looking.

During the second act, while Roly was onstage with Lynne and the girls, Michel had the dressing room to himself. He wasn't on again until the Spanish duet near the end of the ballet. He sat with his feet up comfortably on the edge of the dressing table, his hand resting idle on his groin, drinking mineral water from a plastic bottle and thinking about Primo's inconsolable despair.

He looked up quickly at the Tannoy as the stage manager's voice cut into the familiar orchestral music. "Mister St. Michel to the prompt corner immediately."

Michel jumped to his feet and seized a tunic from the rail and a pair of ballet shoes, sprinting out of the dressing room. When you heard the word "immediately" during a performance you didn't stop to think. Marina was waiting for him at the prompt desk in the wings.

"What is it?" Michel asked, already half into his tunic.

She laid her hand on his arm.

"Don't panic, pet; I just wanted you to see this."

"Is Roly alright?"

"Look!"

Michel ducked his head to see past the lanterns on a scaffolding stand between the flats. His mouth opened slowly as he looked at the stage. Roly was more than alright. He was flying. Beautiful arabesques. Soaring jetés. Every sweep and turn of his body magnificent. He was a different dancer. His emotion and fluidity as he swept Lynne smoothly into his arms and tossed her spinning into the air catching her above his head made Michel's cheeks turn cold.

"My God," he whispered, stunned, to himself and to Marina. "My God, he's got it. He's really got it."

Around him the girls' corps in their white feathery basques were jostling into position between the lantern stands for their final entrance. Michel just stood and stared.

He had never seen such a transformation. Roly's dancing had always been so restrained, so bound, as though a hand were holding him back, stopping him from letting himself go. And suddenly here he was, dancing like a god. And Lynne, coiling like a soft reed in Roly's powerful arms, was a goddess.

Marina wiped the tears from her face with the heel of her hand.

"It's fucking heartbreaking," she growled in a furious baritone. "I hate this fucking profession, I hate it!"

In the back of the hushed auditorium Charles Crown watched the transcendent swan song of the young man who had nothing left to lose with his hands half covering his eyes, unable either to look or not to look. There at last was the flow and beauty of expression that Roly had been fighting for all these years. There was the dancer Roly had always had inside him. It was stomach-turning.

In the interval Roly was as taciturn as he had been before the show.

He sat silently in front of the mirror retouching his sweat-smudged makeup with hard, angry eyes. Neither he nor Michel spoke a word to each other.

Crown popped into the dressing room at the five-minute call, nodding approvingly with downturned mouth, avoiding both men's eyes.

"It's going fine. Don't slacken the second half."

He turned to leave but Roly stopped him. "Charles?" He reached into his bag for the brown bottle. "Do me a favor: stick this somewhere out of my reach till after the curtain, will you? Somewhere no idiot can take a swig."

Crown took the bottle from him and looked down at it in his hand.

"Yes. I'd probably better." He raised his anxious eyes to Roly's face. "Look . . . Roland, son . . ."

"What?" Roly demanded, flaring. He rounded on him with his blue eyes flashing fiercely.

"Nothing," Crown muttered, and he went away.

Michel touched up his eyeliner with raised eyebrows, whistling a tune very quietly to himself.

Roly danced the last two acts as beautifully as he had danced the first two.

In the dressing room, once the show had ended to enthusiastic applause, Michel pulled off his Spanish tunic with a jubilant laugh.

"I don't know what in hell's up with you today, but I'll tell you one thing: that was one serious bloody performance. I knew it, I could feel you were on the verge of a breakthrough. This is it, Roly; you're on your way—Albrecht, *Romeo, Manon, Nutcracker, Don Q;* you're ready to dance them all!"

Roly was sitting at the dressing table looking sadly into the mirror. His eyes were Roly's familiar gentle eyes again. The brown bottle was open in front of him.

"You dance them for me, Shel," he said quietly.

Michel's smile faded. He looked at him in silence. As Roly sat there a large tear welled up on his mascara-coated lashes and spilled over to slide down his cheek, plowing a furrow through his makeup. He looked at the ceiling, screwing up his face in an effort to stop others following it, but a second tear swelled on his lashes and coursed down the side of his nose.

After watching him cry for some seconds Michel picked up the bottle and read the label: morphine. Then he turned the lock on the door and sat down, leaning back in his chair with his knees spread wide, his fingertips tapping against his lower lip.

In the seven years in which they'd spent almost every day together, Michel had never once seen Roly cry. Like everyone else he had always taken Roly's strength for granted. Watching him now hide his face in his folded arms and weep, Michel felt helpless. He tried to make himself speak to Roly or touch him but he didn't know how. Michel himself hadn't shed a tear since he was nine years old. All he could do was sit and watch and tap his fingers against his mouth.

There was a knock on the door.

"Go away!" Michel called.

A minute later their dresser knocked, calling out to them, "It's me; let me in!"

"Leave the costumes out there, darling! I'll bring the washing to wardrobe before I go!"

The longer Roly cried the more frustrated Michel grew at his own inability to do or say anything. At last Roly dried his eyes on a towel, swallowed a mouthful of morphine, raised his eyebrows with a sniff, and told Michel what the doctors had said.

Michel chewed the inside of his mouth as he listened.

"No way at all?" he asked when Roly had told him everything. "Not even if you wait . . . five years?"

"No, I'm finished, Shel. I'll never lift a woman again." He got up slowly from his chair, his eyes puffy from crying, and flexed his aching spine inside his heavy tunic. "Get me out of this, will you?"

Michel stood behind him, unhooking the row of fasteners down his back.

"Does Nettie know?"

"Yeah. Bawled her eyes out when I told her, bless her. Don't worry, Shel, I'm okay. It was the physical pain as much as anything else. That was a tough pull out there for me tonight. God, was I angry. But, oh boy, it felt great to be dancing and not be afraid." He folded his hands on top of his head while Michel unhooked him, smiling wearily at Michel's reflection in the mirror. "Good time to discover that, eh?"

"Not the best," Michel said.

"In fact it's really quite funny when you think about it. Do you realize, until tonight, I've never danced a single step, on- or offstage, without being terrified of injuring myself?"

Michel nodded. He realized it. But he couldn't see the funny side.

"And I'm glad I did that bloody painful show tonight. It's made me see what a good thing it is my back's packed up now while I'm still young enough to start again."

"It's not a good thing," Michel said. "It's an injustice and a terrible waste."

"Yes, it is a good thing. It hurts, of course it does: it hurts like hell. I loved ballet and I wanted it—Jesus!—so badly. And I've worked so damn hard. But the truth is I would always have been afraid, Shel. Always."

Michel turned away to hang up Roly's tunic on the rail. He was glad Roly couldn't see his face.

"What are you going to do?"

"Get my back down: get it fixed; that's my first priority. And once I'm on my feet again I'll pull myself together and start building myself a new career. I'm only twenty-three. I've got my whole life ahead of me."

"What career, do you know yet?"

Roly splayed his hands out and executed a cute little soft-shoe shuffle on the carpet in his ballet shoes like a gawky child doing a tap routine. He spread his hands in a shrug of resignation.

"It's what I always did best. It goes to show you can't blow against the wind."

Michel stopped himself from wincing at the thought of Roly going back to tap: at the thought of the beauty and skill he'd only seen properly for the first time tonight doing the rounds of Butlins and ocean liners in sequined waistcoats and top hats and tails. But whatever Roly did, he'd still be Roly. Nothing would ever take away his optimism or his zest for life. Michel pulled off his black T-shirt and sat down to remove his make-up. He was going to be very lonely without Roly.

"The company will miss you," he said.

Roly's smile was bleak as he slipped his elastic braces off his shoulders and peeled off his white principal boy's tights for the last time. He knew his name would become a pariah in the company: an evil omen. For a fortnight the dancers would talk about nothing else, and then they would never mention him again. Dancers lived with their heads in the clouds. Theirs was a world of beautiful make-believe and deep-hidden fear. No one wanted to remember failures and career-terminating injuries.

"Yep," he said, "of course they will, and I'm going to miss the company." He sat down at the dressing table in his dance belt and picked up a jar of cold cream. "We've had the best times, haven't we? I've adored every minute of it: every class, every rehearsal, every performance; I just wanted it never to end. And I wanted to dance Romeo." He laughed to himself, shaking his head. "Oh Christ, did I want to, you have no idea. But, despite that and despite this bloody pain in my back, would I go back if I could and wipe away everything that's happened to me in the past twenty-four hours? I honestly couldn't say." He looked down at the jar in his hands and unscrewed the lid slowly. "I love her, Shel. I've been in love with her since I was sixteen."

"Yeah," Michel said. "Yeah, I know you have."

"And listen, you're going to do something for me. This next fortnight while you're away in Halifax and Sheffield I'm going to be in hospital. I want you to watch out for Nettie and keep your ears open. You hear anyone try and tell her this is her fault, you jump on them, okay? And you shake her until she believes it's not true. Because it isn't."

"Okay." Michel nodded. If that was the way Roly wanted it, that was the way it would be.

When Roly was showered and dressed, ready to go and meet Annette, he held his hand out to Michel with a firm smile.

"Thanks for being there for me tonight, Shel. You're a good friend and I love you to death; we all do, you know."

Michel looked at him helplessly. Roly's brave smile and affectionate words were more than he could bear. He screwed up his face in distress and turned away from the offered hand.

Roly stared at him in surprise and his eyes softened in sympathy. "Ah, Shel." He put his arms around him and held him as tenderly as he would a woman. "Don't get upset on me, not you. I know you're unhappy about Primo and Nettie; I am too, but don't you worry about me. Trust me, I can handle this; I wouldn't say so if it wasn't true. Come on, you macho bastard, give me a hug. You're going to be a big fucking star, Michel, and I'm so proud of you."

Michel remained uncomfortably rigid in Roly's embrace. After a while he patted the taller man uneasily on the shoulder.

"I'm no good at this male-bonding shit, Roly."

Roly laughed, a huge, open laugh, and let him go, cuffing his head.

"That's more like the Michel I know. Go on, fuck off home to Jonni. And give her a kiss from me. When you get back from Bristol come and cheer me up in hospital. And for Christ's sake don't bring grapes; bring . . ."

They pointed at each other.

"Oysters," Michel nodded, smiling, "yeah, I know." And suddenly they were both laughing, remembering their first week on tour in Margate as seventeen-year-old apprentices when Roly had introduced Michel to oysters in the dressing room before the show and Michel had upstaged the Giant Tomato by throwing up at the back of the stage during her dying solo.

Roly took a long swig from his morphine bottle and then tossed it into his bag with a comical raise of his eyebrows.

"Blimey, it's good stuff that!" He lifted his bag onto his shoulder and headed for the corridor. "Hey, Shel." He turned back at the door and looked at him. "I was great out there tonight, wasn't I?"

"World-class," Michel said, shaking his head slowly. "Absolutely world-class."

Lynne had taken a very long time to get changed after the show. By the time she knocked on Michel's dressing room door he was out of the shower and leaning against the dressing table in his jeans, towel-drying his hair.

He lowered his towel as she came in. Their relationship had been strained lately, though the coolness had all been on Lynne's side, and they looked at each other in uncertainty.

Michel looked at her pale blotchy face and red eyelids.

"He told you then?"

Lynne nodded tightly.

"Yes, after the curtain call."

Michel chucked his towel onto a chair and held out his hand toward her, and she went and threw her arms around his neck, laying her cheek on his naked shoulder.

"Oh, God, poor Roly!"

"He'll be alright, Lynnie. He's got more guts than the rest of us put together." He looked at the wall over the top of her head as he held her. "You danced fantastically for him tonight. You were beautiful; I was watching you."

"Charles helped me; he came and bitched me out before the show. I just can't believe it—and Primo and Nettie too."

Michel laid his hand on her head where it lay against his shoulder.

"It's just the two of us now."

She raised her face to look at him with that strange, bleak look that had haunted her eyes recently. Michel looked down at her and kissed her. It was a long time since there had been any intimacy between them.

"Michel?" She gazed up at him in entreaty. "Kiss me again."

His mouth moved slowly against hers, sensuous and yearning, not for sexual gratification but for release from the knotted discomfort that had been lurking in his chest all day and had worsened with the evening. Lynne clung to his neck as he kissed her. When he lifted his head her hazel eyes gazed up at him plaintively. Michel stroked her light-brown fringe away from her face. He didn't feel guilty about kissing Lynne. She was his natural dance partner; his closest friend in the world.

"How about you?" he asked. "I got made principal. Has Charles talked to you yet?"

She nodded and released herself from his arms, shrinking into herself as she walked across the dressing room to look through the costumes on the rail.

"Yes, he came to see me after the show." Her hands leafed rapidly through Michel's tunics and clean tights. "I'm a fully signed up first soloist."

Michel sat down to pull on his trainers.

"A senior soloist! Hey, that's great!"

"Not a principal though."

"It'll happen."

"Yes, I know." She pulled out the white tunic Michel wore for the first two acts of Siegfried and ran her fingers over the scratchy silver brocade. The tunic smelled of greasepaint and Michel's body. "I'll still be earning more than you this year though."

"Really?" He was doing up his shoelaces. "That's interesting. I don't begrudge it, Lynnie, but I'm surprised. How did you wangle that then?"

"PACT pays better than we do."

He stopped halfway through a double knot and twisted his neck to look up at her.

"What?"

"The Performing Arts Council of Transvaal."

"Yes, I know who PACT is, Lynne. What are you saying?"

Lynne's fingers were trying to smooth out a crease in the shoulder of his tunic.

"I've signed a contract to dance with them for a year. I fly out to Johannesburg on Sunday week."

Michel sat up very slowly and looked at his own reflection in the mirror. His mouth opened as he lifted his hand in slow motion to clasp the top of his head. He didn't believe it.

"No!" he said. He searched his own incredulous eyes for an explanation. "You've betrayed me."

"Me?" She flung his white tunic back amongst the other costumes on the rail so hard that all the coat hangers rattled. "I've betrayed you? Me? Michel, you married her!"

"But, Lynne, we're partners! We're . . . oh, shit, Jesus, Lynne!"

"You married her, Michel."

He shook his head in bewilderment.

"But that's my . . . my . . . sex life; my . . . my relationship. This is different! This is our careers, our lives as artists. This is . . . Lynne, our dreams!"

"Michel, Michel, I love you, don't you understand that? I can't deal with this anymore. You've hurt me, Michel. You've let me down and you've betrayed me."

He turned on his chair to look at her, spreading his hands in uncomprehending appeal.

"Lynne, I never pretended to feel anything for you that I didn't. You knew the sex we had was just part of our friendship. You said you understood. When did I ever deceive you? When? Tell me."

"Every single time you touched me. And every time you kissed me. I thought you couldn't make a commitment. I thought you were incapable of it, and I felt sorry for you. I thought you were giving me what little you had to give. But it was all a lie. You just used me and tossed me aside like all the others."

"Used you?"

"Yes, used me." She looked at him with distraught eyes. "Do you really believe you didn't? How can you? You let me run around after you for more than six years. You let me cry over you. You let me humiliate myself waiting around while you screwed other girls. You used my body—yes, you did, Michel; that's what you do to people: you use them. And when we dance together you're still using me. You feed off my love and give me nothing in return except your physical protection. You just take what you need from me and you throw away the rest—it's true, I'm as much your whore in our partnership as I was in your bed." She shook her head bitterly. "If you had ever loved me—ever, even for a moment; if you had ever cared about my weight for me rather than for our partnership. If you had ever thought about me at all while you were shoving your prick into me . . ."

"Fuck off!" he cried, clasping his hands to his head.

"It's true, Michel!"

"Fuck off out of here!"

Lynne's body crumpled. There it was at last: the reaction, the emotional acknowledgment she had so urgently craved all these years. She knelt on the floor, burying her face in the carpet, and wrapped her arms tightly over her head.

For a long, long time neither of them spoke. When she finally lifted her head and knelt up Michel was looking in his dressing table mirror, running his hand angrily over the top of his head.

"Did Charles tell you about the casting for *Romeo*?" he asked.

"No."

"He wanted you to create Juliet with me."

She pressed her hands desperately to her middle.

"Oh God! Did you want it?"

"Yes, of course I wanted it." He lowered his hand, letting it drop onto his knee. "Change your mind, Lynne."

"I can't. It's too late; I've already signed the contract." Her hazel eyes met his sadly in the mirror. "And I can't dance with you anymore. It hurts me too much."

She got up and put her slight arms around his naked shoulders, resting her cheek on his damp blond curls, still looking at his reflection.

"We couldn't help it, Michel. Neither of us. You would have loved me if you could. Please don't say I've betrayed you. Say you understand."

Michel looked at her coldly in the mirror. He didn't move an inch in her embrace.

"Go away," he said. "Go on, Lynne, just . . ." he waved his hand in dismissal, ". . . go to South Africa."

When he got home to Pimlico Jonni met him at the door of the flat, ready with a kiss for him.

"How did it go tonight?"

He put her away from him with his hands, turning his head to avoid her raised face.

"Not good," he said. "I can't tell you about it now. Go to bed, will you? I need to do some work for my Siegfried tomorrow."

"But, Mike, it's after midnight!"

"Please, Jons, just go to bed."

Primo was sitting, drunk, at the piano playing languid sonatas with empty, melancholy eyes.

"If you want to play, play something useful." Michel threw his jacket on a sofa and kicked off his shoes. "Give me Siegfried's first variation in Act Three."

Primo lifted the score from the top of the piano and opened it at the variation.

"You have a lovely time dancing with your company tonight, amico?"

"Yeah, great. Shut up and play."

And he turned out his hips, pulled up his muscles, spread his arms in second position, and vanished into his work.

21

MICHEL EVENTUALLY CREATED the role of Romeo with Carlotta. And at the start of September, when decorators invaded the studios in the Goswell Road, the entire choreography process, complete with production backup, moved to Michel's flat in Pimlico.

"Are you sure you don't mind?" Michel asked Jonni before he gave his permission to the company, "I mean, this is a big production; it's going to be chaos. You're not going to be able to move for people."

"No, I really don't mind," she said. "It's the only chance of my actually seeing you for more than two minutes in the next month. Besides, it'll be fun."

And it *was* fun. Fun but entirely overwhelming. All day, seven days a week, the flat was overrun by dancers, designers, and administrators, rushing about from early morning until late at night. Costume fitters came and went with big bundles of fabric and tape measures. The production manager tore up and down the stairs ten times a day with production budgets and schedules and pasteups from the marketing manager. The phone rang so constantly that Crown's secretary installed herself beside it, shifting Michel and Jonni's possessions off the hall table to turn it into a desk.

Every corner of the flat was taken over by the dancers. The bathroom was always occupied, often by several people at once. The kitchen became a common room and the room for production meetings. Even the bedroom became the changing room, the room for private quarrels, and the dozing room. Sometimes during the nominal lunch hour as many as half a dozen dancers were cuddled up together on Michel and Jonni's bed trying to catch a few minutes' sleep between rehearsals.

But most of the time they worked and worked and worked. Even when they weren't involved in the choreography, several boys were usually learning the steps in the corner of the studio while the girls worked on their pointe shoes, customizing them to their personal specifications. Sometimes the whole studio became an industrious workshop of snipping, stitching, and daubing of shellac as the girls stockpiled shoes for the busy days ahead.

It was the most fraught working environment Jonni had ever seen, throwing even the intensity of the Paris choreography into the shade. At ten o'clock every morning dancers would line up at the barre—sometimes only three or four, sometimes more than a dozen—and slog with steely discipline through an hour of classwork with Marina before launching into a grueling schedule of rehearsal. The pace of the work was tempestuous. Moves were fought over and debated. Dances were created and scrapped. Squabbles broke out over the musical interpretation. Step by step the mammoth piece struggled groaning into existence amidst flying tempers and injuries.

At the center of all this bedlam was Charles Crown. Every morning at half past eleven he leaped out of a taxi in Warwick Way, straight from a budget meeting or marketing conference, and roared into the flat with his dark eyes blazing.

"Go! Go! Go!" he shouted, even before his jacket was off: "Act Three, the balcony scene, end of Juliet's second variation! Carlotta, go! Michel, go! Andrea, sit down! Primo, play!"

He worked as though driven by demons, his black brows knotted in fiery concentration, barking out commands, flicking feverishly through notebooks, thinking of ten, twenty different things at once, but always focused with laserlike intensity on the thing in front of him.

"Don't you ever rest?" Jonni asked him, bringing him a cup of coffee during a five-minute break in rehearsals.

"Never," he snapped, taking the coffee without raising his eyes from his notes.

Everyone was tired, everyone was nervous, everyone had tantrums; even the choreologist, Andrea, cried when her notation got so confused with all the changes she couldn't tell which steps were the current ones. Only Michel and Carlotta remained calm, working with channeled single-mindedness. When tempers snapped in the studio Michel put his arm around Carlotta and led her out of the room until it blew over. They couldn't afford to get involved in petty squabbles; there was too much at stake for them and for the company.

Michel was intensely involved in the choreography but he was exhausted. He worked almost as hard as Crown, tumbling out of bed every morning straight into class and straight into the creation of his role. It was a great, glorious, impassioned role, and Crown's reworking of the ballet was incredible. Moreover, Michel had underestimated Carlotta; she was a fabulous Juliet. For all her stroppiness and arrogance, the moment she hitched up her tights and walked out to join Michel on the studio floor she was fourteen and vulnerable and in love for the first time.

Jonni watched her husband and his dancing partner grow closer every day, their minds entwining in the excitement of the beautiful choreography that Crown was developing through their bodies. The intimacy and interdependence of their work drew them together. They touched each other all the time, even when they weren't dancing, gravitating instinctively toward one another across the studio. As the trust between them deepened and their work grew more difficult, Michel's arms became Carlotta's home and her waist became his anchor.

"What do I do when I've got her there?" Michel asked, with Carlotta's supple waist clasped to his groin during yet another rethink of the difficult bedroom scene. "I've got to do something with her. Shall I snog her, or what?"

"No, you can't," Crown said, gnawing his lip, "you'd spoil the kiss after her variation. Let her go and she can step back on the beat before you follow her into the lifts."

"Why would I let her go?" He looked into Carlotta's eyes, inches from his own. "Believe me, I wouldn't let her go—no chance."

Crown scratched his head hard.

"Alright then, let's try having you make another move on her. Put your hand up her nightie, St. Michel, and go to kiss her neck."

"Like this? God, they're going to think I'm an animal! Anyway, why would she run away? I've just fucked her. She wouldn't move away."

"I might," Carlotta objected. "Especially if I thought you were going to do it again. I'm only fourteen, you know. That first time hurt." She hitched up the strap of her leotard under her practice frock, looking archly at Michel's pensive face. "Michel, get your hand off my clit, will you?"

He took his hand away, preoccupied; "Oh, yeah, sorry."

It wasn't easy for Jonni to watch Michel and Carlotta creating this choreography; not easy at all. She knew they were playacting. She knew they took physical contact for granted. But when they put the steps together and danced flat out to the music they were so passionate and so sexually explicit it was hard to believe there was nothing between them beyond their professional relationship.

When Michel and Carlotta collapsed laughing in each other's arms, exhausted after a particularly heated rendition of the bedroom scene, Jonni leaped up from the sofa and stormed out of the studio in jealous fury.

"Easy, bella," Primo said, following her into the kitchen. "*Pianissimo,* okay? *Calma ti!*" Primo was sullen and bad-tempered in rehearsals, always with a glass of whisky on top of the piano. He had persistently refused Crown's offers of the post of assistant musical director, agreeing only grudgingly to play for rehearsals because Michel had said he needed him. But he was Jonni's best friend and comfort during the weeks of that choreography. "Bella, that boy ain't got the energy to screw Carlotta even if he wanted to."

"I know," Jonni said glumly, sinking her chin onto her fist at the table. "He hasn't got the energy to screw *anyone* at the moment."

Michel hadn't even noticed that she'd left the studio.

It wasn't just the love scenes that were painful to watch. Jonni saw Michel, time and time again, die a horrible death from poisoning, heartbroken and in agony. She watched him howl in despair over the dead body of his best friend, and she cowered in the corner of the sofa at the sight of his violent rage while he hacked Daniel to death in a brutal, terrifying sword fight.

At night Jonni was usually in bed well before Michel staggered into the bedroom at midnight or one in the morning. When she woke up and tried to talk to him, he hushed her with a weary shake of the head and a gesture indicating that he couldn't cope with the demands of a wife in addition to those of Crown and the choreography.

"But, Michel, you haven't said a word to me all day."

"Don't . . ." He put his hand to his head. "I'm sorry, Jons. I have to sleep. I have to sleep." He crashed onto the bed beside her and went out like a light, only to leap up eight hours later and begin the whole routine again.

As the days passed Jonni found herself more and more neglected. Michel no longer saw her. He no longer kissed her in the mornings. He no longer sought out her face in the studio during pauses in rehearsals to flash her his special smile. There weren't any pauses in rehearsal anymore; Crown hammered and hectored and bullied Michel until he was almost at breaking point. But Michel remained attentive and focused in the studio; it was only in the rare moments he was alone with Jonni that the strain showed. Desolate, Jonni watched his nights become more and more disturbed. He muttered in his sleep, whispering in distressed murmurs, turning over and over to try and escape Crown's persistent criticism. One night when Michel had kicked the bedclothes off, tossing and turning in his sleep, Jonni looked down the bed in the half-light from the window to see his sleeping feet jerking in troubled little entrechats and tendus.

"I wouldn't worry, love," Roly said when she told him about it. Roly often popped in at the weekends or in the evenings. He had been back on his feet for almost three months now and was working as a painter and decorator. "Straight out of one kind of plaster and into another," as Annette wryly put it. When Roly came to the flat she always came with him to sit on his knee with her arms twined possessively around his neck while he watched the choreography.

"Poor old Shel's just trying to sort out the unfinished bits of the choreography in his sleep," he told Jonni. "You wait and see; once the moves are in place and the company goes into regular rehearsal, he'll soon settle down."

"He never has time to talk to me anymore," Jonni mourned.

"Hey." Roly put an affectionate arm around her. "Shel would be lost without you, chicken."

Jonni didn't think so. After all, it wasn't Jonni's eyes that Michel was smiling into so intimately as she watched him across the studio.

The further Michel's mind and body were sucked into the new ballet, the further away from Jonni he grew. By the end of September, when the ballet was finally in one piece, she felt she had lost him completely. Now that he had to combine rehearsals with publicity calls and costume fittings he no longer had even a minute to call his own. He walked past Jonni in the flat as though she were invisible, always with his hand on Carlotta's waist. But Roly was right about Michel's troubled nights: since the last steps were nailed down he was sleeping silently and deeply—so deeply, in fact, that he didn't seem to realize she was there beside him at all.

One afternoon London Weekend Television invaded the flat, lugging a whole truckload of cameras and lighting and sound equipment up the four floors to film a rehearsal. Jonni sat hunched in a corner against the wall—the only place there was room—and watched them filming the balcony scene. Crown had originally intended they should do the bedroom duet, but as soon as the TV director saw the choreography he shook his head; it was far too racy to be shown before the nine p.m. watershed.

The recording which should have taken an hour ran on and on. Crown had LWT's written guarantee they wouldn't broadcast anything unless he had approved it and nothing but nothing Michel and Carlotta could do would satisfy him.

"Okay, move that camera back!" the director shouted. "Mister Crown's not happy with that one either, so we're going again!"

"Shove up, darling," the cameraman said to Jonni, nudging her out of the way with his foot as he took her place. Jonni squashed herself even farther into the corner. She felt like an intruder in her own home.

All afternoon without pause Michel danced and redanced his balcony variation under the excruciating heat of the TV lights, criticized and spurred on by Crown's fierce voice as he flung out the dizzying combinations of leaps and turns.

"I'm sorry," Michel gasped, out of breath, mopping his dripping face while Crown harangued him for mistiming a leap. "Look, I'm sorry, alright? I lost my place for a moment, that's all. Everyone makes mistakes."

"Not in my fucking ballet." Crown turned to the director. "Scrap that last take; the whole thing. He's going to do it again from the start, and this time he better fucking get it right. Let's go!"

"Hey, Charles," Primo said, flexing his powerful hands slowly above the keyboard, "I don't know 'bout Michel but you gotta give me a minute here. Even my chops got a limit, you know?"

Again and again Michel danced the variation until Crown grunted that it was better than nothing and they moved on to the pas de deux. Once, twice, three times Michel and Carlotta danced their massive duet, wilting like cut flowers under the hot lights, their muscles stiffening from all the stopping and starting, while the recording spilled over into the evening, and Crown still wasn't satisfied. This ballet was the biggest thing Crown had ever attempted and by far the most financially perilous. One piece of bad publicity could bring the entire future of the Islington Ballet crashing down around his ears.

"You're still fucking coasting, St. Michel. And why the bloody double after the turns in second instead of a triple? Do it again!"

"Oh God, no!" Michel groaned. "No, I can't."

"Of course you can. Stop arguing and get on with it."

"For Christ's sake!" Carlotta snapped. "Michel was fine last time; leave him alone. I'm tired too."

Crown waved them to silence.

"Look, just once more; that's all. Then you can break while these guys pack up, and we'll work on the second half of the duet tonight before we go back to the bedroom scene."

Michel held up his hands.

"That's it." He tore off his ballet shoes and threw them, one after the other, at the mirror, striding toward the door and pulling off his T-shirt as he went.

"Where are you going?" Crown demanded.

"I'm going to take a shower."

Crown exploded in rage.

"You get the fuck back here, St. Michel! If I say we rehearse all night that's what we do."

"No we don't!" Michel retorted sharply, turning round in the doorway. "It's eight-thirty on Friday night and I haven't had an evening off for three weeks! I'm going to get changed and I'm going to take my wife out to dinner. And when I get back I'm going to take her to bed and make love to her—and I don't want to find any of you here. Not one of you, do you understand?"

As he walked out of the studio everyone looked at each other in silence. No one, including Jonni and Primo, had ever seen Michel lose his cool before. Crown ran his tongue slowly over his lips and looked at the TV director.

"I think we've finished, Gavin."

When Michel and Jonni came home from the taverna in Tachbrook Street the flat was deserted. Someone had even made their bed for them. Michel had been very quiet in the restaurant, still thinking about the choreography, but Jonni was happy just to be with him and to hold his hand across the table.

Jonni stood wrapped in a white bath towel and looked at Michel in the glow of the bedside lamp as he pulled his shirt off over his head. She laid her hand on his bare chest, gazing up into his eyes while he stood there flexing his stiff neck.

"It's okay, Mike. We don't have to. I understand; really I do."

"I'm sorry," he said. "I'm not quite myself at the moment."

"Yes you are. And that's alright. If you weren't obsessed you wouldn't be the dancer Charles thinks you are." She smiled at him softly. "We'll make up for it later, once the ballet's opened."

Michel's tired eyes looked down at her adoring face. It was the first time he had looked at her properly in weeks.

"Have you been feeling neglected? I'm sorry, Jons. You knew what I was when we got together. But you must be bored to tears with this ballet."

"No, I'm never bored." Her eyes lit up. "I love the music. I could listen to it forever. Primo's fantastic; he makes the Steinway sound like an entire orchestra."

Michel stroked her waist. She had found something they could talk about.

"Yes, he's wonderful, isn't he? Charles thinks it's his yelling that keeps us hammering away at that bloody bedroom pas de deux. It's not; it's Primo."

Jonni laughed. "I've watched that duet so many times, if Carlotta's ever ill I could probably go on and do it for her." She looked down at her hand where it still lay on his chest. She was still smiling but her eyes were a little sad. "Though I wouldn't be a very good substitute even if I could dance. The two of you look gorgeous together, Michel. She's so beautiful."

Michel looked down at her face for a long time, watching her humble gaze roam over his chest and shoulders. Eventually he beckoned to her, whispering, "Come with me, Jonni. Come."

He led her silently by the hand into the empty studio and brought her to stand in the middle of the floor, leaving her there as he went to pull back the heavy gray curtain that had been half drawn over the mirrored wall to cut out the reflection of the TV lights. The studio was dark and filled with nighttime shadows, with only the thin lights of the city fanning out from the windows over the white ceiling to soften the blackness.

Going to stand behind her, Michel took off her bath towel and threw it away. He turned her face with his hand to make her look at her naked body in the mirror while his own eyes moved slowly over her reflected image. Jonni looked at herself—at her small, rounded figure with her pointed breasts and broad hips, at her wide mouth and turned-up freckled nose—and she looked at the eyes of the bare-chested man who stood in shadow behind her, and she felt beautiful. As beautiful even as Carlotta.

Michel reached in front of her and took her hands in his. Watching her eyes in the mirror he lifted her hands slowly away from her body, uncoiling her fingers gently with his palms. "You want to know what it feels like?" he asked her. "Okay, keep your back strong." He turned her around and crouched down to wrap one arm carefully around her knees, picking her up with her shins clasped to his chest. Jonni looked down at his face in the semidarkness as he stretched his free hand behind him and spun around very slowly, gazing up at her. As he stopped spinning he let her body slide gradually through his arm and kissed her belly and her breasts while he lowered her inch by inch to the floor.

"Now turn around," he whispered, "and walk toward the mirror."

She crept away from him and he caught her hand, turning her again to face him as he tipped her gently off balance, supporting her in his arms.

"You're fourteen," he whispered, his face very close to hers, "and a virgin and frightened."

Michel's shadowy eyes looked down into her eyes while he led her silently through the choreography at a hundredth of the speed he danced it with Carlotta. His hands were warm on her bare skin, guiding her gently through the steps with an intimacy and eroticism that tightened her chest and left her breathless.

He stood in front of her and raised his hand above her head in invitation. Jonni smiled in wonder as she lifted her own hand to lay her palm against his. His hand was so beautiful; so graceful. He gathered her waist to him and slowly leaned over her in the darkness, bending her naked body against his own as their fingers intertwined.

Nothing that Jonni had ever experienced was as wonderful as being taken, in the silence of the dark studio, into the secret place in Michel's life where his passion lay and from which she had always been excluded. Here his arms coiled slowly around her in yearning love, and desire was life or death to him. She had never felt, even in their most ardent moments, so much emotion and tenderness flow through his body as now when he held her in his arms as his Juliet.

She understood Juliet's trepidation as she backed slowly away from him across the room. There was a hunger and a need in his eyes which she had never seen there before.

Like a panther, a black silhouette against the studio wall, Michel leaped softly toward her, turning in the air and landing without a sound. She caught her breath as he spun her around and held her tightly against him, his chest hot against her back. Their gazes met in the mirror and they watched each other's eyes as he ran his hands slowly down over her breasts to her groin.

"Michel?" she whispered, staring at his reflection.

The eyes that looked back at her unflinchingly from the mirror were Michel's eyes and yet they weren't. She could feel his heart pounding against her shoulder. He turned her toward him and, just as he did with Carlotta, took her face in his hands and looked deeply and passionately into her eyes before he plastered his mouth over hers. Just as he did with

Carlotta, he picked her up in his arms and laid her on the studio floor. And just as he did with Carlotta, he pressed his body onto hers, still kissing her ravenously. Then, as he did not do with Carlotta, he unbuttoned the fly of his jeans and plunged himself inside her with an urgent exclamation that broke the silence of the dark flat, echoing in the empty hallway and reverberating in the vastness of the studio around them.

Afterward they lay together panting on the studio floor with their hands touching. Jonni couldn't move.

"Oh crumbs," she wailed, "I wet myself. That's so embarrassing!"

Michel smiled, still trying to catch his breath.

"No you didn't." He touched her wet thigh and put his fingers to his lips. "It's part of sex. It's part of you."

"I felt it all the way to my fingers and toes. Heavens, do you think poor Carlotta feels this way every time you dance that bit with her?"

"My God, I doubt it. That whole section lasts about fifteen seconds. Even I'm not that sexy." He turned his head to look at her in the faint light from the windows. "Are you worried about Carlotta?"

Jonni turned her own head toward him, smiling a little shrug.

"Not really."

"Jonni, Carlotta and I are going to get a lot closer before this ballet opens. You've got to be prepared for that."

"I know."

He moved his hand to lay it on her damp belly. "Do you want to know what I see in Carlotta's eyes when I gaze into them before I make love to her? Honestly? I see—oh shit—we've got that bloody overhead lift in five bars' time."

Jonni looked at him; at the clean contours of his face and his clear gray eyes.

"And what does she see in your eyes, Michel?"

"She sees thank Christ I got through that bit without dropping you on your head. Now, d'you want to stay here all night or shall we go to bed?"

"You'll have to carry me."

"Oh God, must I?" He sighed. "Alright then."

The next afternoon during a rehearsal of the bedroom pas de deux Crown halted Michel in mid-orgasm, waving to Primo to stop playing.

"Thanks, Primo. St. Michel, I was wondering if we should try having you cry out here."

"I am."

"No, I mean really crying out."

"You mean use my voice?" Michel stared at him in amazement as he climbed off Carlotta to sit on the floor and rub his knees. "You've got to be joking! I'd feel incredibly inhibited using my voice onstage. Besides, this is a ballet; the audience would fall off their seats in shock."

"When has that ever stopped him doing anything?" Carlotta asked tartly, sitting up and pulling her rumpled practice frock back down over her leotard. "Next he'll ask us to sing a ruddy love duet."

"Okay," Crown said, with a rare smile. "Okay, I get the message. It was only an idea."

"No, I think it's a good idea!"

Crown, Marina, Michel, Carlotta, and Primo all turned their heads to look at Jonni in surprise. She tucked her feet further underneath her on the sofa with an embarrassed smile. "Michel does"—she shrugged— ". . . great crying out."

Michel's eyes laughed as he looked at her across the studio.

"My wife has spoken," he said dryly. He turned back to Crown. "Alright, whatever you say. I'll give it a go. You're the boss."

Crown was already doubtful.

"Look, I don't think the audience needs to know about your sexual expertise, St. Michel. Let's keep that particular legend confined within the company if we can. I was talking about a spiritual, emotional crying out, not the sound track to some hard-core video."

"I'll see what I can do," Michel said, adjusting his dance belt through his all-in-one as he climbed back on top of Carlotta.

He looked at Jonni and she smiled at him. She knew he would never dance with her like that again or make love to her like that again. But it had sealed a trust between them and if he cried out in Carlotta's arms she knew it would be for her.

At the end of the first week in October, although the premiere of *Romeo and Juliet* was only a fortnight away, Crown was forced to allow the company the day off to attend the big social event of the season. If he had tried to stop them there would have been a full-scale rebellion. Eventually he even gave in and canceled Michel and Carlotta's scheduled rehearsal.

The Potter wedding was a lavish affair. Three hundred guests assembled on the mown grass outside St. Anselm's church in Hertford in the thin October sunshine, exchanging jovial platitudes in their suits and big floppy hats, snatching a last cigarette before the bride's car arrived.

Annette's fashionable mother had been far from impressed by her daughter's choice of husband. She didn't at all relish the prospect of having it known amongst Hertford's cocktail set that Annette was marrying a painter and decorator, especially one who wasn't at all good-looking (though his body passed muster, she had to admit) and whose mother lived in a council house in Kent.

"Don't be such a snob," Annette protested in disgust. "So his mum went out in the evenings scrubbing floors to put him through his apprenticeship. That's a bloody sight more than you've ever done for me."

"I'm sure they're frightfully nice people," her mother replied smoothly over the rim of her martini glass, pushing her Yves Saint Laurent sunglasses farther up her nose.

But the choice of groom was a mere detail. Helena Potter had only one child and, you'd better believe it, she was going to be married in style. In one respect Roly, though deficient as a fashion accessory, found instant favor in his future mother-in-law's eyes: he was a complete pushover when it came to the wedding. He left everything to Annette and Helena, agreeing in smiling bewilderment to whatever excesses they dreamed up. And now, after months of feverish preparations, the gold-embossed invitations had all been sent out, the aisles were heaving with flowers, three ribbon-trimmed Rolls-Royces were lined up outside the church—Roly had finally put his foot down over the helicopter; he wasn't keen on heights—and the smartest hotel in Hertford was buffing up its silver cutlery and spreading a white cloth over a serving table because its usual wedding-cake stand wasn't big enough.

Helena Potter was strutting ostentatiously up and down the central aisle making sure everyone had a chance to admire her fawn Dior suit and cream silk Hermès scarf before the bride arrived to steal the limelight, and Jonni couldn't honestly blame her; Annette's mother was drop-dead gorgeous. Michel broke off his conversation with Crown and half rose from his seat to look at the bits of Mrs. Potter that were hidden behind the wooden pews. He sat down again with raised eyebrows and a muted whistle.

"No secret where Nettie got her legs from anyway."

At the front of the packed church, in an immaculate gray pinstriped morning suit, Roly was whispering nervously with his best man. He had asked his old flatmate from his stage school days to be his best man: Michel and Primo had both had to decline the job; they hadn't known until two days ago whether they would be able to come at all. Roly turned his head, anxiously scanning the sea of faces in the church until he met Primo's eye. Primo winked at him and nodded reassuringly.

"She'll turn up," Charles Crown whispered to Michel. "I can't see Potter ducking the chance to be center stage in a five-star gig like this one."

When Annette arrived in a cloud of satin and tulle the entire congregation turned in their pews to stare. Hearing the united murmur of awe, Roly twisted his neck to look at her over his shoulder. His mouth fell open and he raised a trembling hand to his breast. Annette stood poised radiantly on her father's arm, majestic in her corseted satin dress with its wide skirt and long train, her dark curls cascading from a coronet of little flowers beneath the haze of her veil, exquisite eyes shining with the knowledge of her own loveliness. It was small wonder Roly stared. She looked stunningly beautiful.

Primo leaned across Jonni's lap to whisper to Michel, "*Cristo,* I don't believe it, she's wearing white!"

"Didn't you know?" Jonni whispered. "She's a born-again virgin."

"No way! How come? They bin living together. You've seen their flat; they only got one bed."

"I know," Jonni said, blushing guiltily at her disloyalty for gossiping. She and Annette had become bosom buddies since Annette started at drama school in September and she knew all the details. "They've been sleeping together but that's all—just sleeping."

"She's kidding," Crown whispered to Michel. "The boy must have a prick of steel."

"I'll bet he has," Michel murmured back.

They all beamed encouragement at Annette as she sought out their eyes, walking triumphantly down the aisle at her father's side in front of a gaggle of pink bridesmaids. It was easy to spot Roly's three sisters amongst the bridesmaids, from their broad smiles as much as their bright, red-gold hair.

Jonni always cried at weddings, although usually she managed to wait until the service had started. This time, seeing the emotion in Roly's blue eyes as he rose to wait for his bride at the altar, she was rummaging in her handbag for a tissue even before Annette was halfway down the aisle.

"I give them six months," Crown whispered to Michel.

In front of the altar rail Roly offered his hand to Annette and she gazed up at him with tremulous devotion, her eyes swimming with happiness as she put her hand in his.

"Okay, a year," Crown whispered.

After the usual preamble—and the awful pregnant pause while everyone waited in irrational fear for someone to jump up and reveal that Roly had a secret spouse stashed away somewhere, or that Annette had several—the vicar lowered his head to look over the top of his spectacles, smiling paternally at the groom.

"Do you, Roland, take this woman, Annette, to be your lawful wife?"

Roly answered that he did.

"And do you, Annette, take this man, Roland, to be your lawful husband?"

There was such a long pause that the congregation began to glance at one another. Roly looked up at the stained-glass window behind the altar, waiting and caressing Annette's hand with his thumb.

The vicar repeated the question.

Eventually, Roly turned his head to look at her. She was absolutely still, staring straight ahead—frozen, like a windup doll who had suddenly stopped working. Roly twisted his neck to glance uneasily at the sea of expectant faces behind him. No one in the congregation moved.

"Nettie?" he whispered at last, aware that his whisper probably carried all the way to the back of the echoing church. "Nettie?"

After another lengthy pause Annette came to herself with a start. She glanced at him sharply before she gave the vicar a rude look.

"Of course I do. I heard you the first time!"

The entire congregation sank back in their pews in relief.

"What in God's name was that?" Crown whispered to Michel. "Eleventh-hour panic?"

Michel clicked his tongue and shook his head—he had seen what happened when Annette panicked and, whatever this had been, it wasn't that.

"Pause for dramatic effect, more likely."

The reception was memorable, less for the quality of the champagne and the caviar-stuffed vol-au-vents than for the conspicuous feuds that raged throughout the banqueting suite between various warring branches of Annette's family. Roly was furious that members of his own family had been strategically placed by Annette—or, more probably, by Helena—to act as human barricades separating the bloodthirsty factions of his turbulent in-laws. But he kept his anger to himself; today was Annette's day and he'd wait until tomorrow to let her know what he thought of the seating arrangements. He did the rounds of the tables, once lunch and the speeches were over, making polite conversation with each of Annette's ex-stepfathers and their current wives, dodging the laser beams of hostility that were sweeping around the room from eye to eye. At least he'd never have to see most of them again.

When he reached the table where Michel was seated with his friends, Roly crouched down between Jonni's and Primo's chairs, smiling at them all as he rested his hand on Jonni's knee.

"Everyone okay? Have you all got a drink?"

Primo looked at him wryly across the table.

"Gettin' to know the happy family, amico?"

Roly rolled his eyes laughingly to the ceiling.

"Apparently this isn't too bad. Nettie says the insult swapping has been going on for years."

"Wife swapping, you mean."

"Yes, that too, by the looks of it. Anyway, Nettie's promised they won't be staying for the evening so it should be more relaxed."

"How is Nettie?" Jonni asked, looking down at him and furrowing her forehead in concern. "What happened in the church? Is she okay?"

"Oh, yes." Roly smiled up into her eyes with affection. For all the hostility amongst his new relatives, there was no mistaking his happiness.

"She's fine, chicken. It was nothing; she was just a bit nervous. It's terrifying going through that in front of hundreds of people. You and Shel did it the right way, I can tell you."

Later, during the lull before the evening disco, when Michel, Marina, and Crown were inevitably discussing the choreography for *Romeo,* and Primo was, equally inevitably, sitting alone at the bar downing one drink after another, Jonni sat with her arms folded on the table amidst the debris of coffee and wedding cake, watching Roly playing football in the hotel garden with his friends from stage school. He was laughing and scuffling over the ball in his shirtsleeves with amazing agility for a man who had spent four of the last eight months up to his neck in plaster.

Jonni got up from the table and wandered slowly out into the large bar area where numerous guests were milling around wearily, their assumed wedding jauntiness set aside as the bride and groom were both temporarily out of sight. Jonni was no better at big parties now than she had been when she first met Michel. In search of a place to hide, she turned the handle on the door to a room where the wedding presents had been stacked prior to being shipped home to Helena's house to await opening and cataloguing after the honeymoon.

As she opened the door and slipped through it, glancing behind her to check she wasn't observed, she stopped short in surprise. Instead of finding seclusion amongst the mountain of white- and silver-wrapped parcels, she was confronted by the unexpected sight of Annette standing there in her wedding dress, her veil wildly askew, ripping the paper off a pastel-blue table lamp complete with fringed blue velvet shade. A brass magazine rack and a toaster were lying on the floor surrounded by paper and ribbon—they looked rather as though they had been thrown there.

"Why would anyone think we wanted this?" Annette demanded savagely, without looking at Jonni as she came in. "I mean, seriously, who in their right mind would give this houseroom?"

Jonni looked at the lamp. Admittedly, it was pretty hideous.

"Well . . . who's it from?" she asked, hesitating.

But Annette had already cast it aside and was pulling the paper off a big rectangular parcel beside it. When she saw the cardboard box inside, containing a king-size duvet, her face clouded still further.

"This is an eight-tog duvet! What's the point of that? If I'd wanted an eight-tog duvet I'd have said so. I asked for a fourteen-tog." She tore open the box and pulled out the duvet, unrolling it and shaking it out. "It's nearly winter; what use is this? And goose down! I can't bear goose down; I specifically said duck!" She searched the discarded paper angrily until she found the label. "One of *his* relatives! I should have known."

Jonni was watching her in unease.

"Nettie, are you okay?"

"And I bet these are bloody well goose too!" Annette attacked another parcel with matching paper and ribbons, looking furious as she yanked the two goose-down pillows out of their packaging. "How can people be so fucking stupid? What's the point of making a wedding list if no one can be bothered to bloody well read it?" She flung the pillows at the wall.

Jonni glanced nervously at the silver-wrapped crystal wineglasses she had bought as a gift from herself and Michel. Luckily they were on a different table on the far side of the large room.

"Why don't you wait until you and Roly can open your presents together?"

When Annette ignored her, tearing the wrapping off a Breville slow cooker with a snort of disgust, Jonni slipped out of the room and went to extract Roly from his football game.

By the time Roly arrived, still pink-cheeked and heated from his game, Annette had done considerably more damage. Unwrapped presents lay all over the tables and floor, surrounded by a chaos of torn paper and ribbon.

"Look at this!" she cried, the moment she saw him. She held up a lace tablecloth, fuming. "A ruddy lace tablecloth!"

He closed the door behind him, taking in the mess with surprised eyes.

"I don't see what's wrong with it."

"Of course you don't. That's so typically male. It's lace, Roly! Lace! Like the kind of tablecloth your grandmother would have in her dining room. And, apart from that, we haven't got a dining room. We haven't even got a dining table."

"Whoever gave it to us probably liked it," Roly said reasonably. "And they weren't to know we haven't got a table."

"Yes, they were!" she declared. "All they had to do was look at the fucking list. Does it say lace tablecloth anywhere on the list? No, it doesn't!" She threw it aside and snatched up a porcelain figurine of a shepherdess in a long frock with bows around the hem. "And what the hell is this? This is from your aunt Greta. Am I seriously supposed to write a thank-you letter for this? And this?" She waved her hand in rage at a flowery teapot. "Look at it! It's all rubbish."

"Love, we don't need any of this stuff," Roly soothed. "We haven't got room for it anyway. The important thing is that people have made an effort. The gifts don't matter, we both know that."

"They might not matter to you but they matter to me!" she snapped, pushing him away as he tried to touch her. Roly had made a mistake trying to reason with her in this mood; she stalked maniacally away from him across the room like Miss Havisham in her disheveled wedding dress, flinging her long silk veil out of the way with her arm as she kicked up waves of crumpled wrapping paper. She seized the eight-tog duvet that had so affronted her from the floor. "Look! This is a duvet!" She hurled it down and grabbed up another duvet, still in its box, ripping the cardboard and pulling it out to show him. "And this is another duvet!" Her green eyes rounded on him, distraught. "Two duvets and both from your relatives! It would be understandable if they were my relatives—none of them are on speaking terms—but you'd have thought your bloody cousins could have communicated on a simple matter like a duvet! That's what comes of marrying someone from a council estate in Kent!"

Roly was beginning to grow alarmed at the intensity of her distress. "What's got into you? For Christ's sake, calm down." He tried to hold her, putting his arm around her waist, and reached out with his free hand to make her let go of the duvet. On the verge of hysteria, Annette yanked it away from him. The duvet tore, sending a cloud of white goose down flying into the air. Even more upset, she flung it back at him, sending up another fountain of feathers.

"Go on, take it," she cried. "You can take it with you when you leave me!" She threw out her arm, indicating the rest of the presents. "You can take it *all* with you when you leave."

"Darling, don't talk rubbish," he said. He tried again to put his arm around her waist and she pushed him off.

"I'm not talking rubbish. Of course you'll leave. You might not have actually picked the date yet but it goes without saying that you'll go eventually." She kicked the train of her dress viciously out of the way, and bent down, like a ballet dancer, without bending her knees to pick up a box of mauve potpourri from amongst the snowfall of goose down on the floor, tearing the lid off to smell it. The pungent, rather artificial smell made her recoil in repulsion.

Roly made no attempt to stop her emptying the potpourri over the floor. His blue eyes were watching her in blank consternation as he took in what she had said.

"Is that what you really think?" he asked her, amazed. "That I'll leave you? Then you don't know me very well, Annette."

"Men always leave," she said, slapping a fierce hand at the front of her white dress to brush off the mauve petals that had stuck to it. "It's a fact of life. I expect it. Once you get what you want from me you'll get bored and, yes, sooner or later, you'll leave."

Roly looked completely dumbfounded as he stood there in his pinstriped trousers, gray silk waistcoat, and shirtsleeves.

"Once I get what I want from you? What are you talking about?"

"You know what I'm talking about."

His eyes darkened as he began to understand her.

"Is this why we've waited eight months to make love: because you think I'll get bored and walk out on you? Jesus!"

The door opened and Roly's youngest sister, Hettie, who was almost ten years younger than he was, froze in alarm as she saw the state of the room. Roly put his finger to his lips. "Go outside, chicken, and don't let anyone in."

When she had gone, closing the door behind her, he stood still, looking into Annette's frightened, aggressive eyes. He realized that with all the fevered preparations for the wedding over the past few weeks she couldn't have had a moment to think about the reality of what they were doing, while he had thought about little else. Poor Nettie, it was hardly surprising she was scared. Thinking about all those ex-stepfathers sitting in the church today and the catalog of abuse and abandonment they represented in her past, it would have been unnatural if she hadn't been afraid. Roly and Annette were far closer than anyone who saw them at this moment would have imagined. There was very little Roly didn't know about her childhood and it had been as much as he could manage today to look those men civilly in the eye.

Surprisingly, given Annette's frantic scowl, he found himself smiling.

"What are you smiling at?" she demanded.

"I thought you kept putting me off because you didn't want to," he said.

Her frown changed as she glared at him. In all those months while she had sat glued to his bedside throughout his painful convalescence and in the months since then while they painted and furnished their Putney flat together she had skillfully avoided the subject of sex, keeping him at arm's length with the breezy assertion of her right to wait until they were married. Now she registered, for the first time, the possibility that he too might have been afraid.

"Didn't want to?" she asked, irritated, as she always was when she felt ashamed. "Don't be stupid; I married you, didn't I? If I didn't fancy you I'd have realized it before now. It's hardly something that would have dawned on me halfway through our wedding vows." She kicked up an angry flurry of goose down with a swish of her train. "I told you that was all you men ever think about! Go away and stop being so vile to me!"

Like an upset child, she stomped over to the edge of the room in her cumbersome wedding regalia and sat down on the floor, on top of the ruptured duvet. She lay down and pulled the other duvet over her head. "Go away!" her muffled voice insisted petulantly.

Roly picked up a pillow, which to his wonderment appeared to have been conveniently provided, and went to join her in her improvised bed despite her protests, propping himself up against the wall with the pillow behind his back.

"You don't need to worry," he said to the amorphous white lump of duvet that was his wife. "I'm not ever going to leave you."

"How do you know?" the white lump wailed.

"I just know. So you'll just to have to trust me."

Her crushed veil and then her hair and eyes appeared over the top of the duvet.

"You'll regret that promise, you know, Roly, once you realize how dreadful my cooking really is."

"I know how dreadful your cooking is."

"I'm going to make you the most awful wife. I'll drive you to distraction. And you'll be terribly disappointed when you discover what a mess I am when it comes to sex—it's true, I'm afraid; I'm terribly mixed-up. All those dozens of wild, passionate flings: I was faking like a trooper through almost all of them."

"It doesn't matter," Roly said, although, if he were honest, this wasn't exactly what he wanted to be hearing on his wedding day. He reached for the other pillow and tucked it behind her as she sat up next to him. "I know I'm inexperienced, Nettie, but I'm not a prude. And we'll get help if we need to."

Annette laid her head on his shoulder and he put his arm around her, moving her veil away from his face with his hand.

"You know," she sighed, "they all think our marriage is doomed. Your sisters, my mum, Michel, Primo, Charles—everyone. They all think I'll chuck you and run off with the milkman or someone."

"Yes, I know they do."

"But they're wrong, you know. I'm not going to."

"You don't have to tell me that. I don't care what any of them think. I know they're wrong." He put out his hand and picked up a box from the floor, turning it upside down to try and see what it was. When he opened it and took out the object inside, his eyes widened. "Oh my God, did you see this?" He showed it to her. It was an iridescent, pink plastic lamp, about eight inches tall, in the shape of the leaning tower of Pisa. "No!" he said in awe. "It must be from my mum's cousin Lucie. She was on holiday in Pisa this year. That has got to be the most phallic thing I have ever seen in my life."

"Let me check," Annette said, unzipping his trousers and putting her hand down the front of them.

"No, don't," he said, pushing her hand away. "That's not fair." When she refused to stop, he added, more firmly, "Annette, that is completely unacceptable."

She wriggled down under the duvet and reappeared, dangling her lacy G-string provocatively on the end of her finger, her green eyes smiling with almost wicked confidence.

"What if someone comes in?" he protested, his pupils dilating wildly.

"Of course they won't. Hettie's as loyal as a tree. I do suggest we get on with it though. She's not going to be able to hold them off all evening."

Roly shuffled down beside her, laughing, and pulled the duvet over them both.

"I've got a terrible feeling this isn't going to take long at all," he said.

When they emerged from the room a little later, both rather tousled, they ran straight into Helena, who had been trying to bully her way past the valiantly resisting Hettie. Roly's face was flushed crimson and he was in a daze. With his dark-gray trousers and waistcoat covered in goose down he looked as though he had been tarred and feathered.

"Oh my God," Helena said, assuming a tragedy. "What's happened? Roland, you look absolutely frightful!"

Roly wasn't listening. "Thank you, darling. You too."

He ruffled his little sister's hair and walked away, light-headed under the tidal wave of sexual revelation that had swept over him, while Helena stared after him, openmouthed. Annette brushed a few pieces of potpourri out of her décolletage.

"If you must know," she said, "he's just had the most beautiful six seconds of his life." She gave her offended mother a cold look. "This is one marriage you aren't going to fuck up, Mummy."

22

THE NIGHT BEFORE THE PREMIERE of *Romeo and Juliet* at Sadler's Wells, Jonni lay awake in bed beside Michel, listening to him breathe.

"Can't you sleep?" she whispered.

"It's alright, Jons. Try and get to sleep yourself. I'm fine."

She laid her hand gently on his thigh.

"Do you want to make love?"

Michel clicked his tongue, moving her hand away.

"I'd better not. It weakens my legs. I need to keep everything I've got for tomorrow."

They lay without speaking for several minutes. Jonni hated the sound of the air moving unevenly in and out of his tense lungs.

"Are you nervous?" she asked in a whisper.

"No," he whispered back. "It's just going round and round in my mind."

The whole company were tense at the Goswell Road the next morning. The secretaries were tense. The press officer was tense. Even Nadia Petrovna was tense as she sat at the front of the big studio watching company class, tapping her walking stick anxiously with her arthritic fingers. After the losses of the previous season there was more riding on tonight's premiere than any of them dared admit, even to themselves. Charles Crown and Nadia Petrovna had gambled everything on this production. The company were dangling by a thread over a financial precipice, and below them was a sheer drop to bankruptcy. The petrifying pre-publicity spend of a hundred and twenty thousand was enough, alone, to put the Islington Ballet into receivership if tonight wasn't a success.

The thirty-three dancers at the barres were rigid and uncoordinated as Crown tried to coax a decent class out of them, struggling to hide his terror. But as with everyone else in the building, it radiated from him like a beacon. Error after error raised the level of tension in the studio to a bristling nervousness.

"Loosen it up, St. Michel," Crown said, pacing beside the barre. "Come on, son, loosen it up."

Michel tried a few more battements and then walked away in the middle of the exercise to grind his feet in the rosin tray. He flexed his back and shoulders slowly under his sweatshirt. Usually, by the time they finished the barre, he had discarded his sweatshirt, T-shirt, and woolen leggings and was dancing in just his all-in-one. This morning his muscles simply refused to warm up.

In the center, the dancers' strain became even more visible. Halfway through the first allegro of little hops and entrechats, Michel's tense feet mistimed a landing and he went over on his ankle. He dropped to the studio floor with a cry of pain, clasping his ankle in both hands.

The exercise crashed to a halt and the whole company froze. Michel sat perfectly still, holding his ankle and staring wide-eyed at the parquet floor. Crown came and crouched down beside him, resting his elbows on his knees. He didn't say a word. There was nothing to say. All they could do was wait.

Seconds ticked by and nobody moved. Peter, watching from the side of the room, turned pale. He wasn't ready for Romeo; he had been too busy working on Mercutio. Erik turned pale. He wasn't ready for Mercutio. Crown folded his arms, still crouching, and rested his forehead on them, closing his eyes. A minute became two and still there was no sound but a few whispers amongst the corps.

Eventually Michel flexed his ankle gingerly and held out his hand for Crown to help him up. He took several slow steps across the studio, stopping to rotate his ankle between each step. After several slow chassés, a cautious pirouette, and a couple of little hops he looked at Crown and nodded. Crown tilted back his head and closed his eyes, thanking God with a deep slow exhalation.

Michel went home to Pimlico after class. When he had eaten a plate of pasta he paced the studio slowly, thinking through the ballet step by step as he walked back and forth, up and down, staring at the floor. Jonni was in the studio with him, calmly absorbed in learning her role for a fringe production of *The Tempest*. She didn't look up at him once while he paced. Primo was sitting beside her, also studiously focused, writing something on a piece of paper.

At last Michel came to stand in front of them with his hands propped on his waist, breaking the silence in the studio for the first time in almost two hours.

"What're you doing, Primo?"

"Hold on, amico. Is almost finished." He rubbed out a couple of pencil marks on the paper and replaced them with new ones. "There. Is a first-night present for you—an adage. Is called 'Ariel.'"

Michel took the paper to the piano and played through the chords slowly, trying to decipher Primo's notation.

"Nah, lemme do it," Primo said, shoving him out of the way. He played through the piece and looked at Michel with a smile. "You like it?"

It was a beautiful melody but right now the only music Michel needed in his head was Prokofiev.

"It's great," he said. He picked up the piece of paper from the piano and looked at it again. "Thanks."

"Who knows, amico? Maybe I write the whole ballet for you one day, eh?"

"Yeah, you do that." He put the page of music down on the coffee table and leaned over the sofa to kiss Jonni. Standing up slowly, he looked at his wife and his best friend and then took a long, deep breath and clapped his hands together decisively. "Okay, I'm out of here." He picked up his bag from the floor beside the sofa, lifting it onto his shoulder, and strode out of the flat.

When the door had closed behind him Jonni and Primo both collapsed onto the cushions of the sofa, burying their faces and shrieking in terror.

The first night audience at Sadler's Wells buzzed with anticipation and curiosity. The monumental publicity spend hadn't yet kick-started the advances at the theater box offices but it had brought the entire ballet world to the premiere. Critics huddled together at the bar conferring over the program and exchanging notes about the dancers they already knew. Charles Crown stood like a statue in his dress suit watching the obese critic, Boyle, who was frowning at the posters of Carlotta and Michel in the foyer, shaking his flabby head disparagingly as he talked to his colleagues with hideously downturned mouth.

In the crowded auditorium, as the lights started to dim with the applause that greeted the conductor's entrance, Nadia Petrovna twisted her stiff neck and looked at Charles Crown across the rows of the stalls. Crown was so terrified that he met her eyes with no expression at all. But she knew. And so did he. The next three hours would decide the fate of the company.

Crown watched blankly as the curtain rose and Michel, Peter, and Daniel romped gaily through the opening scene with the corps. Crown had looked at it so hard and for so long that he could no longer see it. Was it good? Was it bad? Was it terrible? He had no idea. The audience were giving nothing away.

In the interval, when he overheard Boyle praising the choreography of the balcony scene, Crown locked himself in one of the foyer loos and threw up.

At the end of the longest and most terrifying three hours of Crown's life, as the company lined up on the stage to take their bows, he was just about compos mentis enough to understand that his company had done extremely well for him tonight. Everyone had danced at their best. Michel had danced superbly from first to last, pushing each leap and turn in the air to the point of danger like the daredevil he was, sailing through every combination as though nothing were further from his mind than the technical demands of the choreography. But the only thing that had penetrated Crown's numb mind sufficiently to make him realize just how well Michel had really danced tonight was the absolute stillness of the audience around him when Michel dropped like a stone, dead at the foot of Juliet's tomb.

Nothing in Michel's experience had prepared him for the reception that greeted him as he walked out of the wings onto the stage at the curtain call with Carlotta. Within moments the only person in the whole auditorium who wasn't on their feet was Charles Crown. Even Boyle was standing. For a long time Michel just stood there looking at the audience and at Carlotta in blank incomprehension, going through the polite motions of handing his ballerina forward for her solo bow several times before they just stood together hand in hand and looked into the blinding lights. And then slowly Michel smiled—the soft, special smile that Jonni knew so well—and the already elated audience went into raptures.

The ovation went on and on as Crown sat there like a dead man. He looked up as the house manager tapped him on the shoulder.

"They're asking for you, Mister Crown."

Blindly he let himself be led into the orchestra pit and up the stairs to the stage. Everyone around him, both onstage and off, was cheering and calling out his name. Crown looked around in a daze. The orchestra were on their feet, clapping their hands above their heads. The dancers were shouting and stamping their feet. Michel and Carlotta were both applauding him with radiant smiles. Crown stood, dreamlike, unable to understand that this euphoric uproar, the yells of approval from the auditorium, the love on the faces of the cheering dancers, was all for him. Crown had never coveted applause for himself—had never even thought about it. Everything he did was for the company and for the love of dance. But standing here onstage surrounded by the adoring faces of the company he had bullied and hectored and criticized for so many months, and the cheering audience who had forgiven him for all the pieces they had hated in the past, his eyes swam with tears.

That night, after Sir Christopher's formal reception in the foyer, the entire company piled back to Michel's Pimlico flat for a wild impromptu party. Tomorrow was Sunday and a much-needed day off to recover before Monday's performance, but tonight the company was bent on mayhem. Marina and even Charles Crown turned up to wet the head of the company's new offspring and the flat was so crowded it was almost impossible to move.

Michel squeezed through the crowd around the kitchen door, patting one of the Sadler's Wells usherettes on the bottom to move her out of the way, and put his arm around Jonni as she found him amidst the hubbub.

"Were you scared for me while I was onstage tonight?" he asked her.

She shook her head: "Not scared. My heart just went zing!"

"Zing?"

"Uh-huh . . . ZING!"

"Just your heart? Nothing else?"

"No, nothing else," she said, laughing. "But I'm sure it could be arranged."

Everyone was ecstatically happy. The atmosphere soared on adrenaline and high spirits. A group of the apprentices were doing the cancan in a line in front of the mirror—it was just as well the flat below was empty at weekends. The only person who wasn't celebrating was Primo. Michel finally found him sitting alone on one of the low windowsills in the studio.

"What are you doing here all by yourself, Primo?"

One of Primo's feet was up on the windowsill beside him, his arm resting on his knee. As ever, he had a glass of whisky in his hand.

"I'm just watchin' the world go by. Ponderin', you know, amico?"

"Well, stop pondering and come and join us. This production's as much your work as anyone else's."

"Nah, it ain't." Primo sipped his whisky slowly. He looked at Michel with a bland smile. "You did good tonight, Michel. Real good."

"Come on, we need you. A party's only half a party without you."

"You'll get by. There's gonna be hundreds of parties in the future where you ain't gonna notice I'm not there."

"Well, if you don't want to talk to me, come and talk to Roly and Nettie—they've come back from their honeymoon early, especially for tonight. They're both disgustingly brown."

Primo swung his foot down from the windowsill and stood up.

"Nah, I think I'll head home. Say hi to them for me, yeah? You have a good time, Michel. You deserve it." He picked up his jacket and made his way through the crowded studio and out of the flat.

While Michel vanished, shaking his head, back into the exultant throng, one of the boy dancers on the far side of the studio picked up his glass from the coffee table and peeled off a sheet of paper that had stuck to the bottom: a sheet of scribbled music notation, covered with wet rings from other glasses. He screwed it up and threw it away.

Even before the reviews came out everyone in the company knew that this was the evening that would make Charles Crown and would make Michel.

First thing on Monday morning the Islington Ballet phones started ringing. All the radio arts programs wanted interviews. Several national broadsheets wanted to run features. ITN and the BBC wanted footage. After years of having to scrabble for every three-inch column in the regional papers, suddenly the press officer was having to fight off publicity calls. Crown couldn't believe he was actually mulling over a breakfast television interview to decide if it was worth the trouble.

"Sending a car at what time?" Michel asked. "You've got to be joking. I won't even be conscious at half past six, let alone in a fit state to talk to anyone."

"Sorry," said Elaine, the press officer, on the phone. "We really need you to do it. We'll have you back before class."

"What do I say to them? Jesus, a live television interview!"

"Just be yourself."

"Well, don't blame me if I'm rude to them."

And Michel was rude to them. He was incredibly rude. And the studio audience adored him.

"I warned you it was a bad idea," he told Elaine in the press office when he arrived at the Goswell Road. "I didn't mean to be so foul to her but she came out with such stupid questions. I mean, what do I do first thing in the morning? What sort of question is that? I have a crap first thing in the morning. And as for my comment about her . . . you know . . . when she looked down and asked me, 'What do you think of these?' I honestly didn't realize she was talking about the little ballet shoes embroidered on the collar of her blouse." He shook his head with an apologetic smile. "Sorry. You'll know next time to send someone else."

Elaine was new to the company; a fashionable PR girl with dyed black hair cut in an aggressive businesslike bob. She waved her spiral-bound notebook, showing him a page of scribbled notes.

"Check out this!" she said. "Since your interview this morning I've had calls from Channel 4's *Arts Week, London Tonight, Late Review,* and GMTV. Fasten your seat belt, Michel. The next few weeks are going to be hairy."

All these press calls, on top of classes, rehearsals, and performances, were draining for Michel. And the media effect snowballed; as soon as one magazine ran a feature the rest wanted one too. Every interviewer wanted to know, of course, about Michel's relationship to Jacques St. Michel. Was it true Michel was his nephew? Michel had no idea where that rumor had originated but he never confirmed or denied it; he merely said he'd never met Jacques St. Michel and suggested they change the subject.

When the company had been out on the road for a month, performing *Romeo and Juliet* to packed houses, a feature appeared in the *Daily Mail* comparing Michel to Nureyev, although not entirely favorably.

"What cobblers," Crown muttered, turning over the page to read the rest of the article. "The idiots don't know what they're talking about. He's a completely different sort of dancer. Still, it's good publicity, you can't knock that."

Nadia Petrovna looked up at him from behind her desk.

"I'm afraid we're going to lose him, Charles. This company is becoming too small for him. Or rather he's getting too big for it."

"Nonsense, he's perfectly happy here. He knows what he wants."

"Someone will make him an offer that's too good to turn down. He'll be snapped up and taken off to Paris or Milan."

"We'll cross that bridge when we come to it."

"Will we?" The old woman's pale eyes followed him as he walked across the room, still engrossed in the article, to switch on the kettle. "You're becoming an eminent figure in the dance world, Charles. When Michel goes there'll be nothing to hold you here any longer. I shall lose you both."

Crown looked up at her from his newspaper with a frown of surprise.

"You think I'd walk out on this company after all the work we put into creating it and building it up?"

"My dear friend, it's inevitable. All the great companies of Europe are clamoring for your choreography. And once Michel goes, yes, you'll go too."

Crown stared at her incredulously, his black eyes gradually darkening in rage. Seconds passed and he just stared at her.

At last he hurled his newspaper onto the desk and strode out of her office.

"Screw you, Nadia Petrovna," he said, and slammed the door behind him.

Part Three

23

ANOTHER PREMIERE WAS COMING UP, a big one, and Michel had been very quiet for the past few days. His preoccupation made Jonni uneasy.

"I'm making coffee. Want some?"

"Black, two sugars, thanks."

"I do know, Michel. This is your wife speaking. Hello? Remember me?"

He looked up from the sofa where he was absentmindedly thumbing through last month's copy of *The Dancing Times*. His smile was only a half smile and his eyes remained distant.

"Sorry, yes, I'd love a coffee."

He returned to his magazine and Jonni padded out to the kitchen in her bare feet.

When she could muster the self-control to look at the situation logically she knew full well that this was just Michel's reaction to stress and overtiredness in the buildup to the premiere of this new ballet. Poor Michel, everyone wanted their share of him: Charles Crown wanted him, the Islington Ballet's publicists wanted him, London's fashionable society, journalists, TV producers, photographers—they all thought they had a right to a part of him.

She reached down into a cupboard for a packet of arabica beans and hooked her loose hair behind her ear, plugging in the electric grinder. Michel was a rising star: an idol in the dance world. Why should he be interested in her, an insignificant actress struggling in unpaid fringe theater? She pressed the switch on the coffee grinder aggressively. She was dull. Uninspiring. A nobody beside the rich and glamorous throng who vied for Michel's attention day after day. When had they last gone out, just the two of them, or spent an evening alone together like they used to? Or a Sunday afternoon in bed? Why would he want to spend the afternoon in bed with her when there was a pile of love letters six feet high in the Islington Ballet press office from women—and men, of course— offering him undying love, sex, and the use of their yachts at St.-Tropez?

The past three years of Jonni's marriage had been peppered with periodic manifestations of her low self-esteem. For weeks now she had been fretting over tiny signs that her life with Michel was stagnating. In reality their marriage never got half a chance to stagnate. At the first sign of complacency Jonni pounced, and every aspect of their relationship was dissected and despaired over amidst tears and reproaches while the smallest signs of change or apathy were inflated into major disasters. As for Michel, he listened to these outbursts with weary resignation, unable or unwilling to enter into the argument, knowing that ultimately the power to comfort her lay in his arms. Jonni's tantrums invariably ended up in bed where they were forgotten within minutes.

For the past week Jonni's emotional barometer had been falling fast. But Michel was so snowed under with work for the coming premiere she hadn't had an opportunity to voice her frustration and fear. He hadn't even asked her about her two depressing auditions at the start of the week.

"That's it," she thought, as she shook the coffee grounds into the paper filter. "We've stopped communicating."

"How's the ballet going?" she asked, dragging a coaster across the low table and setting a mug in front of Michel.

"Oh, fine." He was still absently scanning the pages of the dance journal.

"The general rehearsal's on Friday, isn't it?"

"Yes, Friday afternoon. I'm watching."

"Oh. Who's dancing it then?"

"Hmm?" He turned to the next page. "Oh, Erik, I expect."

He was as near as dammit telling her to mind her own business.

Jonni remained calm while she sipped her coffee. "Could we go out together for lunch tomorrow? You aren't rehearsing, are you?"

"Tomorrow? No, I'm having lunch in Chelsea."

"Who with?"

"Mmm?" He was frowning at an article about Jacques St. Michel's new double bill in Los Angeles. "Some . . . clients of one of my sponsors." Michel had two highly paid personal sponsorship deals, one with a brand of sportswear and the other with a leading antiperspirant, neither of which he wore.

"I wish to God," she burst out, "you'd put that bloody paper down for a minute and talk to me."

Michel took a deep breath which inflated his chest slowly before he closed the magazine and threw it on the black lacquered table.

"What do you want to talk about? Thanks for the coffee."

"I don't know. Nothing. Anything. I just wish we could talk sometimes."

"Oh, please, Jonni; not this again. Not this evening."

"Again? What do you mean, again? You've barely spoken to me all week. You spent ten minutes talking to those fans on the doorstep; so what about me? What sort of relationship have we got if we don't talk?"

"When you're in this mood you never have anything to say. We just end up talking about talking."

"What else can we talk about when you're so distant?"

"I'm not distant. I've just got things on my mind."

"What things?" she insisted. This secrecy, this unwillingness to let her into his life was tearing her apart. "Michel, if there's something wrong why won't you tell me about it?"

Michel picked up his coffee with a weary grimace.

"There's nothing wrong. I'm tired and I'm trying to think."

"What are you thinking about? You never tell me what you're thinking."

"Jesus, aren't I allowed any privacy? I'm thinking about work."

"Well, I'm sorry if I'm intruding. If I had anywhere else to go I would."

Jonni was getting worked up but Michel was too exhausted to play the game. He leaned against the back of the sofa, closing his eyes and cradled his coffee mug between his hands.

"Jons, couldn't we just have a nice quiet evening?"

"Are you sorry you married me?"

He answered her, "No," with a sigh and then opened his eyes, turning his head against the back of the sofa to look at her. "When's your period due?"

Jonni flew into a rage.

"It must be hell living with me!" she cried. "You knew what I was like from the first time we met, didn't you? Why on earth did you marry me?"

"Because you wanted me to."

"Oh, you really are a charmer, Michel."

He reached for her hand and laid it on his thigh, covering it with his own hand.

"I told you at the time marriage means nothing to me. You know I'm no flatterer, Jons, and if you think I only want you here because we're married, you're a bigger fool than I took you for."

He was being flippant but Jonni was in no mood for humor. She pulled her hand away and stared at him furiously.

"And just how big a fool is that?"

The one-sided quarrel escalated until Michel ran out of patience and put a stop to her tirade, rising swiftly from the sofa to leave the studio.

"For Christ's sake, Jonni, grow up, will you?"

Jonni stared at the door as he closed it behind him. The point at which Michel walked out on her was always the moment when she realized she had overdone it. Michel never exploded; he didn't blow fuses—his temper was protected by a mental trip switch; when she pushed him too far he simply shut down, blocking all attempts at communication until this trip switch was given a chance to reset itself. Jonni waited miserably in the studio for ten minutes, timing herself by the clock above the door. She had no pride where Michel was concerned; she was ready to make an abject apology.

"Do you want me to leave you in peace?" she asked humbly, poking her head around the kitchen door and seeing that Michel was deep in thought.

"Depends what you've come for."

"I've come to grovel. But I can come back and grovel later if you like."

Michel looked ready enough to forgive her. He held out a hand to her and she went to join him where he stood leaning against the sink. She looked up at him sheepishly as he put his arm around her.

"Were you thinking about me?"

"Nope; work again, I'm afraid. In fact, I was thinking about someone else."

She forgot that she was supposed to be groveling and asked him a question which, though she hadn't realized it until now, had been hovering at the back of her mind for weeks.

"You weren't by any chance thinking about the girl you're partnering in this new ballet?"

"Actually, I was. Her name's Louisa."

"I know her name's Louisa," she said. "You haven't talked about anything else since you and Charles started work on this new piece. Louisa's marvelous sensitivity. Louisa's fantastic extension. I've had it up to here with bloody Louisa."

"She's a good little dancer. Charles has made us a couple of knockout pas de deux, especially the love scene after our wedding. Are you jealous?" Michel was teasing her now but Jonni was in deadly earnest.

"I heard Charles saying she's good for you because you fancy her."

"He said I gel with her physically. That's different."

"And do you?"

"What?"

"Gel with her physically."

Michel was noncommittal: "Sure; yes."

"You mean you do fancy her."

"I suppose so."

Jonni's chin shot up suddenly and she stared at him in horror. Michel tilted his head to one side and smiled at her.

"I could lie to you, Jons. I will if you like."

Jonni searched his face, devastated that he was laughing at her. Her whole world was falling apart, or so she thought, and he was laughing!

"My God, you really do fancy her, don't you? You aren't joking."

"So what? It doesn't mean I'm going to do anything about it."

"Don't you want to?"

"No. If I wanted to, I would."

"So why don't you then? Because of me?"

"Yes. I know it would upset you."

"Upset me?" She looked at him in despair. "You mean if you thought I wouldn't mind, you'd sleep with her?"

"Maybe. Yes, probably—I don't know. I told you, it would upset you so I'm not going to do it. But I'd be lying if I said it hadn't crossed my mind."

She put her hands to her head, clenching great handfuls of hair in her fists. She was terribly hurt.

"Do you think of her when you're in bed with me?"

"No." Michel raised one hand to stop her, trying to calm the situation down. "Look, don't start down that road. It's a mild attraction; nothing more. She gets my hormones going when we dance together, which is good for our partnership, but it's purely physical; not mental."

Jonni couldn't see the difference.

"You've never even told me you love me," she wailed, starting to cry in self-pity.

"I shouldn't have to tell you."

"But I need you to."

His face hardened; he wasn't prepared to be manipulated that way.

"Jons, those are just words!"

"Well, do you?"

"I'm not even going to answer that; it's not an issue."

Jonni blew her nose angrily on a piece of kitchen towel. To her it was very much an issue.

"You mean he never once said he loves you? Even in bed?"

Primo was amazed. He was sitting with Jonni in the tiny lounge of his flat in Lupus Street. She had flown there in a torrent of furious tears, shouting to Michel that if he wanted her he could find her at Primo's and slamming the door as she went. For the past two hours she had been pouring out her woes, waiting for Michel to arrive and getting steadily blotto.

"Love!" she mourned drunkenly. "I don't even think he knows the meaning of the word."

"Perhaps you're right," Primo agreed. In his heart, he was sure of it.

Things hadn't been going well for Primo. Since leaving the Islington Ballet three years ago he had been drinking far more than was good for him and the alcohol had intensified his habitual mood swings. He spent days at a time in a state of semicomatose lethargy in the flat, doing nothing, seeing no one. Dirty dishes piled up in the sink, empty bottles accumulated. The place became a pigsty. At other times his energy was frightening; he scrambled out of bed at dawn or earlier and worked like a man possessed until the early hours of the next morning. When this mania of creativity hit him he existed in a state of ecstatic jubilation, bent over the pages of his score on the piano, a glass always at his side, scribbling and laughing to himself. In the past two years he had received letters from all the major dance companies offering him accompanying work but the letters had all gone unanswered. He played for occasional classes at the Royal or the English National to pay his rent and finance his drinking, but otherwise he sat alone in his flat and let the music inside his head gradually devour him.

Since Christmas, Michel had been working almost as hard as Primo in one of his manic phases. But not so hard that he failed to notice how reclusive his friend had become.

"Hey, Primo," he had said, phoning from the Goswell Road during a well-earned break in rehearsal, "when are you coming in to play for class? I need you; I can't take much more of the crap these idiots dish out on the piano."

"I got no time at the moment, amico," came the cheerful reply. High or low, Primo always managed to find a moderate tone when he talked to Michel.

"How about coming round to the flat tonight? I should be through at seven or eight and Jonni would love to see you too. She's down in the dumps about being out of work. Come to dinner."

"I'm writing music. You know me; I'm a-like a cat in a hot roof when I got music pouring out of my head."

"What are you writing?"

"Something big; is a ballet. Is gonna be good."

"Can't wait to hear it. Well, come soon. You know the code for the door."

"You bet," Primo agreed, but somehow time had passed and more than two months had elapsed since he had last brought his lazy Italian smile to the Warwick Way flat.

This evening, when Jonni had rung on his doorbell, shaking and in tears after her quarrel with Michel, she had caught him in a period of transition. The months of frenzied activity had come to an end and Primo was on his way down. His ballet was finally finished—the adaptation of Shakespeare's *Tempest* he had started writing for Michel more than two years ago—and he was slumped in exhaustion. For a week he had done nothing but sit and brood. The manuscript, fully orchestrated, was all there in a folder at his side. It was a magnificent piece of work and he knew it: a labor of great love into which he'd poured every drop of skill, art, and inspiration he possessed. Its completion marked an ending for Primo of more than the work it had involved—a massive full stop on the page of his life. He knew, now his masterpiece was complete, that he would never show it to Michel. The risk was too great; the risk that Michel would reject it as he had rejected every other manifestation of Primo's passion.

Now, as he sat watching Jonni cry, Primo hated Michel. He hated him and loved him. Coldly lucid despite the whisky, Primo realized that he had always envied Michel. He envied Michel's single-mindedness, his unshakable belief in his own ability, the professional respect of his colleagues. He envied the energy and labor Charles Crown had invested in him. He envied Michel's fame; the fame which justified his existence as an artist. Primo's envy, as he listened to Jonni's outpouring, filled him with self-disgust.

He wanted what Michel had. He wanted to be Michel. Most of all, he wanted to run away from himself and not to feel anything.

He lit another cigarette and emptied the remains of a bottle of Scotch into his glass. Another bottle, already opened, sat on the table and he pushed it toward his visitor with a smile.

"Bugger Michel," he said. "I love you anyway."

Jonni was too drunk and too immersed in self-pity to notice just how low Primo really was. She didn't see how quickly the smile faded from the deep-brown eyes; the smile that, for years, had concealed layer upon layer of heartache and bitterness. She didn't see, either, how empty his eyes became once the smile had gone, as though part of him were absent from the room.

"He doesn't love me," she slurred, pouring herself another drink and spilling more whisky on the table than into her glass. "If he did, he wouldn't fancy her. You can't be in love with one person and fancy someone else."

Primo answered that with a mirthless laugh.

"Yes, you can. I've been doing it for ten years. I've got a feeling being in love is a fallacious concept anyway. A big cultural myth. Perhaps it's just another name for desire—or need—or an excuse for a lifetime of habit." He looked with a sigh at the stacks of disarrayed piano scores. "Or something, Jonni. I'm not sure."

Alcohol seemed to have steamed up the windows in Jonni's head. She blinked her eyes carefully and stared at him. It wasn't what he had said that had made her choke on her drink; it was the way he had said it.

"Your accent! Primo, what happened to your accent?"

"It's phony, darling, like the rest of me."

"It can't be; I've known you for years."

Primo shrugged and flicked the ash from his cigarette onto the carpet. "Like so many things, it's just a habit. You don't live in Hackney half your life and Pimlico the other half and still end up talking pidgin English like your parents. But I was like any other kid; screaming for an identity. My accent made me different. It made me feel special."

"You are special," she said. "You're the most special person I've ever known."

Primo threw his cigarette into an ashtray and moved over to sit next to her on the sofa, putting his arm around her. Jonni laid her head drunkenly on his shoulder.

"You haven't been to see us for so long."

"Yeah, I know; I've been busy."

"Primo, why does everything have to be so horrible? I want everything to be beautiful."

"The world's a fucked-up place, Jonni." He caressed her arm slowly, looking at the bottle on the table with embittered eyes. The stinging jealousy he felt toward Michel welled up inside him. "Don't think about the ugliness. You've got to find beauty wherever you can."

She lifted her head and smiled at him with fuzzy affection.

The feel of Primo's mouth against hers was peculiar. He kissed differently than Michel; his mouth moved differently, tasted different. It was rather like being in a play, she decided. His hands, gentle at first, on her waist and under her jumper, made her giggle. Her head was reeling from the alcohol. When he leaned over her, pressing her against the cushions and pulling up her long woolen skirt, the flood of sexual response that swept through her body felt unreal, as though it belonged to someone else. It had to belong to someone else: it was impossible that Primo was kissing her and that she was kissing him back. Impossible that her friend had his hand inside her knickers and that she was murmuring with pleasure. So impossible it was funny. It was only when he unzipped his trousers and pushed her thighs apart with his knees that she realized she had made a dire mistake. Her bleary eyes opened wide in alarm as she felt the unknown shape of his penis pushing its way into her, tearing away the precious hymen of her fidelity to Michel.

Afterward she lay motionless in his arms while her drink-dulled mind shrieked incoherent reproaches at her. Perhaps Primo was miserable too—she tried to look at him but he was holding her face close to his shoulder and she was too drunk to move her head. In fact, she wasn't sure she could move any part of her body.

Physically, once she had understood what was happening, it had been ghastly. Emotionally—well, she had the feeling that they were both going to wake up tomorrow morning with a distinct problem. She felt too dizzy to think about that now.

"We should have used a condom," she said.

Primo's voice was soft as he answered. He was the old Primo again, comforting and brotherly.

"Is okay, bella; I ain't HIV-positive. I know; I checked. When you expect to get the curse, eh?"

"I don't know; a week or so."

"Ai ai." He stroked her hair kindly. "Don't worry, baby. I'll talk to Michel tomorrow. Is all gonna be okay." His reassuring caress was so much like the Primo she knew so well, so like the affection he had always lavished upon her since the days when they had first met, that she nuzzled her face against his shoulder and closed her eyes. The wrongness of being with him was over. All that was left of it were the consequences they would both have to face in the morning.

Primo lay with her, staring at the ceiling, while she drifted into sleep. When she was breathing softly and evenly he shifted her limbs off his body, gently to avoid waking her, and went to crouch beside his record collection in the corner of the sitting room. He flicked through the records slowly. Primo had never learned to like CDs; he still swore by the quality of good old-fashioned vinyl. Eventually, after looking through his entire collection, he pulled out Ashkenazy's recording of Beethoven's fifth piano concerto and tipped the record out of its sleeve, putting it on the turntable.

Jonni didn't stir once while the three movements of the concerto filled the room. Primo listened without moving, sitting on the floor with his legs drawn up and his elbows resting on his knees. When the music stopped at the end of the third movement he turned out the lamps in the room and took his manuscript to the bedroom, closing the sitting room door quietly behind him as he left.

There were a few blissful moments of ignorance when Jonni opened her eyes the next morning. Then her chest tightened in horror. The light crashing through the curtainless window stabbed at her mind.

Her argument with Michel had been a fool's argument. Poor man, he had been shattered after eight solid hours in the studio. She had no business nagging him when he needed rest, especially when he was under pressure with the premiere only a week away. And why shouldn't he have a passing fancy for another girl? It was meaningless. And it was big of him to confess it, too. She knew perfectly well that he loved her and wanted to be with her.

She swung her feet onto the floor. They felt like lead. Oh, that stupid bloody quarrel! Why had she let herself behave so insanely? She put her hands to her splitting head and screwed her eyes tight shut, hoping what she and Primo had done would go away if she willed it hard enough. Desperately she tried to change the events of the night before. She tried to make Michel have come and collected her—or make herself have slinked home to apologize. But try as she might, her bed was still the uncomfortable brown sofa in Primo's flat and there was no Michel beside her reaching out to her forgivingly for a Sunday morning cuddle. What she had done would never go away.

Jonni crawled onto the carpet and held her head wretchedly in her hands. Michel would probably be magnanimous. Oh God, she hoped he wouldn't. She hoped he'd throw the book at her: storm, rage, hit her—anything but forgiveness, at least not for a while.

Primo had left her a note drawing-pinned to his bedroom door—

"Jonni, don't come into the bedroom to see me. Go home and tell Michel to come. I'll explain everything to him. Don't worry, it will be okay. Love Primo. P.S. Tell Michel to bring his keys. I feel too sick to get up and let him in."

Jonni ignored the note and tapped gently on the door. She very badly needed comfort. She wasn't ready for Michel just yet.

Michel had genuinely intended to stroll over to Lupus Street to collect Jonni the previous evening. He thought it might be as well to give her an hour or so to cool off and he stretched out on the bed to wait, dog-tired. The next thing he knew it was broad daylight and the phone was ringing, dragging him reluctantly out of deep sleep.

He thought of class and groaned, burying his face in the pillow—and then came the delicious realization that it was Sunday. But the phone still rang persistently, and he hauled himself out of bed, not bothering to wake up fully as he stumbled into the hallway.

Within thirty seconds he was sprinting bare-chested along Warwick Way through an icy wind. The cold air bit at his throat as he tore between the pedestrians who stepped out of his way on the narrow pavement. Turning left into Cambridge Street he grabbed a young woman by both shoulders and leaped over her small dog to avoid knocking either of them down. The woman recognized him, turning her head to stare after him in amazement.

He hadn't been able to get a single word out of Jonni; only screams from the moment he answered the phone.

"Speak to me!" he had shouted at her. "Darling, speak to me!"

There had been no response except more screaming and then the sound of the receiver being dropped or thrown onto something hard, probably the floor.

Michel's face was expressionless as he raced across Lupus Street, placing a hand on the bonnet of a waiting car as he ran in front of it. His body had taken control. The keys to Primo's flat were in his hand and he turned the key cleanly in the lock, leaving the front door gaping behind him as he bounded up the stairs four at a time.

The telephone receiver was still on the floor a few feet from Jonni's curled-up figure in the small hall of the cold flat. Michel looked from Jonni's staring eyes toward the door of Primo's bedroom. He pushed the bedroom door open, glancing at Jonni again over his shoulder as he walked through it.

Primo was lying on his bed curled up in a fetal position. He was dead. His pale face wore an expression of mild surprise.

Michel stood beside the bed and looked down at Primo's lifeless body and sightless eyes. Then he turned his head and lifted it very slowly to look at the phenomenal quantity of blood that covered the walls and spattered the ceiling. He looked at the brown-stained razor blade on the blood-soaked carpet next to his foot, and at the envelope on the bedside table that bore his name. And as he looked he felt something move inside himself, a slow, grinding movement as though a huge steel door was being gradually closed on massive iron hinges. The movement inside him made him wince in physical pain, but after a moment the sensation passed and he felt nothing at all.

He walked out of the bedroom and picked up the telephone receiver from the floor, pressing the connecting button a few times until the dialing tone was restored.

"Ambulance, please," he said, when the female voice answered. "Actually, no, better make that the police, thanks."

Twenty minutes later the police constable walked out of Primo's bedroom with slow steps, resting his hand on the door frame to support himself, traumatized by what he had just seen.

"Jesus," he said to the woman officer who was leaning over Jonni. He wiped the back of his fist over his mouth. "I've got a son his age."

When the constable had blown his nose and pulled himself together, he turned to Michel. He was a middle-aged man with a soft cockney accent.

"You called in the report, sir?"

"Yes."

"Right." He pulled out his notebook. "The dead man's name."

Michel stood with his hands in his pockets while the policeman painstakingly wrote down Primo's full name and date of birth.

"And your name, sir?"

"Jean-Baptiste St. Michel." He spelled it for him.

"Any ID, sir, just for the record?"

Michel shrugged without taking his hands from his pockets, glancing down at his body. He was wearing not a stitch apart from his loose jogging pants and jazz shoes, and a sweatshirt he had taken from Primo's cupboard. The policeman nodded.

"Alright, it's not important at the moment. As this envelope's been opened, I assume the name Michel refers either to yourself or your wife."

"Yes, to me."

"Have you read it?"

"Yes."

"Mind if I take a look?"

"No, not at all."

The constable had the flattest face Michel had ever seen. It wasn't an unpleasant face, it just looked as though it had been squashed repeatedly by a steamroller. When he had read the note he looked up at Michel, squinting into his emotionless gray eyes. Michel's eyes were blank; no trace of shock or distress.

"Particularly close, were you, sir?"

"Yes, he was my best friend."

"Then I'm sorry for your loss, sir."

While the ambulance team took Primo's body away on a covered stretcher the constable stood tapping the letter pensively against his hand. He glanced at Jonni's huddled body in the corner of the hall and whispered discreetly to Michel, "Mind stepping into the lounge with me for a word, sir? It won't take long."

"Sorry about this," he said, closing the door. "There are just a couple of things I want to clarify so I can explain them to my sergeant. Coroners ask awkward questions about violent suicides."

He looked around the room, glancing over the empty whisky bottles on the table and the shelves crammed with musical scores, and the piles of well-thumbed concerti and sonatas on the battered brown piano.

"Musician, was he?"

"Yep."

"Are you a musician too?"

"Not the way you would define musicianship, no."

The constable looked Michel over with thoughtful eyes. He didn't like this good-looking young man with his impassive face and his matter-of-fact attitude to that bloody mess next door.

"Mind telling me what you do actually do?"

Michel nodded toward a clip frame on the wall and the constable turned his head to look at it. It held a poster advertising a recent Islington Ballet season: a picture of Michel in a flying leap from one of Charles Crown's modern pieces. The policeman's eyes traveled slowly over the picture, over the stretched feet in their ballet shoes, the soaring hands, the naked muscular torso, and then turned back toward Michel to look him dubiously up and down. He plainly wasn't impressed.

"I see. This note; there are things in it that, frankly, I can't make head nor tail of."

"That's because it was written for me to understand, not you."

"Yes, of course, I'm sorry. I don't want to pry into your relationship with the dead man any more than necessary . . ."

"That's okay," Michel said. "Go ahead."

"This passage here, for instance, where he mentions your wife; would you mind explaining what you think he meant by it?"

Michel perched on the back of the sofa and took the note from him. When he had skimmed over the paragraph he handed it back.

"I'd have thought it was fairly plain."

"Well, yes, if it's a statement of fact. It's pretty blunt."

"We were always blunt with each other. If he says he fucked her, I'm sure that's exactly what he means."

"Right. In that case, this paragraph here about his feelings for you . . ."

"He was bisexual."

"And you are . . . ?"

"Heterosexual."

The flat-faced policeman nodded. "I understand." He clearly didn't understand at all. He looked long and hard into Michel's gray eyes and then sighed, shaking his head as he walked away to the window, putting his hand in his pocket. He looked out onto the street where the cold cloudiness of the morning had turned to steady rain. He wasn't a quick-thinking man but he was experienced and thorough.

"There's nothing in this letter to suggest it's a suicide note."

"He probably assumed I'd work that out for myself."

The constable turned around at Michel's flippant reply and studied his face with a frown.

"Mister St. Michel, I'm trying to be tactful with you here. I'm assuming this is not a happy morning for you. But you aren't making it easy for me to be sympathetic."

"I don't need sympathy," Michel said. "I need to get my wife home. At the risk of appearing unhelpful, can I ask you to get on with this?"

"Alright. Just one more question. What does he mean, here in the last paragraph, when he says . . . I have destroyed the only thing I have to give you because I don't want you should still reject me after I've gone?"

"You tell me," Michel said.

Throughout the whole procedure Jonni had remained curled up in the corner of the hall, untouched and undisturbed apart from the offer of a cup of tea from the kindly policewoman. She had merely wailed in reply, burying her head deeper in her arms.

"Drink it, Jons," Michel had said, and she obeyed automatically.

Now they were alone together, away from the scene of Primo's death. They had walked home in silence, Jonni's shoulder occasionally brushing the sleeve of Michel's sweatshirt as they walked side by side along Cambridge Street in the rain. He put a cup of coffee laced with brandy on the kitchen table in front of her. She made a move to lift it in her hands but changed her mind.

"I'm going to be sick again."

Michel held her hair away from her face while she threw up in the sink and then he wiped her mouth with a piece of kitchen towel and led her back to a chair.

"Michel, how did the blood get on the ceiling?"

"It's under a lot of pressure in the arteries."

"Oh." She gazed down at the kitchen table, her eyes unfocused and vague. "Did you know Primo's accent isn't real? He can talk in an English accent if he wants to."

"Yes. He used to talk in his sleep when we shared a room as students."

Michel left her alone for over two hours. Primo's mother had to be told and he couldn't do it over the phone. The police had offered but Michel had shaken his head. He'd go himself. He'd tell everyone who needed to know—except perhaps one person. He didn't want to be the one to tell Crown. The bond between Primo and Crown was a deep one; Michel didn't think he could face Crown's anguish, not today.

"I'll do it." Jonni's trembling voice had come from the corner of the hall. The constable had looked at her hunched figure and then at Michel. Michel nodded.

Once she was alone Jonni brought the telephone into the studio and tucked her feet up beneath her on one of the black leather sofas. Outwardly, she had fallen into step with Michel's calm practicality. She listened to the sounds of car engines and banging front doors in the street below. Sunday in Warwick Way sounded different from other days of the week; there were no workmen whistling, no delivery vans with their back doors rattling as they were thrown open or crashed shut.

She turned her head to examine the studio. She sensed Primo's presence very strongly. He was here on the sofa next to her, over there on the piano stool, in the open space of the room on the parquet floor he had laid with his own hands. He was here in her head. She looked at the red coffee mugs, still sitting on the table since before she'd picked that foolish quarrel with Michel yesterday. Primo had brought those mugs back from his last trip to Rome. This was his home; he wasn't going to go away.

She picked up the receiver and dialed. The moment she heard Charles Crown's voice she fell apart and her first words were little more than a squeal.

"It's me . . . Jonni!"

There was a pause before Crown spoke again, his voice lower by almost an octave. "Okay, tell me, darling. Is it very bad? Is he sick?"

She managed a negative sob.

"Injured? Dead? Come on, my love."

"Suicide," she squeaked.

Crown's voice made several attempts to repeat the word.

"Michel's gone to tell his mother," Jonni said.

"Mi . . . Michel's gone . . . ?"

"To Hackney. I was in his flat last night when he did it."

"Oh Jesus, no." Crown's voice dropped to a whisper. "Sweet Jesus, not Primo." There was another pause and Jonni heard a stream of terrible swearing uttered some distance from the phone in an animal-like howl.

When Michel came back to the flat Crown was sitting with Jonni in the studio, red-eyed and chain-smoking. Together he and Michel spent the afternoon making phone calls while Jonni sat by in silence, marveling at how calmly both men told what must be told, over and over again. She had only made the one call and she had messed it up completely.

Crown and Michel shared the really nasty ones between them. They struck bargains.

"I'll do Marina if you'll do Roly."

"No, if I've got to call Roly, you do Daniel and Carlotta as well as Marina."

"Oh, for fuck's sake; I'll do Roly. But you've got to call Lynne."

"Alright, done."

Eventually it was over. They hadn't been able to contact Lynne in South Africa so they dictated a telegram over the phone. No one could face leaving it until another time when she was available. Crown kept it short and to the point; "Primo is dead stop grief and love Michel Jonni Charles stop we can't believe it either stop."

"Thank you," Michel said as he walked with Crown to the door.

Crown took the hand that Michel held out to him. "Friends, Michel," he said, looking down at the tiled hall floor. He held Michel's hand in both his own for a moment before he left.

Time dragged horribly in the flat. Michel and Jonni sat on a sofa in the studio without speaking, a space of several feet between them. At last, when the gloomy day outside had turned to night and the shadows in the unlit studio had absorbed the silence, Jonni turned her eyes toward him.

"Michel, there's something I have to tell you."

"I already know. Primo told me in the note he left."

"Did his note say anything else?"

"Not about you. Only that it happened."

She looked at his face. His eyes were closed.

"Do you want to talk about it?"

He shook his head slowly as it rested on the back of the sofa.

"No, let's leave it for a while."

That night they lay sleepless together in bed, not touching or talking, and in the morning Michel went to sort out the funeral. Primo's family were all either too young or too distraught to make the arrangements. Jonni stayed in bed while he was gone, only getting up twice to be sick.

In the afternoon they sat with the bereaved mother, listening to her talk unceasingly in Italian as she rocked herself in despair. Only the two youngest of Primo's brothers and sisters lived at home now. Maria and Mauro sat crying on the sofa on either side of their mother; Maria's desolate brown eyes looked at Michel in resentment, as though somehow he should have stopped this happening.

The evening was silent again, apart from the occasional phone call from a colleague or friend.

"I'm going to bed," Michel said. "I've got class in the morning."

"Class?"

"I can't afford to miss another day before Saturday."

Jonni's mouth fell open as she looked at him.

"Michel! You aren't going to do the premiere!"

"What did you expect? Do you think life stops here?"

"But before he's even buried!"

"The premiere won't wait."

"Is the premiere more important than Primo?"

"Primo's dead," he told her. "If there was anything I could do for him I would. But there isn't so I'm going to class in the morning."

Jonni turned her head away and looked at the wall.

"Poor Primo. Not a single sign of grief from the person he loved most in the whole world."

Michel stopped with his hand on the edge of the studio door. His knuckles whitened as he gripped it tightly.

"Don't feel too sorry for him, Jons. He did a selfish, stupid thing. If he'd woken up in a hospital bed and seen what he'd done he'd have been the first to agree."

"I wish he had," she said. "I wish he had. But it was his life; if he couldn't face it anymore . . ."

"Jons, he let you find his mutilated body."

Jonni looked up quickly. "He didn't mean to. You saw the note he left me. He wanted it to be you that found him."

"That too," said Michel, and he went to bed.

Michel felt the eyes of every dancer in the company turn toward him when he walked into the Goswell Road studio the next morning. He kept his eyes on the parquet floor and went to the barre to start stretching. When Louisa appeared anxiously at his side he caressed her arm in greeting but he couldn't manage a smile.

"A short run-in to Saturday," he said. He saw her face flood with relief, even while her brow creased in sympathy.

"I'm so sorry about Primo."

Michel looked down at his foot on the barre and made a small movement with his hand that was meant for a shrug. What could he say?

The whole company did a terrible class. No one felt like dancing. Daniel, who had known Primo since their apprenticeship, and even before that at the Royal Ballet School, walked out halfway through the barre. Michel danced appallingly and, for once, Crown let him get away with it.

"I'll be on form by Saturday," he told Crown, when the class finished.

"Tomorrow," Crown replied. It wasn't a demand; it was a statement of fact.

Marina was standing a few feet away, organizing her rehearsal notes. Her eyes were heavy and sad.

"I know, Michel. I felt the same. It was the music."

Michel rubbed his hands hard over his face.

"Right, what section are we starting with?"

"Let's take a break first. Come and have a coffee, poppet."

"You go ahead, Marina. I think I'll crack on and run through a few of the variations before we start."

24

For Jonni time stopped with Primo's death. For Michel time moved smoothly toward Saturday night's premiere at Sadler's Wells.

While Michel poured sweat in the studios at the Goswell Road, Jonni wandered vacantly from room to room in the flat, too physically traumatized to go out, too distressed to see anyone. While Michel discussed choreography over coffee with his colleagues, Jonni leaned exhaustedly over the loo, propping herself up with a hand on the wall, retching and retching even when her stomach was empty and she had nothing more to bring up. For hours she gazed through the studio windows at the ceaselessly falling rain, as though it could replace the tears she couldn't shed.

She dug out every old photo of Primo she could find: Primo playing the piano for the BNB in evening dress; Primo sunbathing on the roof terrace in Paris; Primo and Michel laying the studio floor together years before she had met them—anything that would help erase from her mind the terrible image of his dead face and all that blood. She spent hours on the floor in front of the VCR with her knees drawn up and her arms wrapped around her shins, watching the same video snippets of Primo dancing or playing the piano over and over again.

In the midst of her sickness and self-torture she wondered about Michel. She wondered what he had done when he first saw Primo lying there. Had he staggered under the force of the shock? Had he wept? Had he doubled up in pain as she had? Since then there had been nothing. Michel was gravely and intently focused on the coming premiere. He was quieter than usual when he was at home, keeping his mind on his work with a self-discipline that was so rigid it scared her. He and Jonni talked about coffee, about food, about visiting the doctor, but otherwise there was no communication between them at all. Michel walked around the flat in a little bubble of his own, isolated with his own preoccupations.

On Wednesday night as Jonni lay clinging to him in her disturbed sleep Michel shook her gently. "Jonni," he whispered. "Jonni, wake up." As she stirred he unclasped her arm from around his neck. "Jons, I'm sorry, you can't lie on me. I need to unwind my body."

"Mmm?" She blinked at him.

"You're pushing me off the bed," he whispered. "Can you move over a bit?"

"Oh . . . sorry." She sat up groggily and scraped her hair back off her face. "Perhaps it would be best if I slept in the studio for a while."

Michel lay flat on his back and closed his eyes. "Yes, maybe. Just until the premiere."

On Thursday, the day before the general rehearsal, Jonni didn't get up at all. But when Michel arrived home from work at midnight she climbed out of her bed on the sofa and followed him into the bedroom. The bedroom was untidy: Michel's unwashed dance gear piled on the floor, T-shirts and underwear draped over the back of the chair and the bedposts, cups half full of coffee on his bedside table. She stood by the window in her toweling bathrobe and watched him undress. It was still raining outside, a steady, monotonous rain.

"Michel, we've got to talk."

"This isn't the right time, Jonni." He pulled off his T-shirt slowly. He was pale from overwork and physical fatigue. "Can't it keep? Please, just for two days? This ballet's so tough. It's the most difficult piece I've ever done."

"I know," she said. "And I know how distressed you must be."

He shook his head and clicked his tongue.

"I'm not distressed. I haven't got time to be distressed."

"I can't wait anymore, Michel. I'm sorry but I can't. We have to talk about what happened between me and Primo."

Michel sat down on the edge of the bed with his back to her and unclasped the strap of his watch.

"Alright. If we have to talk, we have to."

"I didn't mean it to happen," she said. She leaned against the wall and
rested her heavy head against it. Her unwashed hair hung lank over her
face and her unhappy eyes, looking down at his seated figure, were deep-
set and dark-rimmed. "We were both very drunk; I know that's no excuse
but we were. And I know if I hadn't been stupid enough to get worked
up over nothing and let it happen then . . . then he wouldn't . . ." She
shook her head. This couldn't be about Primo; this had to be about her
and Michel. "I don't know how it started or how it went as far as it did.
We didn't even fancy each other. I am so sorry, Michel. I let you down
and I was unfaithful to you. But there was never any question, for a moment, of not telling you, even before . . ." She couldn't say the words.

Michel was rubbing his eyes slowly.

"Yes, I know you would have told me anyway."

"I need to know how you feel about it," she said. She needed, urgently, to know what kind of marriage she had to look forward to once
the present unbearable period of mourning was over.

Michel raised his eyebrows wearily, trying to think. What did he feel?
In the light of what had happened afterward, Jonni's infidelity seemed almost immaterial. He had neither the strength nor the will to try to imagine what his feelings might have been if Primo had told him about it in
person. He searched the sanded floorboards for some coherent train of
thought. He had been right; this was a bad time to talk. They were too
far apart, distanced on the one hand by misery and on the other by tiredness and overwork.

"Did you enjoy it?" he asked at last. "Was it good sex?"

"I truly can't remember. All I remember is realizing what was going on
and being horrified."

"Then it's gone." He snapped his fingers to show how easily a forgiven
wrong could be wiped from the slate. "As far as I'm concerned, it never
happened."

Jonni closed her eyes with a silent sigh. It might be that simple for
him but it wasn't for her. But one thing was clear: the subject couldn't be

reopened until after the premiere. Everything must wait until then. Even grief, it seemed.

On the evening of the premiere Jonni washed her hair and made up her face, and took her seat in the auditorium at Sadler's Wells. She tried not to think of all the times she had sat here before, holding Primo's hand through Michel's terrifying premieres.

Before the performance, Charles Crown, in full evening dress, stepped through the tabs at the front of the stage to address the audience. He was greeted with a cheer but he quickly held up his hand and shook his head. So great was the strength of his authority that there was immediate silence.

"My colleagues and I would like to dedicate this new work to our friend Roberto Vincenti, or I should say to his memory."

He went on to describe briefly the part Primo had played in the life of the company; the rehearsals and performances he had accompanied, the music he had orchestrated. The audience listened with sober faces. The realization of how many lives amongst this knowledgeable, largely invited first-night audience Primo had touched lodged a boulder of granite in Jonni's throat.

The ballet was called *The Seven Ages of Man*. It was a complex, technically demanding piece, kicking off with anarchy from the corps and the birth of a child into a mad, unpredictable universe. Louisa was radiantly lovely dancing the delighted mother while Michel spun joyfully around the stage knocking out seemingly effortless saut de basques and cabrioles fouettés. Jonni's mournful eyes followed his bouncing progress around the stage. How gay and blithe he seemed; like a sunny day in spring; not a care in the world.

Michel's first scene alone onstage, a long solo exploring the inner life of a child, was an extraordinary feat of imagination on Charles Crown's part and an equally extraordinary feat of observation and interpretation on Michel's. Nearly naked, with his beautifully proportioned, muscular body defying all laws of gravity and balance, Michel was a dreamlike creature of the air.

Along with every other member of the audience, Jonni sat with her eyes glued to Michel's flowing form. She felt as though she were watching a stranger. What connection could there possibly be between Jonni and the mind that controlled those movements? How could she possibly fit in with all that beauty? It came from something inside Michel, something to which she had no access. The mystery that had once been fascinating to Jonni, attracting her like a magnet, now filled her with sadness. His portrayal of the development through childhood to adolescence and sexual awakening was magnificent. Despite the maturity of his body, every movement he made breathed youth and teenage angst. As the young lover, too, in his first pas de deux with Louisa, he danced with an emotional openness and vulnerability that made Jonni's sickened heart ache. There was no jealousy as she watched him take pretty Louisa in his arms and kiss her. Too much had sprung from her fit of jealous anger for her not to see its pettiness now.

She felt the uneven, shallow breathing of a woman sitting beside her. Before the performance Jonni had been looking at her; she was in her late thirties or early forties, long-necked and sharp-nosed, probably trained as a dancer. Now Michel had control of this woman's heart. He was giving himself more freely to her than he had ever given himself to Jonni. Jonni tore her eyes from the stage to look at the people sitting around her. The real Michel, the only bit of him which mattered, was common property.

He was a great dancer. Who could doubt it as they watched him glide through Crown's taxing choreography, carrying his partner's performance with him? Jonni looked across the aisle toward the grotesque form of the vitriolic critic, Boyle. His fat hands were resting on the arms of his seat and his double chins were squashed against his collar as his mouth hung open. He was in love.

Jonni understood why it was that Michel had been able to slog away at this ballet all week unperturbed by Primo's death. Nature was protecting her masterpiece when she gave him a heart which couldn't be penetrated by the pains of the world around him. Last night when a terrible plane crash had been reported on the ten o'clock news, Michel had shaken his head, not wanting to know, and gone to bed, willing himself into the peaceful night's sleep which he owed his body if it was going to work hard for him tonight. At the time Jonni had thought him callous. Watching him now, she knew he had been right. It would be a tragedy if the world were deprived of such an artist on account of the death of one man, or even of a hundred men.

It no longer surprised Jonni that he had offered her no word of comfort all week; hadn't held her or touched her. What Michel owed to his wife was nothing to what he owed the strangers in the audience. As Jonni watched him spin and leap and fly he seemed the custodian of some God-given capacity greater than himself. He was a Mozart.

When Michel emerged from the stage door after the premiere with his arm around Louisa, he was instantly surrounded by a wall of journalists and fans who surged forward to engulf him. Over the past two years Michel had made that almost mythical journey out of the dance reviews and specialized magazines and into the public consciousness: a transition usually reserved exclusively for a few top dancers at Covent Garden. No one knew why Michel, amongst all the fine dancers in the country, was suddenly flavor of the month. If there was a recipe for fame, Crown said wryly, someone would have bottled it and sold it years ago. Perhaps it was his dancing, perhaps it was his looks and sex appeal, or the fact he was so rude to the press—perhaps London was just weary of its pop stars and ready for a cult hero to emerge from the backstreets of its classical culture; who could say? But whatever the reason, Michel was up there in the public eye and the tabloids wanted to know what his favorite restaurants were and who designed his clothes.

In the crush of photographers and audience members Jonni was jostled backward until she found herself stranded alone on the dark pavement in the rain. She watched him between the heads of the chattering fans. Michel was high on adrenaline, exhilarated, his eyes bright with post-premiere euphoria and healthy exhaustion as he answered the questions of the press. He posed for photographs with Louisa, exchanged greetings with journalists he knew, and kissed all his regular fans who loaded him with gifts and flowers. Jonni could hear him laughing at a gift from a stocky girl with orange, spiked hair and safety pins in her nose who followed him all over the country—she found out later the gift was a pink, furry jockstrap. Several fans gave him exotic coffee beans imported from Uganda and Ecuador. It was almost two years since Jonni had last found it necessary to buy coffee when she went shopping. Perhaps she could get him to drop into one of his TV interviews that he also adored pasta, whole-meal bread, and nonbiological washing powder.

The journalists, with their notebooks and tape recorders, fired questions at him about Primo. It was frightening how well informed those vultures were.

"Is it true you were the one to find him?"

"Yes," he said, "my wife and I together."

"Just how close were you exactly?"

"We were friends."

"The note was addressed to you, wasn't it? What did it say?"

"I'm not answering either of those questions."

"Come on, Michel; for Christ's sake give us something we can print!"

No one asked why Michel didn't stay for the reception after the premiere. It was as much as he was expected to do just getting up there on the stage under the circumstances. On Monday morning there would be stories in the tabloids about the stoicism of the grieving hero who had stashed away his sorrow for long enough to make his mark, yet again, in the annals of British ballet.

"I'm going home," he said, smiling at the blockade of fans who tried to stop him walking away from the stage door. "Go on, bugger off, darlings. Give me a break, will you? I've had a lousy week."

On the pavement on Rosebery Avenue, sharing Jonni's umbrella, he was silent and withdrawn as he waited for the first illuminated yellow rectangle to emerge out of the rain. Jonni spoke to him but he didn't hear her. In the taxi home, crawling through the rain in Oxford Street, he sat with his eyes closed. He was a million miles away.

This then was the great romantic hero. This was the man that every girl in pink satin shoes and every woman who had ever thrilled to the music of Tchaikovsky wanted to marry. He was beautiful, strong, and sexy; intriguing in his physical power and the secret intimacy of his smile. One glance and you'd be swallowed up by those gray eyes; they would seek out the most tender places in your heart. Sitting beside Michel's withdrawn figure in the back of the taxi, Jonni looked at him as though from a great distance. He was an icon; a storybook character who had no place outside the world of ballet and make-believe.

A gloomy Sunday in the flat—no conversation; a light, steady rain falling from the dark sky outside—and then on Monday morning, the funeral.

The affair was dominated by sobbing Vincentis, gathered around the open grave in the rain, which hadn't let up for five days. All in black with their heads covered, Primo's mother, sisters, and aunts rocked themselves piteously as they keened and wept. To Jonni's hysterical eyes it was a scene straight out of *The Godfather.*

Well back from the family group, she and Michel stood amongst the gravestones with Primo's other ballet friends, silent and still, soaked to the skin, occasionally raising a hand to brush dripping hair out of their eyes.

It had taken all Michel's persuasive powers to wangle a Christian burial for his friend. The Irish priest had been stubborn as he listened to the petition of the handsome atheist who was seated on a hard bench in the vestry.

"You're very adamant," said the priest, when Michel went back to see him for a second time, "but I'm afraid it can't be done."

"Aren't rules made to be broken?"

"Not the rules of the Church."

"Please," Michel urged. "You know that his family are very devout and it would mean acceptance for them. Couldn't you make an exception on compassionate grounds? For their sake if not for his."

"It's been done before," Father Connell confessed, "but never in my parish." He sighed deeply and rubbed his ruddy, bulbous nose. "I liked Primo very much. I knew him when he first came to England as a child, you know. His father was devastated when he made up his mind to go to dance school. He was so proud of Primo's gift; made him work very hard to develop it, expected great things of him. I'm glad Roberto didn't live to see this happen." He raised his eyebrows when he saw Michel's change of expression. "Ah, you're thinking he might have learned something from it. Well . . ." He buried his hands in the pockets of his voluminous black cassock and looked down at the stone floor. ". . . he might, at that. You know, these recent years Primo's given me a hard time. An unholy terror he was for tearing my sermons apart and forcing me to justify every word. In all honesty I don't know how he would have felt about a Catholic funeral."

"He's past caring either way," Michel said. "And if he came to church for his mother's sake while he was alive, why should he object to doing the same for her now? The funeral's for the living."

"You're not a believer then?"

"No."

"Not even an Anglican?"

Michel rubbed his eyes. He didn't have time for this.

"Look, he was my closest friend and I want to do what I can for his family, that's all."

The Catholic priest scrutinized Michel's face. There was nothing there; not anger, not even grief, just deep weariness.

"How are you bearing up yourself, my son? You look tired."

Michel nodded; he was.

"Yes, I've been under a lot of strain at work for the last few months. And my wife's ill; she's taken Primo's death very badly. All my colleagues are upset about it. This is a stressful week for the company anyway. I've been trying to find time, as well, to spend with Primo's mother."

"And added to all that," Father Connell said with a sympathetic smile, "the bloody priest won't stick him in consecrated ground because his death was self-inflicted."

Michel frowned at the stone tiles on the floor.

"It wasn't self-inflicted, not really. He wasn't responsible. I watched him fight depression for years. It was a disease like any other. He tried to self-medicate using alcohol and, in the end, the remedy and the malady between them wore him down and beat him. How can he be blamed? He was let down by everyone; he was left on his own for months when he was ill and needed help. If anyone killed him it was . . ." Michel looked at a fire extinguisher on the vestry wall with a sigh and then closed his eyes, shaking his head. ". . . nobody . . . fate, I don't know."

Now Michel's face was blank as he watched the coffin being lowered into that gaping hole in the sodden earth. Father Connell was uttering incantations at the head of the grave, his words barely audible to the dancers who were taking advantage of what little shelter was afforded by a massive oak next to a gravel path. Annette was standing alone on the grass some distance away in total surrender to grief. It was impossible to tell whether her heaving sobs were silent or not; the sound of the rain drowned out everything.

As the first shovel of soil fell onto the wood, Jonni suddenly felt the pain which had been eluding her all morning. Throughout the funeral she had been sitting, dazed, in the cold church unable to fathom what was in that smooth-polished sealed box. Now she knew exactly what it contained. Fighting off an overwhelming desire to jump into the grave, to cling to the coffin lid and let the gravediggers bury her misery along with Primo's body, she turned away to throw herself into Michel's arms. And then she discovered that you can't throw yourself into someone's arms unless they open their arms to receive you. Michel's arms remained folded squarely over his chest. As she clung to him he moved one of his hands and rested it lightly on her waist. Michel hadn't wanted to come today; funerals were superstitious nonsense, he said. He was only here because he didn't want to hurt Primo's family. Jonni realized that he didn't want her to need him.

After three more lonely days and nights in the flat Jonni got up from her makeshift bed in the studio at two in the morning and went into the bedroom to creep under the duvet next to Michel. He had gone to bed early although there had been no performance tonight and the second cast were dancing tomorrow. As she shuffled toward him under the bedclothes Michel stirred and moved his arm to lay it under her neck murmuring, "Mmm . . . hello."

Jonni whispered to him, not sure if he was awake or asleep or somewhere in between.

"Do you want to make love?"

He was somewhere in between.

"Hmm? No, go back to sleep."

He turned onto his side and wrapped his free arm about her waist, holding her close, not waking from his slumber.

She kept very still, feeling his chest expand and contract against her shoulder, breathing in the comforting smell of his body. His body was hot, roasting under the feather duvet, and she could feel his warm breath in her hair. She lay with her eyes wide open, listening and feeling. The fine blond hairs on the muscular arm under her neck were tickling her cheek.

In the morning she watched him dress as he prepared to leave for class. The coffee he had brought to her bedside table grew cold as she lay motionless, her eyes following him around the room.

She watched him step into his boxer shorts and arrange his genitals so they stayed put. In the middle of pulling on his jeans he paused, frowning slightly and running his hand over his raised foot as though he had felt an unfamiliar twinge. It was something she had seen him do involuntarily a hundred times as he thought of the labors that the day had in store for his body. The thin T-shirt he drew over his head hung from his broad shoulders, emphasizing his slimness as he tucked it in at his waist. He cursed the continuing bad weather and picked up his bag from a chair by the window.

"See you later, Jons."

She heard the click of the front door as it closed behind him.

When Michel came home from class nearly three hours later Jonni was waiting for him in the kitchen. She was sitting with her arms folded on the table, a half-empty jug of coffee still warm beside her.

"How was class?"

"One of Charles's stinkers."

She turned her eyes toward him, expressionless.

"Mike?"

He had dropped his bag on a chair and was fetching a cup from the draining board. Her use of that playful nickname made him smile. He hadn't heard it for a week or two.

"Mike, I'm going to leave."

The hand that was stretching out toward the row of newly washed cups stopped moving.

"Leave?" He looked puzzled, as though he hadn't understood the word.

"My bags are all packed in the bedroom. I was just waiting to say good-bye."

Michel lowered his hand and looked at the windowsill above the sink. Drops of rain were hammering outside, splashing London grime in dirty splodges onto the panes.

"For how long?"

"I don't know. For good, maybe."

"Where are you going?"

"I'm not sure. You can send my mail to my mother's."

He went to the far side of the table, turning a chair so that its high wooden back formed yet another barrier between them as he sat down astride the seat. Her announcement had stunned him. A bewildered frown narrowed his gray eyes while they sought out the meaning behind her cool stare.

"Have you got someone else?"

"No. I'm surprised you care."

He ran his hand slowly through his hair.

"I was thinking you'll be lonely."

They were silent for a few moments, eye-to-eye across the table, and then Jonni abandoned her reserve, turning down the corners of her mouth and wrinkling her forehead in pained supplication.

"It's no good, Michel. You don't need me here and I'm going moldy in this flat with no one to talk to. Things were different before."

"Why don't you try and get some work?"

"The industry's dead. There's no work around, either in theater or TV. It's not like ballet where the money's always there."

"It isn't always there. I'm lucky enough to be in a sponsored company. But even that's not secure these days."

"Is the I.B. in financial trouble?"

Michel shook his head and filled her empty cup with coffee from the pot.

"Everyone's in trouble, thanks to Thatcher. But let's not get distracted; let's concentrate on what's going on here, can we? Tell me the rest."

She snapped at him without meaning to: "So all of a sudden you want to talk!"

Michel's foot tapped gently on the floor under the table.

"Yes, I want to talk."

"There's just no point staying!" she cried, longing to bring the conversation to a climax and finish it one way or another. "I've been cooped up in this place, sick, miserable, and lonely, ever since Primo died. You don't say a word to me, you don't want me to comfort you; you don't even let me know what you feel."

"I don't feel anything."

"Then no wonder Primo killed himself. If I stick around here much longer, I wouldn't be surprised if I end up the same way."

Michel looked down into the cup he was holding and didn't say a word.

"Oh God." Jonni put her hand to her face. "Oh, Michel, that was a dreadful thing to say—stupid. I didn't mean it."

"I know you didn't. So you're really thinking of leaving, then?"

"If you could look me in the eye and ask me not to go—and I could see it would hurt you if I went—I'd go straight back into the bedroom and unpack my bags this minute."

Michel thought for a moment, looking at the table, and then shook his head. He reached across the table for his cigarettes.

"I wouldn't use emotional blackmail to make you stay."

She stacked her two suitcases, along with a mountain of carrier bags, by the door to the stairs.

"I'd better call a taxi."

"Why not take the car?"

"And bring it back later? No, once I've gone I think I'd better stay away."

Michel was leaning against the frame of the kitchen door chewing the end of a pencil as he watched her. He hadn't offered to help with the bags; if she was going to assert her independence she could start here and now. He wasn't going to assist or hinder her.

"Want another coffee before you go?" he asked.

"Thanks, can I have decaf? I've already had so much coffee this morning I've got the jitters."

He made it for her and they talked about the crisis in the entertainment industry while Michel watched her drink. When she stood up to go, gathering her bags in her hands, she found herself smiling.

"D'you remember that fight we had in the bath a couple of weeks ago? It was funny, wasn't it?"

Michel smiled too, back in his position at the kitchen door.

"Yeah, it was funny. Carpet's still damp underneath. Must remember to do something about it."

"We were insane to get married so young, just because we were crazy about each other, weren't we?"

"Looks like it," he replied, and he walked forward to open the front door.

Before he closed it again he asked her for a kiss and she raised her mouth willingly to his, glad he'd asked at least that much.

It seemed to Jonni that the sky had been throwing down torrents for weeks. When she staggered out onto Warwick Way, loaded down with her bags, the rain had stopped but the atmosphere was still gloomy beneath the black sky. The gutters were like rivers and water was dripping from the leafless trees that lined the pavements.

As the taxi holding Jonni and all her wordly goods pulled away from the curb, a break appeared in the clouds and bright sunlight burst through. A luminous glow flooded the street. Jonni didn't want to look at the sunshine. She closed her eyes and listened to the sloshing of water under the tires of the cars, just as Michel had done on the journey home along Oxford Street after the premiere on Saturday night.

25

"Good God, Jonni!" Annette said, startled, when she opened the door of her flat a few cautious inches and saw her there. Roly and Annette's flat in Putney was the only place that Jonni could think of to go. Until last week there had always been Primo's little flat in Lupus Street: a natural refuge for emergencies; her second home.

Annette's green eyes looking around the edge of the door were flustered and unwelcoming. When she saw the suitcases and bags that were stacked behind Jonni in the hallway her face fell and her shoulders drooped.

"Oh, Jonni!" she groaned, "Oh, you didn't!"

It was mid-afternoon but Annette was wearing only a dressing gown, and her hair and makeup were unkempt as she stood, statuesque as ever but hollow-eyed from grief, with her hand still on the door, staring at Jonni's woebegone face.

"I'm sorry," Jonni said. "I didn't have anywhere else to go."

A man's voice, low and questioning, murmured from the bedroom, "Annette, who was it?"

"Is Roly here?" Jonni asked in surprise.

Annette seemed undecided for a few seconds and then she made up her mind. Rising to the demands of the crisis, she dragged Jonni quickly into the flat and closed the door.

"No, he's not back from Manchester until this evening. Just wait here a minute. Don't go anywhere, okay?"

She vanished into the bedroom and Jonni heard her voice whisper, harsh with fury: "Why did you call out? That could have been my fucking husband!"

There was further sotto voce controversy and after a couple of minutes a dark-haired man with a beard strode angrily out of the bedroom, doing up his shirt. Without even glancing at Jonni he bent down to pick up his shoes, which had obviously been kicked off in a hurry. When he had pulled them on, he snatched up his jacket from the arm of the sofa and walked out of the flat, slamming the door behind him.

"Don't mind him," Annette said casually, coming out of the bedroom. "He's a moody sod. Let's get your bags in, lovey. You haven't really left Michel, have you?"

"Yes—Yes, I have." She followed Annette out onto the landing to bring in her cases, gazing in blank-faced amazement in the direction of the mysterious man's disappearance. "But . . . I mean, Nettie!"

Annette put Jonni's case down inside the flat and kicked the door shut with her foot.

"Oh, don't be such a prude, Jonni. He's only an affair."

Jonni looked at her with horrified eyes.

"Does Roly know?"

"Good Lord no. He'd be absolutely livid. Jonni, love, you're trembling and you look like shit. For heaven's sake sit down. I think what you and I both need is a drink."

Annette scooped her glorious curls back into a knot, with the ease of years of practice, and secured it with a clip that was lying on the telephone table next to the door.

"Brandy okay?"

"Yes." Jonni felt dazed. "Thanks."

The flat was spacious and modern, the front door opening straight into the living room which was open-plan to the kitchen. Jonni sat on the edge of the cream-colored sofa, looking vaguely around the untidy room while Annette swanned off behind the kitchen counter to get the drinks.

Annette handed her a tumbler of brandy.

"So what's the story?" she asked. "Is this a strop or have you left him for real?"

Jonni took the drink from Annette's hand with a vacant nod of thanks. "It's real, I think."

"Well, what happened?"

"I can't talk about it; not yet."

Annette sat in a big armchair and tucked her long legs up underneath her.

"Honestly, Jonni, what a time to walk out on the poor bastard!" She sipped her drink. "What are you going to do?"

"I don't know. I haven't thought about anything. I just . . . did it. I haven't made any plans."

"Don't worry." Annette waved a hand, eschewing responsibility for the situation. "Roly will sort everything out. He said they'd probably finish filming at about four so he won't be back before eight."

"What's he doing in Manchester?"

"Oh Christ; something really tacky, I'm afraid. Gold lurex and sequin routines for somebody's telly show. I'm not even sure who—Des O'Connor, or someone. Still, the money's good."

"Have you seen him?" Jonni asked hesitantly. "Since . . . it happened."

Annette looked down at her glass and shook her head quickly.

"He came home to tell me after Michel phoned him but he had to go straight back. He was working all day Sunday too. Poor love, they wouldn't even let him come home for the funeral." Her beautiful round eyes were suddenly huge pools of distress. "Oh God, let's not talk about Primo. I can't handle it. Please, please don't talk about Primo."

Jonni couldn't even bear to think about Primo, much less talk about him. They were silent while they each stuffed their sorrow back into its locked box, breathing their grief slowly back down into their bellies where it had come from. But here, where the flat was full of Annette's deep mourning, Jonni's heart swelled painfully; Annette's emotion was such a contrast to the self-possession she had been looking at in Michel's gray eyes for the past ten days.

She couldn't bear to think about Michel either.

Gazing blankly into space, she took small evenly spaced sips of her brandy and contemplated the man who had walked out of Annette's bedroom when she arrived. Jonni hadn't liked the look of him. There was something cold and aggressive about him.

"That . . . man who was here," she said. "Aren't you afraid he might tell someone about it? Someone who'd tell Roly?"

"Lord, it's not very likely." Annette knocked back the rest of her brandy. "He wouldn't dare. He was our marriage guidance counselor."

"Marriage guidance counselor?"

"Yes, it wouldn't look good, would it?" She smiled, seeing Jonni's stupefaction. "After Roly and I got married we went for counseling to sort out our sex life. It worked too—Steve was terribly good; it was a tremendous help." She laughed shamelessly. "Don't look so shocked. Steve and I didn't start this while we were seeing him professionally. He phoned me up a few months later. I suppose he found our conversation a turn-on. Must have decided I was exactly his cup of tea."

Jonni shook her head slowly.

"I can't believe it. He should be struck off, or whatever."

"I know. Disgraceful, isn't it?"

"It's a total abuse, both of you and Roly."

"Yes," she said with irony, "well, abuse is rather Steve's thing."

Jonni stared at the zebra-striped rug on the pale wooden floor under the coffee table. She was amazed that Annette could find it funny.

"I thought you loved Roly."

"Of course I do. What a silly thing to say. He's the love of my life."

"Then don't you feel guilty?"

"Not a bit. Oh, come on, are you saying you've never deceived Michel? Don't talk rot, Jonni. Don't tell me you've never pretended to be in the mood for sex when you really couldn't be bothered, or made out you were enjoying it when actually you couldn't wait for it to be over."

Jonni would have liked to deny it but she knew Annette wouldn't believe her.

"Well sometimes, I suppose."

"Exactly. So what makes your lies any better than mine?"

To her surprise Jonni didn't have an immediate answer to that.

"But those lies are only to make him happy," she said uncertainly.

"Exactly—ditto me and Roly. All women lie about sex to their husbands. It's on page one of the rule book. We lie about who we really are so they'll love us more." She put her feet up complacently on the coffee table, crossing them at the ankles. "I don't see why I should feel any guiltier than you. Actually, I feel rather virtuous. Infidelity is rather hard work, as it happens."

Jonni thought miserably about her own sexual infidelity; thank God she had been too drunk to remember it.

"Does Roly have affairs too, do you think?"

Annette snorted.

"My God, he'd better not. I'd take a ruddy hatchet to him." She saw Jonni raise her eyebrows and shook her head. "It's not the same thing at all, Jonni. Roly couldn't screw a girl unless he was in love with her. I'm the only woman he's ever had, you know. It's a bit like you and Michel only the other way round. Michel could bonk someone without even noticing he was doing it. But look at you: you're the perfect idealistic wife. If you had it off with another man it would be the ruin of you. No, Roly will live and die faithful to me and that's it."

Jonni looked down at the zebra rug again, cradling her brandy glass against her chest.

"Do you and Roly ever quarrel?"

"Heavens, yes; we have some absolute humdingers. Not very often, though—you know what blokes are like; if I'm itching for a fight he usually just goes to sleep. But we have our moments. Lord, that time last year you came to see the panto with me! I was so furious about that love scene with the brunette I went backstage afterward, while you were all in the pub, and punched him in the eye. Then he really did shout at me, I can tell you. The whole theater must have heard us." She laughed shamelessly at the memory. "I'm afraid the whole theater must have heard us making up as well. D'you want another drink?"

"No. No, thanks—Oh, God!" Jonni jumped up and ran to the sink in the white kitchen, clinging desperately to the rim as she threw up, her stomach heaving and her throat retching, stung by acid, while her eyes swam at the physical pain.

Annette came and leaned over her in sympathy.

"Oh, lovey." She gave Jonni a glass of water and rinsed the vomit from her hair under the tap without squeamishness. "D'you want to go and lie down? I think you should."

Jonni nodded limply and let herself be led away and tucked up under the duvet in the double bed where Annette had been doing God only knew what with that man when she had arrived. It was almost thirty-six hours since Jonni had slept and very soon she started to feel drowsy. As she sank toward sleep the dreadfulness of what she had just done drifted away into unreality. Her unconscious mind went home to the warm Pimlico flat where yesterday's leftover salad was still under clingfilm in the fridge and her duck sponge waited for her beside the bath and Michel's strong arms and familiar gray eyes inhabited every room.

By the time Jonni woke up Annette was dressed and sitting curled up on the sofa studying her script for her latest TV drama, wearing a pair of huge red-framed spectacles. It was inevitable, with her vivid personality and stunning looks, that Annette's acting career had stormed ahead of Jonni's in the few years since she quit dancing. Jonni sat in an armchair and watched her while she learned her lines. She felt like a weedy imposter beside her. The closest Jonni had ever got to TV was a walk-on in *Casualty*.

It was almost half past eight when Roly unlocked the door and walked into the sitting room, dropping his bag on the floor as Annette leaped up from the sofa and ran to throw her arms around him. After the distressing events of the past ten days the meeting between husband and wife was an emotional one and Jonni took herself off to the kitchen behind the counter to allow them some privacy. She could hear them talking about Primo in low voices. Jonni loved Annette but she was flooded with relief at Roly's arrival. She felt, rather than saw, his glance in her direction when Annette told him in a whisper what had happened.

"Jonni, love, what is this?" He crossed the room toward her. "You can't seriously mean to leave Michel; that's nuts. The two of you adore each other. Did you have a fight?"

She shook her head. "No."

His straightforward blue eyes looked down into hers.

"Is this about another girl?"

She shook her head again.

"Then why leave him? He needs you, especially right now."

"He doesn't need me, Roly. He's never needed me. When I told him this afternoon that I was leaving he didn't care."

Roly creased his brow in sympathetic frustration. He was still a big kid in many ways but there was something so reassuring about him, so rocklike. "This is a bad time, Jonni. Really a bad time." He laid his hand on her pale face. "You look ill. I know none of us are in very good shape at the moment but you look absolutely terrible. Have you seen a doctor?"

"Yes." She creased up her face like a small child on the verge of tears. "Michel took me to the doctor last week. He put me on sedatives. But I can't eat; I keep being sick. The doctor said it was trauma and it might last for two months and I can't stand it because it hurts so much every time I throw up."

"Okay—okay." Roly put his arms around her. "Poor babe, this is awful. You and Shel are such a great couple; you've always been our role models."

The irony of this was too much for Jonni and she screwed her eyes tight shut, pressing her forehead against Roly's shoulder as he held her. For the past ten days she had needed so desperately just to be held that she coiled her arms around his neck and wouldn't let go.

Roly stroked her back and looked over the top of her head at Annette. Annette spread her hands in a helpless shrug.

"Alright," he said at last. "Now, first things first. Does Michel know you're here?"

"No."

"Okay, I'm going to take a piss because I've been desperate for one ever since I left the M6, then I'm going to have a stiff drink, and then we'll call him."

Jonni lifted her head, looking up at him.

"I don't want him to know where I am."

Roly shook his head as he walked toward the bedroom.

"Sorry, lovely; people worry about each other when there's been a tragedy. Christ knows, I've been scared to death about Nettie all week and I knew exactly where she was. Shel will be worried sick till he knows you're safe. He won't come here hassling you. And if he tries I won't let him."

Jonni heard Roly peeing in the bathroom; the walls of the flat were very thin. When he came back he poured himself a brandy and picked up the telephone, stretching the long lead across the room as he brought it to the coffee table. "Do you want to call him yourself or d'you want me to?"

"Please," she said, "you do it."

Roly started to dial the number from memory. Halfway through dialing he put his hand on the receiver button and looked up, startled.

"What am I doing? I'm insane! I've got to go to him; he'll be on his own. I was thinking—God help me—I was thinking he'd have Primo with him."

"But Roly!" Annette protested. "You've only just come home!"

"He's my friend." He kissed his wife as he picked up the jacket he'd taken off less than ten minutes ago. "I'll call if I'm going to be very late. Look after Jonni, darling."

Once he had gone, Jonni watched Annette cooking omelettes.

"I'm sorry," she said guiltily. "You must be furious at his having to go away again. It's all my fault."

"Don't be silly," Annette told her, picking eggshell out of the frying pan. "What are friends for, lovey?"

Jonni ate a little omelette but was immediately sick again.

"My cooking tends to have that effect on people," Annette said with a sigh.

As they sat on the sofa attempting to chat, Jonni visualized Michel and Roly at the flat talking about her. They'd be drinking coffee, or maybe brandy—probably in the studio. Despite the cold thread of shock that ran through her at the step she'd taken, part of her mind was already constructing the scene of her return to Pimlico: her own shamefaced smile of apology and Michel's forgiving shrug as he put on the kettle. But not yet. Not until tomorrow, at any rate, when he'd had time to feel how lonely and empty the flat was without her.

Roly was gone for two hours. He came back looking dispirited.

"He was . . ." He rubbed his tired eyes. "He was okay—upset obviously. He said you'd probably need these."

He handed her a checkbook and a pair of spectacles. Jonni looked at them.

"What else did he say?"

"He said he'd transfer some money into your bank account tomorrow. We just chatted, darling. He wasn't very communicative. He sent you his love."

Jonni didn't believe him but she was grateful for the lie.

That night Jonni lay awake in her makeshift bed on the sofa staring sleeplessly at the unfamiliar shadows in the dark living room. Recently her bed had been nothing but sofas: Primo's sofa, Michel's sofa, Roly and Annette's sofa. She was a sofa exile. Through the thin wall she heard Roly go into the bathroom where Annette was in the shower.

"Don't," Annette's voice said, half drowned out by the sound of the running water. "No, really; I'm not in the mood."

There was a squeak of flesh against plastic. Roly's reply was low and irritated. "I don't give a fuck; I've had ten miserable, lonely nights grieving on my own in that bloody hotel room."

"Stop it!"

"Shhh, keep your voice down."

"Go away and take your fucking hard-on with you. Look, piss off!"

Jonni heard a slap—she couldn't tell who hit who—and then more squeaking of bodies against plastic and the sound of further angry whispering. When, after an amazingly short time, Annette's protests turned to liquid wails and Roly began to gasp in synchrony with an unbearable percussion of protesting shower fittings, Jonni pulled the blankets over her head and pressed her fingers tightly over her ears. This was horrible.

In the shower Roly put his arms around Annette and leaned against the tiled wall while they both caught their breath. The hot water hammered onto his face and his closed eyes while he listened to the pounding of his own heart. He hated the aggression Annette so often demanded from him when they made love. It was all unspoken; all subtle signals: a complicated game of guilt-sharing. Any moment now she would ask him to apologize.

"You got my hair wet," she whimpered with her face in his neck.

"I'm sorry," he whispered, stroking her back. If that was what Nettie needed then that's what would happen. "I didn't mean to be rough, eh?"

"Alright. Just don't do it again."

Roly opened his eyes, blinking at the smarting water.

"Yeah, okay. I'll try not to, darling."

When they were sitting in bed together, leaning against the pillows, Annette yawned contentedly and folded her arms behind her head.

"What did Michel really say?"

"Nothing. When I got there he was in the studio working on a contemporary solo. We talked about Charles's new ballet and the work I'm doing up north; that's about it."

"Did you tell him Jonni's here?"

"Yep." Roly pulled one of the pillows out from under his head and threw it on the floor as he lay down. "He wasn't interested. He hardly seemed aware she'd gone."

"For God's sake, he really is an arsehole!" Annette was disgusted but she wasn't surprised. "That's typical of him. I honestly thought, for once, he had let someone in. I should have known better."

"Give the guy a break, darling. He's locked up over Primo—he must be."

"Oh, Roly, come on! I don't care how locked up he is; how can he not notice that his wife's left him?"

Roly just sighed. He wasn't very impressed by Michel's attitude either. Annette wriggled down the bed and turned on her side to look at him, propping her head on her hand.

"He's probably just stopped fancying her," she said. "That's the only thing that ever drives a relationship for him."

"I don't see how a man can stop fancying a woman if he loves her."

"Darling, that's very sweet but I'm afraid it's a bit unworldly."

"No it's not. You aren't a man. You don't know."

"Well, in that case he obviously doesn't love her. God, I'm so angry with him. I wouldn't say so in front of Jonni but he behaved abysmally at the funeral. He looked so bored; he even yawned during the service. I don't think I'll ever forgive him for that. And afterward he let Jonni go home on her own and rushed off to a rehearsal. It's the dance world that's done it to him, you know. Thank God we gave up ballet." She preferred to forget that ballet had, in fact, given up them. "All classical dancers are fucked in the head."

"Charles isn't."

"Yes, he is—completely fucked. He's possessed by it, just like Michel. God, did you see that article about Michel in the *Evening Standard*?"

"No."

"It's ridiculous; I've never seen anything like it outside the Royal. Apparently he's become some kind of gay heartthrob. No wonder he's lost touch with reality. With the whole country in love with your public persona, think how depressing it must be to go home to someone who knows how normal and dreary you really are. That's probably why he never calls us anymore—we know him too well."

"He's busy; that's why he doesn't call." Roly turned his head to look at her. "Phone him, will you, love? Go and see him while I'm in Manchester, on Sunday or sometime. He's going to be very isolated with Jonni gone after what's happened."

"No, sod him." Annette was still seething about the funeral. "He knows where I am. If he likes being alone, let him. He could have stopped her going if he'd wanted to. Oh, it's all so ghastly—all of it."

They moved closer together in the bed for comfort and Roly put his arm around her. Annette laid her head on his shoulder.

"She still loves him, Roly. It's obvious."

"I know she does."

"Poor Jonni."

"Shhh, darling." He touched her arm. "Keep your voice down. Don't forget the walls are thin."

It was too late. Jonni was staring wide-eyed at the black ceiling, her mouth open in despair.

In the modern yellow-papered bedroom, in the light of the bedside lamp, Annette lifted her head from Roly's shoulder and propped herself up on her elbow to look down at his face.

"Roly, you wouldn't ever leave me, would you?"

"Oh, I expect so. I'll probably leave you for someone who does the washing-up occasionally."

"No, seriously." Her green eyes were suddenly tense. "What if something went wrong between us? Suppose something happened to stop you loving me."

"Woah, woah, woah!" He half sat up, turning toward her. "Not this again. What are you talking about?"

"You wouldn't, would you?"

"Of course not. Don't talk balls."

"But suppose—I mean, what if you were ever really angry with me?"

"Then I'd do what I normally do: I'd yell at you. You know perfectly well I'll never leave you so pipe down and stop being such a drama queen. Honestly, you do come out with some shit sometimes."

Annette flopped back onto the pillow beside him with a laugh.

"That's what I love most about you—apart from your big cock, of course. Your infallible instinct for killing a good scene. Anyway, it's your fault if I'm being hypersensitive. You haven't told me once today that you love me."

"That's a lie: I told you on the phone this morning and again when we were in the shower."

Annette had a pouting, little-girl voice that she put on with Roly when she needed reassurance.

"Tell me some more. I'm feeling vulnerable."

"Alright, come here, then."

Jonni threw back the bedclothes and leaped off the sofa, pressing her hands over her ears. She paced the unlit room in her T-shirt and knickers while the couple behind the wall made love again.

In the morning Annette strutted out of the bedroom dressed far more seductively than was remotely necessary for a TV rehearsal.

"This ruddy rehearsal's probably going to run on for hours. Don't expect me back till late, darling."

Roly kissed his wife and told her she looked beautiful.

"I always look beautiful. Bye then, Jonni. See you later."

When she had gone Roly sank into an armchair, propping his elbow on the arm and resting his cheek on his fist. He looked shattered. After a while he lifted his head for a moment to run his hand over his face and then lowered his cheek back onto his hand.

"You okay, Jonni? Want anything?"

Jonni shook her head.

"No, I'm fine, thanks—sort of. What about you? Are you okay?"

He gave her a small smile.

"Yeah, I'm getting by. My back's been hurting a bit. Physio says it's no problem but it tires me out, you know? I'll be alright."

Jonni managed to smile in reply. Roly would always be alright.

They watched each other over the cluttered coffee table. Neither of them spoke for a while.

"So what happened?" he asked at last.

"With Michel?"

He shook his head.

"No, with Primo."

"Nothing. He just . . . I can't tell you."

Roly's blue eyes looked into hers. "I need to know, Jonni."

Jonni was silent for a few seconds, her gaze moving around the room, and then she nodded. "Okay."

Slowly, wretchedly, she told him everything that had happened that evening—starting with the foolish quarrel that had sent her fleeing to Primo's flat. Moment by moment she relived their conversation, the whisky they had drunk, the cigarettes they'd smoked, the things Primo had said as he put his arms around her. She looked down at her shaking hands clasped on her lap. "And . . . and then . . . we had sex on the sofa."

When Roly didn't say anything she looked at him with a pleading frown.

"It just happened. Neither of us meant it to; we were just both feeling miserable. It wasn't even . . . It was awful as far as I remember."

Still Roly said nothing. He just looked at her. Jonni had bitten her fingernails down to the quick so she chewed the skin at the end of her fingers.

"Please say something."

After a pause he said, "What do you expect me to say? If you were my wife I'd have something to say, certainly, but you aren't; you're Michel's wife. And Primo was his best friend."

"If . . . if I was your wife, would you forgive me?"

"Jonni, don't ask me that."

"Michel didn't want to talk about it."

"I'm not surprised. He's probably too angry."

She put her hands over her eyes and told him the rest; everything Primo had said and everything he had done. There was no one else she could tell—ever. When she reached the point in her story when she had opened the door of Primo's bedroom and seen him lying there surrounded by all that blood, the tears that had been locked up inside her since that moment erupted from her eyes and she dissolved into uncontrollable sobs.

Jonni cried for so long she thought it would never stop. Every time her tears seemed to be drying up she burst into a new fit of sobbing, plunging her face back into Roly's already drenched sweater. Roly held her patiently while she cried, looking through the window thinking his own thoughts, occasionally raising his hand to wipe away a tear from under his chin. He had spent so many hours crying over the last ten days, he had few tears left to shed.

When at long last Jonni's head lay exhausted on Roly's shoulder, he laid his hand on her waist.

"Jonni, listen . . ."

She reached for another tissue to blow her nose.

"Don't be kind to me, Roly. Please. I don't want you to."

"Yeah, okay." He patted her thigh to move her out of the way. "Shift your bottom, then, so I can put the kettle on before one of us faints from dehydration."

Jonni had never been alone in the Putney flat with Roly before. It was strange to eat bacon and eggs with him and to watch him doing the washing-up—a week's worth by the looks of it—and other domestic chores while she lay on the sofa after throwing up her breakfast.

"Stay here as long as you like," he told her, stuffing the clothes he'd brought home with him into the washing machine. "I'm only around for the next few days but Nettie's in and out."

"Thanks, but I'm going to go back to Gloucester to stay with my parents." Jonni had decided that last night; the walls in this place were far too thin for her to stay. Her mum would have a purple fit when she heard she'd left Michel but it couldn't be helped.

"Probably a good idea, chicken. Spend a bit of time at home with your folks while you and Shel both come to terms with Primo. You can sit down together and patch things up later." He looked up from the washing machine. "Hey, listen, I know Nettie won't mind my telling you this: she and I had some sessions with a relationship counselor when we got married to sort out a couple of things—well, one thing—and it was really helpful. He got us to open up and talk honestly about all sorts of stuff. He was a good bloke; you could tell he was completely on our side. I can give you his name and a contact number if you like."

"No!" she said frantically, turning her face toward the back of the sofa. "No, thanks, really! That's the last thing I want."

"Okay," he said soothingly. "Okay, you'll work things out in your own way."

Roly insisted on driving Jonni all the way to Gloucester. She wasn't well enough, he said, to take the train. When they had been on the motorway for almost two hours Roly switched off the jazz that was playing on the radio. Jonni continued to stare numbly at the grassy bank that rushed past beyond the hard shoulder, listening to the hum of the car's engine.

"He would have planned it," Roly said.

She didn't respond. Roly looked in his wing mirror and pulled out into the outside lane to overtake a lorry.

"I knew him better than you did, Jonni. In some ways I knew him better than Michel did. The last reason he'd have committed suicide is because he made love with you. He was more intelligent than that. He wouldn't have been afraid of telling Michel; he wasn't a coward. What he did was nothing to do with you."

Jonni turned her head reluctantly to look at him.

"Are you sure?"

"Yes. He'd have been planning it for days, if not weeks or months. You couldn't have killed him, darling, and you couldn't have saved him."

He reached over to the passenger seat, feeling for her hand, and Jonni put her hand in his, resting her face against the cold glass of the window beside her and closing her eyes.

In Gloucester, as he helped her to take her bags into the house, Jonni's mother looked on tight-lipped, her arms folded in disapproval. Bernadette, who was twenty and still lived at home, demanded loudly and complainingly just which bedroom Jonni thought she was staying in and what the hell was she doing descending on the family like this anyway with only a few hours' notice.

During a few seconds when Roly was alone on the front path with Jonni's sister he caught her firmly by the arm and looked her straight in the eye.

"She is sick!" he said emphatically. "And desperately in trouble!"

There wasn't time for any more. Jonni came back out of the house to say good-bye and he got back in the car and left her to her fate.

As soon as the front door was closed her mother started.

"Jonquil, what on earth do you think you're doing? Marriage is for life—and Michel's a very good husband; you've told me so yourself. He must feel terribly betrayed." Michel had been a staunch favorite with his mother-in-law ever since he'd been famous enough for his celebrity to cast a reflected glow on her, elevating her social standing amongst her acquaintances. "It'll get in the papers, you know. How am I going to hold up my head once everyone's reading about my daughter walking out on her husband? I'm a firm believer in parents sticking by their children but there's a point at which that becomes collusion and I want you to know that I'm not happy about this. And who was that man who brought you here?"

Jonni leaned limply against the study door.

"He's just a friend, Mum."

"But you kissed him! I saw you kiss him on the lips, Jonquil. I'm sorry but in my book married women don't go round kissing other men on the lips. It's one thing to pack your bags and walk out on your husband. It's quite another to kiss another man like that, even if he's only a friend. I saw the way that man looked at you and touched you. And I heard him call you his darling. What would Michel think of you kissing this fellow? Or have you ceased to think of his feelings altogether? If you haven't been unfaithful with this man, then in my opinion you're far too . . ."

Bernadette clenched her fists and shouted at the top of her voice—

"Shut up!"

Veronica Kendal looked at her younger daughter in openmouthed disbelief. Bernadette had always been the meek one, the one she could control.

"What did you say to me?"

"Shut up, Mum! For once in your life just bloody well shut up and leave Jonni alone!"

Jonni turned her sad, empty eyes from her mother's startled face toward the sister who had always been her rival and her tormentor.

Bernadette put her hands on her hips with a bad-tempered scowl.

"Do you want a cup of tea, Jonni?"

Jonni nodded slowly.

"Yes," she said. "Thanks. That'd be great."

26

AFTER THE LAST PERFORMANCE of the new ballet at Sadler's Wells, Crown followed his leading dancer out of the stage door into a group of waiting fans. The moment Michel stepped onto the pavement the small crowd surged forward to engulf him.

"Michel, will you sign my program?"

"Hey, Michel, can I have your autograph for my sister?"

They surrounded him but they didn't touch him. Michel was a ballet star and his body was sacred; only his name was public property. Crown waited while Michel scribbled his name, J-B St. Michel, in his tidy, cursive hand a dozen times or more.

"Remember me, Michel? I was here the night before last and on Wednesday."

Michel gave the pretty girl a wan smile as he signed her program— "Yes, hello; nice to see you again."—and passed quickly on to the next one. When he had finished he left them with a wave and grabbed Crown by the arm, dragging him away.

"Come on, Charles, let's get out of here. I'll give you a lift home. Don't get me wrong but, God, am I glad to see the back of your bloody ballet for a few days."

"Me too. I'm going to sleep all weekend."

Both men were dog-tired. For Crown the evenings sitting at the back of the auditorium, shoulders hunched in nervous anxiety while his sharp eyes took in every movement, were nearly as exhausting as they were for

Michel, knocking out triple *tours* onstage. Crown didn't bully his dancers half to death before the premiere and then abandon them to the whims of his ballet mistress. Crown bullied his dancers all the time.

"I want to go over the end of that first solo again," he yawned, climbing into the passenger seat of Michel's car. Michel just grunted in reply.

The pressure on Crown's time and energy had been so immense this week that he had scarcely managed a word to Michel outside the immediate concerns of the new ballet. Now as they drove south down Rosebery Avenue he studied the figure behind the steering wheel with a frown of dawning concern. There were dark rings under Michel's blond lashes, still matted together with traces of mascara, and his usually clear gray eyes were bloodshot and heavy.

"Jesus, Michel, you look fucked. Are you okay?"

"Yes, I'm just wrecked, same as you."

"Well, make sure you eat properly this weekend; have some brewer's yeast and iron pills. Try and get a couple of early nights."

"Yes, sir."

"Don't call me sir. It irritates the hell out of me."

Michel smiled wearily.

"I know; that's why I do it. Did it irritate you when I was a student?"

"No," Crown said, yawning again, "I loved it. It made me feel like God."

Crown's yawning was infectious and Michel yawned too as he slowed the car to a stop at the traffic lights at the Aldwych.

"Tell you what, Charles; let's go back to Pimlico and get smashed. Jonni's not at home."

"Now that's the best bloody suggestion I've heard in weeks. I don't think I've ever seen you pissed."

The lights changed to green and Michel pulled into the right-hand lane to double back along the Strand toward Victoria.

"Yes you have. Primo and I once rolled into your class paralytic after one of Dan's all-night parties. You threw us both out with a smack round the ear."

There was a bleak edge to Crown's laughter. Christ yes, so he had; he remembered now.

They sat in the studio with an open bottle of brandy on the table between them. Neither was a great drinker—the rigor of their lifestyles had allowed little time for practice—and they emptied their glasses very slowly.

Crown was thinking ahead to the national tour which was only a fortnight away. Five grueling months of *The Seven Ages of Man* in rep with a revival of Crown's ever-popular Romeo.

"How many Romeos do you think you can face?" he asked, lighting another of the cigarettes which would no doubt one day be the death of him. "It's a bugger to have to ask you on top of *Seven Ages* and everything else this spring, but the sponsor's on my back about it. They're thinking of bums on seats, as always."

"Oh, I don't care. You know me, I'll do what I'm told. In the heavier weeks I can fill in with the smaller roles—Tybalt or Mercutio, whatever."

"Good God, I wouldn't ask you to do that. You'll have nights off between *Seven* and *Romeo,* of course."

"Nights off?" Michel raised his eyebrows, insinuating that his redoubtable boss had taken leave of his senses. Nobody got nights off in the Islington. This wasn't the Royal Ballet where the dignitaries of the profession graced the stage with their presence once or twice a fortnight and, in between, rested on their laurels while the body of the company did the donkey work. Here, everyone mucked in. Despite its successes of the past few years the Islington was neither large enough nor rich enough for nights off. If a principal needed rest he got it at the back of the corps or, at the very least, hung around looking decorative with a spear in one hand. "I don't need nights off. Who wants to spend the evening sitting around in a hotel in Nottingham? I'd rather turn up and help the dressers backstage."

Crown sipped his drink and fought against the temptation to conduct a postmortem of tonight's performance of *Seven Ages.* The role Michel had danced tonight was the most complex role they had ever created together and even after eight performances Crown's hypercritical mind was buzzing with changes he still wanted to make.

"We need Jonni here to keep us off the subject of work. Where's she gone, by the way?"

"To stay with friends. She wanted a bit of fresh air."

The choreographer nodded and tapped his hand gently on the arm of the sofa. He didn't like Michel being alone at the moment. There was no point asking him how he was coping with Primo's death now three weeks had passed; Michel was handling it as well as he could, just like everyone else. Crown marveled at Michel's self-control; he had channeled his grief and anger into his work with iron discipline. There hadn't been a single crack in his concentration, not a moment's wavering of focus either in the studio or onstage. But he didn't at all like the look of those dark rings under Michel's eyes.

"I'm surprised at Jonni taking herself off for a holiday at the moment."

"She needed some time out. She was in a bad state."

"I'd have thought she'd want to stick close to you for a while."

Michel clicked his tongue as he picked up his glass.

"I'm pretty poor company at the moment."

"That's irrelevant. She might have imagined you'd need a bit of support, with this ballet to worry about on top of everything else."

"Come on, Charles, she hasn't got work to keep her occupied. The flat's been empty all day; she's been lonely as hell."

"Well, now you've got a few days off, give her a call and tell her to get her arse back here. Or better still, get out of London for a couple of days—take her to a hotel somewhere by the sea, why don't you, and spend a morning or two in bed."

"I don't think that's what she wants at the moment."

"Maybe not, but it'd do you both good."

As Crown went on pressing his point, Michel stood up and walked toward the mirrored wall, distancing himself from the persistent hectoring.

"Phone her now," Crown insisted. "It's only eleven-thirty; she'll still be up."

"Okay, stop, Charles!" Michel turned to face him, holding his hand out toward him in appeal. "She's left me, alright? Jonni's walked out of the marriage and I don't blame her. Now will you shut up?"

Crown sat quite still with his mouth open and stared at him. Then he pulled his weight from the backrest of the sofa and leaned forward to stub his cigarette out in an ashtray.

"Rubbish! She'll be back within a week."

"Maybe." Michel was running his hand over the top of his head.

"Come and sit down, will you?"

"Alright."

"When did she leave?"

"Thursday. She went to Annette and Roly; I don't know if she's still there."

"Do you care? Do you want her back?"

Michel heaved a great sigh as he flung himself back onto the sofa. "I honestly don't know. At the moment I seem to be living entirely inside my own head. I should care, I know. I should be thinking about going and bringing her home. But right now my mind just won't focus on it. I just can't seem to make myself feel anything. It's best for her to be out looking for a life of her own. She's very young."

"So she's young. Well, what are you then? For Christ's sake, you're only twenty-six."

"I've noticed the papers have stopped referring to me as young."

Crown brushed this comment away with his hand.

"You stop being a young man to the media once you've got to the top. To them youth refers to potential; you've fulfilled yours."

"I hope not."

"You know what I mean. As far as the press are concerned you've made it. Jonni wouldn't just walk out on you, Michel. The two of you are friends."

For once there was a sour edge to Michel's tone.

"I used to think we had something that was more than a friendship."

"Nothing," Crown said firmly, "is ever more than a friendship. It can only ever be less. And one doesn't just bugger off and leave a friend in the lurch. Friends do not take the easy way out, Michel. Never."

"No?" Michel turned his eyes toward the empty piano stool on the far side of the studio. "Never, Charles? Are you absolutely sure?"

Crown was silent, tapping his fingers against the side of his glass. There was nothing he could say to that. He lit yet another cigarette and dropped the match into an ashtray.

"Did you try to stop her going?"

"Not really; she'd made up her mind."

"I suppose she's waiting for you to ask her to come back."

"I suppose she is."

At her parents' house in Gloucester Jonni read a report of her defection in the gossip column of her sister's *Daily Express:* "Michel wouldn't comment on the rumor his wife has recently left him; thousands of palpitating hearts wait for further news."

"What tosh," Jonni said, as she folded the newspaper and turned her attention with a frown to a boiled egg her mother was putting in front of her. "I told you I don't feel well enough for breakfast, Mum. Don't mollycoddle me. I'm not a child anymore; I'm a married woman."

"Yes," her mother replied sharply, "married. Eat your egg, Jonquil."

Another report, a few days later in the same gossip column, reduced Jonni to tears at the breakfast table.

"When I asked St. Michel whether his actress wife's disappearance was connected with the recent suicide of his longtime friend, Roberto Vincenti, he smiled in that seductive way of his and said, I couldn't tell you; ask her yourself if you can find her."

"Please," Jonni blubbered, blowing her nose, "don't show me any more. I feel ill. I don't care what they say."

"Obviously," Bernadette said as she took back her paper. "I can see you don't give two hoots."

Jonni went back to bed and pulled the duvet over her head. She really was unwell. In the fortnight since her return to Gloucester she had scarcely left her bed except for meals. Sometimes she tried to help her mother with household chores but between her nausea and faintness, and the stifling atmosphere of her mother's tight-lipped disapproval, she rarely managed more than half the washing-up before she crawled back upstairs to bed in exhaustion. She barely slept at all. Instead she lay awake, staring into the empty space Primo had left in the world; the black hole his death had created. That—and not missing Michel—occupied her thoughts day and night.

"Why don't you phone him?" Bernadette asked her, sitting down on the end of her bed one evening with two cups of tea. With unusual tact she had left her copy of the Sunday *Express* downstairs with its photograph of Michel and Louisa smiling intimately together at the BAFTA awards. "Call him on some pretext. Say you've left your spermicide jelly in the bathroom cupboard and you need it."

Jonni shook her head with a sigh and sipped her tea.

"I don't use spermicide jelly; it gives him a rash. And anyway, I don't want to call him. He'll find me if he wants to talk."

The ordeal of Sadler's Wells finally over, the Islington Ballet knuckled down to a fortnight's intensive rehearsal, brushing up *Romeo* and polishing *Seven Ages* before the tour. The weather was more like February than April: cold and gloomy with hours of dismal, spitting rain. Each day the dancers trudged back and forth along the Goswell Road from the tube station, wrapped in winter coats and scarves, under heavy skies. The tour hadn't even started yet and already they were worn out. No one talked about Primo's suicide anymore; they had talked the subject dry in the first couple of weeks. But his loss hung over the company like a cloud, subduing their chatter in the common room and dampening their enthusiasm in the studios.

Michel, however, was dancing superbly. He had been working at full stretch for many months, with two new ballets last autumn and the grueling winter tour, combined with all the weeks of choreography for this new piece, but his dedication never slackened, even when the rest of the company were flagging. Even now, after all the stress and tragedy of the past few weeks, he was intently focused on rehearsals.

"How does he do that?" Marina asked in awe, watching from a chair at the front of the studio while Michel partnered Louisa through the balcony duet from *Romeo*. "My God, look at him! Look at that manège; it's incredible."

Nadia Petrovna was sitting beside her and she nodded slowly, her pale eyes following his leaping figure as it spun in a wide circle around the studio.

"Yes," she murmured, "beautiful. They love dancing well who dance on thorns."

"But where's it coming from?" Marina insisted in a whisper. "How can he dance like that after everything that's happened? How can anyone possibly be that resilient?"

"Oh . . ." Nadia Petrovna thought about that as she watched him. ". . . with a lifetime of practice, I should imagine."

But whether it was practice or just too much pressure at work, Michel simply didn't have time to think about Primo, or to notice Jonni's absence when he arrived home in the evenings, already half-asleep, to collapse into bed. From morning until night he lived and breathed dance. As well as rehearsing his roles for the tour, he was brushing up *Giselle* for a guest performance in Germany next month and working with Crown on three new pieces for a TV special in May, not to mention dashing off in taxis almost daily to interviews and personal appearances all over London. And in addition to all this, he spent every spare moment helping Marina train up new soloists for *Romeo* from within the company. On a rapid-fire tour you could never have too many dancers who knew the roles—and Michel knew them all: Romeo, Mercutio, Tybalt, Paris, Capulet; even Juliet and her nurse.

"No," he said, putting Louisa down after a lift. "Don't move your arms till you get there, remember?"

"Sorry, sorry, I'm a wally—try again." Louisa was an English rose with near-black hair and easily bruised skin, so pale that the blue veins were visible on her throat and temple. Her dark, bright eyes watched Michel's reflection in the mirrored wall. "Are you okay?"

"Yeah, just a twinge. Let's try the lift again from the bourrée."

"Why don't we stop for a while? You've been rehearsing all day. I've only just started."

He retied his shirt around his waist and patted her bottom to move her back into position for the start of the sequence.

"No, let's press on and try and get this pas de deux down this afternoon. Arms in fifth . . . here we go."

He put her down and she watched him rub his foot.

"Are you sure it's nothing?"

"Yes. But maybe we should break for a few minutes. I'll run downstairs and show it to Karl."

Karl Redman had been on intimate terms with Michel's feet for ten years. There wasn't a muscle, ligament, or bone in Michel's body that Karl didn't know. He ran his hand slowly over the foot and twisted the ankle carefully from side to side.

"That hurt?"

"Nope."

"That?"

"No."

"It's not skeletal," Karl said. He had X-rays of Michel's feet, less than a month old, on his desk. "I can't find anything wrong: the arch is fine, the tendons are fine, the joint seems fine."

Michel swung himself down off the high examination table.

"That's exactly what I wanted to hear."

He pulled on his socks and leg warmers while the physiotherapist watched him with worried eyes. No one knew better than Karl that ballet and emotional stress are a dangerous combination.

"Michel, you're going to have to slow down. I know you take care of yourself physically. I know you're aware. But there's a limit to how much your body can take. You know my old maxim: mind over matter doesn't work in dance."

Michel smiled, adjusting the elastics on his ballet shoes.

"Don't worry, I'll keep an eye on it."

"I want to fix up daily sessions for you with a remedial masseur."

"Fine. But I can carry on working, can't I?"

"Carefully," Karl told him. "Very, very carefully."

Three days later Michel was back in Karl's surgery.

"This is absurd, I'm turning into a hypochondriac. My foot's fine but my back feels like someone's been using it for a trampoline."

Karl didn't even stop to examine him. He drove Michel straight to the orthopedic hospital in his own car.

"Where are you taking me now?" Michel asked as they left Harley Street an hour later.

"Home."

"But my car's at the Goswell Road. Besides, I've got rehearsals this afternoon."

"I want you right off your feet until I hear from the surgeon."

"Then I'll watch rehearsals sitting down. Honestly, Karl, what difference is it going to make whether I'm in Pimlico or at the Angel?"

"Home, rest, sleep, food," Karl replied. He wasn't taking any risks with the Islington's number one asset. Michel's was one of the strongest bodies Karl had ever worked with. Over the past ten years there had been a few sprains, a nagging shoulder that had needed physio for a couple of months, one or two problems with his arches when he was eighteen or nineteen—virtually nothing. A pessimist in dance physiotherapy would have said a major injury was long overdue.

"I'll call you when I get the results," he said.

When Charles Crown heard that Karl was waiting for X-rays of Michel's spine he was frantic. All afternoon he paced the foyer in the Goswell Road, hovering around Karl's surgery like an expectant father outside a delivery room. When the large brown envelope was finally delivered by courier to reception he pounced on it.

"At fucking last!" he cried, to the amazement of the mother of one of the new apprentices, who was standing at the reception counter. The pearl-draped woman stared at him in disapproval. She hadn't yet encountered the ogre to whom she had entrusted her precious little Lottie or Abigail.

Karl shook his head over the X-rays.

"What?" Crown demanded; "What?" He watched in anguish while the physio flicked through the surgeon's typed report. "What's the diagnosis?"

"No skeletal injury, thank God. No tissue damage."

"But . . . ?"

"But nothing, Charles. His back's okay. There's nothing to diagnose."

"There had better fucking well not be, Karl, because I don't want another Roland Kovak on my hands, and especially not St. Michel!"

The two men looked at each other stonily. The injury that had cost Roly his career had occurred more than three years ago but it still touched a very raw nerve with them both.

"Forget I said that," Crown mumbled, searching his pockets for his cigarettes. "Kovak was as much my fault as yours; we both know it."

Karl took his glasses off and laid them on his desk.

"This problem with Michel's back, it's just exhaustion or his imagination; it amounts to the same thing. I think we should try and get him to take some time off."

"Alright, I'll cancel his rehearsals tomorrow, and he'll have the weekend."

"No, I mean real time off. Charles, he's killing himself. You've seen the amount of work he's taken on himself; no body can withstand that kind of punishment. This is how accidents happen. He's under way too much stress."

"Stress? We're all under fucking stress. I've got a major sponsor who's threatening to pull out of the autumn season and three new pieces to finish by the end of the month—you think I'm not stressed? He can take a week or two off after the telly recording but, in the meantime, I need him in Cardiff at ten o'clock on Monday morning."

Karl looked at the fiery little man who had been his friend and his colleague for almost fifteen years. He shook his head, speaking very slowly and deliberately.

"No, you don't, Charles. Not if you want him in one piece at the end of the season."

There was no point telling Michel to stop working; you might as well tell the sun to stop rising and setting. Not surprisingly, he dismissed Crown's suggestion that he should take a fortnight's break. Crown couldn't force him. The days when Michel took orders were long gone. Michel was an internationally respected dancer; he was amply qualified to decide for himself whether he needed to rest.

"This isn't the time," he said. "It would screw things up for all of us. Let's just get through the next couple of months. If I need to ease off then, I will."

"I'll be straight with you," Crown told him. "Karl's concerned, with the amount of strain you're under, that there's a real danger of your doing yourself an injury. You have to consider, Michel, that with Primo's death, and with Jonni suddenly leaving—"

"Those have nothing to do with my work," Michel said, interrupting him firmly. "Have you ever known me to bring my personal life into the studio? Ever?" He looked hard into his teacher's eyes. "Ever, Charles?"

Crown thought about it, shaking his head.

"No. You're sure you're alright then?"

"A hundred percent."

Crown trusted Michel's knowledge of his own body; however, he did what little he could. He reshuffled the casting for the first couple of weeks of the tour to lessen the burden on Michel and cut out as many of Michel's press calls as possible. The issue of the press calls turned into a battle with the sponsors. Press was what sold the tour—and the press wanted Michel.

The company were cheerful when they assembled on stage in Cardiff for class the following Monday. The dancers were all relieved to be away from London; they sang and laughed as they jostled into position at the portable barres, repinning hair that had fallen out of buns and pulling up the legs of tights. Michel, too, was in good spirits. He joked with the boys and teased the girls while he warmed up with them at the barre.

That evening, as he stood in the wings waiting to go on as Mercutio, he laid his hand on the breast of his blue tunic. His heart was thumping. It was almost two years since he had danced Mercutio and for the first time since his apprenticeship he felt the cold, clammy fingers of stage fright crawl over his skin.

"Jesus, I feel a bit wired," he said to Ivor who was standing beside him.

"Who, you? Mister invincible?" Ivor was sweating copiously, rigid with preperformance nerves, about to go on for the first time as Romeo in front of his home Cardiff crowd. "What you got to be wired about, boyo? You done this role 'undreds of times."

Michel stretched his back; it was still slightly tender.

"I'm just afraid something's going to go on me while I'm on."

"Is that all? Christ, I'm afraid the whole ruddy audience is going to go on me."

No amount of pain or nervousness could snuff out the flame that illuminated the stage when Michel was dancing. He romped and flirted his way gaily through Mercutio, toning down his big jumps in the trios so as not to humiliate Ivor and provoking screams of terror from a couple of children in the front row as he collapsed in Ivor's arms, impaled on Daniel's sword.

"Jesus, there are kids here," he whispered, while Ivor sobbed over him. "Doesn't the theater know this isn't a kids' show?"

"My daughters," Ivor whispered back. "Sorry, boy, I warned Gwen to cover their eyes while I'm shagging Marcia; I forgot about the gory bits."

Michel gave him a dry glance and spat out his unbroken blood capsule into his hand. He wasn't about to expire with blood streaming from his mouth in front of Ivor's daughters. "Welsh git," he murmured, dying.

The next night, while he waited for the overture of *Seven Ages* to start, he was gripped even more tightly by nerves. The hairs on his arms were standing on end and tension squeezed the air out of his lungs. This time, however, he didn't mention it to anybody. Once was funny—twice was a little alarming; and it was no concern of anyone but himself.

Despite Crown's efforts to lighten Michel's workload, the first few weeks on tour were manic. Crown was dashing back and forth from London to the touring venues, struggling to rescue his ailing sponsorship deal while he scrambled to get the new pieces finished for the TV special. It was choreography on the run: he and Michel created an entire eight-minute contemporary piece in one afternoon in the front-of-house bar in the theater in Nottingham. And the publicity calls were still mounting up.

"*Vogue* want to do a photo shoot," the company manager told Michel. "They'll do it at the theater and provide wardrobe and makeup. All you have to do is show up."

"Shit," Michel sighed, putting his hands on his hips. He was in the middle of a rehearsal for *Seven Ages*. "You don't really expect me to do it, do you?"

"It's voluntary, of course, like any other press call." Then the company manager grimaced. "Yeah, it's an important one; sorry. And another thing; you've really got to get yourself an agent."

"What for?"

"To sort out the fees for your guest performances in Toronto and Madrid and to negotiate with us over the royalties for these two videos we're releasing."

Michel was exasperated. "Why can't I negotiate with you myself?"

"Because you'll accept whatever we offer you and that's not fair. Look, I'll get someone from John Proud's to come up and talk to you; they represent several of the big turns at the Garden."

"Whatever you like," Michel agreed, "but in the meantime can I go on with my rehearsal—or is there anything else you want me to do?"

The company manager raised an apologetic hand, smiling as he backed away off the stage. This obviously wasn't the moment to mention the pop video for *Children in Need*.

Michel worked and worked, performing in the evenings and rehearsing all day when he wasn't tied up with radio interviews or sponsors' lunches. His stage fright had increased to the point where it was becoming more and more difficult to conceal it from his colleagues. Cold sweat smeared his makeup as he put it on in front of the mirror every evening and his bowels turned to liquid in the half hour before the curtain. The deeper his anxiety grew, the harder he worked, determined to beat it. He couldn't understand it; he was in good shape, he was confident about his technique, and the regional audiences greeted his performances with cheering ovations, reassuring him that he was dancing at his best.

In the last week of April Michel flew to Frankfurt to partner Carlotta di Gian-Tomaso in a performance of *Giselle*. She had been stuck for an Albrecht for that evening and Michel had agreed, months ago, to do it as a favor. The Giant Tomato was in great form; the atmosphere and prestige of the bigger company suited her perfectly. In the two years since she'd moved to Germany her stroppy conceit had matured gracefully into the arrogance of a grand diva. She and Michel danced their *Giselle* together after only one day's rehearsal—they had danced this ballet together so many times they could probably have done it completely cold.

"My word," Carlotta said archly once the curtain had fallen, "don't they just love you, darling?" She didn't like her partner receiving a more enthusiastic ovation than her own. "You've become quite the little fashion item, haven't you? *Lovely* dix-es in Act Two, by the way." She tugged off her wig and tossed it carelessly to her dresser, scattering hairpins everywhere. "But you were tight as a flatulent ballerina's arse at the top of Act One. What was wrong? Have I put on weight?"

Michel laughed off her comment. "Bloody right I was tight, all those people on stage. I've never seen such a massive corps; where did they all come from? I thought I was going to fall over someone."

"Poor pet." Carlotta patted his cheek and gave him what was, after all, a very affectionate kiss. "I'd quite forgotten how provincial you are. One gets so used to being chauffeured to and from work in a limo, and to having one's own suite at the operhaus—one simply blocks out the dreadful memories of trying to make art in such Neanderthal conditions."

The next morning Michel flew back to the cramped stage and dressing rooms of the theater in Glasgow. There was no time to worry about the appalling stage fright he'd experienced in Frankfurt; he was flung straight back into touring performances and frenzied last-minute re-hearsals for the TV special. Stage fright was controllable; the nervous energy could be channeled into his dancing. But something else had happened in Frankfurt; something far more disconcerting. Onstage in Frankfurt, for the first time in his career, he had experienced a moment when his mind went completely blank. In the middle of the first scene he had suddenly found, just for an instant, that he had no earthly idea what came next. A glance at Carlotta had told him she was preparing to jeté into his arms and, by the time he had held out his hands to catch her he was back in focus. The moment had passed almost before it happened but while it lasted it had terrified him.

And at the end of the week in Glasgow it happened again.

"Bit of a wobble in the *failli* in the waltz," Crown told him.

Michel sat down at his dressing table and leaned over to pull off his ballet shoes.

"Yup, I had a moment there, you're right."

Crown shrugged. A wobble was a wobble; the best dancers had them. And no one except Crown with his eagle eyes would have spotted it.

"Anyway, I've seen you dance a lot worse."—Which was Crown's way of saying he'd never seen him dance better. "Everything alright? No problems with your back?"

"No, I feel great. It's been very peaceful with you away in London."

"Thanks very much."

It was about that time that Michel began to notice members of the company staring at him as he walked around the theater corridors and whispering about him in huddled groups. It was subtle at first but, every day, their stares became a little bolder and more malevolent, and their whispers acquired a more insinuating tone. Michel tried to disregard it, withdrawing into himself and his work, but it was hard to ignore—so many of them were people he'd known for years, friends, who were now putting their heads together when he walked past, whispering his name and exchanging knowing glances.

"Michel?" One of the younger girls from the corps stopped beside him on the stage, raising her arms above her head, while he was warming up for the show. "Are my pits alright or am I fuzzy?"

He turned and hurried away. "Ask your dresser."

"Crikey!" The corps dancer put her hands on her hips and stared at his departing back. "Well, excuuuuse me, Michel! Forgive me for breathing!"

All through the following week, while he recorded the TV special, the sense of being watched clung to him like an irritating burr, accompanying him to morning classes at the Goswell Road and to the BBC studios in Wood Lane. He wasn't consciously aware of it but it was always there, a physical presence in his chest.

Once the TV recording was over, the company went back out on the road and Michel soldiered on: classes, rehearsals, performance, publicity. He wasn't aware of how withdrawn and irritable he had become. The company still watched him with knowing, sinister eyes. Even Marina's gaze was accusing when she looked at him.

"What?" Michel snapped, looking sharply over his shoulder during a break in a *Romeo* rehearsal in Leicester. "What about Primo, Marina?"

"God!" Marina's shoulders recoiled at his tone. "There's no need to bite my head off, poppet. I was only saying he used to play this scene faster than Max. The girls found the *brisés volés* easier that way."

Michel breathed out tensely, looking down at his feet and then at the wings.

"Yeah, you're right," he muttered. "Yeah, he did play it faster." And he walked away quickly to grind his feet in the rosin tray.

The dancers standing around Marina exchanged miffed glances.

"Bloody prima."

"A few TV chat shows and he thinks he's ruddy God Almighty."

The Islington Ballet on tour was an incestuous, claustrophobic little community. Every week seemed a month. Tiny incidents mushroomed into crises. Sexual intrigue and infidelity abounded, and intolerance flared suddenly into enmity. On tour the dancers, who each had their individual charms and failings, blended into a mob personality. And the company was never more closely united than when the whole body of dancers closed ranks against one of their number.

The dressing rooms began to hum with complaints: Michel was too high and mighty to spend his coffee breaks in the green room anymore. He had walked straight past Ivor in the street without even looking at him. He had started demanding his own private dressing room in every theater, even the ones that were short on space, and he always skulked on his own in the wings until the curtain went up. And had you noticed how he always made Adrian book him into a different hotel from the rest of the dancers—a more expensive one, they wouldn't mind betting.

The change in Michel had been gradual. The dancers didn't see how tense and abstracted he was, nor see the fear in his gray eyes as he faced the curtain every night. They only saw how aloof he had grown; his celebrity alter ego beginning to assert itself. Michel was a star and to a certain extent he was allowed to behave differently from everyone else—in fact it was expected of him—but they drew the line at his refusing to warm up at the same barre as them.

Marina watched him in rehearsals with a puzzled frown but, like the rest of the company, she took it for granted that Michel was invincible. The time to worry about a dancer was when their work started to suffer, and Michel was dancing superbly. If anything, he had excelled himself over the past couple of months.

Michel hadn't noticed how isolated he had become—he had retreated into his head, into his work—but a vague sense of unease seemed to hover around him in the air wherever he went. When the company returned to London for a week of rehearsals at the end of the first leg of the tour, he kept his eyes on the floor of the studio. He didn't like all those mirrors. He wasn't used to them after all these weeks of class and rehearsal on stage.

He spent his evenings alone in the Pimlico flat that week with nothing but his own thoughts to occupy him, walking back and forth between the studio and the kitchen, wishing he were back out on the road. The flat was in a terrible state. The dirty cups and plates sitting on the kitchen table had been there since March, over two months ago. He went out to Covent Garden to watch the Royal Ballet perform a triple bill, but the awed gazes of the fans in the foyer unnerved him. In the past his celebrity had never troubled him but now his skin burned under the barrage of their stares as they pointed at him and whispered. His throat constricted every time some bold member of the audience came toward him to ask for his autograph. Even once the ballet had started, people turned around in their seats to look at him, eager to know what he thought of the dancing.

He left in the first interval.

The next afternoon Roly and Annette arrived home from their local supermarket to find a message from Michel on the answering machine. It was a cheerful-sounding message: "Hi, listen, we're in London rehearsing for a few days, until Monday. If either of you are around, how about meeting up in town for a drink or a meal? Or maybe you could pop over to Pimlico if you feel like it. Anyway, if you're there would you call me? I'm in this evening; call tonight, will you?"

"Good God," Annette said, raising her eyebrows as she dumped her shopping on the sofa. "Since when did Michel bother phoning us? That's got to be a first."

"I'll give him a ring," Roly told her.

"No, sod him; why should you? He buggers off for months on end without contacting us." She still hadn't forgiven Michel for yawning during Primo's funeral. "As far as I'm concerned he can go screw himself after the way he behaved when Jonni left. Darling, you're only home for two days!"

Roly looked guiltily at the phone. If he were honest he could do without a long discussion about Louisa Nicholl's fabulous extension and Ivor's hopeless double *tours*.

"Really, I would rather spend the time with you."

Annette put her arms around Roly's waist with a blissful smile. No amount of reassurance was ever enough for Annette.

"Would you really? For that I'll let you take me out for dinner tonight—Chinese—isn't that nice of me? No, you can take me to Joe Allen's; we haven't been there for ages. I'll phone Michel at the weekend or something, I promise."

Michel lay awake in his bed in Pimlico staring at the shadows on the bedroom ceiling. The flat was very quiet. The silence reverberated through the untidy rooms around him.

He was alright, he told himself. He really was.

It was all controllable: the stage fright . . . the nerve-racking moments of blankness while he danced. Everything was controllable.

He reached over to the bedside table and took a sleeping pill. The important thing was the dancing. Nothing else mattered.

He was alright.

After another two weeks on the road the company opened in Bradford with a flurry of cast shuffling due to the last-minute announcement that the Princess of Wales was coming to see the performance on Thursday night with one or two friends. It was to be a private visit, which didn't stop the tabloids besieging the press office as soon as word leaked out from the theater. It was clearly going to be a media circus and, in terms of exposure for the company, it was a gold mine.

"Tell me," said Crown's secretary, Susan, as they sat facing each other on the Bradford train on Thursday morning, "would you have agreed to mess up our entire schedule for the week if all those cameras and journalists weren't going to be there?"

"Of course I would. I couldn't ignore a request from a member of the Royal family, could I? This is nothing to do with the publicity."

Susan was a plump, sane woman in her early forties.

"Honestly, truly? Cross your heart?"

Crown gave her one of his dark, wry looks.

"That's not a fair question."

Crown walked into the Alhambra Theatre just before lunchtime to be greeted by chaos: an entire lighting department who were ready to walk out in despair.

"Charles, the computerized board's blown!"

"Blown? What d'you mean, blown?"

"I mean blown. Sparks, smoke, sizzled circuits! Barbecued! Someone knocked over a cup of coffee while the top panel was open."

Crown didn't ask who; he didn't care.

"Can't we use the theater's board?"

The chief electrician shook his head. He had been tearing his hair so frantically all morning it was sticking up as though it had been he and not his equipment that had been electrocuted. "Software's not compatible. It'd take days to transfer the plot."

"Fuck!" Crown said. "Fuck! Can we replot?"

"The plans are in the Goswell Road."

"So make up a new one! Sketch out half a dozen general states and knock up as many specials as you can. I can't believe I'm having to tell you how to do your job!"

"A new lighting plot? In six hours?"

"Yes!" Crown snapped. "Six hours. So don't stand there, GO! Not to the box, you idiot! Get the fucking book from the prompt corner!"

Almost six hours later Crown was still in the lighting box where the LX department were frantically programming in cues with the Alhambra's electricians. He had been too busy, all afternoon, to take much notice of what was going on down on the stage—that was Marina's problem—and now only Louisa and one or two of the other girls were doing a last-minute warm-up while Michel did a barre in another corner of the stage.

"How does this look?" the chief LX asked him, bringing up a blue nighttime wash.

Crown was gazing through the glass window at the stage. He didn't answer. Something had caught his attention and transfixed him.

"Charles?"

Still Crown didn't answer. His brow contracted very slowly over his sharply focused eyes. He raised a vague hand.

"Sorry, Mark . . . sorry. Do whatever you think looks okay." He still hadn't taken his eyes from the stage. "I've got to go—now."

Michel had disappeared to his dressing room by the time Crown wound his way down through the front of house and through the pass door to the stage. It was more than a fortnight since Crown had seen Michel and when he walked into his dressing room he was aghast. Michel's face was white and drawn, and his forehead was bathed in sweat. Crown sat down slowly on the arm of a chair, looking at him in the mirror.

"What's the matter?"

"I'm alright. It's just a touch of nerves."

A touch?

"How long has this been going on? Why didn't Marina tell me?"

"Marina doesn't know. She's got the good manners not to come into my dressing room during the half. It's nothing to worry about. I've got it under control."

"You're looking very tense. I was watching you just now from the lighting box."

"Of course I'm tense. It's been stop-start all afternoon with these security checks and sniffer dogs all over the place, not to mention all the faffing about with the lights. And you're surprised my muscles are tight?" Michel squeezed the water out of his makeup sponge and started plastering his face with pancake. "Is there any chance of the curtain going up on time tonight?"

"Not much, I'm afraid. We'll keep you informed. I'm sorry we had to switch your performances around this week."

"No problem."

"I should have put Ivor on last night," Crown said anxiously. He lit a cigarette and stood up to pace nervously behind Michel's chair. "You look very tired. Back holding up alright?"

Michel picked up his eye pencil. "My back's fine. Stop nagging."

His hand trembled as he drew a brown line under each eye. Crown watched a bead of perspiration trickle from Michel's forehead down the side of his face. Crown had never ceased to be aware of the immense physical strain that every performance put on Michel's body but, calm as Michel always was, it was all too easy to forget that the strain it put on his mind was equally immense.

"Look, Michel, if you're not feeling up to this performance . . ."

"I told you I'm okay."

"You don't have to do it. I can put Erik on."

"No you can't. Erik's still not jumping after his ankle."

"Then Daniel . . ."

"He's not warmed up for it. For Christ's sake, stop going on. I'm ready. My body's fit. My mind's on the choreography. I'm fine, Charles."

Crown stopped pacing and looked at Michel's veiled eyes in the dressing table mirror. On a normal day he'd pull a show at a moment's notice rather than put Michel on when he looked like this. His dancers' safety was his first concern. But this wasn't a normal day, and this was one show he couldn't pull.

"Okay," he said reluctantly, "I need you to get through this one. Just tonight. And then we'll recast Saturday and next week and give you some time off."

Michel didn't reply.

Crown walked slowly up and down behind Michel's chair. The lights were on in the dressing room; it was still daylight but the sky outside the frosted-glass windows had turned gloomy, heralding another downpour. Almost three months had passed since Primo's death, and the two men had never discussed it.

"Why didn't you talk to me?" Crown said. "Why didn't you tell me what you've been going through?" Still Michel didn't speak. Crown continued pacing. "Look . . . I know this isn't really the moment to bring up Primo but—" The door opened and Michel's dresser came in. "Go away, darling." She went out again. "It's been on all our minds, Michel. We all have a burden of guilt to carry: you, me, and Marina. I know you feel responsible for the—"

"No!" Michel turned around abruptly on his chair to face him. "No, I do not feel responsible, Charles. And you're right, this isn't the fucking time. It hasn't been on my mind. I haven't been thinking about him; I've been thinking about my work because that's what you pay me to do. The only burden I've been carrying is the burden of getting through this ballet three times a week. Now will you bugger off and let me prepare for this performance?"

"Alright," Crown said, leaving.

"And send me my dresser!" Michel yelled after him.

As the press photographers snapped pictures of the private royal party arriving in the foyer, Michel walked up and down behind the huge curtain on stage trying to loosen his muscles. He wiped the cold sweat from his brow onto the sleeve of his Lycra bodysuit, carefully, so as not to smudge his makeup. It wasn't the VIP out front that made him so tense—he wasn't even aware of her—it was the delay. He turned the stage manager's wrist over to look at his watch: 7:40 p.m. How much longer? He could see the hostile eyes of the dancers watching him from the sides of the stage. It was all controllable. His mouth was dry and he signaled to his dresser in the wings to bring him some water. When the overture started and the working lights overhead dimmed, he adjusted his dance belt through his bodysuit and lay down on the stage beside Louisa, coiling his body around hers in his opening position for the show.

The whole company was on edge. They were always twitchy during the overture for *Seven Ages*. If they had been doing *Romeo* the dancers would have been fooling around, laughing and play-fighting until the curtain rose. But this ballet was different. In the dark Michel could feel the bristling electricity of nervous tension all around him.

Michel was so sick with fear he couldn't breathe. His heart inside his breast was pumping so hard his Lycra costume was visibly jumping. As the last note of the overture died he pulled up his muscles, while the curtain rose, flooding the stage with brilliant light. With his head on the rubber dance floor, below the level of the glaring front-of-house lanterns, he could see the first few rows of the audience clearly. He wanted to look away or close his eyes but he couldn't; the choreography said he must look straight ahead. Thank God he had the first thirty-two bars while the corps danced the opening ensemble before he had to move. What was his first move? The floor smelled strongly of rubber and disinfectant. He lay perfectly still waiting for his thoughts to settle, and stared at the shadowy figures in the audience.

Why were they whispering?

They really were. The audience was whispering; looking at him and whispering.

"Michel?" He heard Louisa's worried voice murmur in his ear and he hushed her with a pressure of his arms.

The moment came for him to move and his mind refused to focus. The spotlight hit him full in the face. He had to move. To dance. He stood up—surely that was correct?—and tried to talk himself through the choreography of the first duet. The first combination was, yes, a series of turns—but which way? That way? No, that way. Then the two supported arabesques into the—what?—supported jeté? Surely there was a supported jeté before the first big lift. The corps were spinning around him to a crescendo from the violins. He could tell from the terrified look in Louisa's eyes that something was very wrong but there was nothing he could do about it. He swept her up in the first overhead lift and, as he felt her slipping through his hands in the air, he instinctively snatched her tightly into his arms. Her cry of alarm seemed to come from a long way away. He put her down and looked around. What came next? Grand jeté en arrière. His head was full of all those staring eyes and whispering voices. But still, somewhere at the back of his mind, was the thought that he had to try to get through this performance. Grand jeté en arrière.

From fourth position croisé devant he transferred his weight onto his front foot and dipped into a demi-plié, springing into the air.

Michel scarcely felt himself falling. Like a child, he sat on the rubber floor where he landed and gazed at the audience beneath the blinding front-of-house lights. They were whispering more loudly now. Louisa ran to crouch beside him trying to hold him, but her grasp startled him and he pushed her away with his arm—he had lost touch with his body and he no longer knew his own strength; she went flying across the stage into the backdrop. Nothing around him was real. The only thing that was real was the hatred in the eyes of the crowd of strangers who were pressing down on him on all sides. The piercing spotlight flashed back and forth into his eyes as the follow-spot operator wavered indecisively.

A dark figure was sprinting through the auditorium toward the stage, and Michel recoiled in fear, trying to scramble to his feet and flee. But a man who vaguely resembled a dancer he had once known had grabbed his arm. "Bring in the tabs!" yelled a frantic voice while Michel struggled to fight off the clawing hands that were holding him.

Someone struck him hard across the face and a hand that he trusted seized the front of his costume.

"It's me!" Crown's voice shouted at him above the clamor of voices inside his head. "Michel, it's me! Me, Michel! It's alright!" Crown turned his head to scream over his shoulder, "Clear the fucking stage! Clear it now! All of you!"

Michel raised his hand and closed his fingers on the lapel of Crown's dinner jacket.

"Charles . . . ?"

"Yes, I'm here, it's okay—someone call an ambulance!"

"You won't tell my mother."

"No, no, I won't tell her."

"I just need to rest a minute. I'll be able to go on in a minute."

"Yes, yes, fine—*and get those fucking tabs in!*"

The journalists in the stalls dived for their mobile phones. They loved it.

27

"Hullo?"

"Jonni?"

"Yes, this is Jonni."

"Darling, it's Charles Crown."

Jonni's voice lit up: "Charles!" Apart from two calls from Roly, she hadn't heard a thing from her London friends for nearly ten weeks.

"Why aren't you in London?"

"Charles . . . are you okay?"

"No, I'm fucking not okay; what do you expect? Listen, I'm on a train to Bradford. They didn't have a bed for him last night so I took him back to London because that's where he said he wanted to go, and Marina and I stayed with him overnight. Marina's with him now but I need her back up north this afternoon so get your backside on a train now, and for Christ's sake be nice to him. I'll be down again as soon as I've sorted out the bloody mess I've got on my hands in Bradford."

"What?" Jonni said. He was going way too fast for her. "What are you talking about?"

"Haven't you seen the papers?"

"The papers? Yes, I flicked through the *Times* at breakfast. I saw that Princess Di came to see Michel dance in your new piece last night—I was glad for you, but . . ."

"Look at a later edition."

He cut her off without another word and Jonni stared at the receiver for a few seconds before she flung it back on the hook and tore out of her bedroom in her dressing gown. Bernadette had left for work a quarter of an hour ago but she had come home again; Jonni met her running up the stairs with a copy of the *Daily Express* in her hand.

"Jonni," she said, breathless, "I know you said you didn't want to know anything about—"

"Let me see that!" Jonni snatched the paper out of her sister's hand. On the second page there was a photograph of a dazed-looking Michel being helped from the stage door of the Alhambra Theatre to a waiting ambulance, shying away from the flashing lights of the cameras. The accompanying article, mercifully brief, said he had collapsed through overwork and that Charles Crown said he would be fine, he just needed rest.

"Get the car!" Jonni cried. "Bernie, get the car! I'll be dressed in one minute. I've got to make the ten-fifteen!"

"We'll make it!" Bernadette yelled, running for her mother's car keys.

On the train Jonni sat with her fists clenched in her lap. A woman sitting opposite her opened a copy of the *Daily Mail* and Jonni stared in horror at the front-page picture of Charles Crown and Marina outside the theater, each trying to fend off the press with one arm while they supported Michel with the other. Crown looked frantic. She looked along the length of the crowded train carriage, at the dozens of open newspapers. The realization that all those gloating headlines referred not to some unknown pop idol or TV personality but to Michel—her Michel—made her skin crawl.

She leaned forward to the woman opposite. "I'm sorry, would you mind if I had a quick look at that?"

The blond woman looked at her with suspicion, but she handed the paper over. Jonni read the front page article quickly. Michel had fallen heavily during the performance and had panicked, knocking his ballerina across the stage and fighting off the colleagues who tried to come to his aid. Audience members had assumed it was part of the show until the orchestra had ground to a halt and the curtain had been lowered. The whole company was said to be shocked, stunned, and saddened by their much-loved star's collapse. An aide said the Princess of Wales had expressed her deep concern.

"Oh, Michel," Jonni groaned. "Oh no!"

The woman opposite was watching her, intrigued by her evident emotion.

"Fan of his, are you, then?"

"Yes." Jonni had no taste for melodrama today. "Yes, I'm a big fan. Thanks." She handed back the paper as the train pulled slowly—too slowly to suit her—out of Swindon station. She thumped the wall of the train impatiently with her fist. "Oh, come on!" she yelled at it in frustration.

When she jumped out of a taxi in Warwick Way and ran up the stairs, her knock was answered almost immediately. Michel must have been standing in the hallway; he was reading a letter as he opened the door. His face broke into a smile of surprise as he saw her standing on the landing outside.

"Now, what about that?" he said, standing back and holding the door open to let her in. "I receive a check for eight hundred pounds for the sale of *Swan Lake* to Japan, and then you arrive, all in the space of two minutes. It's obviously my lucky day." He turned toward Marina, who was coming quickly out of the kitchen, already halfway into her coat. "Marina, look who's arrived."

"Thank God you made it, lovey," Marina said. "I have to dash; I've seriously got to catch the one thirty-five or Charles will fry me." She looked exhausted after a sleepless night, her tan linen trouser suit crumpled and her brown hair tied back in a hasty ponytail. Without her makeup and without her usual flippant good humor, her weary smile was disconcertingly masculine. She gave Michel a hurried kiss as she pulled on her gloves. "Michel, poppet, take Jonni into the studio, why don't you?"

Jonni's heart swelled joyfully inside her as her beloved old home opened its mouth and swallowed her into the hallway. She managed to exchange a few whispered words with Marina before she followed Michel through the open door of the studio.

"How is he?" she asked.

Marina's strained eyes looked earnestly down into hers.

"I don't know, love. If you're worried, my mobile number's next to the phone. Charles'll probably call you every ten minutes anyway; you know what he's like. Look after him, Jonni." She pressed a little brown pill bottle into Jonni's hand. "He has to have one of these every four hours; the next one's due in about an hour. For Christ's sake don't let him have more than one; they're absolutely strong as fuck."

As Marina disappeared, her high-heeled shoes clacking in the echoing stairwell as she ran down the stairs, Jonni closed the front door and went toward the studio door. In the doorway of the studio she stood and looked at Michel. He was sitting on a sofa, smiling calmly up at her.

"Hello," she said at last, her mouth twitching in emotion.

"Hello," he said.

They were both silent for a few seconds, looking at each other, and then her eyes creased up in concern, her mouth puckering in pained sympathy.

"Are you alright?"

He mimicked her tragic expression with comical affection.

"Yes."

"What do you mean: yes?"

"I mean I'm alright, Jons."

"But the papers are saying you collapsed. They're saying you threw some kind of fit."

"Oh, God, that's nonsense. You know better than to believe what you read in the tabloids. I had a fall, that's all, and it threw me for a minute or two. But I'm perfectly okay. Hospital was just a precaution."

She came, at his smilingly gestured invitation, to sit on the sofa opposite. He really did look okay. She had been terrified of finding him a helpless, gibbering wreck—perhaps part of her had secretly hoped it; hoped that at last she would be able to lavish on him the love and tenderness she had always longed for him to need from her. But aside from being unshaven and a little pale, he looked exactly as he had always looked.

"Charles said you were ill."

"Of course he did." Michel folded the check he was still holding and tucked it back into the envelope. And if his hands were a little uncoordinated Jonni didn't notice it. It hadn't occurred to her to wonder whether she could cope with a Michel who was helpless, who had lost control of his mind. But it's possible, although this hadn't occurred to Jonni, that it had occurred to Michel. "It's his job to overreact. If he loses me from the tour he loses bookings."

"Are you . . ." Jonni was unsure of herself now, "going back on tour then?"

"Yes, of course," he said. "I'll be joining the company in Bristol on Monday. I'm not due to dance until Wednesday night but we've got some bloody sponsors' lunch on Monday that I've really got to show up for. Do you want a coffee? I was just about to put some on."

Jonni gazed at his untroubled face, confused. He seemed exactly like his usual self. At last she managed a hesitant smile. Despite the ghastly photos in the papers and the worry she had seen in Marina's eyes, she was really beginning to believe that Michel's collapse had all been the invention of the press.

"Okay. Why don't I make it?" She stood up and looked at him across the low coffee table, her eyes full of her emotion at seeing him again after the ten miserable weeks of their separation. "Do you want it white?"

"No."

She chewed the edge of a fingernail for a few seconds.

"Black?"

Michel looked up at her and his smile broadened.

"Good guess."

Life with Michel seemed to begin and end with coffee. The kitchen was so filthy and cluttered Jonni barely recognized it as she searched among the unwashed dishes for coffee cups. It felt blissful to be washing up mugs in her own kitchen and grinding coffee beans as though the ten weeks of her absence had never happened. She didn't mind the mess; it made her feel needed.

The day had grown gloomy and she switched on the overhead lights in the studio as she brought in the coffee. She didn't see that Michel winced at the brightness.

Michel picked up the cup she put in front of him and started drinking it, oblivious to its scalding heat.

"So you've been in Gloucester, have you?" he asked. "Bernadette still a pain in the arse? Veronica okay? What have you been doing with yourself?"

"Nothing much. I've been feeling pretty lousy. In fact I hardly even go out of the house. Most of the time I just sit around and eat and eat and eat." She looked forlornly down at her figure. "I suppose it shows."

Michel looked her over with a small smile.

"Well, maybe," he confessed. "Just a little."

They talked over the recent gossip from the Islington Ballet—Erik's new fashion designer boyfriend and Marcia's ligament sprain—though, in truth, Michel had barely noticed anything that was going on in the company for weeks.

"I bet the fans have been attentive since the gossip columnists discovered I'd moved out."

"Absolutely," he agreed.

"And I'll bet Daniel's furious."

"Absolutely."

It was just chatter and they both knew it.

"How's Louisa?"

"Alright. Pissed off about the number of shows she has to dance with Marcia being off."

Jonni smiled tightly. "But attentive too, I'll bet."

He picked up a pen and started to doodle on the back of the envelope he had laid on the coffee table. "Skip it, Jons." The pen in his hand moved slowly round and round making circles. Jonni watched him, her eyes becoming glued to the paper as she changed the subject to the new theater that was being built in Cheltenham.

The longer their conversation went on, the longer the gaps grew between Jonni's comments and Michel's responses. Michel was drawing steadily and Jonni saw him narrow his eyes slightly as his lines failed to close up into circles. Each time he missed one he went back over the line and had a second attempt. After watching him for several minutes Jonni became firmly convinced that it was a matter of no small achievement to draw a line which curved around to join up with its origin. Eventually Jonni stopped talking altogether but Michel didn't seem to notice the silence.

As she sat and watched him, Jonni saw, at last, that Michel was not as well as he pretended to be. She watched him for a couple of minutes more, and then moved around the coffee table to crouch beside him.

"Mike, you really are sick, aren't you?"

She laid her hand gently on his thigh and a flood of recognition traveled through her fingers as she felt the warm reality of his body through the fabric of his tracksuit, but she took her hand away again as she felt him stiffen at her touch.

"I told you I'm fine." Michel was still drawing circles, going slowly over the same lines again and again. "I'm perfectly alright."

"No, you aren't." She did her best to hide how hurt she was by his physical rejection. "You freaked out in front of a thousand people, not to mention Princess Diana and half the British press. Really, Michel; really, I'm sorry but that is not being alright."

He put his hand to his eyes to shut out the piercing light.

"Well, you have to see the funny side of it, I suppose," he said.

But Jonni couldn't see the funny side. She couldn't see the funny side of anything at all.

"Nothing's been funny since Primo died."

"Jonni, you haven't got a cigarette, have you?"

She shook her head. She didn't smoke and never had.

"No, I'm sorry, I haven't." She looked down at her knee. "I miss him so much, Mike. Don't you?"

"It's bright in here; could we turn the overhead lights off?"

"It's no good avoiding the subject. If we don't talk about him, it'll always come between us." She looked up at his eyes: his pupils were contracted into tiny pinholes, cold and uncommunicative. "We have to talk about him sometime."

"I don't want to talk about that."

"That? You mean Primo? What, you don't even want to say his name? As though he never even existed? Well, I'll say it—Primo."

"Please, Jons, don't." Michel was struggling but Jonni was too immersed in her grief and anguish and frustration of the past few months to see it.

"Primo, Primo, Primo!"

Michel threw his pen down on the coffee table and scraped his hand through his hair.

"Um, I think I might have forwarded a check to you by mistake; did you get a BBC check for a few hundred pounds addressed to J. St. Michel? It doesn't matter, except that my agent was concerned they hadn't paid me."

"Michel, don't do that!" Jonni cried. "I came here because you're ill and I want to help you and look after you. But how can I help you if all you ever do is shut me out and push me away and away?"

Michel stood up quickly and walked across the studio.

"I need to work now," he said. He picked up a cassette from the top of the stereo and pushed it into the tape player, pressing the play button. Jonni watched distraught as he stood at the barre and began to execute fast mechanical tendus in his trainers, his feet moving in strict rhythm, like clockwork, but against the rhythm of the music. The sound of that taped piano music, with the jarring cross-thread of Michel's feet beating out of time, was unbearable to Jonni. The tape was one Primo had recorded for Michel several years ago and there were moments on it when his laughing voice was clearly audible above the music.

"Michel, turn it off! Please, turn it off!"

He leaned over and turned up the volume until it was deafening to drown out the sound of her voice. The speakers buzzed in protest at the level.

"Stop it!" she cried, jumping passionately to her feet. "Why? Why do you always throw my love for you back in my face as though it offends you?" She picked up Michel's half-drunk mug of coffee from the table and hurled it onto the parquet floor, her rage at his refusal to share her grief over Primo bursting to the surface. The mug shattered, scattering red and white chips of china across the studio. Coffee sloshed every-where. "It's not fair! I'm your wife!"

She snatched up a heavy glass ashtray from the coffee table and flung it on the floor. It refused to break but the ash and cigarette butts from Crown's night of anxious chain-smoking flew across the floor. "Michel, stop it!"

She ran across the studio and jabbed her finger at the stop button on the tape player. Michel stopped moving as the music stopped, standing like an automaton with his hand on the barre.

Jonni stood and looked at him in the silence, her face flushed and miserable. She could see his pain, and she was so desperate to comfort him, but there was nothing she could do to get near him. Her gaze fell piteously to the barre.

"I think I need to go now," she said.

"You don't have to go."

"Yes. I do. You don't need me and I'm just in your way. Once I've gone you'll be able to get on with your work. I'm sorry, Michel. I shouldn't have come without telling you first. I came because Charles asked me to."

"Okay. See you around, then." Michel was looking at her but there was no trace of affection in his eyes, nor almost any recognition. His eyes were empty.

Jonni took hold of his wrist and placed the brown pill bottle in his upturned hand before she walked away.

"You're supposed to take one of these. Apparently they're strong as fuck."

She picked up her coat and handbag from the back of the sofa.

"Would you turn out the light?" Michel asked.

Jonni stopped in the studio doorway and turned to look at him for a few seconds. And then she switched off the lights and left.

Until Jonni closed the door of the flat and began walking slowly down the stairs to the street, she had never, not for one moment, truly believed that her marriage to Michel was really over. But she believed it now. As she waited for a taxi on the corner of Warwick Way she looked at the ash tree that grew under the window of the bedroom she had shared with Michel during the four years in which he had been her lover and husband. She could still see the coldness in Michel's steel-gray eyes as he looked straight through her. It was finished. This was the point where Jonni's heartache would begin in earnest.

She held up her hand to hail a passing taxi and climbed in as it pulled up next to the curb. When it drove off again she turned around on the seat to look through the back window at the house which had been her home for so long, gazing at it as it retreated farther and farther down the road and then vanished.

Crown was so anxious at getting no reply from the phone in Michel's flat that he set off to return to London as soon as Marina arrived in Bradford, shortly after four. It was probably as well he left when he did; fear and lack of sleep had combined to fill him with grievances against the whole world, and he had raged mercilessly at the company all afternoon. The dejected dancers had submitted to his abuse quietly; they were all aware of the scale of the catastrophe that had befallen the company.

It was almost eight o'clock by the time Crown trotted up the four floors of stairs to Michel's flat and rapped on the door. When there was no answer he let himself in. The flat was dark and completely silent.

"Michel?"

He poked his head into each of the rooms in turn. "Jonni, darling, where are you?" When he saw Michel sitting on the floor under the barre at the far end of the studio, he stopped short.

"Jesus Christ, what are you doing there?" He switched on the lights and came into the studio. "What happened?"

There was no response. Michel was slumped against the wall with his head lowered, his eyes invisible behind his blond curls. Crown crouched down beside him and picked up the pill bottle that was lying beside his motionless hand. There were still four capsules in it: the same number that had been there this morning. "Michel, how long have you been here? Where's Jonni?" Crown gave him a shake. "Come on, wake up. Where's Jonni?"

It was a while before Michel responded. His eventual answer was little more than a breath but it was clear enough for Crown to get the gist of it. "Gone."

"Gone? Jesus Christ." He turned his head to look at the broken crockery and mess strewn across the floor. "What made you smash the place up?"

"Jonni."

"Jonni who made you angry, or Jonni who did it?"

"She got in a temper."

"And then she left?" Crown was coaxing each answer out of Michel with the tone of a parent trying to coax the story out of a toddler. He tried not to let his impatience show in the long gaps between each question and the response. "You mean she came all the way here from Gloucester to see you, broke the place up, and then just went away?"

When Crown heard the sound, half whisper, half sigh, confirming his incredulous suggestion, he looked at the window, cursing under his breath. The stupid bitch; what did she think this was: some kind of joke rigged up between the two of them to wind her up? He lowered his head to look up at Michel's downcast face. He wished Michel would look him in the eye.

"Did the two of you talk, Michel? Were you nice to her?"

Michel stirred slightly, shifting his back against the wall; it was the first sign of life since Crown had arrived.

"I tried, Charles."

Crown patted Michel's motionless arm in sympathy. He looked at the drooping shoulders and vacant expression. Michel couldn't stay here alone, that was for certain. He hadn't been this bad before, not even last night in the ambulance. There had been whole half hours since his collapse when he had seemed right as rain—he had walked around, chatted, laughed even—but now it seemed he had vanished into some kind of no-man's-land where nobody, not even his wife it appeared, could reach him.

"Michel, we're going to have to find somewhere for you to go for a while; somewhere you can be looked after."

Michel raised his head a fraction in protest, trying to focus on Crown's face.

"I've got no choice," Crown said. "You're ill; you need to be given proper care."

"I don't want to go anywhere."

Crown grunted in frustration and shook him gently by both shoulders.

"Stand up. Come on, I want you to see something. Stand up!"

Michel obediently allowed himself to be pulled to his feet and led to stand in the center of the studio. Crown threw the heavy curtain aside uncovering part of the mirrored wall.

"Just look at yourself, son. Look at that sick, wretched . . ."

Crown stopped. At the first glimpse of his own reflection Michel turned his back and buried his head in his arms with a despairing cry. Crown shut his eyes tightly, cursing himself, and then drew the curtain over the mirror again.

"I'm sorry, Michel. Okay, I'm sorry. Come and sit down."

After another sleepless night Crown left Michel under the supervision of a neighbor while he went to sort out somewhere he could be looked after. When he returned several hours later Michel was exactly where he had left him, seated on the sofa with his hands in his lap staring at some distant point beyond the floor. He hadn't moved a single muscle, the woman from the flat downstairs said.

Crown crouched down in front of him to look up into his face, hoping for some glimmer of communication.

"Are you ready to go, Michel?"

But Michel's mind had set out on a journey. He was many miles away. Crown snapped his fingers in front of his eyes.

"Hey! Come on, son, I know you can hear me. Are you ready?"

Michel murmured, "Yes."

"Do you want to take anything with you? Shall I get anything for you?"

Michel blinked slowly and raised his empty eyes to Crown's face.

"Tell Primo to come and see me. Tell him, next time he goes away, to let me know first."

Crown sighed and laid a gentle hand on Michel's blond, curly head.

"Poor old sod," he said. "You don't know what you're on about."

28

THERE WAS NO RELATIVE to sign the admission papers so Crown signed them himself, and for the next four days he sat in the private room on the acute ward of the expensive clinic looking at Michel's pale face as he lay with open eyes staring blindly into infinity. Michel had sunk into a stupor now; he said nothing, saw nothing and, as far as anyone could tell, heard nothing. His body was rigid.

Crown had managed to keep this sequel to Michel's collapse out of the papers but the fans had somehow discovered where Michel was—they always found out everything—and the room began to fill up with flowers.

"Take them away," Crown said to the nurse who was attaching a drip to the stand beside Michel's bed. "He can't see them."

"You can't be sure, you know. He might be aware of more than you realize."

"No. And anyway, he wouldn't want them. There must be somewhere in the clinic you can use them. And take that mirror away too."

Crown sat on his straight-backed chair with his head resting against the wall and watched Michel. He could see exactly what had happened: the herculean effort of denial throughout all those weeks, the strain to Michel's body and mind as he fought to maintain the blockade that excluded everything but his work—the violent shock to his system when the pressure inside him had finally blasted through that wall like a tidal wave sweeping everything before it. It was all so obvious. Hindsight was a wonderful thing.

Crown was glad that the Islington Ballet was traveling straight to Bristol from Bradford. He didn't want them to see Michel like this. This wasn't Michel. Those unfocused gray eyes weren't Michel's. The limp open mouth, the plastic bedpan beside the bed; the drip needle taped to the lifeless hand on the blanket—none of it was Michel. Where was he? Where was the darling of the ballet fans; the athlete who brought packed houses cheering to their feet? Where was the artist who had taught that dormant body to speak with a voice of such eloquence? Where had he gone?

Hour after hour Crown sat there watching Michel's inanimate face. From time to time nurses came in to check on his drip, and doctors came to shine penlights into his eyes and to look over his notes, murmuring together about EEGs, dopamine levels, electroconvulsive therapy, and the symptoms of PDS.

"What's PDS?" Crown asked from his chair.

"Permanent disengagement syndrome."

His cheek sank onto his fist.

"Oh. Thanks. I was just curious."

It wasn't the first time Crown had seen a dancer fall apart. Mental breakdown was all too common in ballet. He tried very hard not to dwell on thoughts of Nijinsky and Spessivtzeva and all the other great dancers whose short incandescent careers had been followed by decades spent in mental institutions. There was nothing anyone could do but wait.

Crown wasn't the only person who watched by Michel's bed in those first few days. When he arrived at the clinic early in the morning after a second night of fitful sleep, he found Annette lying in Michel's narrow bed with her arms wrapped around his stiff body, her face buried desperately in his neck and her black hair flowing over the pillow. She'd been there since midnight, the clinic staff said. The nurses couldn't move her. The doctors couldn't move her. Even Charles Crown couldn't move her. She lay there all day clinging to Michel until Roly arrived from Manchester and took her away.

In the evening Roly came back to the clinic alone to sit with Michel, holding his hand, while Crown went home to rest. Even inert and insensible, Roly could feel Michel in that cold hand. He refused to believe Michel wasn't coming back to them. Michel would wake up, Roly knew he would.

"Go back to Manchester, son," Crown told him on the third morning. "You've got a contract to fulfill and a mortgage to pay. Whatever happens here it isn't going to happen quickly."

Roly looked reluctantly at the deathlike figure in the bed.

"Yeah, you're right. Granada are getting pretty pissed off with me. You'll phone me as soon as he wakes up, won't you, Charles?"

For the first time in days Crown managed a strained smile.

"Of course I'll phone you."

Eventually Crown had to go back to work too.

It was a wrench to leave Michel at the clinic but after the humiliating episode in Bradford things were looking bad for Bristol and Liverpool: box-office reservations had been canceled and refunds demanded because St. Michel was out of the picture. And with his first cast for *Seven Ages* incapacitated Crown had to knock his third cast into shape and fast. He had no choice but to go. He pinned his mobile number to the notice board beside Michel's bed, warned the security guard at the front desk there'd be hell to pay if any of the fans bluffed their way past him, and scrounged a lift to Bristol with the company press officer.

Twelve days later, in the corridor outside Michel's room, he stopped and rubbed both hands hard over his weary face. His daily phone calls to the clinic had yielded encouraging reports but he dreaded the sight of those glazed eyes and that prone, stupefied body.

When he looked through the small pane of reinforced glass in the door he saw Michel sitting, large as life, in an armchair in a white toweling dressing gown, with his hand on the waist of a very pretty nurse.

"Stop touching up the bloody nurses!" Crown bellowed as he strode into the room.

Michel was still very pale and the drip needle was still taped to the hand that rested on the arm of his chair, but he was awake and his mouth twitched in response to Crown's greeting.

"Yes . . . thanks," he said slowly, "I feel much better."

"Don't give me that shit, St. Michel. You've no idea the fucking nightmare I've just been through with Liverpool."

"Please, please," protested the nurse, deeply embarrassed at being caught in such close quarters with Michel by this intimidating little man. "He must have complete quiet!"

Michel looked at her rosy face and said—again very slowly, "Not much chance of that with sir here." He gave her a slow wink. "Come back once he's gone and give me a sponge bath."

As the nurse went away Crown sat down on the edge of the bed.

"She seems to have taken quite a shine to you. Only you could flirt with a bloody great needle stuck in your hand."

Michel rested his heavy head against the back of his chair. His movements, like his speech, were unnaturally cumbersome.

"It passes the time."

"Bored?"

"Not really."

"You should watch telly—God knows, you're paying for it."

"I can't. It won't keep still." Michel's eyes turned toward him. "How's Ivor doing with *Seven Ages*?"

Crown pulled a face. "Want me to tell you?"

"No, not if that look is anything to go by." He ran his dry tongue slowly over his lips and made a small gesture with his fingers toward a jug of water on the bedside cabinet. "Can you give me some water?"

Crown poured out a glass of water and gave it to him, guiding his hand to the glass.

"Everyone in the company sends their love."

Michel nodded his thanks vaguely but it meant very little to him. The clinic was such an isolated environment it was difficult to imagine people out there in the real world thinking about him and being affected by his absence. He lifted the glass with effort to his mouth.

"What sort of hospital is this?"

"A bloody expensive one so for Christ's sake hurry up and get better."

"Why do they have cameras watching us?"

Crown looked at the closed-circuit monitor on the ceiling. Michel really didn't know what this place was.

"What have the doctors told you?"

Michel was silent for a long time but it was a pause for thought, not the mindless space travel of a fortnight ago. "They said I'd had an acute traumatic episode. Is that bullshit for a nervous breakdown?"

"I suppose so."

"That's what I thought. Roly thought so too." He took another laborious sip of water. "And they said I was experiencing cognitive disorientation."

"Cognitive who?" That was the first Crown had heard of it. "What's that then, when it's at home?"

"I don't know what it means." His voice was getting fainter as he grew tired. He closed his eyes. "You look it up in a French-English dictionary and tell me, okay?"

"What's this about a cognitive problem?" Crown demanded, slamming the door of the consultant's office behind him. "And why wasn't I told about it on the phone?"

"There was nothing to tell you, Mister Crown. Have a seat and I'll explain. Smoke if you like; it's okay in here. Coffee? Filter or espresso?" The consultant was expert at handling bad-tempered managers; he had been a specialist in the psychiatric treatment of the rich and famous for nearly two decades. "Brenda, two filters, please. It's difficult to diagnose and even harder to pin down into the exact form of its manifestation."

"So . . . what? He hallucinates, is that it?"

"Well, perhaps, after a fashion. As I said, it's not easy to be precise. We're talking about the mind here. It's not an exact science. Your friend went very deep, and at the moment he's still fighting his way back to the surface. It seems that some of those submerged images, wherever he's been, are coming back to the surface with him, that's all, and he's having a little difficulty readjusting to reality. I've seen this before. I'm sure, once I reduce the dose of his medication on Monday or Tuesday, the problem will diminish. In the meantime he's not aware of this condition—and more important, these imaginings, or whatever they are, don't seem to frighten him. I really don't think you should worry, Mister Crown."

Crown nodded his thanks distractedly to the secretary as she brought in the coffee. There was a question that had to be asked, although he was afraid of the answer.

"Will he—I mean, what do you think his chances are of making a complete recovery? Will he ever be as strong mentally as he was before?"

The psychiatrist looked at the drawn face of the man sitting opposite him. Crown's dark eyes were hollow and strained, and his skin was sallow from exhaustion. The consultant believed in the clinic's policy of absolute frankness but his job was to alleviate mental suffering, not create it.

"I think there's every chance. This is an acute case, not a personality disorder or a depressive nature. I'm perfectly confident Mister St. Michel will be himself again very soon and back on his feet dancing."

"Is he really going to be alright?" his secretary asked once Crown had gone. "The dancer chap in number seven: the pink elephant case."

The consultant shook his head, leafing through his appointments schedule for the next few days.

"Buggered if I know, Brenda." He closed his diary with a sigh and reached for his coffee. "I'm buggered if I know that about any of these nutters."

On his way out of the clinic Crown stopped in the corridor and looked through the little window in the door of room number seven. Michel was lying on his back in bed with his eyes closed, only his lips moving slightly.

Crown stood there for a few minutes and watched him. What did he think about while he was lying there on his own? Was he torturing himself about Primo? Was he thinking about his broken marriage? Or Lynne? Or the parents he didn't know? Or, like Crown, did he escape from unhappiness into dance: music flooding through him, spirit soaring; his muscles twitching with the physical recollection of the choreography?

Crown rubbed his tired eyes slowly and went away.

The doctor's prognosis of Michel's rapid recovery might have been a shot in the dark but it seemed to have been a lucky one. At the end of June Michel left the North London clinic free from medication and with a clean bill of mental and physical health.

When Crown called into the Pimlico flat on his way back from Exeter he found Michel stretched out idly on a sofa in the studio watching cricket on the television.

"Well, at least somebody's enjoying themselves," Crown said with a sardonic grunt. "This tour's turning into something out of Hitchcock while you're lying here living the life of Riley. The dancers are tearing each other's throats out and the sponsors are all over me like leeches—I'm glad you find it amusing, St. Michel."

Michel's smile came more quickly and his face was less pale than the last time Crown had seen him.

"Don't blame me, Charles. I've got to rest: doctor's orders."

"Oh, really. Well, did Attila the Hun say how long your lazy arse is likely to be glued to that sofa?"

"I've got to see him again on Tuesday but he said I can probably start getting back in shape in a few weeks' time."

Crown groaned. He was knackered too, wasn't he? How come no one told him he could put his feet up for the next three weeks?

"Give me a coffee, then—or is the poor invalid too fucking frail to make it as far as the kitchen?"

The kitchen was spotlessly clean. Crown had sent his own cleaning lady to tidy up before Michel left the hospital. He sat on the edge of the table and watched while Michel filled the kettle and spooned instant coffee into two cups. Michel was still very subdued. He seemed to have aged a great deal over the past few months.

"Why don't you call some friends?" Crown asked him. "What's Roly up to; still in Manchester?"

"Yes, for another ten days."

"Why not give Louisa a ring? She isn't on in Dartford till Friday. Her evenings are free this week. It's Jonni's lookout if you hook up with someone else while she's off playing the injured housewife."

"I don't fancy Louisa."

"Liar."

Michel leaned over to take a pint of milk from the fridge.

"Alright, I do fancy her, but not enough to give her the runaround."

Crown snorted incredulously.

"Mellowed in your old age, have you?"

"I'd rather watch the cricket, to be honest."

Crown humphed. He knew Michel too well.

"Don't tell me—sex just slipped your mind, has it?"

"Yep. My libido's about as flat as Ivor's feet. The only thing I've got on my mind is whether Croft and Fraser can notch up another twenty-three runs between them before some bastard of an Australian in the slips catches one of them out."

"What about my bloody tour then?"

"That's your problem."

Crown took his cigarettes out of his pocket and then put them away again. If there was one good thing to have come out of Michel's time in hospital it was that he had given up smoking.

"So have you thought yet," he said, trying to sound as though the question wasn't of crucial importance, "how soon you might be ready to come back to work?" When Michel made no immediate reply Crown went on, "Of course we'll take it very slowly. You'll have as much time as you need to get your technique back in and build up your stamina. It'll probably be best for you to begin in the Goswell Road; do class with the apprentices—that ought to give them a kick up the arse if nothing else does. Then we'll start you off easy: one or two shows a week, no press calls, no interviews; total privacy between shows—you can write your own rehearsal schedule." He looked at the back of Michel's head. "Any idea when?"

Michel was stirring the two cups of coffee on the counter. He looked down at them as he took the spoon out and tapped it on the edge of Crown's cup.

"Don't hold your breath, Charles."

The Islington Ballet tour limped dismally through the last few days of June and into July. It was the most depressing tour the company could remember; the weather was dull, the dancers were fractious—bickering and sullen by turns—and for once the regional critics had been bloody. Everyone was impatient for the end of July and the monthlong holiday. Crown was almost as keen to see the back of the dancers as they were to be rid of him and his irascible temper.

Crown left the company to Marina's supervision as much as possible, spending most of his time in London beating his apprentices into shape. Between the time he'd spent on tour and Michel's illness there was a lot of lost ground to be regained with the apprentices. There was also the next season to organize with all its associated problems and, to add to

Crown's troubles, Nadia Petrovna was ill. The pain of her chronic arthritis had finally got the better of her obstinacy and she was forced to stay at home in bed for all but one day a week. The atmosphere in the Goswell Road was almost as gloomy as it was amongst the dancers out on the road. Nadia Petrovna's absence left as big a hole at the company's headquarters as Michel's absence did on tour.

Only now that the bulk of Nadia Petrovna's workload had landed on his shoulders did Crown fully comprehend how much the old woman had accomplished locked away in her office on her own for all those hours. He had always known she worked hard but this was unbelievable. There were grant applications to sift through, correspondence with sponsors, invoices, apprentices' reports, even legal actions. He sat at her desk trying to sort through all the paperwork, scratching his head in bewilderment while cigarettes burned away forgotten in the ashtray at his elbow. There was enough work here for a dozen Nadia Petrovnas.

Michel was resting peacefully at home and that suited Crown fine for the moment. It wouldn't hurt him to have a complete break until mid-September when rehearsals for the next season started. It was a long time since Michel had had anything like a decent holiday; last summer Crown had taken him to Stuttgart to make a piece and the previous year Michel had spent the August break guesting in Denmark—no, he hadn't; he had been performing at the South Bank festival, Denmark must have been the year before. And the year before that was *Romeo,* and the year before that . . . Crown looked up from the mountain of paperwork on Nadia Petrovna's desk. Come to think of it, it was a very long time since Michel had had a holiday. Well, let him enjoy a month or two of peace and quiet now; he had earned it. Right now Crown had other things to worry about.

On a Monday morning at the end of July, Crown was giving class to the five apprentice boys in the big studio. The building was half-empty as always when the company was away on tour.

"Undisciplined," he was yelling at them, "ragged . . . lazy . . . stupidity!"

Nothing had changed. The boys were cowering at the barre, their hearts sinking, one and all, into their ballet shoes.

"You need intelligence to dance and, if that allegro was anything to go by—"

"Charles? Er, Charles?"

He stopped in the midst of his tirade and turned his head. Adrian, the company manager, was standing at the studio door waving an A4 sheet of paper.

Crown glared at him in irritation. "What?"

"Charles, I think you should see this. There's a problem."

Crown left his browbeaten students—he'd probably said enough anyway—and went over to the door. He nodded, frowning, toward the paper in the administrator's hand.

"What's that?"

"It's Michel's contract for the coming year. He sent it back unsigned."

"What does he say about it?"

"Just a note pinned to it saying he's sorry."

"What the fuck d'you mean you're sorry?" Crown roared, facing Michel in the hallway of the flat in Pimlico. Michel looked away; he couldn't meet Crown's eye.

"Come on, Charles, you must have half expected it."

Michel was right; he'd been half expecting it for years.

"So who's it to be?" he demanded. He was so furious he could barely speak. "Come on, let's hear it. The Royal? British?" He thumped the hall wall in rage. "English National?"

"Don't be ridiculous."

"The Rambert? Paris? New York?" He flung his hand in the air. "The fucking Kirov?" Crown's gestures, like his guesses, were becoming wilder by the second.

Michel waved a hand to calm him.

"I wouldn't leave you for another company without consulting you first and you know it. I'm not dancing next year; at least I haven't made my mind up yet."

"Okay, I'll make it up for you. Here's a pen."

Michel shook his head. "I'm not signing, Charles. I need more time."

"There isn't any more time. The contracts are due in this week and I've got to make plans for next season; I'll give you till Friday."

"I won't know on Friday—or the following Friday. It might be months before I'm ready to dance again. You'll know as soon as I do. If I've missed the boat and you don't want me that's my own lookout."

"You selfish tick!" the choreographer spat. "You know you've got me over a barrel. Take your month or your six months and I hope it bores you shitless. And it had better bloody well be me and not Anthony Dowell you phone when you're ready to get off your backside and go back to work."

Michel pulled a wry face.

"I'll bear that in mind."

"Call me when you've come to your senses," Crown said, striding out of the flat with a face like a thundercloud. He was convinced it wouldn't take more than a fortnight. Michel was born with his hand on the barre and his feet in fifth position. He wasn't the fellow to sit still for long.

The afternoon had worn into glowing, golden evening. It looked like they were going to have some kind of a summer after all. Michel opened one of the huge sash windows in the studio and climbed out onto the sill, sitting with his back against the white stonework and his knees drawn up to his chest.

The windows of the buildings opposite glinted brilliantly in the low sunlight. Despite the carbon monoxide and lead belching from exhaust pipes on the street below, the air up here smelled fresh and clear.

It was a haven on the fourth-floor window ledge: nobody to disturb you, nothing to break up your thoughts. Somehow the world looked more manageable from up here. Michel never went out of the flat these days in case someone stopped him on the pavement recognizing his face. He was afraid of all those strangers who knew him.

He was relieved that the showdown with Crown was over. He had been dreading it ever since he sent back that unsigned contract. Over the past few weeks it had gradually dawned on him that he wouldn't make it back onstage and he had been racking his brains for a way to let his mentor down slowly. Let Charles go on thinking it was just a matter of time. He'd work out the truth sooner or later.

Michel smiled at the idea of phoning Anthony Dowell at the Royal Ballet. What would Dowell want with a dancer who was afraid to look in the mirror?

He tilted his head, still smiling, as a pigeon arrived to investigate a sandwich he had brought with him onto the windowsill.

"Come on then, fella. Come and get it if you want it."

The mottled pigeon looked at him askance as though he were some kind of exotic bird and then accepted his invitation delicately, keeping a dubious eye on him as it sidled toward him.

"So what do you think?" Michel asked it as it pecked at the bread on the warm sill. "Would you care to live if you couldn't fly anymore?"

The pigeon ignored him and continued with its meal.

"Do you just fly to eat, or do you only eat so you can fly?"

At this his guest turned its back on him and flew off into the sunlit sky with a piece of crust in its beak. Michel leaned over the edge of the sill and looked at the busy street far beneath his perch. It didn't cross his mind to jump; he merely enjoyed the exhilarating thump of adrenaline that rushed through his body as he looked down.

The weeks became months and still Michel stayed alone in the flat, lost in thought. He didn't yet know what he was going to do but he knew what he wasn't going to do: he was finished as a performer, at least for the foreseeable future.

It was fear that had led him to this decision. Fear had always been a part of his life. It was part of every dancer's life. Fear of injury. Fear of growing older. Fear when he twisted an ankle on a curbstone or felt his partner slipping through his hands as he caught her in the air. All these fears he understood. But this fear was different; it had no origin that he could pinpoint but it squeezed the air out of his lungs and landed like a lump of iron in his stomach when he thought about appearing onstage again. Someone or something was trying to tell him he was through.

Standing in the studio gazing down through the window at the pedestrians on the street, Michel tried to envisage a life without dance. It was easy to let go of the trappings he had gathered around his career—the acclaim of the press, the clamor of the fans, the applause, the invitations, the fancy clothes. But a life without classes and rehearsals, without the echo of piano music in the live acoustic of a dance studio, without the breathless hush in the auditorium as the curtain rose . . . He rested his shoulder on the white window frame, still gazing at the street below. It must be possible. All those people down there managed it.

"Do you still miss ballet?" he asked Roly, interrupting him in the middle of an anecdote about Des O'Connor.

"Yeah, of course I do." Roly wasn't at all thrown by Michel's abrupt change of subject. "I still wake up most mornings in a sweat thinking I'm late for class. But would I rather be dancing Siegfried in Glasgow tonight than at home in bed with Nettie?" He looked at the ceiling and whistled. "Tough one, that."

"You wouldn't go back to it then, if you could?"

Roly was sitting on the arm of a sofa with his long legs jiggling slightly as his feet tapped out a cheerful rhythm on the wooden floor. His truthful eyes smiled at Michel easily.

"No, I don't think I would; not now. I'm happy doing tap. I was devastated when I had to give up ballet, absolutely gutted, you know I was. I thought ballet was the only thing in the world; I thought the universe revolved around it. But since then I've discovered there are lots of other things out there." He laughed at Michel's doubtful expression. "I know that doesn't make sense to you, Shel. You're different from the rest of us. Ballet's in your soul."

Michel looked at Roly's serene blue eyes, remembering the desperate tears he had shed after his last ballet performance. Roly was one of the unsung heroes of the dance world. As boys, it had always been Michel and Primo who were the gifted ones; the ones who were special. Roly was just an everyday lad. But in fact, of the three of them, Roly had by far the most valuable gift. He could turn anything around, however bad, and make it into a reason to be happy.

Michel thought about the waste of his own gift. What did he feel about it? Was he sad about it? Angry? Glad? He wasn't sure he'd recognize any of these emotions in himself even if they were there. He seemed to feel nothing about it at all.

"Roly, do you think it's possible I don't have any feelings?"

"No, not for a moment." Good old Roly; nothing shook him.

Michel sat down on the sofa, rubbing his eyes.

"I sometimes wonder."

"You should get out of this flat more, Shel. All this time alone isn't good for you. I've seen you reduce entire audiences to tears, myself included. How could you do that if you didn't have feelings?"

"But that's only acting."

"Of course it is. If you danced with real emotion you'd fall flat on your face on the first arabesque. But you can't express with your body things you don't understand with your heart. No one can."

Michel gave him a faint smile.

"Is that why you were never any good at tragic roles?"

Roly's fair eyebrows rose in surprise. "Wasn't I?"

"Not very."

"Oh." It took him a few seconds to digest this piece of information. And then he laughed. "Lucky for me, then, there's not much call for tragedy in tap. Rather hard to imagine a tragic tap number, isn't it?"

"The thing is I don't feel myself feeling anything."

"So let your feelings take a break—I know I do." He looked at the studio door as Annette breezed in. "If I ever get the chance." Roly was being facetious; his love for Annette was written all over his face.

"Did I miss anything good?" she asked. Her hands were full of takeaway cappuccinos and doughnuts. "Michel, darling, for God's sake have a shave. I absolutely refuse to kiss you with all that stubble. Besides, I'm only ever unfaithful to Roly when he's away."

Roly and Annette had been Michel's most constant visitors in the three months since his breakdown but, in truth, he was relieved when rehearsals for Annette's new West End play and the renewal of Roly's contract with Granada brought their visits to an end.

He liked his daytime solitude in the flat. He liked to let his mind wander. And where it wandered to was nobody's business but his own. He liked to watch the patterns the sunlight from the studio windows made on the floor; the different areas of space they created. And he liked to watch the movement of the dust in the air. He rarely thought about Jonni; that life was gone forever. Occasionally his thoughts strayed to the Islington Ballet and the new piece they were creating without him— Crown told him the dance press had gone bananas when they discovered Michel was out of the new season. Michel didn't care. That too was part of a world he no longer inhabited.

He was never lonely in the flat. His cleaning lady came twice a week to keep him in order and do his shopping—and he had other company too. Often, at night, Primo came to chat to him. They sat talking together for hours about the laughs they'd had as apprentices and the mischief they'd got up to out on the road. Primo was still as moody as ever. The one time Michel had tried asking him about his suicide Primo had refused to speak to him for almost a week. Since then Michel had left the subject alone; he couldn't abide Primo when he was sulking.

After a few months Primo's nocturnal visits became less frequent. But just when Michel was wondering where he'd been for the past few evenings, he was shaken out of his bed in the middle of the night.

"Hmm?—What? What is it?"

"You gotta get up. We got work to do."

Michel buried his head under the duvet.

"Go away; I'm asleep."

Primo was insistent, nagging and tugging at the bedcover until Michel dragged himself out of his slumber and sat up reluctantly in bed blinking his bleary eyes.

"Okay, you relentless bugger; I'm up. What now?"

"You gotta come to the studio with me. Come on, amico. Get your shoes out the cupboard."

"Oh, no; not again! Primo, for Christ's sake, it's . . ." he picked up his watch from the bedside table and looked at it in the dim light which came from the street, ". . . it's two in the morning."

"Five to, actually. So—what, you gonna sit there arguing till half-past? Hey, I came to play for you!"

"I don't care," Michel said, disappearing under the duvet again. "I'm trying to sleep."

Primo laughed and yanked the duvet off him.

"Get up, you lazy motherfucker, or am I gonna have to make you?"

There was no getting away from the tyrant. Michel staggered out of bed and pulled on a dance belt and an all-in-one. He dug a pair of flat-spin shoes out of the cupboard.

At the bedroom door Primo stopped and planted his hands frustratedly on his hips. His brown eyes looked Michel's dance gear over in exasperation.

"Man! You gonna put on a sweatshirt or what, Michel? How fuckin' stupid can you get? You wanna tear a muscle, is that it?"

"Yeah, yeah, okay. Don't be such an old woman." Michel picked up a sweatshirt and pulled it over his head as he followed Primo through the door. His body wouldn't be cold for long; Primo would work him like a slave until daybreak. Crown's classes were a picnic by comparison.

29

As the months passed it gradually dawned on Crown that Michel had no plans to return to dancing. With slow rising dread the choreographer realized that his devoted toil of the past ten years, the work of glorious creativity in which he'd invested so much love and energy, might come to nothing. How often was it that a man found a thing so special he was prepared to cast aside his own ambition for it, to nurture it, feed it, and bring it to fruit? Michel, the talent and beauty he had possessed at the age of sixteen, had been that thing for Charles Crown.

And what had happened to Crown's labor of love? It was rotting away in a flat in Pimlico while the world was lusting to see Michel dance, lusting for the technical virtuosity and passion of his work. What right had Michel to turn all that passion in on itself, to let it swallow him up instead of pouring it out onstage where it belonged?

"For the love of God," Crown said to him, "stop beating yourself up about Primo. You've punished yourself enough."

"I'm not punishing myself."

"Yes, you are. And I want to know how long you're going to hide away here like a recluse, because this morbid bloody self-flagellation of yours is beginning to seriously piss me off. How long? The end of the autumn season? The Christmas tour?"

Michel didn't know how to tell him the truth.

"I don't know, Charles. I just know I'm not ready yet."

"Then when?" Crown insisted. "When? When? When?"

Crown had almost given up his visits to Michel's flat. They only ended in frustration. He wanted Michel back in the studio, and soon, but the answer was always the same: he needed more time. Five months had passed already, and every day Michel's technique and the condition of his body was slipping a little further. A year, or maybe two, and it would start to fade irreversibly.

Crown took his fears to Nadia Petrovna's bedside. Nadia Petrovna was bedridden all the time now but she still played an important part in the life of the company, if only as Charles Crown's constant ear and adviser.

She lay propped on pillows with a jug of water and a bottle of analgesics at her side, a pale, thin wraith, nothing but skin and bone. But though her body was so weak she could scarcely move, the old fighting spirit still glinted in her failing eyes as they watched Crown pace back and forth at the foot of the bed.

"Ten long, hard years of effort," he said bitterly. "A whole decade's labor wiped out!" He flung out his arm in front of him as he paced, sweeping away all the wasted years and wasted work. "Gone! Obliterated! I've broken my fucking back to turn him into a world-class dancer and now look at him: shut up alone in that bloody flat, pasty-faced and withdrawn, getting more introverted by the day. I wouldn't mind if he'd gone to another company; at least he'd be dancing." Crown wasn't the man to insult Nadia Petrovna's courage by tempering his vocabulary to the gravity of her condition. "It makes me fucking furious."

Nadia Petrovna's voice was very faint, forcing him to slow his steps to listen.

"And what about him, Charles? What about his needs? Do you care only for the dancer? Do you not care about the man himself?"

Crown sighed, "Yes, yes." Of course he loved Michel. But he couldn't separate Michel from his dancing—that's who he was: a dancer. "It's the work, Nadia Petrovna. I've strained every fiber in my body, every brain cell, fighting to get the best out of him; to make him what he is. I believed in him."

The old woman's opaque eyes were still following his pacing figure.

"Are you the only one who has worked? Are you the only one who has invested time and effort in his talent?"

Crown threw up his hand conceding her point.

"Yes, of course you've played your part; I didn't mean you hadn't. And the others, Marina and Lex and the rest, but not to the same degree that—"

"Charles!" The frail hand moved impatiently on the white embroidered bedspread. "I'm not talking about myself or Marina. I'm talking about Michel. He too has worked tirelessly all these years."

"And so he should. Hard graft is a dancer's life. I wore the soles off my feet when I was a kid and I don't doubt you did too."

Nadia Petrovna lay there in her antique Italian bed and thought about all the hours Michel had spent struggling with his technique as a boy, sweat pouring from his face, teeth gritted in determination as he pushed his young body through the pain barrier time and again. Oh, that pain barrier. She knew it so well: that great wall of rock that seemed to grow higher each time you climbed it.

"I used to spy on him," she said, "when he didn't know I was there—working away at his pirouettes and *tours* in the evenings. So much quiet determination. So much ambition."

"Ambition?" Crown shook his head. "If he was driven by ambition he'd have left the Islington years ago. He's never been hungry for fame or money."

"No, I know that." She moistened her colorless lips with her dry tongue. "But all ambition is the same. All soul-destroying. Oh yes, Michel was ambitious. I watched him, Charles, practicing alone in the studios while the other boys were out enjoying their youth, slaving over his technique, working and working to try and achieve a standard that would please you."

"Me? What do you mean?" Crown stopped pacing and looked at her with an appalled frown. "Are you saying it's my fault? Are you saying I pushed him over the edge?"

"Yes, in part: you and his own desire to succeed."

"But everything that's happened! Primo's suicide and Jonni walking out on him—"

"People's friends die, Charles, and their wives leave them. Those things aren't sufficient to bring someone like Michel to his knees. I'm afraid he has been heading toward this crisis for a long time."

Crown sat down slowly on the foot of the bed. Her words had hit home. He wondered if he had spent the last ten years driving Michel to destruction.

"Great dancing always exists under tension," Nadia Petrovna said to the back of Crown's head. "You know that. You were complaining at Christmas that Michel's style had stopped developing. Perhaps this breakdown was what he needed to enable him to move forward."

"Move forward?" Crown laughed despairingly. "He's not even a shadow of what he was at Christmas. I just don't get it. You and I both had breakdowns in our time, and when they were over we picked ourselves up and got on with our work."

Nadia Petrovna's white eyebrows rose.

"When did you ever have a breakdown, Charles?"

"When I was nineteen, when Rotterdam sacked me because I was too short. And fuck all sympathy I got too. You told me I had flu and to go home to bed and quit whining."

She smiled slightly at the memory.

"You were a sweet boy when you were nineteen."

"Sweet my arse! Bitter and angry is what I was, and I made bloody sure everyone knew it too. I had some of the best technique on my body of my generation—I still do—and yet I always had to sit around and watch while some limp second-rater who was taller than me and better looking got the principal roles."

The old lady half closed her eyes with a touch of the old prima ballerina grandeur.

"Rotterdam was really a most dreadful mistake."

"You're not wrong there."

"Oh, I was glad when we left Rotterdam. That company had absolutely no élan. They dressed the corps in lime-green toots for *La Belle au Bois,* do you remember? Quite frightful. And the girls all had chunky thighs; it was most distasteful."

Crown put his head in his hands.

"Nadia, I've lost him. He won't come back now."

She looked at him in silence for a while.

"You said you once believed in him. Do you still?"

Crown sighed. "I don't know. Oh, I believe in his talent. I believe in his capacity."

"Then what has always been our motto?" The ancient ballerina's clouded eyes flashed with fiery courage. "Fight for what you believe in." She closed her skeletal hand into a determined fist on the bedcover. "Fight, Charles! Fight! Fight! Fight!"

He smiled. He couldn't help it. She was singing the same song he had been hearing her sing for the last forty years. But it wasn't going to bring Michel back to the company. Nothing could do that.

When Crown returned to the Goswell Road his heart was very full but it wasn't anxiety about Michel that weighted his spirits, it was his love for the brave woman whose bedside he had just left. She was dying and he knew it.

Seated at the great mahogany desk which had until recently belonged to Nadia Petrovna, he thought of the years in Paris and the Netherlands when he had been her student. What a taskmistress she had been. And what an arrogant little shit he had been. He remembered all those times she had exploded over his faulty technique, slapping his offending arm or leg. But he had never protested; he had been too terrified. She, above all his male teachers, had put the fear of God into him.

A sponsorship application lay half written on the desk while Crown sat deep in reverie. His pen lay motionless in his hand. Had Michel ever been afraid of him? he wondered. He didn't think so. But if not, what had prevented him from rebelling? Michel had received some heavy punishment at his hand, he admitted it, and not just gentle taps to correct his port de bras. There'd been times when, enraged, he had struck Michel full in the face—not hard of course, just sharp punitive slaps, man to boy, but humiliating all the same. And yet Michel had never mutinied, not once.

There was a grinding noise from the old clock on the wall as it struggled past the hour and Crown glanced up at it, forcing his attention back to his work. If he had been less hard on Michel he would never have become the great artist that he had been. But perhaps, in all honesty, it might have been fairer to have left him to a career of mediocrity. Crown had a horrible feeling that it would.

When the grant application was nearly written Crown was inter-rupted by a firm knock on the door—not a dancer; their knocks were al-ways timid.

"Yup? Come."

He looked up with the expression which said that he was busy, ex-pecting one of the secretaries to walk in. His visitor was a stranger: a sturdy middle-aged man with a briefcase and the flattest features Crown had ever seen.

"Hullo . . . ?"

"Mister Crown?" The man looked uncomfortable. "My name's Thomas Roper."

"Oh yes?"

Crown's response wasn't rude but he was keen to get to the point. He searched his memory for the name Roper amongst his professional con-tacts. However, not many people in the dance world were Cockneys.

"I'm a policeman, sir."

"I see."

Crown gestured to him to sit down and covered his mouth thought-fully with one hand while he watched the man ease his sturdy figure into a narrow chair. Crown didn't like visits from policemen, especially police-men out of uniform and carrying large black briefcases.

"Actually, I'm not here on regular police business," the man said. He indicated his brown tweed jacket. "You see I'm off duty. I would have called first instead of barging in on you like this but it's not something I wanted to discuss on the phone."

"Look, Mister . . ." Crown made a movement with his hand, ". . . I'm sorry."

"Roper."

"Mister Roper. Is this visit a police matter or not?"

"Well, yes and no." He shifted uneasily in his chair; Charles Crown was a very intimidating little man. "It's—well, it's rather difficult to know where to start, sir."

"Just dive straight in, why don't you?"

"The thing is I'm really not sure whether I should have come—I had almost made up my mind I wouldn't. But in the end my wife told me to."

Crown's face remained expressionless.

"Your wife."

"Yes, that's right." Mister Roper ran a nervous hand over the knot of his brown tie. He had never been in a place like this before. The atmosphere of elite culture, the refined voices and manners of the people who worked here, made him feel like a cod in an aquarium of delicate tropical fish. He looked doubtfully up at a framed photograph on the wall of Nadia Petrovna standing regally beside the Queen. "I'm not really one for highbrow, sir. I don't know anything about art and that. I had no idea Mister St. Michel was a big shot. It was my wife told me. She'd seen him on the telly. Me, I wouldn't know ballet from how's-your-father but my wife likes that sort of thing. She's seen them all; the one with the swans and everything. She said I should have got this St. Michel's autograph but you can't do that really, can you? I mean not as a policeman."

Crown thought the man was dithering and told him so in as many words. At this, Thomas Roper sucked his flattened top lip into his mouth and nodded slowly.

"To be frank, I'm going a bit wide of the rules in coming to see you. In fact, in some lights it could be seen as downright illegal."

"Mister Roper, I don't care which side of the law you walk on. If you've got something to say to me then say it."

"It's a difficult matter to explain, sir. I'm in a quandary. I've been sitting on this problem for six months turning it round and round in my head and it's still not clear. You see, it concerns St. Michel."

Crown reached for his cigarettes with a frown, keeping a wary eye on the policeman.

"Alright, take your time."

"About six months ago St. Michel called 999 to report the suicide of a man called Vincenti—I don't know if you knew him."

"Yes." Crown looked down to pull a glass ashtray a few inches toward him. "I knew him very well indeed."

"The poor young fellow was a mess—I'll spare you the details but, take my word for it, it wasn't a pleasant sight. Anyway, there was a note left for St. Michel by the dead man and, when I read it, it worried me. Violent suicides always worry me, sir. Of course I can't tell you exactly what was in the note."

Crown nodded to show he understood. He'd have given his right arm to know what Primo's note had contained but he was glad to see this self-confessed bent copper had at least some principles.

"Go on."

"Well, there was something in the note, you see: a reference to something which could have constituted a motive if St. Michel had wanted to do Vincenti harm."

"If you've come here to tell me Michel wanted Primo Vincenti dead you're wasting your time."

"Oh, no, no; it's nothing like that. But I did have to wonder; it was my job to wonder. And I'll be straight with you, I didn't like St. Michel at all. He was so cold-blooded; I mean to see your best friend lying there dead in all that blood and not bat an eyelid—God Almighty, I was more upset than he was. I thought St. Michel was scum. And when I got home and my wife said he was a big star I despised him even more."

"Yes," Crown said, "I do understand." He tapped his fingers slowly on the arm of his chair, forcing himself to be patient. He had no idea at all where this conversation was going.

"You see, there was something else Vincenti mentioned in the note he left." Roper rubbed the top of his flat head with his stubby hand. "He talked about something he'd destroyed: something he'd originally planned to give to St. Michel. I didn't know what he might have meant by that and nor did St. Michel. So after St. Michel took his wife home I thought I'd take a look around, check the bins and so on, just to ease my mind."

"And?" Crown's dark eyes were attentive now.

"Well, there was nothing in any of the bins. I had a look through a few cupboards and drawers—the place was a tip; he wasn't a tidy fellow—but there was nothing significant there as far as I could see. And then on my way out, when I was heading back to the nick, I saw a woman putting a plastic bag into a rubbish skip outside the back door, so I thought I'd just have a quick look. And in the middle of all these bags of rubbish I found what I was pretty sure was the thing Vincenti had wanted to destroy."

"What was it?"

"It was this huge folder—massive. Big as a couple of telephone directories. It was nothing but music, sir; hundreds of pages all covered with music."

"Jesus Christ."

"Yes, sir. That's just what I thought. I knew right off that was it, from the handwriting and the inscription. And I knew I should leave it to be cleared away with the rubbish; that was what the dead man wanted, after all. But I couldn't make myself do it. The amount of work he'd put into it, it must have taken him years. His note said it had been meant for St. Michel and at the last minute he'd been too afraid to give it to him. That made me sick, I can tell you. I hated that guy, I really did. All that work for someone who didn't care about him. So I took it home and just sat on it, so to speak." He rubbed the top of his head again in anxiety. "My sergeant would skin me alive if he knew."

"Have you got it here?"

"Yes." Roper picked up his briefcase and opened it on his knee. "I don't even know if it's worth anything to anyone. I didn't know what to do with it but it's been on my conscience, sir, especially since I read about St. Michel's breakdown in the papers. In the end my wife said to me: Thomas, it's your job and your duty to protect the rights of the dead but, more important, you went into the Force to do good to the living. And I reckon a man can't argue with that."

Crown took the huge, heavy manuscript from him and laid it on the desk, opening the cardboard cover. It was a ballet score: a full-length adaptation of Shakespeare's *Tempest*. Enormous. Fully orchestrated. The first hundred pages contained the complete ballet, scored for piano, and the rest was hundreds of pages of orchestral scoring, violas and all.

Crown's cheeks turned cold and his forehead grew hot. His eyes smarted at the knowledge of what he held in his hands.

"It's unbelievable," he said, flicking through the pages of densely annotated music.

"Yes sir," Roper agreed. "You think it might be any good then?"

"I think it might be something quite exceptional."

His eyes skimmed over the pages as he turned them. In the margin of each page there were verses of Shakespeare's text and, between the staves, informal pencil notes crammed together in Primo's untidy handwriting.

Some were choreographic notes suggesting interpretations of specific passages or showing where he wanted the steps to move at a different pace from the music. Others were instructions to the musical director, not all of them very polite. Crown was astounded by the sheer scale of it. It must have been several years' work at the very least.

Crown was so engrossed in examining the manuscript he completely forgot the man who was sitting silently opposite him, watching him with worried eyes. After a couple of minutes the policeman adjusted his position in his chair.

"Mister Crown, you look like an intelligent man and a man of integrity."

"Yes," Crown said distractedly, "I'm both."

"Did I do the right thing bringing this to you? Was it right of me to take it out of the bin?"

Crown lifted his eyes from the manuscript and looked at him, contemplating him for the first time not as a rather slow-thinking public servant but as a scrupulous man who had spent six months wrestling with a moral dilemma and trying, with the limited resources of his own conscience and his wife's advice, to arrive at a compassionate and ethical decision.

"Yes, Mister Roper, you did do the right thing. What's more, you have my complete respect and, believe me, that isn't easily won."

Roper's heavy face lightened in relief as he got up from his chair. At the door of the office he hesitated and looked back at him awkwardly.

"Is . . . Is Mister St. Michel going to be alright, sir?"

Crown hadn't been sure of the answer to that question for a long time, but he was sure of it now.

"Yes he is. He's going to be just fine."

Once Roper had gone Crown rubbed his hands hard over his whole face and then opened Primo's manuscript again at the first page, starting to read. He wished his musical sight-reading was better. His guess was this was probably the explosion of genius Primo had been trying to suppress all his life. Crown knew what kind of music had flowed from inside Primo; he had heard him improvise hundreds of breathtaking melodies for exercises in class—beautiful outbursts of passion which had vanished, never to be heard again, as one exercise ended and the next began.

He stopped at a page titled "Ariel: for Michel" and jumped to his feet, carrying the folder with him out into the foyer. As he stalked toward the ground-floor corridor he ignored the receptionist who tried to stop him with a query.

"Oh God, he's off on one of his benders," the receptionist whispered to the tour booker.

The apprentices were working on a choreography project in the big studio and Crown threw them out unceremoniously, stopping their accompanist, who rose to follow them.

"Sit down, Max; I want you to play for me. Can you play this?"

He laid the heavy score on the ledge above the keyboard of the piano and Max gave it a quick glance.

"I should think so. What is it?"

"Just play."

Max was used to Crown's eccentricity. He began to play with a look of resignation. By the time he was ten bars into *Ariel* his brow was furrowed in surprise and concentration. Outside in the corridor the apprentices fell silent to listen. At the end of the variation Max turned to the next page without a word and continued playing.

Halfway through *Ariel*'s pas de quatre with the Elements, Crown snatched up the score from the music rest.

"Thanks," he said, "that's all I wanted to know," and he stalked back down the corridor to the office. Now he had no choice but to take Nadia Petrovna's advice and fight. It might take years but Michel would dance Ariel. He had no doubt about it.

He stuffed the score into the bottom drawer of Nadia Petrovna's desk and then changed his mind. He'd have the whole thing photocopied and stuff that in the bottom drawer instead. The original would go to his bank.

Michel finally plucked up the courage to tell Crown that he was through with dancing for good.

"Fine," Crown said, folding his arms and perching on the arm of the sofa in the studio. "At least you've made some kind of positive decision."

"I'd dance if I could, Charles, but I've lost my nerve and I'm not going to get it back. Even walking down the street scares the shit out of me."

"I said that's fine. You don't have to justify yourself to me."

"I don't?" Michel looked at him doubtfully. Primo had warned him this interview was going to be difficult.

Crown shrugged and shook his head. "If you've lost it, you've lost it. You're not the first. Any idea what you'll do instead?"

"I don't know yet. I haven't really thought."

"Well, you've got plenty of time. You aren't skint, are you?"

"No, loaded." Michel had never spent much money and he was still earning royalties from video sales and overseas broadcasts of television appearances.

As Crown strolled toward the door of the flat Michel followed closely behind him.

"Charles, do you think—I mean maybe sometime in the future—that I might be any good at teaching?"

"Teaching?" Crown raised his eyebrows and contemplated that for a minute. "Yes, why not? You could give it a go. You've certainly got the technical expertise. It might not be a bad idea at all."

Once he was alone Michel puffed out his cheeks and stared at the hall wall. He had no idea why he'd said that to Crown. Teaching? He must be crazy. He could no more walk into a studio full of people and mirrors than he could fly. Crown's placid response to his confession had startled him out of his common sense for a moment or two, that's all.

His thoughts were interrupted by the telephone ringing. It was only his mother again, calling to ask him what she could do about a wasp's nest in the wall of the barn.

"I don't know, Carrie. Call the fire brigade."

"Are you serious?"

"Yes—no, hang on, I think that's only in France. Have you tried the pest control people?"

"No, I'll do that."

"Where's the nest, at the house end or the field end?"

Carrie's calls were the bane of Michel's life. For years he'd been virtually out of touch with her and now, all of a sudden, she was on the phone every other day with some household crisis. What was wrong with the woman; didn't she know he was sick?

He put his hand over his eyes and tried to concentrate on her wasp problem. It wasn't her fault; of course she didn't know he was ill; how could she? In a funny way these tedious calls from Carrie, always purely practical, were one of the things which helped him to keep a hold on reality. It was irritating to have to emerge from some distant daydream to apply his mind to drains or roof tiles but it did give him a sense of perspective. Michel had no reason to doubt his sanity—although instinct warned him not to confide Primo's visits to anyone; after all, people might be jealous.

"I'm not too good on wasps," he said. "But I think the local council should be able to tell you what to do."

Things were gradually changing for Michel in the solitude of the Pimlico flat. The change which struck him most forcibly was the return of his sexuality. After six months in which sex hadn't crossed his mind he was suddenly flooded with erotic thoughts and sensations; it was as though his libido was making up for lost time.

Everything made him think of sex; toothpaste squeezing out of its tube, door handles, the soft gray velvet of the curtains that always covered the studio mirrors, even soap—or perhaps if he were honest, especially soap. His bodily sexual needs were no problem; it was an abstract lust which plagued him. He didn't want company; he didn't want intimacy; it was a hunger for sensuous activity which dogged him.

Michel's fantasies all centered around kissing. He would spend hours lost in daydreams where he was holding a woman in his arms and kissing her, always gently, never tempted to burst the bubble of his imagination by expanding his thoughts into anything too sexy. He fantasized about kissing lots of different women. He had dreams about kissing Jonni— never memories, just an image of her warm mouth pressed against his— and Lynne and Annette and Louisa, and the pretty girl who walked along the pavement opposite at a quarter to nine every morning and then back again between six and half-past.

All these flights of fancy were getting under his skin. He walked about the flat looking for something he could physically do; something his body could respond to.

Carrie phoned again the following morning. The council had sent someone to smoke out the wasps but now the idiots up at the sawmill had sent her a whole winter's supply of six-foot logs instead of faggots and they refused to take them back because they said the mistake had been hers. Five tons of six-foot logs! What was she supposed to do with those?

Michel rubbed his eyes with a sigh.

"Okay, Carrie, keep your shirt on. I'll come and chop your wood for you."

"Oh, that's kind of you, Michel. Thank you. I'll clear the beets and onions out of the spare room."

Michel threw a couple of tracksuits and half a dozen pairs of socks into a bag. Heavily camouflaged by a respectable blond beard, he walked out of the flat and caught the tube to Paddington. At the ticket office in Paddington station he stopped the girl behind the counter from printing out his ticket.

"I'm sorry, I've just remembered I've got a car. I think I'll go and see if it still works."

He left the station and caught the tube back to Pimlico thinking about the freckle-faced girl in the ticket office. What would it be like to kiss her? he wondered.

30

JONNI HAD A NEW BOYFRIEND: a doctor named Ieuan.

"If you want to know how it's pronounced," she wrote in one of her frequent letters to Maggie Lane, "ask a Welshman."

Jonni's correspondence with her old friend Maggie had grown out of the discovery that she too was trying to survive the breakdown of her marriage. It must be even worse for Maggie; she had been married for twenty-five years and there were fierce legal battles over property. Jonni didn't have the trials of a bloody divorce to contend with; her worst nightmare was the silence. Her letters to Maggie, pouring out her fears and regrets onto paper without reserve, were the only vent for her periodic bouts of despair.

There was no one in the house to confide in. Bernadette had become a cautious ally but she was compulsively flippant; she couldn't possibly understand Jonni's heartache. Her father was passively sympathetic but he wasn't someone she could talk to. Week in, week out, Jonni sat in front of the television watching old black-and-white films or lay on the sofa reading romantic novels and eating chocolate biscuits. She hadn't felt well since Primo's death but on days when she wasn't too sick or weary she went shopping in Gloucester and helped her mother with housework. Without Maggie's letters, which dropped through the letter box onto the hall carpet every few days, she would have been tearing out her hair.

Jonni met her young doctor in the waiting room of the dentist's surgery. They started chatting about the state of the NHS and talked away happily until a dental nurse with frighteningly perfect teeth came to escort Jonni to her doom. When she reappeared twenty minutes later, with a white face and two new fillings, Ieuan was waiting for her.

"What would you prescribe for an advanced state of shock?" she asked limply, smiling when she saw him still standing at the reception desk.

"Coconut and banana milk shake. D'you know Rodney's Café on the corner of the High Street?"

Since then their friendship had graduated to evenings at the cinema and quiet dinners in country pubs. Ieuan was every inch the gentleman; keen but never pushy. And his sense of humor was irresistible. While he walked her home at night along the footpath beside the river, the old embankment walls rang with their laughter as he described the events of his day at the hospital. It seemed rather sick to be howling with merriment over some poor soul who had slipped in a cowpat and broken both collarbones, but the laughter was cathartic. If Jonni could laugh at someone else's misfortune she could laugh at her own. "At least you can do something to help," Jonni said.

"I dunno," he replied. "Sometimes. Did I tell you about the time a farmer brought in a goat at three in the morning because it had eaten six feet of nylon rope?"

Over the weeks their cheerful conversations progressed to holding hands and eventually to the young man placing a shy kiss on her lips as he left her at her front door after an evening in her local pub.

Maggie thought Jonni's new "beau" was the best thing that could have happened to her. The letters which still came regularly from London were packed with smutty insinuations that made Jonni splutter with laughter at the breakfast table as she read them, much to the detriment of her mother's digestion.

"You asked me what he looks like," Jonni wrote in answer to one of Maggie's epistles. "Well, he's no oil painting but he's got a very jolly face. When he laughs it crinkles up like an apple that's been left in a fruit bowl for a month. He's got bright-red hair but he makes up for it by being tall and having rather a good physique (though of course it's not in the same league as you-know-who). And he's nice, Mags; oh God, is he nice!

Though, I have to be honest, I think niceness is overrated. Give me a bloke with a good healthy temper any day.

"But anyway, I like him. He's got a few things definitely in his favor: he doesn't swear in front of my mother, he only works evenings every other week, and he doesn't give two hoots about ballet."

Jonni was sitting in the Pied Martin watching Ieuan rotate a beer mat slowly with his forefinger. It was an afternoon in mid-July and the sun was pouring through the colored glass in the pub windows, making patterns on the polished wood of the round table between them. It was hard to be serious on such a sunny afternoon but Jonni was chewing her lower lip pensively, waiting for Ieuan to speak. She hated taking advantage of him professionally. It must be bad enough having to listen to this all week without being burdened with his girlfriend's medical complaints on a Saturday.

"You ought to be feeling better by now," he said at last. "Have you been eating, sleeping, getting exercise, all the usual things?"

"On and off. I don't exercise much; I'm always too tired. The doctor I saw when I first came down here said that the sickness and exhaustion might go on for a couple of months after my friend's suicide." She still couldn't say the words without tears springing into her eyes. "It's been over four months now."

"Do you feel bloated?"

"Bloated and fat and horrible. I've put on over a stone—and most of it's up top where I could really do without it."

Ieuan rubbed his chin thoughtfully.

"Are your periods regular?"

"Oh, I stopped having them when Primo died. The doctor said that was quite normal."

He raised one eyebrow and then tilted his head, looking at her quizzically with a small smile. Jonni frowned for a moment and then jumped out of her chair.

"I can't be!" she cried. "Four and a half months?"

"Unless you've been with anyone else since you left your husband. I for one regretfully protest my innocence on that score."

A dreadful possibility occurred to Jonni but she sat down slowly, murmuring a negative response to his implied question.

Once the tests had confirmed Ieuan's diagnosis Jonni was hurled instantly into a chaos of antenatal clinics and fetal scans. Thank God for Mum and Ieuan: they had both brought enough babies into the world to know exactly what needed to be done. As for Jonni, she didn't have a clue.

"How can I have a bloody baby?" she wrote in turmoil to Maggie. "I'm a baby myself. How can I take responsibility for another human being?"

Ieuan was wonderful. His face creased into a huge grin when she told him the tests had been positive.

"I'll deliver it," he said, delighted. "We'll find out when it's due and I'll wangle myself into obstetrics for a couple of weeks." And then later he said, "But don't you think you ought to tell the father?"

Jonni just sighed. She couldn't tell him there was a good chance the father of her baby was dead and buried. At the end of a long afternoon stroll through the neighboring fields of the quiet residential area where her parents lived, Ieuan tucked her arm under his and turned his smiling face toward her.

"Tell me, Jonni, do you still love your husband?"

She gazed sadly at the pylons crossing the field and shook her head, clicking her tongue gently.

It was sex which finally brought the relationship between Jonni and Ieuan to an end. She was six months pregnant and she felt misshapen, hideous. Her unsuspected pregnancy had turned her body into a bugbear; there was no time to get used to the idea before her belly swelled like a balloon and her hormones went berserk. Ieuan thought they should wait but Jonni was adamant they should go to bed together. She needed reassurance that she was still attractive, she said—that her body didn't disgust him. But when he took her home with him to his little flat at the hospital, the invasion of her flesh by the kind, gentle young man made her cringe and weep with self-loathing. She hated herself for stringing him along. She didn't want to be loved. She wanted to be punished.

Ieuan drove her to the station in the morning. She was going up to London to look for a flat with Maggie.

"No, I don't really understand, love," he said, "but, if you've made up your mind it won't work then you can bet your life it won't."

She hesitated as she opened the door of the car, not sure if she should kiss him good-bye. The London train was rolling slowly into the station.

"Hey, Jonni!" he called as she walked away. "Don't be a stranger, eh?"

She turned and waved although she hadn't heard him. Her ears were already humming with the roar of London traffic: the screeching brakes of the black taxis and the rumble of buses.

Jonni had told her mother she needed to be in London to look for work. It wasn't true. Who wanted an actress who was six months pregnant? And besides, there was no work to be had. Theaters were closing down all over the country and television had been taken over by management consultants who flooded all the channels with repeats. No one in the business was working; even an established actress like Maggie couldn't find a job.

"The only people who've got work," Maggie grumbled while they had lunch in a Kensington pub between flat viewings, "are a few protected species in their gilded government cages. The RSC and the opera houses."

"And the ballet companies," Jonni agreed. "And the only reason they're protected is because they're on their way to extinction."

"Good Lord, how cynical we both are. A cheerful pair of flatmates we're going to be, aren't we? To hell with art, let's order some more Chardonnay."

"I'd better not," Jonni laughed. "My bump starts doing the cancan after a couple of glasses. And we might be in for a long afternoon."

But the first flat they looked at after lunch turned out to be ideal.

"This is the one!" Maggie cried, throwing open a window which overlooked the Thames. "Terra-cotta tiles in the kitchen and gurgly plumbing. It's so splendidly bohemian."

The flat wasn't strictly a flat: it straddled the top two floors of a narrow Victorian house on the edge of the green that ran down to the river at Chiswick. From a rustic kitchen-diner with chunky pine work surfaces, one door led to a cozy sitting room and another to a short flight of stairs that ran up to the attic bedrooms above. The place had heaps of character. It was fully furnished. It wasn't far from the tube. The rent was double what they could afford. They decided to take it on the spot.

"There's even a tiny bedroom for the nipper when it comes," Maggie said with glee.

Jonni smiled, shuddering. By the time the baby was born she was going to be extremely glad Maggie had had three children of her own.

The first couple of months in the Chiswick flat were a riot. The two marital fugitives spent their days messing around in the kitchen, kicking up the piles of autumn leaves by the river, and shopping for baby things in the quaint villagey shops nearby. They were both unemployed, both wondering how life could be so unfair, both "bitter and twisted" as Maggie declared dramatically, and they were having a wonderful time. They painted their sitting room yellow to cheer themselves up—and then painted two of the walls crimson to stave off the arrival of winter.

"I think that looks jolly tasteful," Maggie said, wiping her hands on her overall as she surveyed their handiwork. Jonni looked at the crimson and yellow walls a little dubiously. Then she looked at Maggie. Then they both looked at the walls again before the pair of them collapsed on the settee in hysterical laughter.

"We can't subject a newborn baby to this," Jonni howled. "It'd grow up to be some kind of psycho."

The paint had cost a small fortune but it couldn't be helped. They dug into their pockets again and made the trip back to the DIY shop. This time they came home with pale pink.

"This'll be awfully chic, Jons. Peach sunrise. This baby's going to be a connoisseur of color coordination."

"Whatever it looks like, we'll have to live with it. You realize we've just blown our monthly chocolate budget on that paint."

"What, all of it?" Maggie asked in despair.

"Well . . ." the thought of a month without chocolate was appalling, ". . . let's say half of it."

Money was tight but they weren't penniless. Each month, as if by magic, a sum of money appeared in Jonni's bank account. In fact it wasn't magic at all; it was a standing order Michel had set up soon after Jonni had left. All summer Jonni hadn't touched the money—she hadn't needed much and she'd been happier to live off her parents' generosity. But since the news about the baby she felt perhaps Michel owed her something after all. Unless, of course . . . but she would cross that bridge when she came to it. At the moment the money was extremely useful.

At night Jonni sat on the end of her bed and looked at herself in the full-length wall mirror—at her flushed cheeks and her lank auburn hair tied in a straggly ponytail at the nape of her neck. She laid her hands on her huge swollen belly and thought about how the baby had got inside her. Sometimes, when she remembered Michel's silent, almost pained ecstasy as he ejaculated into her, or remembered the earth falling into Primo's grave in the rain, tears trickled down her face and dropped onto her bump. But not very often. Mostly she thought about them both calmly and told her unborn baby about them in a whisper.

A fortnight before the baby was due Jonni went home to Gloucester, leaving Maggie to water the geraniums and feed Osborne, the cat. Her mother fussed and fidgeted over her from the moment she arrived, flapping about vitamins and liquid intake and breathing exercises. Within twenty-four hours Jonni was ready to scream.

The happiest thing about her return to Gloucester was the renewal of her friendship with Ieuan. There were no hard feelings between them, just the affection of two friends for whom it might have worked out if things had been different.

Ieuan delivered Jonni's baby on the first of December and, two days later, drove them both home to the waiting clutches of the proud grandmother.

"I'm sorry I had to cut you up," he told her in the car.

"Oh, I don't care. I'm just over the moon to have my body to myself again."

"So long as you don't hold a grudge against the little one. She didn't ask to spend nine months cooped up in there, you know."

Jonni laughed and caressed the minute creature in the baby chair beside her on the backseat.

"How could anyone bear a grudge against such a sweet darling?" She kissed the tiny wrinkled head. "You're my little matey, aren't you?" Jonni's heart sank as the car turned into the avenue and she saw her mother waiting impatiently on the doorstep. "All I want now is my soul back again too. When can I go home to London?"

"Give the stitches a week or so to heal. There's no reason you should stay after that."

Jonni and the well-wrapped bundle in her arms, which was called Caroline, caught the train to London ten days after the birth. Maggie took the sleeping baby from Jonni's arms and looked at it closely. She knew why Jonni was gazing at her with such earnest question in her eyes.

"I don't know, Jons. All babies look the same to me. But she's got your ears."

Two weeks later, just before Christmas, the very last thing that Jonni had expected to happen happened. She got a phone call from London Weekend Television.

"I don't believe it," she said, stunned, putting down the phone. "They want me for an audition."

"Hallelujah!" shouted Maggie. "What's it for?"

"Telly. A new comedy series with Guy Dakin."

"My oh my! We can set up a club, only for people who've really fucked up their marriages in style. How on earth did they get your number?"

"From Spotlight."

"But you haven't got an agent. Who put you up for it?"

"I haven't a clue," said Jonni. She was still in a daze.

The next day she washed her hair, drying it upside down to try and fluff some life into it, made up her face, and went to the audition in South Kensington. She expected to see a queue of actresses stretching out of the door of the studio and down the street but there was only her.

She read for the director, she read for the producers—she even read for Guy Dakin, which would have been horribly humiliating if he hadn't been grinning at her with a wicked sparkle in his eye from the moment she walked in.

"How d'you think these people got hold of me?" she asked him when he took her to the canteen for a coffee after the reading. He really was a very handsome fellow if you liked that sort of thing; his deep-blue eyes were quite startling, especially in conjunction with his dark-brown cropped hair and cheeky smile. A couple of big box-office films and a highly publicized love affair or two had turned him into the man of the moment. He could also boast one of the briefest marriages in Hollywood history—slightly under a fortnight if the *News of the World* was an authority to be trusted.

"They didn't get hold of you," he said. "I did."

"You? How? Why?"

"Contacts."

"What contacts? I don't know anyone in the theater anymore."

"We couldn't find an actress who was right for Samantha. An old buddy told me to give you a call. We have a mutual friend—in fact we've met before. I guess you don't remember."

Jonni listened to his soft American accent but his words didn't make sense to her. How could she have met him before? Had he perhaps seen *Forty-Love* more than four years ago? Unlikely.

"It wasn't . . ." she braced herself, ". . . it wasn't by any chance Grant Noble who recommended me, was it?"

Guy Dakin raised his eyebrows.

"Who the fuck's Grant Noble?"

Jonni decided she was going to like him.

"So spill the beans: what's Dakin like?" Maggie asked as Jonni arrived home and picked up the baby from her cot.

"Oh, fun—arrogant."

"Did you find out who put you up for the job?"

"Yes, it was Roly. They were at stage school together—I never knew that. But I do remember now, he was sitting at the next table to ours at Roly's wedding. He was modeling for catalogs then, can you believe it?"

"Did they offer you the job?"

Jonni's face broke into a huge grin as Caroline set up a hungry wail. "Yes."

"Oh, Lordy! This calls for champagne, and bugger the cost!"

Jonni laughed and rocked Caroline in her arms to quieten her. While Jonni fed her, the two friends talked over the pros and cons of accepting the job.

"I can't leave the poor little mite; she's only three weeks old."

"Are you saying I won't make a good nurse?"

"But what if you get a job too?"

"Then we'll be rich and we can afford the best nanny going to look after our baby during the day."

"Oh, Mags. I don't know what to tell them."

"Frankly, if you don't phone and tell them yes, I'll do it for you."

And so it was decided. Jonni signed a four-month contract to make twelve episodes of a new situation comedy starting at the end of January. LWT had already commissioned the outlines for a second series. With Guy Dakin in the leading role they had no qualms about jumping in at the deep end.

31

MICHEL DROVE HIS PEUGEOT between the crumbling stone gate-posts of his mother's farm in the cold gray light of October dusk. The chalky Devon soil between the courtyard flagstones had turned to mud after several days of autumn rain, and the air smelled of mossy damp woodland. He climbed out of the car and listened to the silence. It was deafening after the constant hum of traffic in Pimlico.

Warm lights glowed in the kitchen windows of the farm cottage. Carrie must be cooking. Even from across the courtyard Michel could see streaks of condensation dripping down the inside of the steamed-up panes. He picked up his bag and slammed the car door with a thud, enjoying an inexplicable satisfaction in shattering the hushed calm of the countryside.

Carrie greeted him with a nonchalant but cheery smile as he ducked under the low oak beam just inside the kitchen door. When he put his bag on the floor and stood up straight the smile faded from her lips. She regarded him blankly, with an air of not quite liking what she saw.

The last time Michel and Carrie had met was when he had brought Jonni down for a weekend not long after their marriage. The weekend had been a pleasant one—Carrie and Michel found it easier to be together in the presence of a third person—and they had occasionally talked of repeating the visit, in fact Carrie had invited them several times, but as Michel's workload had rocketed his free time had vanished, and suddenly it was more than three years since he had found time to see her.

Carrie had aged noticeably since then. The fine wisps of hair which escaped the neat plait at the back of her head were beginning to turn gray. Her eyes were still fine and bright—he watched them as they moved slowly over his face—but her cheeks had lost their youthful bloom and the lines which creased her face when she smiled remained after the smile had vanished.

"I couldn't have imagined you with a beard," she said at last, trying to retrieve her smile.

"Doesn't it suit me?"

"Oh, I don't know. What do you think?"

He pulled a chair out from the huge farmhouse table and sat down.

"To be honest I haven't really looked."

"I've made coffee. Would you like some?"

"Please."

"Did you have a good drive down?"

"Not bad. I got lost in Tiverton."

"Yes, it's tricky, the new one-way system. I should have warned you. Help yourself to sugar."

Michel stirred his coffee in silence. After months of solitude he had grown unused to conversation. Carrie seemed to share his distaste for talking; she pottered quietly at the far end of the kitchen, stirring saucepans while he nursed his cup and watched the reflection of the kitchen lights in the misted windows. The world outside had turned dark very suddenly.

The next morning Michel was up shortly after dawn. That day and the fifteen days following it he spent all the hours of daylight swinging an axe in the barnyard behind the house. There was a mountain of wood to chop; the wood-burning Rayburn in the kitchen heated the whole house and the hot water, as well as being used for cooking. He enjoyed the labor; it got his muscles working and satisfied his need for physical activity. He didn't care if he was ruining his hands in the process. There were no ballerinas to complain about his rough skin laddering their pink tights.

Carrie left him alone and plied him with mountains of food three times a day. That and the clean country air swelling his lungs as he sweated over the woodpile was ample reward for his toil. The fields and clumps of woodland that stretched away over the low hills were very tranquil and the misty autumn days touched a soothing chord in his memory. Once the wood was chopped he set about retiling the end of the barn and, after that, repairing the fence around the chicken hutch and digging a pit for a new septic tank. To his surprise he found he had both a talent and a taste for manual work which he had never suspected. He even managed to replace a worn washer in an outdoor tap, which brought the first spontaneous smile to his face for many months.

"Look at that," he said in wonder, turning it on. "It actually works."

Soon Michel found he had been in Devon for four weeks, and the lifestyle suited him. His health had improved and his face was no longer the pale, gaunt mask it had been when he arrived. These days, if Carrie came home from shopping in the village with a funny anecdote, he sometimes even laughed out loud.

Part of him would have liked to tell her about his illness. But another part, much stronger, was glad she knew nothing about it. Surely though, she must have noticed his absentmindedness, his introverted behavior— or at least wondered why he was here instead of touring or rehearsing in London. But that first month passed without her asking a single question about his health or about his career or his wife—or anything concerning his life beyond the walls of the farm. Neither of them had mentioned dance. It was a subject of unspoken tension between them.

He walked into the sitting room in the early afternoon and put another log on the open hearth. For the past couple of days the torrential rain and a stinking cold had kept him indoors and he was beginning to grow restless.

Carrie was sitting at the piano playing a selection of Chopin études and Michel spoke to her across the room while he crouched down to build up the fire.

"Those were the last pieces you gave me to learn when I was a child, before I went to France."

"Really? I don't remember."

She carried on playing but a moment later she glanced up while she turned the page of her score.

"Do you ever practice now?"

He stood up and reached into his pocket to pull out a handkerchief. "Almost never. I played a bit while I was a student but it must be over a year since I last sat down at a piano."

"You were talented." Her hands were running steadily over the keys. "You should take it up again."

"No, I've seen real skill on the piano since those days." He corrected himself quickly, seeing her raise her eyebrows at his words. "I mean including you."

"You forget," she said, "you brought your Italian friend here once when you were on tour in this area. I do know a real pianist when I hear one, Michel."

He turned back toward the fire. He hadn't meant to offend her. But it did answer one question: he'd been trying to work out how Primo had followed him here from London. Of course—they had been here together in the days when they were both dancing in the corps.

Carrie left the Chopin score on the piano when she stood up to go and roll out the pastry for this evening's steak and kidney pie. Michel seated himself on the stool, raising it six inches to suit his height, and started to play through the first few études. He was surprised at how well his fingers remembered those pieces; he had thought his brain would have long since swept away that early tuition to make room for all those hours of complex choreography. Gradually, as he played, the natural musician in him—the musical core without which he would have been nothing as a dancer—began to wake up and flow through his hands.

From that afternoon, whenever the weather was too wet for outdoor work, he sat at the piano and practiced for hours on end. Carrie began to offer him helpful criticism, always from a distance; always casually as she breezed through the room busy with some household chore. He accepted her criticism with alacrity; it was the only platform upon which their interests had met for the past nineteen years. His month in his mother's house had become two months and still, apart from music, their conversation was limited to the work that needed doing on the farm and impersonal chatter about the daily goings-on in the village.

Only once during the time he had been there had Carrie confronted him on a more personal level.

"Michel?" she said cautiously, opening the sitting-room door one night to find him sitting alone beside the smoldering hearth. "Who were you talking to?"

He looked up, surprised to see her standing beside him in her dressing gown. The clock on the wall told him it was after three in the morning.

"No one. I'm sorry, was I keeping you awake?"

"Yes you were. And I want to know who you were talking to."

"I was just muttering to myself. Go back to bed, Carrie. I'll be quiet."

Michel could remember very little of the childhood years he had spent with Carrie; he certainly couldn't recall ever seeing her angry. But now her temper suddenly flared.

"Night after night I hear you sitting here talking to ghosts! Talk to me if you must talk, but don't sit here talking to the wall!"

"I'm not talking to the wall."

She grabbed his head between her hands and turned his face toward the mirror above the fireplace which reflected the whole room. He tried to pull away but, small as she was, she was strong in her anger and she had the advantage of surprise.

"There's no one here, Michel! Do you understand me? Nobody; just you and your overstretched mind. Look in the mirror! There's no one here!"

She was gone from the room before he had time to lower the involuntary hand he had raised to block his view of his reflection in the mirror.

In the morning there was nothing in Carrie's manner aside from a slight deepening of her habitual reserve to suggest that anything unusual had passed between them. Michel attempted to apologize.

"Carrie, last night . . . I hope I didn't—"

"Blast!" She interrupted him, lifting a saucepan from the Rayburn and laying her hand on her hob. "I can't seem to get the temperature up on this thing. Would you mind bringing in a few logs from the yard before breakfast?"

And he knew the subject was closed.

At the beginning of December, Carrie called to Michel while he was on the roof fixing a new hood to the top of the chimney.

"There's a man on the phone for you!"

Michel paused in his work, deciding it was almost certainly Charles

Crown. He was the only person other than Jonni who knew how to contact him here. From his position on the apex of the roof he could see the humps of the red hills rising out of the woodland to the west and the beginnings of a crimson-streaked winter sunset. It was very peaceful up here; a good place to let your mind wander. But Carrie was still waiting.

"Okay!" he called. "Can you tell him I'll ring him back?"

"No, Michel; I think you should talk to him now!"

Michel climbed reluctantly down from the roof and wiped his grubby hands on his shirt before he strolled into the kitchen to pick up the receiver.

Carrie had been right to call him down from the roof. He hadn't heard from Crown since he had come to Devon and this was no routine call.

"The old lady's dead," Crown sobbed down the line. "She died this morning."

"No!" said Michel, shocked out of his daydream. "I thought she would live forever."

"So did I. I was with her when she went. I sent her your love but I don't know if she could hear me."

"Thank you. Listen . . . are you alright? Do you need me up in London?"

"I need you back in the fucking company, Michel, but that's another story."

When Crown had rung off Michel dropped slowly onto a chair at the kitchen table. Nadia Petrovna couldn't die; she was an institution in the dance world. The Islington Ballet without Sekova would be a ship without a rudder. It was impossible. Michel wished he'd been to see her in the summer when Crown had suggested it. Now it was too late.

"One of your colleagues?" Carrie asked, letting curiosity get the better of her restraint. She had been watching him from the far end of the kitchen where she was kneading bread.

"Yes, a teacher. One of the great old Russian ballerinas. We were close when I was a student. She was like a mother to me."

He saw Carrie's mouth tighten into a pinched line. Her green eyes regarded him coldly.

"I mean she was there when I needed someone."

That was even worse. Michel looked down at the table. There was no way out of that so he stood up and left the room.

The Islington Ballet underwent huge changes following Nadia Petrovna's death. The Board of Governors tried to persuade Charles Crown to take over as administrative head of the company in addition to his role as artistic director. Crown declined. It had never been part of the bargain that he should deal with the business side of things. He didn't have the time and, besides, he'd make a lousy job of it.

The board brought in an administrator of their own to replace Nadia Petrovna—not someone from the dance world, a management consultant—and within days the new man and Crown were at loggerheads. It was pistols drawn almost from the moment he walked into the building.

The new administrator knew nothing but he wasn't content to watch and learn. He set about making staff cuts and changes, and introduced time sheets for the non-dancing employees.

Crown was at his wits' end. The new man even expected him to fill in a time sheet. Him! The artistic director!

"Look," he complained to the board, "you cannot rationalize a dance company. It's not a car factory. And I'm sorry but I shouldn't have to explain to the director of a ballet company why dancers can't perform on a concrete stage."

Unfortunately for Crown the board didn't know the answer to this any more than their administrator so his point was lost on them.

"And why, for Christ's sake, did you allow this *dickhead*,"—the dickhead raised his eyebrows—"to book us to appear at an Easter gala in Regent's Park?"

"It's a question of finance," the administrator insisted.

"No, it's not. It's a question of bloody stupidity. If they dance outdoors in March they'll rip every muscle in their bodies." Crown held up his hands in surrender. "But go ahead; don't let that stop you. Just remember to cancel the rest of the spring tour first."

Late in the evening when the building was all but deserted Crown walked into the big ground-floor studio. He looked at the empty space and silent barres in the reflected light of the streetlamps on the Goswell Road. What had happened to his and Nadia Petrovna's dream? Sixteen years ago this studio had represented to Crown a glorious empty space waiting to be flooded with influences and ideas from all over the world—waiting to be filled with a magnificent future for modern dance. Now it just seemed like an empty space.

Crown leaned against the barre and looked up at the rows of lights embedded in the high ceiling. He and Nadia Petrovna had achieved a lot in the sixteen hard years since they set out on this ambitious adventure together. Their little company had fought the system, struggled to reinvent the classics for the modern world—had helped produce a new generation of young dancers bursting with passionate creativity. It had won widespread renown, enjoyed the brief blaze of Michel's brilliant flame; it had survived critical and financial disaster. What should the company be striving for now that Nadia Petrovna was gone? His gaze traveled slowly over the mirrors and the expanse of the wooden floor, worn smooth by a decade and a half of dancing feet. He wished she had told him what to do before she had died and taken the dream with her.

On the twenty-eighth of December, Crown called Michel and told him that the Islington Ballet was to have a new artistic director.

"I couldn't stick that twit of an admin bloke a day longer. Lex is coming back down from Scottish to take over—unless you want the job, that is."

Michel laughed: "No thanks. But what about you?"

"Me? Oh, I'm moving up in the world. Phone call out of the blue from the BNB. Martyn's going to the Beeb as head of cultural entertainment. You're talking to the new artistic director of the British National. In fact, now I think of it, perhaps you'd better start calling me sir again."

Michel was staggered; things were really happening out there in the world. No wonder Crown was sounding so pleased with himself.

"Charles, you hypocrite, you abhor the BNB! You've always said their whole ethos and repertoire stank and the dancers were in lousy shape."

"I abhor what the BNB is now, not what it'll be in a year's time."

"My God, the poor buggers aren't going to know what hit them."

"Too damn right. And I'm looking for a ballet master I can trust—not someone with a weak stomach either. I need someone who understands where I'm coming from and who can handle my pace. Any ideas?"

Michel sat warming his hands on a mug of hot coffee at the kitchen table.

"Maybe I ought to go, Carrie."

He ought to go, he thought, if only to stop Charles knocking the stuffing out of every dancer in the company.

That pinched, cold expression came back into Carrie's averted eyes.

"Go then, if that's what's important to you."

"No . . . you're right; perhaps it's not a good idea. Perhaps I should stay here."

"Oh, for heaven's sake, go back to your ballet in London!" She jumped up from the table and started to clear away the lunch dishes, clattering them together noisily. Michel shifted his weight uncomfortably in his chair.

"Maybe it would be better to wait a few more months."

"Go, Michel. Just go."

And so he went.

In the flat in Pimlico Michel threw up the blinds and opened the studio windows to let in the freezing air of New Year's Eve.

"What the hell are you doing?" Crown shouted, letting himself into the flat, paper-wrapped bottles tucked under his arm. "It's like a fucking icebox in here!"

"I'm cleaning out the cobwebs."

"Well don't; you need them for insulation."

The two men saw the new year in together in the studio. Three whole months had passed since they had last met.

"I was thinking how much brighter you're looking than the last time I saw you," Crown said, when they found they were staring at each other.

"I was thinking the opposite about you."

Crown was looking washed out. Despite his new post at the BNB the past months had been very tough for him.

"God, I'm glad you're back, Michel."

"I'm glad to be here."

"It's been a god-awful year for both of us. Let's leave all that behind and see what we can make of this one. We're going to grab the BNB by the balls, right?"

"Right, if it's got any."

"Partners?"

"Partners."

They raised their glasses to the start of a better year.

32

DURING THE WEEK BEFORE the official announcement of Crown's appointment, Crown and Michel walked around the corridors of the British National Ballet with Martyn Greene in their smartest suits and gold tiepins, learning about the immense managerial and public relations engine that drove the BNB.

In the few days Michel had spent with the company five years ago he had formed an impression of a larger, wealthier version of the Islington Ballet, but the reality was very different: the infrastructure was vast, with links in very high social and political places and tactical intrigue of international proportions going on behind the scenes. Michel couldn't take it all in; it was mind-boggling. Like all dancers, he had assumed that every ballet company revolved around its performers. Now, for the first time, he realized the dancers were merely a small cog in a very large machine.

Even the building was strange to him. The company had moved from its cavernous old headquarters in Fenchurch Street to spanking new premises in Victoria, not far from Buckingham Palace. There were modern sculptures in the foyer, huge smoked-glass entrance doors, and shining brass handrails lining the sweeping beech staircase that ran up to the air-conditioned offices on the upper floors.

Crown and Michel sat at the front of the main studio watching the girls' morning class.

"Christ Almighty, look at them," Crown said under his breath. "You'd think they had weights strapped to their wrists and ankles."

The standard amongst Europe's major ballet companies was so high that the distinction was a subtle one, but Crown was right; the condition of the dancers was very poor. And worse was the uniform lethargy on their faces as they plodded through the exercises.

"Lovely, darlings!" the ballet mistress called to them. "I can feel the radiance . . . lovely . . . lovely!"

Michel sat looking at the rows of identikit girls, all dark-haired, all between five foot three and five foot five. The atmosphere in the studio reeked of discontent. At the Islington the dancers had all known each other intimately; they quarreled, made up, had tantrums, slept together, slapped each other; they were one big happy family. At the Islington there was no one-upmanship or scheming, just the simple understanding that Charles Crown was God and below him all men and women were equal. But here, where the corps alone numbered forty-nine, the air was thick with animosity between warring factions. From his seat in front of the mirror Michel could pick out at a glance the troublemakers, the swollen egos, the ones who were out of their heads on narcotics or painkillers, the disillusioned ones.

"How the hell do we cope with this?" he whispered to Crown.

"We come out fighting. I'm going to put a rocket up this company's arse that'll blast it out of its complacency. If we go down in flames, we go down together, agreed?"

On the very first day of his official reign as artistic director Crown detonated an explosion of outrage by sacking both the ballet master and the ballet mistress.

"But they've been with the company for years," the chairman protested, in the emergency board meeting that followed the announcement. "Ivan's been ballet master for more than a decade."

"It's time for a change," Crown said. "The dancers' discipline is pitiful and they're in lousy shape."

"Can't you just tell Ivan and Tiffène what you want?"

"No, I can't. I need my own team who understand my methods."

"Your methods?" Sir Andrew Holtham blanched; this was a traditional company; a white tights and tutu company. "Well . . . okay, but St. Michel—no offense to you, Michel—is too young to be chief ballet master of a major national company." The harassed baronet neither knew nor really cared whether Michel was up to the job. It was the PR aspect that terrified him. "Of course I've seen St. Michel dance many times—we all have—but the press simply won't buy him in this role. A change of creative leadership's a media tightrope as it is."

Crown wasn't budging an inch. "I'm the artistic director of this company and this man is my ballet master, end of story. And I want a contract drawn up for my assistant ballet mistress, Marina Walker. She's staying on at the Islington to cover the handover to the new team but she'll be joining us in a few weeks."

The board, made up of aristocrats and business bigwigs, exchanged glances with raised eyebrows.

"I don't know this Marina Walker," Sir Andrew replied—his face said that anyone he hadn't heard of was ipso facto not good enough for the BNB. "You're bringing her in to teach the girls, I presume."

"As it happens, for reasons I won't go into, I'll be putting her in charge of the boys."

"The boys?" Sir Andrew's smooth eyebrows soared in disbelief. Surely even Crown wasn't lunatic enough to expect the men to put up with a female teacher.

"And Michel will be teaching the girls until we've arranged a rota of female guest teachers. He's had a great deal of experience with girls."

Michel choked on his coffee. He hadn't had any experience with them at all—at least not the kind of experience Crown meant.

"We'll be upping the number of classes," Crown went on, "for both men and women to six a week. And I'll be introducing a compulsory contemporary class which I'll be taking myself."

"Oh," said Sir Andrew, dumbfounded. "Oh . . . right. But this list of dancers whose contracts you want terminated. Eight dancers! Three of them soloists! I mean, surely it's far too early . . ."

"I want them out of the building now. Today. I can do *Coppélia* without them and I'll build up the numbers as I find new ones." Crown looked the appalled chairman square in the eye. "Look, Sir Andrew, why did you and the Governors offer me this post?"

"Because you were Martyn's recommendation."

"Okay, you've trusted Martyn's judgment for twelve years. Why can't you trust him now?"

"Charles," Michel whispered as they emerged into the fermenting uproar in the studios, "I've never taken a class in my life."

"Keep your cool," Crown murmured back, "and bluff like buggery."

As Sir Andrew had predicted, the press slated Crown's appointment to the BNB, and his initial binge of hiring and firing sparked an even fiercer controversy. Several of the national papers hinted with almost libelous clarity at a sexual liaison between the new artistic director and his ballet master. Every national dance critic doubted Crown's ability to maintain the profile of the company. The Royal Ballet and English National were rubbing their hands in glee.

But if the response outside the BNB was bloodthirsty that was nothing to what was going on inside it. Hair was standing on end. The dancers were on the verge of full-scale insurrection.

Crown faced the assembled company in the main studio, staring them out with a fierce frown.

"Equity says you have to attend four classes a week," he said. "In my company you attend six if you want your contracts renewed next year. And injured dancers will come in to watch classes unless I've told them not to—no one uses aching feet as an excuse to stay in bed. From now on, rehearsals will start at two o'clock sharp. Anyone who's late will be fined."

The dancers didn't even have to look at each other. Their bristling indignation radiated through the air in the studio, passing like electricity from skin to skin. In the principals' corner it was almost possible to see steam bellowing from dilated nostrils.

Crown's piercing eyes swept slowly over their faces.

"You've all heard the rumor that I'm a nasty piece of work. Well, it's true. Fuck with me and you're out of a job. Don't make the mistake of thinking the Governors can protect you; I have absolute power over who does and who does not dance with this company. I can sack you if I don't like your attitude, I can sack you if I don't like your dancing, I can sack you if I don't like your face. That goes for principals too. No one's indispensable here."

"That was awesome," Michel told him afterward. "You had me scared."

Crown sat back in his chair and closed his eyes. Most of what he had said to the dancers had been bravado; he certainly didn't have the power to sack the ballerinas, much to his regret.

"You realize one of the principals will take that straight to some buddy in Fleet Street. I'll be quoted, word for word, in tomorrow's *Telegraph*."

Unexpectedly, amidst all the negative publicity surrounding Crown's appointment, the BNB's patron decided to throw her weight publicly behind the new regime. Her arrival, in a police-escorted limousine, came at such short notice that Crown and Michel barely had time to button their shirt collars and straighten their ties before they were precipitated into her presence in front of a crowd of TV cameras and journalists.

"I'm very grateful to Her Highness," Crown told the press. "What I need now is for you lot to back off and give me and my staff a chance to start knocking this ragged company into some kind of shape."

Sir Andrew cringed. If it weren't for the TV cameras he would have put his head in his hands and wept.

At the end of that first turbulent week Crown was "invited" to an urgent meeting with the BNB's main sponsor in Nottingham.

"You bugger!" Michel cried, when Crown told him. "You're leaving me to cope with the boys as well as the girls? Can't we get in a guest teacher for the boys?"

"No—Christ no. If we don't keep control of the situation between us now we're mincemeat." They were sitting in Crown's first-floor office drinking the tepid sludge that came out of a machine in the corridor calling itself coffee. Compared to his little broom cupboard in the Goswell Road, Crown's office was palatial. Michel had his own office a few doors along the corridor—near enough to be called in a hurry but not so near he'd hear the heads rolling once the fun really started. "You'll have to take both classes."

"If you insist. God, we really must get a kettle in here; this stuff's evil."

"Don't push the boys too hard; keep it simple. Concentrate on line and ensemble, and don't worry about the allegros."

Michel wasn't concerned about the teaching; it was survival that worried him. The girls were sullen in his classes but they submitted to his authority with no worse display of hostility than a few scornful sneers from the principals. The boys were another matter entirely.

"They're going to eat me alive," he said, sighing.

He wasn't far wrong. Without Crown's controlling presence in the building the following morning the mood amongst the male dancers was patently carnivorous.

"Oh Christ, it's Shirley Temple," a voice muttered audibly as Michel walked into the studio. Michel ignored the barrage of malignant looks that assailed him from the groups of men stretching on the floor and went to lay his folder of schedules on top of the piano.

John, the accompanist, looked up at him wryly from the piano stool. "Showdown time, huh?" John was an outspoken, loud-laughing Canadian: one of Michel's few allies in the company. He thought the Crown–St. Michel revolution was the best thing to happen to the BNB in years. "Let the cocksuckers know who's boss."

"I'll do my best," Michel said.

The boys' hostility toward Michel ran far deeper than the resentment they felt against Crown. Underlying their scorn for Michel there was real, though subconscious, fear. The dancers' world was a cloistered, idealized one, and Michel brought the perils of the real world too near. Here was a dancer who had everything. He had been born with it all—the perfect body, the perfect facility, more sheer talent than half the boys at the BNB put together—and it had broken him. He was their worst nightmare come true.

There wasn't a single man among the BNB dancers who had not, at some point, sat in an auditorium watching an Islington Ballet performance and marveled enviously at Michel's style and technique. Michel as he was before his breakdown, they would have showered with aspiring homage. The real man—the beaten man—they rejected, averting their gazes in superstitious horror from the ominous shipwreck of a great dancer's career.

Michel knew all this, and what he didn't know he understood instinctively. As the boys lined up at the barres their eyes glittered in readiness for battle. He pushed up the sleeves of his sweatshirt and opened his notebook.

"Okay. Let's plié, shall we? You, darling—sorry, what's your name?"

"Melanie."

"What are you doing here?"

"Oh God." Melanie's eyes were round with fear. "I overslept and missed the girls' class. Please don't tell Charles."

"No, okay. But if you're going to stay, get rid of all those things you've got tied around your waist, will you? And whatever that is around your neck so I can see your body."

"Would you like the rest of us to leave?" one of the boys asked rudely.

"No, that won't be necessary."

The class started cautiously. The boys were tense with aggression and Michel was equally tense. Each exercise, as Michel set them and the boys danced them, was conducted in an atmosphere of bristling animosity. It wasn't a question of whether there was going to be trouble—it was a question of when and who.

At the start of the first adage in the center Michel gave a correction to a junior soloist.

"Hold on a sec, John." He raised his hand to stop the music. "Before we start: Robert, you need to walk into the exercise firmly. Don't tiptoe in like a fairy."

"Oh fabulous," singsonged a voice belligerently from the back of the studio. "Our new ballet master doesn't like queers, loves."

There was a universal squaring of shoulders and raising of hackles from the homosexual majority in the room. Michel dismissed the accusation with a half-amused shake of his head. He'd been part of the dance world far too long to fall for that homophobia claptrap.

"Don't be such a hypersensitive bunch of old queens; I meant the kind of fairy you find at the bottom of your garden. But now you mention it, don't walk like any kind of fairy. You need to walk like men."

"You're telling me how to walk?" asked Rob.

"That's right."

"Michel, I've been dancing for twelve years. I don't need to be told how to walk."

Michel sensed the anticipation of the men all around him as they waited for the outcome of this first direct challenge. He caught John's eye at the piano. They both knew if he backed down now he was breakfast.

"Yes you do, or I wouldn't give the correction. It's a mental block that makes you think you have to walk gracefully so get rid of it. You don't look graceful, you look camp."

"You're accusing me of being gay?"

"Oh Jesus, I'm not accusing you of anything, Rob. I don't care about your sexuality. I'm here to give a dance class."

"And you're qualified to correct me? You're an expert?"

"That's the idea."

Rob was very young and very sharp. He flicked his long blond fringe off his forehead looking at Michel evenly.

"So when did you last do class then?"

There were murmurs of protest from a few of the more mature men but Michel waved them to silence. Rob had asked a fair question.

"May; ten months," he said.

Rob was still gazing at him. With the uncanny perception born of deep personal insecurity he pinpointed Michel's fear exactly.

"And you're the big star. You're better than all of us. Alright, you corrected my failli earlier, so show me how to do it. Come on, Michel, turn around and face the mirror and give us a demonstration."

Michel looked into Rob's eyes, trying to find a suitable response. After a few moments he looked away.

"I can't."

"Oh, I'm sorry." Rob laid his hand on his chest with ironic sympathy. "You're injured, are you?"

The other boys exchanged glances. This was going way too far.

"No, I'm not injured. I just can't do it."

"Fine. So don't tell me I've got a mental block. It's not me who's lost my balls. There's only one mental problem in this room," he tapped his own forehead, "and it isn't here."

There was a stifling silence while Michel examined the herringbone arrangement of the parquet floor tiles. At last he looked up.

"Rob, I think we should do this adage before everyone gets cold, don't you?"

Rob walked slowly back into his place for the start of the exercise, still watching him.

For the last half hour of the class there was no sound at all apart from the chonking of the piano and the scuffing of suede shoes on the wooden floor, and Michel's calm voice counting out the beats of the exercises.

When the boys had gone Michel folded his arms and leaned on the top of the piano, looking down at John. For some time the two men just gazed at each other. John's grimly puckered mouth said it all. Eventually John hoisted his shoulders in a shrug.

"Cured the cocksucker's walk, anyhow."

Michel laughed grimly. "Yeah, you're right; it did at that."

After lunch the atmosphere in rehearsals was deadly. Melanie had taken the story to the girls' changing room and female sympathy had swept like a tidal wave in Michel's favor. All afternoon the girls practiced their mazurka under Michel's instruction without addressing a word to their partners. It was silent warfare.

"What the hell's been happening here?" Crown asked him, when he returned from his harrowing meeting with the sponsors to find the air in the building crackling with animosity. "It's like *High Noon* in here."

"Oh . . . power games between the girls and boys."

"Really? That's interesting. Who won?"

"I'm not sure, but I certainly lost."

"Did you?" Crown frowned at him in concern. "So what happened?"

"I had a bit of a run-in with the boys."

"Who started it?"

Michel shook his head. He knew how anxiously Crown wanted to get this right and how fragile his hold on the situation was. If Michel gave him a name the culprit would disappear from the company. The dancers would turn up for class tomorrow morning and the troublemaker simply wouldn't be there.

"No one started it, Charles. It was just one of those things—all in a day's work in this place."

Each night when he got home Michel planned his class for the following morning and then fell exhausted into bed. His health was greatly improved since the autumn but he had lost the physical stamina and the power of prolonged concentration of earlier days. Sometimes as he drifted into sleep he wondered where Primo had got to. But the shadows in the Pimlico flat were undisturbed. He was simply too tired to entertain nighttime visitors.

Things grew easier once Marina joined the company. As well as her practical experience and solidarity she brought her own unique take on the situation.

"Loves, this place is a ruddy diva-ocracy. It's not Martyn who's been running it, it's the ballerinas. Feed Marie Gillette's gizzard through the shredder in Sir Android's office, is my advice."

"I'd love to," Crown said, checking that the intercom to his secretary's desk was switched off. He'd like nothing better than to end the stranglehold that Marie and Tatjana had had on the company for the past decade but the two ballerinas had the Governors in their pockets. "I don't think it'd go down well with the suits, unfortunately."

"Michel, poppet, I see you haven't wasted any time getting the rest of the toots wrapped round your little finger. Still got the old magic touch, eh?"

Michel smiled at that. The girls had certainly been accommodating since that ruck with the boys. He linked his hands behind his head and put his feet up lazily on Crown's desk—over the past few weeks he had come to the conclusion that a bit of healthy disrespect for the property of the BNB was the only way to stop an animal this size getting on top of him.

"That's down to the boys: I get the girls' sympathy vote."

"Well, I'm glad the boys are good for something. Yikes, what a limp bunch: not a pair of bollocks between the lot of them."

"You and I can share their classes," Crown said. "We'll take it in turns to try and hammer some oomph into them."

"Oh no," she said, flapping a hand mischievously, "let's confuse them, Charles; it'll be much more fun. I'll tickle their egos one day—that's the gorgeous thing about being in my position, I can flirt with both camps—and you whip them up into a fury of indignation the next. There'll be so much testosterone flying round that studio that by the time we open in Liverpool the boys' ensemble will be like something out of the Chippendales."

"It's worth a try," Crown said, picking up his cigarettes and then putting them back irritably on his desk again—he was trying to cut down. "Who knows, it might even work. And if they get complacent"—his mouth twitched—"we can always rope Michel in to teach the odd class, pump up the testosterone levels a bit higher."

"Don't," Michel said. "That's not even funny."

Crown strolled into Michel's cozy first-floor office on Thursday evening while he was working out the rehearsal schedule for the following week. Michel looked up at him with a smile.

"Almost there, Charles. Give me two minutes."

Crown perched on the corner of Michel's desk, watching him while he chopped half an hour off a corps rehearsal to squeeze in a call for the male principals. Michel looked more animated than when he started this job six weeks ago. His posture was straighter and his face and gestures were more youthful. Even the pitch of his voice was a tone higher. But there was a gravity in his gray eyes, a reserve that hadn't been there a year ago. His breakdown was behind him but it had scarred him.

"This hostility the boys have toward you," Crown said. "I think it might be a good idea if you come and join my class with them tomorrow morning."

"I can't do that."

"You and I both know they're intimidated by your situation. If they see that you're okay, that you can still turn out a decent double *tour*, you'll seem less vulnerable to them."

Michel was frowning at him in surprise. Do a company class? The idea had never crossed his mind. He hadn't danced a single step since before he went to Devon, and even then only in the privacy of his flat. Do class with the boys . . . he rotated his pen between his fingers, thinking uneasily about the mirror.

"And it wouldn't hurt you to get a bit of exercise," Crown said. "I need my staff to be in shape physically."

Michel went back to his near-completed schedule.

"Let me sleep on the idea, Charles."

"D'you suppose Michel's gay?"

"He's married, isn't he?"

"I thought he was Charles's totty."

"It was in the papers last year when his wife left him, just before his breakdown."

"Poor duck."

"Perhaps he's bi."

A group of the girls were sitting on the low benches in the changing room after class. They were pulling off their tights and wrapping the ribbons around their pointe shoes before putting them away in their lockers.

Melanie shook out the rolled-up socks she had taken off before class. She had a wide, open face and eyes which were just too far apart to be pretty.

"How could anyone leave a guy like Michel? He's far too nice."

"And far too mmmmm," agreed Lizzi, a young soloist, with a hum like the contemplation of a forbidden chocolate sundae. She unpinned her ballet knot and shook out her hair, studying herself critically in the mirror. "Charles says I can go back to blond if I want. I wonder if I should. D'you reckon Michel likes blondes?"

Melanie wiggled her misshapen toes.

"I'll bet you a fiver Fiona's still down in studio two with him pretending she needs help to sort out her supported pirouettes."

"I heard that, Mel," said a voice from the other side of the row of lockers. "As it happens, he couldn't stay. He went off to do class with the boys."

"No; Michel in class? You're kidding."

"Oh my God, I saw him in *The Seven Ages of Man* last year at the Wells! Fancy getting an eyeful of those saut de basques close up!"

"And those pecs!"

"This I have to see."

But the girls were disappointed when they crowded into the doorway of the big studio to watch. Aside from its effortless musicality Michel's dancing was very mediocre. That he was fabulously musical they already knew; his hands, marking out the steps for them in class every morning, were unerringly precise—every beat accounted for, like a metronome. But he was extremely unfit. His line was undistinguished and his extension low.

The girls watched glumly from the side of the studio. Whatever the other boys did, Michel did less. He wasn't even trying. If the boys made four turns he made one. If they performed entrechat huit he did a single beat. When they cabrioled he didn't even attempt it, substituting a simple chassé for the leap and marking the beats of the feet with his hands. Even his body was a letdown. He was the last of the boys to discard his woolly leggings and sweatshirt, and when he did his muscles looked untoned, only half pulled-up. If there was anything to suggest he had ever been possessed of a particular gift it was in an occasional unconscious gesture; his head would turn toward his upstretched arm, his eyes projecting the motion into the distance, and for a moment, to the watching girls, the space around him seemed to expand. But these rare glimpses of the old Michel were gone almost before they occurred.

Crown didn't dare correct Michel's shaky technique, nor direct a single comment to him. As he paced the front of the studio in agitation, snapping his fingers sharply at the other boys, he tried not to watch Michel's sluggish limbs moving mechanically through the exercises. "Look in the mirror," Crown prayed under his breath. "For Christ's sake, look in the mirror."

When the class was over Crown heard the whispers of the men as they gathered their possessions together.

"I thought his feet would be better than that."

"Why didn't Charles correct his batterie?"

"No point, is there? He's past it now."

Rob's comment was loud enough even for Michel to hear.

"He must have started losing it before he cracked up. No one could deteriorate that much in ten months."

"Did you enjoy it?" Crown asked Michel, meeting him at the studio door.

"No, to be honest. I didn't really."

Crown pondered for a few seconds, pursing his lips thoughtfully.

"Do Marina's class tomorrow anyway."

On Sunday afternoon Michel was lying stretched out on a sofa in the studio of his Pimlico flat. Mild February sunlight gently warmed the room. He was gazing at the white ceiling, thinking about the classes he had danced this week, about how empty the steps felt to him.

His thoughts drifted away from class to the Los Angeles Festival Ballet, which had been performing at Sadler's Wells this week. He hadn't been to watch them; he never went out to see dance anymore. But even after all these years, whenever he knew Jacques St. Michel was in London, he couldn't help wondering, just wondering, if perhaps this time Jacques would call. He closed his eyes. Surely he should have learned by now.

He jumped up from his comfortable repose, booted off the sofa by a burst of irritation with himself, and kicked off his trainers, moving to the middle of the studio in his socks. With his eyes fixed on the gray curtain that concealed the mirror he launched himself into a series of pirouettes. They were horrible pirouettes—he was out of practice and not warmed up—but they unwound some of his irritation. Again he tried it, and again, faster and faster, his head whipping around after his body with each turn. On his tenth or eleventh attempt he found his balance and just for a moment, before he wound to a clean halt on the spot where he had begun, he felt he was flying.

"Shit!" he said to the wall in surprise. "Eight bloody pirouettes! That's not bad."

He walked out of the studio whistling and went to run a hot bath.

In the bath he squeezed the water slowly out of Jonni's yellow duck-shaped sponge, remembering how dancing had once made his spirit soar. They had been good times. His hands opened and he watched the duck sponge gradually recover its shape. The duck sponge was headless; it had been accidentally decapitated in a crazy bath fight he'd once had with Jonni. Those had been good times too.

He put the duck sponge on the ledge beside the bath and sank down under the water, submerging himself completely. There was no point remembering. What was lost was lost.

Over the next couple of weeks things began to settle down at the BNB. The national papers had lost interest in the story and the atmosphere within the company became calmer as the dancers grew accustomed to the new regime.

The BNB's premises in Victoria were only a fifteen-minute walk from

Michel's flat. No one disturbed him as he strolled along Belgrave Road in the mornings. Despite the dance world's sense of its own importance, very few people in the streets knew or cared about it, and even those who would once have recognized Michel's face from the television or the papers had forgotten him now.

The BNB no longer seemed so vast and unmanageable. Michel knew all the dancers' names now; all their strengths and weaknesses. The boys were still hostile—he was aware that blond Rob stirred up bad feeling against him in the changing room—but they were civil to him in rehearsals and listened to his instructions, which was all that mattered.

Crown was buried in plans for his debut choreography with the company but he kept a concerned eye on Michel's progress in the classes he still reluctantly attended with the other boys. It took all Crown's reserves of self-control not to pounce on Michel and tear his sloppy technique to shreds, but he mastered his impatience and left him alone.

"How was Michel in your class this morning?" he asked Marina, pretending to be preoccupied with a memo from Sir Andrew.

Marina wasn't fooled by his nonchalance for a moment.

"There's no change, Charles. He has no image of himself; no relationship with the mirror. He's lost heart."

Crown sighed.

He stood at the front of the main studio watching a dozen of the boys perform an adage which he had thought up, as always, on the spur of the moment. The adage involved no travel, just slow arabesques and développés flowing smoothly from one to another. Crown's sharp eyes moved slowly over the rows of boys. He spotted a few wobbles—it was a difficult adage to pull off—but there was a distinct improvement since his first classes with them. Their technique was crisper. They were fighting harder.

"Okay, that's not a bad effort," he said, as the boys cleared the floor to make way for the next dozen.

While he watched the next group perform the exercise his fingers closed into fists and his jaw locked tightly. The first casualty, when Crown was tense, had always been his temper, and now the weeks of suppressed frustration boiled over into fury. As the last notes of the accompaniment faded he pushed roughly past the first two rows of dancers to stand over Michel, who had sat down on the floor to adjust his shoes. Crown's eyebrows met in a knot of black rage above his furious eyes.

"What was that?" he demanded.

Michel looked up in surprise and smiled at the long-absent ferocity in his old tormentor.

"I don't know; you set the thing."

But Crown was in no mood for banter.

"Yes, I set it. And I didn't set it so that you could slouch through it with shoddy technique and a couldn't-give-a-shit look on your face. That wasn't dancing; that was marking."

"Easy, Charles." Michel glanced around uncertainly at the other dancers. "The adage was for the company boys. I'm only doing class for the exercise and for the fun of it, you know that."

He started clambering to his feet and Crown grabbed him by the front of his T-shirt, pulling him forward as he shouted into his face, "Nobody does my fucking classes for fun, St. Michel!"

Crown's aggression toward Michel had never been calculated or deliberate. If it had, their relationship would never have worked. Crown's anger was spontaneous and uncontrolled. And it was this very lack of control—this honesty—that made Michel yield to his will now, as he had in his student days.

"Okay," Michel said. "I hear you."

"You come to my classes to work, understand?"

"Yes."

Crown yanked Michel roughly to his feet and then pushed him away so that he staggered backward a couple of paces. As ever, Michel offered no resistance but let it happen.

"Only you know how much you can or can't do," Crown yelled. "But what you do, you do properly! None of this fucking about. What sort of example d'you think you're setting the other men?"

Michel nodded. He had a point.

The dancers were watching their two superiors in astonishment. They didn't see why—couldn't believe that Michel was taking this from him. What kind of Svengali was Charles Crown that a grown man, a full head taller and almost certainly stronger, would allow him to shove him around like that?

Michel felt the humiliation of submitting to this castigation in front of the men who were under his authority. But they would learn a lesson in humility if nothing else. He and Crown held each other's eyes; Michel's passive, Crown's aggressive—they were on familiar ground.

Crown drew in a deep breath and nodded.

"Alright. Now what was that shit you were doing to my adage? Show me a balance in second."

"Sorry?"

"A balance in second, St. Michel. I know you're supple enough. Show your colleagues how to do a balance in second."

Michel ran his fingers through his hair, gazing at the floor. And then he moved into first position and raised his eyes to look over the top of Crown's head at the wall. The company boys looked on in silence.

As Michel's arms opened into second position his face wore a look of puzzled concentration as though he were feeling his way through a memory. His hands rose in an arc above his head as his right foot swept very slowly up to the side, through ninety degrees and upward until it was somewhere above his right ear. Crown watched him with folded arms.

After a pause Michel's supporting foot rose onto demi-pointe and he arched his back, leaning farther and farther away from his raised leg. The line of his body, foot stretched to its limit and arms falling backward with the arc of his spine, never wavered for a moment.

"Now that," said Crown, pausing to emphasize the word, "is a balance in second."

The boys were motionless. It certainly was.

33

At the end of February a hundred and thirty-nine girls crowded into the smaller of the two ground-floor studios at the BNB.

"How the hell are we going to sift through that lot?" Michel asked, standing with the artistic director at the door.

"Swiftly and ruthlessly," Crown answered.

Michel looked over the mass of blond and brown heads in the studio. He had never been to an audition in his life—unless you counted his Académie audition at the age of eight—and the frantic hope on the faces of this sea of young women appalled him. Unlike the Royal and the English National, which employed their own graduating students, the BNB had no school of its own and so recruited dancers from schools and companies all over the world. Almost every dancer in the BNB had been through this ordeal before they joined the company but it was foreign to Michel. He could almost smell the fear which filled the room.

One two-inch advertisement in *The Dancing Times* had brought all these girls. And each one would give everything she possessed for a place in this high-profile company.

"Don't think of them as people," Crown advised. "Just see which ones can dance and note down the numbers."

"But so many. How can I possibly assess all these dancers just from one class?"

Crown lit a cigarette in defiance of the Board of Governors' rules.

"It'll be easier than you think. You'll find half of them can't dance for toffee. Give them a few exercises to get over the worst of the nerves and then start pruning drastically."

"I won't know where to start."

"Don't think about it too hard. It'll feel random but it won't be. We'll meet at noon for a mutual nervous breakdown." If Crown winced, cursing himself for that inadvertent tactless remark, he needn't have done. Michel hadn't even noticed it. He was too busy dreading the next two hours.

Crown walked to the front of the studio and waved his clipboard to attract the attention of the all-female crowd.

"Morning, ladies. Those of you numbered one to seventy follow me to studio one. The rest of you stay here."

A girl standing close to Michel began to stammer in confusion as she saw the great tide of bodies begin to flow out of the studio. Some who tried to remain stationary found themselves jostled along until the tide passed and dropped them like pebbles near the studio door.

Michel touched the arm of the girl who seemed lost.

"*C'est quoi ton numéro?*"

"*Cent-trois.*"

"*Reste ici.*"

With an effort he stopped himself being too friendly. It would only make it harder if he had to kick her out in five minutes' time.

Left alone with almost seventy auditionees and two administrators, who were shuffling CVs into piles on a table, he walked to the front of the studio and raised his voice to direct the girls toward the barres. Two rows of free-standing portable barres on iron T-stands had been assembled for the occasion but space was very limited. However, it wouldn't be overcrowded for long. Michel exchanged glances with John at the piano and then called out the sequence for the first exercise.

The mass of heads, spread across the room at the barres, began to rise and fall in unison. There were a few heads not quite in time with the rest but Michel tried not to notice which they were; it would be unfair to start making judgments so early. He crouched down to retie his shoelaces and let them get on with it unobserved. Who was more nervous, he wondered, the girls or him?

After maintaining an ostentatious indifference throughout the pliés and first tendu exercises he began wandering between the barres watching the dancers carefully. John was grinning at him from the piano, making surreptitious throat-cutting gestures as he played. Michel widened his eyes in alarmed reproof; he hoped the girls hadn't noticed.

A few minutes later he made his first selection. It was one of the most unpleasant things he had ever had to do; he tapped a dancer gently on the shoulder as he walked past.

"Thank you very much."

The unfortunate girl deflated, disappointment flooding her face, and crawled away to one of the small studios to change into her clothes and slip away. Michel hated every moment of it.

At first he was careful to throw out only the ones whose technique wasn't up to scratch. He fought to keep personal taste out of his judgment. But when the barres were cleared away to begin work in the center he abandoned this attempt at fair play. They were going to have to go at some stage so he swept away all the girls whose bodies or faces he found unattractive.

By the time they reached grand allegro he had narrowed the class down to twenty-five, and during that last exercise he whittled away a final ten including the little French girl he had spoken to before the audition.

"Thank Christ that's over," he said to Crown when they were back in the office.

"It isn't. Put the kettle on, will you? The difficult bit's still to come. Got the numbers of your fifteen?"

Michel threw the list he'd taken at the end of the morning onto the desk.

"They're all there. One of them hardly speaks a word of English."

"Which one?"

"One two four, I think."

Michel spooned instant coffee into two cups while Crown rifled through his pile of CVs.

"Is this her: Minako Soko? Japanese, right?"

"That's the one. Fantastic turns. She's like a bloody top once she gets going. I asked them for thirty-two fouettés—it's lucky she can count or we'd probably all still be there."

Crown was right: the afternoon was where things really started to get difficult. The standard of the thirty girls who'd come back willingly for more punishment was very high. They were only looking for two.

They had agreed to throw out twenty and select the final two from the last ten. But where to start?

Between them, conferring at the front of the studio, they threw out five of the girls who were slower than the others at picking up the exercises; there was no room for slow learners in the BNB. They set contemporary exercises and threw out a few more. Jazz; a few more.

When they had their ten they went back to classical ballet and just watched. What to go on now? Instinct? Sex appeal? All the girls had something but those somethings weren't necessarily comparable. Some of them were extremely musical, others technically excellent, some had beauty, some poetry, some charisma.

"Where do our priorities lie?" Michel whispered.

"In our guts," Crown whispered back.

Eventually Michel pointed out a girl of medium height with bright blond hair and radiant eyes which shone out of a glowing face.

"She's alive, Charles."

Crown nodded. "And she's intelligent."

She got the job; she and the Japanese girl who had been in Michel's group before lunch.

"Funny," Michel said, "Minako's the one I'd have picked within the first two minutes this morning."

Crown yawned, throwing the pile of audition forms into a drawer of his filing cabinet.

"Same's true of the American girl; I knew I wanted her before I'd even seen her tendu. Still, at least this way we know we were right."

That night, while Crown was in a deep dreamless sleep, the two new members of the BNB were celebrating, each according to her own culture. Lisa, the golden-haired American, turned on the TV, opened a huge tub of yogurt straight from the freezer, and ran up a gigantic phone bill calling her parents and friends back home. Minako sat on the carpet of her small hostel room in Vauxhall with her legs stretched out in second position. She drank a cup of green tea and gazed into the distance while her toes pointed then relaxed, pointed then relaxed in a slow, even rhythm long into the night.

Michel lay on his back, looking at the shadow of the ash tree on the ceiling of his bedroom. He could still see the dozens of hopeful smiles which had lined up at the barres this morning. One by one he had wiped the smiles off those faces. What were they feeling now, all those girls? Were they wondering if all those years of training had been a waste of time? It was a dreadful feeling; he knew it well.

Lisa Parfitt sat in Crown's office on the first floor of the BNB building. She declined his offer of coffee—"What, caffeine? Gee, no thanks!"—and scrutinized the framed photos on the walls while he searched through his files for copies of the rehearsal and tour schedules. The photos on the wall were all of past stars of the company in famous poses from the classics. It wouldn't be long, she reckoned, before she'd be right up there on the wall with them.

"I suggest you just sit in on rehearsals this afternoon," Crown said, still rummaging through files on his desk. "We'll start fitting you in as soon as we have the time."

"I guess I can pick up this stuff pretty quick. In America you're expected to get a ballet like this together in a week. I looked in on the girls' class this morning . . ."

"Did you?"

"Yeah, I just kinda wandered in to check it out. Who was that, like, vague woman who was taking the class?"

"A guest teacher: Galina Nikolayeva. She'll be giving class here several times a week."

"I'm not sure she's real qualified. She didn't seem awful competent."

"Yes. Well. Why don't you give her the benefit of the doubt—based on her forty years' teaching experience in some of the top companies in Europe?"

Lisa flashed Crown her sunniest smile. He was just typically English, she decided; real serious about everything and kinda formal with it. He must be repressed; you could tell from the veiled way he was looking at her and the way his lips remained tightly closed when he wasn't speaking.

To Lisa it had been inevitable she would get picked to join the company. False modesty was a strictly British trait. With the standard of training they received in the States and her European style, why wouldn't she be the best dancer at the audition? She had seen Crown looking at her right from the beginning of the class, which had only reinforced her confidence.

There was a brief knock on the office door and Michel stuck his head hurriedly into the room.

"Charles, have you seen the—hi there, darling; sorry to interrupt—the tape of *Coppélia?*"

"Sorry, yes, it's here."

Crown handed him a videotape and Michel gave Lisa another brief smile before he dashed off down the corridor.

When he had gone Lisa's head remained turned toward the closed door for a moment before she pushed her loose blond curls behind her shoulders and tucked one foot underneath her on her chair.

"That was St. Michel, wasn't it?" she said.

Crown plonked a company brochure on top of the pile of papers in front of the girl.

"*Mister* St. Michel—or, better still, just Michel. He's the ballet master here."

"I saw him at the audition and I recognized him right off."

"Did you now." It wasn't a question; it was a clear statement that he couldn't care less. However, Lisa didn't understand the nuances of British intonation.

"Why, sure. He looks just like I expected him to only kinda more solemn and better-looking. I knew he'd have that arty look about him you get with real talented guys."

It had always been Crown's policy that he never interviewed dancers before he offered them a job. A dancer's work should speak for itself; that and the basic information contained in their CV. Now he was beginning to see serious loopholes in the wisdom of this approach.

"I'd like you to watch Michel's rehearsal with the girls' corps at three o'clock," he said—"Quietly."

"Me? Oh, I'll be as quiet as a mouse. I'll just kinda sit there and store it all up in the computer."

"You do that. Now, darling, if you don't mind I'm sure you can look after yourself for an hour or two."

He had found copies of all the schedules for her and now he wanted her out of his office. He didn't really care where she went—just away, that was all he asked. He buried his nose in his new ballet score which had just arrived from Antwerp and waited for her to get the hint. She didn't.

"You want to know why I'm so thrilled to work with St. Michel—I mean Michel? It's just the wildest thing; I bet you can't guess."

"I've really no idea."

"Parfitt's my mother's maiden name. I started using it when I went to ballet school; you know, for anonymity. My real name, like the one on my birth certificate, is St. Michel too."

Crown raised his eyes slowly from the page.

Lisa beamed at him.

"I'm his cousin."

He narrowed his eyes as he scrutinized the face which was glowing with satisfaction at the significance of this announcement.

"Jesus Christ; you are, too."

He could see it now—the keen intelligence of those striking gray eyes, the shape of her nose, her smile, something in her expression when she was surprised. He would never have seen it unless he had looked for it but it was there alright. There was no doubt of the truth of her claim. He ran his fingers slowly along the edge of his desk.

"Is that why you wanted to dance with this company?"

"Hell no, but I was sure curious to meet him all the same. He seems real nice."

Crown was careful as he chose his next words.

"He is nice. Very helpful to all the girls. Did you hear he'd been unwell?"

"Yeah, that's too bad. He's through performing, isn't he?"

"Yes. Yes, possibly. Listen, Lisa, I know you're excited to meet a new cousin but Michel's very sensitive about his family. He never talks about the St. Michel connection."

"Yeah, I never met his dad, my uncle, but I heard he's a real bastard. I heard his dad disowned him."

"That's right. That's what I understand too. So I'm afraid it might upset him a little—in his present state, you understand—to be suddenly confronted with a cousin he never knew existed."

Her face fell.

"I guess you mean I shouldn't tell him."

"I shouldn't mention it to anyone; not for a while. You know how these things get around. Michel's doing very well. His health and his spirits are improving daily. It would be a shame if a surprise like this set him back."

"Oh, gee. Yes, sure; I understand completely. I'll just be as nice as pie to him."

"I—uh—wouldn't be too nice to him, Lisa. He might—well he might suspect there was something behind it."

He sent her away with an encouraging smile. He was sure Michel wouldn't be at all upset to find he had a cousin, but this particular cousin might be a bit too much. Crown didn't want to give her any excuse to be more of a nuisance than she was clearly going to be already.

He lit a cigarette and rested one foot on an open drawer of his filing cabinet, blowing the smoke pensively into the air. It was strange to see similar facial expressions and mannerisms in two members of a family who had never met. Could it have been that undetected likeness which had drawn him to her so quickly yesterday? He was reassured by the fact that Michel had selected her too; he'd be the last person to have been influenced by the resemblance. Even so, it was bizarre—bizarre to think how small the world was, especially the world of dance.

"How did you get on with the new girls?" he asked, after class the following morning.

Michel raised his eyebrows and nodded.

"Yes, fine. They both did very well. The American girl's got a hell of a mouth though. I had to shut her up pretty sharply."

"Good for you. But go as easy on her as you can—new culture and all that. We don't want her to feel she can't fit in."

"She'll fit in," Michel said, laughing. "In fact I'd say she'll make damned sure of it."

Michel had grown fond of the girls in the company. Their individual personalities were very different from the ugly mob personality he'd encountered when he first arrived. There were the funny ones, the rude ones, the insecure ones, the bitchy ones—each had her own set of quirky idiosyncrasies. He got used to Melanie blowing her nose all the way through class, and Dana singing along to the piano, and Josie hiccupping whenever she did bourrées.

It was a new experience for Michel being responsible for other people. He liked it. His performing career had focused his attention obsessively on himself and cut him off from the people around him. Even Primo and Jonni had remained at a distance. The years of Crown's bullying hadn't touched him; he had viewed it all as if through a window. Now for the first time he felt himself being penetrated by tiny threads from the people who surrounded him. He felt needed. Whatever he could give the dancers of his time, his experience, his judgment, and his skill he was happy to give. As long as it wasn't for himself they needed him. As long as they asked nothing of him emotionally.

Watching the women run through the first exercises in class, Michel made a mental note to have a chat with Fiona about her weight. She'd been looking lumpier in classes recently. He looked across the studio at Hilary, one of the soloists, who was crouching on the floor with her arms stretched above her head, gripping the barre.

"What's up, darling? No, carry on, the rest of you." He walked toward her. "In pain?"

Hilary kept her head down, grimacing miserably.

"It's okay, Michel. You wouldn't understand."

"I've lived with girl dancers all my life, and been married. Go on; off you go. You can put your feet up in my office if you like. There are aspirin in the top drawer of my desk if you need them."

Hilary nodded and crawled away while Michel set the next exercise. This week was going to be trying; when one of the girls got her period they all did. It was like that in every company.

Shortly after class Michel found Lizzi curled up in the corner of one of the small studios, crying. He strolled over with his hands in his pockets to stand over her. As she hadn't heard him coming he nudged her gently with his foot.

"Hey."

"Who is it?"

"Michel."

"I don't want to talk about it."

He sat down on the floor beside her, resting his back against the wall, and took Crown's cigarettes from his pocket—he was always finding Crown's cigarettes and lighter left lying around the building. He lit a cigarette and passed it to her.

"I can't smoke in here," she sniveled. "I'll get shot if Evelyn catches me."

Evelyn was the sharp-eyed vulture of the company office who roamed the studios looking for evidence of transgressions just such as this.

"You're alright with me here." He didn't like to encourage the dancers to break the rules but once in a while it didn't hurt to be a bit irresponsible.

"So what's the story?" he asked as he watched her smoke and cry by turns.

"It's that fucking American bitch again."

He closed his eyes with a sigh. What had Lisa been up to now? He'd been wrong when he said she would find a way of fitting in. In the two weeks since she came on board she'd been rocking the boat from every possible angle.

"She says I'll never get past dancing second solos."

"Does she really? What makes her think that?"

"She says I haven't got the imagination to take on a major role. She said I was colorless. Fucking colorless, I ask you!"

"So if you think she's talking crap what are you doing sitting here bawling your eyes out?" It wasn't really a fair question; any dancer would be hurt by such a damning comment, whether they believed it or not.

"I just felt . . . felt . . ." and she was off again, holding her cigarette at arm's length while she covered her eyes with the other hand and sobbed. Michel watched her. Even in tears, Lizzi had a natural elegance. She was one of the company's few long-muscled girls: strong-featured, rather punkish since she'd cut her hair short to let the brown dye grow out to return to her natural blond.

"If you want an opinion on your dancing, ask me or Charles."

"Do you think I'm colorless?"

He thought about that. The question called for tact, and tact wasn't Michel's forte.

"This knee of yours is still on your mind. You've got to put the operation behind you; you can't dance expressively while you're hung up about an old injury." He patted her knee. "It's healed, Lizzi; it's not going to let you down. Your pointe work's getting stronger every day. You're a different dancer to the one you were two months ago. A leap of faith is all you need now."

She sniffed and wiped her eyes.

"My turns are getting steadier, aren't they?"

"Oh God, yes. Hey, what about those piqués in class this morning? They were something else. And those fouettés in the last allegro." He spread his hands in a shrug. "What can I say?"

Lizzi managed a feeble smile.

Michel looked in on Crown's rehearsal on the ground floor.

"Lisa, darling, can you come and see me in my office when Charles is finished with you?"

She waved and flashed him a big smile but Crown stopped him as he turned to leave.

"Take her now," he said, and added, with just enough emphasis to raise smiles from the rest of the dancers, "please."

In his first-floor office Michel perched on the windowsill. With his feet crossed at the ankles and his hands resting idle in his pockets, he watched the young woman make herself comfortable in the low armchair by the door. How old was she—nineteen? Twenty at most. He marveled at her relaxed self-assurance. No wonder she put the other girls' backs up.

"So how are you settling in?" he asked at last.

"Oh, I guess I've come to grips with most of the ensembles. I'm pretty smart, you know. I've just finished learning the steps for—"

"You misunderstand me. I can judge for myself how well you're picking up the choreography. I meant how are you settling into the life? How do you feel you're fitting in with the rest of the company?"

"You pulled me out of Charles's rehearsal to ask me that?"

"I didn't pull you out of rehearsal; it was Charles who suggested you come now. Do you want a coffee?"

He stood up and moved over to the kettle while she shook her blond mane adamantly.

"I never touch caffeine."

"You will once things start getting tight. That is, you will if you've got any sense. Out on the road the working day gets extremely long."

"Did you drink coffee when you were a dancer?"

"I'm still a dancer. If you mean when I was a performer then the answer's yes; I drank a vast amount of coffee all the time and I don't think it did me any harm." He switched the kettle off before it came to the boil. "Charles probably wouldn't agree, though." It had been a running battle between them for the past ten years. Even now Crown occasionally told him to cut down on the coffee just for old times' sake.

Lisa's gaze was fixed intently on Michel's face. It was the first time she had ever been alone with him and she was looking for a connection between them that didn't exist. He was real laid back, she decided, studying his eyes, and so calm it was almost scary. She had read all those sad things about him in the papers back home—they were just wild about European ballet stars over there. He did seem a bit somber sometimes, like the way he was looking at her now. But he looked strong and self-controlled too—he was her cousin, after all.

"What are you smiling about, Lisa?"

"Oh, nothing—just a private joke between me and my alter ego."

"You were going to tell me how you feel you're fitting in here."

"So I was. Well, not so good to be honest. They're sure unfriendly, the guys in this company."

Michel carried his coffee back to the windowsill. By "guys" he assumed Lisa meant all the dancers and not just the boys.

"It takes time to get to know people; you can't expect to make friends all at once."

"I've tried real hard to get them to like me but I guess they don't care for colonials."

"Perhaps you're trying a bit too hard."

"I kinda think they might be jealous—the girls, I mean."

"Of what?"

"Well, of me; of my ballet." She pronounced it ball-*ay*.

Michel raised his eyebrows, scratching his cheek.

"Maybe you should show the girls how good you are, rather than telling them. Every dancer here's ambitious; they all dream of making it to the top. I don't think you'll make friends with them by telling them how much better than them you are."

Lisa laughed as though he had been teasing her.

"But I'm only saying what I think. Come on, I saw you pick me out at the audition. Why did I get the job, huh?"

"Because you were good. Every dancer in this company has been picked out of an audition because they were good."

"So why was I made soloist right off instead of going into the corps like the other girls?"

"Because you're non-EEC and you wouldn't get a visa if you went into the corps; exactly the same as Minako."

"That's not what Charles told me."

"He probably didn't want to hurt your feelings. Perhaps he should have been more frank."

"Are you saying I'm not good enough to be a soloist?"

"Of course you are." Michel didn't want to hurt her feelings either. Besides, it was true; she was certainly good enough.

"Well there you are then. I'm good and I'm smart—and I'm attractive, aren't I?"

Michel smiled despite himself. She was about the most thick-skinned creature he'd ever met.

"Now there's a question," he said.

"Don't you think so?"

"You have a pretty face and a lovely figure, if that's what you're asking."

Her gray eyes opened wide in hurt surprise.

"Don't you think I'm attractive?"

He waited for a moment and then shook his head, puckering his lips and clicking his tongue gently.

"Jesus!" Lisa gasped. "You were so like my Pa when you did that!"

Michel looked at her startled gray eyes. It seemed the thought of her father had driven her enthusiastic conceit out of her head for a moment.

"What made you come to Europe to dance?" he asked, after a pause. "There must be plenty of work in America for a talented dancer."

"My style's pretty European—I guess you noticed. I studied at the Cecchetti School. I'm half French, you know."

"Really? Speak the language?"

"Pretty good. My accent's ghastly. Do you ever get over to France to see your dad?"

Michel looked at his coffee cup as he lifted it to his mouth.

"My father doesn't live in France."

"I thought he did. Is he—"

"I don't want to discuss my family, Lisa."

Lisa blushed at the sharpness of his tone. Charles Crown was right; he sure was sensitive on the subject. She looked down at her leg warmers sadly. She guessed she knew how he felt. Her own family life had always been lonely and insecure. Her parents' marriage had been falling apart for years—they never did anything together except fight. Neither of them cared about her. Ma had been all too eager to pack her off to Europe. And Pa had only tried to stop her going because he hated England and everything it stood for. She had come to England to spite him.

Things were so different over here. She adored the culture and the people. The problem was they didn't seem to adore her.

Michel put his coffee cup down on the windowsill beside him.

"I didn't mean to upset you, Lisa. It's just not something I want to talk about. That's not your fault."

She raised her face to look at him. She was thick-skinned but she wasn't stupid. She knew he was only being kind because he was a kind person. He didn't like her any more than the rest of them did.

"I guess I'm a bit lonesome in London," she said.

"Don't you have any family over here at all?"

A pause. "No, none."

"You'll make friends quick enough. We British are easy to scare off. Try not to push yourself forward quite so much."

"But that's the only way to get ahead."

"Not in this company, I promise you. I don't know how these things work in America but Charles casts dancers in the roles they're best suited for, whether they're loud or quiet, confident or shy, likable or unlikable."

She looked at him with resolution.

"Okay, I'll do whatever you say. When I'm being un-English you let me know and I'll take your advice."

"Mine? Why?"

"Because I trust you. And I want you to like me. Do you think you could like me, just a little, if I learn to behave like a proper English ballet dancer?"

Michel smiled. "I think it's just about conceivable. How about a piece of advice for starters?"

"What?"

"Put your hair up for class and rehearsals."

"Why?"

"It's conventional. And it gets in the way if you don't."

Lisa stood up, understanding from his tone that the interview was at an end.

"Consider it done," she said. "I vow never to darken your studios again without my hair tied in a prim European ballet knot."

"Good girl. Oh, and Lisa?"

She waited with her hand on the door to see what his parting comment was going to be.

"You're wrong about Lizzi, you know. She's going to make it someday."

"Me too," she said, and she left.

34

MICHEL WAS SITTING in the boys' changing room. He had been in the building since eight o'clock, mulling over the exercises he would give the girls later in the morning, but now he was changed and ready for Marina's class—ready, that is, apart from one shoe on which the elastic was coming loose.

The other men began to drift into the changing room half-asleep and they greeted Michel with civil nods. His relationship with the boys was improving slowly.

"Vy don't you t'row dose old things away?" Anatoly asked him, looking at the worn flat-spins in Michel's hand. Anatoly, a hot-tempered Russian, was in his late thirties and already so plagued by arthritis that he rarely appeared in anything other than character roles. He retained the title and wage of a principal; once you'd earned that distinction no one was going to take it away from you while you were part of the company. Anatoly Kalinin had been a considerable star in the ballet world. He still was.

"I don't get a shoe allowance like the rest of you sods," Michel said in answer to Anatoly's question.

"Don't dey pay you to do dis job?"

"Leave my shoes alone. I like old shoes; I just didn't sew the elastics on properly first time round." He glanced up as Rob came in. "Morning, Rob."

Rob gave him a curt nod, avoiding his eye. By now a good dozen of the men were stripping off and clambering reluctantly into jockstraps and Lycra garments of varying shapes and colors.

"Hey, Michel," called one of the boys from the far end of the room, "weren't you married to Jonquil Kendal?"

"Still am," Michel said. He raised his needle to eye level while he threaded it, "sort of."

"Saw her snogging with Guy Dakin last night. Very sexy."

"Who's sexy?" Anatoly asked. "Dakin or Jonquil Kendal?"

"Both, as it happens."

Michel sewed the elastic onto his shoe with a frown of concentration as he called out casually to the dancer who was hidden behind a row of lockers.

"So where did you see them, Paul?"

"On the box. In that new sitcom about the couple living on a barge in Hampton Court. Can't remember what it's called."

One of the boys suggested it should be called *Wet Dreams.*

"No, I saw it," someone else yelled over the lockers. "It's called *Sinking Feelings.*"

Michel bit the thread off his now-secure elastic and followed the boys down the corridor to the studio. He couldn't imagine how Jonni had come by a job like that. And yet he'd always known she had something special. He sat down on the floor to stretch and parted his legs into second position. She must be living in London if she was filming at Hampton Court. His chest sank slowly onto one extended knee as he clasped his ankle with both hands. It was strange to think of her being here in the same city as himself.

From that morning, he often turned his head as he walked through the West End, his eyes following the figure of some small russet-haired woman on the other side of the street. He didn't think of Jonni consciously as he did it; it just became one of the things he did automatically, especially on sunny days.

Michel was in the kitchen of the flat in Warwick Way. It was a Sunday afternoon and he was replying to one of Lynne's long letters from South Africa. The days when Lynne, Primo, and the gang had spent every Sunday creating mayhem here in the studio seemed very distant.

He valued the privacy of his evenings and Sundays at home but he was glad those endless weeks of sitting here alone were over. Looking back on his months of solitude, he was amazed he hadn't gone crazy.

"Dear Lynnie," he wrote, "another ten days and we are out on the road. The company is in pretty good shape; God knows it ought to be the way we've worked these past weeks. The new American girl is still a major pain in the arse; she's started contradicting me when I give her corrections in class. She even contradicts Charles, which sends him into convulsions, as you can imagine. I've never seen him lose his temper with her though—I wonder what she's got that I haven't. He's still a bugger with me in classes; anyone would think I was still dancing in the company.

"To answer your question, no, I haven't seen anything of Jonni since last March. In fact, Charles told me that she came to see me at the end of April but I don't remember. I do know that she's working though. She's doing a telly series with a teen idol called Guy Dakin—I don't know if he's reached South Africa yet but he's all the rage here.

"Talking of all the rage, did you—"

He put down his pen as the telephone started to ring.

"Yup, hello?"

A woman's voice, rich and mature but uncertain of itself.

"Is that Michel?"

"Yes."

"I don't suppose you'll remember me: Maggie Lane."

"Maggie Lane . . ." He searched his memory without success. He was on the wrong track; he was looking for a Maggie in the mental directory marked "ballet."

"A friend of Jonni's."

The fog cleared instantly.

"Maggie! Yes, of course. Good God, how the hell are you?"

"Unemployed, divorced, skint. How are you?"

He laughed. "I don't think I can beat that. Listen, Maggie, I'm afraid you won't reach Jonni here. I don't have an address for her but I can give you her parents' number and they'll be able—"

"I'm not looking for Jonni—I live with her!"

"Oh!"

It was hard to tell who was more astonished. From her tone it was clear Maggie had supposed he knew all about the Chiswick flat.

After a moment Michel was startled out of his surprise by a different thought.

"Is something wrong?"

"No, no, she's fine. She's got a marvelous job."

"I've seen the show; it's not bad at all."

Maggie sounded as though something had suddenly thrown her into haste.

"Michel, could I possibly pop into town and see you sometime?"

"Sure. It'll have to be this week though; I'm going on tour the week after. Let's meet for dinner."

"So long as you're paying; I haven't got a bean."

"With pleasure. I don't have anything else to spend—"

"When and where? Quick."

He said the first thing that came into his head.

"Da Bruno's in Eaton Place. Tuesday, eight o'clock?"

"Tuesday's fine, Doris. Thanks for calling. Don't forget the pattern for that sweater." And she hung up very quickly.

Michel went back to his letter, thoroughly bemused.

"Talking of all the rage . . ." He frowned blankly at the unfinished sentence on the page. He couldn't for the life of him remember what he'd been going to write.

Jonni laid Caroline in her cot in the living room and unbuttoned her jacket. She had left the pram in the hall downstairs when she came in from her walk.

"What did Doris want, Mags?"

"To give me a new knitting pattern. I'm going to meet her on Tuesday."

"Couldn't you just get it from her when she comes to clean on Wednesday morning?"

"I'm going to arrange to be out walking with Caroline on Wednesday; I don't want her to know that I never knitted up the last one she gave me. I haven't the heart to admit to her I'm a hopeless knitter."

Maggie started tidying away cups and glasses to hide her blush. This must be just like having an affair, she thought: getting caught on the phone and having to lie your way out of it. Acting was one thing—lying was quite another. She felt wildly out of control. Any second now Jonni might ask a question that would leave her stymied. Or worse still, Doris might phone up and offer her a new knitting pattern.

Once she was certain she could conceal her guilty conscience she brought two glasses of white wine into the living room and sat down on the sofa opposite Jonni.

"What are you thinking about, Jons? Still feeling miz about that article in the *Guardian*?"

"No, I'm trying to psych myself up to go over lines this afternoon."

"I'll hear them for you."

"Thanks but I don't know them yet. I've got to sit and swot for a while first." She sighed and lowered her cheek onto her hand. "That was a nice photo, wasn't it?"

"Every picture of him is stunning, love. He's photogenic, that's for sure."

"It's not that he's photogenic; that's just the way he looks. He looked well, didn't you think? Better than when I last saw him. Oh, Mags, I was so vile to him."

"That was a whole year ago. From all you say he doesn't sound like a chap who could bear a grudge for a week, much less a year. At most it would take an apology to wipe it all away."

Jonni cursed the tears which, yet again, threatened to well up in her eyes. For the past few months the pain of losing Michel had been getting worse, not better. Now the pain was no longer dull; it was sharp: sharp and relentless, stabbing at her chest every time she thought of him or heard his name. What did she want, she asked herself? Was it the old life they'd had together? That was gone for good; Primo had taken it with him. Did she miss Michel's masculinity; his protection? Surely not. Or sex? Well yes, okay—but that couldn't account for this persistent ache in her heart. Was she homesick? Homesick, she thought. Homesick. The word stuck in her mind.

"It was just that photo," she said. "It'll pass. I'll feel better by this evening."

Maggie leaned forward insistently.

"Jons, there's always something. An article, a chance comment from one of the people at London Weekend, a place you remember going with him, an old poster on the tube. If it's going to pass I'd like to know when."

When? That was something Jonni would very much like to know herself. There was nothing she could do about it. All she could do was wait and hope the pain would go away. It was too late to go back to Michel.

The article in the *Guardian* said he'd made a new life for himself and no doubt that life included women. He wouldn't want her now: her or her baby. She'd wreaked havoc in his life and now she was paying for it.

Maggie couldn't bear seeing Jonni so low. It had been like this, on and off, for too long. At first the new telly job had taken her mind off her grief but it had crept back slowly over the past few months.

"Jonni!" Maggie said, slapping the palm of her hand on the coffee table, "for God's sake why don't you just pick up the phone and call him? You can use Carro as an excuse if nothing else."

"Oh, I expect he wouldn't be in."

"He might be. He might well be. It's worth a try."

"I'm pretty sure he's away on tour."

Maggie bit her tongue. What could she say—he told me ten minutes ago he's not going on tour till next week? She steeled her mind to patience. At least she had set something in motion.

At eight o'clock on Tuesday evening Maggie slunk into Da Bruno's Restaurant in one of the expensive side streets between Pimlico and Chelsea. Actress to the core, she was wearing dark glasses and had turned the collar of her fake fur up over her earlobes. She felt like a spy. She also felt rather foolish so she turned down her collar and whipped her specs into her handbag as one of the waiters approached her.

"It's okay, thanks awfully. I'm looking for someone. Oh, I see him at the bar."

Her heart sank. At the far end of the long bar Michel was deep in conversation with a young couple. There was no mistaking Michel, even after meeting him only once five years ago. If his striking face and blond curly hair hadn't been so distinctive, his natural grace would still have marked him out as the object of her clandestine rendezvous. Drat the boy; what was he doing here with friends? This was supposed to be a tête-à-tête.

She handed her coat to the waiter and made her way between the crowded tables to the bar. The restaurant was a mixture of expensive London kitsch and phony rural Tuscany: marble tabletops, stucco archways, clusters of dangling Chianti bottles nestling amongst trailing vines.

This was a haunt for artists, she decided; working artists. She recognized her own kind in the self-consciously animated faces and strident voices which surrounded her. She prayed she wouldn't meet anyone she knew; especially if they were among Jonni's new acquaintances.

"Michel?" she said at last, when she finally reached the bar. "It is you, isn't it?"

Michel's face lit up with pleasure as he recognized her.

"Maggie! Yes, I think it's me."

"My God, you're even handsomer than the last time we met."

"Older and wiser, that's all."

"Wiser?"

"Well, older anyway. You look marvelous. Maggie, this is Daniel and this is Louisa. Daniel and I were students together."

Daniel knocked back the rest of his gin and tonic and set his glass down on the bar.

"You two will come and join us, won't you? The waiters can squeeze another two onto our table."

Michel laid a hand on Louisa's arm to prevent her adding her enthusiastic entreaty.

"Next time, thanks. I haven't seen Maggie for about three centuries. We've got a lot to catch up on."

Maggie invoked a silent blessing on him. Mind you, she hadn't realized she'd aged quite as much as that.

At their corner table Michel glanced over the wine list.

"What d'you think of the restaurant?" he asked her.

Maggie's eyebrows rose as she looked around, nodding earnestly.

"Oh, interesting. Original. The vines add heaps of atmosphere."

Michel looked at her dubiously and then went back to the wine list with a chuckle, which Maggie, after a few seconds hesitation, shamefacedly joined in.

"You're right," she said. "It is pretty ghastly."

"I'm sorry, it was the first place that came to mind. At least the food's good. Damn, I forgot that knitting pattern, by the way."

"Oh, don't take the piss, Michel. It isn't funny. I feel like such a rat."

"I take it Jonni doesn't know you're meeting me."

Maggie shook her head. "No."

When he had ordered the wine Michel sat back and looked at Maggie with a smile. She looked great. Fifty if she was a day and she still looked like a dispossessed Italian countess, albeit a little plump. Italian countesses ought to be plump, he thought. It didn't matter that her dark red hair owed its shine to the contents of a bottle; she was still the most naturally sensuous woman he'd ever met. But her expression of shrewd amusement at his scrutiny couldn't hide the fact that her eyes had lost some of the sparkle he remembered from their single meeting long ago in Jonni's Stratford dressing room. He guessed that life had dealt Maggie some hard blows in the past few years.

"You're divorced," he said. "That's a shame."

"Oh, I know." Maggie's eyes swept dolefully upward to the vine-covered ceiling. "He shacked up with a production assistant at the BBC."

"Then he's out of his mind. Believe me, if you weren't such a good friend of Jonni's I'd offer my services like a shot for revenge in kind."

Maggie laughed. "Be careful what you say. If I weren't such a good friend of Jonni's I'd probably take you up on it."

"I should be so lucky."

She looked into his smiling gray eyes. The extraordinary thing was he meant every word of it. For the first time since her divorce she began to feel that perhaps she wasn't old and ugly after all.

"Michel, has anyone ever told you you're an appalling flirt?"

"It's certainly been said. But I really don't know why; what's wrong with my telling a beautiful woman I find her attractive? Shall we order? The lobster here's great."

While they waited for the lobster they chatted about work and the general lack of it. Maggie wished he would ask her why she was here. He must already know, anyway. If it were left to her they could pass the whole evening without broaching the subject.

"Oh Lord," she said, watching him fill her wineglass, "I'm getting dreadfully cold feet."

"This should warm them. Is it okay? The eighty-six is usually very drinkable."

"Mmm, yes, it's lovely. This is awfully kind of you, Michel. Meeting me like this and buying me dinner."

"Pleasure's entirely mine. Now let's stop being so bloody polite to each other. I know you're dying to tell me what's on your mind."

"Shall I be horribly frank with you?"

"Yes, as horrible as you like. Tell me about Jonni. She seems well as far as I can see from the telly. She's lightened her hair."

"Because Guy Dakin's dark; the producers insisted."

"Is she coping with him okay?"

"Barely. She comes home from work fuming half the time; he winds her up something rotten."

"I bet she winds him up just as badly."

Maggie laughed but she didn't want to talk about Guy Dakin.

"Tell me about yourself, Michel. Have you got a girlfriend?"

He shook his head. "Jonni's the only girlfriend I've ever really had. Other women always seem to be passing through on their way somewhere else."

"Is anyone passing through at the moment?"

"No. Too busy. I've been working flat-out for months."

Maggie lifted her hands from the table as a waitress laid a shelled lobster in front of her. She waited for the young woman to go away before she continued.

"Do you still love her?"

There was a long silence while Michel tore apart a piece of bread on the table. Love was a subject he'd never discussed in his life, not even with Primo. He'd been asked questions as personal as this many times but he had always managed to sidestep them, usually by answering with another question. But Maggie had put him on the spot deliberately and directly.

"I don't know," he said at last. "I think about her."

"What do you think about her? Do you miss her?"

"I don't have much time to miss anybody but when I do, yes, I suppose I must miss her. I got used to having her around."

"You must have been in love with her at some point."

That was a hard one. "I'm honestly not sure."

"What went wrong between you?"

"I'm not sure about that either. I was surprised when she left; it was the last thing I was expecting. I haven't really thought about why she did."

Maggie peered at him determinedly, a little shocked at her own temerity.

"Then think about it now, Michel."

"Well . . . a friend of ours died." The bread under his hand was virtually in crumbs by now. "It came at a time when I was under a lot of stress at work. Jonni and I stopped talking. We stopped sleeping together. I suppose the truth is she needed me and I wasn't there for her." He looked at Maggie with a smile. "I'm a hopeless case, I'm afraid."

"Absolutely tragic." Maggie planted her elbows firmly on the table. "Now listen to the opinion of an interfering old woman for a moment, will you? I think you still love Jonni, whatever you say. All that noncommittal twaddle about being too busy to miss her just proves it. For pity's sake, why don't you go and see her and tell her?"

"Tell her what?"

"That you love her."

He turned his head to look at a crowded table nearby. A girl with a blond perm and deep suntan was gazing at him languishingly. He wasn't sure whether she had recognized him or she was just ovulating.

"That wouldn't solve anything," he said.

"If you ask me it would solve a lot. Women need to be told that they're loved. And you didn't tell her—did you?"

"Those are just words, Maggie. I'm not going to suddenly wipe away a whole year's separation simply by telling Jonni that I love her."

"You'd be surprised."

"It's just not something I'd say."

"Do you mean you couldn't?"

"It amounts to the same thing."

"No, Michel, I'm sorry but it doesn't."

The conversation had become uncomfortable on both sides. They didn't know each other well enough to be talking like this. On the other hand, that's what they were here for. They picked up their forks and started eating their lobster in silence, each following up the conversation in their minds.

Michel mulled over this obsession with talking about love that seemed to preoccupy everyone. If people loved each other why did they have to discuss it? Why didn't they just get on with it? He thought of all those times Jonni had clung to him in bed after sex whispering to him that she loved him while he pretended to be asleep. He could still hear the emotion in her voice as she whispered the words, over and over again, until he was so tense he could scarcely lie still. The mere memory made his chest tighten in physical discomfort. He laid down his fork. He had lost his appetite.

Maggie's perceptive eyes watched him with compassion.

"Michel, why don't you go and talk to her?"

"I don't suppose she'd want me to."

"Oh, for goodness' sake. I phone you up secretly and arrange to meet you in town. I sit here asking you whether you still care for her. I almost beg you to go and see her. Doesn't that tell you anything?"

"You mean she's spoken about me?"

Maggie rolled her eyes. "Honestly, you men are the most idiotic creatures. What on earth do you think Jonni and I discuss: knitting? Of course we've talked about you. She adores you. When your name comes up in conversation her whole body droops. She doesn't dare look at photos of you; they make her cry."

"Cry?" He frowned in astonishment. "After all this time?"

"All what time? A year! Michel, she's not just some old flame. She's wearing your wedding ring on her finger. She's your wife and she wants you back. Go and see her."

Maggie was delighted to see how dumbfounded he was. She thought she had been rather eloquent, in fact. Michel's startled gaze moved slowly over the marble surface of the table, looking for something familiar to fix upon.

"I didn't know," he said.

"Of course you didn't. The two of you are as bad as each other. I'd like to see you back together again. You should settle down cozily and have a family."

"A family? What would we do with one of those?"

"Whatever you like. Enjoy it. Will you come and see her?"

"Out of the blue?"

"Why not? Turn up one evening; I'll make myself scarce."

"Turn up one evening," he repeated. He was still dazed. "Where do you live?"

"Chiswick."

She scribbled the address on a piece of paper and changed the subject to the lobster. For the rest of the evening, over brochette of lamb and zabaglione, they chatted about restaurants and theaters and the shocking state of the Arts Council. It fell to Maggie to provide most of the conversation but she didn't mind at all. She was very pleased with her night's work.

Maggie was humming a breezy ditty as she opened the door to the flat shortly after eleven-thirty. When she saw Jonni making coffee dressed in nothing but a long T-shirt, she felt herself flush guiltily. She wasn't sure how to explain the fact she'd come home without a knitting pattern but it didn't matter; she could improvise something.

"Hiya, Mags!" Jonni called through the open door of the kitchen. "Want a coffee? How was your evening?"

"Yes, please. It was fine. You know Doris; same old stories about the Blitz."

Jonni seemed cheerful too. She rinsed out another cup in the washing-up bowl while Maggie peeled off her coat and draped it over a kitchen chair. Maggie looked up quickly with a frown. Why was there a man's leather jacket on the back of a chair? And why was Jonni making three cups of coffee?

"Jons? Who's here?"

"Guy. He's upstairs. I just came down to make a drink."

"Guy? Guy Dakin? What's he doing up there?"

Maggie looked at Jonni's half-naked body and tousled hair and knew exactly what Guy Dakin was doing up there. She closed the door to the bottom of the stairs and squeaked in a high-pitched whisper, her eyebrows nearly touching the roots of her hair, "Jons, what are you doing?"

"Don't you think it's great?"

"The man's a professional wolf!"

"I don't care. It's fun and I like him. Oh, Mags, be happy for me."

"But—but what about Michel?"

Jonni threw her arms out in a gesture of release and freedom.

"I'm over it. I've finally got him out of my system. It's wonderful. I don't give a damn about him."

"Since when? You were crying over him all weekend."

"Since yesterday morning. I woke up and I just knew—that's it, I'm over him. I must go back up to Guy; he's waiting for me. You've been nagging me to find a boyfriend for months. You should be glad."

"Oh, I'm glad," Maggie said nodding. "I'm glad." She was slowly sinking into an abyss. "I just hope he won't hurt you."

Jonni's face was a picture of joy.

"Don't worry, I've got my eyes wide open this time. Be happy for me, Mags, please."

"I am."

Maggie listened to Jonni's feet tripping lightly up the stairs to her bedroom. She was happy for Jonni—very happy—but she wasn't too happy for herself.

Michel walked along the corridor from the main studio after class. He was explaining a point of contemporary balance to Fiona, who was at his side hanging on his every word and watching the illustrative gestures of his hands.

Evelyn, the company termagant, descended on him like a bird of prey.

"There's a call for you, Michel. A woman; says it's important."

"Thanks. Can you put it through to my office? See you later, Fee."

He bounded off up the stairs. When he picked up the telephone and heard the distress in Maggie's voice he dropped onto a chair and propped his feet against the edge of the windowsill.

"I've been trying to get you all morning," she said, "but they wouldn't let me talk to you. I said it was urgent."

"They should have come and found me in the studio. I'll have a word with them about it."

"I've done the most dreadful, awful thing in the world. I'm so sorry. I'll never forgive myself."

There was nothing for it but to blurt out the truth in one long rambling sentence, heavily punctuated with expressions of remorse. Maggie was sitting curled up in an armchair in Chiswick, with the cord of the telephone stretched tightly across the room. She'd been sitting there all morning since Jonni, and of course Guy, had left for work.

Michel took the news calmly—at least Maggie thought he did; it was difficult to tell. When she reached the end of her miserable confession he laughed.

"Not to worry, Maggie. It was a nice try anyway. Tell you what; how about that steamy romance between you and me after all?"

"Oh, Michel," she groaned, "for Christ's sake, don't be so bloody nice about it."

Charles Crown looked into Michel's office a minute later and saw that he had just finished a conversation on the telephone.

"Good. Michel, I need you to give the English National a ring about those—"

"Give me a cigarette, will you?"

Crown hesitated. What had become of the chirpy mood Michel had been in all morning?

"I thought you'd given up."

Michel took the cigarette which Crown held out to him and lit it, not taking his eyes off the wall of the office.

"Can you give me five minutes, Charles?"

"What the fuck's happened?"

"Five minutes."

"Did someone phone you up and—"

"Charles, for once in your life will you bugger off and leave me alone when I ask you to?"

Put like that the request was difficult to refuse. When the door had closed behind Crown, Michel stood up and walked the five paces from one wall of his office to the other and then back again. He finished his cigarette, threw the butt into the wastepaper basket, made quite certain that it wasn't still alight, and then opened the door and walked down to Crown's office.

"You wanted me to . . . ? Matt, I'm glad you're here; I've got that sword from the Royal for you to try. Sorry, Charles, you wanted me to phone English National about what?"

There was a lot of work to be done before the tour started on Monday.

35

Jonni turned over groggily and laid her arm across Guy's chest. She was at the edge of the double bed and one of her legs was sticking out from under the duvet. Any moment now she was going to fall off onto the floor.

"Darling," she said, not opening her eyes, "did I have a lot to drink last night?"

"Hmm? I don't know, hon. Go back to sleep."

"I think the bed's collapsing."

"Probably."

Guy opened one eye and looked over her shoulder.

"I guess I'm either hungover or the pictures on the wall are crooked. Hey, sweetheart?"

"Yeah?"

"Sweetheart?"

"What?"

"We're sinking."

She sat bolt upright and screamed. "Bobby!"

"That'll do," the director said. "Cut there. I don't think we got your boobs that time."

The dresser brought Jonni a dressing gown and she scrambled out of bed and jumped off the bedroom truck. The truck had been built four feet above the studio floor on a massive hydraulic lift so it could be tilted when necessary. At the moment it was sloping at a very rakish angle.

Mark, who was the third director already to be in charge of the series, told them both to take a break for half an hour.

"Are we still going out this afternoon?" Guy asked, pulling on his clothes.

"The crew won't be ready at Hampton till two o'clock. I want to level off the truck and do the last scene of the episode before we leave."

Jonni wriggled into her jeans and accompanied Guy to the cafeteria.

When they were seated face-to-face across an orange Formica table and two Danish pastries, Guy reached for her hand. She gave him a secret smile.

"I don't feel up to all this swimming this afternoon. We should have got a bit more sleep."

"Are you a good swimmer?"

"Mmm," she screwed up her nose, "so-so."

"Don't worry, I'll rescue you. That's what the script says anyway."

"Chauvinistic crap."

"Don't blame me, honey. I'm a victim, same as you. I only speak the lines; I don't write them."

Guy had been quite easy with Jonni last night; no embarrassment, no apologies, no emotional challenges. He was just as easy with her now. She was certain she'd done the right thing in starting this affair with Guy. Who knows, it might turn into something serious but she wasn't banking on it. It was the perfect way to celebrate her release from the agony of loving someone who no longer loved her. So Guy's lovemaking hadn't been that great, who cared? It was fun. It was freedom.

"Say, listen," he told her, "I'm meeting Roly and Annette for dinner tonight; why don't you come with us?"

She shook her head quickly.

"I couldn't ask Maggie to spend the evening babysitting at such short notice."

The thought of having her new romance scrutinized by friends, and Michel's friends at that, was alarming. She hadn't got used to the idea of Guy as a boyfriend yet. It was far too early to think of publicizing it. And that's just what it would amount to; oh, not Roly and Annette—they were both perfectly discreet—but Guy's face was so well known people recognized him wherever he went. It wouldn't be long before somebody saw them and put two and two together.

"You're just being paranoid," Guy said, when she voiced her reservations. "We work together; people expect us to be seen in the same places."

Jonni hesitated. It had been so long since she'd seen Roly and Annette. Annette's infidelity had stuck like a barb in her mind. Still, that had been a year ago; a lot had changed in her own life—who was she to judge?

"Alright. I'll go and call Maggie."

"Good girl. I won't tell Roly you're coming; it'll be a surprise."

"Talking of surprises, you won't mention Caroline to them, will you?"

"Why the heck not?"

"It's . . . well, my ex," she said, her ears turning pink at the lie. "He doesn't want his friends to know about her."

"Jesus, you weren't joking, were you? The fellow's one real cold son of a bitch."

Jonni spent the afternoon falling off the side of a sinking barge in Hampton Court and then drying her hair in the makeup wagon so she could do it all again. There were long, frustrating pauses while the crew and actors paced the concrete wharf waiting for the sun to go in for the sake of continuity. By the time filming finished for the day Guy was in a foul mood. He grumbled all the way home to Jonni's flat and all the way into town, grinding the gears of his Jaguar.

But the moment he caught sight of Roly across the crowded Belgravia restaurant his bad temper evaporated.

Roly had phoned Jonni a number of times while she was living in Gloucester and she had exchanged postcards with Annette. But to see them in the flesh and to feel Roly's arms around her as he picked her up, laughing with delight, to kiss her made her ache with happiness. It was like waking from a bad dream.

Annette was looking radiant. She had just finished playing the lead in a West End production of *Helen of Troy*. The play had been a disaster but that wasn't her fault.

"The director was a wool-brained fop," she said disdainfully, reaching for the wine. "Honestly, that man couldn't tell passion from a smack round the face with a wet haddock."

"Hey, each to his own," Roly objected. "I've met a couple of very alluring haddock in my time."

Roly smiled at Jonni across the table as he put his arm around Annette, resting his elbow on the back of her chair. Roly's career was at last beginning to take off; he had a principal role in a tour of *42nd Street* coming up at the end of April and was already booked for a panto up north at Christmas.

"You look marvelous, Jonni—doesn't she, darling?"

"Blooming," Annette agreed. "Guy, my love, you must be better in bed than I imagined." She bit the end off a breadstick, ignoring Jonni's startled blush. "I'm absolutely starving. If they don't take our order soon I'm going to start eating the vines. Have the lobster, Jons—it's fab here."

Jonni looked nervously at Roly, afraid of his disapproval. Roly's blue eyes had narrowed in concern at Annette's comment, but when Jonni caught his eye he smiled at her. Roly was too generous to disapprove for long of anything that made his friends happy.

Jonni sipped her wine and listened while Guy chatted to Roly about life on the telly series. It was strange to see her past and present brought together so suddenly across the table of the noisy Italian restaurant— strange to think that Roly had been Guy's friend long before she had met either of them. She only had the vaguest recollection of meeting Guy at Roly and Nettie's wedding: an indistinct memory of a dark-haired fellow with a soft American accent, rather innocent-looking. But, of course, that had been before he became the national number one heartthrob of the under-twelves.

"So the director stuck two fingers up at the producers and walked out in the middle of episode three," Guy said, attacking his lobster.

"I expect it was your fault," Annette told him. "It usually is."

"Hell no, it wasn't anything to do with me."

Jonni cupped her hand around her mouth to stop Guy lip-reading and mouthed to Roly, "It was."

Jonni was so glad to see Roly and Annette, and so pleased to see them both looking so happy and so much in love. But it was painful too. It was so like old times, when it had been Michel and not Guy who had been sitting beside her with his hand on her knee, and when there had always been five at the table rather than four, that the past hung heavily over the occasion for her. It wasn't until her glass had been refilled many times that she was able to sit back and enjoy the evening.

"Mmm . . . oh my God," Annette groaned, swallowing a mouthful of gooey chocolate cake. "Ecstasy! That's absolutely the best thing about not being a dancer—fresh cream cakes."

Roly smiled at that. "Are you telling me you didn't eat cream cakes when we were dancing together?"

"Of course I didn't." She gave him a guilty, pouting sideways glance. "Well, only when you were nasty to me."

That made Roly laugh. "When was I ever nasty to you, Annette?"

She picked up her glass, looking at him with raised eyebrows.

"What about that time you lamped me? That was pretty nasty."

"Lamped is a bit strong, isn't it? It was only a light slap."

"Light my eye! You walloped me."

"Darling, if I had walloped you, you wouldn't have got up again for a very long time." He helped himself to a forkful of her chocolate cake. "Anyway, you know perfectly well it'll never happen again."

"Oh, yes it will," she said complacently. "Any man who can hit a woman once can always do it again. One day you'll get so mad at me you'll take a swing at me." She winked at Jonni. "Don't worry, I expect I'll have it coming."

At the end of the long meal, as Roly helped Jonni on with her coat while Annette and Guy went off in search of the loos, she smiled at him awkwardly, trying to sound casual.

"Have you seen anything of Michel?"

"No, not recently, chicken; not since last summer. I've left a couple of messages but he's been busy. You know how he is."

"You won't tell him, will you?—if you see him—about me and Guy."

"Of course I won't. Why should I?" He put his arm around her, his kind eyes looking down into hers in concern. "Guy's a nice bloke, Jonni, and he and I go back years. But you probably already realize he isn't the most reliable of men."

Jonni's wide mouth curled up wryly.

"I work with him, remember. Don't worry, I know what I'm getting into. I'm not about to get my heart broken again."

When she staggered into the flat, well after midnight, Maggie was sitting curled up on an armchair nursing the telephone.

"Where's lover-boy?" she asked blankly.

"Don't be nasty about him, Mags. He went home; we had a very long day and we both need some rest. How's Carro?"

"Sound asleep. D'you want the good news or the bad news?"

Jonni stopped dead and stared at Maggie; she was behaving very oddly. Come to think of it, she'd been extremely odd ever since last night.

"Both."

"The bad news is Caroline threw up all over your next two episodes. The good news is . . . my agent phoned this afternoon."

"And?"

"I've got a seven-month tour playing Polina in *The Seagull*."

Jonni put her hand to her forehead.

"Oh, my God! When?"

"Rehearsals start the end of next week."

It was almost too fabulous to be true but, over the next few days as they scrambled to find a nanny for Caroline, Jonni realized that the months ahead were going to be very lonely. True, she had her new relationship with Guy to keep her busy but somehow she couldn't imagine the flat without Maggie. Jonni dreaded living alone—Caroline was no substitute for adult companionship, adorable as she was. Jonni's spirits plummeted.

"Can't you come home for the weekend?"

"From Northern Ireland? I shouldn't think I'll make it home until we start touring England in June."

"Oh." Jonni watched her climb into a taxi from the step below the front door. She was holding Caroline in her arms and the baby girl began to cry as her mother raised her voice above the noise of the traffic: "Watch the bombs then."

"I'm more scared of the bloody airplane," Maggie yelled, and she waved as the taxi set off toward the airport.

Alone in the flat Jonni cuddled Caroline disconsolately. The deserted rooms felt terribly empty around her. Perhaps she should have tried to get a live-in nanny—but, no, she would have had to ask Maggie to give up her room and that was unthinkable.

"It's just you and me now, matey," Jonni said to the wailing baby who was dribbling onto her shirt. "Shall we phone Guy and tell him to come and cheer us up?"

The cat, Osborne, came and rubbed his sleek black neck against her ankles and she smiled bravely as she pushed him gently out of the way to carry the baby to the telephone. Of course she wasn't lonely. She was surrounded by life.

Guy wasn't answering the phone. Jonni hung up with a wistful sigh. Lonely—who was she kidding? Even the geraniums on the windowsill looked droopy and pathetic. She settled Caroline in her cot, shoved a Billie Holiday CD in the stereo and picked up a tattered copy of *Pride and Prejudice* resignedly. At least someone was reliable. Jane Austen was always good for a reread.

Michel decided to take his car on tour. The logistics of moving nine tons of scenery, seventy-one dancers, a full symphony orchestra plus their instruments, a physiotherapy unit, eighteen technicians, and a whole lorry-load of costumes from one city to another were frightening. He and Crown, along with the accompanist, John, and Crown's PA, Helen, drove up to the first venue in blissful ignorance. The move was the transport manager's problem. Michel and his passengers would have plenty to worry about once the whole shebang was assembled in Liverpool.

Company class on the stage of the Liverpool Empire was a nightmare. The stage was cluttered with scaffolding and flats. The dancers spilled into the wings, making do with winch handles and water pipes where there were no barres, while the crew and electricians, working against the clock, tried to maneuver around them.

Michel shielded his eyes with his hand and squinted up into the lighting grid high above the stage.

"Sorry, guys!" he called. "You'll have to leave it out while we're doing class!"

He was answered from the grid by a stream of foul language, but the overhead work stopped.

The dancers could barely hear the music from the piano, let alone the exercises Michel was setting for them. All morning, although there was no longer a danger of anyone being hit on the head by a falling lantern, there was a deafening cacophony of hammering and electric drilling from the dock behind the stage and, to add to the chaos, they were treated to disco lights as the chief electrician, banished from the grid, tested the front-of-house rig from the lighting box at the back of the auditorium. Every so often there was a shout of "Going to black!" and the stage would be plunged into total darkness for several seconds.

"I didn't see those last battements," Michel joked, during a welcome lull in the sound of drilling, "but I'll assume they were perfect. Don't worry, we'll get them to stop messing around when we get to the jumps. Now here's your fondu; watch closely if you can't hear at the back."

"This is disgraceful," said a female voice from the side of the stage.

"This is touring, darling."

"In the States you'd never have to work in conditions like these."

"Yes, I know; America's wonderful. Now will you shut up and fondu? We're already twenty minutes behind schedule."

The three days in Liverpool before they opened were bedlam. But by the time the overture started on Wednesday night the interests which had raged in conflict throughout the fit-up had converged: the dancers knew where to enter and exit from the wings, the costumes were pristine, the set was in place, the lights were focused—and all with at least twenty minutes to spare.

Hidden at the back of the packed stalls, Crown, Michel, and Marina sat anxiously watching the critics as they studied their programs. The critics were out for blood. They'd been waiting for tonight ever since Crown's appointment to the BNB and they had come from London in their dozens, anxious not to miss out on the massacre.

"Sweet Jesus," Crown whispered, closing his eyes.

"Amen," Michel murmured.

"And if that fails," whispered Marina, "there's an ad in this month's *Dance and Dancers* for three people to teach ballet to the under-fives in Alaska."

The first performance passed without mishap, and the reviews, which came out over the following few days, were grudgingly favorable. The critics admitted that the corps was looking better than it had for years, and most of them even reluctantly praised the production. It had been part of Crown's bargain with the Governors that his first ballet with the company would be a classical one and, true to his word, his production of *Coppélia* was strictly traditional. The critics who had come to Liverpool expecting a toy shop seething with lust and psychological angst went away disappointed.

At the end of the first week in Liverpool, heaving a sigh of relief, Crown returned to London with his PA, leaving Michel and Marina behind to keep the dancers up to scratch.

"Phone me if you have any problems," he said, searching in his briefcase for the train ticket Helen had given him only five minutes ago.

"In your jacket pocket," Michel told him. "I'll see you in Bristol if we get that far without a disaster."

The prospect daunted Michel. Practical problems he could pass on to the stage management, likewise any major breaches of discipline, but the real business of the tour—what took place onstage—was his responsibility and his alone. Marina could share the burden of the work but the buck stopped with him.

Things went surprisingly smoothly. The dancers were in high spirits, buoyed up by the good reviews. Barring inevitable minor injuries and a few tantrums, the vast machine of the BNB trundled successfully through the two weeks at the Liverpool Empire and a week in Bristol before it returned to London for a week's rehearsal and then moved on to Manchester and Bradford.

At the Alhambra Theatre in Bradford Michel sat alone at the back of the stalls watching the first act of *Coppélia.* The performances in Bradford bore a creepy significance for him. It was here in this same theater, just over a year ago, that he had last attempted to dance in public.

When the curtain came down at the interval he slipped through the pass door from the auditorium to the wings. Most of the dancers were still milling around on stage.

"See if you can lift the second half," he told them. "You were great last night; don't start drooping on me now."

"Is it no good?" Marie Gillette asked in her forlorn French accent.

"You were fine, darling. It's just the ensemble that's a bit ragged." He raised his voice to take in everyone on the stage. "Pull everything up a bit, okay?"

They mumbled assent as they wandered away sulkily to their dressing rooms. They didn't like being told they weren't wonderful. Praise from the ballet master was their food and drink; it was for him they stretched their feet and kept the beats precise. Ultimately of course they did it for the audience, but the audience couldn't come backstage at the interval and tell them they were doing fabulously.

Michel put his hands in his pockets and turned around to see what Lisa's loud American voice was complaining about now. She was snapping at one of the dressers, who was on her knees with her hand under the hem of Lisa's hooped skirt.

"What's the problem?" he asked.

Lisa made a gesture of disgust while the dresser patiently told her to keep still.

"This darned girl keeps on insisting on fiddling around with my costume. She was messing about with it halfway through the folk dance and she's at it again now. How can I concentrate with this going on? It can wait till after the show. I've got to fix my makeup and change my shoes."

The dresser looked up at Michel. She was a chubby northern girl with huge breasts and a plain, no-nonsense face.

"This hoop's broken, sir. Millie told me to tape it up." Millie was the wardrobe mistress. "You see, this end's sticking out."

"Don't call me sir, darling, my name's Michel. Millie's right, Lisa. I'd rather risk losing your concentration than one of the boys' eyes. Let her do her job."

As he walked away he heard Lisa snap at the dresser to darned-well hurry up.

"For Christ's sake," the girl snapped back, exasperated. "I would if you'd keep still, you stupid bitch."

"Goddamn it! You're just a common dresser; how dare you talk to me that way?"

Michel turned around and watched them while the girl finished stitching Lisa's skirt. When she snipped off her thread and climbed to her feet he took a hand from his pocket to scratch his ear with a smile.

"Thanks, darling."

"You're welcome," she said. "And my name's not darling, it's Sarah."

He raised his hand in good-natured submission.

"Thank you, Sarah."

As the two girls turned to march off in opposite directions Michel caught Lisa by the arm to stop her leaving. The dimly lit stage was empty now apart from two electricians who were changing the gels in a few lanterns and one of the crew who was sweeping the rubber dance floor with a wide broom. From the far side of the vast curtain came the hum of chattering amongst the audience. Lisa twisted her neck to see why he had stopped her.

"Don't do that again," he said. "Not in a company where I'm in charge."

"Do what?"

"The way you spoke to that girl."

Lisa's gray eyes widened in disbelief.

"The way I spoke to her? Jesus, she called me a bitch!"

"You can fight with her as much as you like, but on equal terms."

"You're mad because I called her a common dresser?"

"A girl with less sense than Sarah could have the union up in arms over a comment like that. I've seen full-scale technicians' walkouts over smaller incidents . . ."

"Aw, for Pete's sake, lighten up. Don't be so pompous and English."

". . . But that's beside the point; I won't have any member of this company spoken to like that. And don't tell me to lighten up, Lisa. This isn't an informal piece of advice I'm giving you here."

Lisa drew herself up to her full five-foot-four and looked up at him boldly from beneath her long false eyelashes.

"Are you giving me a professional telling-off, Michel?"

"That's right." He nodded, looking into her indignant gray eyes. "If this gets back to the company management I intend to tell them it's already been dealt with. Look in your company handbook; you'll see you're entitled to two verbal warnings and a written warning. This is your first verbal warning, Lisa."

He saw, through her thick stage makeup, that a scarlet flush appeared beneath her eyes and spread rapidly over her face, but he continued to stare her out.

"I want you to find Sarah after the show and apologize to her, okay?"

Lisa nodded, her eyes filling with tears. His hold on her arm had been quite gentle but when he let her go she raised her hand to her wrist defensively, as though he had hurt her. Michel stood and watched her run toward the dressing room she shared with nine other girls. She wouldn't get much sympathy there, he thought, and he was right.

Never had Michel met anyone who wanted so desperately, yet failed so dismally to be popular. Professionally he had to admire her; she was quite a dancer, as well as being lively and sharp-witted. It was just a pity she had the sharp tongue to go with it. It wouldn't hurt her to shed a few shameful tears—and he knew that's what those tears were for; Lisa was above pitying herself for his harsh words.

In the second act, Michel sat in the darkened auditorium and watched the corps perform their mazurka. They'd perked up a lot—good girls. Lisa was dancing with her usual strong, crisp technique, her face glowing with her love of movement, no trace of the mortification he had seen in her eyes fifteen minutes ago.

As he watched the girls' mazurka he found himself thinking about the last time he had danced on that stage—or any stage. What a curious spectacle that must have been. His recollection of it was hazy; he remembered a sensation of losing touch with his body. He remembered hearing the orchestra fade to silence. What else had happened? He glanced over the rows of heads in the stalls; was there anyone here tonight who had been here to see his humiliation? It didn't matter if there was. The public had forgotten him by now.

After two long, grueling months on the road and a fraught week in Barcelona the company returned to London for a brief season at the Coliseum. The Coliseum was the big one; the venue upon which their reputation depended.

At lunchtime during rehearsals, when the dancers had vanished to their dressing rooms, Michel stood alone on the stage of the Coliseum under the vast proscenium arch. His arms were folded peacefully as he gazed up at the tiers of empty seats and the ornate ceiling of the auditorium.

His pensive gray eyes came to rest on the top tier of the distant balcony. How far away this massive stage had looked from there in the days when he and Primo used to sit there as students watching the world's great ballet companies perform. The dancers had looked so mysterious and untouchable from those seats up in the gods. The youthful ambitions of every apprentice at the Islington Ballet had centered on the sprung boards beneath Michel's feet. This was the stage where he and Lynne had always dreamed of dancing one day. It had embodied all their hopes. They were going to dance *Giselle* here together . . . and *Manon* . . . and *Romeo*.

In a seat near the front of the stalls Crown was sitting with a folder of cast lists on his knee, watching Michel's face thoughtfully. The stillness of that solitary figure touched him. He saw a small smile illuminate the dreamer's eyes.

"That's right," Crown murmured under his breath, "you go ahead and wander through those forgotten castles in the air. Take a good look at them, Michel. They'll be there waiting for you when you wake up."

When the fortnight's stint at the Coliseum was over, the company was granted a three-week holiday before the start of next season's rehearsal period. Crown tried to persuade Michel to go abroad.

"Why don't you fly somewhere hot and just fall asleep for a week or two? You must have saved a fortune over the past five months. Go and spend some of it on yourself; you look tired."

Michel shrugged at the idea. He could fall asleep just as easily in the flat in Pimlico. But Crown was right, he had money to burn at the moment. At the start of the tour he had received a note from Jonni asking him to cancel his standing order at the bank. The note had been civil, nothing more, and she had given her mother's address in Gloucester although it was postmarked Chiswick.

Michel stayed in London for those three weeks catching up on paperwork in his office, going to open classes at the dance colleges, and walking in St. James's Park. He phoned Carrie in Devon and asked her if she'd like a new car to replace her beaten-up Morris but, no, she didn't need anything from him. Oh, except could he pick up a copy of Delia Smith's new cookbook in London and send it to her?

The summer rehearsals were to focus on Crown's choreography of a new full-length ballet. The musical score and libretto were more or less finalized—he planned a ghost story about a man who was haunted by his past—but the title hadn't yet been decided. As usual Crown's mind was teeming with complex themes he wanted to explore and ideas for new systems of movement. He had three months in which to create, rehearse, and stage the ballet, which seemed a tall order.

Crown agonized over his choice of dancers to create the roles. There was only one dancer he wanted in the central role but that dancer he couldn't have.

"What about Rob?" Michel suggested, when Crown asked his opinion.

"I know; I've thought about it. He's got the imagination and the intelligence but he's only a junior soloist."

"Since when did that stop you?"

"I have to be a bit cagey with the BNB. It's not like the Islington where I could play God and get away with it."

"You're getting soft in your old age, Charles."

"Who the fuck are you calling old? And as for soft, you can stuff that right up your dance belt. If I want Rob I'll bloody well have him."

Michel and Marina were in charge of putting together the other ballets for the autumn and winter seasons: Balanchine's *Prodigal Son* to run as a double bill with Crown's *Brainstorm,* which he had choreographed on Michel two years ago, and a new production of *Giselle.*

There wasn't much for the female corps to do in Crown's new ballet so the bulk of the women were at Michel's disposal. Three weeks into rehearsal he lost Ruth, one of his three Giselles, to an emergency operation on an ankle. It was the last thing he needed.

"There's Lizzi but I don't think she's anything like ready," he said to Marina when they were sitting in conference with the artistic director.

Crown rubbed his hand thoughtfully over his jaw, feeling the places he had missed in his hurry to shave before coming to work this morning.

"I think you should teach the role to Lisa."

"But she doesn't know the ballet at all. She's never done it."

"She's quick. She can learn it."

"Yes, unfortunately she probably is the best of the soloists." Michel looked at Marina. "What do you think?"

Marina answered with a glum nod; "Governor's right as usual. Her head will probably explode once she hears. Just don't make me have anything to do with her, I beg you. I can't exchange two words with that girl without wanting to wring her neck."

"It's alright," Michel said, "I can handle her. I've wrung her neck a couple of times already. She's wary of me by now."

"You wrung her neck without inviting me to watch? What kind of friend d'you call yourself?"

Crown waved them to silence.

"Lisa's not a bad kid. She just needs some teaching."

Michel raised his eyebrows. "Since when were you such a fan of Lisa's?"

Crown folded his arms and sat back in his chair.

"I wouldn't go that far. But you've got to admit she's got her good points."

"Like what?"

"Well . . . she's intelligent, she's punctual, and she can dance, to name but—"

"Them all," Marina interrupted.

Crown smiled grimly. "Yes, you're probably right."

"Which of the boys would partner her?" Michel asked.

"None of them for now. We'll have World War Three on our hands if we ask one of the principals to work with her. Just teach her the role as a backup. Once the ballet opens she can cover the other two women until Ruth's back on her feet."

Michel scratched his blond head and puffed out his cheeks.

"Okay, Charles. I'll teach her *Giselle* if that's what you want. But to be quite honest I can think of ways I'd rather spend my free time."

Marina smiled sweetly. "Like sticking your head in a threshing machine?"

36

THE JUNE AFTERNOON had become unexpectedly gloomy and storm-laden. Michel switched on the lights in the big studio and continued with the girls' rehearsal while the sky outside became black and heavy. The air prickled with tense anticipation.

"Ladies, can you try to settle down? Let's try the bourrées again without the music; steady and much lighter."

How could anything be light under the massive weight of that atmospheric pressure? Even Michel's voice sounded harsh and disembodied in the strange stillness which had suddenly descended in the studio. The dancers felt hot and sticky. The hairs on their arms tingled with electricity.

The cluster of twenty-four women glided across the floor making quick, tiny steps on the pointes of their shoes. As they moved, their toe blocks pattered against the wooden floor with a sound like falling rain, eerily preemptive, magnifying the silence of the dark street outside. The noises which drifted in through the open windows were distorted; footsteps on the pavements had a ringing echo, while the traffic passing the end of the alley sounded ominously distant and hushed. The impending storm was making the girls nervous.

Michel wiped the cold perspiration from his face with the back of his arm.

"This weather's giving me the willies too."

At last a massive streak of lightning broke up the sky, immediately followed by a crash of thunder. One of the girls screamed.

"It's okay!" Michel called. "Calm down! No, keep away from the windows."

Another flash and explosion and the inevitable rain burst from the clouds. Michel closed the windows himself and attempted to proceed with the rehearsal but the tempest drowned out everything. It was impossible to concentrate.

"Forget it!" he called, gesturing to them to stop. "Let's wait half an hour for the worst to pass!"

Lisa felt a strange excitement as she sat on a chair at the side of the studio to untie the ribbons of her pointe shoes. She had always loved storms. Nothing was predictable when the skies were raging like this. Normality was suspended; everything seemed possible. Once, when she was sixteen, she had been sheltering from a violent storm in a doorway on Fifty-eighth Street and she had been kissed by a man she'd never met. For Lisa, freak climatic conditions invited the surreal.

Michel walked over to her chair. Even with all the windows closed he had to shout to make himself heard from a distance of only a few feet.

"Come up to my office! I want to talk to you!"

She grimaced and made a sign to say she'd follow him up there.

What had she done now? She racked her brains to think of any transgression she had committed over the past few days. All Lisa's attempts to make friends with Michel had met with failure; he was too honest to hide the fact that she irritated him. He couldn't know, of course, how urgently she wanted him to pay her special attention.

"Are you frightened of lightning?" he asked, when she appeared in his office in answer to his summons.

"No, I love it."

He invited her to sit down and closed the door behind her. In this cozy room the noise of the storm was less intrusive and they could talk at their normal volume, except during the loudest bursts of thunder.

Lisa settled comfortably in the low armchair and tucked her feet underneath her. Even if she was destined for a lecture she was glad to be close to her cousin. His office, surrounded by the havoc outside the windows, felt isolated and womblike.

"I'm taking you out of that little solo in the second act," he told her without prelude. "Charles wants you to learn *Giselle;* do you think you can manage it?"

"*Giselle?*"

"Yes, *Giselle.* But don't let it go to your head; you'll be third cast, just a cover. I can't even guarantee you'll be put on."

Lisa was too stunned to speak. It took a great deal to knock the wind out of this particular young woman but his words had done it. *Giselle?* Her? Why, the biggest role she'd ever danced was the pas de trois from *Swan Lake* in her last year at college. Michel had broken the news to her as if he were asking her to run down to the corner shop for a paper. This was the kind of stuff which only happened in the movies.

"Why?" she asked.

"Ruth's got to have part of the bone removed from her ankle."

"But why me?"

"Do you think you can do it?"

"I don't know."

Michel shook his head with a smile. That was about the most sensible thing he'd ever heard her say.

"You'll have to sit down with a video for the next week or so. As soon as I've got time I'll start coaching you and you can join in the rehearsals behind Marie and Tatjana."

"Is Matthew going to be partnering me?"

"No, you won't have a regular partner. I'll teach you the pas de deux myself. The principal boys have all done this ballet several times; they can't be expected to go back to the basic steps."

She listened while Michel talked about the practical difficulties and the long evenings of work ahead as though it were merely a profound inconvenience to them both. Outside the window the gloom had begun to lighten and the thunder was sounding farther and farther away. To Lisa, looking from her cousin's clouded face to the clearing sky beyond, it was as though a hand had reached down through a temporary hole in the universe and grabbed her by the scruff of the neck. Life was giving her a chance.

"And, Lisa," she heard Michel say as he wound up his instructions, "try and behave yourself, okay?"

———

Lisa sat in her rented studio flat in Maida Vale watching the video of Nureyev and Lynn Seymour that Michel had lent her. The role was huge. Glorious and huge. She had called her parents the moment she ran in from the fresh, wet street but Mom didn't understand her excitement and Pa, as usual, hadn't been home.

After watching the whole ballet for the second time she scraped her yellow curls back into a ponytail and stood in the middle of the small room kicking off her shoes. With her finger on the remote control of the video she watched the first entrance of Giselle again and then marked out the steps with her hands. Over and over she watched and counted until she could pace out the whole solo in the narrow space between her bed and the sofa. Her body ached to try the steps for real.

The next afternoon, as she took up her position amongst the corps for an ensemble rehearsal, she saw Michel look at her and murmur something to Marina in amusement. Lisa was furious with him, cousin or no. How dare he imagine she was arrogant enough to stop turning up for corps rehearsals because she had been cast to understudy a principal role? She was so offended she couldn't get up onto pointe as the corps started their bourrées. She clumped across the studio in her place like an angry goblin while the other girls floated daintily around her.

Toward the end of the week Michel asked her how she was getting on with her video watching.

"Yeah, okay. I sneaked some time in one of the small studios to try a few things out." She laughed. "Melanie and Fiona came in while I was there; I reckon they thought I was getting kinda above myself going through *Giselle* solos when no one was looking."

"Why didn't you tell them you've been cast in the role?"

"I guess they'll find out from the rehearsal schedules like people usually do."

He frowned at her meditatively. She was a funny girl. Unpredictable.

"Alright, let's see if we can fit in some rehearsal time next week."

There was certainly some talk amongst the company when Lisa's name appeared on the schedules as a cover for Giselle.

"I expect Michel fancies her," Rob said to the boys' changing room with his usual flair for stirring trouble. "He's probably got his leg over with her already."

"I don't blame him. I wouldn't mind giving her one myself if I could tape her mouth shut first."

"As long as he doesn't expect me to dance with her," said Matt. Matt was the dispossessed Albrecht who had been rehearsing, until now, with Ruth. He would develop a hernia if anyone suggested he should partner Lisa.

On Saturday afternoon Michel caught up with Lisa as she was leaving the girls' changing room.

"Good, you're still here. Want to go over some of the groundwork now?"

She looked at him in astonishment.

"At half past four on a Saturday? You're kidding."

"I'm sorry but that's the way it's going to be. Evenings and weekends; I warned you."

"I was— Ah jeez, forget it!"

She had been going to say she was thinking of his free time, not her own, but she scowled instead and stomped off to change back into her dance clothes and pointe shoes.

Michel was impressed by how much of the role she knew. If she'd learned all this herself with nothing but a video for guidance she must have been putting in some serious work at home. Sitting on a radiator at the side of the studio with his arms folded, he watched her attempt the little jumps from Act Two. When she had finished he nodded to show she'd done well.

"Just a few mistakes; you've got most of the basic steps. What are you doing in the evenings next week?"

Her face lit up. "Rehearsing with you?"

"Take a look at the Act Two pas de deux before Monday if you get the chance." He unfolded his arms, standing up with a smile. "You know, you've made me quite look forward to doing a bit of partnering again."

She tried to laugh that off but there was no way she could hide the two bright pink spots his compliment had brought to her cheeks.

Being partnered by a dancer of Michel's caliber was unlike anything Lisa had ever experienced. When he was marking the steps at her side he was authoritative and reassuring. When he was dancing flat-out he was breathtakingly wonderful. He picked her up in arabesque and held her high above his head in a straight-arm lift.

"How d'you feel up there, Lisa—frightened?"

"Hell no, it's just like going up in an elevator. Jeez, you're strong. I feel like that girl in *King Kong*."

Michel laughed as he looked up at her: "Don't forget, while you're insulting me, you're at my mercy up there."

He lowered her effortlessly to the floor and off they went into the rest of the huge Act Two pas de deux.

Lisa couldn't bear to think that Michel was never going to perform on stage again. Watching him sail through Albrecht's taxing enchaînements, she was heartbroken at the idea of his virtuoso talent being buried forever in company classes and rehearsals. Michel was a creature of dance. His purity of line and technical mastery were God-given.

From her place in the corps during company rehearsals Lisa watched the tall fair-haired man who was directing operations from a chair in front of the mirror. Why, you could take him just as he was, body relaxed and hands curving gracefully as they described the movements to the dancers, and stick him straight on stage in the middle of a ballet. With his natural beauty and unconscious fluency of movement he wouldn't look a mite out of place.

Lisa looked at her own reflection in the mirror behind Michel's seated figure. It was hard to believe she and Michel were related by birth. She couldn't detect any direct similarity—sure, they both had blond hair but hers was much yellower and finer. And yet people had often said she looked like her dad and Michel was the dead spit of him, except that Michel's mouth was soft while Pa's was hard. Michel was better-looking than Pa had ever been too; she had to admit it.

She wished she knew what had gone wrong between her dad and Michel. She didn't understand why Pa had come to England so many times with the Los Angeles Festival Ballet without ever seeing his nephew dance—even after spending all that money on his education. And Michel wouldn't talk about his uncle. On the one occasion when Lisa had mentioned Jacques St. Michel's choreography to Michel he had interrupted her with a sharp instruction about her port de bras and she had never tried to renew the subject. He was real touchy about it. Pa was kinda touchy about Michel too. Perhaps there'd been some kind of quarrel. Perhaps they had fallen out over Michel's father. She wanted to know. This was her family and she wanted to be a part of it. Sometimes she felt as though she had no family at all. Pa was too busy with his work and his mistresses to care about her, and Ma had only phoned once to tell her she was filing for divorce. It wasn't fair. Giselle was the most important challenge she had ever faced. She needed someone to care.

Lisa wasn't the only junior dancer in the BNB facing a challenge that summer. Since Rob had been chosen to create the central role in Crown's new ballet he had become insufferable. He never left Michel alone. Wherever Michel went Rob hounded him. Each time he came out of a room Rob seemed to be just walking in. If he went to the library or the canteen or the front office Rob was always there watching him across the room with hostile eyes. If he was coaching Lisa in the evening in studio two Rob was in the gallery looking down at him with a knowing smile.

On Monday morning, when Michel was in the first-floor canteen writing changes to the afternoon's rehearsal schedule on a whiteboard on the wall, Rob sauntered in and leaned against the counter a few yards away. Michel went on with his task, ignoring him.

"You're busy these days, Michel—coaching Lisa in her big role."

"Busy with lots of things, Rob."

Rob's forearm was propped nonchalantly on the counter and his boyish face wore its usual derisive smirk.

"You think Charles has shown pretty poor judgment in choosing me to make this ballet on, don't you?"

Michel was still writing. He consulted the printed schedule in his hand while he wrote out the altered timetable.

"Actually, I recommended you for it. Not that Charles needs my advice; he's perfectly capable of deciding for himself who he wants to create on."

"But, of course, I'm not the dancer he's used to working with. It must be rather satisfying to you to know he's always comparing me to you in his mind."

"He isn't comparing us, Rob. He doesn't expect you to be me; he's got more sense than that. And it does him good to have to work with new dancers, as long as they've got the technique and the imagination to keep up with him."

Rob's ironic smile became even more blasé. He picked up a salt shaker from the counter and rotated it casually between his fingers.

"So do you think I've got the technique and the imagination then?"

"The imagination, certainly. Your technique's not bad. You've got a few . . ." Michel turned his head and looked him calmly in the eye, ". . . mental blocks that get in the way. You know what they are." He went back to his writing.

Rob shifted his position against the counter and watched him for a while gnawing a fingernail. Then he folded his arms.

"You think I could get over them if someone was prepared to coach me?"

"If you managed to find the right person; I expect so."

"You mean you won't?"

"I mean it has to be someone you trust."

Rob looked down at the floor, his face screwing up with the anxiety he had been trying to conceal.

"This choreography's a nightmare. He's so fucking demanding. It's like he expects me to be fucking . . . Superman or something."

"I know; I remember. Those first few pieces he made on me—the fear of failure, the continual confrontation with your own limitations. The feeling that every time you take a step you're letting him down. You aren't the only one who's felt that way."

Rob shook his head slowly in desperation. He was a young man urgently in need of a mentor.

"Please, Michel, will you help me?"

Michel snapped the lid onto his marker pen and stepped back to examine his completed schedule on the board.

"All you had to do was ask."

A month before the new season was due to open at the Coliseum, Charles Crown crept into the doorway of the ground-floor studio to watch Michel and Lisa working on her role. Michel was dancing in a gray BNB T-shirt and loose jogging trousers but he was still the *danseur noble* Crown remembered from the old days at the Islington Ballet. Michel seemed to be thriving on his extra workload: two or three evenings a week coaching Lisa and every other evening locked away in studio four with Rob—it was supposed to be a secret but Crown had rumbled it almost immediately; the change in Rob's technique and confidence was an instant giveaway.

Michel filled in Albrecht's variation between two sections of the Act Two pas de deux, spinning and flying through the choreography which he knew like the back of his hand. He threw in a triple *tour* just for fun. Crown rubbed his chin pensively—he was looking wonderful. And so was Lisa. She laughed at Michel as he collected her hand to lead into the next partnered section.

"Seven pirouettes! You big-headed bastard!"

"It was six—no, concentrate; don't lose your line."

"It was seven."

"I can . . ." he lifted her into a jeté, ". . . count . . ." he lifted her again, ". . . thank you very much."

Crown smiled to himself. They could have been made for each other. She was small and compact, balancing his long, muscular build perfectly. Their faces weren't alike and yet there was an extraordinary harmony between them—like two Christmas cards from the same box set; different but designed by the same hand. Crown took a step forward so his shadow fell onto the floor of the studio. Michel pressed the off switch on the CD player. His face was glowing with healthy sweat.

"Charles, you sneaky bastard! I thought you'd buggered off after rehearsals."

Crown gave Lisa a wry smile. "This is how he talks to me, darling, once the dancers have gone home. I stayed to talk through the designs for *Ghosts* with Russell. Don't let me interrupt; you two carry on."

"I think we've just about finished for the evening. Wait for me, Charles; I'll walk down to the station with you."

Michel was full of praise for Lisa's grit. She'd been working like a demon to catch up with the two principal women.

"I hope you'll at least let her have one go at it," he told Crown as they strolled through the alley toward Victoria Street.

"She's looking lovely. The role suits her."

"One or two problems to be ironed out but I think she'll be alright. I'd like to see her try it with Matt if we can persuade him."

"Is she confident?"

"Seems to be. You know Miss America; nothing takes the wind out of her sails."

"Still a pain in the arse?"

Michel turned his head to check for traffic before stepping out onto a zebra crossing.

"Only when she feels I'm disappointed in her."

"And are you?"

"No, far from it."

Crown paced around his office like a caged lion, puffing on a cigarette, while Lisa gazed at him expectantly from her seat in front of his desk. This was the first time she had been summoned into the great man's presence since the day she joined the company. Since then she had learned just how great he really was—and how volatile. She wondered if she hadn't been just a little free with him on that previous occasion. Like Michel once said, she had been trying too hard. Now she just sat and waited.

"How are you getting on with Michel?" he asked eventually.

"Great. He's been real good helping me learn the role."

"Nice fellow, isn't he?"

"Why wouldn't he be? He's my cousin."

Crown squinted as a cloud of smoke drifted into his eyes and rubbed the back of his neck. He'd been overworking recently and he was run-down. However, this was Crown's most productive state. There was a lot riding on his first creation for the BNB but that wasn't what was making him pace the floor in such agitation this morning.

"What do you think of Michel as a dancer?"

Lisa sat up straighter in her chair and her eyes shone. For the first time Crown caught a glimpse of the radiant personality she had kept hidden from the company for so long.

"Gee, did you ever see anything like the way that guy turns? Why, he makes it look so easy. And the lightness—do you know what I mean?"

"Yes, I do know what you mean."

"I'll bet he was something when he used to dance Albrecht on stage, wasn't he?"

"Yes. Yes, he was certainly something." He paused, not certain how to commit himself. "Look, Lisa, I expect you'd like to see Michel back on his feet—as a performer, I mean."

"I'd give anything. But I asked him. I asked him if he thought he'd ever dance again in public."

Crown stared at her intently. "What did he say?"

"He said he hasn't got what it takes anymore. He was smiling when he said it—you know, like he does. He says he's past it as a performer."

"Do you think he's past it?"

"Hell, no. It's all in his head."

"That's right. It's all in his head. Listen, Lisa, I want to . . ." He unclenched his fist slowly, searching for the right word, but there was no right way of putting it. "I want to try and . . . *con* Michel into dancing the premiere of *Giselle.*"

She jumped to her feet in horror. He couldn't do that! It was cruel to manipulate him like that after he'd been through a mental breakdown! He might have a relapse! He might leave the dance world altogether!

"Will you help me?" Crown asked.

She sat down again quickly.

"Anything. Tell me what I can do and I'll do it."

Crown had been planning this from the day he had accepted the directorship of the BNB. Lisa was the thing which had convinced him the time was right—Lisa, and Michel's undoubted improvement in spirits over the past six months. Even when Michel was at his lowest and Crown had been tearing out his hair at Nadia Petrovna's bedside, he had always believed in his heart that Michel would perform again one day. Now, with the help of this girl, he was almost certain he could pull it off.

It had to be Albrecht. Albrecht was perfect. It was a role Michel knew backward and he also knew he had been brilliant in it. Crown had considered a smaller role but it might be unsettling for someone who was used to large, concentrated sections of dance. Everything about Albrecht was right: it started with ten minutes of pure mime which would give Michel plenty of time to get over any initial stage fright, and it was technically difficult enough to give him the shot of adrenaline he'd need to get himself out onstage. It also had to be the premiere. A less high-profile occasion—less pressure on him—and he'd simply back out at the first moment of self-doubt.

"If it works and we can make him do it," Crown said to Lisa when he had explained all this, "your reward will be to dance the premiere of *Giselle* alongside him on the stage of the Coliseum."

She shook her head: a minute gesture but one that indicated a very firm negative.

"If I can get him to do it my reward will be to see my cousin, a dancer I truly admire, back up there onstage where he belongs. If I dance the premiere alongside him it'll be because I've worked hard enough and I'm a good enough dancer to do the role justice. If I don't dance the premiere on my own merits I don't dance it at all. Is that a bargain?"

Crown hadn't anticipated that. He looked at her with dawning respect and nodded. It was a bargain.

Lisa was excited and frightened by the challenge Crown had set her, but for the time being there was very little she could do about it. For as long as Michel would agree to coach her in the evenings she would work her socks off to please him, and the fairy-tale scenario of dancing the premiere with him stayed far at the back of her mind. She had meant what she said to Crown and she was determined not to be disappointed when the inevitable happened and Marie or Tatjana was cast as Michel's partner for the big night. Lisa was a romantic; the idea of being instrumental in bringing about her cousin's return to the stage had captured her imagination. She was only twenty; her time would come. She labored and sweated over her Giselle in rehearsals, inspiring Michel's passion for dancing to the best of her ability.

Michel turned his head to wipe the sweat from his eyes onto the shoulder of his T-shirt. That pas de deux had been their best yet—Lisa was coming on in leaps and bounds.

"Sore feet?" he asked, breathless.

"Yeah, ouch; just a little. Darned if it's going to stop me though. Want to see the hunt solo again?"

"Have you been working on it?"

"How d'you think I got these blisters, watching the video?"

"Go on then."

He watched her prance through the solo. What must it be like, he wondered, to hop along on pointe with enormous blisters to cushion her toes against the blocks in her shoes? Yes, she certainly had grit. Her steady technique had developed into a lovely lightness and freedom; there was a tremendous cheekiness in the way she flirted through those hops. But there was something else underlying her joyful energy. She had a definite fragility—not of body, which was strong and graceful, but of personality. It was most visible in the tragic Act Two pas de deux, but he could see it too in the way she danced the gay first-act solos. Lisa's Giselle had a deep vulnerability which begged for tenderness.

"Where the fuck's your left foot?" he said, interrupting her. "I thought that was something we sorted out last time."

Lisa was aggrieved. "Oh, we did and I've worked on it. I honestly thought I had it."

"Do that again, will you?"

"Sure."

She brought the offending foot under control by an effort of will-power and earned a grunt and a nod as a reward. Lisa put her hands on her hips and glared at him. Michel was never impatient with her but he sure liked to pretend he was sometimes.

She saw he was thinking of calling it a night—it was Saturday, after all—and she caught him by the arm in supplication.

"Can we try the first pas de deux once more?"

"Again? You really are a glutton for punishment."

"Oh, please. I want to try it for real; all the mime and everything, just so I can get the feel of it."

She thought she was pushing her luck but, to her surprise, Michel shrugged and pulled off the sweatshirt he had put on only a moment ago.

"Alright then; we'll give it a go. Bring a couple of chairs over for a bench. If you go wrong just make it up. I'll tell you what to do as we go along."

Ever mindful of her undercover mission she had one more plea to make.

"Couldn't we do it facing the mirror? Just this one time." She tilted her head with a pleading smile. "Please?"

"No, we'll do it facing the windows."

"But why?"

"There's no mirror onstage. Put those chairs over here, will you?"

Lisa resigned herself to a partial victory; she could make him dance for the mirror another day.

They went through the whole pretty mime scene; Michel chasing her, she slipping out from his grasp. He raised his hand to make the dance sign for a vow of fidelity and looked over his shoulder in surprise when Lisa was nowhere to be seen.

"Hey, where are you? I'm trying to swear undying love to you."

"Shit! Shit!" She ducked quickly under his arm. "Sorry!"

Michel put his arm around her waist and held her close against his body. He felt her stiffen.

"What's wrong?" he asked her. His gray eyes smiled down at her. "You're safe with me—keep counting: seven, eight: go."

He knew his way round this ballet as well as he knew the first five positions.

When they reached the end of the duet Lisa sat down to untie her shoes, groaning as the blocks pulled away what felt like half her toes.

"Is there any chance of getting in here tomorrow?"

"Precious little, not on a Sunday. Don't you think it'd be better to give those feet a day off anyway?"

"I'm afraid they'd seize up. I want to work. I guess I'll go to an open class in Shaftesbury Avenue."

"No, don't do that," he said. He didn't want her thrown off track. Lisa was a very impressionable dancer and Shaftesbury Avenue had some extremely flaky female teachers. "Tell you what, come round to my place in the afternoon. We can work on some of those solos if you like."

"Your place?"

"I've got a studio."

"In the house where you live?"

"In my flat."

"Oh, wow!"

"Oh, wow!" Lisa said, when she walked through the open door of the studio in the Pimlico flat. It was four in the afternoon and the light was slanting through the half-open blinds, making modern art of the plain white walls and wooden floor. "Did you do this place up yourself?"

"With a friend. Years ago."

She was pleased to see Michel was wearing dance gear. His face was glowing with perspiration; he had obviously been working. He strolled into the kitchen, leaving her to follow or stay behind as she chose.

"Do you want anything? Mineral water, orange juice—anything else if I've got it."

"Oh, whatever you're having."

"Coffee."

"Yeah, that's fine."

She swept her eyes around the hallway and through the open door of the neat bedroom before she joined him in the huge kitchen.

"Do you really live here—alone?"

Michel laughed. "No, I live at the BNB; I just come here for the odd evening and Sunday."

"Oh, why, you shouldn't leave that plant in the kitchen window! It'll die in the direct sunlight. Can I move it?"

"Eat it for all I care. I've been trying to kill it off for months. Its owner should have taken it with her."

Lisa carried the plant lovingly away to a shady spot at the back of the kitchen work surface.

"Jeez, you're cruel. How could you eat a poor plant?"

He laughed as he poured coffee into two red mugs.

"Spoken with the impeccable logic of a vegetarian."

They did a barre together for twenty minutes and then had a second cup of coffee. Lisa decided she rather liked the stuff after all. Back in the studio they went to work on the Act Two adage pas de deux: her last great stumbling block. Michel held her hand as she tilted forward into arabesque. She fell off pointe. And then she fell off pointe again.

"What's the matter, tired?"

"Don't know. I guess I'm just a bit wobbly. I'll try again."

A second attempt and she began to flutter nervously.

"Jesus! What is it? I've got the shakes."

Michel put an arm around her; she really was trembling.

"Try taking a few deep breaths. Feel any better?"

"Some. My heart's pounding."

He laid his broad hand on her leotard under her breast.

"Certainly is. How much coffee have you had today?"

"I never tasted coffee until this afternoon." She looked at him with reproachful eyes. "Oh, you bastard! You told me it wouldn't do me any harm."

After half an hour in which Lisa was good for nothing, she looked up from the sofa forgivingly. Michel was leaning against the piano smoking a cigarette.

"Do me a penance?" she asked.

"What's that?"

"Albrecht's solo from Act One."

He clicked his tongue. "No, no."

"Oh, please; just once. Please, Michel; I swear I'll never mention coffee to you again. Please?"

Nothing she could say would persuade him. She had to make do with being criticized, niggled, and picked at over her dying solo. Michel didn't see any reason to inform her that he'd been going over Albrecht's solos, just for old times' sake, that afternoon before she arrived.

At the end of their practice session Michel nodded in the direction of the bathroom when she asked if she could have a shower.

"Go ahead. You'll find a towel in the cupboard next to the sink."

"Wow! You're real tidy for a man," she called from the bathroom.

"I've got a Peggy who comes in twice a week," he called back.

When she came back into the studio, fresh and smelling of soap in ski pants and a yellow sweater, Michel was still standing where she had left him with his hands buried in the pockets of his tracksuit bottoms and his thoughts deep in abstraction.

"Say, that's a great shower. Listen, it's really good of you to spend all this time coaching me on . . . Michel? Are you okay?"

He seemed reluctant to be dragged from his reverie. Several seconds passed before he tore his gaze from the skirting board and turned his head toward her with a smile.

"Yes, sorry; I'm fine. Lisa, would you mind if I kissed you?"

"Huh?"

"I won't do anything else to you. Would you mind?"

He was her cousin but she guessed she didn't mind. She guessed she didn't mind at all. When she came obligingly to stand in front of him, looking up at his face in curiosity, he laid his hand on her waist and lowered his mouth to hers without further preamble.

"Michel." She pulled away from him gently. "I'm sorry; my neck's cramped; I'm not as tall as you."

He led her to the piano where he perched on the closed lid, bringing his eye level down to hers, and passed the hand he was holding into his other hand almost as if he were partnering her in a ballet. Then he closed his arms around her and pulled her to stand between his parted knees.

Lisa's mind emptied. She barely even felt the slow movements of his mouth against hers. If she were conscious of anything it was of his hands spread one across her back and the other over her waist, and the warm masculine smell of his body.

When at last he moved his head away he looked calmly into her eyes and ran his fingers over her pink cheek.

"I should have shaved a bit closer."

Lisa's legs felt even wobblier than they had after the coffee.

"Boy, you're a great kisser, Michel. I'd say you were one real hungry man."

He raised his eyebrows dubiously and then laughed and patted her waist to move her out of the way. Her comment had reminded him of a bowl of potatoes he had sitting in the fridge, so he took her into the kitchen and made her a potato salad, using low-fat dressing as a concession to her dietary scruples.

"Your Giselle's really coming on," he told her as he walked with her to the door. "This week I'm going to arrange some calls to fit those solos in with the corps."

"Let's do it," she agreed. "If you think I'm ready then so do I."

Lisa grew accustomed to Michel kissing her. He kissed her in the studios of the BNB in the evenings when he had finished his coaching, perched on a radiator or a windowsill to avoid cramping her neck. He never alluded to those kisses while they were working together—never acknowledged by a single glance, even when they were alone, that there was any intimacy between them beyond simple professional courtesy. It was only in the quiet moments at the end of the day, when the other dancers had gone home and the building was silent, that his gaze fell from her gray eyes to her lips.

"I've got a rehearsal with Rob at seven. Shall we stop a few minutes early?"

"Sure, whatever you like."

Lisa saw his kisses as an encouraging sign: an outbursting of his frustrated sensuality. It was a sign he was ready to dance again, she was sure of it.

Michel saw those kisses for exactly what they were. An abuse of his position and Lisa's vulnerability.

37

Two weeks before the premiere at the Coliseum, Crown called Lisa into his office first thing in the morning and closed the door behind her.

"Brace yourself, darling; this is going to be bloody difficult."

Her eyes widened. She had known Michel must be tackled soon if it was going to happen at all but she had hoped for at least a few more days.

"Can't you wait just a little longer?"

"No. I wish I could but the publicity department have been all over me for a week screaming for principal cast lists to get out to the press. I can't hold them off anymore."

"How are you going to tell him?"

"I'm not. I've decided to let him find out for himself; give him time to think it over properly before he talks to me."

He heard the sound of a door banging shut along the corridor and of steps approaching.

"Jesus!" he whispered. "You're on your way out."

Lisa jumped to her feet.

"Hi, Michel; I'm just on my way out."

Michel raised a distracted hand in greeting, not taking his eyes from the sheaf of papers in his hand. When she was gone he held out the papers to Crown.

"What's this bullshit, Charles?"

"Cast sheets for the three weeks at the Coli."

"I can see they're cast sheets. Speak to me. What sort of insane joke is this? I hope to Christ no one else has seen these things."

"Think about it, Michel. Think about it before you say no."

Michel looked at him in astonishment. Crown was serious. Did he think it was that easy? Did he think he could put his name on a cast list and transform him, just like that? Would Michel's name appearing on a typewritten sheet turn back the clock by eighteen months? He spread his hands in affectionate appeal.

"Charles, I can't. If I could I'd do it for your sake if for nothing else, but I really and honestly can't."

"Just think about it for an hour or two."

"Don't tell me to think about it. I think about it all the time. I've thought about nothing else day and night for the past year and the answer's always the same: I couldn't do it. The very idea of stepping out onstage in front of an audience makes me nauseous. My career as a performer is finished, Charles; you have to understand that. It's over for me."

Crown would have been helpless but for a quick glance he saw Michel cast toward the papers in his hands. He might be certain that he couldn't do it but there was something at the back of his mind tugging him the other way.

"Wouldn't you even like to try?"

"Yes, okay; to be honest, I'd like to try. I'm sure I'd fail but that doesn't stop me wishing. You know yourself that no dancer lets their career go without a wrench. But dancing in front of an audience isn't something you do with the prior knowledge that you'll almost certainly flunk it." He held up the cast sheet again, laughing at the preposterousness of it. "And a premiere at the Coliseum? Charles, you're out of your mind."

Crown had enough to go on. He decided to strike while the iron was at least tepid.

"Let's not talk about it now." His tone was deliberately abrupt. "Come and see me this evening once you've thought it over."

"I'm not doing it, Charles."

"I'm your employer and you've signed a contract."

Michel shook his head. He knew his contract had an "if called upon to do so by the artistic director" clause in it somewhere but there was no way Crown was going to use that to get him onstage.

"I appreciate your wanting me to do this but—"

"I said later!" Crown shouted. "I'm not telling you to commit yourself now. I've told you to think about it and that's what I expect you to damned well do."

"It's a waste of time. There's no point."

Crown grabbed Michel by the front of his sweatshirt and squared up to him furiously. "If I tell you to think—you think! That's in your fucking contract too! We won't discuss it anymore until this evening!"

Michel looked into Crown's dark-brown eyes, some inches below his own, and then slowly down at the hand that was clutching his sweatshirt.

"Take your hand off me, Charles."

Crown let go of him at once.

Before Michel left the room he turned back to look at Crown. His hand, still holding the sheaf of cast lists, fell to his side.

"Tell me something: is Lisa part of this scheme of yours?"

"Yes."

When Michel had closed the door behind him Crown took a handkerchief out of his pocket and wiped his face. He wasn't sure how it had gone but he refused to give up hope. One thing was certain; it wasn't easy manifesting nonexistent anger. He felt like a cheap cheat. It couldn't be helped; he'd done what he could. The rest was down to Lisa.

"Are we rehearsing this evening?" Lisa asked Michel during a break in rehearsals that afternoon. Michel answered without raising his eyes from his notebook.

"Talking, not rehearsing. Just you and me. My office, six o'clock."

She waited a few moments to see if he would say anything else and then went away to shuffle into her place in the Act Two ensemble, watching him surreptitiously through her blond fringe as she bent down to tuck in her ribbons. Michel had been unusually brusque and withdrawn ever since the start of class that morning. Generally, in class, he would look around the studio and exchange smiles with each of the girls in turn. This morning he had remained buried in his notebook, looking only at the girls' feet and bodies when necessary.

Lisa popped into Crown's office to find out, as far as possible, what her meeting with Michel this evening was likely to involve.

Crown was sitting at his desk, engrossed in the study of a pile of photographs. He glanced up briefly to see who had knocked so timidly on his door. Timid wasn't Lisa's usual style.

"How did it go?" she asked, almost in a whisper.

"Hard to tell, darling. Has he said anything to you?"

"Not a word. He wants to see me later in his office."

"Look at this one." Crown held out a black-and-white eight-by-ten photograph toward her. "Nineteen eighty-six. He was eighteen."

Lisa took the photo in her hand and smiled. It had captured a very young and free-spirited Michel in arabesque, with one long leg stretched out behind him and his chin and wrist reaching for the sky. He couldn't have been aware of the beauty of his line and the sheer dance quality of that posture. From his uplifted face you could see that the movement flowed unconsciously all the way to his hands and feet.

"Looks like he'd just won a trip to the moon," Lisa said, handing it back. Crown looked down at it again, smiling wryly as he recalled the day of that photo shoot.

"I remember, in fact, he'd just been clipped round the ear and told to stop pratting about and get into arabesque." He threw the photograph back on the pile. "Listen, Lisa, I'm afraid I had to tell him that you're in on the plan."

She laid her hand flat on her chest. "Jeez! Why?"

"Because he asked."

"Couldn't you lie to him?"

"No."

"But what if . . ." Her gray eyes darkened in anxiety. "Jeez, he said he wants to see me alone; what if he's real mad at me? What if he loses his temper? It runs in the family."

"He won't, Lisa, I promise you. If it was me you'd have something to worry about, but not Michel. He might make you feel like an absolute shit but he won't lose his temper."

Lisa stood in front of the closed door inside Michel's office. Her arms were folded defensively over her waist and her eyes were fixed on Michel's. He hadn't said one word to her yet.

Michel was motionless; perched on the edge of his desk with one hand supporting his elbow and the other hand covering the lower half of his face. He was gazing into her eyes, deep in thought.

Was he thinking about her? she wondered. Or was he contemplating something else entirely, gazing through her eyes to some distant place beyond them? The intensity of his transfixed stare unnerved her.

At long last Michel stood up abruptly, like someone waking suddenly from a deep sleep.

"Okay," he said, and he touched her shoulder abstractedly as he walked out of the room. A few seconds later he knocked on Crown's door and went in.

"Charles, I'm sorry. I've thought it over. Just the mere idea, the sight of my name typed on a cast list, makes me sick to my stomach. I can't do it."

"Are you sure?"

"Yes."

Crown nodded reluctantly, lowering his eyes to the jumble of papers and files on the desk in front of him.

"Alright. I accept that. Just do one more thing for me. Sleep on it tonight and give me your final answer in the morning."

Michel looked wearily at the man who was not only his employer but his closest friend.

"Do you really need me to do that, Charles?"

"We won't talk about it tomorrow. If you come to me in the morning with the same answer I'll drop the subject and I'll never raise it again. You have my word."

Michel sighed and agreed with a small nod. "Okay. If that's what you really need me to do."

Lisa lay awake all night in her bed in Maida Vale, trying to sleep, trying to settle her mind, turning over and over on her mattress wondering what Michel was thinking now—wondering what she and Charles Crown had done to him.

In the morning Michel walked into Crown's office and dropped into the chair in front of his desk. He looked exhausted.

"Alright, I'll do it if you want me to."

Crown clenched his teeth and shook his clenched fist in triumph.

"I knew you would! I did! I knew it!"

For the past week the company had been haunting the notice board in the foyer waiting for the cast lists to go up. It was the big question that hung in the air over rehearsals: who was to dance the premieres of the three new productions this summer? The biggest question surrounded *Giselle*. This was the prestige event: the Royal gala launch of the company's new season.

Things weren't easy in any dance company at the time of casting announcements. Someone was bound to be disappointed. At the Islington it had been understood that you kept your disappointment to yourself. Crown's decision was law; it would brook no argument. You were honor bound to congratulate the first cast heartily and take your tears home to the privacy of your digs—or if you couldn't hold out that long, to a corner of the changing room where hopefully no one would see you.

At the BNB there were ructions every time the cast lists went up. Sulking and tantrums were the order of the day. The two principal ballerinas, Marie and Tatjana, had been absolutely charming to each other all week, both knowing full well that one was destined to hate the other bitterly before the week was out.

That morning, when Crown strode into the common room and pinned three sheets of paper on the noticeboard over the Fire and Safety regulations, a crowd of dancers gathered instantly around him. Even before Crown had beaten a hasty retreat, Marie and Tatjana were staring at each other in stunned silence, their recent intimacy still very much intact.

The news spread through the company within minutes. In every corner of the building there were whoops of incredulous delight at the news about Michel, just as there were gasps of incredulous outrage at the news that he was to partner Lisa.

Michel shied away from the congratulations of the boys who surrounded him in the changing room before class. He had grown unused to being the center of attention. One thing, however, took him by surprise: the boys' handshakes and slaps on the back were sincere and enthusiastic, but none so sincere and enthusiastic as those of the three men who had each hoped themselves to be chosen to dance the premiere. The prospect of seeing a dancer of Michel's quality healed and restored to the stage touched something in them that lay deeper than personal ambition. Rob had turned scarlet with the effort of hiding his elation. In a few short weeks Michel had become his idol.

After Marina's class with the boys—a class in which Michel worked with focused concentration—he met Lisa in the corridor between the changing room and the canteen. Her yellow hair was tied in a ponytail and she was dressed, as usual, in ski pants and a BNB sweatshirt.

"Michel," she said, "are you speaking to me? I hope you are because no one else seems to be. I couldn't sleep all night for worry. How do you feel?"

Michel stopped beside her and nodded. "Good. A bit crazy."

"I'm all in a spin." She rubbed her cheek with a sleepy smile. "Real happy but kinda dazed."

"Well, you've made a chance for yourself. Congratulations. But listen, Lisa, no more secret schemes with Charles, okay? Not till the premiere's over at any rate. This one's paid off for you though. I'll see what I can do to help you make the most of it."

His manner hadn't been unkind and yet as Lisa watched him walk away she felt she had alienated him somehow. Her brain was ticking over very slowly this morning. When it dawned on her that he put everything she had done over the past weeks down to her own ambition—all her eager overtime, all her coaxing, all her efforts to win his friendship—she crouched down against the wall of the corridor folding her arms tightly over her waist and burst into tears. No doubt he even thought she had tolerated his kisses only to further her chances of securing her place in the premiere.

Dancers of both sexes walked past Lisa in the corridor, seeing her distress and ignoring it. They'd all seen her buzzing around Michel like a bee around a honeypot these past weeks, persuading him to give her special coaching after hours. Now they knew exactly what she'd been up to. If she was crying over some bitchy comment from Tatjana or Marie, well, she probably deserved it.

Lisa clenched her hands into fists and jammed them against her eyes. She felt miserable, mistreated, and humiliated but she must and would defy her emotion. "Come on!" she commanded herself furiously. "Are you Dad's daughter or what? Think, girl! Think about Michel. Get these angry feelings under control, Lisa, or you're going to blow the whole thing."

She took herself to the ladies' loo on the ground floor and locked the door, determined not to let herself out until she was prepared to see reason.

———

The thousand duties which ought to have filled Michel's every moment simply melted away. Unexpectedly a guest teacher arrived for a fortnight to give class to the girls. Out of the blue there was an offer from one of the great Danish ballerinas, crippled by arthritis and crabby with age, to supervise the run-throughs of *Prodigal Son*. The steady daily stream of dancers' problems and complaints dried up. Most bizarrely of all, costumes, sets, and lighting designs seemed to be taking care of themselves.

"All under control," the wardrobe mistress said cheerily to Michel, "just your costumes to sort out, duck, and we're ready."

"Bang on schedule," said the production management.

"Done," said the lighting designer.

Charles Crown had been wielding an iron hand. But despite Crown's powers of persuasion miracles like this didn't happen without the goodwill of everyone involved. The plot to get Michel back onstage had become the joint conspiracy of the entire company.

There was no way of knowing what was going through Michel's mind during the two weeks leading up to the premiere. He attended long hours of rehearsal every day without betraying anything apart from businesslike concern about the steps. Morning and evening, he traveled between his flat and the BNB in taxis, vigilantly escorted by the company's security staff from the building to the taxi door. The press couldn't get near him.

Michel seemed to have forgiven Lisa for using him to advance her career—or else he found it perfectly understandable. He continued to coach her in her role with the same even temper and patience as before. As they worked together on their partnership a natural intimacy grew up between them—except that he never kissed her now. When Albrecht kissed Giselle in rehearsals it was with exactly the same passion that he wiggled his fingers at her to indicate her arm needed to be higher in arabesque.

Lisa's confidence, in those two weeks of intensive work, was indestructible. She seemed to have nerves of iron and an ego the size of an elephant. No amount of criticism shook her composure. No mistake got her down. She breezed through rehearsals with so much airy self-assurance that very few of the female dancers were still on speaking terms with her.

If anyone was unable to control their fear about the premiere, now only a week away, it was Crown. He grew more irritable every day, his dark eyes watching Michel nervously in classes and rehearsals. In his state of agitation he had to bite his tongue constantly to stop himself lambasting Michel's technique. Instead he vented his spleen on Lisa.

"For Christ's sake, there are twenty-four women here dancing in perfect ensemble! Why does there have to be one person behind the beat? And why does that one person have to be you?"

Lisa laughed his criticism off lightly.

"Why, I guess it's because I'm at the front. Forget it; I'll get it right next time. I was too busy pretending to be a ghost."

The four rows of women behind her lowered their faces toward the floor and gave each other sideways glances through wide, dangerous eyes.

Of all people it was Lizzi—of "too colorless to make a soloist" fame—who found it in her heart to remain on speaking terms with Lisa. She too had a big challenge coming up in the premiere on Saturday; she was cast to dance Myrtha, the ghostly queen of the Wilis. It was a wonderfully grand and mysterious role, and Lizzi had the height and the long limbs to suit it.

In the changing room when the other girls had gone home Lizzi pulled off her tights and waved her free toes in the air thoughtfully. She was sitting on a low wooden bench wearing nothing but a cotton G-string.

"Do you think Michel's okay?" she asked.

Lisa folded her towel to stuff it in her locker.

"I guess. Charles says he's always real calm when he's working up to a big performance."

"I find his coolness a bit scary. Did you hear what happened last time? I read he just completely weirded out after the curtain went up. The paper said he threw his partner right across the stage. Jesus; imagine if it happens again!"

"It won't."

"Aren't you worried?"

"What, that Michel'll screw up? No way."

"No, I meant about doing *Giselle*."

Lisa looked at the other girl in uncertainty. She wondered if Lizzi was offering her the confidentiality of friendship. It was hard to tell; Lizzi could be very pally to someone's face and then tear them to shreds behind their back. Better not to risk it.

"Sure, I have the odd quaky moment but, hell, I'm just going to go out there and do my damnedest. What about you? You scared?"

"Absolutely peeing myself. I know I was only given the premiere because Marie and Tatjana refused to dance with . . . I mean if they weren't in the lead role."

"That's not so. You were given the premiere because Charles wants you to do it. You were born for Myrtha, anyone can see that."

Lizzi's expressive eyes appealed to her in anxiety.

"You don't think I'll get panned by the press?"

Lisa sat down to rub liniment on her aching calves, smiling sympathetically. There was no dancer so confident in their ability that they didn't need a boost sometimes, least of all Lizzi. With the premiere coming up Lizzi needed all the reassurance she could get.

"The press are going to be knocked out by you. Jeez, Liz, you're so majestic. I wish I had your elegance—and your nose."

"I thought I was colorless."

"You might as well know I got hauled over the coals by Michel for saying that to you. And what's more he was right. You know darned well what a good dancer you are. You're going to be an absolute prima on Saturday. I heard Marina and Charles discussing how terrific you look in the part."

Lizzi took Lisa's shot in the arm in the spirit in which it was intended. It had been a long unsatisfactory day with tears over her adage solo, which wouldn't come right, and frustration over the costume, which was at least two inches too short. Now Lizzi perked up and, in the best tradition of the theater, attempted to reciprocate.

"You've got such a lot of guts, Lisa. All the flak you take—the girls sending you to Coventry and Charles laying into you the way he does—I'd have fallen apart long ago. I admire you for knowing what you want and sticking to it. You must be chuffed to bits to have nabbed Michel as a partner."

Lisa laid her head to one side and gazed at the peeling lino under Lizzi's bench.

"Oh, I guess I piss him off some. My inexperience kinda shows when he's dancing with me. To be honest, I'll be sort of glad when this premiere's over."

"Rubbish. I can tell you're having an absolute whale of a time."

Lisa knew the voice of encouragement when she heard it.

"Yeah," she said, stifling a sigh, "I'm having a whale of a time."

Michel woke up with a sudden start. Something had pulled at the cotton sheet that covered his body, and he felt the mattress move slightly. When he saw the shadowy figure sitting on the edge of the double bed he ran his hand over his face and propped himself up on his elbows.

"Oh, it's you. I didn't hear you. I must have been asleep."

Primo folded his arms and shifted his position so his face was turned obliquely toward Michel, just catching the dim light from the window.

"I was very quiet coming in. You glad to see me?"

"Well . . . yes. I'm always glad to see you."

"Is very brave you doing this premiere on Saturday, amico. I'm lookin' forward to it."

Michel rubbed one eye with the back of his hand.

"It's only *Giselle* again. Nothing brave about doing a ballet I've done dozens of times."

"Yeah." Primo wrinkled his nose. "Easy. Funny thought though, ain't it? Perhaps you're gonna get out on that stage an' you can't dance, eh? Is gonna be quite a sight: the great St. Michel in a premiere at the Coliseum. Quite a sight you standing there in front of two thousand people an' you can't move a muscle."

"Don't think about that. I'll be okay."

"All those people staring at you. Oh, you ain't gonna be able to see them with the lights, sure, but you're gonna know they're out there."

Michel closed his eyes to shut out the image of Primo's taunting face.

"I've danced in front of large audiences before. This one's no different."

Primo laughed and it sounded unlike him: a bitter, scornful laugh.

"Everyone out there's gonna be looking at you, wondering is he gonna make it or not. You ain't seen all the fuss in the papers. Charles has been hiding them from you. They're all waiting to see you fail."

"I don't care what the papers are saying."

"Sure you don' care. An' you don' care what they gonna say afterward if you don' make it."

"No, I don't."

"An' you don' care if Jonni's out there reading about how you were left standing there like a baby in front of all those people."

"Primo, will you shut up, for Christ's sake? I'm going to be fine. Leave me alone."

Primo jumped to his feet and started to move around the dark bedroom. Now he was standing by the window, now he was pacing at the foot of the bed.

"You don' want me here, eh? You don' reckon you owe it to me even to listen to what I got to say? Great; Primo's out the way now; I don' have to take no notice of him no more."

Michel sat up and leaned against the pine headboard, propping a pillow behind his back. Yes, he owed it to Primo to hear him out. And if Primo's words were spiteful, hadn't he earned it?

"Go on, Primo. I'm listening."

"What you want to do this for anyway? I thought you liked your job. Hey, I'm glad you're havin' a good time. I don' want you should care that I died."

"Primo, please."

"You got over it pretty quick. And now you're all better an' you're goin' back onstage to be a big star. Is good, amico. *Buonissimo!* Forget all about Primo Vincenti."

"Why are you doing this?"

Primo was the picture of wounded innocence.

"What I'm doing, eh? I'm just telling you the truth. There ain't no point your going back onstage. Who are you doing it for? Jonni left you because you cared more about dance than her. And I'll tell you something, amico; she ain't never coming back. She's in bed with another man. So who's gonna care if you make it or not? Me? I'm dead, Michel. And your mamma don' give a fuck what you do—she never has. So who's gonna care if you become a big star? Who, amico? Tell me."

Michel threw the sheet aside and swung his legs over the edge of the bed. It was unbearably hot in the bedroom. He lit a cigarette with trembling hands.

"I'm only doing the ballet for Charles. He's struggled for months to get me back in shape for this. I can't back out now. I owe it to my partner to see it through, as well. She's worked hard for this chance."

Primo smiled and leaned against the window frame. With his back to the window his face was in deep shadow.

"Ah, *si*, of course. The little Lisa."

"What do you mean?" Michel didn't like his tone.

"You can't hide nothing from me, amico. She's pretty cute, hey? Poor Jonni."

"That's bullshit, Primo. Lisa's a good dancer. I don't think about her like that."

"I don' believe you. You like the way she looks at you as though she's gonna make everything okay for you. An' she's got a nice arse, eh?"

"I haven't noticed."

Primo snorted with laughter. "You haven't noticed. Okay, amico, have it your own way. Enjoy your premiere. I hope you don' crack up. I tell you it's gonna be quite a sight if you get out on that stage an' can't move. Don' say I didn't warn you."

Primo breezed out of the room whistling one of the melodies from *Giselle*. It was a tune that had been bugging Michel all evening. Michel drew on his cigarette and pushed away the wet curls which hung over his forehead. They were drenched in perspiration.

"It's going to be fine," he said to the empty room.

38

Jonni sat on the floor in the living room of the flat in Chiswick. She was holding a rag doll and making it dance for the little girl who was sitting just a few feet away, laughing and reaching out for the toy. Once she learned to crawl, Jonni thought, life would be chaos. The flat was a death trap to an inquisitive pair of grasping hands like those.

It was early afternoon on Saturday and the radio was blaring out pop music to keep Jonni company while she played with Caroline on the floor. She was no more used to living without adult companionship now than she had been on the day Maggie left, over four months ago. Today she felt especially isolated. Liane, her bright-faced nanny, had left her for another post. Jonni would miss her cheery chatter in the mornings. There wasn't even work to look forward to on Monday. Assuming the rushes for yesterday's filming came out okay, she had just finished shooting the very last episode of *Sinking Feelings*.

The producers had been all for a second batch of the successful comedy but Guy had other ideas; he was negotiating a major film role with one of the big Anglo-American studios. Jonni couldn't blame him; they'd had fun making this show but the world was out there waiting for Guy Dakin. She wasn't desolate; there were lots of possibilities in the pipeline. Her new agent said he'd had availability checks from several TV production companies; something would crop up.

She looked for her watch and realized she'd left it upstairs by the bed. Guy was coming to pick her up at one-thirty and she hoped the girl from the ground floor who'd agreed to babysit wasn't going to be late. Well, if she wasn't here when he arrived he'd just have to wait for once and have a drink. Jonni didn't like to keep Guy waiting; he didn't mind keeping people waiting himself but he was always bad-tempered if anyone did the same to him.

A Whitney Houston song faded out on the radio and the radio presenter told Jonni in her honeyed, sensuous voice that it was one-seventeen p.m. Sacrificing the rag doll to a good chewing by her daughter, she reached for her shoes.

"Are you going to behave yourself for Josephine, Carro?"

The baby gasped as if in amazement, opening her big eyes until they were nearly round and then gave her a huge joyous grin. When she wasn't teething Caroline was the nicest baby in the world.

"That's my matey," Jonni said with a wink. "I bet you'll be a bugger for her once I've gone, though. Shall we go and see if we can find you a snack? How about a nice piece of . . . ?"

Her words dwindled away as the soothing chatter on the radio caught her attention. ". . . And at the Coliseum tonight, for those of you with more conservative tastes, the stage is set for the return of Jean-Baptiste St. Michel in the opening of the British National Ballet's *Giselle* after a week of intense media speculation about his long absence from performing. He was my guest a couple of years ago on my breakfast show, and what an irresistible charmer he is. So good luck for tonight and if you're listening, Michel, this is for you . . ."

Jonni scooped Caroline up in her arms and switched off the radio as an introduction to a song on slide guitar began to play.

"Stupid," she snapped in irritation. "Michel doesn't like Country and Western anyway."

Michel didn't hear the good wishes of the radio presenter. He was working his way through a very unsatisfactory class in the big studio at the BNB.

Halfway through the first floor-work allegro he threw up his hand in a gesture of frustrated defeat and walked away to the back of the studio to prop his elbows on a windowsill and bury his fingers in his hair.

Charles Crown's sharp eyes followed him. He let the other boys finish the exercise and then snapped his fingers briskly.

"Come on, Michel, let's see you do it. Crisp beats on all the brisés volés and good clean feet on the sixes."

Michel fixed his gaze on a block of reinforced concrete which was being lifted by a crane on the building site across the road. "I can't do it, Charles. I can't give you what you want."

"All I want from you, son, is that you do as you're told. Juan, David, Yuri; you three do the exercise again with him. Better feet, all of you."

If Michel hadn't already been stiff with tension the anxiety of the other boys would have seen to it that he soon was. Every eye was turned nervously toward him. "Jesus, he's losing it," one of the corps whispered under his breath to Rob.

"No, he fucking isn't," Rob whispered back more savagely than he intended to.

"Alright," said Crown at the end of the exercise. "I've seen you all do those steps better but we'll pass on."

At the end of class Crown walked over to stand beside Michel. Michel was leaning over the barre with his face buried in his folded arms, breathing quickly.

"Too fast," Crown said. "Slower and deeper." Michel stood up with his eyes closed and put his hands on his hips, focusing on his diaphragm. Gradually his chest stopped heaving and his waist began to expand and contract steadily. When he opened his eyes Crown was still beside him.

"Are you alright?"

"Yeah. Crap class; sorry."

"It was fine, Michel, fine. What do you want to do now? You're a bit pale. I should eat something if I were you."

"Yes, I will. How were the girls this morning?"

"Not bad. Lizzi was a bit highly strung; cried over her fouettés: couldn't get them going."

"There aren't any fouettés in Myrtha."

"No, but she took it as a bad omen; you know what she's like. It was my fault; I shouldn't have set the girls fouettés this morning. Lisa did a storming class. She's raring to go. You were right about her grit."

Michel rubbed his eyes.

"I'm sorry I couldn't get those sautés together after the—"

"Forget class," Crown interrupted. "Put it behind you. Think about how you're going to spend the time between now and seven-thirty this evening. What time are you going over to the Coli?"

"I think I'll wander over now."

"I'll get Evelyn to call a cab. I'll come with you."

"I fancy the walk if you don't mind. I'll go through the park and get some lunch on the way."

Crown nodded. "Go out the back way and get one of the security guys to walk up to Buckingham Palace with you." If Michel wanted to be alone he was better being alone out in the sunshine than cooped up either here or in the theater. "And for Christ's sake don't get run over," he called after him as he walked away.

Michel stooped to pick up his sweatshirt from under the barre and draped it over his shoulder, shaking his head slowly as he headed for the door.

"That's the least of my worries," he said.

In the plush dressing room backstage at the Coliseum, Michel stretched out on the floor and tried to relax. The dressing-room window was propped open and the afternoon sunshine sloping across the echoing Charing Cross alleyway outside was refreshing and optimistic. He had turned down the Tannoy to shut out the threatening presence of the enormous, historic stage. Technicians and wardrobe staff clattered along the corridor outside his dressing-room door. Musicians whistled as they strolled past. Dancers twittered about the premiere as they walked between the dressing rooms and the luxurious green room. The Coliseum was like a self-contained city within the heart of London.

Michel heard the resonant voices of several of the girls' corps in the corridor.

"There'll be a right to-do if he doesn't make it."

"What'll Charles do?"

"He's got Tatjana and Matt lined up in costume in their dressing rooms, just in case. Marina's all set to bung them on if the worst comes to the worst."

"Hey, Mel, Fiona!" Michel called out. "Guess where the principal boys' dressing room is!"

There was a murmur of whispered curses and then a tap on the door.

"Michel, are you in here?"

"Yup, come in."

They poked their heads round the door, shamefaced, and saw him lying flat on his back on the carpet with his eyes closed. Mel came to kneel beside him, leaning over him on her hands and knees with her hands beside his shoulders.

"Sorry, I'm a prat. I know you'll be fab; I was just jawing."

Michel reached up to feel for her face.

"Don't worry. Give me a kiss and go and be nice to Lisa."

"She doesn't need being nice to. She's cocky as hell." But she willingly granted his other request and then went away, shooing the other girls out of the room in front of her.

Michel sat up reluctantly as the phone on his dressing table started ringing.

"Yup," he muttered into the receiver. It was Roly.

"Shel! How are you doing? All set for the big one?"

Michel scraped his hand through his hair. "I'm as sick as a pig. I've got the shits and I've been puking up all afternoon. Can't work out which end to point at the loo. Oh, and I think I've just had a coronary."

"Jolly good. Glad to hear you're flying fit. Listen, do you want company?"

"No, I'm better on my own. Where are you?"

"Leeds, unfortunately."

Michel puffed out his cheeks in relief. "Thank Christ for that. I thought you were about to announce you were coming to the show."

"Can't. No chance of getting away from the theater in time. I just spoke to Nettie. She's got a tech for the new play this evening but she sends her love. And I got a postcard from Lynne. She said she'd heard you were going back on; asked me to send you a hug."

"Miserable cow," Michel said, with a grim smile. "She could've sent me a card as well."

"Oh, you know how it is. She's cracking away at *Swan Lake*—did you see the review in *The Dancing Times*?"

"Yes, I must send her congratulations; you're right. I've been so busy doing this thing. Have you heard anything from the others: Daniel and Louisa and the rest of the Islington gang?"

"Not much. I saw Dan at an open class in Shaftesbury Avenue; he's got his fingers crossed for you tonight."

"I need it."

"You'll be fine. Nothing'll go wrong."

"I don't know, Roly. I really don't know. Christ, the thought of that auditorium stuffed with people all waiting to see me fall apart."

"Oh, bollocks! Just get out there and give it your best shot. If you forget what you're doing, make it up. By all accounts this kid you're partnering's got the common sense to busk it if there's a shaky moment or two. Give her a kiss from me, by the way."

Listening to Roly's confident voice Michel began to feel slightly better. He sat down on the chair in front of his dressing table and tried to coax himself into a smile. God knows, he'd done enough *Giselles* in the past, and with far less reliable partners than Lisa. He could get the better of this terror. Once in his life, and only once, he had gone out onstage and lost his nerve. There was no reason why it should happen again tonight. What was it Roly always used to say about his own first-night nerves? More risk is more life.

"What are you going to do now?" Roly asked.

Michel looked at his watch. Quarter past five.

"I don't know. Try and rest, I think. Maybe do a barre."

"Leave yourself plenty of time to get ready, Shel. The last thing you want is to end up in a rush to get your makeup and kit on. I bet you need a shave."

Michel ran his trembling hand over his jaw. Yes, he did; Roly was right. That was the problem with so rarely looking in mirrors; it was easy to forget things like that.

When the receiver was back on the hook he riffled through his washbag for his razor and went to the basin to cover his face with shaving foam. As he fixed a new blade into the razor with unsteady hands, something made him glance in the mirror at the reflection of the room behind him. Primo was standing leaning against the dressing-room door with his arms folded, watching him.

"Hey, amico, you din' think I was goin' to let you go on tonight without comin' to wish you luck, did you?"

Michel stared at the shadowy figure in the mirror. After a long silence Primo's mouth curled into a knowing smile.

"*Si,* you're right, amico. That's the only way you're gonna get out of doin' this tonight; there ain't no other way."

"What way?"

Primo nodded toward the razor in Michel's hand. Michel looked down at it, his face falling gradually, appalled.

"Christ, I was shaving! That's all: shaving!"

"It ain't so bad. I did it."

"Yes, and you fucked up a lot of people's lives."

"You just got to make sure you do it the right way. You remember you looked and saw how I done it? You wanted to do it then, didn't you?"

"I'd never do it; never. Think what it'd do to Charles. Get out of here!"

Primo held up his hands to pacify Michel, laughing off his friend's agitation.

"I was jokin', amico. Sure, you got work to do. You gotta shave an' put on your makeup. Then you gotta do a barre an' get into your costume. An' all the time you're gonna be shaking like a jelly coz you ain't gonna know if you're gonna make it till the moment you get out on that stage. Is true, isn't it? There's no way you're gonna know."

Crown didn't see Michel before he went out to the front of house to meet the sponsors. They had a shouted conversation through the door of the en-suite bathroom in the dressing room.

"How do you feel?" he yelled. He was relieved not to have a face-to-face meeting with Michel at the moment; he didn't want Michel to see how petrified he was.

"Coping, thanks!"

"Right. Best of luck then!"

"Thanks. I'll see you after the show!"

"Not if I see you first!"

It was as well Crown didn't hear Michel's gentle repetition of the word "if" tacked on to the end of his parting comment. It was also as well he hadn't seen the blank terror on the face of his leading man, who had just thrown up yet again.

Lisa came into the dressing room a few minutes later and found Michel sitting in a low armchair staring at the floor. He was very far from being ready to go onstage, dressed only in white tights held up to his armpits with elastic braces.

"Michel, shouldn't you be getting your face on? It's half past six."

She was already made-up and her hair was tied on top of her head with an ingenious squishy invention which would allow her to release it with one tug during the mad scene. She looked fresh and lovely, even in her old blue dressing gown, and if she was pale it wasn't visible under all that foundation.

"Gee, what happened to your cheek?" she asked.

Michel looked up and gave her his best attempt at a smile.

"Cut myself shaving. It's just a nick. Bled a lot, though."

"You okay?"

"Fine. How about you?"

Lisa didn't answer. Instead she sat on his knee and buried her face in his neck. Michel put his arms around her and rested his cheek against her blond head, closing his eyes.

"We're going to be great," Lisa whispered. "Really the best."

He stroked her arm and whispered encouraging words in his turn while she nestled against him, forgetful of her false eyelashes.

"Michel, you're shaking a little."

"Uh-huh, I'm nervous a little."

"Me, I don't know if I'm nervous or not. I just feel cold; frozen like an ice pack. Right now I'd rather spend the evening here than go out there and face all those people."

Michel drew his arms closer around her and kissed her forehead.

"That's from my friend Roly," he said, and she lifted her face to smile at him.

"Sweet of him, whoever he is."

"And this is from me."

Michel tasted of strong mouthwash and fear.

———

When Lisa had gone to repair her makeup and perform cabalistic rituals over her shoes, Michel lowered himself onto the chair at the dressing table and opened his makeup box for the first time in nearly a year and a half.

He forced himself to look at his reflection in the mirror and he was startled by what he saw. Surely those frigid gray eyes, the color of steel, couldn't be his eyes. His face looked unmasculine; spineless; weak. Did that quivering mouth belong to him?

His hand shook as he rubbed a damp sponge over a dried-up block of pancake foundation. Always his mind was on the great gulf of the proscenium arch which he must face within the hour or spend the rest of his life wondering if he could have done it or not. That wouldn't be a life worth living. He would fail if he must but he would fail making the attempt. It would be a tough end to Lisa's first crack at glory, but there it was; it couldn't be helped.

It felt strange to be covering his face with foundation and drawing brown lines around his eyes. There must be a knack to eyeliner; if there was he'd definitely lost it. Time was, when Michel had sat at any dressing table in any theater and thrown all this stuff on his face without giving it a moment's thought. Today he felt as peculiar as he had at the dress-run on Thursday when he'd first pulled on a pair of white tights. He thought of the millions of men out there who would find the idea of wearing tights and mascara preposterous. For once it seemed preposterous to Michel too.

When his makeup was done—and well done; it was like riding a bike, he decided—his dresser came to fasten him into his tunic. It was short-waisted, black and gold, tailored to fit him perfectly. It seemed excessive to have gone to all that work and expense for a garment that would appear on stage for no more than a minute. At the Islington he had been used to dancing in any old tunic that could be altered to make it wearable. One that was made to measure was an absolute luxury.

"Have you got the quick-change tunic?" he asked the dresser.

"Yeah, yeah. It'll be there, and me too." The girl didn't like the implication that she didn't know her job. But then, she supposed he wouldn't be a dancer if he didn't fuss about his cos'ies. "I've got the cloak an' all. D'you want to take it with you or shall I bring it onstage at Beginners?"

Her bland "just another show" air was reassuring for Michel. If she had been one of the BNB's dressers, buzzing round him full of a sense of occasion, he'd have hated to have her with him now. As it was, she was dull but efficient. If she had noticed that he was really a very handsome man, she didn't show it. And if she had noticed that he was limp with terror, she didn't show that either.

Lisa stood in the cavernous wings gripping a portable barre as she shuffled her feet in a tray of rosin. She stepped out of the powder, which crunched beneath her shoes, and pummeled the ground with her pointes like a horse impatiently waiting to be led out to the paddock. Dancers milled quietly around her, stretching their limbs and hitching up their tights as they thought of the ordeal that lay ahead. The first night of a new production was nerve-racking for everyone.

Through the open door to the prompt-side corridor she heard the quiet booming of a Tannoy as the half hour was called. Any minute now the massive red tabs would come down to cover the front of the stage before the house was opened to the audience. Lisa decided to take one last look at the challenge that lay before her.

She had danced on this stage before in the corps of *Coppélia* in May. Now as she stood on the rubber floor between the great chunks of scenery, she gazed up at the distant rows of seats in the galleries. All those seats would be filled within the next thirty minutes. Filled with two thousand people—four thousand critical eyes—all staring straight at her. No Michel to click his tongue and tell her, "Take that adage from the start again; it was all over the place." In the past she'd been content to get it right second or third attempt. There were no second chances tonight. No one was going to make allowances.

The chief electrician up in the box was checking each of the lamps in turn before the show. He flicked the switch marked "red-38" and Lisa was picked out on the stage by a sharply focused spotlight. A voice from the flies shouted, "Heads on stage!" and the heavy crimson curtain rolled slowly down, snapping out the light as it crossed the path of its beam.

———

The dresser tugged on the folds of Michel's tunic as she tried to fasten the row of hooks down the back. Beyond the frosted-glass window, half-open to let in the air, the evening was still bright and golden.

"Keep still a sec; I can't do 'em up."

"Sorry."

"So who are you playing in this, then?"

"A nobleman—a duke, I think. I disguise myself as a peasant to seduce the heroine. She kills herself with my sword at the end of Act One when my fiancée turns up."

"Nasty. D'you actually have it off with her before she does herself in?"

"History doesn't relate. Can you put it on the second row of hooks? I need more room at the top; sorry to be a pain."

"Yeah, okay. So if she's dead by the interval, what are all the white frocks in Act Two?"

"Ghosts who get revenge on men by dancing them to death."

"Nice one. Do they get you, then?"

The dresser was doing her bit by keeping him talking. At least it would keep the poor love's teeth from chattering.

There was a hurried knock and the door opened before Michel had time to answer it. The stage manager thrust a tense face into the room.

"Michel, can you come? We've got problems."

"Problems?"

"Lisa. She's fallen apart. Marina can't get a word out of her."

"Oh, Jesus."

Michel grabbed his white ballet shoes and dashed out of the dressing room, hopping on each foot in the corridor as he pulled them on in his haste.

"Where is she? In her room?"

"Wings; prompt side."

Michel found Lisa huddled in the corner of the wings next to the theater wall. Her arms were covering her head as though she were defending herself from physical assault and she was shrieking hysterically. For the past month she had beaten all thoughts of herself out of her mind with iron self-discipline but, at the last hurdle, she had seen the reality of her situation in one great, ghastly moment of revelation.

Michel could see it all as he stood watching the ballet mistress's helpless attempts to comfort her. Marina was trying to catch hold of one of her arms but she fought like an injured animal at the slightest touch. The sight repelled him.

Michel was self-centered—because his life as a principal dancer had taught him to be—but he wasn't blind. He knew how far Lisa had stuck her neck out for him. Yes, she'd been keen to dance the premiere but she'd been keener still to nurse him through a safe run-in to the show, putting aside all her own doubts and insecurities for his sake. He had let her do it, hadn't he? Because it made it easier for him. And look at her now.

It was the perfect let-out. Sorry, Charles; sorry, all you gawping, bloodthirsty critics in the front rows of the stalls; I was perfectly able and willing to go on but my ballerina funked it at the last minute. Come on, Marina; off you go and dig out Tatjana and Matt from their hiding places in the first-floor dressing rooms. Good evening, Your Royal Highness, ladies and gentlemen. Owing to the indisposition of Miss Lisa Parfitt the roles of Giselle and Albrecht will be taken by . . .

It was really that easy. Thanks, Lisa darling.

Marina looked around at Michel in panic as the quarter-hour call echoed in the corridor next to the wings. A crowd of dancers had gathered behind him murmuring in awed delight; not delight because it was Lisa but delight because they loved a good drama.

Michel waved Marina away from the cringing heap of blond hair and netting in the corner and walked over to her.

"Get up, Lisa. You'll crush your costume."

Her only response was a frightened howl.

"Come on, up you get!"

More howling. He tried a softer approach, dodging her flying arms with his hand as he tried to caress her face. "Hey, darling, take it easy." Lisa fought him off. He tried three times to catch hold of her arm, encountering increasingly violent resistance with each attempt. What would Charles do in this situation? He'd probably thump her. God, he wished Charles was here now.

"Okay, Lisa, that's enough!" Somehow, because he was a great deal stronger than her, Michel managed to force his way through her defensive, curled-up posture to seize her, none too gently, under her arms and hoist her to her feet. It was the first time in his life he had ever laid a hand roughly on another person, least of all a woman, but he was determined. "You've come this far; you're not going to let yourself down now."

The crowd of onlookers stepped back to make room as he dragged her toward the stage. Marina had already flown to alert the backup team on the floor above. When Lisa saw where he was taking her she struggled, shrieking, to free herself. Michel picked her up and carried her bodily onto the stage.

Behind the red curtain the stage was crowded with dancers, all waiting to see the outcome of this unexpected crisis. Already Lisa was a hundred percent more popular than she had been five minutes ago. As he put her down Michel threw out his arm to order them away from the center of the rubber dance floor.

"Right; up on pointe, Lisa."

When he relaxed his hold on her she tried to flee, and he grabbed her. She was wailing quietly—which was just as well; at their earlier volume her screams would have been clearly audible in the auditorium from the spot where they were standing now.

He lifted her by the waist until she was balanced on pointe. It was a start but it wasn't going to get her through two hours of grueling choreography.

"Pull up your muscles," he ordered. Nothing happened so he smacked her thigh. "Pull them up. Come on; up!" He was prepared to slap her face if necessary but a second smack on her thigh did the trick. She tightened the muscles in her shaking legs and let him coax her into part of the pas de deux from Act Two.

"Okay, again," he said when they had limped through it once. She tried to escape, sobbing pathetically as he caught her by the waist.

"Please, I can't!"

"Rubbish! Again!"

"I can't!"

"Again!"

"No!"

He raised his open hand, threatening her with his eyes. Lisa recoiled in instinctive fear. After a few seconds her shoulders fell and her tears ceased as she looked at him miserably, shaking her head.

"You're just like my dad," she said. "Go ahead and hit me."

Michel lowered his hand slowly and she buried her face in his shoulder. As he held her he looked over her shoulder at Marina's anxious face, nodding in response to her gesticulated question. Matt and Tatjana were standing beside Marina in their makeup and costumes, both looking extremely worried.

"Come on, Lisa," Michel said. "Shall we run through something? What would you like to do?"

"The grape pickers," Lisa whispered.

Michel sent a dresser for Lisa's makeup and a mirror, and then beckoned the watching corps into their positions for the folk dance.

"Do you mind?" complained one of the girls. "The ruddy overture's about to start. This is no time to call a rehearsal."

"I'm still ballet master here, darling. Get into your place with the others. We're bound to go up late. Premieres always do."

If Charles Crown could have seen what was going on behind the closed tabs as the orchestra started tuning up in the pit he would have burst a button off his starched dress shirt. With his vivid memories of Michel's last performance in Bradford, and the sponsors breathing down his neck in the crowded VIP lounge in the foyer, his buttons were under quite enough strain already. He had never needed a cigarette so badly in his life.

39

A CROWD OF GIRLS bundled Lisa away as the overture commenced. All enmity and jealousy toward her was forgotten in the common interest. They huddled around her protectively in the wings while Michel made his way upstage.

At the back of the stage, Rob was waiting for him. He was playing Albrecht's squire, and he gave Michel a thumbs-up sign as he appeared behind the scenery. It looked as though Michel might be going to make it after all. Michel looked at him with a small smile as he held out his arms for his dresser to wrap his cloak about him: a monstrous, swirling thing, the type of costume loved by designers but hated by dancers, more than likely to get caught on a flat as he walked onstage.

"Thanks, darling; I'll see you on the o.p. side in about three minutes' time if everything goes okay."

"Why shouldn't it?" the girl demanded. "I intend to be there and if you ain't I'll bleedin' come on and get you."

She walked off just as the curtain rose on a dozen of the corps who were waving to one another and skipping offstage with village-maideny smiles. Rob braced his muscles to follow Michel onto the stage but as he started moving he saw Michel stiffen. Michel turned his head sharply, snapping in a whisper, "I wish to Christ you'd get off my back!"

"What?" Rob whispered.

Michel laid a hand quickly on his arm.

"Not you, Rob."

There wasn't time for explanation; they were on.

Lisa watched from behind the cottage flats with Lizzi and Connie, who was playing Giselle's mother, as Michel walked out of the wings with Rob trailing in his wake. She expected to see him glide on like a proud ballet dancer but, instead, he struck out boldly for the front of the stage with a spring in his stride and his eyes full of spoiled mischief.

All the dancers were crowded into the wings behind the taped sight lines, watching as Michel chucked his cloak to Rob and stood with his hands on his hips while Rob struggled hopelessly, falling over his own feet, to disentangle himself from it.

"Jeez, what's he doing? He's making this up. This is pantomime," Lisa whispered to the other women.

"Don't knock it, duck," Connie whispered back. "It's better than the original."

Connie opened the cottage door and swept out, broom first, onto the stage. Lisa looked past her to where Michel was ripping off his tunic with the help of his dresser in the opposite wing. His smile had vanished and he was frowning in sober concentration.

Time slowed to an interminable crawl as Michel, only just hooked up in time, bounced back on the stage intent on romantic adventure. To Lisa, waiting behind the flat, it seemed to take him forever to get rid of his servant and decide to come knocking on her door. And yet before she knew it she was on, leaping and hopping around the stage searching for her lover. She felt merry and springy and light. This was Giselle.

When she had completed her first little solo she started pacing diagonally backward across the stage. One, two, three, four . . . she stopped breathing—where was he? Suppose she walked right past him! Suppose he wasn't even there! She felt her shoulder make contact with a large solid object. It was okay; Michel was in charge.

She turned her head to look up at him and her eyes widened as sparks of electricity flew between them. Her mouth opened slowly in astonishment at the intense sexuality in his gray eyes. All of a sudden, as they stared at each other, she believed in all-consuming, overpowering love. In the pit the conductor saw exactly what they were about and waved his hand frantically to pull back the tempo. Bloody dancers: they were always having good ideas at the wrong moment.

Toward the back of the auditorium Charles Crown was sitting surrounded, for moral support, by Michel's friends. He had been sitting like a statue since the curtain had gone up. When Michel led Lisa into the first passage of dance-mime he lowered his head and shielded his eyes with his hand, running his thumb under his eyes to wipe away the first tears he had shed since Nadia Petrovna's death. He wished she were here with him now; it was she who had told him to believe in Michel.

A broad, strong hand reached over the right-hand arm of Crown's seat. He looked down at the offered palm and grasped it in his own. Roly smiled, a firm, confident smile, as he gripped his old teacher's hand in a gesture of solidarity and congratulation. A small hand stretched from the seat on Crown's left to join with the two larger masculine ones. Crown turned his head to smile at Lynne, not at all ashamed of his emotion. Lynne was crying like a baby.

As Roly rested his free hand on Annette's knee she leaned in front of Guy to whisper to Jonni, who was twisting her wedding ring with a look of terror on her face.

"It's alright, lovey. He's found his feet. Nothing on earth's going to stop him now."

Daniel, on the other side of Jonni, put one arm around her—to Guy's annoyance—and the other around Louisa, who was also crying.

On the stage Michel launched into a circuit of huge spinning leaps. He looked like he was dancing on a trampoline.

At the interval Lisa went straight to her dressing room. She had her shoes and costume to change, as well as her hair and makeup to fix.

"Oh my God!" gabbled Lizzi, following her in. "What about that! Wasn't that wild? What did Michel say?"

Lisa climbed out of her dress and sat down to untie her ribbons.

"He didn't say anything, except in the grape pickers he reminded me a couple of times to breathe." She grimaced in pain as she pulled off her shoes. "Ah, jeez, that hurts! Heck! Did you see my left foot go haywire in the little hops?"

"Did I, bull! You were right on top of it all the way through." Lizzi was beside herself with excitement and nerves. She hadn't been on yet; she was all dressed and ready in her white netting dress and ivy crown. "Michel's just incredible, isn't he? Oh shit, they're going to hate me! If they don't hate my dancing, they'll hate me for condemning Michel to death. Did you feel how sorry the audience was for him while he watched you dying?"

"I'd have hoped they felt a bit sorry for me, as it happens."

"Of course they did. But, oh, you should have seen him; the way he just stood there and gazed at you knowing it was all his fault. It was so awful. Did you see his face when he turned and walked offstage?"

"How could I see his face? I was dead."

Lizzi turned to frown at the mirror, adjusting the wreath of ivy leaves that encircled her brown wig.

"Oh yes, so you were."

"Thanks," Lisa said. "Thanks for the sympathy; thanks for nothing!"

"Well, you were a wally to do yourself in. When you found out about his fiancée you should have kneed him in the balls and gone back to your boyfriend like any normal person. That's what I'd have done."

"What about Act Two, then?"

"Sod Act Two; I don't mind giving it a miss. We could all go to the pub instead."

Lisa stood up to take off her tights and the two girls looked at each other.

"Oh my God, Liz," she whispered, wide-eyed. "We're dancing principal roles in the damn Coliseum!"

And they shrieked with laughter and terror and happiness.

At the end of the ballet Michel walked with Lisa through the small parting in the tabs to acknowledge the audience's applause. As he stood beside her in front of the red curtain, dripping with sweat, he cast his eyes slowly over the vast auditorium, listening to the cheers and whistles of the two thousand people in the crowd. Although he couldn't see them because of the blinding spotlight, Michel had that strange gift: the ability to convince every individual in the house that he had given them a special look just for themselves. Jonni shrank down in her seat as she felt him look at her, gazing right into her eyes.

He handed Lisa forward to make her curtsy to the guest of honor in the Royal Circle. She was in agony, whispering to him that she was dying from a cramp in her calves. Flowers rained from the boxes above. It was clear from the volume of the applause that the crowd were digging themselves in to break the BNB record of twenty-two curtain calls. But Michel wasn't to be bound by convention. After only seven bows he told the audience with a wave and a smile that he was taking his partner away because she was exhausted. He winked at the Royal Circle and handed Lisa back through the gap in the curtain, signaling to the prompt corner for the house lights to be raised.

Thankfully, there was no sponsors' reception tonight. The dancers had that chore to look forward to tomorrow night. Michel dried his face with a towel while his dresser unhooked the back of his tunic.

"Darling, remind me of your name."

"Michelle."

"Thank you, Michelle."

"Yer welcome, Michel. Aren't you doing any more?"

"Maybe next Thursday. We'll have to wait and see how my partner feels. This is for you." He handed the girl two twenty pound notes but she shook her head quickly, refusing to take them.

"No, you don't have to—"

"It's not a tip," he said, taking her hand and closing it around the notes. "It's a present. I was in serious shit tonight and you saw me through like a trooper. I'd like to go out and buy you an enormous bunch of roses but the shops are closed." There was a knock on the dressing-room door. "Bugger off, whoever you are!" he called. He wasn't ready to see anyone.

When Michelle had left him he sat down at his dressing table in his dance belt and closed his eyes. He had been ill for a long, long time and suddenly he felt wonderful. He couldn't remember a single second of his time onstage but it had left him drained—drained and yet somehow free. When he opened his eyes Primo was sitting in the armchair beside the dressing table. Michel had been expecting him.

"How could you do that to me?" Primo groaned, with tears streaming down his face. Michel laid the palms of his hands together and pressed his fingers against his mouth.

"I'm sorry, Primo. I'm sorry."

Primo's hurt brown eyes looked into his with deep reproach. "You think I want you to ruin your life over me? You think I want to see you broken and humiliated?"

"No, I was being crazy; I knew it. I needed someone to blame because I was afraid."

"Jesus, you think I tell you to kill yourself! Is that the kind of friend I was to you? What kind of memories you got of me, eh?"

"I told you I'm sorry. I know how much you would have wanted tonight to go well for me."

Primo dried his eyes with a sniff and a grudging smile.

"They're all goin' to be waitin' for you out there, amico." His eyes flickered with a spark of the old mischief. "Hey, you showed them gits in the boys' corps Michel's back in town, eh?"

As Michel walked toward the stage door he was accosted by the stage manager.

"Champagne on stage, Michel."

He turned and smiled wearily.

"Really, Andy, I'm knackered. I think I'll just—"

"Oh bullshit. Get in there. Everyone's waiting for you."

He allowed himself to be given a friendly push toward the door to the stage.

Onstage, behind the red tabs, he was greeted by a riot. He didn't know where to look first; his colleagues crowded around him bombarding him with congratulations and shouting his name. He was smothered on all sides by hugs and kisses. For a moment, he was overwhelmed. "Thanks, Fee," he said, "Mel . . . Hey, you too, Rob. Lizzi, let me kiss you . . . Sian, yes, thanks . . . Bless you, Connie . . . What? No, knackered . . . Shit, Roly, you sod! And Annette! Daniel! Christ, what is this? Louisa!"

Louisa hugged him and shouted above the din to tell him that Jonni had seen the show but had rushed off.

"She had to get home for something! She said to tell you: Zing!"

Michel nodded, smiling.

He felt a pair of hands reach up from behind to cover his eyes and he laughed in surprise. It could have been any one of the girls—it was a small woman, he knew that much.

"Give me a clue."

There was a pause, amidst much giggling, while a shoe was discarded on the floor of the stage and a small foot curled around Michel at an impossible angle to hang fully stretched in front of his nose. When his eyes were uncovered he looked at the foot and his face fell in amazement.

"My, God, I don't believe it. I'd know those bunions anywhere."

He spun round and picked Lynne up in his arms, crushing her against his chest. As he clung to her he felt an unfamiliar discomfort in his throat and a stinging in his eyes, which he mistook for symptoms of surprise. When the sensation had passed he put her down on the floor and accepted two glasses of champagne from the company manager, passing one to her.

"How long have you been in London?"

"This morning," she said. "Roly picked me up from the airport."

Michel smiled. "Roly! The bastard phoned me this afternoon—said he was in Leeds."

"I was with him when he called," she admitted.

"Where?"

Lynne gestured toward the red tabs with her thumb. "Front of house."

They toasted one another, laughing silently, and sipped their drinks. Lynne's eyes sobered suddenly as she surveyed the mayhem of celebration on the stage.

"All this happiness; it doesn't seem the same without . . . without . . ."

"I know," Michel said. He felt it too.

Around them, dancers were shrieking and dousing each other in champagne, wild with adrenaline. If Primo had been there, he would have been the wildest of them all.

While the backstage party was still in full swing, Michel glanced across the stage to where Crown was standing chatting to Rob. Probably talking choreography for *Ghosts*. Michel and Crown had more or less avoided each other since the end of the ballet tonight. There was nothing to say. Or rather, there was too much to say and this wasn't the time or the place.

Crown looked up and caught Michel's eye, nodding toward the prompt-side wing and raising his eyebrows significantly. Michel thanked him with a nod.

In the corner of the dark wing, only a few feet from the scene of her terrified retreat before the show, he found Lisa quite alone, sitting on top of an enormous metal flight case. Her face was in deep shadow but he could hear from her uneven breathing that she was crying.

Michel stood in a path of dim light that leaked into the wing from the stage through a gap in the scenery. He tucked his hands comfortably into his trouser pockets and rocked gently on the balls of his feet, throwing his weight forward as he stared at the floor. It was hard to know what to say to her after everything they'd been through together in the past few weeks.

"Quite an evening," he said at last.

She sniffled softly to herself without replying. Michel rocked on the balls of his feet for a while.

"Nothing wrong with crying, Lisa."

"I feel just awful."

"You're exhausted, that's all."

"I let you down. I wanted to make everything easy for you."

He had raised his head to look at her in surprise.

"You let me down? What are you talking about?"

"Before the show started."

"You didn't let me down. You pulled yourself together in no time."

"You pulled me together, you mean."

"We pulled each other together. It was good for me; it took my mind off my own problems."

"But I meant to be so supportive."

Michel smiled. She was a sweet girl. "So you were. But you couldn't help me get through this performance. No one could." Somehow Michel's quiet words were audible to Lisa above the loud hum from the stage. "They were my own demons. I had to face them alone. Of course you should have been thinking of your own performance. You're a young dancer just starting out in your first solo role."

"Was it okay for a first attempt?"

He laughed. "Oh, I should say it was okay for—a third attempt even. Charles was very impressed."

"Did he say so?"

"No, and he won't. With Charles you've got to learn to make a little praise go a long way. But you've every reason to be proud of yourself."

"But I want you to be proud of me."

"Me? Because I taught you the role? Darling, it was you that danced it."

"No, I want you to be proud of me because . . . well, I just do."

Michel paced slowly up and down in the thin path of light and then stopped and looked up at an illuminated green Fire Exit sign above Lisa's head.

"It'd be very easy to say almost anything at the moment. Dry your eyes and when you feel better come and find me, eh? I want to introduce you to my friend Lynne. She's come all the way from South Africa to see tonight's show. She and I were partners for years."

Lisa nodded and laid her hands on the cold steel of the box at her sides. "Yes, go back to her. I'll see you later on."

Still with his hands in his pockets, Michel bent to kiss her cheek in the darkness.

"And next time we rehearse," he said, "I want to see what that left foot's up to in the little hops, okay?"

Guy climbed into bed next to Jonni and put his arms around her but she pushed him gently away.

"I'm sorry, Guy. I'm all upset after seeing Michel tonight."

"Then why did you insist on going, honey?"

"I couldn't have borne staying at home while he was doing the premiere, not knowing what was happening. I'd have gone crazy."

"I think it was kinda understanding of me to take you."

"Oh, I know it was. Don't think I was talking about any regrets. It was just odd to see all those old friends again; so many people I haven't seen since before he and I split up."

Guy put an arm around her neck and they lay together quietly in the dark. After a while he turned his head toward her, whispering.

"Are you asleep?"

"No."

"You know that fellow, your ex?"

"Uh-huh?"

"I thought you said he didn't have any feelings—that he was a real cold fish."

"Oh, he's not cold exactly. He does have feelings. It's just that he never shows them. Except onstage."

"Oh."

"All that heavy emotion tonight," Michel said, setting two cups of coffee on the kitchen table at his flat, "all those people in tears and gushing about how moving it all was; it made me bloody uncomfortable."

"It always did," Lynne replied. She took a packet of sugar-free sweeteners out of her bag and popped three into her coffee.

"At least Charles had the sense not to go overboard."

"Dear old sir; I can't get used to the pair of you being bosom pals. It makes me feel as though the whole world's gone topsy-turvy in my absence."

Michel swung his leg over a chair and sat down facing her. He looked tired but elated. And he had every reason to be both.

"Lots has changed. Lots and lots. But look at you; you look tremendous."

"Four years, Michel. I can't believe it." Her eyes filled with tears despite herself. Michel frowned and tilted his head to one side.

"Lynnie, I'm not the same person I used to be. But we all change as we get older. How about you? Married and a principal at PACT. Now that's something."

She smiled. But it was true; he had changed. She had seen it and wept over it during his performance in the ballet tonight. There had been a depth of grief and torment in his dancing that she had never seen before. Now, as she looked into his affectionate gray eyes, she saw all that pain close-up, even as he smiled at her.

"That little girl you were dancing with tonight; she suited you. You should try her out in a few of the other classics. I rather fancy her as your Juliet. You were very sensitive with her."

"Do I detect a hint of jealousy?"

"God, yes. Come to SA, Michel; I need you. The chap I'm dancing with at the moment, Jason; he's got hands like chisels. You've spoiled me for any other partnership."

"Not what I read in *The Dancing Times*. Lisa's got promise, though, hasn't she? She's very young yet. Did Charles tell you this was an absolute first for her?"

"It's just like Charles to stick his neck out with a new soloist. He's made a good choice for you."

The telephone rang and Michel twisted the loose metal watch strap on his wrist to look at the face. Twenty past midnight. He pulled himself up from his chair wearily.

"Now who in God's name is that?"

To his immense surprise it was his mother. He felt ashamed when he heard her voice; it was more than four months since he had last called her.

"Michel? Oh, I'm ever so sorry to call you at this time of night but I know what late hours you always keep."

"Not at all, Carrie. I was up anyway, chatting to an old friend. Everything alright there?"

"I've got a bit of a domestic crisis, actually. That's why I'm phoning. The header tank in the attic's overflowing. It's already pouring through the light fitting in the front bedroom."

Carrie was impossible; she'd lived alone for nearly twenty years and she was still thrown by a blown fuse or a blocked drain. He scratched the back of his head and tried to form a mental picture of her plumbing system. He must have turned the water off when she had the new septic tank installed last year. Nothing like a call from Carrie to bring him down to earth.

"Do you know where the stopcock is?"

"No, I've never had any reason to look for it. I'd call someone out but it's far too late."

"Follow the pipe from the tank along the wall to the back of the attic. I think there should be a tap behind the joist which runs under the window. You might need a bit of oil; as far as I remember, it was quite stiff."

"I'll go and have a look. Can you hang on?"

"Sure."

He smiled at Lynne, who was staring at him with puzzled, incredulous eyes.

"My mother's header tank is overflowing," he said.

He drank his coffee during the long wait while Carrie climbed up the ladder to look for the stopcock under the roof. At last she came back on the phone sounding breathless.

"Found it," she gasped. "Thank heaven for that. I'm awfully sorry, Michel, I really am."

"Don't be silly; call me anytime. Listen, don't turn on the light in the spare room, okay? It might be worth getting someone in to check it out. I'm no electrician."

"I will. And I'll get a plumber in the morning . . . Oh no, damn, it's Sunday. I'll have to wait till Monday. Well, thanks very much. I hope you're well and having a good time."

"Yes, fine. Carrie, I . . . Tonight I danced at the Coliseum in the premiere of a new production of *Giselle.*"

"Oh, that's nice."

When Michel and Lynne stood up, shortly after two-thirty, to turn in for the night he put his arms around her with a smile as she came to hug him. Lynne stayed in his embrace far too long and held on to him far too tightly. She felt his groin move against her but still she didn't pull away. She lifted her face to look up at him, her gaze shifting between his two cautious gray eyes, and ran her hands slowly over the muscles of his lower back.

Michel turned his head away toward the wall, taking several slow, deep breaths. The tap of the kitchen sink was dripping and he closed his eyes, listening to the steady ticking of water falling against metal. Her fingers touched him softly.

Ever so gently, he stroked her arm as he held her.

"I'd love to, Lynnie; I really would. It's been . . . God knows how long since I've had a woman. You're as sexy as you always were. But you're married and so am I."

She laid her face against his shoulder.

"You're not really married anymore."

"No. That's true. But you are. You'd always regret it."

"It'd be worth it."

He took a step backward and kissed her softly.

"No, it wouldn't."

Lynne sat down on the edge of the table, folding her arms with a wistful sigh; "You're right, I suppose."

"What are friends for?"

"You always did tell me how to behave."

He laughed as he went to turn off the dripping tap.

"That's an utter lie. I never did any such thing."

"Well, you should have done. Oh God, can I come and sleep with you anyway?"

Michel sat in bed with his arm around Lynne's shoulders. She had thrown off her clothes with as little ceremony as in the old days but Michel, mindful of his own limitations, had stripped only as far as his tracksuit bottoms before he stretched out his long legs under the duvet beside her. She laid her hand on his shoulder and then rested her chin on her fingers.

"Know what?" she said, "you should take your little partner, what's-hername, to bed. I can tell she adores you."

Michel pulled a face that was intended as a shrug.

"Maybe. She's only a kid; twenty, at most."

"God, she's American; that makes up for it. Reckon she's a virgin?"

He shook his head and leaned across her to turn out the bedside light. No, Lisa was no virgin but he certainly hadn't noticed any romantic involvement between her and any of the boys at the BNB. Poor Lisa had probably frightened them all off. It was strange how abrasive she appeared; her heart was as soft as her pretty red mouth. Unfortunately she opened that mouth just a little too often.

Michel leaned over to kiss Lynne as she settled down beside him with her head on the pillow. She was very far from sleep, lying there looking at his sharp, clean profile in the low light from the window. Everything was familiar: the peaceful clarity of Michel's face, the warmth of his body; even the shadows of the furniture in that room struck a chord in Lynne's memory. Only the ash tree beyond the window was bigger than she recalled. It was five years since she had last lain with him in this bed. It could have been yesterday. Michel sat staring at the far wall of the room. He looked distant and thoughtful.

"You know you can't wait for Jonni forever," she said quietly.

"Shhh."

"I should have married you when I had the chance. I let you get away too easily."

He touched her face with his hand.

"I thought you were happily settled with Jerry."

"Oh, I am but it's not the same. You're family. I won't ever get over losing you, really."

"You haven't lost me. I'll always be here."

"Michel, I won't ever forgive myself for not coming back to England after Primo—"

"Hush. It never crossed my mind that you should. Don't ever regret that you and I didn't marry, Lynne. You need far more than I'd ever know how to give you. If anyone could have stuck with me it was Jonni, but I couldn't even give enough to keep her. It's better as it is, all round."

"I love you, Michel. You know that, don't you?"

"Shhh."

40

LYNNE PLANNED TO SPEND the following evening with her parents in Cambridge before flying back to Johannesburg on Monday morning. Michel drove her to King's Cross in the early afternoon and put his hand over hers as she sat in the passenger seat beside him.

"I wish I could drive you up there but I've got this bloody reception this evening."

"Things never change, do they?" she said. "That's the price of fame, my darling. And the price of living in this stupid country where the government doesn't give a shit about the arts. That's one good thing about PACT: no kowtowing to pigheaded industrialists who don't know the first thing about dance."

Michel shrugged; "A bit of kowtowing doesn't hurt occasionally, as long as they keep putting up the funds."

"Then don't be surprised if their photographers ask you to pose *en attitude* on top of a washing machine at this reception tonight."

"If they ask me to pose on top of a washing machine, or anywhere else for that matter, I shall politely tell them to go screw themselves."

Lynne hooted with laughter. He would too.

When he kissed her outside the forecourt of the train station his eyes creased up in affection.

"It's not going to be another four years, right? If you don't make it back here, I'll fly out to see you in the spring."

"You never know. As I said, Jerry's got a lot of dates lined up with orchestras all over Europe and I'm not going to stay in SA forever. I might start touting for a principal post in Germany or Scandinavia once this season's over."

"I'll partner you again one day, Lynnie; wait and see."

"Yes you will. What'll we do?"

"Onegin."

"Manon."

"Lilac Garden."

Lynne's hazel eyes looked yearningly into his and her mouth turned down in a plaintive smile. *"Romeo."*

Michel arrived at the reception, at a gilt-paneled and chandeliered Mayfair hotel, wearing a cream linen Valentino suit and Gucci shirt. He resented having to shave on a Sunday.

Charles Crown appeared at his side in impeccable black tie, and shook his hand vigorously, muttering through clenched teeth, "We're in for a fucker of an evening, I'm afraid. They've set this whole thing up as a massive press conference. The place is swarming with photographers and journalists."

Michel's fixed smile didn't waver for a moment. He raised his eyebrows in acknowledgment of a greeting from a rubber-faced businessman he'd never seen before.

"Bless their hearts," he said.

"For Christ's sake go and rescue Lisa before they get their clutches on her. She's around here somewhere; look for a mass of violent orange."

Michel skirted the edge of the function, skillfully avoiding a cluster of notebooks which were heading his way. He spotted Lisa under siege on the far side of the room. She too was sporting the regulation smile—along with the very orangest garment he had ever seen. Through a momentary gap in the crowd he saw that the extraordinary color belonged to a clinging velvet creation, decent in its length but outrageously low-cut; her breasts looked ready to pop out of the strapless bodice at any moment. As he caught her eye across the room her lashes batted out a desperate SOS.

Michel swooped down on her and whisked her away.

"Stick close to me, darling, and for Christ's sake don't lift your arm to wave at anyone."

He escorted her across the room, his hand securely on her waist, to the safe haven of a huddle of dancers near the buffet. Michel and Lisa were in the spotlight tonight and a waitress appeared instantly at their side, demanding to know what they wanted to drink.

"What would you like, Lisa?" Michel asked.

"Orange juice, thanks."

"I'd have something stronger if I were you. You're going to need it."

"Oh, I never use alcohol."

"Orange juice then. At least if you spill it on your frock it won't show."

Lisa bridled. "Don't you like my dress?"

"I should have worn sunglasses." He smiled at the waitress, fishing a packet of cigarettes out of his pocket. "A Scotch for me, thanks."

As the waitress went away Lisa glared at him. "You've got all the vices, haven't you, Michel? You smoke, drink . . ."

"Gamble," he said nodding, "snort coke, bugger schoolboys, sell pornography." He was still wearing a studied smile, reminding her they were here to keep up appearances. "I even do a bit of pimping on my days off. Want to make a few extra quid on top of your salary? That little orange number would suit the purpose admirably."

She pursed her lips, planting her hands on her hips.

"Want to know what your worst vice is?"

"Love to."

"You're so darned honest."

Michel managed to persuade one of the girls from the corps to part with a pretty purple jacket, which went splendidly with Lisa's color scheme. At the same time he swapped his red tie for Rob's mauve one.

"Okay, darling," he said to Lisa, once they no longer clashed hideously and she was safe from any danger of indecent exposure, "let's go and sparkle for the press, shall we? At least we won't offend them before we've even opened our mouths."

Lisa had never experienced being the center of media attention before. She was overwhelmed by the constant barrage of questions as the journalists tried to sniff out the personal angle, the human interest story that would secure them a good spot in the first half-dozen pages of their paper. Even Michel found their ducking and diving taxing but he kept his hand firmly on his partner's orange waist and chaperoned her safely through interview after interview.

Together they posed for photographs; one sharp-eyed photographer caught them in touching juxtaposition, with Lisa's gray eyes raised in helpless confusion to the smiling eyes of her tall partner. The readers of tomorrow's *Evening Standard* wouldn't know she had just been asked by an impertinent reporter whether she was embarrassed by her lack of academic education.

"Ask him if he can spell saut de basque," Michel whispered savagely into her ear, still smiling.

When they moved away from one crowd of flashing cameras—for a brief respite before the next descended—she clutched his arm, gasping at the unexpectedness of it all. She wanted to hide her head under the lapel of his jacket and stay there until everyone had gone away.

"I want to go home," she wailed. "Please, please let me go home."

"Trust me, the very first second we can leave without upsetting the sponsors we're out of the door. Now put your smile back on, darling; here comes another one."

Michel drove Lisa home to her flat in Maida Vale and accepted her offer of coffee. He was surprised she permitted that dangerous substance over the threshold of her abode.

It was a nice little flat in a purpose-built block, ugly and forbidding from the outside but cozy once you closed the door on the grim concrete stairwell. There was one good-sized room—a combined bedroom and sitting room—and a tiny kitchen and bathroom. The window above the kitchen sink overlooked a jumble of dark courtyards at the back of a row of Victorian houses.

"Why did you refuse to talk to the press about your family?" Lisa asked as she read the instructions on the jar to see how many spoons of coffee she should put in the cups.

Michel unbuttoned his jacket and tucked his hands in his trouser pockets.

"Because I haven't got a family."

"What, none?"

"None to speak of." A twinge of guilt pricked him as he remembered the months he had spent last year with Carrie, but he put it quickly out of his mind. "And, by the way, I don't think you should have said that about your parents."

"Heck, I only said Mom and Dad didn't care too much when I called to say the premiere went okay. What's wrong with that?"

"They'll find a way to twist it round and make something out of it. You're the youngest dancer ever to have starred in a premiere with this company; the press will play that up as far as they can. If they can make a sob story out of it they will. You're a novelty."

"A novelty? Gee, that doesn't sound too flattering. Don't you think I've got the potential to be more than that?"

"Plenty of potential. But you've got lots of work ahead of you. One good performance doesn't make a ballerina. There are pitfalls all the way from here to the top."

Lisa looked very crestfallen as she stood looking at him with a pint of milk in one hand. Several thick strands of blond hair had fallen out of the pile on top of her head and she blew them away from her face sullenly.

"You're real hard, Michel, you know that? You're always bullying me."

"Do I bully you? I hope not; that's dreadful." He meant what he said. He was frowning at her in surprise.

"Well, no, I guess you don't exactly bully me. But you always make me feel real immature. Like I'm nothing but a dumb kid. You're always in control. Nothing ever flummoxes you."

"I was pretty flummoxed yesterday."

"Sure, but you were so darned grown-up about it. You didn't need anyone else to lean on. You just took charge and sorted it all out."

Michel followed her into the sitting room and hung his jacket over the back of a chair, loosening his tie and undoing the top button of his shirt.

"I'm a lot older than you, Lisa. I've danced more than a dozen different principal roles and I'm ballet master at the British National. You've only been a pro for six months. I'd be worried if I didn't make you feel inexperienced."

"Does Charles ever make you feel stupid?"

"Invariably."

She laughed and curled up in the corner of the sofa while he sat down beside her with his coffee. Michel's cool reserve, along with his brilliance as a dancer and his cult stardom, made him extremely fascinating to all the girls at the BNB. Lisa felt she had come closer to penetrating that reserve than any of her colleagues. The deep vulnerability of his Albrecht last night might have been only acting but he had looked into her eyes and given himself to her completely for those two brief hours on stage.

When Michel put his arm around her and kissed her, leaning over her on the sofa, his hand traveled to her orange velvet neckline, his fingers stealing under the soft fabric.

"I thought you didn't like me anymore," she said, drawing away, suddenly coy now that his approach was openly sexual.

"No, it wasn't that at all. I just . . ."

He got up from the sofa and went to stand next to a tall bookcase crammed with books on self-improvement and dietetics, rubbing the back of his head and looking at the floor. How could he possibly explain that all those times he had kissed her after rehearsals had been nothing to do with her? She had been no more than an object to him, available and compliant—a young woman under his authority and dependent on his help in her first major role.

"I shouldn't have taken advantage of you," he said.

Lisa stood up and went to put her arms around his waist, her gray eyes smiling up at him confidently. He was taken aback by the trust he saw there.

"I didn't mind," she said.

"You didn't mind?"

"No, I liked you taking advantage of me. I didn't think you cared for me at all but it was nice to know you found me kinda attractive and I guess I felt like you were confiding in me."

He rested a hand on each of her hips and looked thoughtfully down at her face.

"Perhaps I was."

"Are you going to take me to bed?" she asked.

He glanced at the divan in the corner of the room.

"I think it's rather up to you. It's your bed, after all."

Lisa watched Michel pull off his tie and unbutton his blue shirt. She was in awe of his physique, and she prided herself on being something of a connoisseur.

"Jeez, Michel, you're real beautiful."

"Well, what can I say to that? So are you. Take your dress off, why don't you?"

"You know you could have your pick of the girls in the corps."

"Could I now?"

"Sure. They all fancy you."

"Do they indeed?"

"Yeah, I've heard them—"

"Lisa"—he paused and looked up at her as he pulled off his shoes—"you do know I'm married, don't you?"

She stopped struggling to undo the back of her dress.

"Why sure. But you're separated."

"Not legally, but yes. I just wanted to check you knew."

"Do you sleep with a lot of girls?"

"I used to; quite a few. None since my wife."

"Then what are you waiting for? Help me with this darned zipper."

After eighteen months without sexual contact the feel of the soft parts of Lisa's body under his hands was intoxicating for Michel. Lisa gasped for breath, lying naked in his arms on the bed, as he kicked the duvet onto the floor and buried his face in her belly, devouring her with his hands and mouth.

Lisa enjoyed sex, and she thought herself experienced, but she had never encountered anything like this. For her, sex had rules—courtship, foreplay, intercourse—but Michel didn't follow the rules. At times the ferocity of his lovemaking was almost frightening, and at other times he gazed into her eyes, quiet and intimate, watching for her response to his experimental caresses. Looking into his eyes in the half-light from the open bathroom door, Lisa could see every flicker of hunger and sensual awareness that passed through them while he made love to her gently. She was transfixed by his eyes. Her body melted at the combination of raw eroticism and tenderness of his slow movements inside her.

At last, involuntarily, Michel closed his eyes. And with the rare permission he granted himself to abandon his physical restraint came an even rarer explosion of uncontained emotion. Lisa saw his face contort in anguish as he pressed her body tightly against his in the darkened, unfamiliar surroundings of her flat.

For Lisa, too, orgasm brought an unexpected flood of emotion. Mingled inextricably with the breaking wave of her sexual pleasure was the knowledge that the man who was ejaculating into her with such urgency was her cousin—her older, wiser cousin, to whom she belonged in a way that went far beyond physical desire. They might not always be lovers but he would always be there to love and protect her once he knew of their blood relationship.

Michel reached over to the chair near the bed and took his cigarettes out of his jacket pocket.

"You don't mind if I smoke, do you?"

"No, go ahead. Use that saucer on the table for an ashtray."

She lay with her arms under her head and watched him light up, the flame of his lighter glowing bright blue and orange in the semidarkness. His back was toward her as he sat on the edge of the bed. She wondered what he was thinking. Suddenly she laughed quietly to herself.

"What's funny, Lisa?"

"Oh, nothing. They say girls are supposed to go for men who are like their fathers. I guess this must be a case in point."

"Yes? What's your father like?"

She looked at the ceiling. "Oh . . . he's kinda tall, with blond curly hair—well, kinda mousy hair really—and gray eyes. He's not so handsome as you and of course he's a lot older."

Michel blew out the smoke from his cigarette.

"What's it like having a father? Is he nice?"

"Oh, I don't know; he's just Dad. He's always working—forgets all about us half the time. He's rough too; used to hit me and Mom when things weren't going well at work. Him and Mom have split up now. Say,

Michel, I didn't mean it yesterday when I said you were like my dad. I know you wouldn't have hit me."

Michel stretched back a hand and felt for her arm.

"I might have done. I don't know."

"It doesn't matter. You want to know why I agreed to help Charles persuade you to dance the premiere?"

"You're ambitious. There's nothing wrong with that."

"No, that wasn't it; I had a better reason. It was . . ." she turned onto her side, propping her head on her fist and looking at him expectantly, ". . . because you and I are cousins."

The back that was still turned toward her didn't show much interest in her revelation.

"What do you mean?" he asked, his voice expressionless.

"Your uncle is my father."

He flicked the ash from his cigarette into the saucer.

"No he isn't. My uncle's dead. And, anyway, he was a homosexual."

Lisa lifted her head, supporting herself on her elbow. "Why then, who paid for you to study at the Paris Académie?"

"Lisa, I don't want to—"

"Wasn't it Jacques St. Michel?" She pronounced the name Jacques to rhyme with shark and not to rhyme with shack the way they did in Europe. Michel drew in a breath like a slow sigh.

"Yes, it was Jacques St. Michel."

"My real name's St. Michel too. Parfitt was Mom's maiden name. I took it when I went to ballet school because I didn't want people only to see me as Dad's daughter."

"And your father is . . . ?" His tone was suddenly uneasy.

"Jacques St. Michel, the choreographer. Isn't he your uncle?" Lisa just couldn't understand why Michel was being so dense.

Michel turned quickly around to look at her and ran both his hands through his hair. His cigarette burned away forgotten on the saucer next to the bed.

"Jacques St. Michel is my father," he said.

Lisa stood in the middle of the room, stark naked with her hands over her ears, and screamed. Nothing Michel could say would calm her.

When he tried to put his arms around her she just screamed all the louder—and he couldn't really blame her.

People from the neighboring flats were hammering on the door and he scrambled into his trousers, wrestling with the zip.

"Lisa, Lisa, for Christ's sake shut up! They'll call the fucking police!"

He was still doing up his fly button with one hand as he threw open the door. A crowd of worried faces peered into the room and he stood back to let them see that the screamer was in one piece and physically unharmed. They looked from her naked hysterical figure to the half-dressed body and sober face of the man just inside the door.

"It's okay," he said, searching for a plausible explanation. "She's just had a bit of rather bad news about a relative."

41

MICHEL SAT IN CHARLES CROWN'S OFFICE on Monday after company class; a welcome return to the normality of daily routine. Tonight and for the next three weeks there were performances at the Coliseum but for Michel the agony was over. He could perform or not perform. He was cured of his fear.

Crown's postmortem of Saturday's premiere was practical and unemotional. This morning's reviews were spread on the desk in front of him and he picked them over discriminatingly.

"'St. Michel dances with pathos and conviction,'" he read, "'but one feels that his prodigious technical virtuosity undermines the piteousness of Albrecht's plight'—now what the fuck does that mean? Either you stretch your feet in a cabriole or you don't. The prat doesn't know what he's talking about."

"Perhaps he's calling me smug," Michel suggested, fiddling with the corner of a folder of schedules.

"Sounds like the voice of envy to me. Written by some no-hoper who never got beyond the corps, I expect."

"What do they say about the partnership?"

"Good on the whole. Most of them love it. *Telegraph* complains about lack of contrast."

"Might have a point, seeing I coached Lisa on it myself."

Crown swept the reviews carelessly into a pile, indicating his contempt for their judgment.

"Will you dance the show on Thursday?" he asked, pretending not to care either way. Michel smiled at Crown's assumed nonchalance and then sat back in his chair, tapping his foot slowly.

"I don't know. I really don't know."

"Why not? The premiere was a sensation. A second crack at it can only do you good. Lisa too."

"I've got other work to do. I need to focus on getting your new piece on next week." Michel was still tapping his foot. "Look, I'm going to have to talk it over with Lisa. We've had a falling-out. It's hard to tell how it'll affect our partnership."

"A falling out?"

"Yes." He rubbed his eyes, sighing. "It transpires that Lisa's my sister."

"Your cousin, you mean."

"No, my sister. Her father is Jacques St. Michel."

"Christ, are you sure? When did you find this out?"

Michel flung his folder of schedules exasperatedly onto the desk.

"After I fucked her." He saw Crown's eyes crinkle up and the corners of his mouth turn down. "Please don't laugh, Charles. It isn't funny."

"No, you're right, it isn't. It's atrocious." He was still trying not to smile. "Actually, I'm sorry but it really is a bit funny."

Michel sat in his own office, staring through the window with a cup of coffee in his hand. It was a relief to have a few minutes to himself after his long morning in the studio.

On the building site opposite, a group of construction workers were putting a roof on a low office block and Michel watched them with fascination. When he'd first come to work here they'd been halfway through building that block. Eight months later they still hadn't finished it and yet before class this morning there had been a gaping hole where the roof should have been. Now it was two-thirds covered. It was September and the sky was gray. He was glad to think of that building having a roof for the winter. That same dreary, unchanging view from his window had been causing him unconscious frustration for months.

Michel couldn't think about the past few days. Too much had changed too quickly. He told himself he should be thinking about Lisa but his mind rebelled, persisting in its steady contemplation of the prosaic but satisfying act of creation going on over the road.

Lisa knocked on the door, as he had known she would.

He turned his revolving chair briskly to face her as she entered and greeted her with businesslike courtesy.

"Come in, Lisa—close the door and sit down. D'you feel better?"

It seemed peculiar to Lisa to be walking into the ballet master's office, watching him tidy the papers on his desk into a neat pile as she closed the door. She half expected him to break into a lecture on punctuality and the importance of regular classwork.

"I'm sorry I missed your class this morning," she said.

He waved aside her apology.

"Won't kill you for once in your life. We need to have a think about our partnership. Charles is asking me if we want to perform on Thursday."

She frowned, puzzled. Why was he being so curt with her? Properly speaking, he should be on his knees.

"I guess it's up to you, Michel."

"As professionals I don't think we ought to let a personal upset interfere with the company's schedule." He folded his arms into a firm knot. The room was full of what had happened physically between them last night, and he struggled to banish it from his mind, focusing his frown on Lisa. "It's not ideal, of course, but I'm prepared to partner you if you want me to."

She pulled a face of pained disbelief and shook her head at him.

"I can't believe you're being so nasty. Are you angry with me because I overreacted last night?"

"I don't really think, under the circumstances, that you did overreact. You were distressed; it's understandable."

"Can't you be a bit . . . nicer? I came in here all prepared to be real positive about it. You just make me feel like you don't want me here; like you want to pretend it never happened."

"Yes, I think that's probably best."

Lisa was still traumatized by last night's revelation; she hadn't prepared herself for the further shock of his rejection. Her gray eyes searched his face, disbelieving.

"Don't you even want to talk about it?"

Michel turned his chair slowly back to face the window. The burning anger he felt toward Lisa gnawed at him with a carnivorous hunger. It was a physical presence in his chest. He didn't understand this anger himself and he was certainly not about to try explaining it to her.

"Do you see those iron girders going up on that crane?" he asked. "It's amazing to think that each one is big enough to reach right across the width of that building."

"Michel?"

"Uh-huh?"

"Do you hate me or something?"

"Don't be silly, darling. Why should I hate you?"

She sat on the chair in front of his desk, relieved, and tucked her foot underneath her on the narrow seat.

"You know, you're the only relative I've got in Britain and the only one in the world I really respect—well, I've got an aunt in Iowa but she's an awful stick-in-the-mud. I guess I respect her because she knows her own mind but I'd never confide in her; she's still in the dark ages. Mom's so wrapped up in her own problems that she doesn't have time for mine; I suppose she thinks I'm grown now and I can take care of myself. You're an only child too, aren't you? At least you thought you were, huh? Gee, I've always wished I had a brother. It was pretty terrible, us finding out about each other like that, but I'd rather that way than not at all."

Michel tapped his mouth with his fist. Her unquestioning trust in their relationship made him extremely uncomfortable.

"I hardly know you."

"Sure, but you'll get to know me. I'm your sister."

"Half sister."

"Oh, don't be picky. A half sister's a sister when you're as short on family as we are."

"Listen, Lisa . . ." Michel paused. It was difficult to find the right words to tell her that there simply wasn't room in his life for someone to come in off the street and start setting up house. He didn't want her there. He didn't want the responsibility of being an emotional prop for her, or of supervising her dance career. He felt trapped: she was asking him to make a commitment to her, to love her purely on the strength of a chance family link. She was a nice enough girl but he couldn't afford to let her need him.

He turned back to face her, forcing himself to be patient.

"Lisa, we're going to have to take some time to think this through. A brother-sister relationship isn't something you create overnight. A brother is someone you grow up with, someone who shares your background, someone whose experiences and attitudes somehow relate to yours. He may have different tastes and opinions to you but they're rooted in the same family setup. Now, your father . . ."

"Our father," she corrected him.

"No, yours," he insisted, frustrated at her naiveté. "Let's talk about your father for a moment. He may have his faults but at least he's part of your life and always has been. The very fact he lied to you about me shows he thinks of you as his only child."

She gazed at him, baffled. Knowing nothing of his childhood, it was impossible for her to understand the force and complexity of his feelings about Jacques St. Michel.

"But that's just him, Michel, not us."

"But he's the only link between us. He chose to bring you up as his daughter; that's fine. He chose not to have me as a son and that's also fine. Lisa, I haven't met the man, not since I was three or something. He's not my father. And if I don't consider him to be my father, how can his daughter be my sister? It's not a problem for me; I just don't think you should read any more into the relationship than necessary."

Lisa's brow puckered in supplication. Her eyes were very pale, reflecting the cloudy daylight outside the window.

"Can't you just forget about Dad? I'm here; now. This is me. I can't help it if you and Dad don't have anything in common."

"But that's exactly my point." Michel held out the flat palm of his hand for emphasis. "To you he's Dad. To me he's just some Franco-American bloke with the same name as me. That's all. When he was rocking you in his arms I was on my own in Paris trying to survive amongst a bunch of other kids who all had homes and families. When he was driving you to school Charles Crown was tossing my student reports in a filing cabinet because there was no one to send them to. When he came to watch your graduation from ballet school I was on my own in a fucking mental hospital."

"What about your mother?"

"She doesn't come into it. She had her own life to lead. Listen, none of this is your fault. I wouldn't have wanted it any other way—in fact, for your sake, I'm glad it worked out that way round. But it does make a difference, Lisa. And there's nothing we can do to change it."

She looked down at her hands, knitted together on her lap, and nodded to indicate her comprehension.

"In short, you have no sister."

He breathed in slowly. "In short."

"Fine."

"Look, I've never placed any importance in blood relationships. Why should I? I'm more interested in who you are as a person. Why would I care more about a sister, about whom I know nothing, than about my dance partner? Obviously I can't care for you as a woman—and you know perfectly well I'm sorry about what happened, without my saying so. I'm not going to waste time pretending I feel something for you which I frankly don't. But I do enjoy working with you. I do care what happens to you within this company. And I think that's the basis upon which our relationship should continue."

Lisa sat gazing downward, perfectly still, her eyes widening as her stare became unseeing fixation. There was a long silence during which Michel's resentment subsided back into his belly, having expressed itself more clearly than he intended, and Lisa's resentment came bubbling uncontrollably to the surface.

Michel stood up and walked over to the kettle.

"Want a coffee?"

"No, thanks."

Strange, it seemed to Lisa, that such mundane words were possible in the face of the anger and humiliation which beat at her mind. When he sat down again she lifted her head high with a fierce courage.

"Do I get to say my piece?"

"Certainly."

"I think you're evil."

Michel closed his eyes and rubbed them slowly with his fingers.

"Okay, and the rest, Lisa."

"I don't think it's anything to do with whether I'm your sister or not. I think you're just terrified that, given half the chance, I might just come to care for you. No, you don't like the sound of that, do you? Nothing scares you quite so much as being confronted by the idea of love, does it? Oh, it's okay onstage where nothing's real; you can show as much emotion as you like and no one can use it against you. With all those people out there watching, you're quite safe; no danger of anyone taking it personally.

"And there's sex of course. Let's not forget sex. Just for one brief moment you let the barriers down and it feels great, doesn't it? It's just a pity there has to be someone else involved. So you turn your back and shut out the possibility that the girl in bed with you might just have seen what really lies under that shell of yours. Why screw a girl you have to face in the morning, Michel? Why not go to prostitutes? Better still, become a necrophiliac. And your wife stayed with you, what, three years? Brave woman. She must have a taste for cripples."

Michel pressed his eyelids hard as he rubbed them. When he looked at Lisa he saw flashing multicolored halos instead of her face.

"Have you finished?"

"No I haven't. I think you're a pervert. Your perversion is the worst type there is: cruelty. And I think you're jealous. All that stuff about being glad it was me who had a father and not you; I think it was all complete bullshit. It makes you mad, doesn't it? Or were you lying to yourself as well as to me? Well if it's any comfort to you, Michel, you didn't miss a darned thing."

She ran out of steam very suddenly. After a pause Michel turned toward the window again.

"Charles has asked me for an answer by this evening," he said. "Do you want to dance on Thursday night?"

Lisa sprang to her feet and looked defiantly at the back of his head. Sitting there like that with his ankle resting on his knee and his arms folded, he might almost be her father.

"Fuck you, yes I do."

"Right. Rehearsal of the Act One hunt solo tomorrow, two-thirty in studio four."

"I'll be there," she said and she strode out of the room.

Michel heard the door close and rested his head against the high back of his chair, looking at the ceiling. It had been the worst possible time to try and make sense of the situation, with the memory of their erotic encounter, less than twelve hours ago, still so vivid in both their minds. Michel's body was still exulting in its release from sexual frustration, his attraction to her not yet fully doused despite all his guilty assurances to himself to the contrary.

He hadn't meant to hurt her but what could he do? How could two people make a relationship out of a label? Brother, sister, husband, wife, mother, father; they were all just meaningless names to Michel. Lisa was just Lisa, sister or no sister, in the same way that Jonni had just been Jonni on the day he had brought her home from the registry office, proud of her new title and expecting him to look at her through different eyes now that she wore his gold ring.

"Cripple," he said, running both his hands slowly over his blond head.

Lisa leaned against the cool plaster wall next to the closed door of Michel's office. She was shaking, flabbergasted by the venom she had poured out at him. She tried to remember the exact words she had used. What had she said to him?

Her heart thumped noisily against her breast, blotting out all coherent thought. Pervert, she had called him; cruel pervert. Angry words she had often longed to hurl at her father. Now she had found a different target for them—different and yet not so different. She closed her eyes in an agony of confusion.

That Michel was her brother was incomprehensible to her now. All night she had been turning over in her mind the concept of the relationship, coloring it with the permanent emotional bonds that she had seen and envied in the sibling relationships of all her friends back home. That concept had fragmented and collapsed in a few short minutes. What she had tried to build in one sleepless night, her friends and their brothers had constructed over many years of close proximity and tolerance.

All she knew was that the caresses she and Michel had shared last night had been no expression of love or even of friendship. Instead, the gratification of his physical appetite and her own emotional neediness had created a monster between them that would never go away.

Standing with her back to the painted wall she felt a warm, hideous trickle between her thighs as the last of his seed dripped out of her defenseless body. Her father's son! She cringed when she thought where she had allowed him to put his hands. And not just his hands, either.

Michel and Lisa met to rehearse the following afternoon under Crown's supervision. Her mouth turned down involuntarily as Michel held out his hand toward her to lead her into the first duet, but after only a moment's hesitation she put her hand in his and stepped up on pointe to test her toe blocks. What was done was done and what was said was said, and now they had a performance to prepare for Thursday evening.

Michel walked through the park and up Charing Cross Road on Thursday afternoon. His peaceful stroll was very different from the journey his faltering, petrified feet had made along that same route last Saturday. There was nothing to fear for his performance tonight. He had complete confidence in Lisa. She had shown herself possessed of a common sense that far exceeded his expectations.

Their rehearsals over the past few days had certainly been awkward but the awkwardness had been on Michel's part, not Lisa's. He had never noticed before how much he was in the habit of touching women. When he talked to a woman he would unconsciously rest his hand on her waist, or her back if they were walking together. It was a protective habit— sexist really, he supposed—and came naturally in an environment where everything revolved around physical contact. With Lisa, since the implicit sexuality in such gestures made them taboo, Michel found himself folding his arms defensively as they talked over the details of their work. This alone had made their discussions together seem stilted. Otherwise, their relationship had been businesslike; they hadn't once looked one another in the eye, except to read each other's timing for the launch into a lift or partnered move.

Now, walking along Charing Cross Road toward the newsagent's, Michel was thinking of other things.

It was a beautifully bright afternoon. The rich September sunlight gave the West End an atmosphere of vibrancy. Michel loved London. The bustle and the architecture still held the thrill of the foreign for him after all his years living here. He looked up at the stone-carved buildings above the shops. How magnificent they were, these old buildings.

As he walked, Michel found himself remembering warm evenings when he had strolled along this road with Primo and Jonni, bound for favorite pubs or restaurants in Soho. He could almost hear their voices and laughter beside him. It seemed that the cars passing on the road and the tourists meandering slowly around him were the same cars, the same tourists, which had been there then.

"Excuse me; aren't you Jean-Baptiste St. Michel?"

Michel stopped and wrote his autograph on a page of the young woman's sketchbook at her blushing request. He took the trouble to think back to the matinee of *Manon* she had seen at Sadler's Wells almost two years ago.

"God yes, I do remember all those screaming kids in the audience . . . No, only in the quiet bits; we have very loud speakers in the wings blasting fold-back from the orchestra at us. Marcia and I got the giggles terribly in her death scene . . . Oh, I'm glad you didn't—the artistic director certainly did."

As he continued on his walk his thoughts returned instantly to Primo and Jonni where he had left them strolling gaily by his side in happier times. He tried to visualize Jonni's face, a whole series of snapshot images presenting themselves to his mind for inspection: Jonni chattering cheerfully across the kitchen table, Jonni looking up at him from the bath, Jonni reaching out to him tenderly in the semidarkness of their bedroom, Jonni crying over some imagined slight. He could picture her body perfectly, clothed or naked, but her face—and especially her eyes—remained out of focus. He stared up at the stone façade above a snuff shop, screwing up his face in his effort to complete the evasive portrait.

Something made Michel glance down at the pavement opposite, to where Jonni was standing on the curb outside Leicester Square tube station. It was almost as though the sheer force of his mental exertion had achieved her physical manifestation. Her back was half-turned toward him. She was checking her watch, looking for a taxi. Guy Dakin was standing beside her.

Michel stopped on the pavement and stared at her. Jonni's appearance had changed a great deal. She looked fashionable and self-confident in a light summer raincoat, its sleeves pushed up to her elbows, with the hem of her cashmere skirt covering the top of smart, expensive boots. Huge silver earrings dangled beneath her cropped, copper-tinted hair and her face was carefully made-up. Her wide mouth, curling in frustration at the lack of taxis, was painted bold red.

Slowly, as though an irresistible magnet were pulling her gaze, Jonni turned her head to glance across the street and she found herself looking straight into the eyes of her husband.

For Jonni, it was as though someone had punched her very hard just below her rib cage. It couldn't be Michel—he belonged to another world. And yet there he was.

They held each other's eyes. Neither of them registered anything in their faces except blank surprise. They just looked. When it became impossible to look any longer without some form of communication, Jonni turned away quickly.

"Guy, can we go? I'd rather walk."

"What?" Guy frowned in surprise. "Hon, it was you insisted we wait for a taxi. We've been here five minutes; we might as well—"

"Please, I'd really rather walk."

She grabbed his arm and hurried him away. It wasn't that she particularly wanted to avoid Michel; it had just been so unexpected. The shock to her system had been too great to allow her time to think.

Before she had dragged Guy ten paces down the road she regretted her reflex reaction. She turned her head back to look at the spot where Michel had been standing but he was gone. There was no sign of him across the street. She twisted her neck to scan the pavement behind her hopefully but he wasn't there either.

In his dressing room behind the stage of the Coliseum, Michel chucked his newspaper onto a chair and handed his dresser a very pretty bunch of irises. She took them with a gasp, stunned that he had thought of her.

"I'm gobsmacked," she said, with her hand on her chest. "God, they're gorgeous. Where did you get them?"

"Shop in Charing Cross Road; I saw them in a bucket outside on the pavement and thought of you."

"Can I put them in your sink while I sort out the cos'ies?"

"Go ahead."

Michelle turned on the cold tap, separating out the blooms carefully before she laid each one in the basin.

"Such purple. Did you get some for Lisa too?"

Michel stopped dead in the middle of pulling off his jeans.

"Jesus, you're right. I didn't think of it." He liberated his foot from his jeans and threw them on a chair before reaching for his dance belt. "Mind you, I don't think she'd exactly jump with joy if I gave her flowers."

While Michel put on his makeup in the peaceful half hour before the call for Act One Beginners he looked at Michelle's robust, honest face in the mirror of his dressing table.

"Darling, tell me something; have you ever run into someone you knew from the past and ignored them?"

"How d'you mean ignored them?"

"Met someone's eye, across a street say, and just turned away before they could react to seeing you."

Michelle laid his sword belt on the settee and stood up straight, scratching her wrist and frowning at his reflection as she contemplated his question.

"Yeah, I did," she said at last, as though his mentioning it had been a remarkable coincidence. "Yeah, I once saw this bloke I knew on the other side of a pub up in Covent Garden. I looked at him and he looked at me. Then I just picked up my drink and carried on playing the fruit machine like I never recognized him."

"Who was he?"

"A real dickhead. An ugly git I met at a party. He went round telling racist jokes all night and trying to get into the girls' knickers. Then he threw up on my friend Tracy's coat and passed out."

"Oh," said Michel.

"Yeah, I wouldn't have ignored him if I didn't hate him."

"No," said Michel, leaning close to the mirror to draw pencil lines under his eyes, "I don't suppose you would."

He popped into Lisa's dressing room just before the quarter-hour call to check that she was all set for the performance. She was standing in front of the mirror while a dresser hooked her into her bodice.

"Coming onstage for a final warm-up?" he asked.

"I think I'll do it here. I've got bad memories of warming up out there."

"Right then. See you at Beginners."

She gave him a chilly nod, beautiful in her peasant dress and bright makeup with tiny silk flowers in her hair. Michel pressed his lips together in a flat smile, returning her nod as a gesture of solidarity.

"You'll be tremendous," he told her.

"You too."

Several minutes into Act One, when Lisa turned her head to look into the eyes of her aristocratic seducer, the conductor raised his baton high, ready to pull back the tempo. And then he very quickly hurried the tempo on again. Fucking dancers! He wished to God they'd make up their minds!

At the back of the auditorium Charles Crown raised his eyebrows meditatively. Yes . . . nice, he thought after a few moments' consideration; but different: chaste and yet flirtatious.

At the moment when Albrecht captured Giselle and placed his lips on hers, the first half-dozen rows of the audience could have sworn they saw a shudder pass through her body. Or maybe they just imagined it.

42

WHEN THE TWO-WEEK RUN at the Coliseum finally came to an end
the entire company flew to New York for three performances of *Coppélia*
and then buckled down to a fortnight's rehearsal before the start of the
autumn tour.

They were all tired. Marina, in particular, was shattered. With Michel
tied up in performances, she'd been working so hard she hadn't even had
time for her regular sessions with her beauty therapist and a fine beard
was starting to reemerge on her pale cheeks.

"Take the rest of the week off," Michel told her. "Phone in sick. I'll
cover your classes and rehearsals."

Marina was too weary even to argue. She sloped off home and collapsed back into bed.

Crown was exhausted too, but high on caffeine and nervous energy.
His new piece, *Ghosts,* had been well received by the press, with only a
few disapproving grumbles from shocked traditionalists and one or two
outright snubs from critics who'd been waging personal war against
Crown for years. Boyle, surprisingly, gave both the ballet and Rob an un-
reserved thumbs-up.

Michel enjoyed rehearsing the lead role in the new ballet—it was
quirky and melodramatic—but he argued with Crown ceaselessly about
the interpretation.

"Of course you're bloody well frightened," Crown insisted, during a session which had fallen apart because choreographer and dancer couldn't agree on motivation. "I ought to know; I made the sodding piece."

"Why would I be frightened? I'd be pleased to see her; I'd want to touch her but she'd be scared of me."

"Michel, you're talking balls. You murdered her, okay? Her ghost walks in through the French windows and you're scared shitless."

"But the audience don't know I killed her until the flashback. If I turn into a jelly when her ghost appears in Act One, they'll just think I'm spineless."

Crown smacked the palm of his hand against his forehead in frustration.

"You murdered your wife. You're mad with guilt. She comes back to haunt you and you're petrified of retribution. What the fuck's wrong with that?"

Michel was obstinate. "No, I'd want to see her. You said yourself I'm insane. It doesn't alter the moral argument of the piece. Later, if you like, when I face the reality of what I've done, then I can be scared."

Crown pursed his lips.

"Big of you, Michel."

"Let's just try it, yeah? What do you think, Lisa?"

She waved a hand to show she didn't care either way. She was keeping well out of this one.

"Alright," Crown sighed. "You're telling me the combination into the arabesque is him reaching out to touch her, not him trying to fend her off?"

"Yes."

"Okay, we'll give it a whirl as there's clearly no other way of shutting you up." Crown turned to Lisa. "Can you do that, darling? Pull back as though you're horrified by the thought of him touching you."

"Oh, yeah. I can do that."

Lisa and Michel exchanged very quick glances; caustic on Lisa's side, irritated on Michel's. Crown caught the significance of the exchange but said nothing as they moved into position to try the new version of the pas de deux. The estrangement between the two dancers was extremely contained; that glance was about as nasty as it ever got.

The autumn tour started in Birmingham and moved on to Liverpool. Michel and Lisa danced a few *Giselle*s and concentrated on pulling together their partnership for *Ghosts*.

Michel had turned the whole piece upside down; if he was glad to see the ghost of his wife in the first scene, then his following anguished solo must be one of grief at losing her again instead of fear that she'd destroy him. And so on. Crown watched Michel pick his masterpiece apart with grudging curiosity. Michel seemed pretty certain he knew what he was doing.

"There are four critics booked in to see you dance this piece next week," Crown told him. "I bet you a fiver every one of them hates it."

"Okay, you're on," Michel said.

Michel badly needed his absorption in his work at the moment. Despite his joy at performing again and the high morale amongst the company, he was burdened by unwelcome thoughts: nagging images that spiraled around in his mind and wouldn't leave him alone.

At night, when he should have been sleeping, he sat in his featureless hotel rooms in Birmingham, Liverpool, or Bath thinking about Primo, about the months before his suicide when Michel had been too engrossed in his work to notice how deeply his friend had sunk into despair. And if he had noticed it, what then? Would he have stretched out his hand to Primo and tried to pull him out of the abyss? He hoped the answer was yes. The alternative didn't bear thinking about.

He knew that Primo's visit to the dressing room in the Coliseum after the premiere had been his last. He would never see Primo again.

Sometimes, lying awake in his hotel room, Michel thought about Lisa. The memory of making love to her still troubled him, catching him out with unwanted erotic images as he tried to bury his guilt. Once he even leaped out of bed, flinging back the bedclothes, and poured a glass of cold water over his head to dispel a discomfiting picture that lingered in his mind.

His decision to continue partnering Lisa had been a practical one. None of the other male principals would work with her and there was no woman in the company whose style suited him so well. But the sexuality in the roles they danced together fed the demon that lurked between them. In rehearsals Lisa was calm and professional—she knew those were the only terms under which Michel would dance with her—but Michel was well aware how deeply he had hurt her and how bitterly she loathed him. There would be no reconciliation with Lisa. He had seen parts of her and touched parts of her that made friendship between them impossible.

Many of his sleepless hours were filled with thoughts of Jonni. His mind endlessly replayed their nonmeeting in Charing Cross Road. How self-possessed she had looked. And how happy. And the confident, good-looking man beside her—he had recognized Guy Dakin from the television. Jonni's life had moved on while his own . . . had he moved backward? Sideways? Not at all?

Michel lay in his uncomfortable bed in the fake-pine-paneled hotel in Liverpool vainly chasing sleep around inside his head. He gazed at the ceiling, remembering all those sleepless nights before his breakdown. Sooner or later something was going to have to give. He couldn't survive without sleep forever.

After Michel's first performance of *Ghosts* in Bath, Charles Crown came into his dressing room and perched on the arm of a heavy sofa. Michel was drying himself, just out of the shower.

"What did you think, then?" Michel asked, throwing his towel over the costume rail and reaching for his boxer shorts.

Crown took a five-pound note out of his wallet and held it out to him.

"No," Michel said, "keep it until the crits come out. I want to know what you thought."

The choreographer lit a cigarette and tossed the match into a bin next to the full-length mirror.

"You were right, of course. It made perfect sense. The flashback scene where you murdered her was horrific."

Michel flicked his T-shirt off the back of a chair with a smug smile. "Yes, I thought you'd like it."

"Lisa was great. Sheer bloody terror. Marvelous."

At that, Michel's smile became a sardonic one. He'd felt that terror as he bore down on her, hands outstretched to encircle her throat.

"Bit of method acting there, I think."

Crown shook his head and drew on his cigarette.

"I'd be scared of you coming at me with all that evil on your face. I thought you were really going to strangle her for a second."

"She seems to have survived; even squeezed my hand in the curtain call. Let's see if we can persuade her to come to the pub. You'll have to ask her, though, Charles."

Crown nodded and smoked in silence while he watched Michel dress. No, he hadn't been wrong; that air of repressed tension about him hadn't just been nerves leading up to his first go at *Ghosts*. Something was definitely wearing him down.

"You look tired," he said, as Michel crouched to tie his shoelaces.

"I am. Not been sleeping very well. All these lumpy bloody hotel beds."

"Anything on your mind?"

"Lots of things; nothing special."

Michel and Lisa danced their fifth performance of *Ghosts* on the BNB's last night in Southampton, a Friday in early November.

There were twelve whole days before the next set of dates in Manchester and Edinburgh, and the whole company breathed a sigh of relief as the curtain came down on Friday evening. They were ready for a few nights off. But, all the same, there was a touch of melancholy in the atmosphere backstage as the dancers cleared out their dressing rooms, bundling possessions into bags and stacking their makeup boxes by the stage door to be loaded into the wardrobe lorry. However glad you were to be going home it was always sad to leave a theater. These places became home in a few short days.

Crown's voice echoed through the dressing rooms over the Tannoy—"okay, girls and boys, because I'm such a softhearted bugger, class tomorrow at two p.m."—and a universal cheer went up around the theater. The past six weeks had been long and hard. They deserved a lie-in.

Michel was dressed in his jeans and a sweater, packed up and ready to go but still sitting on the chrome-framed chair next to his dressing table. One of the younger girls was sitting on his knee, an unthinkable liberty if they were back in Victoria where he was a figure of authority but permissible here in the theater where they were all equals.

The dressing room was long and narrow, almost hygienic in its Formica-paneled symmetry. The chairs were angular and uncomfortable, and the shelves were lacquered metal. Even the small window, high up on the end wall, was framed with aluminium. Glaring strip lighting, brown carpet tiles, and utterly neutral paintwork all added to the impersonal atmosphere of the room. In these sterile surroundings Michel and Fiona were engaged in quiet conversation.

Michel's elbow was resting on the dressing table and his head was propped on his fist as he looked up at her face.

"It's all on here," he said, patting her thigh.

"I know. I've dieted and dieted but it doesn't do any good. I'm just fat."

"No, you aren't. Look at the rest of you; skinny as anything. I don't think you're working properly in class at the moment."

"I don't like Nikolayeva's classes; she's too—"

"Uh-uh," Michel interrupted, "don't blame Galina. She's not the only one who takes classes. I'll have a look at what you're doing tomorrow. Maybe you need to pull things up a bit more. You're sometimes lazy, you know."

"Lazy?" Fiona's bright eyes frowned from her childlike, freckled face. "I work much longer hours than most of the—"

"I mean the way you use your muscles. Listen, can you," he shifted her slightly on his knee, "can you stop wriggling like that? It's turning me on."

She sat still and looked into his eyes, holding them for a long moment with an expression of daring invitation. Michel lifted his head from his hand and raised his eyebrows dubiously. Then he smiled and shook his head. Fiona's mouth twitched a wistful little shrug.

They were interrupted by the familiar crackle of the Tannoy and a booming announcement from the stage door: "Visitor for Miss Parfitt; Miss Parfitt to the stage door, please." Hearing the name broadcast through the speaker, Fiona looked at the ballet master in curiosity.

"Do you fancy Lisa?"

He clicked his tongue and frowned.

"Nope. What makes you think that?"

"Oh, I don't know: the way you don't seem to get on anymore. It's like you deliberately avoid each other. Mel swears the two of you have slept together but the rest of us don't think so."

"You girls are impossible. Tell the fishwives in the changing room that Lisa and I haven't slept together, we aren't going to, and that's the end of the story."

"So why aren't you friends then?"

"Has she told you we aren't?"

"No, she says you get on . . ." Fiona imitated Lisa's broad American accent, ". . . just peachy, but—"

"Then you have your answer."

There was a hurried knock and someone called out to him through the closed door. "Say, are you still there?"

Fiona and Michel exchanged glances. Michel smiled at the blush which stole over the girl's cheeks as he turned his head toward the door.

"Come in, Lisa."

When he saw his partner's face, pale and deeply worried, he tipped Fiona quickly off his knee and stood up.

"Off you go, Fee. I'll see you in class tomorrow."

Fiona trotted away, eyeing Lisa inquisitively as she left the room, while Lisa stood and stared at Michel in motionless alarm. For a few seconds they just looked at each other. Michel's mouth opened in silent question. It was the first time they had been alone together since that memorable interview in Michel's office more than two months ago.

He shook his head. "What is it? Are you okay?"

She was totally disarmed, raising her hand softly to her throat almost as she had earlier this evening when he had murdered her onstage.

"It's Dad," she whispered. "He's here and he wants to see you."

"Dad? Your father?"

She nodded blankly.

"Jacques St. Michel is here?" He too had lowered his voice to a whisper.

Michel held the dressing-room door open for Lisa to walk out ahead of him. As he followed her into the corridor he laid his hand unconsciously on her back and she threw him off with a vigorous shake of her shoulders. Michel lifted his hand away with an exaggerated gesture, annoyed at her pettiness. The last thing he needed right now was hostility from his partner-sister-lover. Lisa must have known how badly he would be shaken by her announcement. For once she might have moved just one step closer to him.

He could hear his own heart thumping. It was a good thing he hadn't known about this before the performance; he would have been a nervous wreck. For more than a decade he had avoided speaking or even thinking about his father, hiding from himself and everyone around him how much it still hurt that Jacques could spend time in the same city as him without making any effort to see him. He declared unmixed antipathy toward him, scoffing at his choreography—though secretly he admired it—and laughing at the rumors of his bad behavior. And then there had been all those years when he had denied the relationship, even to Charles Crown.

But Michel had kept his ears open despite himself, and paid attention to articles about the choreographer when they appeared in the dance literature. If the name St. Michel leaped to his attention when it cropped up in the media it wasn't because there was a fifty-fifty chance it was referring to himself. Michel could no more disregard his unknown father than he could pass by a reference to Jonni in the glossy magazines that littered the theater green rooms.

Ever since he could remember, he had maintained in his mind the certainty that he would meet his father one day—by chance or in just such a situation as this. Now that the longed-for and dreaded meeting was at hand he was terrified. What could he say to the man? A whole lifetime of news to exchange. A whole lifetime of grudges. A lifetime of need.

Lisa had slipped away to her dressing room and Michel caught up with Crown, who was strolling along the corridor with the stage manager, Andy.

"Charles, do something for me, will you?"

All expression vanished from the artistic director's face when he saw the intensity in Michel's eyes and the unusual flush which colored his temples. Crown had never met anyone less excitable than his protégé and yet there was no question that some uncommon apprehension—or enthusiasm—had gripped him now.

"Name it."

"How are you getting up to London?"

"Andy's driving. I'm going with him."

"Take Lisa with you. See her safely home."

Crown nodded and tried to question him with his eyes but Michel turned back toward his dressing room after only a very brief glance of acknowledgment.

Thirty seconds after the door closed behind him there was a firm knock. Crown or St. Michel?

"Yup. Come in."

It had never occurred to Michel that his father might be shorter than him. He remembered—or thought he remembered—the man to have been a giant.

Jacques St. Michel stood in front of the door, which closed slowly behind him on sprung hinges. He smiled as he looked at the younger man in wonder, through gray eyes that were frighteningly familiar.

Michel returned his stare numbly. There he was, finally, after all these years: the man for whom he had given up his home and his childhood. Now that they were face-to-face the similarity between them was astounding. His father might be five or six centimeters shorter but the proportions of their bodies were exactly the same. And his curly hair, the color of dusty straw. The shape of his face. He was older of course—fifty perhaps—but they might both have been turned out of the same mold. Only his mouth was different; Michel's was soft and wide while his father's was a thin, hard line, despite his smile.

The thoughts which preoccupied both men during the long silence evidently followed the same lines. Michel saw Jacques St. Michel glance at his own reflection in the full-length mirror just inside the door, confirming the extraordinary resemblance. And then he laughed almost silently, returning his gaze to his son's face.

"Eh! Te voilà, Jean-Baptiste."

Michel saw him move to embrace him and quickly preempted the gesture by holding out his hand. As they shook hands formally Michel smiled and attempted to explain away the awkwardness which had left him hitherto speechless.

"Je suis bouleversé. Vous m'avez surpris."

His father drew himself up in reproof. *"Ne me vouvoie pas!"*

Michel didn't know what to say. Brought up in the strict environment of the Académie, he found it hard to use the informal "tu," as his father requested, when he was speaking to a stranger and a man nearly twice his age. He moistened his lips, looking at his father without replying.

"Perhaps you would like that we should talk in English," Jacques said. He spoke with a very strong French accent combined with long American vowels. "I speak very good English."

"Yes, if you like."

The older man smiled and looked around him, indicating the setting for their meeting with a wave of his hand.

"So, Jean-Baptiste, you are in number one dressing room. Very good."

"Everyone calls me Michel."

"But it is me that has given you your name. It is a good name."

Michel smiled again. "Whatever; I don't really mind." If Jacques St. Michel wanted to call him Jean-Baptiste, that was his privilege. But Michel couldn't help feeling that it widened the gulf already existing between them.

His father seemed unaware of any possible embarrassment or discomfort in the situation.

"Would you like to go and talk over a drink? I detest the English people but I love English pubs."

"Sure. I'll show you one of our locals."

They left the theater together—it was more or less deserted by now—and walked across the unlit car park toward The Jolly Sailor on the waterfront. Michel had deliberately chosen a pub that wasn't frequented by members of the company. The barman looked from Michel's face to the face of his father and smiled before he turned away to pour the drinks. Their relationship was instantly apparent, even to a perfect stranger.

"Did you see the show tonight?" Michel asked, trying not to betray how much he cared about his father's answer as he set his drink on a beer mat on the small corner table and shuffled along a bench to sit opposite him.

"Yes, I did. I do not like Crown's choreography but it is an interesting ballet. The steps, of course, are nonsense. Childishly emotive. But you are a very remarkable dancer, eh?"

Michel looked down at his beer glass with a smile. There were a hundred reasons why he should loathe the man who had just bought him a drink but, irrationally, he wanted Jacques St. Michel's approval more than he had ever consciously wanted anything. Michel felt his own disloyalty in not sticking up for Crown's choreography but, after all, St. Michel was a choreographer of equal renown. They were entitled to be rivals.

"I should think it's rather hard to judge my work from this piece. It's not as technical as some."

"I have seen videos."

Michel looked up at him.

"Of my dancing?"

"Oh, yes. *Swan Lake*. Cabrioles which cut the air like scissors, eh? And this and this." He made several movements with his hands in the air imitating Michel's virile port de bras, turning his head sharply and raising his chin to indicate a particular nobility of posture. "What a dancer!" he said. "What a dancer!"

Michel's face changed color in a rare blush. After so many years spent craving his father's notice, he was absurdly pleased. His dancing had earned much praise from different quarters over the years but it had rarely been delivered to his face, and never by someone whose good opinion mattered so deeply to him. He found himself comparing his father's zeal and warmth to Crown's cool approbation.

"Lisa's fantastic, isn't she?" he asked, looking down at his glass again as he diverted the conversation modestly. "You must be incredibly proud of her."

The choreographer made a dismissive gesture. "Very technical; very lively. But you have that special thing, Jean-Baptiste." His pale-gray eyes lit up in excitement. "You are much better dancer than I ever was. What you have comes rarely but, when it comes, then you have a dancer who is not only good but also great. You have genius."

Michel spread his hands, laughing. "That means nothing to me. Yes, if you're talking about Makarova or Baryshnikov but, for myself, I just get on and do the steps. All I can tell is whether my feet are stretched and my turns are under control." He paused, still grappling with his father's compliment. "Do you mind if I smoke?"

"No, do as you please; I'll have one too. Thank you. Your training has been good. Henri was the right teacher for you, no?"

Michel lit both their cigarettes.

"Christ, I can hardly remember. Charles Crown has taught me for so many years."

"Yes . . . Crown. Well, he has made good work of it. But Henri has built a strong foundation—he studied at the Opéra, you know, and went on to dance with American Ballet Theatre. I knew him there very well. I made my first pieces on him."

Michel sat smoking for several minutes while Jacques talked with animation about dancing and dancers. His enthusiasm was magnetic and yet Michel gradually found himself withdrawing from the conversation. It felt increasingly strange to be sitting there listening to Jacques talk about the differences between American and European ballet as though they were unconnected strangers with nothing in common apart from dance. The longer he talked, the harder Michel found it to understand why this man asked him no question about his life. He longed to say something which broached the connection between them but he was tongue-tied.

Eventually the choreographer sat back in his chair and surveyed the interior of the traditional saloon bar, smiling dryly at the image of provincial Englishness that surrounded him. At half past ten on a Thursday night the pub was half-empty. A few couples sat quietly under the frosted windows chatting over pint glasses and metal ashtrays.

"So restrained," Jacques said, watching them with amusement. "So very British and discreet."

Michel thought back to his father's earlier comment about British pubs. This supercilious Anglophobia was beginning to get on his nerves.

"If you hate the English what made you marry an Englishwoman?"

Jacques looked at him and raised an eyebrow.

"My wife is American."

"But . . . my mother."

"Caroline and I were not married."

"Not married?"

His father shook his head and clicked his tongue.

Michel was dumbstruck. Carrie had never mentioned Jacques St. Michel as her husband but then she had never mentioned him at all. Michel had just assumed it was so. No wonder Uncle Jim had regarded the alliance with such disapproval. Despite his own sexual non-conformity, Uncle Jim had believed in keeping up appearances.

"I didn't realize," he said.

Jacques looked at him with wry interest, examining him with the same air of casual superiority he had applied to the interior of the pub a few moments ago, aloof from any personal involvement. After a while he exhaled heavily through his nose and nodded.

"I expect you want to know why I have come here."

Michel's eyes darkened in surprise. It hadn't occurred to him that his father needed any reason to come. He had imagined he merely wanted to see what kind of dancer—and what kind of man—existed in his son.

"Why have you come?"

"I want you to dance in America. I am making a ballet for the summer season. I want to create it on you."

"I'm tied up here," he said, frowning, not clearly understanding.

"Your contract runs from January to January. So you will finish this season and then come. That's time enough."

Michel began to shake his head slowly, his rib cage squeezing his chest tightly as the truth began to dawn on him that there was no personal interest in Jacques's appearance here in Southampton, no paternal impulse; not even curiosity. He was only here for the dancer.

"I appreciate your wanting me," he said, "but I'm just getting settled into performing for the BNB. Charles has new projects coming up for me. I can't walk out on him."

"First thing they teach you at the Académie," Jacques said with a smile. "Is no such word as can't."

"Sorry?"

Jacques raised his hands in a shrug. "Jean-Baptiste, you have gone your own way always. Never in this life does one get something for nothing. I ask you to come to America for one year; you owe me that much."

Michel's mouth fell open. He stared thunderstruck at the unabashed face of the man opposite him.

"I owe you?"

"Your education was very expensive. Seven years you studied in France; that was not for free, you understand?"

Michel couldn't believe he was hearing this. He laid his hand incredulously on his chest. "I . . . owe . . ." he pointed at his father," . . . you?"

"Exactly."

The two men looked at each other expressionlessly.

"No," Michel said. There was no way Jacques St. Michel was going to turn up in his life after twenty-four years of absence and get away with that. "No! I don't owe you anything. You paid for me to go to dance school in Paris; it was the least you could do. It was nothing. Less than nothing."

"It cost me a great deal of money."

"I didn't ask you to send me to Paris. If you didn't want me in your life you should have left me alone."

"What would you be now if I hadn't arranged for you to be trained, eh?"

"A farmer, perhaps, or a builder or a piano teacher—whatever Carrie wanted me to be. I'd probably be a happy man. And she might be a happy woman. She didn't want me to go to ballet school."

"Yeah, yeah, I know. She wrote to me letters full of anger after you were living in France."

Michel's throat contracted with the pain of remembering all those years of hurt and rejection.

"It would have been better for us both if you had left us in peace."

Jacques St. Michel scoffed.

"Look at you. Look; you are a great dancer. You would push aside anything which got in the way of your dancing, I know. Dance is your whole life. You owe that to me, Jean-Baptiste: your whole life."

"And what do you owe me?" Michel demanded. "More than that. You brought me into the world. I didn't ask to be born."

"Ah, don't give me that shit."

"But it's true. And you owe me. You owe me and you owe Lisa, that poor little bitch who was sobbing her eyes out in the car park because you couldn't be bothered to say one bloody word to her about her performance on the stage tonight."

Michel was sitting up straight on the bench, his hands resting flat on the table as he glared at his father. Jacques St. Michel seemed amused.

"Ah yes, Lisa. So you have a sister, eh? You like her?"

"Like her? What d'you mean, do I like her? You told her I didn't exist. You made her believe I was your nephew."

"Nephew, son; what's the difference? Her mother is New England Baptist. She would not have married me if she knew I had an illegitimate son."

Michel screwed his face up, baffled. "But you must have known she'd find out."

His father tossed his hand in the air.

"Of course. It doesn't matter anymore. The marriage with Lisa's mother is over. Yes, I knew she'd find out, especially when Lisa joined the British National where you are *maître de ballet*."

Michel leaned forward over the table, lowering his voice as he said through clenched teeth, "So you thought you'd let it come to light by itself. Well that was a fucking stupid piece of thoughtlessness, wasn't it?"

Jacques laughed. "Yeah, she told me about that."

Michel frowned in disbelief at the callousness of the man before him.

"How can you find it funny? I screwed her. Your daughter, fucked by her own brother: don't you even care? I abused her—made myself anathema to her"—he caught the flicker of incomprehension in Jacques's eyes—"*elle m'a en abomination.* And you let me do that to her! Jesus Christ, that girl is your daughter!" Michel pointed at the door of the pub, indicating that Lisa was out there somewhere, abandoned by her father and defiled by her brother. "Doesn't that mean anything to you at all?"

Lisa sat in the back of Andy's car for the whole journey between Southampton and London with Charles Crown's arm around her shoulders and her face buried in his soft leather jacket.

"What do you think they're saying to each other?" she asked in a tiny voice. Crown tightened his arm about her.

"Oh . . ." He rubbed his hand over the steamed-up window beside him and looked out into the darkness, at the bare hills and the cold, black soil of the fields whizzing past the motorway. ". . . just catching up on all those lost years, I expect."

———

When Michel saw that the cool smile remained unaltered on his father's face, the energy drained from his reproach and he propped his elbows on the table, resting his forehead on his hands.

"I screwed my own bloody sister."

"So, she'll get over it. She's tough. She's got a good body, yeah?"

"Oh Jesus. Don't."

Jacques St. Michel shifted in his chair and folded his arms.

"I don't like women much—except for fucking. I don't even like them so much in dance, you know. Lisa's got a good figure: small, compact, strong like Margot Fonteyn, no? She's got a cute ass and she knows how to use it. If she makes herself sexy she's going to get laid. Don't worry, it's nothing so surprising for her. At least it proves you aren't a faggot."

Michel looked at his father blankly.

"You don't like women but you lived with Carrie, what . . . five years? And you married Lisa's mother."

Jacques smiled. "There's always sex. You like women or you hate them, there's still sex, eh? I used to be . . . romantic, I think you would say. I used to think if you want a woman bad enough it means you love her. There's been no room in my life for sentiment. I live a life in dance." He widened his eyes expressively and nodded at his son. "You know."

Michel tried to tell himself that he didn't know; he didn't know at all. He looked at the hard face and the ruthless stone-gray eyes. There was strength and resilience in those eyes but also experience. Jacques St. Michel hadn't achieved his success without paying a heavy price.

"I remember you," Michel said with a bleak half smile.

"Do you?"

"Yes, a little. Just from dreams I've had since I came to England."

"You remember I taught you how to stand *en attitude*? You only just learned to walk."

The idea was a strange one to Michel. He wondered if his father had ever held him in his arms and rocked him to sleep, ever kissed him, ever played and laughed with him.

"No," he said. "I only remember you quarreling with Carrie; hitting her."

Jacques put down his drink and, for the first time, his face clouded with defensive anger.

"She made me mad. Always she tried to interfere with my work. You know how it is with women; they are all the same—Lisa and her mother too. I couldn't stay with Caroline. I was a dancer. I couldn't be listening always to complaints: I was not caring enough, I spend too much time at the studio. She even wanted me to skip class every time the fucking baby got sick and had to be . . ."

He stopped. After a moment he made a small gesture of apology but Michel shrugged. It didn't make much difference anymore.

"You've gone through your whole life without loving anyone?" Michel asked.

Jacques St. Michel no longer appeared superior and remote. He leaned forward in his chair to talk to his son, man to man, dancer to dancer. His reply was accompanied by insistent movements of his hands, reinforcing every word.

"When you are committed to a life in dance, Jean-Baptiste, there is not room for anything else. When you are not onstage or in the studio, still you are working in your head. Nothing must be allowed to stop you. You have a career in dance . . . or . . ." he slammed his hand on the polished surface of the table for emphasis, ". . . you have a life with a family and people you make sacrifices for. You do not have both. You ask me if I have ever loved. Yes, I have loved faithfully. Dance."

Michel stood up to leave.

"I've got to take class tomorrow; I haven't prepared anything."

"Will you come to America?"

"No."

The choreographer shrugged and waved him away with his hand. "Then *au revoir.* Good-bye, Jean-Baptiste." He smiled and added with irony, "Look after your sister, eh?"

Michel met his cold gray eyes with the uncomfortable sensation of gazing into a mirror.

"I will," he said.

43

THROUGHOUT THE DRIVE BACK TO LONDON, Michel's mind was empty apart from an occasional image of his father's face or involuntary recollection of a word or a gesture. He kept his eyes focused on the road and pulled into the outside lane to overtake the slow, articulated lorries. He had timed his journey badly; heavy rain slowed the traffic down and sent up great fountains of spray from the back wheels of the trucks.

His mouth felt dry and he was having trouble staying awake. Driving through rain in the dark always made him sleepy, and his long wakeful nights were catching up with him. He pulled into the services at Fleet to fill up with petrol and drink a cup of coffee but once he was back on the motorway he began to feel drowsy again. The extra concentration needed with the poor visibility made his eyelids feel heavy, and the rhythmic sloshing of the windscreen wipers lulled him.

"No room for sentiment." He could hear the strong French-American accent clearly in his ears. "*You* know."

Michel shook his head to wake himself up. He turned on the radio and listened to pop music until he turned off the M3 at Sunbury.

As soon as he hit well-lit streets his sleepiness passed. He was nearly home. His mind was blank; so blank he took a wrong turning and found himself crossing Wandsworth Bridge instead of Chelsea. How many times had he driven this route? Come on, he told himself, just get yourself home. He slammed on his brakes as a woman with an umbrella stepped out from the pavement on the King's Road without warning—at least he assumed it had been without warning; he certainly hadn't seen her.

He closed the door of the flat and stopped to think, filling his mind with anything that would keep out the memory of his meeting with his father. Coffee. Of course there was no milk but he could have black. He preferred it that way. The flat was warm; Peggy must have been in to switch on the heating. Dear old Peggy.

He opened the fridge. Milk. Pints of it. Bless her. He must remember to pay her for it when she came in tomorrow. Post; there must be post. Only a couple of bills and a postcard from Roly saying he was in panto up in Newcastle. The rest of his post had been forwarded to Southampton.

Michel took his coffee into the studio and turned on the overhead lights. He smoked two cigarettes in succession, pacing the floor with his cup in his hand. Then he put down his empty cup on the Steinway and pulled back the heavy gray curtain which covered the mirrors; pulled it right to the end of the rail until the whole length of the studio was reflected in the smooth glass, doubling its size.

He stood in the middle of the room and looked at his own reflection. This was everything he possessed: his body and his face. Nothing was missing from the picture of Michel's life. No single tie connected him to any other living being.

"A career in dance . . . or . . . a family and people you make sacrifices for." He pictured his father's collusive smile. "*You* know."

Slowly Michel straightened his spine and turned out his hips as he did at the barre every morning. He stretched out one arm and glided into a gentle series of chassés, following the movements through with his hands gracefully, always watching the mirror. "Yes, I have loved faithfully. Dance."

Walking toward the mirror, Michel looked into his own eyes. He'd rejected every word that man had said to him but it rang very true, didn't it? He had made his choice . . . when? When he was eight and he'd left Carrie standing alone on the platform at Charing Cross? When he'd allowed Primo to drift out of his life? When he'd watched Jonni walk away and not called after her?

He stood within a foot of the mirror and studied his face. He saw his father's face there: the face of an isolated, successful man. Success for whom? For what?

Jacques St. Michel had thrown in the towel and walked out on his home, his country, his child, and the mother of his child. As Michel looked at his reflection he realized his father would have been almost exactly his own age at the time. He thought of his own broken marriage. Thank Christ at least there was no child.

What his father had been when Michel was four years old, Michel was now. What his father was now, Michel would be in twenty years' time.

He covered his face with his hands—not the face he could touch and feel but the face in the mirror—stretching his arms out in front of him. When he closed his eyes he could still see his father's face, and he knew that his own face, so similar, remained behind his hands inside the cold glass.

Michel clenched his hands into fists and slammed them, using the whole of his weight, onto the reflection of his face. The mirror shattered, shards of glass cascading to the floor with a violent tinkling clatter. He raised his arms above his head and brought down the rest of the mirrored panel with a further furious barrage from his fists.

When it was reduced to a pile of sharp fragments on the floor he destroyed the panel next to it, raining blows in rage; rage at himself and at his stupidity for letting Jonni go, the one really good and valuable thing he had managed to seize hold of in the midst of this emotional wasteland he called his life. But each time he demolished the face of the man who had squandered his marriage so carelessly, the same face reappeared beside it in the mirror. He roared at the reflection he couldn't obliterate, wiping it out again and again.

Michel's rage was out of control. As he annihilated his reflection in the mirror, time after time, he was annihilating the man who had come so close to destroying his own sister. He was annihilating the egotist who had allowed Lynne to break her heart over him. He was annihilating the child who had turned his back on his mother for the sake of the unknown father he had spent his whole childhood trying to emulate, and who had now become the single person on earth he most wanted *not* to resemble. Most of all, as he demolished himself in the mirror, he was annihilating the unfeeling monster who had gone to his best friend's funeral—the friend who had died because of his negligence—and not shed a single tear.

At last, as he raised his fists to bring the last unbroken piece of mirror crashing to the floor, he stood still and let the shattered glass rain over his hands. When the noise of destruction had ceased he remained there, breathing heavily and looking at the wall that he hadn't seen for almost twelve years.

All around him lay the results of the last ten minutes' work. He wiped his face with his forearm and walked away from the mountain of broken glass into the hallway. There was a radio on the table in the hall and he kicked it hard, sending it flying against the wall where it smashed to smithereens.

But he had only kicked it for fun. He felt great.

He staggered, exhausted, into the bedroom and collapsed onto the bed. Within ten seconds he was sound asleep.

He was woken by a piercing shriek which sent him flying out of the bedroom and across the hall. If he hadn't, by chance, fallen asleep in his jeans he would have been standing in the studio, stark naked, face-to-face with his cleaning lady.

Her horror-struck eyes turned from the bare, blood-spattered studio wall toward him, incomprehension deepening the wrinkles in her care-worn face.

"It's alright," he said quickly. "It was me, Peggy. There's nothing to worry about."

For Michel, the sight of all that broken glass brought an instant flood of satisfaction. Peggy nodded blankly, unable to take her eyes off him.

"What happened to your face, dear?"

Michel crouched down and looked at himself in one of the angular shards of mirror which had fallen propped against the bottom of the wall. A very unpleasant picture greeted his eyes: copious blood smeared with dust and sweat. He raised his hand and touched his cheek just below his eye. He was beginning to become aware of odd stabs of pain awakening in different parts of his body.

"It's just a small cut," he said. "It won't look like anything once I've cleaned it up." He glanced at the chaos around them. "Leave all this. Tell you what; you go and make us both a cup of coffee while I have a shower. Would you turn the taps on for me?"

Peggy was the best sort of cleaning lady. She asked no questions and never made a drama out of a domestic crisis. She sat calmly in the kitchen drinking her coffee—heavily laced with the brandy she always kept with her for emergencies—and smiled at Michel's freshly showered face over the rim of her cup.

"It's going to take a good few black plastic bags to clear up all that glass, isn't it?"

"Don't you touch it, Peggy. I'll get someone to come in and sort it out. I'm sorry about the mess."

"Oh, I don't mind, dear. If you want to smash up your flat that's your affair."

It was after half past one by the time Michel set out toward Victoria and the BNB, striding quickly along the pavement, late for once in his life.

The November day was glorious: crisp autumnal sunlight, bracing and cold, which made Pimlico feel like the middle of the countryside. Today the road seemed wider and the trees, usually gray and corpselike, seemed vibrant and awake, tolerant of all the concrete and stone around them. Even the birds had forgotten the threat of winter, just around the corner.

Michel slowed the pace of his brisk walk and sniffed the hazy air. The BNB would just have to wait. As he strolled along he puzzled over the quality of the light which brightened everything in the street. He felt as though he had made the beautiful day all by himself.

And the despair he had felt driving back from Southampton last night? He searched for it inside himself but without success. A young woman passed him, running down the street holding on to her wide-brimmed hat as her large Alsatian took her for a much faster walk than she had intended. The animal had obviously been infected with the same joyful energy that made Michel's grin broaden as he followed the progress of dog and owner down the road with his eyes.

Michel felt an inexplicable sensation of lightness. He found he was quite unable to dwell on his meeting with Jacques St. Michel last night. So his father had turned out to be no father at all—except in the sense of the one brief physical act that had sparked Michel's existence. After years of obsessing about him, tormenting himself with the idea that he had somehow done something to anger his father, sitting through torturous performances of his ballets when his company came to Europe on tour, suddenly none of it mattered anymore. He threw out the thought of Jacques with a shake of his head as he turned down Belgrave Road toward the class that awaited him.

The women were already lined up at the barres when Michel strode into the studio. The bright sunshine outside flooded in through the windows and the women smiled because he was smiling, squinting into the blinding light which bounced off the mirrors.

"Sorry to keep you waiting, my darlings," he said. He took up his place in front of the mirror with his feet in a solid second position and his hands behind his back. "I'm afraid I haven't given your class a moment's thought so you'll have to put up with whatever I can come up with on the spur of the moment. How about some of Charles's Bolshoi exercises?"

There was a universal groan. A number of glances were exchanged. No one had expected to see Michel so bright and chirpy this morning. Rumor had it there'd been a scene between him and Lisa last night. Mel had certainly seen Lisa crying outside the theater and someone had said that Jacques St. Michel had been in the audience. Nobody was quite sure about anything.

"Who are we missing?" Michel asked. "Carla—typical. Tatjana, Lisa . . . anyone seen her? No, right . . . Josie?"

"Here, here!" Josie came scampering into the studio.

"Good. Let's do this thing. Fiona, come down here where I can keep an eye on you."

Michel's class that afternoon was full of laughter. He set a whole string of villainous exercises, calling out the steps without moving from his spot in front of the mirror, bombarding the women with cheeky insults to put them off.

At the end of the class Fiona approached him, still giggling breathlessly from the last horrendous allegro.

"Could you see whether my muscles were . . . Gosh, what happened to you?"

She touched her own face to indicate the cut on his cheek.

"It's nothing, Fee. I scratched it on a piece of broken glass."

Fiona decided immediately that it had been Lisa's doing, but Michel changed the subject to her overweight thighs and she didn't dare question him about it further. She couldn't wait to tell the girls.

On the way out of the studio she caught sight of his lacerated hands. Within ten minutes the entire company knew that Michel had been in a punch-up.

Lisa came into the canteen during the half-hour break between class and the first rehearsal of the afternoon. She was called for a rehearsal of *Ghosts* at four o'clock.

On the far side of the canteen she saw Michel surrounded by women from the corps. He was sitting with his hands in his lap being fed coffee from a plastic cup by Lizzi.

"Liz, you swine!" he cried, spluttering with helpless laughter as she spilled coffee all down the front of his T-shirt. The unexpected scene of merriment brought Lisa up short just as Michel spotted her through the queue for the drinks machine.

He wiped his chin on the shoulder of his shirt and stood up, still laughing, to go and meet her.

"Hi, darling; where were you? We missed you in class this morning."

She frowned at the unusual sparkle in his eyes and then lowered her gaze to his hands. As her eyes darted back to his face in fear Michel shook his head quickly, lowering his voice.

"No, no, I only hit the wall."

He held his hands out to show her the damage. They were hideous, puffy balloons, cut to ribbons and a deep purply blue where they weren't covered by thick, clotted blood.

"What happened?"

"I was on my own. I was just letting off steam."

Lisa took his hands very gently in hers to look at them. There was no tenderness in the way she held them but only a true sadist could have touched those hands with anything other than extreme care. Michel felt a sudden yearning to put his arms around her; she looked so young and confused as she stood staring openmouthed at his mutilated knuckles.

"You hit the wall? Jeez, your poor fingers."

"They'll heal. Look, I can still move my thumbs . . . well, that one, at any rate."

She gazed up into his eyes.

"Did the two of you quarrel, Michel?"

He dismissed the meeting with deliberate flippancy, smiling.

"No, we got on famously. You'd have thought we were father and son."

"Screw you." Lisa was incensed at his glibness; she'd been awake all night worrying. "Just forget I damn well asked. I really don't care."

She turned in a temper to leave but Michel called after her, "Wait a moment!" This was only the second time in nearly a year that Lisa had missed class. Her face was scarlet and her eyes were deep-set and glazed. He laid his wrist on her forehead. It was burning.

"I think you should go home to bed."

She shook her head in irritation.

"I'll get by. It's just a chill."

"I don't care what it is. Home you go; you shouldn't have come in at all."

"I've got rehearsals. Listen, Michel, you aren't my darned nursemaid so skip the phony concern. It doesn't suit you."

"This is your ballet master speaking, Lisa. You can't dance with that temperature. Go home and phone your doctor. Get Evelyn downstairs to call you a taxi; tell her I said to charge it to the company."

As he watched Lisa walk away, swaying slightly on her feet, his eyes creased up in sympathy. What sort of father wouldn't congratulate his daughter on a performance like the one she'd given last night? Jacques St. Michel was a bastard, he thought; he really was.

Charles Crown was furious when he saw Michel's hands. Michel had known he would be.

"You irresponsible prick," Crown said, looking at the hands which were spread before him on the desk. "How long's that lot going to take to heal? Are any of your fingers broken?"

Michel lifted his hands away and laid them carefully in his lap.

"Don't know. A couple, I should think. I'll get Physio to take some X-rays."

"Marvelous. How did you manage that, then?"

Michel smiled and rocked his chair on its two back legs, resting his feet against the side of the desk.

"I smashed up the studio at the flat. Actually, I enjoyed it."

"All the mirrors?"

"Yup. Fifty-six years' bad luck coming my way."

"Serves you right—stop rocking your chair; you'll break your neck. Well, I don't suppose you'll be doing much partnering in the next couple of months, will you? Tokyo and Sydney are going to go ballistic."

"Let them. Dancers get injured, it's in the rules." Michel felt no remorse about his wild rampage of the previous night. It was strangely gratifying to think of all that broken glass on the floor of the studio back home. The pain in his hands was nothing—in fact, his whole body hurt from the jarring violence which had shaken it but he didn't care.

"So what about Jacques?" Crown asked, standing up and turning his back to look for his provisional cast lists in the filing cabinet. "Did you get on alright with him?"

"Uh-huh. He didn't think much of your piece, I'm afraid. He liked your principal danseur, though."

"Did he now? Yes, I thought he might."

"Wants me to spend next year in the States, as a matter of fact."

Crown was still flicking through the files.

"Next year . . . really."

"Yes, from January. He wants to create a ballet on me."

"And what did you tell him, eh?"

"What d'you think? I told him where to stick his bloody ballet."

Crown turned around. "Did you?"

"Yes, of course." When he saw Crown's expression Michel's face fell in astonishment. "Charles! You can't seriously have thought I was going to defect to LA. Come on! That's ridiculous."

"Well, it did cross my mind. He is your father."

"What absolute tosh."

Crown pulled a wry face. "And you have been avoiding me all day."

"Too right, I have; I knew bloody well you were going to kick my arse when you saw my hands. How could you imagine I'd run off to America to work for someone who can't make the effort to contact his son once in twenty years? The man's an arrogant shit."

Crown sat down with the cast lists in his hand, rubbing his nose.

"Did your meeting get nasty?"

"Not really. We both made our feelings pretty clear to each other.

This," he said, raising a purple, swollen hand, "wasn't about him. He isn't worth it."

Crown agreed completely, but he didn't say so.

"Anyway, it's just as well I'm out of this season," Michel said, rocking his chair again. "I can't partner Lisa anymore. It's not right. If I'm going to dance from January you'll have to look me out a new tutu."

Crown folded his arms and nodded, raising his eyebrows.

"Take your pick."

"Not Marie or Tatjana."

"What's wrong with them?"

"Nothing technical but—you know what it's like—partnering them's a bit like masturbating: very pleasurable physically but not something you'd want to do in public. There's just no chemistry there."

"But there's chemistry with Lisa?"

"With Lisa it's not chemistry that's the problem, it's history. Find me someone like Lynnie, Charles. Someone who's got some fire and guts, and who isn't my sister. I know"—he folded his battered hands on top of his head and leaned back in his chair with a smile—"steal Sylvie Guillem from the Royal for me."

"I would if I could, believe me."

"But anyone will do. As long as she's a technical genius with blistering sex appeal, ultra-musical, with a body like Claudia Schiffer and feet like Darcey Bussell, and doesn't put me through psychological torture every twenty-eight days, I'm really not at all fussy."

Crown sat with his hand over his mouth, watching Michel with a pensive smile. Whatever Michel had been through last night it had wrought a remarkable change in his state of mind. Crown wasn't sure he had ever seen Michel quite so exuberant and extroverted. If he had, it certainly wasn't at any time since Primo's death. If it had been rage which made Michel smash up the studio in Pimlico it had left him high on adrenaline. You'd never think to look at him that he'd just buggered up the entire next two months' casting by injuring himself out of the running.

"Will you phone the glaziers for me later?" Michel asked, as he stood up to leave.

"Phone them yourself."

"Oh, I'll talk to them; I just need you to dial the number for me."

He raised his grotesquely swollen hand in salute and breezed out of the office. This was the glazier's lucky day. Two thousand pounds it had cost Michel to mirror the studio, and that had been over a decade ago.

On Monday, Crown and Michel went to Nottingham for a meeting with the BNB's big sponsor, leaving Marina behind in London to cope with rehearsals.

"I suppose we'll have to take the train," Crown grumbled. "You're not driving anywhere with those hands."

Michel yawned. It was eight in the morning and they were in Michel's flat in Pimlico. Crown had arranged to meet him there on the understanding that they'd take Michel's car but that was out of the question now.

"It's about time you learned to drive, Charles."

"Don't you start. I passed my driving test before you were born. I'm just not cut out to be a driver."

Michel was changing into smarter clothes on Crown's insistence. This was going to be a tricky meeting where appearances were vital.

"Why don't you drive my car?" he asked, strolling out of the bedroom in a gray silk suit with his tie dangling from his collar. "Do this up for me, will you? I'll keep an eye on you; make sure you don't hit anything."

Crown furrowed his brow trying to visualize a half Windsor tied from the front. "I haven't driven for fifteen years. We can work out what we're going to tell these big shots while we're on the train."

They took the tube to Euston and caught the 8:46 to Nottingham. It was another bright autumnal morning. Michel sat opposite Crown in the first-class compartment, looking through the window across gardens and rooftops.

"We're going to have to make this look good," Crown said. "Somehow we've got to convince them our plans for the summer are worth two hundred thousand to them."

"What are your plans for the summer?" Michel asked. He was distracted, gazing out at the speeding landscape of Hertfordshire.

"Well, the rep we've already planned, of course: *La Fille, Mefistofele,* our *Romeo.*"

"And the new piece?"

"Hmmm," said Crown musing. "I've been thinking about attempting a full-length ballet of *The Tempest*."

"Oh . . . yes."

Michel was barely listening. He was hearing, instead, strange whispers and half-remembered melodies inside himself. He wanted something and he didn't know what it was. He wanted lots of things. He felt frustrated, euphoric, anarchic—it was like watching an emotional fireworks display; high-energy sparks shooting off aimlessly into space.

"Charles, can I—"

"I want to—"

They both stopped.

Crown was reaching for his briefcase and he drew back his hand.

"Sorry, go on, Michel; you first."

"No, it's not important."

"No, really, you go ahead. Mine wasn't important either. Really."

Michel looked thoughtfully into his teacher's eyes.

"Charles, how come you've never given up on me?"

"Come again?"

"You. You're the only person who's never given up on me. I've alienated everyone who's ever come anywhere near me apart from you."

Crown frowned and ran his hand over his jaw. He looked at Michel, shaking his head.

"We're colleagues . . . friends. Give up on you? There's never been a question; I don't know what you mean."

"Everyone, Charles. Everyone except you. Jonni gave up on me. Lynne couldn't take me anymore; disappeared to South Africa. My mother gave up on me God knows how long ago. Primo gave up on me. Lisa detests me and I don't blame her. Even Roly and Annette don't call anymore."

Crown's piercing black eyes narrowed. "Are you saying they all gave up on you or that you drove them away?"

"Yes, as I said, I've alienated everyone. But you, Charles; you've stuck by me through thick and thin—picked me up and set me back on my feet when I was ready to let myself go to hell. So why haven't I alienated you?"

Charles Crown lit a cigarette and rested his head against the back of his seat, looking at Michel reflectively. He realized he probably knew this reserved young man better than anyone else did. Yes, Michel had isolated himself. Was the fact really only staring him in the face for the first time now?

He blew out a calm stream of smoke.

"I think," he said, "you'll find it's because I've never tried to tell you that I love you."

Michel turned his head away, immediately recognizing the truth in what he'd said. Even as Crown spoke the words he felt gates crashing shut inside him; bolts being driven home and locks turned. Already he could feel himself shifting Charles Crown's friendship into the past, erecting a barricade against the sentiment he'd just expressed.

"You'll find I'm not an easy man to drive away, Michel."

Michel forced himself to look Crown in the eye. They looked at each other for several long, difficult seconds. And then Michel turned his head again, back toward the leafless landscape racing past the window. A young woman with a buffet trolley stopped in the aisle beside them, asking Michel if he wanted tea or coffee. When Michel made no reply Crown answered for him, catching the young woman's eye and shaking his head.

Crown smoked his cigarette while he watched slow tears slide, one at a time, down Michel's face. Michel's tears were private, silent, and painful. Now and then he lifted his swollen hand to brush it over his jaw, but otherwise he was still.

"You know," Crown said, after a while, "the other night when you went off after the show with Jacques; yes, I was afraid he'd whisk you off to Los Angeles; and, yes, I was afraid he'd hurt you—and he did hurt you, I know. But more than that, I was so fucking jealous I didn't know what to do with myself."

Michel sniffed and wiped his eyes on his cuff, laughing. He smiled at Crown. "Hi, Dad."

Crown folded his arms with a sardonic grunt and looked out of the window.

"Don't give me any of your fucking lip, St. Michel."

When the train pulled into the station in Nottingham, Michel stretched his shoulders and neck before he stood up.

"I've got a bloody awful headache."

"Dehydration," Crown said, picking up his coat and briefcase. "We've got over an hour before this meeting. Let's go and find a coffee."

"Crying's a horrendous thing," Michel said, when they were sitting in a café across the road from the station. "Why on earth do women do so much of it?"

"Don't knock it," Crown told him. "We men spend the first twelve years of our lives learning not to cry and the next fifty trying to remember how."

The café was ugly and run-down. Red chipped Formica tabletops adorned with huge plastic pots of mustard and ketchup. Everything was peeling: the lino tiles on the floor, the yellow paint on the walls, the paper menus glued above the counter, handwritten by a dyslexic waiter.

Crown shook the glass sugar jar, tapping it to unclog the metal spout.

"You talked about all the people who've given up on you," he said, but Michel brushed the subject away with his hand. That conversation was in the past.

"Don't let's go back over that. Tell me about this new ballet."

"No, wait. I think you're being rather hasty, Michel. I think you might find none of those people have given up on you at all."

Michel raised his eyebrows and gazed into his weak coffee. He couldn't understand how it was possible to make coffee that looked and tasted so exactly like dishwater.

"Give it some thought," Crown insisted. Michel nodded but he wasn't convinced. He wondered about Jonni, whether Charles was right and there was a chance she might still think about him, or perhaps even, at some level, regret leaving him. He stirred his coffee and laid down the spoon with a sigh that inflated his cheeks.

"It's too late for thought," he said. "I wore them down, Charles. God knows, some of them tried hard enough but I slammed the door in their faces once too often."

"Perhaps they're distant because you keep them that way. What makes you so sure they gave up on you?"

Michel laughed grimly at that.

"Well, Primo, for instance. He didn't say so in so many words; he didn't really have to."

Crown wasn't smiling. He wasn't smiling at all. He frowned intently into Michel's eyes from under his knotted brow.

"Self-pity, Michel. If you're angry with Primo for committing suicide that's fine, but don't go attributing your own feelings to other people like that."

Michel blinked at him. "Are you angry with me?"

"Yes, I am. We all know that Primo gave up on himself but who are you to say he gave up on you? I happen to know he didn't."

"He didn't," Michel repeated.

"No."

Crown reached for his briefcase and laid it on the table, popping up the catches. "I've got something in here that belongs to you. I've had it for months. There never seemed to be a good moment to give it to you, and I wasn't sure whether you were ready to handle it. I was going to show it to you on the train. There's no need to discuss it at this meeting but I'd like to know how you feel about it before we go in."

He took a bound copy of Primo's score out of his case and laid it on the table in front of Michel.

Michel looked at the score, his face expressionless. Primo had first spoken about the full-length ballet he planned to write several years before he died. During the past two years Michel had vaguely wondered if any of it still existed—if any of it had ever been written—but he had imagined it as one of Primo's unfulfilled pipe dreams. Abandoned dreams had littered the path of self-destructive inactivity that had led Primo slowly downhill toward suicide.

"*The Tempest,*" he said, after flicking through the pages clumsily. "How much of it is there?"

"It's complete. Massive. Fully orchestrated. I got Max to play some of it for me; it's incredible."

"What are you going to do with it?"

"It's yours, Michel."

"Mine?"

"Look at the title page."

Michel turned to the front page and read the dedication. *For Michel. This is in return for that time you gave me your crossbow in* Swan Lake *so I wouldn't get in trouble with Charles and you got smacked round the head in-*

stead of me—you remember, amico? I can't say it in words so I have tried to write in this music what your friendship has meant to me. I hope you can forgive me that I won't be there to play it for you.

Michel wiped his eyes with the back of his hand.

"Jesus," he said referring to his tears, "once you get started with this stuff, it's hard to stop, isn't it? This is a photocopy; where's the original?"

"In my bank. The policeman who dealt with Primo's suicide found it in a rubbish skip and brought it to me. It seems Primo had second thoughts about giving it to you at the last minute."

Michel remembered the unexplained passage in Primo's letter. "I don't want that you should still reject me after I'm gone." The memory made his stomach turn.

"I think I need another cup of coffee," he said.

Crown and Michel put it to the sponsors that they were working on a spectacular new project which would take the dance world by storm.

"Best fff . . . blooming ballet score since Prokofiev," Crown said. "We're going to choreograph it jointly, St. Michel and I."

The sponsor's representatives looked at each other doubtfully. St. Michel was bankable as a ballet star—very bankable—but as a choreographer they weren't sure.

"I'm sure you've heard of Jacques St. Michel," Michel told them. "Obviously you have; he's a world-renowned choreographer, and I'm sure you also know that the press have been asking me for years what my relationship is to him. When I tell them that Jacques is my father, the balletgoing audiences of Europe and the States are going to be very interested indeed to see what I can come up with."

He felt Crown's intense surprise and, while the sponsors assimilated this piece of information, he scribbled a few words on a piece of paper, sliding it discreetly along the table toward him: *"Why not? The bugger owes me."*

44

JONNI FOUND HERSELF in a tricky situation.

She was in the kitchen of her flat in Chiswick and there was a strange man—a large, strange man—bearing down on her with a cup of tea in his hand and a menacing glint in his eyes.

She bared her teeth in a frantic smile and took a step backward toward the fridge. It was her own stupid fault; she shouldn't have allowed him through the door, let alone offered him tea. She'd been so pleased with herself for selling Guy's car to the first person who'd phoned about the advert. He'd paid cash; a great wad of it—she should have guessed he was dodgy from that alone.

As he edged toward her she sidestepped the fridge and sought refuge in front of the geraniums on the window sill. Until he made a move that was definitely threatening, she would feel foolish if she ordered him out of the flat.

"Hope the tea's alright," she said with a fixed smile.

She took rapid stock of her position. The front door was open; if necessary she could zip through it. But that would leave her outside and him inside with Caroline. Flight was out of the question.

Guy was away in the States until Monday, so no hope of rescue from that quarter. And Maggie was in Exeter on tour. Roly was back from Newcastle for the weekend but she knew he wasn't home now; he and Annette had called round earlier on their way out to lunch.

"What's a nice girl like you doing living alone with a kid, then, eh?"

She had no choice but to resort to time-honored feminine bluff.

"I don't live alone. In fact my husband should be home any minute."

Another step closer. "Thought you said the car was your boy-friend's . . . and he was away for the weekend."

"Oh!" How could she have been such an imbecile? "Well, when I said boyfriend I meant husband; it's his agent's name on the logbook, you see. And he's not away exactly; that is, he's going away but he's not away yet . . . and he's coming here before he goes away for the rest of the week-end. If you see what I mean."

"I've read about you in the papers. You and your husband split up."

Damn! Jonni grabbed a geranium and clutched it to her chest. "Ah, yes, well, you see we did but then we got back together again and, well, we didn't want to let anybody know about it because—no, please don't come any closer—you know what the press are like and basically . . . he's very jealous."

My goodness, this was hard work. Any moment now he was going to be on top of her. She needed a contingency plan urgently.

"Jealous, is he?" Her guest smirked. "Oh, he won't mind you being a bit friendly now, will he?"

"Oh, yes, yes, yes; he'd mind terribly." Jonni heard a car pull up to the curb on the street below the kitchen window. "I expect that's him now—don't do that. No, look really! Get your hands off me! I tell you my hus-band's awfully . . . oh, don't, please."

There was a ring on the doorbell two flights down.

"Come in; it's open . . . darling!" Jonni yelled in panic. Whoever it was probably wanted the floor below; they usually did. "My husband," she said, shrinking away from the hand which was creeping across her shoulder.

"Always rings the doorbell, does he?"

Michel stood in the open doorway looking into the kitchen. His eye-brows rose slowly as he took in the scene which confronted him. He had just had time to catch the look of desperate supplication in Jonni's eyes before her face collapsed completely. The solidly built man in front of her moved away when he saw Michel's figure at the kitchen door.

Michel smiled at the stranger. The man was considerably bigger than he was.

"Hello," Michel said. "Is everything alright here?"

"Yeah, fine," the car dealer replied quickly.

"Has my wife been making a nuisance of herself again?"

"Nuisance? No, she's . . ." The stranger looked perplexed. "Everything's cool. I was just having a cup of tea. She sold me your Jaguar, you know."

"Yes? What did you pay for it?"

"Three thousand; cash."

"Fair enough. You're sure she wasn't out of order with you?"

"No, mate; straight up. She was just being civil."

"I mean, just say the word, you know?"

The car dealer looked at Michel's split knuckles as he picked up the car keys and logbook. He glanced at Jonni as though she were out of her mind.

"Thanks for the tea, love. I've got to meet someone." He was out of the flat quicker than Michel could say, "Don't forget to check the tire pressure."

As the new owner of Guy's Jaguar disappeared, Jonni burst into a furious stream of expostulation at the cheek of the man and at her own stupidity. She stared frantically at the kitchen floor, wallowing in the shock of the stranger's behavior rather than face the far greater shock that had followed it.

"I walked right into it; I can't believe I was such a numbskull! What a nerve! Who the hell did he think he was, trying to jump me in my own kitchen? Men like that assume any woman who's alone is fair game. It's because he's seen me on TV—my agent warned me about that; how people take more liberties if they recognize your face. My God, he could have murdered me! Or worse! I should report him. I should phone the police. I should hire someone to rip his testicles off. Or put him up against a wall and . . . and . . ."

She realized she was being ridiculous and her harangue trailed away to nothing. Finally registering the bombshell of Michel's sudden appearance in her kitchen, she looked up and her eyes met his with the expression of one who had finally been caught out, resigned to arrest and imprisonment.

"Hello," she said.

"Hello." Michel was smiling. "Did I come at a bad time?"

Jonni glanced helplessly at the door and spread her hands in a shrug. "No, you came at a great time. Thanks."

Michel stood looking at her. She seemed different from the glamorous creature whose sudden appearance had so surprised him in Charing Cross Road. Her hair had grown into a fashionable bob and her clothes were comfortable and sloppy: baggy T-shirt tucked into jeans and a droopy cardigan hanging from her shoulders. Her face was in full bloom with those glowing green-brown eyes and her soft, childlike mouth. She was more natural today; more recognizable.

"How did you find me?" she asked. Her expression was pained and apologetic. "Did Roly tell you where I was?"

"Roly?" Michel frowned slightly. Did she really think he'd find it difficult to track her down? He pictured her leaving instructions with her agent; London Weekend Television; her parents; her friends—"If my husband asks where I am, for God's sake don't tell him." The thought hurt him but he smiled and shook his head.

"I've had your address since the spring. Maggie gave it to me."

"Maggie?"

"Yes, I met her in town for dinner."

Jonni twisted her lower lip in her fingers and avoided Michel's gaze. Maggie had betrayed her. And yet it didn't make sense; if he'd known where she lived since the spring—gone to considerable trouble to find out by the sound of it—she didn't understand why he had waited until now to contact her. Suddenly she started in surprise, her face falling in horror.

"Your hands! Michel, your beautiful hands!" She realized she had been staring at them for the past ten or twenty seconds without really seeing them. He lifted one hand and turned it over to look at his broken knuckles as though he'd only just noticed them himself.

"It's a long story," he said.

Jonni made coffee for them both. More than eighteen months had passed but she still resorted to coffee in a crisis. They sat on tall chairs next to the counter in the kitchen and looked at each other in silence.

Now that she'd got over the initial shock of Michel's arrival, Jonni couldn't take her eyes off him.

"You look great," she said at last. "Really well."

He looked older. The features of his face were no longer unnaturally perfect; his face was beginning to look a little lived-in. The strains of the past two years had started to engrave themselves around his mouth and eyes. She suddenly remembered he would be twenty-eight next week. Twenty-eight!

"You look well too," he said.

Michel was wondering where to begin inquiring about her life; wondering how much he could ask without intimidating her. This was an awkward, painful meeting for them both.

"How's Guy?" he asked, succeeding in not sounding churlish.

"Guy? Oh, he's fine." Their faces were strained as they tried to read each other's eyes. "He's negotiating a film to start shooting in the States in January. It should be good for his career."

Michel smiled and nodded. "You get along well?"

Jonni smiled and nodded. "Yup. Yup, we get along okay."

There was a pause while Michel ran the fingers of one hand slowly over the palm of the other.

"You working?"

"Yup: bits of telly now and then. I did a commercial last week."

"That's good. I stopped dancing for a year or so but I'm performing again now—well, I was until . . ." He rubbed one of his injured knuckles. "Of course, I forgot, you saw the premiere of *Giselle*."

Jonni was still looking into his eyes.

"Michel, I'm sorry I couldn't stay to congratulate you that night. I really was very glad that it all went well for you." She licked her lips. "And that day in Charing Cross . . . I was startled, you know?"

Michel gave her a reassuring smile. The longer he spent with Jonni the more he liked being with her and the more he liked looking at her. His purpose in coming here had been as much to gauge his own feelings as to discover hers and, now that he was here, gazing into her expressive eyes, he had no doubts at all. Jonni smiled at him hesitantly in reply.

Within a few minutes they were friends and Jonni wondered why they hadn't done all this long ago. It was so easy to talk to him about her work and the flat and even about Guy. Only one thing was making Jonni extremely nervous and, every so often, she cast surreptitious glances toward the closed door of the living room. With any luck Carro would remain asleep until after he left. She normally slept for two or three hours in the afternoon. There was a baby cup and a pile of bibs on the counter a few feet behind Michel's elbow and she scooped them swiftly into a drawer as she went to top up the coffee jug.

"So what about you?" she asked. "Any nice girlfriends?"

He laughed briefly and scratched his head. "Just one, very short-lived. Actually, it was a disaster. Nobody really; I've been too busy."

"Gosh, yes, you must have been. I've been busy too."

She told him about her six months making *Sinking Feelings* and he told her about Primo's ballet which was being scheduled for next year. She told him she'd been having singing lessons and he told her about Lisa—not the unpleasant parts, just that she was his sister. Bit by bit they filled each other in on the events, trivial and major, which had made up the past eighteen months of their lives.

"I see quite a lot of Roly and Annette," she said. "It must be difficult for them with us . . . well, you know."

Michel nodded. "Yes; I haven't spoken to them since the premiere. Are they okay?"

"Oh yes, in great form. But Guy's worried that Nettie's been seeing other men while Roly's away. I'm afraid it's true."

"Roly's a big chap. He can take care of himself."

"I suppose so. How about everyone else? Charles well?"

"Thriving; stormy as ever. He's been a good friend to me. I've been through some . . . difficult things, Jons."

He looked at her earnestly, wanting her to understand. Her eyes fell to the cup in her hand and she bit her lip.

"Michel, I was a bitch to you when—that time I came to the flat. But you were horrible to me too, you know."

Osborne, the cat, had jumped onto the counter and Michel gently stroked the animal's sleek black fur. "Was I horrible? I don't remember."

"Don't remember? How come?"

"I was very sick. I can't remember anything that happened before I got out of the hospital." He saw her puzzled frown. "It was a psychiatric hospital," he said. "Charles managed to keep that part out of the papers."

Her mouth curled down in distress and she held her mug of warm coffee against her cheek for comfort. "Are you alright now?"

"God, yes. Fine. Really fine. So how about you?" He made a gesture of cheerful admiration of her surroundings. "What about this place? It's great. Are you happy living here on your own? I'll bet it's taken some getting used to."

She nodded, grateful that he'd lightened the conversation. "I went through the pits when Mags first went away. Guy was around a lot but he kind of does his own thing; doesn't like to be tied down. I was so lonely for about six months I thought I'd die of it sometimes. But, you know," she looked at him brightly, "just the last few months I've started to really like living this way; I like my own company. I like being able to do anything I want to without . . ."

A noise from the living room made Michel turn his head.

"What's that?"

All the breath seemed to drain out of Jonni in one long sigh. Her shoulders fell and she twisted the hem of her cardigan around her fist.

"It's a baby," she said.

Reluctantly she followed Michel into the living room. He was smiling dubiously. When he saw the sleepy little face that smiled up from the cot in front of the television he laughed aloud.

"Hello, there," he said. "Who are you, eh?"

Jonni's chest tightened when she saw Michel lift the child to look at her. Now that he was here, now that he'd seen her, she would have to tell him the truth. But she didn't want him touching her baby.

She took her quickly from his hands.

"Her name's Caroline."

"Caroline? Now there's a thing. She's a darling little tot. Whose is she?"

"She's mine," Jonni snapped, more defensively than she intended.

Michel looked at Jonni. He closed his eyes for a moment and then he opened them again, raising his eyebrows. "Yours? You're her mother?"

"Yes, she's mine."

Michel stood quite still for some seconds, his bruised hand covering his mouth, while he thought this one out. Jonni's baby. A baby belonging to Jonni. Jonni had a child. A baby. He could go on forever and still not quite understand what he was telling himself. Okay, slowly . . . he hadn't seen Jonni for a year and eight months, as far as he could remember. Sometime in the intervening period she'd conceived, given birth to and become a mother to this baby. This was her baby. Right, he'd got it.

"I see," he said. "Who's her father?"

"She hasn't got a father."

Michel nodded sober comprehension.

"No, right; no father. How old is she?"

Jonni buried her face in Caroline's soft curly hair. Caroline was laughing and gasping happily, burbling away in a language of her own.

"Nearly a year old."

"A year." Michel ran his tongue over his lips. This was getting more bizarre by the second. "Yes, I see."

Jonni's mind was clawing at the walls. She wanted to be out of here, away from him; she and her baby. She allowed Michel to take Caroline in his arms again but, as he did so, a voice inside her head was screaming in protest. She couldn't bear for him to touch her—she couldn't bear for him to have any part of her. The force of her own possessiveness shocked her.

Michel was looking at the baby. He held her quite gently; Jonni had no fear of her coming to harm. It was the huge grin on the little girl's face as she reached out to Michel with her tiny hands that struck terror into Jonni's heart. She glared at Michel savagely.

"Yes, look at her, Michel! Any fool can see who fathered her. But she's my baby. Mine, you understand?"

Michel walked a few paces away from Jonni across the room, to think and to gaze at Jonni's child.

Michel had met very few babies in his time. Occasionally some acquaintance in the ballet world would produce one at a social gathering and he'd make polite noises about it and hurry away before the squealing object could puke on him. One of the pianists at the Islington had produced two at once—or rather his wife had—and Michel had been unsure whether he was expected to offer congratulations or commiserate. He had nothing against babies in principle but he had never understood why so many of his female colleagues had thought it worth swapping a life in dance for a life of dirty diapers and constant noise. But this baby was different. She wasn't a baby, she was a person.

Caroline had the clearest, brightest, smiliest, most giving eyes he had ever seen in a baby: warm gray eyes framed by soft blond lashes. The blond hair that covered her soft head was thick and curly. Her mouth opened into a huge grin of amazement as she showed him her new teeth and her eyes fixed themselves on his, widening into deep pools.

Michel's gut understood the full story of the child's parentage some seconds before the understanding reached his head. When he comprehended that he was the father Jonni claimed didn't exist, he sat Caroline carefully on the floor and walked toward his wife.

"I don't believe you never told me. It's impossible." His voice was strangely calm: not the offhand, immovable calmness which had so tried Jonni's patience during their marriage but a deliberate effort of self-possession while he tried to make sense of the truth.

"I couldn't tell you. You weren't around."

"You knew my phone number."

"Michel, you can't just phone up a man and tell him he's a father. You were sick; you said so yourself. How could I land you with that out of the blue?"

Michel shook his head slowly. How could she? His mouth was half-open and his eyes were fixed on hers as though Caroline's mesmerized stare had grafted itself onto him. Jonni's mouth turned down at the corners and she broke the hold of his gaze, focusing on the front of his sweater as she began to talk rapidly, taking quick, noisy breaths between phrases.

"I didn't know that I was pregnant for . . . more than four months. I was afraid . . . the baby might be . . . Primo's. And when she was born I still didn't know. I wanted to tell you. I really did. But then after I had slept . . . slept with Primo . . . and I was angry with you because . . . because I knew you wouldn't want the baby, even once you knew she was yours."

A blinding light seemed to flash in front of Michel's eyes and he slammed his hand against the frame of the open door. The pain that shot through his hand only inflamed his anger further.

"How dare you do that to me? What right have you? My own goddamn child!" Jonni backed away in fear as he shouted at her, drawing himself up to his full height, tensing every muscle in his powerful body. "My flesh and blood! Jesus, d'you think it's a kindness to tell a man he's the father of a child? Do you? Well, it isn't; it's a basic fucking human right! How dare you abuse me like that?" A glass candleholder from the mantelpiece flew across the room and smashed against the wall.

"What did I do to earn that from you? Okay, so I was a fucking awful husband." He aimed an outraged kick at a wooden chair, sending it flying. "I was a failure as a husband. I let you down in just about every possible way. But I didn't deserve this. What was it, did I starve you? Beat you? Did I ever lay a hand on you in violence? Did I turn you out of the flat? Tell me what I did that gives you the right to do that to me. Did I humiliate you, Jonni? Take you into my bed against your will? Did I force myself on you?"

"Please, Michel, don't!" But he couldn't hear her.

"So you were angry; well, now I'm bloody angry! You expect me to apologize because you fucked my best friend? You blame me for that? Primo died with a note beside him addressed to me"—he hurled a book furiously at the wall—"so does that make me responsible? Is that it? You blame me for Primo's death?"

"No, no!"

"Well, so do I but it's too late to change that now. There's nothing either of us can do to bring him back. So you're punishing me: what about the kid, you punishing her too? You want her to grow up thinking the man who brought her into the world didn't give a shit? Because it's going to hurt her, Jonni, and don't tell me it isn't because I know better!"

There was a wail of terrified misery from the floor several feet away. Michel's rage evaporated. He stood with his mouth open, his chest heaving as he caught his breath. The wail became a scream but Jonni didn't move. She was standing hunched against the wall in the far corner of the room with her arms over her head.

Michel bent to pick up the petrified baby and she resisted his outstretched hands with shrieks of alarm. He held her tightly to his chest, resting his mouth on her fragile head as her tears soaked his sweater.

"I'm sorry," he said. "Shhh, I'm sorry. I won't do it again, I promise. Shhh, I didn't mean to frighten you."

"What about me?" Jonni whimpered.

He glanced over at her grudgingly, his eyes still tense with anger.

"Were you frightened?"

"I'm shaking from head to foot."

He didn't look very sympathetic but he shifted the screaming baby into one arm, sighing heavily, and held out his hand toward her.

"You shouldn't have been afraid," he said as she came and buried her face, sobbing, in his shoulder. "There's no need." He put his arm around her and gazed at the wall behind her. "Okay, girls, calm down now. Both of you. It's all over. Everything's going to be alright."

45

Michel stood for several minutes while the sobbing of the two unhappy females in his arms gradually subsided.

Caroline was more easily pacified by warm, comforting arms than her mother; the baby was already dozing against his shoulder by the time Jonni stopped crying. As he held Jonni he became increasingly aware of the closeness of her body, and the softness, after all these many months of separation, of her arm under his slow caressing hand.

He nudged her forehead with his chin until she lifted her face a fraction. Then he lowered his head and nudged her nose with his nose until she lifted her face a little more. Her mouth tasted of salt tears. Her lips were tight-shut and ungiving.

"Come on, Jons," he whispered, "please," and she parted her lips a little, slackening her defenses to let him in. As he kissed her Michel felt his body being sucked into the warmth of her mouth. He dropped his hand to her waist to press it against his groin and she didn't resist.

Sharp pain was pulsing through the hand which Michel had smashed against the door, but it only increased his desire as it had previously inflamed his rage—doubtless, as Jonni had always maintained, there was a streak of masochism in every classical dancer. He left her standing alone and carried the baby to the playpen in the corner of the room.

Before he set her down Michel lifted Caroline so her face was level with his own and had a private, quiet word with her. "You just sit there quietly, okay? Your mum and I are going to lie down for a little while, so you behave yourself like a good girl, eh?"

Jonni watched him helplessly. It wasn't going to be easy to get rid of him now. He was besotted.

Reason told Jonni that what seemed to be happening here was a very bad idea. She was only storing up more misery for herself once he had gone again. But reason was drowned out by emotion and the momentum of the situation, and when Michel came back to her side she took him by the hand and led him toward the stairs.

They lay in Jonni's bed together. Michel's hand rested between her thighs where the feel of her warm skin soothed the smarting discomfort of his bruised fingers.

"Where did you learn to do that?" he asked, panting.

"What?"

"With your pelvic floor muscles."

She laughed at his anatomically correct description.

"Did you like it?"

"Christ, yes."

"Guy taught me."

"Oh. Guy."

She turned her head a fraction on the pillow to look up at his face out of the corner of her eye.

"Don't tell me you're jealous."

Michel thought about it. He'd swear he didn't have a jealous bone in his body. No, he wasn't jealous, he just felt an irrational urge to tear this Guy fellow apart, limb from limb.

"He's welcome to you," he said, smiling, still breathing heavily. "After what I've just been through, if he can handle you, good luck to him."

Jonni laughed again, looking at the lamp shade above her head in exhaustion. Her body felt so floppy she couldn't move, her arms and legs lying like lead on the mattress, exactly where they had fallen when he rolled off her.

Sex with Michel had been a revelation. She had forgotten she liked sex; she did it with Guy for the sense of belongingness it gave her. Making love with Michel just now had been wild. Extraordinary. Better than in the days when they had lived together. She wasn't sure whether it was she who had matured or he, or perhaps both of them.

"You obviously like having Guy around," Michel said. "Is he nice to the kid?"

"Don't call her that. Yes, he's okay with her. He's never cruel to her or anything, he just doesn't take her very seriously, that's all."

He wiped the back of his wrist over his sweat-drenched face.

"Do you love him?"

A warm red glow filled the attic as the afternoon light filtered through the red curtains Jonni had drawn across the window. She closed her eyes to shut out the light.

Did she love Guy? She hadn't expected that from Michel. Since when did the topic of love crop up on his agenda?

"Guy suits me at the moment," she said. "We're both pretty wrapped up in our careers. We keep each other company."

Michel lay still and thought about how Jonni had changed. It seemed all her romantic notions about unalterable love had flown out of her head. She was tougher, more independent. If anything, Jonni had gone to the other extreme: she wanted space and freedom. Her relationship with Guy suited her precisely because it was shallow and required no commitment. This was the grown-up Jonni had always wanted to be. Michel thought he preferred the childlike, impulsive woman he had married.

He stretched his arm out toward her and Jonni moved her head to allow him to lay it under her neck. He had forgotten how warm her skin felt against his. The cream-covered duvet smelt of sex and the familiar woody, sensual odor of her body—a smell he'd forgotten—but there was another smell too: the sharp, spicy tang of a man's aftershave. Again Michel felt a stab of jealousy. He rolled over and looked at her without speaking.

Lying there with his strong arm under her neck, Jonni was intensely aware of his gray eyes watching her and his gentle breath on her face. The power of movement was gradually returning to her limbs but she continued to lie motionless with her eyes closed, trying to hold on to the moment, to shut out the future. She didn't want to think about what would happen in ten minutes' or half an hour's or an hour's time.

"Did you ever think of me after I left?" she asked. There was no co-quetry in the question. She was thinking of all the countless hours she had spent crying over him and wanting him, even after she had come to live here.

Michel smiled and touched her face with his broken knuckles.

"The face that launched a thousand masturbatory fantasies."

Jonni tried to shove him away, grinning and digging him in the ribs with her elbow.

"In that case I wouldn't mind betting it wasn't my face you were thinking of."

"You're probably right," he confessed. And after a few moments' silence he said, "Will you think about coming home?"

Home? Jonni's eyes opened wide, and she stared at the ceiling. She hadn't anticipated that at all. Her eyes grew round in confusion and she turned her head away to gaze at the curtained window. The bright afternoon outside had faded into an early dusk as a dark cloud passed over the sun, making the room feel colder. Michel took his arm from beneath her neck and turned onto his back to give her time to answer.

"Let's go down and have another coffee," she said. "Poor Carro will be getting fed up by now."

Caroline had been remarkably patient, sitting quietly in her pen playing with squishy colored cubes and her half-eaten rag doll, Judith. However, she was happy to see her parents and held up her arms to Michel with a squeal of delight when he came to pick her up. She had forgiven him for his vile behavior earlier in the afternoon.

Michel sat on the sofa and let the little girl clamber all over him while Jonni made the coffee.

"What do you think?" he asked her, aware that Jonni was listening from the kitchen. "D'you think you and your mum should come back to Pimlico and live with me? I don't think she's really sure about it but . . . No, sweetheart, don't stand there . . . ouch! What about you, eh? Would you like to come and run around in the studio? It'd be a few years before you could reach the barre, I'm afraid."

"She's not going to be a dancer," Jonni said tightly, bringing two cups of coffee into the living room.

"Of course not. Why should she?"

"I don't want her having anything to do with it."

Michel's brow furrowed as he took the cup she held out to him, nodding his thanks. Her talking like that reminded him of his mother.

"If she wants to take up ballet when she's five or six there's no harm in it. It's good for a child's posture and balance. It doesn't mean she has to make a lifetime's occupation of it."

"I can decide what's best for her, thanks."

She stooped to pick up the book he had thrown across the room and gather up the broken pieces of the candleholder. The book was Guy's—an anthology of erotic extracts from literature. She laid it down on the shelf behind the television. It was ridiculous how guilty she felt about going to bed with Michel, her legal husband, when Guy slept with anyone he pleased. Guy was a "free agent" as he called it. Her own sexual freedom—or lack of it—had never been put to the test but she instinctively knew he would be furious. For the first time in her life Jonni planned to lie to a man about having slept with someone else.

She sat down on the arm of an armchair and watched Michel sip his coffee while Caroline made determined efforts to pull his cup out of his hand. Jonni already deeply regretted having allowed him to make love to her—she couldn't admit to herself that she had played every bit as active a part in their encounter as he had. After twenty months of slow, painful healing, putting one day at a time between herself and the agony of losing him, she could feel, even now, the old wounds reopening, tearing away the emotional scar tissue that she relied on to get through each day. She couldn't believe she had allowed him to do this to her. She couldn't believe she had done it to herself.

"There's more coffee in the pot," she told him. "Do you want another cup?"

"No, that's plenty, thanks."

Michel looked over at her as he unclasped Caroline's fingers gently from the handle of his cup. Jonni's face was still open and soft from their lovemaking upstairs, her eyes still cavernous. He couldn't tell how she felt about the idea of a future shared with him but, based on the deep, defenseless emotion of her response when they had made love, he was hopeful.

He lifted the little girl off his lap, sitting her on the sofa beside him, and leaned forward to put his empty cup on the coffee table, looking expectantly into Jonni's eyes.

"So how about it?" he asked. "How about coming back to live with me?" When he saw that her expression didn't change he went on quickly, "Or if you don't want to live in Pimlico we could buy a house. Somewhere with a garden—maybe around here; lots of the dancers commute from Chiswick and Richmond. Whatever you like."

Jonni got up from the arm of the chair, turning away on the pretext of going to collect one of Caroline's toys from the playpen. She stooped to pick up the doll, gripping her lower lip hard between her teeth.

"Michel, would you give me a divorce if I asked you to?"

He laid the back of his hand over his mouth, his face creasing up in distress, and lowered his gaze to the carpet beyond his feet. That hadn't been the response he was waiting for. But he supposed it answered his question, more or less.

"Yeah," he said after a pause. "Yeah, of course I would."

She stared down at the doll in her hands.

"I don't want anything from you, money or whatever. I don't even know if I can be bothered to get divorced. I'd just like to know I could if I wanted to."

Michel nodded. She was making him very unhappy.

"You don't want to know about the possibility of a future with me?"

Jonni couldn't look at him—couldn't bear to feel his disappointment filling the room between them. She had known, from the moment he had asked her while they were upstairs, that she couldn't live with him again. It wasn't that she didn't feel anything for him anymore. On the contrary, she felt too much. If she went back to him, sooner or later he would cut her out of his life again; it was inevitable. And she didn't think she could survive losing him a second time.

"It's no good. Too much has changed. I'm different now: I've made a life for myself; I'm happy living here with Carro—and Mags when she's around. And you're a dancer, Michel, first and foremost. That's the one thing that isn't going to change."

"Okay," Michel said, blinking. "Okay." He didn't want to hear any more but Jonni needed to justify herself. A lump swelled in her throat in sympathy with the tears she saw beginning to gather on his blond lashes. She couldn't cope with the sight of Michel in tears. That wasn't the image she associated with him at all.

"What we had before wouldn't be enough for me now," she said. "I couldn't live within that obsessive setup again, always coming second to your career. And we'd just end up being in your way, Carro and I. It really is better this way."

Michel nodded, pulling his hand away from the baby who was gripping the knuckle of his forefinger painfully.

"Uh-uh," he told the little girl. "That hurts. Let's not talk about it anymore for now, Jons." He was angry with himself for having rushed her, trying to push her into such a big step after one afternoon together. "Let's wait and see how things develop. Your feelings may change."

She shook her head slowly from side to side, her eyes wretched.

"They aren't going to change. You have to believe that, Michel. I have to do what I think is best for Caroline."

"This isn't about Caroline. This is about you and me."

"No!" she stopped him, suddenly fierce. "Everything that happens in my life is about Caroline; that's what you don't understand—everything! That's the difference between us, Michel. You think it might be amusing to have your baby crawling about in the studio but what happens when you find yourself faced with a conflict? What happens when you have to choose between picking her up from toddler group and an emergency rehearsal because some principal's sprained their ankle? You know bloody well what would happen: the first call from Charles and you'd be off." She scooped the baby quickly up from the sofa and held her against her chest, glaring at him. "What do you know about being a parent, Michel? How can you say the decision has nothing to do with her?"

"I didn't mean that it was nothing to do with her," he said in frustration. "I meant that it's a different issue from your feelings about me."

"There are no feelings, Michel. It's too late." She made a firm gesture with the hand that had been resting on Caroline's back, forbidding any doubt on the subject. "I don't feel anything about you. I got over you a long time ago."

He stared up at her steadily from the sofa.

"Then what just happened between us upstairs?"

"That was just . . ." She shook her head and then buried her mouth in Caroline's soft curly hair, leaving the sentence unfinished.

"Just sex," he said, finishing it for her. He looked at her, and when Jonni refused to meet his eye he said, "Well, I hope I gave satisfaction."

"Oh, how can you be such a hypocrite?" she demanded, her head shooting up. She didn't raise her voice because of the baby in her arms but her tone was tight with anger. "How many times have you had one-off sex with someone?"

"Plenty of times, but not with my wife."

"I'm not your wife. I stopped being your wife when you stopped thinking of me as your wife; when you stopped noticing I was even there. Look, we're too different, Michel. I'm me and you're you and the two just don't go together. There's no point grieving over something we never even really had. I thought for a long time that I was wrong to leave you, but I wasn't; I was absolutely right."

Gazing at her eyes, whose language he knew so well, Michel could see that she meant what she said. She had had twenty long months to think it over. He got up from the sofa.

"I'd better go, Jons. I'll be in touch with you about the child."

"What do you mean?"

"About when I can see her."

"See her? She's mine, Michel. I don't want a father for her. She and I are a family all on our own."

Michel wasn't prepared to fight about it. He picked up his jacket.

"I'll see her when I can. It won't be very often; probably not much more than once every few months. I'm away on tour a lot of the time. I'll give you a call before I go to Australia in February."

"Michel, I don't want to see you. Don't you understand?" She didn't think she could bear the torture of putting herself through this again.

"I can take her out somewhere or back to the flat. She'll be quite safe."

"If I try to stop you . . . what?"

"Then I'll take you to court."

"I see." Jonni looked at her daughter, who was gurgling away happily on the sofa. "You'd win," she said. "Your name's on the birth certificate."

Michel stood with his hand on the open door, waiting for Jonni to look up at him, waiting to say good-bye to her. After waiting almost a minute he went out and closed the door quietly behind him.

In Monday morning's class the women of the BNB were aware of a deep despondency in the ballet master who was standing in front of the mirror setting them exercises. This wasn't the withdrawn weariness of spirit which had dogged him through his convalescence; this was an open, tangible sorrow which affected them all.

"Come on, my loves," he said, looking at the lazy feet sweeping up in a long, uneven line at the barre. "This is dreadful. Pull yourselves together. I know it's Monday morning but you can do better than this."

John, at the piano, beckoned Michel over. When Michel leaned across the top of the upright piano John half rose from his seat to whisper to him.

"What the fuck's up with you, Michel? You're grinding the whole class into the floor. How can they get going when you're this flat?"

"Am I?" Michel asked. John nodded.

Michel closed his eyes and rolled his head around slowly, stretching his neck. John was right. If he couldn't be bothered with class this morning, how could he expect the dancers to pull their weight?

"Hold on, ladies," he called out. "Stretch for a minute or two while I just nip upstairs."

A few minutes later Marina came into the studio to finish the class by a mixture of improvisation and what she could fathom from the hieroglyphic notes in Michel's classbook. No one made any comment but glances were exchanged all around the studio. Lisa, back at work for the first time after her brief spell of fever, kept her eyes on the mirror and executed her battements in strict mechanical rhythm.

Sitting in his office, hours later, at the end of a long afternoon of rehearsals, Michel twisted his revolving chair slowly from side to side.

Since his meeting with Jacques St. Michel—or since smashing up the studio, he wasn't sure which—he was suddenly aware of all the things that were missing from his life. His conversation with Charles Crown on the way to Nottingham stuck in his mind. Charles loved him, was the

{712}

father he'd always longed for; his stern, chastening father. It had been true for years but he only realized it now. It was worth something, that realization. And Primo's score: that was worth something too. Primo was giving him a chance to redeem himself.

He folded his hands on the desk, tapping his fingers against his fractured knuckles. His hands were healing at a remarkable rate. They were the shape they ought to be now and the bruising had turned yellow.

Michel couldn't drive away the feeling of bereavement that filled him every time he thought of Jonni. Jonni and the child. Two days and three showers later the smell of Jonni's body still lingered in his nostrils. His bed, *their* bed, felt so empty without her, and he realized that it had felt empty every night since the day she left. He closed his eyes in frustration. He wanted her desperately and he couldn't have her. If he thought it stood half a chance of succeeding, he would march over to her flat in Chiswick and carry her off in his arms, baby and all. But she would run away again. And she would keep running away until, finally, he let her go for good.

He tried to picture himself with Jonni and their daughter; the three of them as a family. What did he know of family life? Jonni was right, he'd be a terrible father. The problem didn't lie between him and Jonni. The problem lay in his estrangement with Carrie—Carrie, his mother. He had no concept of a relationship between parent and child, child and parent. Added to which, he was an extremely prominent dancer— already, since his comeback in September, he'd received invitations to give guest appearances all over the world and offers of several very lucrative sponsorship deals. The responsibility of a child would weigh him down. Jonni had seen it all very clearly.

As he sat at his desk tapping his fingers slowly against the back of his hand, his mind ran over all the people he had lost: not just Jonni and the baby, but Carrie . . . Lynne . . . Primo . . . Lisa. With no one to come home to at the end of a tour, he wondered what the point of it all was. What drove him to get through each day? But he already knew the answer. No matter who or what it cost him, the thing that got him out of bed in the mornings was still, and always would be, that seven-thirty deadline when the curtain went up in the evening, and all the hours of physical and mental preparation that had to be done before then.

Disheartened as he was, he steeled himself to make the best of what was left to him. He really had no other option. He wanted Jonni's breath on his face when he woke in the mornings. He wanted the hot, sexual summer nights he had shared with her during their marriage. He wanted to chat to her over breakfast. But the BNB was going back out on the road in two days' time. There were rehearsals to take, schedules to organize, dancers to chastise for sloppy work. Michel had made his choice years ago. It seemed it was too late to go back on it now.

He looked up as Fiona knocked on the door and poked her head into the room.

"Can I come in?"

"I thought Charles was having a late rehearsal. Shouldn't you be there?"

"I'm going in a minute." She came in and closed the door behind her. "I just wanted to ask you if you'd seen Mel recently."

He frowned at the wall for a moment.

"Yup, she was in class this morning. Is there a problem?"

"Some of us are worried about her. I know she's always been a beanpole but these last few weeks she's turned into a skeleton, and Gunter—who's been partnering her in *Ghosts,* you know—says she doesn't weigh anything like what she did at the start of the season. I heard her being sick in the changing-room loos this afternoon when we were both supposed to be in your rehearsal; I'm almost certain she was doing it on purpose. The others say we shouldn't tell anyone but I don't agree. It's not safe what she's doing and I don't want to be a party to it, so I thought you ought to know."

Michel scratched his ear. Life goes on, he thought.

"You were right," he said. "Do me a favor and ask her to pop up and see me, would you?"

"Now? In the middle of Charles's rehearsal?"

"Yes, I think so. Charles won't mind if he knows it's me that wants her."

"But she'll know it was me who snitched on her."

"No, she won't. You can tell her I called you in here to rocket you about missing four classes in a row last week."

Fiona's shoulders drooped.

"Oh arse. Am I in trouble?"

He looked at her with raised eyebrows and nodded.

"I'm really sorry," she pleaded. "Let me off this once. I had a compulsive attack of the lie-ins."

"Alright," he said, "just keep it under control."

"I'll buy a rosary and say fifty Hail Marys."

"Buy a new alarm clock; that's much more to the point. Go on, or you'll be in trouble with Charles too. And do me another favor, will you? Ask Lisa to come up and have a word when the rehearsal's over."

Melanie didn't appear in Michel's office so, after waiting fifteen minutes, he went downstairs to the big studio and leaned against the barre watching the women practicing Crown's ensembles. Fiona caught his eye from her place in the ranks and gave him an expressive shrug.

When the rehearsal paused Fiona walked over to him, adjusting her leotard straps as she clumped over the wooden floor with her feet in her pointe shoes splayed out like flippers.

"Lisa said she wouldn't come either," she told him. "She said she takes her orders from Charles, thank you very much."

Michel glanced at Lisa. She was sitting on the floor retying her ribbons with a sour face.

"Will you ask her again?" he said to Fiona. "Tell her . . ." He thought for a moment, tapping his fingers against his mouth, and then looked at Fiona. "Tell her—will you?—it's not an order but a polite request from her brother."

"Yikes, are you sure? She's not going to find that amusing, you know."

"I don't expect her to. It's not a joke." He started walking away but he stopped and looked back at her. "There's no need to gawk at me like that."

Fiona was staring at him with a very silly smile.

"You are pulling my leg, aren't you, Michel?"

"Not at all. Why should I be?" He went and extracted the protesting Melanie from her place in the ensemble.

"Fiona, get the fuck back in line!" Crown yelled. He was having a bad afternoon with these women.

Outside the door to the studio Michel looked at Melanie's sullen face. It wasn't as pretty as it had been in the summer. She was gaunt and sallow-skinned.

"What do you weigh, darling?"

There was no answer so he gave her a gentle shake. Her shoulder felt twiglike under his hand. She'd had some tough knocks this season. Her boyfriend in the corps had jilted her for a soloist, and Crown and Michel had both come down heavily on her technique in class and rehearsals.

"Seven-stone-twelve," she sang reluctantly.

Michel caught her beneath her arms and lifted her up. He expected it to hurt his hands but it didn't; she scarcely seemed as heavy as his daughter. What did she weigh? Six stone? Six and a half?

"Okay," he said, "upstairs to my office. Let's talk it all through."

The next hour was a heavy one, with tears and recriminations from Melanie, but at least she understood what was at stake. Michel gave her the number of the counselor who had helped Lynne all those years ago, and promised her if she gained half a stone by Christmas he'd put pressure on Charles to renew her contract next year. It was the best he could do.

When Lisa knocked on the door of his office he was leaning back in his chair, gazing at the wall and thinking of Jonni.

"Yup, come in!"

Lisa's blond hair was falling out of the bun at the back of her head. She looked at him warily as she stood in the doorway. She had never once entered this loathed office since the memorable day of their quarrel.

"Thanks for coming up," he said, straightening himself in his chair. He looked from her suspicious eyes to the oppressive walls of his small office and shook his head. "Let's get out of here."

"Where to?" Her voice was mistrustful.

"I'll buy you dinner."

"No."

"Don't argue. I'm not in the mood." He picked up his jacket and pushed her ahead of him out of the office. He had made up his mind. It might be too late to save his marriage but he intended to save what he could of the rest of his life.

46

It was after eight o'clock by the time Michel opened the door of a vegetarian restaurant in Soho and followed Lisa in from the cold November street. The restaurant was warm inside and so crowded that the front windows were steamed up.

The basement was less crowded. "How did you find this place?" Lisa asked as she walked down the spiral staircase in front of him.

"An old haunt from my student days. It was one of the few places we could afford. We used to come here whenever one of us was flush."

"Sounds like good times."

"Oh yes, they were. It's gone way upmarket since then."

Lisa allowed him to take her coat and install her at a small table near the stairs. It was a trendy, wholesome-looking place, with rush-seated chairs and red candles in earthenware saucers on round pine tables. Lisa stretched out her hand to touch the frilly leaves of a large fern in a pot on the floor.

"Gee, these are real. They must have daylight bulbs on in here overnight."

Michel sat down opposite her with a smile.

"I used to have a friend who compared the plants in here to the fish you get in tanks in expensive restaurants in Italy. He said he was always expecting the chef to run out of the kitchen with a pair of shears and decapitate one."

She opened the menu, raising her eyebrows.

"Another of your ex-friends, huh?"

Michel didn't answer. He put his foot up on the rung of the chair beside him and took his cigarettes out of his pocket. When he saw a red no-smoking sign on the wall he put them back again with a muttered curse. That was something else—as well as the prices—that had changed here.

"Those things'll wreck your health," Lisa told him curtly. "You'll regret it, you know, when you're an old man."

"I already regret it. Anyway, I'll never be an old man. My body's taken too much of a hammering for that."

"Well, I intend to live to a hundred."

"I'm sure you will."

A spiky-haired waitress with nose and eyebrow rings was making her way over to their table and Michel nodded to Lisa to direct her attention to the menu.

"What are you going to have, Lisa?"

"Just a green salad, nothing else."

"Have you already eaten today? You need to eat after your flu."

"I always have grains for breakfast."

"Grains?" Michel didn't like the sound of grains at all; it sounded hideous. "That's not enough; you'll waste away."

"Look, don't get so darned protective all of a sudden. I can take care of myself. I told you."

Michel sighed. He'd have to look out for Lisa; he didn't want another Melanie on his hands. It occurred to him it might be a good idea to ask Lisa to keep an eye on Melanie: it might do them both good. They were both isolated within the company. Neither of them would be doing much dancing between now and January.

"I'm afraid I've more or less blown the rest of this season for you," he said, once the waitress had taken their order and disappeared to the kitchen. He raised a bruised hand in illustration. "I'm sorry about that."

Lisa avoided his eyes. "No, you aren't. Charles told me you don't want to partner me anymore."

"Well . . . yes." He shifted uneasily in his chair. "That's true. You know it isn't right for us to dance together. It's just not appropriate. Besides, it can't be good for you always to dance with someone so much more experienced than you."

"Boy, and modest with it!"

"I'm just being truthful. You need to put your time in doing the spadework in smaller roles while your strength and style mature."

"It's okay," she said, picking red candle wax off the saucer on the table. "Actually, I'm glad we're not going to dance together again. I hate for you to touch me."

Michel rolled up his napkin slowly with one hand. "We'll have to find you someone else to work with. I thought maybe Rob."

She broke a stalactite of wax self-consciously off the candle, her cheeks flushing pink in the glow from the candle's flame. "Why Rob?"

"Why not? He's strong and you're well suited heightwise. You looked good together in the rehearsal you did in Southampton—I thought it worked very well. And you seem to get on okay; Rob told me he called round to see you while you were sick." He saw the faint blush that was spreading over her throat and raised his eyebrows with a smile of surprise. "Christ, don't tell me there's actually something going on in this company that's escaped the notice of Rumor Control!"

"Sure," she said with sarcasm, picking at the candle. "Like the romance of the century. Forget it, Michel. He's not interested in me. I'm not the type of girl guys have relationships with. Or hadn't you noticed?"

Michel frowned. "What are you talking about?"

"I'm a once or twice type of girl." She was attacking the candle mercilessly now. "That's just the way men see me."

"Rubbish; you're a beautiful woman. Any man would be proud to have a girlfriend like you."

"Uh-uh, I'm an easy lay. Men don't see a future when they look at me. They see a pleasant hour, half hour, whatever."

"Oh, that's just bollocks, Lisa."

"Yeah?" She looked up at him sharply. "You're pretty darned sure of yourself. So what kind of relationship did you have in mind, Michel, when you were screwing me, huh?—I mean before it came out about our being related."

Michel looked down at the table. He stopped himself denying her implied accusation because it was true. He hadn't intended to make anything serious of his affair with her. In fact she was spot on: he had seen it, very definitely, as a once or twice thing, and he had taken it for granted she had seen it that way too. He couldn't even make the excuse that he had always conducted his sex life that way, because that wasn't the case. It might have been true before Jonni but it wasn't true now. He rolled up his napkin again.

"Not all men are bastards," he said.

"Oh, yes, they darned well are!"

The waitress arrived with their drinks and they remained rigidly mute after she had gone away. The behemoth of their sexual encounter had been present in every word they had exchanged since the morning after it happened, every step they had danced together, every instant of eye contact, but this was the first time either of them had spoken about it. Now that Lisa had thrown the problem that lay between them so openly onto the table they were both reduced to silence. Michel could feel Lisa's rage and hostility radiating from the other side of the table. He found himself thinking about Crown's insistence that none of the people in his life had given up on him. He had been wrong about Jonni and it wasn't looking too good with Lisa either. Michel, however, had no intention of giving up on Lisa without a struggle.

"Do you want to talk about it?" he asked at last.

"Nope."

After another long pause he sipped his wine and then put the glass down, twisting the stem.

"So what's it like growing up in America?" he said. "Tell me about your family."

"Why do you want to know?"

"Because I'm interested."

She began tapping the end of her fork against the table.

"There's nothing to tell."

"Okay, then talk about something else. Tell me about where you lived, or your ballet school, or your friends."

"Why?" she demanded. "Why do you care about my past?"

"You're my sister; why wouldn't I?"

She slammed her fork down in irritation. So all of a sudden he wanted to know about her, did he? Of all the darned hypocrisy. Okay, she'd tell him.

"Alright, Michel, the first time I got fucked I was in eleventh grade.

The guy screwed me standing up in a closet. He didn't even bother to take my panties off before he shoved me against the back wall and pulled the door to. He fucked good and hard, just like you, bro."

Michel rested his head on his hand and looked at his shoe on the rung of the neighboring chair. Lisa was glaring at him in triumph, the defiance in her eyes sharp and bright.

Eventually Michel looked up at her flatly and nodded.

"Alright, if that's what you want to talk about then we will. How old were you? Eleventh grade means nothing to me."

Lisa was suddenly bored with the subject. "Forget it."

"No, go on," he insisted, lifting his head. "Who was he? One of your friends' brothers?" He leaned toward her over the table. "A boy from school? Did you ask him for it? Did you press yourself against his cock in pas de deux classes, eh? Flash your tits in his face the way you used to do to me? Come on, Lisa; you want to talk dirty, let's do it." Michel was looking at her steadily and angrily. Lisa turned her head away.

"Alright," he said, "let's talk like civilized human beings. Don't try to humiliate me, because two can play it that way."

She scraped a strand of her blond hair sullenly behind her ear.

"Okay, I'm sorry."

A couple, eavesdropping from the next table, were staring at them through the ferns—forkfuls of broccoli suspended in midair. Michel turned his head and looked straight at them and they went hurriedly on with their meal.

"Tell me about Jacques St. Michel," he said.

"I don't want to talk about Dad."

"You said he was rough. Did he ever hurt you?"

"He got pretty mad sometimes, like I told you. He never hit me very hard." She twisted her mouth into a grimace. "Except one time when I was little and I wouldn't stop crying he smacked me across the room and fractured my arm. I guess he didn't mean to."

"Jesus."

"Don't fret for me, Michel. I'm tougher than you think."

He looked down at his wineglass, shaking his head. Yes, she was tough—and thank God for it—but some of her toughness was a direct result of all the blows that had been inflicted on her, physically and morally, throughout her young life. He thought about what he'd done to her himself; the double betrayal of violation and rejection.

"I'm glad I didn't know about that when I met him," he said.

"Why?" she asked, her expression and her tone both cynical. "What would you have done? Would you have hit him?"

"No. I'd have been afraid of killing him."

Lisa laughed. Macho talk like that sounded absurd coming from Michel. "He's real strong," she suggested. "I guess he might have killed you first."

"Perhaps." He took another sip of wine, looking at her evenly. "So what was he like the rest of the time? Did you do things together? Did he make time for you?"

She folded her arms in discomfort. She didn't want to have this conversation.

"Look, he did his best, okay? I guess he tried when I was small. In fact, I know he tried real hard. It wasn't easy for him. Once he got appointed artistic director at the LAFB and we moved to California he was scarcely home at all." She looked into Michel's gray eyes ironically. "You and I both devoted our childhoods to dance, trying to get his attention. I guess we were both wasting our time."

"Perhaps it wasn't wasted," he said with a half smile. "We got each other's attention."

She screwed up her face. "Jeez, that's supposed to be a consolation? Oh my God. Look, what is this, Michel? Did you bring me here on some kind of guilt-expunging mission or something?"

"I just wanted to talk to you. To see if it's possible for us to be friends."

"No. No, it isn't. So let's just save ourselves the aggravation."

"Listen, I handled things wrong, okay? When we talked that morning in my office I was surprised—upset too. And I was probably deceiving myself a little. I . . . felt . . ." This wasn't easy for Michel to say, however he was determined to get this right. He rolled his table napkin up again, clutching it tightly in his fist. "I had a lot of confused feelings about our father, Lisa: things that are much clearer to me now that I've met him. I reacted to the discovery about our relationship badly and I want to try and fix that. And, yes, of course I feel guilty about what happened between us that night. I wish it hadn't happened. I wish to God I could just—I don't know—cut my dick off or something and make it go away. If there's anything I can do to make it up to you, I will. So tell me. Tell me what I can do."

Lisa had not anticipated that. She stared at the table for a while, thinking it over, and then sat back on her chair with a heavy sigh.

"Look, forget the sex. It doesn't matter. We could have got past that if you'd been a little kinder. It was an accident; we didn't know what we were doing. Hell, I had no business sleeping with you without letting on I thought we were cousins, anyway. If you need my forgiveness for the sex, it's okay. I forgive you."

He looked at her anxiously.

"And for the rest?"

She shook her head. "No. Not for the rest." Her eyes filled with resentment. "I could have loved you so much, Michel. Jeez, a brother of my own—I could have worshipped you; you have no idea. But when you told me you wanted none of the relationship, that I was no sister to you, you hurt me more than anyone's ever hurt me in my life." She looked away with a bitter little laugh. "Jesus, you'd think after growing up with a ballet star for a father, I'd have known what to expect."

Their conversation stopped short as the spiky-haired waitress arrived with their food and laid the plates in front of them. Lisa pushed her plate away as soon as the girl had gone, but Michel picked up his fork and toyed with his moussaka.

"The things I said that day don't have to be binding, Lisa. I can be different."

"I don't think so."

He looked up at her.

"People can't change?"

"Sure they can. Perhaps some even do. But not you, Michel. You've got too much to lose."

"Have I?"

"Oh yeah. You'll never change. You only want to change the way things are on the outside: the way you relate to people. But it just isn't that easy: you don't just get to wake up one morning and decide you're going to do your relationships better. It takes balls to make changes like that; you've got to look at what's going on inside, rebuild from the ground floor up. And you aren't going to go digging around inside yourself and risk disturbing that delicate balance that makes you such a great dancer. Trust me, you wouldn't jeopardize that for the sake of my happiness or anyone else's—not even your own." She exhaled a sharp puff of air in scorn. "Jeez, you're so full of shit. You don't even want to change. You want me to change things for you."

The two pairs of gray eyes watched each other. Michel waited to see if her expression of anger and finality would fade, but it remained there, frozen in her eyes.

At last he looked down with a shake of his head and a small smile.

"Be quiet and eat your salad."

"I'm not hungry."

He laid down his fork. "Me neither. Shall we go?"

He called over the waitress and she came, smiling.

"Everything alright, is it?"

"Fine. But we've decided not to eat after all. Would you bring me the bill?"

"Not eat? Why not?"

"Don't worry, we're dancers. We're just like that."

"Ohhhh." She rolled her eyes and nodded significantly. "Dancers . . . I see." She made out the bill and handed it to Michel. Lisa reached for her purse as Michel opened his wallet and took out his credit card.

"I'm paying for this, darling."

"I'll pay my way, thanks."

"I earn a great deal more than you do, so put your money away."

"It's mine; I can do what I like with it."

"For once in your life will you do what you're told?"

"I will not."

Michel looked at the waitress in exasperation.

"What would you do with a sister like this?"

"Let her pay," the spiky-haired girl said firmly. "Male financial subjugation is a form of political repression."

Michel threw up his hands in defeat. "It's a conspiracy."

He drove Lisa to Maida Vale and then went home to the empty Pimlico flat, sitting down at the kitchen table with a strong black coffee and a much-needed cigarette. His failure with Lisa depressed him more than he felt it should. It was for her sake he had made the effort, wasn't it? Not for his own. If Lisa preferred to keep him at arm's length it was the better for him. The responsibility of a younger sister shadowing his footsteps in the dance world was a burden he could well do without, especially one as needy as Lisa. And yet it was with a sigh of dejection that he exhaled the smoke from his cigarette and followed it with his eyes as it spiraled above his head.

His mind wandered to the afternoon's rehearsals; to Melanie's thin, downcast face, and the sections of the ensembles he needed to tidy up before Manchester. And then his thoughts turned to Jonni, Jonni and the baby, and there his reflections revolved ceaselessly, without progress like a stuck record, until he got up from the table and took himself to bed. Even there the memory of Jonni's warm presence haunted him, driving away sleep and deepening his sense of isolation.

Michel's twenty-eighth birthday fell on the BNB's last day in Manchester. After the evening performance he sat with Crown in a quiet pub near the stage door of the Palace Theatre talking over plans for *The Tempest*. Outside on the street the massive scenery lorries were being loaded up for the overnight move to Edinburgh by an army of technicians. The get-out at the Palace would still be going on well after midnight.

Crown sat back in his chair with his Scotch and soda.

"Twenty-eight, eh? Well, you're as old as you feel."

Michel smiled grimly. "Good God, I hope not. What time's your train? For Christ's sake don't miss it."

He was disappointed Crown wasn't staying with them for the rest of the tour. A month on the road without him—the cold, gray month of December—was going to be a long haul. Crown had a million things to occupy him in London: the Tokyo and Sydney trip in February to organize, along with the details and publicity for the British spring tour.

The two men shook hands outside the pub and Crown slapped his ballet master encouragingly on the back.

"Let Marina do her share of the work, eh?"

"Oh, bullshit, Charles; she works her tits off already. Any chance of seeing you in Newcastle or Liverpool?"

"If I can get away. I don't know yet. I'll be in touch about *The Tempest.*"

"Yes, okay."

But Michel was finding it difficult to muster any enthusiasm about the choreography of Primo's score. The music was so stunning he didn't feel he could add anything to it. It stood alone. He left it to Crown to decide on the rehearsal dates and designs.

The performances in Edinburgh and Leeds were sold out in advance in the rush of pre-Christmas social euphoria. The BNB was in excellent condition. In less than a year since Crown had taken over it had been transformed—there was no sign now of lethargy amongst the corps or the notorious weakness of the boys. From the moment the curtain rose, every twitch of a foot, every bat of an eyelid was crisp and professional.

Michel and Marina watched over Crown's hard-won achievements jealously. Morale within the company was high. The dancers sang around the theater and arranged nights out in local clubs and restaurants, swarming out of the stage door after the show in laughing groups, warmly wrapped up against the northern winter cold. The BNB hadn't been so happy a troupe for decades.

Rehearsal by rehearsal, show by show, Michel's spirits sank lower. He thought about Jonni constantly. His breath condensed on the biting air as he walked through the city center between the theater and his hotel, watching couples window-shopping hand in hand under the Christmas lights. He concealed his frustration from the company, even from Marina, and withdrew slowly inside himself thinking over the many mistakes he'd made. In classes and rehearsals he was as focused as ever. Only occasionally, when a dancer's laughter brought an image of his daughter's smile to his mind, he would stop in the middle of setting an exercise and pass his hand over his face. A moment later he would be smiling again and marking out the combinations of jumps and turns with his hands.

The more he thought about his life, the more hollow and superficial it seemed. Rebuild from the ground up, Lisa had said—well, she was right: it just wasn't that easy.

"How did you decide?" he asked Marina over breakfast in the hotel, where they had met to discuss cast changes in the wake of the usual mid-tour spate of dancers' injuries. Marina, if anyone, understood what it meant to rebuild a life from scratch. "How did you make the decision to give up your career as a dancer after all those years?"

"I didn't decide," she said, sticking her fork into her kedgeree. "There was no decision to be made. I didn't have a choice." She gave Michel a sad smile; his question was a personal one but they were old friends. "The only way I could dance was by continuing to live inside a stranger's body, and I couldn't do it anymore. It was killing me. But giving up dancing killed part of me too."

She ate a mouthful of rice, chewing it slowly.

"D'you know, I once worked out that, by the time I stopped dancing, I must have spent more than six thousand hours in class? Six thousand hours of pain. You could only do that if you loved dancing with every atom of your being, if it was right there in your heartbeat. I mean that's what we're all doing here, isn't it?" She put down her fork and picked up the evening's cast list to check it over. "No dancer ever gives up his career through choice, poppet—time and injury take it from us all too soon. Any dancer who did would be a bloody fool."

Michel absently tore a croissant to pieces on his plate. She was right, of course.

In Newcastle, halfway through December, Michel called into the Grand Theatre to see Roly. An hour or two with Roly would lift anyone's spirits.

Roly's name was painted in large letters above the theater entrance surrounded by lights and brightly painted cutouts of beanstalks and cows. When Michel rapped on the door of dressing room number two and walked in, Roly jumped up from his dressing table with a cry of delight.

"Michel, you bugger! What are you doing here? Of course, for God's sake, there are posters for the BNB all over town. Hang on, I'll buy you a coffee if I can find my jeans." He searched through the costume rail. "My dresser's a sweetie but he keeps my life in far too much order."

Michel laughed. Roly never changed.

"They're on the back of your chair under your jacket."

Roly looked wonderfully well, if a little tired. Physically, he was unrecognizable as the same person who had retired from the Islington Ballet five years ago with a broken back. His manner was easy and confident, and he no longer had the obsessively upright posture and turned-out feet of a ballet dancer. Instead he had the relaxed, ambling gait of a tap dancer, which suited him much better.

It was snowing as they stepped out of the stage door together. Michel waited with folded arms while Roly crouched down amongst the melting snowflakes to sign autographs for the crowd of children. It was a novel experience for Michel to stand outside a stage door and not be recognized. He rather liked it.

"What time have you got to be back?" he asked.

"Six twenty-five," Roly groaned, laughing. "Remind me never to sign another contract to do twelve shows a week."

The café off the main street was different from the scruffy local cafés they used to frequent in Islington. The chairs were just as battered and the tables just as scratched but the shabbiness here wasn't a symptom of neglect. All the damage had been done deliberately. The Newcastle café wore its dilapidation with an air of fierce pride.

Roly sat opposite Michel, at a table near the gas heater, stirring his tea as he looked at his friend across the table with enthusiastic affection.

"So how the fuck are you, Shel?"

"I'm good. Injured out of the tour with two broken fingers."

Roly didn't ask how. "So what's this I hear on the grapevine about a sister turning up at the BNB?" News traveled fast in the theater world. "That pretty girl you partnered in *Giselle,* isn't it?"

"Yes, Lisa. She's my half sister."

"That's crazy. I could have sworn you fancied her."

Michel winced at that. "Too close for comfort," he said. "How's Nettie?"

"Wonderful. Working at the Beeb until February." He either hadn't heard the rumors about her sexual indiscretions or he didn't care. "That's the worst thing about being up here without weekends off; I miss her like hell. We stop doing Monday shows after the New Year; I might take the train down to London one Sunday night and surprise her. Otherwise I won't see her till February. So what's new with you, then?"

Michel reached for the sugar with a sigh. There wasn't much he couldn't tell Roly. There also wasn't much Roly didn't already know.

"I saw Jonni a few weeks back."

"Yes, she told me." Roly's blue eyes were sympathetic. "You saw the nipper then. She's a real pet."

Michel nodded. "It's dragged me down a bit. Jons's boyfriend is a friend of yours, isn't he?"

"We were at stage school together and we've kept in touch over the years."

"He's younger than us, isn't he?"

"Twenty-six. He's done really well for himself. Looks like he's off to Hollywood next."

The subject of Guy Dakin irked Michel but it was like his broken thumb; he couldn't leave it alone. "What's he like, then?"

"Decent bloke," Roly said. "But his ego gets in the way a bit. Sometimes lets his cock do his thinking for him. And he's rash sometimes. Says things without thinking of the consequences. But he never means any harm. Had a bad time with his marriage a couple of years back but I think he's pretty entrenched with Jonni at the moment. He seems to make her happy."

Michel nodded flatly. If he were honest it was the last thing he wanted to hear.

Roly tactfully changed the subject, chatting about his dangerous exploits climbing up and down the beanstalk, and a near miss when he'd been accidentally gored in the groin by the pantomime cow. As he talked Michel watched him, envying him and loving him. Roly's happiness was infectious. His funny, irregular face creased up in laughter as he described the panto's hopeless Bulgarian conductor, who either took the music so slowly it was impossible to dance or so fast it was murder.

"Christ, I know that one," Michel said. He drained his coffee cup and looked at Roly, shaking his head. "I don't believe you, Roly. I mean look at you: you've taken more insane risks than anyone I've ever met. You spend all those years waiting for one girl rather than hedging your bets like the rest of us. You break your back and then dive like a lunatic straight back into tap. And here you are married to one of the most beautiful women in the country, with your name up in lights above one of Britain's top provincial theaters. You should be arrogant as hell, but you're just as much a crazy schoolkid as ever."

"Too busy having a good time to be arrogant," Roly said, laughing. "And as for the risk, well, you know my motto. All the same, I get a kick thinking back to the days of dingy digs in Scunthorpe and hard labor in the back row of the ensembles. I get a kick out of knowing I made all this happen."

Michel sat back in his chair and looked at him pensively. After a few moments he smiled into his eyes.

"Listen, Roly, if you do decide to go down to London one Sunday, let Nettie know you're coming, eh? If you surprise her she's bound to be out somewhere and you'll have a wasted journey."

Roly thought about that and then nodded, looking into Michel's eyes with a grateful smile.

"Yeah. You're right, Shel. Better to let her know. I'll call her first."

In his featureless hotel room in Newcastle Michel sat in bed and thought about Roly. Seeing Roly now, anyone would say he'd been destined for success but Michel knew better. Everything Roly had in his life he had fought for tooth and nail.

He thought of all the years Roly had spent struggling to make his way in ballet despite the fact that every ballet school in Britain had refused him a place. And even when his body had failed him he still hadn't lost faith. All the other dancers Michel knew who had moved from ballet to musical theater were bitter and envious, seeing it as a humiliating step down. But Roly had none of that snobbery. Roly was proud of his success, and it was only just beginning. He would go on and on, making his way to the very top of the profession. That was one certain thing about Roly: anyone who worked with him would always want to work with him again.

Michel lit a cigarette and threw the bedclothes onto the floor; these expensive hotels were always monstrously overheated—he'd open the window but it was right over the main road and the noise of traffic was deafening.

What about his own success? He'd achieved a lot in his twenty-eight years too. He was a bloody good dancer; other dancers took him seriously and that counted for a lot. His thoughts ran through his early creations at the Islington: *Swan Lake* and *Romeo,* the rave reviews that had catapulted him into the limelight, the principal roles and guest appearances all over the world since then. A lot had happened to him in the last ten years.

After a few moments he stubbed out his cigarette in disgust in the white china ashtray beside the bed and rubbed his hands hard over his face. That was it, of course; that was the difference between Roly and himself: it had all just happened to him. Roly had struggled hard for everything he had—his career, his marriage, his home—whereas Michel had had it all handed to him on a plate. His whole career; that had been Charles Crown's doing—all Michel had really had to do was to show up at the barre in the mornings. His partnership with Lynne, his flat in Pimlico, meeting and marrying Jonni, even little Caroline; they were all things that had just landed in his lap. The only time Michel could ever recall making a conscious, life-changing decision for himself was on the day, when he was eight, that he had locked himself in the barn refusing to come out until his mother agreed to let him go to ballet school.

The weather in Newcastle had turned wintry. Michel walked quickly between the theater and his hotel through freezing snow, with his coat collar turned up against the wind and his gaze fixed on the pavement. On the stage of the Opera House he stood with his hands in his trouser pockets, watching the boys whip through the ensembles from *Ghosts.* All these boys had, to some extent, made their destinies for themselves. They'd auditioned for the BNB, if nothing else, which was more than Michel had done.

Michel was growing desperate. These days on tour, with their classes and rehearsals, meetings and performances, dragged on him, hanging like chains around his neck. Images of Jonni ran again and again through his mind. Jonni and Caroline. Loneliness twisted his intestines in its relentless grip. He felt as isolated as he had at the age of sixteen, in those first few terrible weeks after he moved to London.

As he sat in the dressing room that served as a company office, writing his signature on the show reports for the past week's performances, he looked into the mirror, thinking about Carrie: about the withdrawn sadness he had seen in her eyes each time she looked at him since his childhood. He stared beyond the mirror, through the reflection of his own eyes, wondering whether it was too late to salvage that relationship. Was there a chance, if he had the courage to ask her, that she might be able to care for him again? His eyes darkened and he broke the hold of his reflected gaze, looking back down at the show reports on the dressing table in front of him. There was no point thinking about Carrie. He was a dancer and, as long as that remained the case, she wouldn't want anything to do with him.

In the next hotel room in the next city he lay in bed envisaging his future. The future of a dislocated ballet star: an entry in *Who's Who* and a BBC documentary after his death. Lisa had once accused him of cruelty and he knew it was true. He had known it even at the time. His was the cruelty of neglect; of putting his egotism as a dancer before the needs of the people around him—the egotism that would one day turn him into another Jacques St. Michel: an insular, embittered man.

In the theater foyers, during performances, Michel was still surrounded by fans demanding his attention. Fame had always been unimportant to Michel; it gave him leverage within the dance world, and was a pull to investors—perhaps, if he were honest, it had appealed to his vanity. But now, suddenly, he found its spotlight intolerable. In regional TV interviews, during the inevitable publicity calls, he stared at the well-groomed interviewers blankly, unable to fathom how they could possibly find anything in him of interest. Even the teenage girls with their autograph books irked him. They all looked at him as though they knew him, as though there was a special bond between them, and their mistaken belief in that illusory intimacy made him feel his isolation even more deeply. Once, in a state approaching panic, he even took one of the teenage girls up to his hotel room in the hope that he might find something real behind the spurious adulation of fan worship. But he couldn't see it through. As he watched the busty seventeen-year-old unbuttoning her Lycra top—ready to prostitute her body in exchange for the kudos the escapade would win her tomorrow amongst her friends—he closed his eyes with a sigh and shook his head. What in God's name was he doing? She probably had to get up for school in the morning.

He called a taxi and sent the girl home.

Michel was at his wits' end. He had tried everything he could think of, been down every emotional blind alley, but he couldn't see a way out of the hole he had dug himself into. At lunchtimes he paced the city centers—all identical, with the same shops, the same winter-wrapped pedestrians carrying carrier bags of Christmas presents—trying to walk off his desperation. At night he tossed and turned in his hotel room, thinking of Jonni. Jonni's body. Jonni's laughter. Jonni's listening eyes.

At last, in Liverpool, the last port of call for the autumn tour, the company manager brought Michel his contract for the coming year.

"I'll need to glance over it," Michel said.

"Yes, yes, keep it," waved the administrator. "Sign it and bring it back to me by the end of the week, will you?"

"Yeah, thanks."

Michel laid the printed contract on top of the black, shiny grand piano in the orchestra pit where he had been working with the conductor. He leaned over the instrument, resting his weight on both his hands, and closed his eyes tightly, thinking intently. When Marina came to his side and laid her hand inquiringly on his shoulder, he stood up slowly and sighed, with the contract in his hand.

"I think I'd better go to London to see Charles," he said.

47

THE PREMISES OF THE BNB in Victoria were deserted when Michel walked through the double doors at nine o'clock the following morning. Without thinking about it consciously, he had somehow pictured the BNB buzzing with activity and crammed with bustling dancers while he was away on tour. The only signs of life this morning were the heads of the receptionist and two other administrators bobbing up and down behind glass panels in the general office. Evelyn, the office manager, waved to Michel cheerfully as he passed the main desk on his way to the stairs.

He stopped in the corridor outside Crown's office and stood with his hands in his trouser pockets, closing his eyes. "Wait," he told himself. "Wait until you know what you're going to say." He had come this far without hesitation but the difference between this side of Crown's office door and the other was so immense this last obstacle seemed almost impassable. Once through that door his world would turn upside down. Rooted to the spot, he waited for someone to take that final step for him. But no one could help him do it. He was on his own.

Still with his eyes closed, he rested his forehead against the cool, painted plaster of the corridor wall.

And then he opened his eyes, removed his hands from his pockets, and walked into the artistic director's office without knocking.

———

Crown looked up from the mountain of paperwork on his desk and his face lit up with relief.

"Michel! Thank Christ you're here; I'm being hounded to death by the press office. I've had to cobble together a schedule for next spring; I need your okay on the projected dates for *The Tempest*. Look; what do you think of this?"

Michel drew a chair up to Crown's desk and sat down, listening to him blankly and staring at the large watercolor design that was thrust under his nose.

"This is the rough idea Marc's come up with for the set; I've already told him there's too much fucking greenery interfering with our floor space. Christ, you wouldn't believe the shit that's been flying my way from the sponsor; they want me up in Nottingham on New Year's Eve to give a press conference—New Year's Eve; would you fucking believe it?"

Michel opened his mouth to speak but no words came out. Crown's unsuspicious chatter and the warmth of his welcome only made matters worse. He licked his lips and waited until the choreographer noticed his unnatural stillness and silence.

"So what's wrong?" Crown asked at last. "A problem with the dancers?"

"No."

It became apparent to Crown, over the next few seconds, that Michel was having great difficulty deciding how to phrase whatever he had to say. Crown sat back in his chair with a slight frown, watching him and waiting.

"I think," Michel said at last, pausing to clear his throat, "you're going to have to find a new ballet master."

Crown's frown deepened. "Of course, it's already done; we've discussed that. Anatoly's retiring from the company after Christmas; he'll be assisting Marina from New Year. I wasn't expecting you to manage rehearsals while you're choreographing and performing."

"Charles," Michel leaned forward and rested his forehead on his fists. "I want to leave the company. I want to give up dance."

"Oh, don't talk crap."

"Charles, listen!" The intensity in Michel's voice brought the artistic director up short. Crown sat and looked at him, the animation draining from his face.

"I really think I have to," Michel said quietly.

There was a silence while Crown chewed on a paper clip, gazing at Michel expressionlessly. Michel's gray eyes roamed across the junk that littered the desk, searching for a way to escape the pain he was causing this, his most constant friend. So much this man had given him that Michel could never repay, even in a lifetime of work and self-sacrifice. And despite this debt, Michel was proposing to lay waste the work of twelve long, hard years of Crown's life.

"Give it some thought," Crown said, almost under his breath.

Michel pressed his teeth into the knuckle of his forefinger, leaving a row of uneven dents, before he answered. He really didn't know if he was doing the right thing. The thought of a life without dance made no more sense to him now than it had done during the months after his breakdown when he had believed he would never have the nerve to go back onstage. He only knew he couldn't go on like this. Tears stung his eyelids.

"I have thought about it."

"What brought this on so suddenly?"

Michel held up his hand for a moment, indicating that he couldn't reply. He fought to control his voice while Crown watched him impassively.

"I've thought of nothing else for the past month. I just can't think of any alternative."

"Give up . . . altogether? For good?" Crown's eyebrows had risen as though this was a mild curiosity; a joke.

"Charles, I've got nothing left. I've lost Lisa. I've lost Jonni. And the father I've spent all these years wanting to impress doesn't even exist. I've got no family at all—I've messed everything up: all of it. The only possible solution I can think of is to go back to the beginning and try and start from scratch, and I can't do that while I belong to the dance world."

Crown took in a deep breath and then exhaled slowly.

"I think you're making the wrong decision, Michel. I honestly think this is a mistake."

"Listen, Charles, this is what I need to do but . . . I can't go unless you let me. If you tell me to stay and dance for you, then I will. It's up to you. I'm asking you to let me go . . . go and try to find something that will give me some sense of direction . . . a sense of worth."

Michel's gaze had rooted itself onto the cord of the telephone but he heard Crown begin to drum his fingertips lightly on the arm of his chair. Almost a minute passed while the drumming remained steady and rhythmic and then Crown thumped his fist down on the desk and jumped up with a cry of despair and rage.

"Get out! Get the fuck out of my office! Get out and don't come back until I've calmed down. I'll hear your reasons when I can look at you without wanting to break your neck—or mine."

Michel backed toward the door and Crown stared at him through stricken eyes, gripping the edge of the desk in his hands and tipping it up violently so that papers, books, cups, telephone, and ashtray were thrown across the floor of his office.

"Get out!" he screamed. "Get out!"

Michel closed the door of Crown's office and went down the corridor to his own office, where he sank into a chair and pressed his fists over his eyes.

Charles Crown looked out of the window at the dull December day. It was early afternoon and, since Michel had left his office this morning, he had been sitting in the same position smoking and staring at the deserted building site across the street. The new office blocks were nearly finished now; the builders had hung Christmas decorations behind the freshly installed glass panes in the windows. In another month, or even less, there'd be companies moving into those offices; the empty carcass which had taken shape so slowly over the past year would come to life.

Crown closed his eyes. He was fifty-four and he felt like chucking it all in: the whole frustrating business. Worthless. Wasn't that what Michel had said; something that would give him a sense of worth? Crown thought of all the effort and all the tears he had poured into his profession over the last four decades. What did he have to show for his forty years of toil in the dance world? Like Michel, should he think about getting out now and trying to find some point to it all before it was too late?

A voice whispered in his ear from somewhere deep in his memory. It was his own voice a hundred years ago—more like a dozen in reality— speaking to the boy that Michel had been then: "There's nothing at the end of a life in dance but certain heartbreak."

He thought of the option Michel had given him. He could veto Michel's decision on a whim. No, Michel, you may not walk away from everything I've taught you: twelve years of hope and work and pain; no, you may not throw away all that talent, yours and mine.

Crown knew all too well that Michel had meant what he said. If he was forbidden to go he would return to his work, he would choreograph Primo's ballet, he would perform brilliantly onstage and pour sweat every day at the barre until his body gave out and he was too old to dance—no sulking, no reproaches; he would do the best he could. This was the worst evil that confronted Crown as he opened his eyes and stared out of the window lighting another cigarette.

Running his hand through his hair, Crown wondered what degree of emotional control a man of fifty-four ought to possess. He felt like a helpless child—racked by indecision. Nadia Petrovna had taught him to fight for what he believed in. It had been her tireless litany over all the decades he had known her.

When Michel had been worn down by mental fatigue, too ill to dance, Nadia Petrovna had told Crown to fight, and he had fought and won. But this was different. Michel wasn't sick now, he wasn't hovering on the brink of insanity. Michel was whole and strong and scared stiff of squandering his life like the rest of cringing humanity. Michel had made this decision by long and careful thought; it didn't matter what his reasons might be.

Crown's heart sat in his breast like lead. Yes, he must fight for what he believed in. He believed in Michel as an unparalleled dancer and as an artist. But more than that he believed in a man's right to freedom of choice. He picked up the telephone from the floor and dialed down to reception.

"If you see Michel, would you tell him to call me or come up to my office? Thanks."

In the late afternoon the two men walked across St. James's Park together. It was dark by half past four and the air was crisp and cold. Brown leaves crunched under their feet and the bare black branches of trees stood out in the pink haze of the city lights against the clouds.

Michel walked with his hands in his pockets and his head bowed, watching the unvarying tarmac of the path passing beneath his feet. Crown strode beside him with his chin held courageously high, rubbing his hands together in the chill wind.

"What will you do?" he asked.

Michel puffed out his cheeks and sighed.

"I'm not good for much. I might try manual work; building, farm laboring, something of that kind."

Crown bit his lip but nodded encouragingly.

"You'll find something to suit you better than that. What about the immediate future?"

"I'm going home to Carrie; my mother in Devon."

"Ah, I see."

"She never wanted me to dance; she took it very hard when I went off to Paris. It was twenty years ago but I'm going back to her to do what I can."

Michel tried to explain it to Crown and, while he talked, he was explaining it to himself.

"It's as if . . . everything I've done—all the relationships I've ever had—have vanished into some kind of bottomless pit. Like watching my life being sucked into a black hole, you know what I mean?"

"Yes, I know exactly what you mean."

"And I started asking myself where that hole had come from; how it had appeared. And I realized . . ." he looked up at Crown, not sure of himself, ". . . I made that hole for myself right back in the beginning when I first took up dancing. I cut myself off from my mother and it left a huge gap. And since then everything's just slipped through my fingers into that gap: Jonni, Lynne, Primo, the baby . . ."

"Baby?"

"Yes, Jonni's got a baby; a nice little thing; she's mine. I don't know what made Jonni name her Caroline, after my mother, but it set me thinking."

Crown smiled; he was beyond being amazed by anything.

"Perhaps she thought the child might do the trick for you: plug the gap, so to speak."

"No," he rubbed his eyes so Crown wouldn't see the regret in them, "Jonni doesn't want any of me—as a man or as a father to her child. It's not her fault; she's got her own life now."

They turned onto The Mall, heading toward Trafalgar Square for no particular reason, and Crown breathed in sharply, feeling the sting of the icy air in his nostrils.

"Go back to your mother, Michel. Go and find what happiness you can. Better to do it now than leave it till you're too old to start again. It's a hell of a thing to walk out on a career as successful as yours, even if you know it can't make you happy. I wish you luck."

"Thank you."

"Shall I be hearing from you?"

"God, yes. There's Lisa; I'll be around to keep an eye on her from time to time. And I'll be anxious to see what you do with *The Tempest*."

"Ah, yes, *The Tempest*. Who do you think I should get to dance Ariel?"

"Rob? He's probably your best choice."

Crown raised his eyebrows and nodded. "Primo would be disappointed, you know."

"I think he'd have understood."

"Maybe, maybe." Crown held out his hand to Michel. "I would offer you my friendship but I don't think it would do you much good, not out there in the real world."

Michel took the offered hand and screwed up his face.

"Charles, that's a dreadful thing to say."

"I know. But I'm not going anywhere; you know where to find me if you need me." Crown smiled and waved Michel away. "Go on. Off you go."

Michel tried to smile, nodding in farewell, and walked away in the direction of Admiralty Arch, leaving Crown standing alone on the dark pavement of the wide tree-lined avenue. Behind him lay the regal austerity of Buckingham Palace, with its forbidding wrought-iron railings and grim masonry. In front of him lay the seething mass of Christmas shoppers passing through Trafalgar Square on their way home or out to office parties. Crown watched until Michel's retreating figure was swallowed up by the crowd.

48

THREE DAYS BEFORE CHRISTMAS, Michel drove to North Devon.

The past week, finishing off the tour in Liverpool, had been dream-like and full of uncertainty. On the one hand, there he was, giving class and dealing with routine problems and cast shuffles; carrying on with the only life he knew. On the other hand, the future beyond Saturday was a blank. It was like a cliff face viewed from above; a sheer drop.

That week in Liverpool had been so like every other week out on the road that Michel had almost succeeded in shutting the future out of his mind. Squinting at the girls' feet from the back of the auditorium or rolling his eyes to the ceiling of the rehearsal room because one of the dancers had left the rehearsal tape back in their digs, he concentrated on each performance as it came. But all the time butterflies danced in his stomach reminding him of the huge upheaval that awaited him; the change and the opportunity. And the overwhelming loss.

The motorways around Birmingham were overburdened with holi-day traffic and Michel drifted patiently down the outside lane at fifteen miles an hour. His face was blank; his eyes flitting mechanically from the bumper of the Land Rover ahead to his rearview mirror. His thoughts were on yesterday's ballet class.

He had asked Marina to give company class on the last day of the tour. Joining the other boys at the barre, Michel had done class like he had never done class before. Every exercise had been an emotional wrench. Week in, week out, he'd practiced pliés, glissés, battements; daily

{741}

for the past twenty years. The year of his illness had been nothing but a brief interlude. Sweeping his extended foot away from the floor into a développé and knowing it might be for the last time had been almost unbearable. His last ever double *tour,* his last ever entrechat, his last ever arabesque.

The traffic thinned out as he turned off onto the M5. There was no point thinking about what he was leaving behind. He pulled into the first service station to fill up with petrol and coffee, and paused next to the line of payphones outside the cafeteria. Should he phone Carrie? he wondered. No, he didn't know what he could possibly say to her on the phone that couldn't be said better face-to-face. He remembered how Crown had once described a character in one of his ballets; a man who was facing the greatest turning point of his life. "He's a man balanced on the edge of the void," Crown had said. Michel had been acclaimed by the critics for his interpretation of that role but he realized now how little he had understood it.

It was three-thirty by the time Michel drove between the weathered sandstone gateposts into the courtyard of his mother's farm. Already the afternoon sky had descended into gloom; darkness would not be long coming now at this time of the year.

The low farmhouse was in shadow and the yard seemed spookily barren. Denuded of their leaves, the cherry trees on either side of the door looked jagged and unwelcoming.

He experienced a moment of doubt as he stood beside the car with his hand resting on the cold metal roof. It was more than three months since he had spoken to Carrie. Turning up unexpectedly like this just before Christmas . . . perhaps she was away, or had visitors. He was tempted to get straight back in the car and go home to London. Now that he was here he was suddenly very afraid; afraid of what, he couldn't tell, but his chest and stomach were tightly knotted.

When he thumped on the back door Carrie's voice sang out a summons from the kitchen as though she had been expecting him. It was possible, he supposed, that she had spotted the car passing the kitchen window before he'd turned into the yard.

She hadn't.

When Michel appeared, ducking under the beam near the door, his mother's face fell in astonishment, almost in the same way that Jonni's face had fallen when he'd appeared in Chiswick.

"Good God! Michel!"

She was standing at the sink with her hands immersed in water but she spun around, facing him with a carrot in one hand and a peeler in the other. Michel saw her eyes dart furtively around the kitchen in alarm, as though he had caught her in the act of some gruesome crime and she was afraid she might have left a bit of evidence lying in view.

"Michel . . . why, what a surprise."

He had, in fact, caught her in the act of thinking about him.

"My tour finished yesterday. I wanted to see you; I hope you don't mind."

"No. No, of course not. Come in. Put the light on, would you?"

Michel flicked the switch on the wall and closed the door behind him, crossing the stone-tiled floor to pull back a chair from the long pine table. Carrie threw her carrot into the sink and wiped her hands on her skirt; it was one of her scruffy, calf-length working skirts. She seemed agitated; disturbed almost.

"So, you've come from London, have you? Or were you working in this area anyway? It's nice of you to think of popping in."

"I was in Liverpool," he said, sitting down. "I left this morning but the traffic was dreadful."

"Oh, Liverpool, I see; then I expect you'll want coffee."

Michel watched his mother fill the kettle and open a drawer next to the sink.

"Damn, I'm out of filters. Oh! No, I'm not; I've got some in the larder." She vanished through the door next to the fireplace and reappeared a few seconds later tearing a packet of paper filters open with her teeth. "I knew I had some. I remembered last time I went into town. Oh, sugar! You take sugar, don't you? Blast! Well, you'll have to make do with castor; you won't mind, I'm sure."

Michel had never seen Carrie so flustered. He had always thought of her as unflappable. His eyes followed her back and forth as she fussed over the coffee, chattering incessantly, but she never once looked in his direction.

"Are you expecting someone?" he asked.

"What? Oh, yes; only Margery. She's driving up to the village this afternoon. She said she'd pop in for tea. I thought you were her when you knocked on the door."

Margery was a very old friend of Carrie's: one of Michel's old primary school teachers. He hadn't seen her since his early years in Paris when he'd spent Christmases and summers at home. Once or twice, she had phoned when Michel was here during the months of his illness. Michel had always liked her.

"I'm sorry to burst in on you like this. If you like, I'll take myself off and come back later."

"Don't be silly; Margery would love to see you. Are you staying?"

"Only if you've got room. I'd like to."

"Can you stay for Christmas?"

"It depends on your plans, Carrie."

"Oh, you know me; I never do anything about Christmas."

Carrie's tone was artificially light and her hands fidgeted as she shook ground coffee into the filter. Michel thought of the purpose which had brought him here and wondered how many weeks and months it would take to penetrate her hardened reserve. And once he'd broken through her armor of restrained pleasantry, what then? What if she didn't want him in her life at all? If she had never bothered to inquire into his health, his work, his personal life in the past, how was he to interest her now?

"Carrie, I would like to stay for a while; to stay and . . . talk with you."

"Yes, surely," she replied, setting two cups of strong black coffee on a woven mat. She seemed scarcely to have registered what he'd said.

"It's not about anything in particular. I just felt it would be nice to . . ."

There was a tap on the door and Carrie, halfway into a chair, jumped back to her feet in evident relief.

"Margery? Is that you? Just a sec; I'll get the latch."

The short, stout figure of Margery bouncing cheerfully into the kitchen seemed to illuminate the whole room. She had a red, rosy face and lively eyes which beamed energy and youth, defying the gray that had crept into her once rich-brown, curly hair.

Margery held out a huge bunch of holly and Carrie took it with a laugh.

"Oh my goodness, is that from your garden? You must have brought the whole bush."

"Nothing like; it's taking me over; I'm glad to be rid of the stuff."

She stripped off her coat and gloves while Carrie deposited the holly gingerly on the farmhouse table.

"You remember my son, Michel, don't you, Marge?"

"Heavens, yes, of course. What an absolutely splendid surprise!"

She turned her enormous smile toward him and he stood up to greet her, heartened by the warmth of her personality. Carrie watched, blank-faced, as he laid his hand on Margery's shoulder and leaned over to kiss her cheek.

"Dear old Marge," he said, smiling. "You haven't changed a bit."

She reached up to take his face in her plump, freezing hands, shaking him affectionately.

"Why, just look at you, boy. You're huge. And so grown-up and handsome. The way Carrie talks about you, I imagined you still a young whippersnapper. Are you well? You look tired."

Michel glanced at his mother but she had turned away to top up the kettle so he looked down at Margery, smiling.

"I'm as well as can be expected in an old man, pushing thirty. No need to ask how you are, though; you look wonderful."

The three of them had a merry tea party: Michel and Margery laughing together; Carrie and Margery laughing together. When Margery questioned Michel about his life touring with the BNB Carrie looked on stonily. Michel tried to steer the subject back to Margery's work on the town council.

"So do you get nervous when you go onstage?" Margery asked.

"No, rarely; just for first nights and really tricky things. How about you when you have to make speeches in the town hall?"

"Pshaw! Chicken feed. I hear from Carrie your big premiere at the Coliseum was a tremendous success."

Michel looked up at Carrie as she stood up to refill the teapot. Before she moved she caught the question implicit in the turn of his head and she spoke frigidly from her position in front of the stove. "Yes, there was rather a good review in the *Times*. Vera in the post office pointed it out to me."

There was a moment's awkward silence, and then Margery plowed on with her merry chitchat until she looked at her watch and rose reluctantly to go.

"I've got a meeting of the PCC tonight. Mince pies and the vicar's wife's problems choosing a carpet for the vestry." She shuddered. "It's been lovely to see you, Michel. I know it must be a marvelous surprise for Carrie; she would never have invited me if she'd known you were coming."

Carrie looked embarrassed by this comment but Michel merely smiled with a touch of guilt. It must have been dreadful for Carrie having him at the farm when he wasn't fit to be seen. For months he had lurked here, morose and taciturn, making her drive away all her friends. It was small wonder if she had been ashamed of him.

Once Margery had gone the awkwardness between Michel and his mother deepened. He had come here to open his heart to her, to try to repair the rift in their relationship, and he was tongue-tied. He couldn't say a word.

It was Carrie who managed to sustain some semblance of conversation beyond Margery's departure.

"You'll be needing me to clear out the front bedroom—no, don't worry, it's no bother. I'll make up the bed in two ticks. I've got it covered in newspaper stacked with beets at the moment; it won't take long to shift them to the barn."

"But if it freezes?"

"Oh, it won't. This winter's ridiculously mild; I was outside pulling up onions today in just a sweater."

"I'll come up with you and help you move the beets. Did you sort out the leak in there, by the way?"

"No, they're in a box in the utility room."

"Ha?"

They looked at each other for a few seconds, both aware that something had gone awry. Michel frowned and then smiled cautiously.

"The leak from the header tank; it was running through the light fitting in the front bedroom."

Carrie remembered the leak with a sudden jerk of her shoulders.

"Oh, the header tank; of course. Yes, it's fine; no more problems, thank goodness. I think after all, if you don't mind, it might be better to put you in the orchard room. The ceiling's rather low for you but you won't mind."

The orchard room was a tiny bedroom overlooking the aged apple trees behind the house. It was like a bedroom in a doll's house, with rosebud wallpaper and a miniature casement window set into a recess in the sloping ceiling. He would feel like an ungainly giant in that dainty apartment but it was cozy and, besides, he didn't care; anywhere would do.

"The orchard room's fine," he said.

"Good. I'll go up and bring down the turnips, then."

For two days Michel stayed in the farmhouse with his mother. Their restrained, impersonal chatter was interrupted by seasonal visits from Carrie's friends and a few relatives who were unknown to Michel. Invariably these guests had the advantage of him; they were sufficiently well informed about him to inquire in maddening detail about his career. Michel replied in mumbles. For the first time his renown was a curse—everyone in Devon seemed ballet mad. He only hoped they didn't plague Carrie with vexatious questions on the subject when he wasn't around to be a focus of interest.

At night he lay in bed, feeling like Alice in Wonderland or Gulliver in his minuscule room, staring at the rosebuds on the wall. His anxiety and frustration increased by the hour.

He felt powerless to effect any change in his relationship with Carrie. Every time he tried to clear a space in the day to sit down and converse with her she managed to fill it with an urgent chore or a trip to town that couldn't wait because of the bank holidays coming up. When she caught him looking pensive she would break his train of thought with an abrupt request to run over to the barn and bring in a couple of pounds of potatoes.

It was twenty years since they had exchanged even a momentary intimacy. What was he doing here? The mother who had caressed him with such tenderness—he could scarcely even remember her—and the boy who had run so unhesitatingly to his mother's knee; they had been different people. He had given up his career in dance to come home and be the son Carrie wanted. He was kidding himself.

He thought of Charles Crown—the devastation in the man's eyes when he had broken the news to him—and turned over to bury his head under the pillow.

On Christmas Day Michel and Carrie ate lunch together in the kitchen. It was a strange, silent meal, eerily reminiscent of the same day a year ago when Michel's heart had been empty and his mind a blank. But the resemblance was superficial; now Michel's heart was agonizingly full and his mind was churning, turning the same thoughts over and over.

They sat on opposite sides of the table: a woman of forty-seven—with sharp, bright eyes and an unshakable, cold reserve—and a man of twenty-eight, with a graceful, solid body and a wary, contemplative manner. Each, to the other, was an enigma. The feelings that hung in the air over their shared meal were more simple than they imagined; it was the inability to express those feelings that created the deep rift between them. Carrie watched his uncommunicative face with guarded eyes, looking down at her plate often. After two decades in which Michel had pushed her away at every turn, keeping her at arm's length, she was so frightened of being driven yet further away she didn't dare try to hold his gaze for long.

When their silent meal, punctuated by occasional attempts at desultory conversation, was finished, Carrie stacked the dishes by the sink. Michel rose from his chair, congratulating his mother on her culinary skill as he rolled up his shirtsleeves.

"No, leave the washing up," she said. "We'll do it later. Sit down; I'll put on the coffee."

He turned on the hot tap and fitted the plug into the steel rim.

"I might as well get it over with. If we leave it, it'll be you who ends up doing it; it always is."

Carrie snapped at him in irritation.

"Oh, for heaven's sake, will you leave it alone, Michel?"

He looked up from the suds, out of the window where the somber afternoon was darkening rapidly and uneventfully into night, and turned off the taps, returning to his seat at the table.

He watched Carrie make the coffee. She didn't like him interfering with her domestic independence. He supposed that was understandable.

They both remained mute while the kettle's hiss rose on the stove. The battered grandfather clock at the far end of the kitchen had become a monster, clonking out the seconds with jerky metallic thuds instead of its usual unobtrusive ticking. Carrie brought the coffee jug with its filter to the table and left it to drip while she sat down.

"So what did you want to talk about?" she said.

"Sorry?" He looked up blankly.

"You said, when you arrived on Sunday, that you wanted to talk."

"Oh . . . yes." He rested his arms on the table and stared at his hands. She had taken him completely by surprise; the opportunity he had been seeking ever since his arrival, now forced upon him unexpectedly, shocked all his prepared speeches out of his mind.

"Yes . . . yes, I'd like to talk with you."

"Talk, Michel; I'm listening. What would you like to talk about?"

"Oh, anything. How about you? Tell me your news, Carrie."

Her voice remained very cold.

"I don't have any news."

He made a small sound which was almost a laugh. No news in twenty years?

"Okay," he said. "Let me see; last time we spoke, you were having trouble with the plumbing. How about starting there? Did you get it seen to professionally? What about the front room; did the water damage the plaster?"

"It was a lie," she said bluntly.

"A lie?"

"Yes, there was no leak in the header tank. What else would you like to talk about?"

Michel looked at her face for a moment; it was hard and expressionless but she was looking at him determinedly.

"I could tell you some of my news," he said. "I've had some changes in my life recently. Would you like to hear about me?"

Carrie pursed her lips. What did he think?

"Say whatever you want. I told you, I'm listening."

"Right, well . . . well, let's see." He rubbed his nose with the back of his hand. "When I came to stay here last year, to help out around the farm, I was . . . I had been ill. You must have wondered why I wasn't working at my job in London. I had a . . . what the doctors called a mental breakdown."

"Oh dear. Well, you're over that now, I can see."

Michel sniffed and nodded enthusiastically; he was having a very hard time of this.

"Yes, yes I'm fine." He searched his mind for other news. An hour ago—ten minutes ago, even—there had been so many things he had wanted to tell her. Where had they gone? "Oh, yes; you're a grandmother," he remembered suddenly. "Jonni—you remember the girl I married—she had a baby; a little girl. Jonni named her Caroline after you."

Carrie removed the filter from the jug and poured out the coffee. It was too huge a piece of information to be absorbed all at once.

"A daughter? That's nice. Is she pretty?"

"Oh, yes; she's a sweet little thing . . . but . . . Jonni and I are separated, I'm afraid."

"That's a pity; she seemed a bright girl. But these things happen, sadly."

"It was my fault. It was very complicated. We had a friend who died . . ." He cleared his throat. ". . . Died. Do you remember Primo, the friend I brought here once?"

"Yes, I do. He's dead; that's a great shame."

"Yup." Now Michel was running his hand incessantly over his mouth and jaw. "Carrie, I saw Jacques St. Michel."

For the first time his mother's face colored a fraction but she remained placid. Her eyes rested on the handle of her cup.

"Did you speak to him?"

"Yes, we had a long talk."

"Did you like him?"

"No."

"He may have changed a lot. He was very likable when I knew him."

"He can't have been easy to live with."

"No, not always; I really can't remember."

"He's married now—well, married and divorced. He's got a daughter."

"Yes, I knew about that. When I wrote to him while you were at school in France, he wrote back telling me not to write again. His wife wasn't to know you were his son, something like that. He did mention he'd had a little girl . . . Lisa, I think her name was."

Michel looked up at her and she avoided his gaze.

"Well, I wish to God you'd told me about it," he said.

"Why?" Her lips pursed into a bitter smile and her intelligent green eyes regarded him cynically. "Did you want a sister? Should you like to go to America to meet her?"

"She's not in America. She's a dancer with the British National Ballet. We were working together without even knowing we were brother and sister."

"How extraordinary. Yes, I can see that must have been very strange for you both. Is she nice?"

He made a gesture of frustrated helplessness.

"Carrie, I took the girl to bed."

"Oh, my God!" Carrie's hands flew to her face and she looked at him, wide-eyed.

Michel took a deep breath and sighed, raising his eyebrows. "It was a pretty unpleasant experience for her—I mean when she found out. She'd got it into her head we were cousins. And, on reflection, I could probably have been a bit nicer about her mistake."

"Are you friends—now, I mean?"

"No. We dance . . . danced together regularly but she can't stand the sight of me."

Carrie stared at the tablecloth, shaken by the knowledge of her own guilt. She hadn't wanted him to go to the States and seek out this sister; she hadn't wanted him to be involved with that other family. She blushed in shame at what her selfishness had done to them both.

Slowly, she looked up at Michel's face. How like Jacques he was. The same eyes, the same bone structure, same nose. The same hands. She thought about Michel, her son, as a sexually active man and the idea made her flush deepen. He was her child; had he really held a woman in his arms and looked at her with that same intense desire she remembered so well in Jacques's gray eyes? Did he touch women the way Jacques had touched her?—and other men since Jacques; she'd had her share of boyfriends over the years, hiding them from Michel through a perverse form of jealousy.

The idea of Michel as a lover was disturbing, but another image, a memory of Jacques that became a vision of her son, was more disturbing still. She raised her hand involuntarily to a little scar that just touched her lower lip. They were so very alike. A picture had presented itself, coming suddenly before she could forbid it, of an angry, heartless Michel towering over a woman—his wife, maybe—holding her roughly, raising his hand and bringing it down hard across her face, splitting her mouth; no mercy, just a violent impulse and the brute strength of his powerful hands.

Her eyes smarted and her gaze traveled frightenedly to Michel's hands, which were resting on the table. The knuckles of both his hands were faintly bruised and bore the scars of painful splitting. She bit her lip until it bled. There must be lots of ways a dancer could fall and scar his hands like that. Mustn't there?

Michel was deep in thought. As though he read her mind, he ran his thumb lightly over the knuckles of his left hand and looked up at her. He too was chewing his lip.

"Carrie, listen. I have to try and explain something to you." He was shifting uncomfortably on his chair, hounded by emotions he didn't understand and the clock beside the hearth, which was taunting him ruthlessly. "I'm a miserable guy. Twenty-eight, successful, well off; I should be in my prime, full of plans and ambition. But I've lost myself somewhere along the way. I don't know how much potential there is left in me to become someone worth being but this is it; I'm here and I'm going to give it a try."

"What are you saying, Michel? You're speaking in riddles."

"I used to think I could be many things. I've tried to be lots of things but failed. A husband, a friend, a father, a brother; I'm none of those. I'm not even a dancer anymore. I want to be the one thing that could have made all those things possible except that it's probably too late. Do you understand? I want to be a son."

Carrie was frowning at him in perplexity and alarm.

"No I don't understand. What on earth are you talking about?"

His gray eyes looked at her in appeal.

"I've given up dancing. I've come home to try to make up for what I stupidly threw away twenty years ago."

"You've given up dancing?"

"Yes, I'm through for good; completely—dancing, teaching, choreography: everything. I'll find something else. I could work here on the farm. Or I could go to college if you like. I can afford it; I've got plenty of money."

"You've given up dancing?" Carrie's face was a picture—and not an encouraging one.

Michel hesitated. "Well . . . yes."

"What a stupid, stupid thing to do!"

Michel grimaced in distress and clenched his fist, pressing it against his mouth. The only thing he could offer her had been this, the one real sacrifice he could make, and she had rejected it in one short, angry outburst.

"What does Charles have to say about this?" Carrie asked curtly.

"Charles?" He looked up at her in surprise at hearing his forsaken mentor's name on her lips. "Crown? Do you know him?"

"I've never met him," she replied ungraciously, "but we've spoken on the phone a number of times. I'm sure he's not too pleased about your defection. What on earth put such an idea into your head, Michel?"

"Well . . . you. I want to get to know you. You hated my going away to France, I know. I was just being a stubborn kid. Why didn't you stop me? Why didn't you let Uncle Jim take his belt to me and make me do as I was told? I realize you were being unpossessive, liberal—you didn't want to stifle me the way Jim tried to stifle you; I appreciate that, but look what it did to us . . . I mean me."

"Oh, Michel." She sounded disgusted at his words.

"I know I remind you of Jacques. Yes, I do, Carrie; don't shake your head. I've seen it in your face when you look at me. You look at me and see him. But I'm not him. I'm nothing like him. I'm no wife batterer, for a start; I've never hit anyone in my life. I'm not a violent man, Carrie. I'm not a bully. Yes, okay, I betrayed my wife but I didn't walk out on her and I wasn't unfaithful to her. I don't hate women; I'm not a misogynist."

"Misogynist?"

He raised a hand. "Forget it. I'm not Jacques; that's all I'm trying to tell you. I'm me. You resented my dancing right from the start. You've never wanted to hear about it, never cared if I made it or if I didn't. That's fine; I understand. You were angry with me for leaving you to study in France; angry that I wanted to be like my father. Look, I made a mistake when I was too young to know better and now I'm trying to rectify it."

Her face was stony. "So you've come here to accuse me of not loving you enough."

He looked at her imploringly.

"I've come here to show you that getting to know you again is more important to me than my dancing. And to ask you to learn to love me if you can."

Her temper snapped.

"Are you the only one who's allowed to have suffered? Do you think I don't know what it is to regret the past? Why do you think I lied about the water tank? Do you suppose I suddenly find myself, one night when you happen, by coincidence, to be making your first appearance on stage after an illness of eighteen months, with the urge to phone you up at midnight and lie to you that my blasted header tank is overflowing? Are you stupid? Is it true that all ballet dancers are congenitally dumb? I think not; you are my son, after all."

Michel was blinking numbly in the face of her anger.

"Do something for me!" she ordered. "Go upstairs to my bedroom. There's a bureau in the corner, next to the bed. In the bottom drawer there's a big square book with a black cover. Bring it down here to me."

Michel stood up obediently. Twenty-eight he might be, but he felt more like the bewildered eight-year-old who had walked away from his mother's comforting hand into that unknown world of the Paris Académie, dazed and abandoned. This was not working out at all as he had hoped.

It was many years since he'd had occasion to go into his mother's bedroom. He crossed the old carpet, which had once been white, and crouched down to open the bottom drawer of the antique oak bureau. The drawer was heavy and unevenly grooved; he had to jiggle it gently to pull it out far enough to lift the wide, heavy book from its place on top of a pile of papers.

Resting the book on his knee, he reached out to lift up one of the documents which had been squashed underneath it. It was his apprenticeship report from his first year at the Islington Ballet, written partly in

Crown's hand, partly in Nadia Petrovna's. He skimmed over it quickly, wondering how it had come to be there, and dropped it back into the drawer.

As he adjusted his balance to rise to his feet he lifted his head and looked up. Above the bureau, on the wall, was a framed poster from one of the Islington Ballet's seasons several years ago. The photograph of Michel in an expressive, tortured posture had excited considerable acclaim at the time. He supposed it was a good photo—and without doubt his feet and the line of his body looked great or you could be sure Crown wouldn't have allowed them anywhere near a poster—but all the same, he had felt a little self-conscious about appearing half-naked all over the London Underground.

He turned his head and looked behind him. Above the dressing table was another poster: himself and Carlotta very passionate in the first staging of Crown's *Romeo*. There was a framed black-and-white poster too: a sexy shot where his head was turned obliquely toward the camera as if caught out in a moment of guilty thought, and the muscles of his arms and shoulders were highlighted by sharp contrast of light and shade.

He stood up and walked slowly to the door of Carrie's room. There were half a dozen snapshots resting against the back of the dressing table, all of Michel as a child. One picture showed him as a toddler in his father's arms. He glanced at it briefly and then carried the book downstairs to his mother.

"Now, sit down, Michel. I want to show you something."

Michel sat down and Carrie laid the book on the table in front of him, standing beside him with her arms folded as he laid his hand tentatively on the book's cover.

"Go ahead," she said. "There's nothing in there you haven't seen before."

The first press cutting was from a French dance journal. It was a picture of Michel looking very lanky and, to his own eyes now, horribly arrogant at the age of twelve when he had won the Junior section of the *Concours National*. He remembered how cocky he had been coming home to the Académie with his gold medal. It was just as well he hadn't known then how much work and sweat and physical pain were in store for him.

The next cutting was from the *Telegraph,* a vicious review by Boyle, describing in gloating detail Michel's falling flat on his backside during one of the ensembles on an opening night when he was eighteen.

They were all there: every review, every article, every photo, every cheeky mention in the gossip columns. Michel looked at an article torn roughly from a magazine six or seven years ago. The edges of the paper had been covered with doodles; grim, agitated squiggles and hard lines, pressed into the paper. Someone had spent a lot of time looking at that particular page.

He skimmed through it quickly. One paragraph had been underlined repeatedly in black ink: *"Michel has nothing to say about his background or family. He shrugs and tells me, I'm not involved with my parents at all. We live totally separate lives."*

It had never occurred to him that Carrie might see that interview. He had always assumed she read nothing and heard nothing of his work as a dancer. He looked up at her and she glared at him, her eyes harsh and her mouth set in an angry line.

"Keep going," she said.

He glanced through the rest reluctantly: reviews of his performances, the mentions of his name in connection with Primo's death, the gossip about Jonni's defection. When he got to the photo and front page article about his breakdown, Carrie slapped her hand down quickly on the page to prevent him from turning it over. She pointed to the printed date at the top of the page.

"May twenty-third," she said fiercely. "I was in the village buying bread when Vera ran across from the post office to show me this. I'd have been on the first train to London if Charles Crown hadn't phoned and said that you—yes, *you,* Michel—had specifically told him you didn't want me there." Her voice rose almost to a shout. "How do you think I slept that week, eh?"

She snatched her purse out of her old leather handbag on the table. It was the kind of purse that folds round on itself, and she pulled the catch open and hurled it on top of the open scrapbook, faceup, so he could see the photograph of himself, cut from a magazine, that filled the clear-plastic pocket designed for a bus pass. She opened one of the wooden kitchen cupboards and grabbed a big jar from the back, hidden behind the pots and pans, turning it upside down and covering the table in a confetti of white, pink, blue, and green paper; ticket stubs from dozens of Islington Ballet performances spanning more than a decade.

"What else can I show you?" she cried passionately.

She ran to the far end of the kitchen and flung open the cupboard where she kept everything from shoe polish to aspirin, pulling out a pile of videos. She threw them on the table, one by one. Jean-Baptiste St. Michel in the Islington Ballet's *Romeo and Juliet.* Jean-Baptiste St. Michel in *Swan Lake.* A BBC video featuring St. Michel dancing in excerpts from the Islington Ballet's current season. The last video was home-recorded and Michel recognized Crown's handwriting on the box: "Bits of rehearsals for *Giselle* and *Le Corsaire.*" Crown had scribbled on the bottom in pencil, "Please ignore dreadful fall toward end of tape; worst injury incurred was a clip round the ear from me."

Michel ran both his hands through his hair and looked at the window, wondering how long it had been pitch-dark outside. Christmas night. What sort of Christmas was Charles having? he wondered. The full force of his own stupidity hit him square on.

After a few seconds he turned wretchedly back to face his mother. She was still glaring at him, her breast rising and falling quickly.

"Don't you tell me I'm not interested!" she yelled suddenly. "Don't you come here telling me I don't care enough! You think I look at you and see your father? Don't you ever dare tell me I don't love you, Michel. You're my son! Do you think I stopped loving you just because you went off to France and never bothered to write to me, or phone me, or visit me? Have you really had so little faith in me all these years? Who stopped loving who, Michel?"

He stood up and spread his hands wide in entreaty. He was speechless. After staring at his helpless face for a moment Carrie flung herself at him, hitting him with her fists and sobbing uncontrollably.

Michel looked up at the oak beam above his head, opening his mouth in disbelief. The blows which his mother struck against the solid muscle of his chest were painless but his heart twisting and compressing inside him felt as if it were about to explode. If Michel's heart were ever to break it would be now. Tears of pain spouted from his eyes.

"Oh, God," he said. "Oh, Mum."

Gradually the pain eased and Michel's body relaxed. He closed his arms gently around his mother's neck and shut his eyes. It was the first time they had touched each other with affection in twenty years.

"It's alright, Carrie. Come on, hush now or you'll hyperventilate. Let's sit down and finish our coffee."

49

At eight o'clock on the morning of New Year's Eve, Charles Crown buttoned up the front of his only decent overcoat and let himself out of the front door of his Victorian ground-floor flat in Kennington. It was a chill, overcast morning, not yet fully daylight. His head was lowered, his eyes fixed on the pavement, as he closed the front gate and set off toward the tube station with his briefcase in his hand.

"Charles!"

He looked up. He hadn't seen Michel's car parked next to the curb outside the house. He stopped on the pavement, watching without expression while Michel wound down his window.

"Hello, Charles—Jesus, it's cold!" Michel blew on his hands and rubbed them together. "I thought I'd give you a lift up to Nottingham. I thought you might want some help pitching our plans for *Tempest* to the Board."

Crown didn't reply. There was a pause while Michel looked into his eyes, waiting for him to speak. Around them, as commuters left home for work in the semidarkness, front doors banged and car engines started.

"I tried to call you over Christmas," Michel said at last. "I couldn't get through."

"It's been off the hook. I didn't want to talk to anyone."

For a long time the two men remained motionless, the searching brown eyes and the anxious gray ones looking at each other through the mist that their breath formed on the gradually lightening air.

Eventually, Crown flexed his shoulders with a sniff, and walked around the car to the passenger door. He climbed in with his briefcase, slamming the door, and reached for the seat belt.

"I hope to Christ you brought a tie," he said. "This press conference is going to be a fucker."

Michel started the engine.

"Of course I brought a bloody tie. What the hell do you take me for?"

The meeting with the sponsors and the press conference that followed it were as arduous as Crown had predicted. It was almost dark again—cold, murky dusk—by the time they returned to London in the late afternoon, hitting solid rush-hour traffic at the Angel. They had been discussing the choreography process for *The Tempest* ever since they left Nottingham. With only three weeks until rehearsals started, there was a lot to discuss.

"I suppose there's no question of Lisa creating Miranda," Crown said, frowning through the window as the car crawled past the Islington Ballet. Michel shook his head. Primo had written three duets—beautiful duets—for Ariel and Miranda, and he couldn't create them either on or with Lisa.

"No. It'll have to be Tatjana, I'm afraid."

"Unless you'd prefer to make it on Gillette, of course."

Michel took his eyes from the road and turned them in Crown's direction for just long enough to let Crown see exactly what he thought of that idea. Crown screwed his mouth into a twisted smile in reply. As ever, with the two ballerinas, it was a question of the devil and the deep blue sea.

"Tatjana didn't do too bad a job on *Ghosts*," Crown conceded with a sigh. "Anyway, we need to put together a provisional rehearsal schedule so we've got something to give the company. Let's head back to Victoria and see if we can cobble something together tonight."

"I can't this evening," Michel said. "Carrie's in London at the moment; I'm taking her out to dinner at the Ivy."

Crown looked at him with the same concerned, questioning frown that had been in his eyes, on and off, all day. "Oh, she's here, is she? And she's staying with you?"

"No, she's staying in the hotel a couple of doors down from me; you know, the one with the window boxes." He paused as he turned right off the Goswell Road, trying to escape the traffic. "We drove up from Devon together yesterday. She's planning on staying for a while; do a bit of sight-seeing and shopping. She might even try and get some work."

Crown's eyes moved slowly over Michel's face, studying him closely. "Was it her idea that she come to London or yours?" he asked, which was as close as he would ever come to asking him what had taken place in Devon.

Michel smiled, pulling on the hand brake in another traffic queue. "I'm not sure; we just kind of developed the idea between us," which was as close as he would ever come to telling him. "Look, Charles, forget about the rehearsal schedule; come out with me and Carrie tonight."

"No, no, no." Crown shook his head. "The two of you go out together. Besides, I need to get this work done."

"Bullshit. It's New Year's Eve. The restaurant will fit us in." None of London's top restaurants would refuse to alter their seating plans for Michel, even on New Year's Eve—especially if it was to accommodate the artistic director of the BNB. "Come on, Charles, you're even dressed for it for once—you cut quite a decent figure in that suit. It's about time you and Carrie finally met face-to-face. Besides, you might be able to give her some ideas about finding work. She's an accompanist," he added, in not altogether as offhand a tone as he hoped. "She used to play for classes and rehearsals at the *Opéra* Ballet when she was a student at the Conservatoire." He cast a nonchalant sideways glance toward Crown. "Did I ever tell you that?"

Crown turned his head away with a small smile to look out of the window, amused. "No, you never told me that."

They were silent as they crawled, stopping and starting, through drizzle along the Clerkenwell Road. When Michel pulled up at the lights at the junction with Farringdon Road, Crown looked at him, folding his arms and said, "Look, if I come out with you tonight you've got to spend tomorrow in Victoria doing these schedules with me—that's the deal, okay? And you've got to sign your fucking contract for this season."

Michel laughed; Crown drove a hard bargain.

"Yes, alright." But he dreaded to think what the company would say when he rolled into class on Thursday morning, less than a fortnight after supposedly going into permanent retirement. "How do you think the dancers will react?"

"They won't react at all," Crown said. "They don't know anything about it."

"They don't know?" Michel was surprised. "You didn't announce my retirement to the company? How did you manage that? I mean what about the performances at Wembley last week? They must have wondered where the hell I was."

It was Crown's turn to try to sound more nonchalant than he felt.

"Oh . . . I told them you were in Helsinki giving a master class. I thought I'd leave it for a while before I told them and announced it to the press. Until I was absolutely sure."

Michel frowned slightly, smiling at the same time, as he looked at his teacher.

"You knew I'd be coming back?"

"No." Crown shook his head. "No, I didn't know." He rested his elbow in its dark suit sleeve on the narrow rim of the car window and propped his cheek on his hand. "I suppose if you want something badly enough, you're never quite ready to give up hope, are you? You always think you'll just give it that one last chance."

Michel looked out at the wet traffic junction, watching a couple of ballet students crossing the road from the Central School of Ballet toward the station—it was easy to spot them amongst the other pedestrians, with their designer-label dance bags and their feet turned out at forty-five degrees. Was that true? he wondered. If you really wanted something, did you never altogether give up hoping? He stared thoughtfully at the traffic lights, mulling that over.

"Why Helsinki?" he asked.

"It was the first place that came to mind."

Michel's first task, when he went back to work, was to train his body back into condition in preparation for the choreography of *The Tempest* and rehearsals for *La Fille* and *Romeo*. He stood at the barre in his old all-in-one and threadbare black leg warmers with his sweatshirt tied around his waist, one hand on the barre and the other gripping his heel, stretching his foot up, up until his working leg was vertical, his whole body rejoicing in the movement, his chest expanding with the stretch. In class, turning and leaping through one exercise after another, he reveled in the familiar atmosphere of the studio—the stridency of the echoing piano, the presence of that illusory parallel world behind the mirror, the worn, warm wood beneath his feet, the resonance of the teachers' voices.

Michel was scarcely aware of how wonderful it felt just to be dancing after two months off with his injured hands; there was too much work to do to allow time for introspection. Every day was filled with meetings and rehearsals, and Michel stood among his colleagues in the studios and offices, his back straight and hands propped on his turned-out hips, a T-shirt or a towel slung over his shoulder, every millimeter a ballet dancer.

The whole company was in a fever of excitement about the forthcoming choreography of *The Tempest*. For the first time in years there was a feeling that the BNB was undertaking a project that would put them at the forefront, the cutting edge of world dance. One afternoon in December the whole organization had crammed into the big studio—dancers, musicians, administrators, press officers, technicians, shoe dyers, transport chief, wig makers, cleaners, even Sir Andrew and the Governors—to sit on chairs or lie on the floor and listen while the company pianists, between them, played the whole ballet—all two hours and thirty minutes of it—from start to finish. And since those electrifying two and a half hours, the company had been on fire.

The greatest single burning topic of discussion was the casting of the lead roles—and most specifically, who would create the prestigious central role of Miranda opposite Michel's Ariel. Wherever he went, the soloists and principals stared at Charles Crown, as though they could read the information through the back of his head. Marie and Tatjana squabbled like cats in the soloists' changing room. But day followed day, and Crown wasn't giving anything away.

"I know what you've been thinking," Crown said to Michel, as they talked it over in the privacy of his office. "But the truth is it would be an expensive, difficult thing to buy a principal out of a contract with PACT."

Michel jiggled his foot slowly on the rung of his chair, folding his arms. He didn't ask how Crown had known it had been on his mind; he supposed it was obvious. Crown moved a pile of letters carefully from one side of his cluttered desk to the other, then he moved them back again.

"However," he said, "Johannesburg is going to get back to me tomorrow on whether they're prepared to make a deal."

"No!" Michel sat up straight, his eyes opening wide in eagerness. "You're kidding! You never said a word! When did this happen?"

"Lynne and I have been speaking over the past week. She's absolutely wild to come back and do it."

"When does she arrive? When can we begin work?"

"Don't count your chickens," Crown cautioned, holding up a restraining hand. "Even if they're willing to negotiate, there'll be hell to pay at this end. I'd have to get it past the Governors for a start."

"They can't stop you," Michel said avidly.

"They can. They can sack me anytime they like."

"What, and have you take *The Tempest* with you to the English National or the Royal? I don't think so."

"Okay, maybe not, but they're the ones who've got to come up with the money. I'm afraid it's no money, no go."

The next afternoon, once the crucial call had come from South Africa, Crown wrote a nervous memo by hand to the Chairman and President of the Board asking them to approve, with extreme urgency and absolute secrecy, the funds for buying Lynne Forrest out of her contract with PACT. He handed it to his PA.

"Make me two photocopies, darling, and courier them, sealed, straight to Sir Andrew and Lord Harrington-Gibbs. And, whatever you do, don't let anyone see this; don't talk to anyone about it; don't even drop a hint. All our jobs are on the line here."

Within half an hour Crown was in heavy negotiations on the phone with Sir Andrew, fighting off accusations of subversion and bargaining hard for the money, watched with anxious faces by his council of war: Michel, Marina, and Helen, his PA, who was now in on the plot. Eventually, by agreeing to waive his royalties for the coming production of *Romeo,* Crown brought the Chairman round.

"Now there's just Lord H.-G. and the board to convince," he said grimly. Sir Andrew controlled the purse strings, but the ballerinas controlled the board.

"What on earth did he mean by subversive?" Marina wanted to know. "What did you say to him in your memo, for God's sake?"

"Haven't you seen it?" Crown asked. He glanced over the papers strewn over his desk, moving one or two aside, and then looked up at Helen. "Where's the original, darling?"

Helen frowned, thinking for a moment, trying to remember where she had put it when she came back from the photocopier. Then her eyes suddenly grew round in horror, her hand rising to her open mouth.

"The original!" she yelped. She was on her feet and out of the room, flying along the corridor, before Crown, Marina, and Michel had time to realize what had happened. But she was too late. When she reached the photocopier and threw up the cover, there was no sign of the original memo.

She put her hands to her head, plunging her fingers into her blond hair, and wailed, "F*uuuck!*"

So efficient were the wheels of communication within the BNB that the only person in the building who didn't already know the contents of Crown's memo was Marie Gillette, the self-styled *prima ballerina assoluta* of the company, because no one dared break it to her. When Tatjana finally told her, hands on hips, that a dancer was being bought in from South Africa not only to create the lead role in the new ballet but to become the new fairy on the top of the BNB Christmas tree, there was a long, piercing scream of rage from the soloists' changing room and the few dancers who were hanging around in the corridor outside exchanged ominous looks and then, by tacit mutual agreement, dived for cover.

The shock wave from the bombshell was even more catastrophic than Crown had foreseen. By the end of the afternoon almost the entire Board of Governors had assembled for an emergency meeting with the dancers, who were boycotting classes and rehearsals, while the press office was besieged with requests for a press conference. In a dramatic showdown the next day, which threw even the tempestuous scenes of Crown's first few weeks at the BNB into the shade, the Governors were finally forced to go into hiding alone in the boardroom to decide the future of the company and its artistic director. When the message finally came from the board-room that the Governors would back whatever decision Crown made, Marie and Tatjana both cleared out their lockers, touched up their make-up, and marched in high fury out of the company, straight into the arms of the media, who had gathered outside the huge smoked-glass doors of the BNB, waiting to hear the outcome of this latest storm in the nation's cultural teapot.

Charles Crown summoned a conclave of his inner circle behind the locked door of his office. Michel, Marina, Anatoly, and the quaking Helen all stood in front of his desk, watching him with worried frowns. The tension that pervaded the building had affected them all.

"I wanted you to be here too, Helen," he said, rubbing his hands slowly together, "because if it hadn't been for that memo getting into the dancers' hands, we would probably have been able to square all this with-out Marie and Tatjana going so far as to walk out." He leaned over and reached into the voluminous bottom drawer of his massive desk, pulling out a bottle of Moët Special Reserve and plonking it on his desk. "So get the glasses out of that cabinet over there. It's a crime to drink this warm but, under the circumstances, who gives a damn?"

The tempest within the BNB blew over almost as soon as the two bal-lerinas had left the building. By the end of the day nothing remained of the hurricane that had raged in the studios and corridors overnight except for a few disgruntled mumbles from the ranks of the female soloists—and even those evaporated when Lisa pointed out to her col-leagues the obvious corollary that, with Marie and Tatjana gone, some of the other women in the company might finally get a look in on casting, and perhaps a few of the longest serving might even be promoted to prin-cipal. The press, of course, had their forty-eight-hour field day with the story of the ballerinas' departure and Lynne's expensive purchase from PACT, making much of the fact that the usurper was an ex-lover of St. Michel's and accusing Crown of blatant cronyism. But all in all, it was a happier, somehow more frank and relaxed company that welcomed Lynne when she arrived for morning class at the start of the following week.

When the dancers watched Michel and Lynne partner one another in the first rehearsals for *Romeo*—saw how naturally their bodies flowed together even after all this time—heads were shaken in wonder and eyes softened at the beauty of the shapes the two intertwined figures made as they moved through the choreography. Even Lisa's eyes glinted with an unexpected green tinge of jealousy as she watched them, so intimate and trusting of each other.

Michel and Lynne were so blissfully happy to be dancing together that they were unaware of the eyes that watched them in the Victoria studios or back at the Pimlico flat as they worked on the pas de deux while Lisa and Rob learned the steps beside them. Ten years had passed, and more heartache than either of them cared to think about, since they had first shared the dream of one day dancing *Romeo and Juliet* on the stage of the Coliseum together.

Meanwhile, the Pimlico flat was once again developing a life of its own. Lisa came almost every evening to dance or to chat with Carrie. She came, the first time, only because Carrie personally and pressingly invited her. Michel would never know what the two of them said to each other that evening in the studio while he and Rob were banished to the kitchen, but Lisa had become devoted to Carrie. She would even put up with Michel's company for the sake of Carrie's friendship and counsel. Lisa had changed since Christmas—she was brighter-faced and less self-conscious—and it was easy to see what had caused the change. Lisa was in love, and Rob was equally, if not more smitten.

It wasn't just Lisa and Rob who came to Warwick Way in the evenings. In addition to Crown, Marina, and the few others that Michel brought home to meet Carrie, people seemed to have started inviting themselves. There was usually someone playing the piano: either Carrie or Jerry, Lynne's husband who had accompanied her from South Africa to assist with *The Tempest* between his European concert engagements. Dancers from the BNB, and some who had known Lynne at the Islington, arrived with bottles of wine and gossip. The beautiful studio with its gleaming new mirrors, which had been virtually a mausoleum for the past two years, was suddenly filled with conversation; and the Steinway, untouched and silent since Primo's death, was pouring out music again. Even on the evenings when Michel had to stay late at the BNB to work, there were always at least half a dozen people in the studio by the time he got home.

Annette was among those who visited the flat, delivered to the door one evening in a bright-red twelve-cylinder Pontiac by a blond Neanderthal of a man in police sunglasses. Drawn to the studio windows by the deafening roar of the car's engine, Michel and Lynne looked down at Annette's long legs emerging from the car onto the pavement. When they saw her hulking escort kiss her and squeeze her bottom, Lynne looked at Michel with raised eyebrows and Michel rolled his eyes.

"Oh Lord," Lynne said. "Don't tell me she's bringing him up here."

"Well, I don't fancy trying to stop him, do you?"

But luckily, having deposited her on the doorstep, the burly man got back into his American sports car and thundered off, leaving a cloud of black smoke behind him.

Late that night, when Michel had gone to bed and Jerry was walking Carrie back to the hotel, Annette and Lynne sat curled up on the black sofas in the studio, talking.

"We've had some times on these sofas, haven't we?" Annette said, kicking off her shoes and putting her feet up on the coffee table.

Lynne looked around at the room in which so many of the best and worst hours of her life had been spent. She had even lost her virginity on one of these black leather sofas—although she couldn't honestly remember which one, they had been moved around so often over the years.

"My God, just think," she said, "you and Roly have been married more than four years; that's so bizarre."

"What, bizarre that we've stuck it out so long?" Annette asked, laughing, though she knew that wasn't what Lynne had meant. She wiggled her toes, which were still misshapen from all those years of punishment, and sighed noisily, looking at the ceiling. "He's still got another three weeks in Newcastle, the bugger. Why do pantos have to drone on into ruddy February? Why can't they just wrap it up after Christmas?"

Lynne smiled. "You miss him."

"Oh yes, of course I do."

"Then, Nettie," Lynne shook her head uncomprehendingly, "why Piltdown Man and the batmobile?"

Annette snorted at that.

"Piltdown Man: I'll tell him that. He'll think it's a scream."

"I'm sure he will." But Lynne was in earnest. "Netts, seriously, Roly's bound to find out—surely. Michel said you've been seen all over town with who knows how many men."

"Oh, don't you start on me," Annette grumbled, curling her toes in irritation. "Why are all my friends so fucking paranoid? Roly has the least suspicious mind in the world. He trusts me completely. If he walked into our flat and found me in bed with Helmut he'd laugh and say, Christ, if I didn't know better I'd think you two were up to something under there."

Lynne's hazel eyes looked into Annette's bold, green ones in the low light from a single standard lamp next to the piano. The studio looked warm and shadowy in the light that glowed from behind the paper shade. There was something very unsettling in Annette's airy self-confidence.

"Don't you think you're being rather unfair on Roly?"

"No, not at all. It's up to every couple to work things out the way that best suits them, isn't it? And what Roly doesn't know can't hurt him." Annette raised an arch eyebrow. "Are you so sure you'd never be unfaithful to Jerry? I take it extramarital sex with Michel's out of the question, then."

"Of course it is!" Lynne retorted stoutly. Then she looked down at the table, remembering a certain conversation she had had with Michel when she visited last summer and thinking that perhaps she had no call to sound quite so sanctimonious, after all. "Besides," she added a little guiltily, "I think his sentimental attentions are engaged elsewhere."

"No, really?" Annette's head rose, her ears pricking up at the hint of gossip. "You don't mean it! Who is she?"

Lynne creased up her forehead, tilting her head in reproach.

"Oh, Nettie, for God's sake, who do you think?"

The following afternoon, while Michel and Lynne were sitting in the BNB canteen, sharing a solitary cup of coffee because they didn't have enough change for two, she asked him—

"Do you think there's any chance you'll patch things up with Jonni?"

Michel tucked the heel of one ballet-shod foot up on the seat of his plastic chair and rested his arm on his knee. He took a sip of coffee and passed the cup over the table to her—it was pathetic: two senior princi-pals of one of Europe's top ballet companies and they couldn't rustle up sixty pence between them.

"No, I don't think there's really any chance." He rubbed his stiff knuckles. "She cut loose, Lynnie. She didn't have any choice; she had to put her life back together and move on."

Lynne handed the coffee back to him, her eyes narrowing in sympathy. "You still think about her, don't you?"

He took the coffee and sipped it, looking across the room toward the whiteboard where Anatoly had written up the changes to the afternoon's rehearsal schedule. "Yup. I think about her all the time. That's the thing, isn't it? You never altogether give up hope. And, who's to say? I might . . . you know," he turned his eyes back toward her and smiled slowly, "give it one last try after all."

That Sunday afternoon Michel parked his car in the small Chiswick road, finding a space by pure luck as a Japanese Jeep crammed with a cargo of children and dogs pulled away from the curb in front of him. Jonni had raised so many objections when he phoned—Caroline looked like she was getting a cold, there was dreadful traffic because of the road-works in Chiswick, and she really was terribly busy with Guy just about to leave for California—that he would have backed down if he hadn't felt he would be setting a dangerous precedent in their negotiations concern-ing his right to see the child.

Jonni had clearly meant it when she said on the phone that she didn't want him in the flat. She met him at the door to the street with Caroline, warmly wrapped in her winter coat and woolly hat, clutched protectively in her arms.

"It's too cold," she said anxiously. "I don't think she should be out."

Michel glanced at the gray sky. It wasn't at all cold: it was a mild, slightly misty January day.

"She'll be fine. I'll only be an hour. I'll walk down to the river with her." He nodded toward the riverside green at the end of the road.

"Do you want the pushchair?"

"No, I'll carry her."

He moved closer to her to take the baby, who was staring at him in fascination, and Jonni shrank backward, taking care that their hands didn't touch as she reluctantly allowed him to take Caroline from her.

"Don't take her too near the river," she said, her face taut.

Michel's answer to that was simply to give her a long, fixed look, and she looked away with an apologetic twitch of her mouth. "Alright, I'll see you in an hour," she said.

Michel walked along the grass-flanked path beside the Thames, talking to the baby who was perched in his arms, showing her the trees and houseboats and the few rather bedraggled ducks who drifted glumly on the smooth surface of the water. Caroline seemed to find everything funny—except his refusal to let her eat the snowdrops he gave her to hold. There were a number of people on the green, walking their dogs in the mild Sunday afternoon air, and some of them smiled at the sight of the beautiful man with his beautiful child.

Eventually, with the fresh air on her face and the gentle rhythm of his slow stroll, Caroline fell asleep. Michel sat down on a green bench facing the river, propping his elbow on the armrest at the end as he held her. It felt marvelously peaceful after the chaos of these past hectic days at work and the emotional and practical upheaval of the last few weeks just to sit here without moving and gaze at the stone-gray river, listening to the baby's quiet breathing as she slept on his chest. His eyes were grave as he sat there thinking about Jonni, but if his thoughts weren't happy ones, they were at least tranquil.

Michel had no idea how long he sat there holding the sleeping baby. He didn't think of the time at all until his meditation was suddenly broken by Jonni's voice behind him, sounding both angry and relieved.

"Oh, God, I thought something had happened! Michel, if you say you're going to be an hour, I expect you to be back when you said you will."

Michel turned his head to look at her over his shoulder.

"I'm sorry," he said, keeping his voice low so as not to disturb Caroline. "She fell asleep; I didn't want to wake her."

Jonni wasn't accepting any excuses. "I was really worried."

Michel carefully extracted his left hand from beneath the sleeping baby's arm and looked at his watch.

"It's been an hour and ten minutes," he said. "She's been asleep about half an hour. Do you want to wake her now?"

Jonni hesitated. She was at a disadvantage. She longed to snatch her baby out of his hands and take her home, but it would be unfair to wake her just because Jonni had a personal problem with her choice of pillow. She looked down at the path and pushed her hair behind one ear with her finger.

"She'll probably wake up in a few minutes. I might as well wait."

He watched her for several seconds and then glanced at the bench beside him.

"Why don't you sit down?"

She came and sat at the end of the bench, as far from him as possible, without looking at him.

When they had sat there for a little while in the warm, damp air, both gazing at the reflection of the dull sky on the water, Michel turned his head to look at her.

"How are you?" he asked quietly.

Her uncomfortable gaze remained fixed on the river. "I'm alright, Michel."

"Are you really?"

"Yes, I am."

Michel's eyes, reflecting the diffused gray light of the clouds, were soft as he looked at her, and his tone was unchallenging.

"Things are good with me," he said. "Much better than they've been any time since Primo died and you left." Perhaps, if he were honest, better even than before those events, although he couldn't expect her to understand that. "Lynnie's home, you know; she flew in a week ago with her husband to join the company. We start rehearsals for *The Tempest* tomorrow."

Jonni looked down at her knee.

"I'm very pleased for you," she said, closing her mouth tightly after she had spoken.

Michel rubbed his ear slowly and then laid his hand on the baby's back again. He noticed that Jonni's wedding ring was no longer on her finger.

"Does it hurt you, my talking to you like this?" he asked.

"Yes," she said, and closed her mouth again to stop her lips moving involuntarily. Her averted eyes were tight with unhappiness. "Yes, actually it does."

"I'm sorry," he said, and it was true, he did feel genuinely sorry for the distress he was causing her, but if he were ever going to tell her how he felt, it had to be now. He turned his head away again to gaze in anxiety at the river, chewing the inside of his mouth, and then puckered his lips thoughtfully, trying, like Jonni, to make this look easier than it was. After a while he looked down at Caroline's curly head where it lay on the breast of his jacket.

"She really is terrific, Jons. I could get quite into kids. I wouldn't mind having a whole houseful of them."

"I'm sure you will if you want to."

He looked at her again.

"But I don't want to have them with anyone but you."

She made no answer to that, continuing to stare at the gray water. Michel's eyes creased up seriously as he gazed at her.

"We could make it work," he said, lowering his voice. "I realize that I can't give you and Caroline what you need from me at the same time as living completely wrapped up in dance; I know there just aren't enough hours in the day. But I've thought about it a lot, and I can reorganize things at work: stop touring and just do the London performances and a few international dates a year. If I go freelance there'll be enough work around the companies just in London to keep me employed most of the time. It's not that great a sacrifice. In any case, I'd only have another ten years at the top, and that's if I were lucky. Really, Jonni, my priorities have changed."

He watched her face expectantly, so intent on her response that he stopped breathing as he waited. Jonni turned her tense eyes in his direction, looking not at him but at the baby still asleep on his chest.

"I wish I could believe that, Michel; I really do." She frowned at Caroline's curly head and the fingers of her hands on her lap, intertwined, twisting slowly, painfully together. "But I'm afraid I can't. I think you'll find they're not as different as you'd like to believe they are."

He urged her quietly. "Couldn't you take that risk, Jons? You know how Roly always says that risk is life."

She raised her eyes finally to his, shaking her head, not attempting to hide the sadness in them.

"No, I couldn't. It's all very well for me, but I couldn't take that risk on Carro's behalf; I don't have that right. And even if you meant it and you were really prepared to sacrifice so much of your career for us, you'd be frustrated and miserable."

His eyes smiled now that she was looking at him.

"No," he said, "and, anyway, that portion of the risk would be mine to take." He saw that the sorrow remained unaltered in her eyes and, for a moment, he indulged in a fantasy about taking her home and holding her body against his in bed to comfort her, but the fantasy was an emotional, not a sexual one—or at least not predominantly sexual. After digesting the ache that came with the realization that it would most probably never be more than a fantasy, he looked down at the green wooden slats of the bench between them and frowned hard.

"Would it help if I told you I love you?" he asked.

"Oh, no," she pleaded. "No, Mike, please don't do that to me."

"Alright," he said, still frowning, and looked away, shifting his position on the bench. "Alright."

The baby stirred in his arms, disturbed by his movement.

"I'd better take her," Jonni said, standing up and reaching out for her. Michel passed his daughter carefully into her mother's hands.

They walked the few hundred yards back toward Jonni's house together, side by side, not talking at all. When they reached his car, Jonni stopped on the pavement and forced herself to look at him.

"Michel, please don't ask me again to come back to you."

He looked steadily down into her eyes.

"Are you absolutely sure?"

"Yes." She nodded. "Absolutely."

He nodded in his turn. "In that case, okay, I won't."

"Good-bye, then."

"Good-bye, Jons."

Once she had vanished through the front door, he sat behind the wheel of his car looking at the front of the house, visualizing her inside it, talking to the child—perhaps feeding her or playing with her. After staring at the first-floor windows for a long time he thought of Lynne and Jerry waiting for him at the Pimlico flat to rehearse the balcony pas de deux, and Carrie giving Lisa a promised lesson in cooking proper English bread-and-butter pudding, and he started the car engine and drove off.

50

JONNI SAT ALONE ON A TRAIN from Gloucester to London on a cold, gray Saturday at the start of February. She twirled her hat on her forefinger, gazing at a landscape that was so bleak and hazy it seemed barren, and wondered why anyone should choose to be married in this depressing season.

She had pleaded Caroline as an excuse for leaving before the reception. A fictitious baby flu served as a let-out for any occasion. She had been happy for Ieuan and his pretty, shy bride. If anyone's marriage should survive it was theirs. But weddings were drab events to Jonni's disillusioned eyes; they left a bitter taste in her mouth. She was glad she hadn't stayed. As always, when she invented an illness for Caroline as an excuse, she phoned the babysitter from Gloucester station in a panic of guilty fear. Carro was fine, Josie said; gurgling happily away on the settee and chewing her rag doll.

As fine drops of rain started to spatter on the train window she wondered what the weather was like in California. Perhaps Guy was on the beach now, sunbathing or sitting under an umbrella sipping gin and tonic. Perhaps he was in his rented apartment studying lines for his film. Another three days and she'd be there with him; she and Carro.

A new world. A new start.

A world away from the rain and the loneliness, and where she'd never have to worry about Michel trying to infiltrate Carro's affections or her own. The lawyers said she wouldn't even have to see Michel. Once she'd signed the papers for the divorce proceedings on Monday that would be it. Gazing through the window, she leaned her arm despondently on the narrow sill, remembering that day back in November when he had turned up unexpectedly at the flat and wishing for the thousandth time she hadn't made love with him that afternoon. It had been thoughtless and unnecessary to hurt him like that—not to mention the heartache she had caused herself. She was like an addict who, after eighteen months in recovery, had slipped off the wagon just once, and found herself back at square one, drowning in the misery of losing him all over again.

She thought about the risk Michel had asked her to take. She just didn't see how she could; not after all the pain he had put her through—the despair of those seemingly interminable months after their breakup, when her heart had leaped into her throat every time the telephone rang. Loving him was simply too dangerous. She watched the gloomy Cotswold hills whiz past the window. Was it possible, she wondered, that a man like Michel, so entrenched in his career and beloved by the fans, could ever really change enough to make room in his life for a family? No, the risk was too great. And, anyway, it was too late: she had already made the only sensible, safe decision. Guy was sensible because he didn't pretend to be in love with her, and safe because, whatever happened, he couldn't hurt her.

The dark gray contours of the landscape outside the train were growing gradually more indistinct as the light faded. Already the trees on the hills looked like grim beasts in the dull afternoon. It would be pitch-dark long before she reached Chiswick. The flat would be solitary and cheerless tonight once Carro was asleep. Perhaps she should ask the babysitter to stay to supper. She still hadn't forgiven Maggie for her treachery in going back to her husband.

The train wheels rattled beneath her with relentless monotony as the fading British landscape flew past. Britain had let her down badly. It was time for a new beginning.

As Jonni sat watching the day vanish she felt very old and very world-weary for her twenty-five years. There was no sunset at this time of year, and no dusk. The day simply slipped away.

———

On Monday evening Jonni walked around her bedroom in the Chiswick flat doing a last check of all the cupboards and drawers. There was nothing left in the flat apart from the furniture; the shelves and wardrobes were empty, the beds were stripped; everything she and Carro owned was crammed into two large suitcases and a holdall next to the door. All their other possessions had been either thrown or given away over the past couple of weeks.

Carro was sitting on the floor behind her in her pajamas playing with a stray flip-flop Jonni had found under the bed. It was past Carro's bedtime but, with no cot to put her in, it was hard to convince her that she was ready to sleep. At least if she was tired she should sleep on the plane tonight. Their plane was due to take off from Heathrow at eleven-thirty and fly through the night.

Jonni closed the wardrobe door and pulled open the drawers of the desk, one at a time, putting a pen lid and a couple of two-pence pieces in her pocket. At the back of one of the drawers, wedged between the back and the bottom, she found an old photograph and pulled it out, turning it over to look at it. It was a picture of her, taken during her Pimlico days: standing between Michel and Primo at her twenty-first birthday party. She recognized the event by her dress: she had been so pleased with herself in her new off-white silk minidress. Inevitably, by the end of the evening it had been splodged indelibly with red wine and chocolate.

She stood looking down at the picture in her hand, straightening out one corner that had got folded at the back of the drawer. Primo and Michel were both smiling at her, both amused by something that had just been said—rude, by the look of it. As ever, the body language of the two friends mirrored each other's; they were both standing, leaning with their backs against the barre, their hands in their trouser pockets and their feet crossed lazily at the ankles. They both looked healthy and happy. They looked beautiful. Gazing at that frozen moment in time from her past, Jonni wondered which of them she was really going all the way to California to escape. She put the photo on the empty bedside table, propped up against the wall. She decided she would leave it there when she left—just that one object to say, "I was here."

With the maternal eyes that she had developed in the back of her head she saw that Caroline had made her way out through the bedroom door and was contemplating a spectacular descent of the stairs. Jonni went and picked her up, laughing as she put her on the bed, plonking her in the middle of the bare mattress.

"You've got no fear at all, have you, you little daredevil? I know who you take after. No, come back here, you!" Caroline had set off again, undaunted, crawling toward the edge of the bed, and Jonni pulled her onto her lap, wrapping an arm around her to keep her there. She picked up the photo from the bedside table again, the laughter fading in her eyes as she looked for a while at Michel's smiling face. Even laughing at a bawdy joke, there was something tranquil and still about him. "You'd take the risk, wouldn't you?" she asked her babbling daughter.

Very gently, Jonni ran her fingers over the picture of Primo's glowing face and figure. In the past couple of months she had finally accepted that she was never going to see Primo again; never hear his voice; never look into his brown eyes; never feel the resonance of his personality in the room around her. As her fingers traveled lightly over the glossy photograph to touch Michel's image she realized that, in all probability, she would never see him again either. When she had signed the papers that morning, the solicitor had told her that, assuming Michel didn't contest the divorce, it might only take a matter of weeks.

Sitting on the bed on which Michel had, on one occasion, pressed his naked body so ardently against hers, and with his child on her lap, she gazed down at the photograph and ran her fingers slowly over Michel's image a second time. The flat around her was completely silent and, from outside, there was no sound except the low medley of traffic on the main Chiswick roads and a distant wail of a police car or ambulance, sounds so omnipresent in London that she no longer even heard them. After staring at the photograph for several minutes, she put it down on the bedside table decisively and stood up, lifting the little girl up to her own eye level to look into her eyes.

"Let's go and call a taxi, shall we?"

The warm, bright kitchen of the top-floor flat in Warwick Way was filled with the buzz of conversation as copies of Primo's score for *The Tempest* went back and forth across the table and different editions of

Shakespeare were passed from hand to hand. Michel was surrounded by the people he loved and talking about the work he loved.

In an atmosphere of intense but chaotic concentration several discussions went on at once around the crowded table and hands rummaged between the empty dinner plates and full glasses for notebooks and cigarettes. At one end of the table Charles Crown and Marina were deep in choreography with Michel and Lynne.

"Here," Crown said, tapping his finger hard on the score halfway down a page. "Here, Lynne, we'll break the pas de deux and give you sixteen fouettés."

"Oh God," she laughed, putting her hand to her head, "Primo always hated my fouettés."

Michel frowned at the score and rotated his hand in the air, trying to hear the music in his head. He looked up shaking his head in frustration and his hand rotating turned into a gesture of beckoning.

"Carrie?" he said. "Come on, Carrie; get out of the sink. That's not your job. Can you read me this?"

Carrie left the washing-up, drying her hands on a tea towel as she came to lean over the back of Michel's chair. She looked at the section he pointed out to her and sang through it, dum-de-dumming the melody and tapping the rhythm gently on his shoulder.

"See?" Crown insisted. "It's joyous; it's absolutely perfect!"

"Yeah, you're right." Michel laid his hand over his mother's on his shoulder in thanks. "It does sound like fouettés. What's this here on the score above the stave?"

"What?"

"This gray mark. Is it an annotation?"

"I haven't got anything," Jerry said.

"No, nor me."

"Nor me," Crown said. He stood up and leaned over the table, trying to turn his head upside down to see the faint smudge Michel was pointing at on his score. "It's probably just the photocopier buggering around. There aren't any notes in this section; I'd have seen it. Hi, Rob?" he called down to the far end of the table. "Pass us up the original, will you?"

Crown took Primo's score as it was handed to him and leafed through it, frowning in surprise as he found the page.

"Jesus, there is a note here! Well, I'm buggered; I'd have sworn there wasn't. It's a pencil scribble: M . . ." He scratched his head hard and then shook it, defeated. "No, I can't make it out."

Michel held out his hand. "Pass it over. I know his handwriting." He narrowed his eyes, grimacing as he deciphered the words slowly: "M don't let . . . C give L . . . fouettés here . . . you do them."

He looked up and they all stared at each other, openmouthed. One by one they laughed in breathless disbelief.

Lynne's cheeks turned cold and she put her hands to them, her eyes filling with tears of surprise and joy.

"He knew! Oh, Michel, he knew I'd come back to dance this with you!"

"Of course he did," Crown said, and he glanced up at the ceiling: "Cheeky sod."

As Michel reached across the table to squeeze Lynne's hand, Carrie smiled at him quizzically with her hands on her hips, still holding her tea towel.

"If it's not a rude question, can you actually do fouettés, Michel?"

"No," he laughed, "not the way the girls do them, anyway—we do them straight-legged. I suppose I could always learn, though."

While they continued talking about the fouettés there was a yell from the far end of the table.

"Say, Michel!" It was Lisa.

"Hmm?" He turned his head toward her.

"Michel, who's that?"

He looked up and stopped moving. His face cleared as his preoccupied frown fell away. Jonni was standing in the open doorway of the kitchen, her face pale and nervous, with Caroline, wrapped in a rug and sound asleep, cradled against her chest. Her eyes found him and she looked at him in frightened hope as the conversation in the kitchen fell to a hum and died.

Every eye in the room turned toward Michel as he gazed at her across the crowded table.

"Hello, Jons," he said in the silence.

"Hello," she said, her voice as nervous as her face.

Lisa leaned toward Rob with a loud stage whisper—

"What's that woman doing here?"

Michel's eyes, looking into Jonni's, were asking the same thing but in a very different manner. As his gray eyes stared into hers everyone else in the kitchen vanished and, for a moment, there was no one there at all other than the two of them and the tiny person asleep on Jonni's breast. Eye to eye across the room, they both read the answer to Lisa's question in each other's gaze.

Jonni's mouth turned down and her eyes filled with plaintive emotion. "This is where I live," she said.

Michel's eyes smiled slowly as he turned his head in Lisa's direction without breaking the hold of Jonni's gaze. "Lisa, this is Jonni . . . my wife. And our daughter, Caroline."

"Oh my Gawd!" Lisa screamed, and leaped up from her chair. "Oh Gawd, it's my niece!" She ran around the table to Jonni and jumped up and down in frenzied delight, flapping her hands excitedly. "Oh, let me look! Oh Gawd, isn't she gorgeous? Oh, Jonni . . ." Lisa clasped her hands together desperately, ". . . please, please, please let me hold her!"

Jonni looked at Michel in uncertainty. When he nodded, smiling, she turned, still trembling slightly, and handed the sleeping baby to her aunt. Lisa carried Caroline tenderly away like a thief to have her all to herself in the corner of the kitchen.

"Oh my Gawd," she whispered, looking up with radiant joy, "I can't believe it; she looks like me! Carrie, doesn't she look like me?"

Carrie leaned over her granddaughter and gently stroked the soft blond curls as the baby began to wake up.

"Yes, she does. Though she's got Michel's eyes. She's adorable."

Carrie took her from Lisa's arms, jiggling her gently to hush her as she started to wail, and put her into the arms of her father. When Michel looked down at the fretful baby and touched her hot cheek with his finger, Caroline seemed to recognize him and her frown dawned into a grin which became a huge yawn. Michel kissed the sleepy little face and turned toward Jonni.

"Let's put her in the bedroom. That way, if we go into the studio for any reason, we won't disturb her."

"Okay." Jonni managed her first timorous smile. "We'll have to put her on the floor though. She's starting to walk."

"Is she?" Michel laughed. "Oh Christ." He stood up with Caroline in his arms and looked over his shoulder at Crown. "Carry on, Charles; we'll be back in a minute. Rob, fill up Nettie's glass, will you?"

And the conversation rose again to a noisy hum as Michel and Jonni went to put their child to bed and to put their arms around each other quietly in the shadow of the ash tree from the dim yellow light of the streetlamp across the road. The white walls of the square bedroom, with the familiar shapes of the furniture silhouetted against them, and the warm orange-brown floorboards underfoot gave the room its special nighttime atmosphere of tranquillity and safety.

Much later in the evening when several of the dancers had gone home exhausted, Jonni sat on Michel's knee in the warm kitchen with her head resting against his, listening while they discussed the choreography for *The Tempest.* Michel's hand lay on Jonni's waist while he and Marina argued with Crown about the meaning of the last solo and, beside them, Carrie, Jerry, and Lisa discussed the music.

When Michel and Crown grew heated in their disagreement Lynne leaned back in her chair and grinned at Jonni across the table.

"Nothing changes. I'm glad you're home, Jons. It didn't seem right without you. Now it really does feel like the old gang again."

Jonni felt Michel's hand gently squeeze her waist and she drew her arm closer around his warm neck, smiling at Lynne.

"I know," she said. "There's someone missing though."

Crown looked at her, shaking his head.

"No, he's here, Flotsam. And not only is he here but he's sticking his oar into my fucking choreography."

Jonni laughed.

"I believe you. That sounds just like him. But I wasn't thinking about Primo." She smiled, closing her eyes. "I was thinking of Roly."

Michel and Crown exchanged quick glances.

"Jons, listen—"

"No, it's alright!" Annette raised her head from her wineglass. Since Jonni arrived she had been sitting morosely at the table hidden behind a large pair of very expensive Gucci sunglasses, saying little and drinking steadily. She took off her sunglasses slowly.

"It's alright," she said again. "I'm drunk."

Jonni lifted her head and looked at her, her face falling in horror at the sight of Annette's two black eyes and a livid cut, carefully stitched, below her eyebrow.

"Nettie! Oh no! What happened?"

Annette took another sip of wine, staring straight ahead at the far kitchen wall. Everyone had fallen so silent that the low hum of the refrigerator filled the room.

"Hasn't Guy told you?"

"Guy? No, he hasn't said anything; he's in California."

Annette inhaled sharply through her nose.

"Roly came down from Newcastle to see me a week ago. He called to let me know he was coming but I hadn't been home for a couple of days so I didn't get the message. When he arrived on Sunday night I wasn't there. So he called Guy on his mobile—in California, I suppose. Guy told him about the other men I'd been seeing. Not just recently but all of them, going right back to the time before we were married. I don't know how he knew. Perhaps everyone knew. Except Roly. When I got home late on Monday evening . . ." She paused to sip her wine and the fridge hummed loudly in the silence. ". . . he was raging drunk, waiting for me." She took another sip of wine. "He smashed up the flat and knocked me about a bit. And told me he'd see me in hell before he ever set eyes on me again."

Annette ran her wrist slowly up over her forehead. Her voice was trembling. "He caught the train back up to Newcastle. Somehow he found his way to the theater in time for Tuesday's show; God knows how. He went on stage so drunk he could hardly stand up, in front of a thousand children, with a glass of whisky in his hand. At the start of the first number, with his radio mike turned up full, he threw his glass of whisky in the conductor's face, called him a cunt, and walked offstage. No one knows where he's been since."

As Annette's breast heaved in a sudden involuntary gasp, Michel moved to shift Jonni from his knee, but Annette stopped him with a shaking yet clearly raised hand.

"No, Michel. I'm okay. Leave me alone."

She put her sunglasses back on slowly and continued to stare at the wall. Jonni gazed at her in appalled silence.

"We'll find him, darling," Crown said.

Annette just shook her head minutely.

Crown and Michel looked at each other and Michel raised his eyebrows in a reluctant shrug. There was nothing they could do for her.

"Okay," Crown said, picking up his train of thought abruptly, "where were we? Oh yes, the last solo. You're talking bollocks, Michel: Primo's left it up to us to decide on the ending, I agree, but with all this grandeur in the string section, I tell you it's about Ariel snuffing it from loneliness."

"Bullshit, Charles; the strings are for his freedom, or else why hasn't Primo brought back the bloody oboe?"

"I agree," said Marina. "Ariel's a spirit of the air and spirits can't snuff it."

Their debate babbled on, arguments bouncing back and forth across the table.

After half an hour Crown noticed Michel's hand caressing Jonni's thigh as she sat dozing on his knee. He looked at the rest of the group in the kitchen, closing his copy of the score.

"Look, I think we should call it an evening. Come on, folks, let's clear off and give Michel and Jonni a bit of space."

"No, stay," Jonni said drowsily, shifting her cheek against Michel's head. "Stay and work, all of you. Stay late into the night. This is where you belong."

Crown caught Michel's eye and they exchanged smiles.

"Alright." Crown opened his score again at the last page. "Now this epilogue—suppose, for the sake of argument, we say we're going with your happy ending."

Michel slapped his hand on the table triumphantly.

"I knew you'd come round!"

"I haven't fucking come round. I'm giving you a starting point. Now convince me."

"Okay." Michel started flipping through his score. "Let's go right back and start with the first scene."

Lynne flopped back in her chair, laughing.

"Oh, my God." She raised her wineglass from the table. "Here's to the pair of you mad buggers!"

Lisa picked up her orange juice, thrusting it joyously high: "Here's to us!"

"To Roly," Annette said bitterly. She picked up her wine and pursed her lips. "Wherever he is, the bastard."

"Okay," Crown said, "if we're raising our glasses, I'll raise mine to *The Tempest.*"

They clinked their glasses in companionship, eye meeting eye around the table. Outside on the street, where one man huddled heartbroken in a drunken stupor, it had started to rain. But the Pimlico kitchen was warm and filled with bright hope for the future.

"To family," Jonni said, looking into Michel's eyes.

Michel touched his glass against hers.

"And to Primo."

Primo was raising his glass to them all.

About the Author

REBECCA HORSFALL grew up in a theater family in London. Her father is an actor and her mother is an actor-director from America. Like her parents, Rebecca has worked in the theater as a director, production supervisor, and script editor. She also spent a year as a company manager and wardrobe supervisor for two ballet companies. This experience gave her great insight for *Dancing on Thorns*, her first novel, which she worked on for ten years. She lives in a remote house in the Lincolnshire hills with her husband, and is now working on her second novel. For more information, visit *www.rebeccahorsfall.com.*

ABOUT THE TYPE

This book was set in Garamond, a typeface originally designed by the Parisian typecutter Claude Garamond (1480–1561). This version of Garamond was modeled on a 1592 specimen sheet from the Egenolff-Berner foundry, which was produced from types assumed to have been brought to Frankfurt by the punchcutter Jacques Sabon.

Claude Garamond's distinguished romans and italics first appeared in *Opera Ciceronis* in 1543–44. The Garamond types are clear, open, and elegant.